DOCTOR DOLITTLE

VOL. 4

The COMPLETE COLLECTION

READ ALL OF
DOCTOR DOLITTLE'S ADVENTURES!

DOCTOR DOLITTLE

VOL. 4

The COMPLETE COLLECTION

Doctor Dolittle in the Moon ✳ *Doctor Dolittle's Return*
Doctor Dolittle and the Secret Lake ✳ *Gub-Gub's Book*

HUGH LOFTING

Aladdin

NEW YORK LONDON TORONTO SYDNEY NEW DELHI

This book is a work of fiction. Any references to historical events, real people, or real places are used fictitiously. Other names, characters, places, and events are products of the author's imagination, and any resemblance to actual events or places or persons, living or dead, is entirely coincidental.

ALADDIN

An imprint of Simon & Schuster Children's Publishing Division
1230 Avenue of the Americas, New York, New York 10020
First Aladdin edition November 2019

For information about special discounts for bulk purchases, please contact Simon & Schuster Special Sales at 1-866-506-1949 or business@simonandschuster.com.
The Simon & Schuster Speakers Bureau can bring authors to your live event.
For more information or to book an event contact the Simon & Schuster Speakers Bureau at 1-866-248-3049 or visit our website at www.simonspeakers.com.
Cover designed by Karin Paprocki
Interior designed by Mike Rosamilia
The text of this book was set in Oneleigh Pro.
Manufactured in the United States of America 0719 FFG
2 4 6 8 10 9 7 5 3 1
Library of Congress Control Number 2018959983
ISBN 978-1-5344-4900-8 (hc)
ISBN 978-1-5344-4899-5 (pbk)
ISBN 9781-5344-4901-5 (eBook)
These titles were previously published individually with slightly different text and art.

CONTENTS

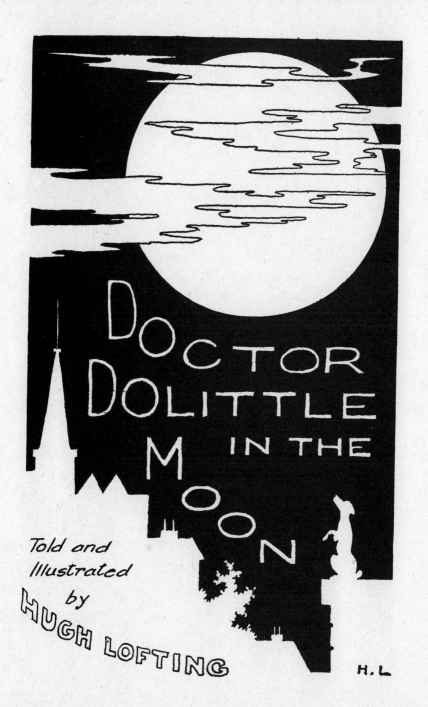

Contents

We Land Upon a New World

IN WRITING THE STORY OF OUR ADVENTURES IN the moon I, Thomas Stubbins, secretary to John Dolittle, MD (and son of Jacob Stubbins, the cobbler of Puddleby-on-the-Marsh), find myself greatly puzzled. It is not an easy task, remembering day by day and hour by hour those crowded and exciting weeks. It is true I made many notes for the Doctor, books full of them. But that information was nearly all of a highly scientific kind. And I feel that I should tell the story here not for the scientist so much as for the general reader. And it is in that I am perplexed.

For the story could be told in many ways. People are so different in what they want to know about a voyage. I had thought at one time that Jip could help me; and after reading him some chapters as I had first set them down I asked for his opinion. I discovered he was mostly interested in whether we had seen any rats in the moon. I found I could not tell him. I didn't remember seeing any; and yet I am sure there must have been some—or some sort of creature like a rat.

Then I asked Gub-Gub. And what he was chiefly concerned to hear was the kind of vegetables we had fed on. (Dab-Dab snorted at me for my pains and said I should have known better than to ask him.) I tried my mother. She wanted to know how we had managed when our underwear wore out—and a whole lot of other matters about our living conditions, hardly any of which I could answer. Next I went to Matthew Mugg. And the things he wanted to learn were worse than either my mother's or Jip's: Were there any shops in the moon? What were the dogs and cats like? The good Cat's-Meat-Man seemed to have imagined it a place not very different from Puddleby or the East End of London.

No, trying to get at what most people wanted to read concerning the moon did not bring me much profit. I couldn't seem to tell them any of the things they were most anxious to know. It reminded me of the first time I had come to the Doctor's house, hoping to be hired as his assistant, and dear old Polynesia the parrot had questioned me. "Are you a good noticer?" she had asked. I had always thought I was—pretty good, anyhow. But now I felt I had been a very poor noticer. For it seemed I hadn't noticed any of the things I should have done to make the story of our voyage interesting to the ordinary public.

The trouble was of course *attention*. Human attention is like butter: you can only spread it so thin and no thinner. If you try to spread it over too many things at once you just don't remember them. And certainly during all our waking hours upon the moon there was so much for our ears and eyes and minds to take in it is a wonder, I often think, that any clear memories at all remain.

The one who could have been of most help to me in writing my impressions of the moon was Jamaro Bumblelily, the giant moth who carried us there. But as he was nowhere near me when I set to work upon this book, I decided I had better not consider the particular wishes of Jip, Gub-Gub, my mother, Matthew or anyone else, but set the story down in my own way. Clearly the tale must be in any case an imperfect, incomplete one. And the only thing to do is to go forward with it, step-by-step, to the best of my recollection, from where the great insect hovered, with our beating hearts pressed close against his broad back, over the near and glowing landscape of the moon.

Anyone could tell that the moth knew every detail of the country we were landing in. Planing, circling and diving, he brought his wide-winged body very deliberately down toward a little valley fenced in with hills. The bottom of this, I saw as we drew nearer, was level, sandy, and dry.

The hills struck one at once as unusual. In fact, all the mountains as well (for much greater heights could presently be seen towering away in the dim greenish light behind the nearer, lower ranges) had one peculiarity. The tops seemed to be cut off and cuplike. The Doctor afterward explained to me that they were extinct volcanoes. Nearly all these peaks had once belched fire and molten lava but were now cold and dead. Some had been fretted and worn by winds and weather and time into quite curious shapes; and yet others had been filled up or half buried by drifting sand so that they had nearly lost the appearance of volcanoes. I was reminded of "The Whispering Rocks," which we had seen in Spidermonkey Island. And though this scene was different in many things, no one who had ever looked upon a volcanic landscape before could have mistaken it for anything else.

The little valley, long and narrow, which we were apparently making for did not show many signs of life, vegetable or animal. But we were not disturbed by that. At least the Doctor wasn't. He had seen a tree and he was satisfied that before long he would find water, vegetation, and creatures.

At last, when the moth had dropped within twenty feet of the ground, he spread his wings motionless and like a great kite gently touched the sand, in hops at first, then ran a little, braced himself and came to a standstill.

We had landed on the moon!

By this time we had had a chance to get a little more used to the new air. But before we made any attempt to "go ashore" the Doctor thought it best to ask our gallant steed to stay where he was awhile, so that we could still further accustom ourselves to the new atmosphere and conditions.

This request was willingly granted. Indeed, the poor insect himself, I imagine, was glad enough to rest awhile. From some-where in his packages John Dolittle produced an emergency ration of chocolate that he had been saving up. All four of us munched in silence, too hungry and too awed by our new surroundings to say a word.

The light changed unceasingly. It reminded me of the northern lights, the aurora borealis. You would gaze at the mountains above you, then turn away a moment, and on looking back find everything that had been pink was now green, the shadows that had been violet were rose.

Breathing was still kind of difficult. We were compelled for the moment to keep the Moon Bells handy. These were the great orange-colored flowers that the moth had brought down for us. It was their perfume (or gas) that had enabled us to cross the airless belt that lay between the moon and the earth. A fit of coughing was always liable to come on if one left them too long. But already we felt that we could in time get used to this new air and soon do without the flowers altogether.

The gravity too was very confusing. It required hardly any effort to rise from a sitting position to a standing one. Walking was no effort at all—for the muscles—but for the lungs it was another question. The most extraordinary sensation was jumping. The least little spring from the ankles sent you flying into the air in the most fantastic fashion. If it had not been for this problem of breathing properly (which the Doctor seemed to feel we should approach with great caution on account of its possible effect on the heart), we would all have given ourselves up to this most light-hearted feeling that took possession of us. I remember, myself, singing songs—the melody was somewhat indistinct on account of a large mouthful of chocolate—and I was most anxious to get down off the moth's back and go bounding away across the hills and valleys to explore this new world.

But I realize now that John Dolittle was very wise in making us wait. He issued orders (in the low whispers that we found necessary in this new clear air) to each and all of us that for the present the flowers were *not* to be left behind for a single moment.

They were cumbersome things to carry, but we obeyed orders. No ladder was needed now to descend by. The gentlest jump sent one flying off the insect's back to the ground where you landed from a twenty-five-foot drop with ease and comfort.

Zip! The spring was made. And we were wading in the sands of a new world.

"Zip! The spring was made."

THE SECOND CHAPTER

The Land of Colors and Perfumes

WE WERE AFTER ALL, WHEN YOU COME to think of it, a very odd party, this, which made the first landing on a new world. But in a great many ways it was a peculiarly good combination. First of all, Polynesia: she was the kind of bird that one always supposed would exist under any conditions, drought, floods, fire, or frost. I've no doubt that at that time, in my boyish way, I exaggerated Polynesia's adaptability and endurance. But even to this day I can never quite imagine any circumstances in which that remarkable bird would perish. If she could get a pinch of seed (of almost any kind) and a sip of water two or three times a week, she would not only carry on quite cheerfully but would scarcely even remark upon the strange nature or scantiness of the rations.

Then Chee-Chee: he was not so easily provided for in the matter of food. But he always seemed to be able to provide for himself anything that was lacking. I have never known a better forager than Chee-Chee. When everyone was hungry he could go off into an entirely new forest and just by smelling the wild fruits and nuts he could tell if they were safe to eat. How he did this even John Dolittle could never find out. Indeed, Chee-Chee himself didn't know.

Then myself: I had no scientific qualifications, but I had learned how to be a good secretary on natural history expeditions and I knew a good deal about the Doctor's ways.

Finally there was the Doctor. No naturalist has ever gone afield to grasp at the secrets of a new land with the qualities John Dolittle possessed. He never claimed to know anything, beforehand, for certain. He came to new problems with a childlike innocence that made it easy for himself to learn and the others to teach.

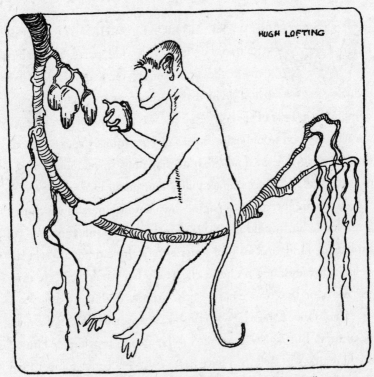

"By smelling he could tell if they were safe to eat."

Yes, it was a strange party we made up. Most scientists would have laughed at us, no doubt. Yet we had many things to recommend us that no expedition ever carried before.

As usual the Doctor wasted no time in preliminaries. Most other explorers would have begun by planting a flag and singing national anthems. Not so with John Dolittle. As soon as he was sure that we were all ready he gave the order to march. And without a word Chee-Chee and I (with Polynesia who perched herself on my shoulder) fell in behind him and started off.

I have never known a time when it was harder to shake loose the feeling of living in a dream as those first few hours we spent on the moon. The knowledge that we were treading a new world never before visited by man added to this extraordinary feeling caused by the gravity, of lightness, of walking on air, made you want every minute to have someone tell you that you were actually awake and in your right senses. For this reason I kept constantly speaking to the Doctor or Chee-Chee or Polynesia—even when I had nothing particular to say. But the uncanny booming of my own voice every time I opened my lips and spoke above the faintest whisper merely added to the dreamlike effect of the whole experience.

However, little by little, we grew accustomed to it. And certainly there was no lack of new sights and impressions to occupy our minds. Those strange and ever-changing colors in the landscape were most bewildering, throwing out your course and sense of direction entirely. The Doctor had brought a small pocket compass with him. But on consulting it, we saw that it was even more confused than we were. The needle did nothing but whirl around in the craziest fashion and no amount of steadying would persuade it to stay still.

"*The Doctor had brought a compass.*"

Giving that up, the Doctor determined to rely on his moon maps and his own eyesight and bump of locality. He was heading toward where he had seen that tree—which was at the end of one of the ranges. But all the ranges in this section seemed very much alike. The maps did not help us in this respect in the least. To our rear we could see certain peaks that we thought we could identify on the charts. But ahead nothing fit in at all. This made us feel surer than ever that we were moving toward the moon's other side, which earthly eyes had never seen.

"It is likely enough, Stubbins," said the Doctor as we strode lightly forward over loose sand that would ordinarily have been very heavy going, "that it is *only* on the other side that water exists. Which may partly be the reason why astronomers never believed there was any here at all."

For my part, I was so on the lookout for extraordinary sights that it did not occur to me, till the Doctor spoke of it, that the temperature was extremely mild and agreeable. One of the things that John Dolittle had feared was that we should find a heat that was unbearable or a cold that was worse than the Arctic. But except for the difficulty of the strange new quality of the air, no human could have asked for a nicer climate. A gentle steady wind was blowing and the temperature seemed to remain almost constantly the same.

We looked about everywhere for tracks. As yet we knew very little of what animal life to expect. But the loose sand told nothing, not even to Chee-Chee, who was a pretty experienced hand at picking up tracks of the most unusual kind.

Of odors and scents there were plenty—most of them very delightful flower perfumes, which the wind brought to us from the other side of the mountain ranges ahead. Occasionally a very disagreeable one would come, mixed up with the pleasant scents. But none of them, except that of the Moon Bells the moth had brought with us, could we recognize.

On and on we went for miles, crossing ridge after ridge and still no glimpse did we get of the Doctor's tree. Of course, crossing the ranges was not nearly as hard traveling as it would have been on earth. Jumping and bounding both upward and downward was extraordinarily easy. Still, we had brought a good deal of baggage with us and all of us were pretty heavy-laden; and after two and a half hours of travel we began to feel a little discouraged. Polynesia then volunteered to fly ahead and reconnoiter, but this the Doctor was loath to have her do. For some reason he wanted us all to stick together for the present.

However, after another half hour of walking, he consented to let her fly straight up so long as she remained in sight, to see if she could spy out the tree's position from a greater height.

"Jumping was extraordinarily easy."

Thirst!

SO WE RESTED ON OUR BUNDLES A SPELL while Polynesia gave an imitation of a soaring vulture and straight above our heads climbed and climbed. At about a thousand feet she paused and circled. Then slowly came down again. The Doctor, watching her, grew impatient at her speed. I could not quite make out why he was so unwilling to have her away from his side, but I asked no questions.

Yes, she had seen the tree, she told us, but it still seemed a long way off. The Doctor wanted to know why she had taken so long in coming down and she said she had been making sure of her bearings so that she would be able to act as guide. Indeed, with the usual accuracy of birds, she had a very clear idea of the direction we should take. And we set off again, feeling more at ease and confident.

The truth of it was of course that seen from a great height, as the tree had first appeared to us, the distance had seemed much less than it actually was. Two more things helped to mislead us. One, that the moon air, as we now discovered, made everything look nearer than it actually was in spite of the soft dim light. And the other was that we had supposed the tree to be one of ordinary earthly size and had made an unconscious guess at its distance in keeping with a fair-sized oak or elm. Whereas when we did actually reach it we found it to be unimaginably huge.

I shall never forget that tree. It was our first experience of moon life, *in* the moon. Darkness was coming on when we finally halted beneath it. When I say *darkness*, I mean that strange kind of twilight that was the nearest thing to night which we ever saw in the moon. The tree's height, I should say, would be at least three hundred feet and the width of it across the trunk a good forty or fifty. Its appearance in general was most uncanny. The whole design of it was different from any tree I have ever seen. Yet there was no mistaking it for anything else. It seemed—how shall I describe it?—*alive*. Poor Chee-Chee was so scared of it his hair just stood up on the nape of his neck, and it was a long time before the Doctor and I persuaded him to help us pitch camp beneath its boughs.

Indeed we were a very subdued party that prepared to spend its first night on the moon. No one knew just what it was that oppressed us, but we were all conscious of a definite feeling of disturbance. The wind still blew—in that gentle, steady way that the moon winds always blew. The light was clear enough to see outlines by, although most of the night the earth was invisible, and there was no reflection whatever.

I remember how the Doctor, while we were unpacking and laying out the rest of our chocolate ration for supper, kept glancing uneasily up at those strange limbs of the tree overhead.

Of course it was the wind that was moving them—no doubt of

"It was different from any tree I have ever seen."

that at all. Yet the wind was so deadly regular and even. And the movement of the boughs wasn't regular at all. That was the weird part of it. It almost seemed as though the tree were doing some moving on its own, like an animal chained by its feet in the ground. And still you could never be sure—because, after all, the wind *was* blowing all the time.

And besides, it moaned. Well, we knew trees moaned in the wind at home. But this one did it differently—it didn't seem in keeping with that regular, even wind that we felt upon our faces.

I could see that even the worldly-wise, practical Polynesia was perplexed and upset. And it took a great deal to disturb her. Yet

HUGH LOFTING

"The Doctor kept glancing up uneasily."

a bird's senses toward trees and winds are much keener than a man's. I kept hoping she would venture into the branches of the tree; but she didn't. And as for Chee-Chee, also a natural denizen of the forest, no power on earth, I felt sure, would persuade him to investigate the mysteries of this strange specimen of a vegetable kingdom we were as yet only distantly acquainted with.

After supper was dispatched, the Doctor kept me busy for some hours taking down notes. There was much to be recorded of this first day in a new world. The temperature; the direction and force of the wind; the time of our arrival—as near as it could be guessed; the air pressure (he had brought along a small barometer among his instruments) and many other things which, while they were dry stuff for the ordinary mortal, were highly important for the scientist.

Often and often I have wished that I had one of those memories that seem to be able to recall all impressions no matter how small and unimportant. For instance, I have often wanted to remember exactly that first awakening on the moon. We had all been weary enough with excitement and exercise, when we went to bed, to sleep soundly. All I can remember of my waking up is spending at least ten minutes working out where I was. And I doubt if I could have done it even then if I had not finally realized that John Dolittle was awake ahead of me and already pottering around among his instruments, taking readings.

The immediate business now on hand was food. There was literally nothing for breakfast. The Doctor began to regret his hasty departure from the moth. Indeed it was only now, many, many hours after we had left him in our unceremonious haste to find the tree and explore the new world, that we realized that we had not as yet seen any signs of animal life. Still, it seemed a long way to go back and consult him; and it was by no means certain that he would still be there.

Just the same, we needed food, and food we were going to find. Hastily we bundled together what things we had unpacked for the night's camping. Which way to go? Clearly if we had here reached one tree, there must be some direction in which others lay, where we could find that water which the Doctor was so sure must exist. But we could scan the horizon with staring eyes or telescope as much as we wished and not another leaf of a tree could we see.

This time, without waiting to be ordered, Polynesia soared into the air to do a little scouting.

"Polynesia soared into the air."

"Well," she said on her return, "I don't see any actual trees at all. The beastly landscape is more like the Sahara Desert than any scenery I've ever run into. But over there behind that higher range—the one with the curious hat-shaped peak in the middle— you see the one I mean?"

"Yes," said the Doctor. "I see. Go on."

"Well, behind that there is a dark horizon different from any other quarter. I won't swear it is trees. But myself, I feel convinced that there is something else there besides sand. We had better get moving. It is no short walk."

Indeed it *was* no short walk. It came to be a forced march or race between us and starvation. On starting out we had not foreseen anything of the kind. Going off without breakfast was nothing after all. Each one of us had done that before many a time. But as hour after hour went by and still the landscape remained a desert of rolling sand dunes, hills and dead, dry volcanoes, our spirits fell lower and lower.

This was one of the times when I think I saw John Dolittle really at his best. I know, although I had not questioned him, that he had already been beset with anxiety over several matters on the first steps of our march. Later he spoke of them to me: not at the time. And as conditions grew worse, as hunger gnawed at our vitals and the most terrible thirst parched our tongues—as strength and vitality began to give way and mere walking became the most terrible hardship, the Doctor grew cheerier and cheerier. He didn't crack dry jokes in an irritating way, either. But by some strange means he managed to keep the whole party in a good mood. If he told a funny story it was always at the right time and set us all laughing at our troubles. In talking to him afterward about this I learned that he had, when a young man, been employed on more than one exploration trip to keep the expedition in good humor. It was, he said, the only way he could persuade the chief to take him, since at that time he had no scientific training to recommend him.

Anyway, I sincerely doubt whether our party would have held out if it had not been for his sympathetic and cheering company. The agonies of thirst were something new to me. Every step I thought must be my last.

Finally, at what seemed to be the end of our second day, I vaguely heard Polynesia saying something about "Forests ahead!" I imagine I must have been half delirious by then. I still staggered along, blindly following the others. I know we *did* reach water because before I fell and dozed away into a sort of half faint, I remember Chee-Chee trickling something marvelously cool between my lips out of a cup made from a folded leaf.

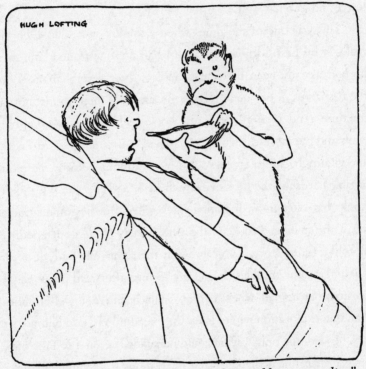

"*I remember Chee-Chee trickling something cool between my lips.*"

Chee-Chee the Hero

WHEN I AWOKE I FELT VERY MUCH ashamed of myself. What an explorer! The Doctor was moving around already—and, of course, Chee-Chee and Polynesia. John Dolittle came to my side immediately when he saw I was awake.

As though he knew the thoughts that were in my mind, he at once started to reprimand me for feeling ashamed of my performance. He pointed out that after all Chee-Chee and Polynesia were accustomed to traveling in hot, dry climates and that so, for that matter, was he himself.

"Taken all in all, Stubbins," said he, "your own performance has been extremely good. You made the trip, the whole way, and only collapsed when relief was in sight. No one could ask for more than that. I have known many experienced explorers who couldn't have done nearly as well. It was a hard lap—a devilishly hard lap. You were magnificent. Sit up and have some breakfast. Thank goodness, we've reached food at last!"

Weak and hungry, I sat up. Arranged immediately around me was a collection of what I later learned were fruits. The reliable Chee-Chee, scared though he might be of a moving tree or a whispering wind, had served the whole party with that wonderful sense of his for scenting out wild foodstuffs. Not one of the strange courses on the bill of fare had I or the Doctor seen before. But if Chee-Chee said they were safe, we knew we need not fear.

Some of the fruits were as big as a large trunk; some as small as a walnut. But, starving as we were, we just dived in and ate and ate and ate. Water there was, too, gathered in the shells of enormous nuts and odd vessels made from twisted leaves. Never

HUGH LOFTING

"Some of the fruits were as big as a trunk."

has a breakfast tasted so marvelous as did that one of fruits that I could not name.

Chee-Chee!—Poor little timid Chee-Chee, who conquered your own fears and volunteered to go ahead of us alone, into the jungle to find food when our strength was giving out. To the world you were just an organ-grinder's monkey. But to us whom you saved from starvation, when terror beset you at every step, you will forever be ranked high in the list of the great heroes of all time. Thank goodness we had you with us! Our bones might today be moldering in the sands of the moon if it had not been for your untaught science, your jungle skill—and, above all, your courage that overcame your fear!

Well, to return: as I ate these strange fruits and sipped the water that brought life back, I gazed upward and saw before me a sort of ridge. On its level top a vegetation, a kind of tangled forest, flourished; and trailing down from this ridge were little outposts of the vegetable kingdom, groups of bushes and single trees that scattered and dribbled away in several directions from the main mass. Why and how that lone tree survived so far away we could never satisfactorily explain. The nearest John Dolittle could come to it was that some underground spring supplied it with enough water or moisture to carry on. Yet there can be no doubt that to have reached such enormous proportions it must have been there hundreds—perhaps thousands—of years. Anyway, it is a good thing for us it *was* there. If it had not been, as a pointer toward this habitable quarter of the moon—it is most likely our whole expedition would have perished.

When the Doctor and I had finished our mysterious breakfast we started to question Chee-Chee about the forest from which he had produced the food we had eaten.

"I don't know how I did it," said Chee-Chee when we asked him. "I just shut my eyes most of the time—terribly afraid. I passed trees, plants, creepers, roots. I smelled—Goodness! I too was hungry, remember. I smelled hard as I could. And soon of course I spotted food, fruit. I climbed a tree—half the time with my eyes shut. Then I see some monster, golly! What a jungle—different from any monkey ever see before—Woolly, woolly!—Ooh, ooh! All the same, nuts smell good. Catch a few. Chase down the tree. Run some more. Smell again. Good!—Up another tree. Different fruit, good just the same. Catch a few. Down again. Run home. On the way smell good root. Same as ginger—only better. Dig a little.

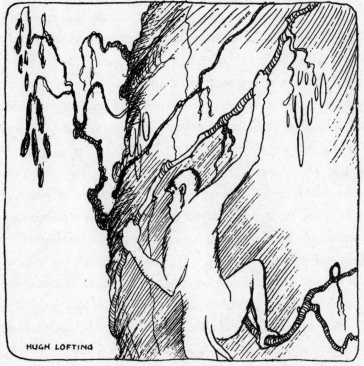

"I climbed a tree."

Keep eyes shut—don't want to see monster. Catch a piece of root. Run all the way home. Here I am. Finish!"

Well, dear old Chee-Chee's story was descriptive of his own heroic adventures, but it did not give us much idea of the moon forest that we were to explore. Nevertheless, rested and fit, we now felt much more inclined to look into things ourselves.

Leaving what luggage we had brought with us from our original landing point, we proceeded toward the line of trees at the summit of the bluff, about four miles ahead of us. We now felt that we could find our way back without much difficulty to the two last camps we had established.

The going was about the same, loose sand—only that as we approached the bluff, we found the sand firmer to the tread.

On the way up the last lap toward the vegetation line we were out of view of the top itself. Often the going was steep. All the way I had the feeling that we were about to make new and great discoveries—that for the first time we were to learn something important about the true nature of the mysterious moon.

On the Plateau

INDEED OUR FIRST CLOSE ACQUAINTANCE WITH the forests of the moon was made in quite a dramatic manner. If it had been on a stage it could not have been arranged better for effect. Suddenly as our heads topped the bluff we saw a wall of jungle some mile or so ahead of us. It would take a very long time to describe those trees in detail. It wasn't that there were so many kinds, but each one was so utterly different from any tree we had seen on the earth. And yet, curiously enough, they did remind you of vegetable forms you had seen, but not of trees.

For instance, there was one whole section, several square miles in extent apparently, that looked exactly like ferns. Another reminded me of a certain flowering plant (I can't recall the name of it) that grows a vast number of small blossoms on a flat surface at the top. The stems are a curious whitish green. This moon tree was *exactly* the same, only nearly a thousand times as big. The denseness of the foliage (or flowering) at the top was so compact and solid that we later found no rain could penetrate it. And for

HUGH LOFTING

"We approached the bluff on whose brow the vegetation flourished."

this reason the Doctor and I gave it the name *Umbrella Tree*. But not one single tree was there which was the same as any tree we had seen before. And there were many, many more curious growths that dimly reminded you of something, though you could not always say exactly what.

One odd thing that disturbed us quite a bit was a strange sound. Noises of any kind, no matter how faint, we already knew could travel long distances on the moon. As soon as we had gained the plateau on top of the bluff we heard it. It was a musical sound. And yet not the sound of a single instrument. It seemed almost as though there was a small orchestra somewhere playing very, very softly.

"The Umbrella Tree"

We were by this time becoming accustomed to strange things. But I must confess that this distant hidden music upset me quite a little, and so, I know, it did the Doctor.

At the top of the bluff we rested to get our wind before we covered the last mile up to the jungle itself. It was curious how clearly marked and separated were those sections of the moon's landscape. And yet doubtless the smaller scale of all the geographical features of this world, so much less in bulk than our own, could partly account for that. In front of us a plateau stretched out, composed of hard sand, level and smooth as a lake, bounded in front by the jungle and to the rear of us by the cliff we had just scaled. I wondered as

I looked across at the forest what scenery began on the other side of the woods and if it broke off in as sharp a change as it did here.

As the most important thing to attend to first was the establishment of a water supply, Chee-Chee was asked to act as guide. The monkey set out ahead of us to follow his own tracks which he had made last night. This he had little difficulty in doing across the open plateau. But when we reached the edge of the forest it was not so easy. Much of his traveling here had been done by swinging through the trees. He always felt safer so, he said, while explaining to us how he had been guided to the water by the sense of smell.

Again I realized how lucky we had been to have him with us. No one but a monkey could have found his way through that dense, dimly lit forest to water. He asked us to stay behind a moment on the edge of the woods while he went forward to make sure that he could retrace his steps. We sat down again and waited.

"Did you wake up at all during the night, Stubbins?" the Doctor asked after a little while.

"No," I said. "I was far too tired. Why?"

"Did you, Polynesia?" he asked, ignoring my question.

"Yes," said she, "I was awake several times."

"Did you hear or see anything—er—unusual?"

"Yes," said she. "I can't be absolutely certain. But I sort of felt there was something moving around the camp keeping a watch on us."

"Humph!" muttered the Doctor. "So did I."

Then he relapsed into silence.

Another rather strange thing that struck me as I gazed over the landscape while we waited for Chee-Chee to return was the

"'Yes,' said she, 'I was awake several times.'"

appearance of the horizon. The moon's width being so much smaller than the earth's, the distance one could see was a great deal shorter. This did not apply so much where the land was hilly or mountainous; but on the level, or the nearly level it made a very striking difference. The *roundness* of this world was much more easily felt and understood than was that of the world we had left. On this plateau, for example, you could only see seven or eight miles, it seemed, over the level before the curve cut off your vision. And it gave quite a new character even to the hills, where peaks showed behind other ranges, dropping downward in a way that misled you entirely as to their actual height.

Finally Chee-Chee came back to us and said he had successfully retraced his steps to the water he had found the night before. He was now prepared to lead us to it. He looked kind of scared and ill at ease. The Doctor asked him the reason for this, but he didn't seem able to give any.

"Everything's all right, Doctor," said he—"at least I suppose it is. It was partly that—oh, I don't know—I can't quite make out what it is they have asked you here for. I haven't actually laid eyes on any animal life since we left the moth who brought us. Yet I feel certain that there's lots of it here. It doesn't appear to want to be seen. That's what puzzles me. On the earth the animals were

HUGH LOFTING

"'You bet they were not!' grumbled Polynesia."

never slow in coming forward when they were in need of your services."

"You bet they were not!" grumbled Polynesia. "No one who ever saw them clamoring around the surgery door could doubt that."

"Humph!" the Doctor muttered. "I've noticed it myself already. I don't understand it quite—either. It almost looks as though there were something about our arrival that they didn't like. . . . I wonder . . . Well, anyway, I wish the animal life here would get in touch with us and let us know what it is all about. This state of things is, to say the least—er—upsetting."

The Moon Lake

AND SO WE WENT FORWARD WITH CHEE-Chee as guide to find the water. Our actual entrance into that jungle was quite an experience and very different from merely a distant view of it. The light outside was not bright; inside the woods it was dimmer still. My only other experience of jungle life had been in Spidermonkey Island. This was something like the Spidermonkey forest and yet it was strikingly different.

From the appearance and size of that first tree we had reached, the Doctor had guessed its age to be very, very great. Here the vegetable life in general seemed to bear out that idea beyond all question. The enormous trees with their gigantic trunks looked as though they had been there since the beginning of time. And there was surprisingly little decay—a few shed limbs and leaves. That was all. In unkept earthly forests one saw dead trees everywhere, fallen to the ground or caught halfway in the crotches of other trees, withered and dry. Not so here.

Every tree looked as though it had stood so and grown in peace for centuries.

At length, after a good deal of arduous travel—the going for the most part was made slow by the heaviest kind of undergrowth, with vines and creepers as thick as your leg—we came to a sort of open place in which lay a broad, calm lake with a pleasant waterfall at one end. The woods that surrounded it were most peculiar. They looked like enormous asparagus. For many, many square miles their tremendous masts rose, close together, in ranks. No creepers or vines had here been given a chance to flourish. The enormous stalks had taken up all the room and the nourishment of the crowded dirt. The tapering tops, hundreds of feet above our heads, looked good enough to eat. Yet I've no doubt that if we had ever gotten up to them they would have been found as hard as oaks.

The Doctor walked down to the clean sandy shore of the lake and tried the water. Chee-Chee and I did the same. It was pure and clear and quenching to the thirst. The lake must have been at least five miles wide in the center.

"I would like," said John Dolittle, "to explore this by boat. Do you suppose, Chee-Chee, that we could find the makings of a canoe or a raft anywhere?"

"I should think so," said the monkey. "Wait a minute and I will take a look around and see."

So, with Chee-Chee in the lead, we proceeded along the shore in search of materials for a boat. On account of that scarcity of dead or dried wood that we had already noticed, our search did not at first appear a very promising one. Nearly all the standing trees were pretty heavy and full of sap. For our work of boat-building a light hatchet on the Doctor's belt was the best tool we had. It looked sadly small compared with the great timber that reared up from the shores of the lake.

But after we had gone along about a mile I noticed Chee-Chee up ahead stop and peer into the jungle. Then, after he had motioned to us with his hand to hurry, he disappeared into the edge of the forest. On coming up with him we found him stripping the creepers and moss off some contrivance that lay just within the woods, not more than a hundred yards from the water's edge.

We all fell to, helping him, without any idea of what it might be we were uncovering. There seemed almost no end to it. It was a long object, immeasurably long. To me it looked like a dead tree—the first dead, lying tree we had seen.

"What do you think it is, Chee-Chee?" asked the Doctor.

"It's a boat," said the monkey in a firm and matter-of-fact voice. "No doubt of it at all in my mind. It's a dug-out canoe. They used to use them in Africa."

"But, Chee-Chee," cried John Dolittle, "look at the length! It's a full-sized Asparagus Tree. We've uncovered a hundred feet of it already and still there's more to come."

"I can't help that," said Chee-Chee. "It's a dug-out canoe just the same. Crawl down with me here underneath it, Doctor, and I'll show you the marks of tools and fire. It has been turned upside down."

With the monkey guiding him, the Doctor scrabbled down below the strange object; and when he came forth there was a puzzled look on his face.

"Well, they *might* be the marks of tools, Chee-Chee," he was saying. "But then again they might not. The traces of fire are more clear. But that could be accidental. If the tree burned down it could very easily—"

"The humans in my part of Africa," Chee-Chee interrupted, "always used fire to eat out the insides of their dug-out canoes. They built little fires all along the tree, to hollow out the trunk so that they could sit in it. The tools they used were very simple, just stone scoops to chop out the charred wood with. I am sure this is a canoe, Doctor. But it hasn't been used in a long time. See how the bow has been shaped up into a point."

"I know," said the Doctor. "But the Asparagus Tree has a natural point at one end anyhow."

"And, Chee-Chee," put in Polynesia, "who in the name of goodness could ever handle such a craft? Why, look, the thing is as long as a battleship!"

Then followed a half-hour's discussion, between the Doctor and Polynesia on the one side and Chee-Chee on the other, as to whether the find we had made was, or was not, a canoe. For me, I had no opinion. To my eyes the object looked like an immensely long log, hollowed somewhat on the one side, but whether by accident or design I could not tell.

In any case, it was certainly too heavy and cumbersome for us to use. And presently I edged into the argument with the suggestion that we go on farther and find materials for a raft or boat we *could* handle.

The Doctor seemed rather glad of this excuse to end a fruitless controversy, and soon we moved on in search of something which would enable us to explore the waters of the lake. A march of a mile farther along the shore brought us to woods that were not so heavy. Here the immense asparagus forests gave way to a growth of smaller girth; and the Doctor's hatchet soon felled enough poles for us to make a raft from. We laced them together with thongs of bark and found them sufficiently buoyant when launched to carry us and our small supply of baggage with ease. Where the water was shallow we used a long pole to punt with; and when we wished to explore greater depths we employed sweeps, or oars, which we fashioned roughly with the hatchet.

From the first moment we were afloat the Doctor kept me busy taking notes for him. In the equipment he had brought with him there was a fine-meshed landing net; and with it he searched along the shores for signs of life in this moon lake, the first of its kind we had met with.

"We used a long pole to punt with."

"It is very important, Stubbins," said he, "to find out what fish we have here. In evolution the fish life is a very important matter."

"What is *evolution*?" asked Chee-Chee.

I started to explain it to him but was soon called upon by the Doctor to make more notes—for which I was not sorry, as the task turned out to be a long and heavy one. Polynesia, however, took it up where I left off and made short work of it.

"Evolution, Chee-Chee," said she, "is the story of how Tommy got rid of the tail you are carrying—because he didn't need it anymore—and the story of how you grew it and kept it because you *did* need it. . . . *Evolution!* Proof!—Professors' talk. A long word for a simple matter."

It turned out that our examination of the lake was neither exciting nor profitable. We brought up all sorts of water flies, many larvae of perfectly tremendous size, but we found as yet no fishes. The plant life—water plant, I mean—was abundant.

"I think," said the Doctor, after we had poled ourselves around the lake for several hours, "that there can be no doubt now that the vegetable kingdom here is much more important than the animal kingdom. And what there is of the animal kingdom seems to be mostly insect. However, we will camp on the shore of this pleasant lake and perhaps we shall see more later."

So we brought our raft to anchor at about the place from which we had started out and pitched camp on a stretch of clean yellow sand.

I shall never forget that night. It was uncanny. None of us slept well. All through the hours of darkness we heard things moving around us. Enormous things. Yet never did we see them or find out what they were. The four of us were nevertheless certain that all night we were being watched. Even Polynesia was disturbed.

There seemed no doubt that there was plenty of animal life in the moon, but that it did not as yet want to show itself to us. The newness of our surroundings alone was disturbing enough, without this very uncomfortable feeling that something had made the moon folks distrustful of us.

Tracks of a Giant

NOTHER THING WHICH ADDED TO OUR sleeplessness that night was the continuance of the mysterious music. But then so many strange things contributed to our general mystification and vague feeling of anxiety that it is hard to remember and distinguish them all.

The next morning, after breakfasting on what remained of our fruit, we packed up and started off for further exploration. While the last of the packing had been in progress, Chee-Chee and Polynesia had gone ahead to do a little advanced scouting for us. They formed an admirable team for such work. Polynesia would fly above the forest and get long-distance impressions from the air of what lay ahead while Chee-Chee would examine the more lowly levels of the route to be followed, from the trees and the ground.

The Doctor and I were just helping each other on with our packs when Chee-Chee came rushing back to us in great excitement. His teeth were chattering so he could hardly speak.

"What do you think, Doctor!" he stammered. "We've found tracks back there. Tracks of a man! But so enormous! You've no idea. Come quick and I'll show you."

The Doctor looked up sharply at the scared and excited monkey, pausing a moment as though about to question him. Then he seemed to change his mind and turned once more to the business of taking up the baggage. With loads hoisted, we gave a last glance around the camping ground to see if anything had been forgotten or left.

Our route did not lie directly across the lake, which mostly sprawled away to the right of our line of march. But we had to make

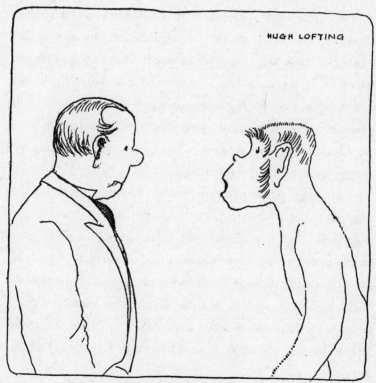

HUGH LOFTING

"'What do you think, Doctor?' he stammered."

our way partly around the lower end of it. Wondering what new chapter lay ahead of us, we fell in behind Chee-Chee and in silence started off along the shore.

After about half an hour's march we came to the mouth of a river that ran into the upper end of the lake. Along the margin of this we followed Chee-Chee for what seemed like another mile or so. Soon the shores of the stream widened out and the woods fell back quite a distance from the water's edge. The nature of the ground was still clean firm sand. Presently we saw Polynesia's tiny figure ahead, waiting for us.

When we drew up with her we saw that she was standing by an enormous footprint. There was no doubt about its being a human's, clear in every detail. It was the most gigantic thing I have ever seen, a barefoot track fully four yards in length. There wasn't only one, either. Down the shore the trail went on for a considerable distance; and the span that the prints lay apart gave one some idea of the enormous stride of the giant who had left this trail behind him.

Questioning and alarmed, Chee-Chee and Polynesia gazed silently up at the Doctor for an explanation.

"Humph!" he muttered after a while. "So man is here, too. My goodness, what a monster! Let us follow the trail."

Chee-Chee was undoubtedly scared of such a plan. It was clearly both his and Polynesia's idea that the farther we got away from the maker of those tracks the better. I could see terror and fright in the eyes of both of them. But neither made any objection; and in silence we plodded along, following in the path of this strange human who must, it would seem, be something out of a fairy tale.

But alas! It was not more than a mile farther on that the foot-

"An enormous footprint"

prints turned into the woods where, on the mosses and leaves beneath the trees, no traces had been left at all. Then we turned about and followed the river quite a distance to see if the creature had come back out on the sands again. But never a sign could we see. Chee-Chee spent a good deal of time, too, at the Doctor's request trying to find his path through the forest by any signs, such as broken limbs or marks in the dirt which he might have left behind. But not another trace could we find. Deciding that he had merely come down to the stream to get a drink, we gave up the pursuit and turned back to the line of our original march.

Again I was thankful that I had company on that expedition.

It was certainly a most curious and extraordinary experience. None of us spoke very much, but when we did it seemed that all of us had been thinking the same things.

The woods grew more and more mysterious, and more and more *alive*, as we went onward toward the other side of the moon, the side that earthly man had never seen before. For one thing, the strange music seemed to increase; and for another, there was more movement in the limbs of the trees. Great branches that looked like arms, bunches of small twigs that could have been hands, swung and moved and clawed the air in the most uncanny fashion. And always that steady wind went on blowing—even, regular, and smooth.

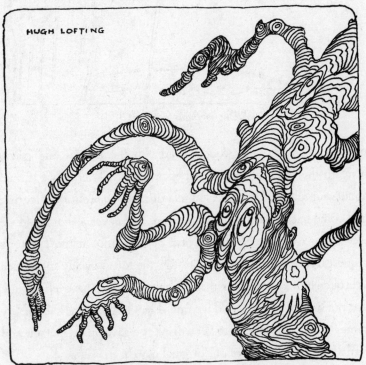

HUGH LOFTING

"There was more movement in the limbs of the trees."

All of the forest was not gloomy, however. Much of it was unbelievably beautiful. Acres of woods there were, which presented nothing but a gigantic sea of many-colored blossoms, colors that seemed like something out of a dream, indescribable, yet clear in one's memory as a definite picture of something seen.

The Doctor as we went forward spoke very little; when he did it was almost always on the same subject: "the absence of decay," as he put it.

"I am utterly puzzled, Stubbins," said he, in one of his longer outbursts when we were resting. "Why, there is hardly any leaf-mold at all!"

"What difference would that make, Doctor?" I asked.

"Well, that's what the trees live on, mostly, in our world," said he. "The forest growth, I mean—the soil that is formed by dying trees and rotting leaves—that is the nourishment that brings forth the seedlings which finally grow into new trees. But here! Well, of course there is *some* soil—and some shedding of leaves. But I've hardly seen a dead tree since I've been in these woods. One would almost think that there were some—er—balance. Some *arrangement* of—er—well—I can't explain it. . . . It beats me entirely."

I did not, at the time, completely understand what he meant. And yet it did seem as though every one of these giant plants that rose about us led a life of peaceful growth, undisturbed by rot, by blight, or by disease.

Suddenly in our march we found ourselves at the end of the wooded section. Hills and mountains again spread before us. They were not the same as those we had first seen, however. These had vegetation, of a kind, on them. Low shrubs and heath plants clothed this rolling land with a dense growth—often very difficult to get through.

But still no sign of decay—little or no leaf-mold. The Doctor now decided that perhaps part of the reason for this was the seasons—or rather the lack of seasons. He said that we would probably find that here there was no regular winter or summer. It was an entirely new problem, so far as the struggle for existence was concerned, such as we knew in our world.

The Singing Trees

INTO THIS NEW HEATH AND HILL COUNTRY WE traveled for miles. And presently we arrived upon a rather curious thing. It was a sort of basin high up and enclosed by hills or knolls. The strange part of it was that here there were not only more tracks of the Giant Man, just as we had seen lower down, but there were also unmistakable signs of *fire*. In an enormous hollow, ashes lay among the sands. The Doctor was very interested in those ashes. He took some and added chemicals to them and tested them in many ways. He confessed himself at last entirely puzzled by their nature. But he said he nevertheless felt quite sure we had stumbled on the scene of the smoke signaling we had seen from Puddleby. Curiously long ago, it seemed, that time when Too-Too the owl had insisted he saw smoke burst from the side of the moon. That was when the giant moth lay helpless in our garden. And yet—how long was it? Only a few days!

"It was from here, Stubbins," said the Doctor, "that the signals we saw from the earth were given out, I feel certain. This place, as

HUGH LOFTING

"It was sort of a basin."

you see, is miles and miles across. But what was used to make an explosion as large as the one we saw from my house I have no idea."

"But it was smoke we saw," said I, "not a flash."

"That's just it," he said. "Some curious material must have been used that we have as yet no knowledge of. I thought that by testing the ashes I could discover what it was. But I can't. However, we may yet find out."

For two reasons the Doctor was anxious for the present not to get too far from the forest section. (We did not know then, you see, that there were other wooded areas beside this through which we had just come.) One reason was that we had to keep in touch with our food supply, which consisted of the fruits and vegetables of the jungle. The other was that John Dolittle was absorbed now in the study of this vegetable kingdom, which he felt sure had many surprises in store for the student naturalist.

After a while we began to get over the feeling of uncanny creepiness, which at the beginning had made us so uncomfortable. We decided that our fears were mostly caused by the fact that these woods and plants were so different from our own. There was no unfriendliness in these forests after all, we assured ourselves—except that we *were* being watched. That we knew—and that we were beginning to get used to.

As soon as the Doctor had decided that we would set up our new headquarters on the edge of the forest, and we had our camp properly established, we began making excursions in all directions through the jungle. And from then on I was again kept very busy taking notes of the Doctor's experiments and studies.

One of the first discoveries we made in our study of the moon's vegetable kingdom was that there was practically no warfare going on between it and the animal kingdom. In the world we had left, we had been accustomed to see the horses and other creatures eating up the grass in great quantities and many further examples of the struggle that continually goes on between the two. Here, on the other hand, the animals (or, more strictly speaking, the insects, for there seemed as yet hardly any traces of other animal species) and the vegetable life seemed for the most part to help one another rather than to fight and destroy. Indeed, we found the whole system of life on the moon a singularly peaceful business. I will speak of this again later on.

We spent three whole days in the investigation of the strange music we had heard. You will remember that the Doctor, with his skill on the flute, was naturally fond of music; and this curious thing we had met with interested him a great deal. After several expeditions we found patches of the jungle where we were able to see and hear the tree music working at its best.

There was no doubt about it at all: the trees were making the sounds and they were doing it *deliberately*. In the way that an Aeolian harp works when set in the wind at the right angle, the trees moved their branches to meet the wind so that certain notes would be given out. The evening that the Doctor made this discovery of what he called the *Singing Trees,* he told me to mark down in the diary of the expedition as a Red Letter Date. I shall never forget it. We had been following the sound for hours, the Doctor carrying a tuning fork in his hand, ringing it every once in a while to make sure of the notes we heard around us. Suddenly we came upon a little clearing about which great giants of the forest stood in a circle. It was for all the world like an orchestra. Spellbound, we stood and gazed up at them, as first one and then another would turn a branch to the steady blowing wind and a note would boom out upon the night, clear and sweet. Then a group, three or four trees around the glade, would swing a limb and a chord would strike the air and go murmuring through the jungle. Fantastic and crazy as it sounds, no one who heard and watched could have any doubt that these trees were actually making sounds, which they *wanted to make*, with the aid of the wind.

Of course, as the Doctor remarked, unless the wind had always blown steadily and evenly, such a thing would have been impossible. John Dolittle himself was most anxious to find out on what scale of music they were working. To me, I must confess, it sounded just

"Spellbound we gazed up at them."

mildly pleasant. There *was* a time: I could hear that. And some whole phrases repeated once in a while, but not often. For the most part the melody was wild, sad, and strange. But even to my uneducated ear it was beyond all question a quite clear effort at orchestration; there were certainly treble voices and bass voices and the combination was sweet and agreeable.

I was excited enough myself, but the Doctor was worked up to a pitch of interest such as I have seldom seen in him.

"Why, Stubbins," said he, "do you realize what this means?— It's terrific. If these trees can sing, a choir understands one another and all that, *they must have a language.* They can talk! A language in the vegetable kingdom! We must get after it. Who knows? I may yet learn it myself. Stubbins, this is a great day!"

And so, as usual on such occasions, the good man's enthusiasm just carried him away bodily. For days, often without food, often without sleep, he pursued this new study. And at his heels I trotted with my notebook always ready—though, to be sure, he put in far more work than I did, because frequently when we got home he would go on wrestling for hours over the notes or new apparatus he was building, by which he hoped to learn the language of the trees.

You will remember that even before we left the earth, John Dolittle had mentioned the possibility of the Moon Bells having

HUGH LOFTING

"For quite a long while he sat watching certain shrubs."

some means of communicating with one another. That they could move, within the limits of their fixed position, had been fully established. To that we had grown so used and accustomed that we no longer thought anything of it. The Doctor had in fact wondered if this might possibly be a means of conversation in itself—the movement of limbs and twigs and leaves, something like a flag signal code. And for quite a long while he sat watching certain trees and shrubs to see if they used this method for talking between themselves.

The Study of Plant Languages

BOUT THIS TIME THERE WAS ONE PERSON whom both the Doctor and I were continually reminded of, and continually wishing for, and that was Long Arrow, the famed naturalist whom we had met in Spidermonkey Island. To be sure, he had never admitted to the Doctor that he had had speech with plant life. But his knowledge of botany and the natural history of the vegetable kingdom was of such a curious kind we felt that here he would have been of great help to us. Long Arrow, the son of Golden Arrow, could tell you why a certain colored bee visited a certain colored flower; why *that* moth chose *that* shrub to lay its eggs in; why this particular grub attacked the roots of this kind of water plant.

Often in the evenings the Doctor and I would speak of him, wondering where he was and what he was doing. When we sailed away from Spidermonkey Island he was left behind. But that would not mean he stayed there. A natural-born traveler who rejoiced in defying the elements and the so-called laws of nature, he could be looked for anywhere in the two American continents.

And again, the Doctor would often refer to my parents. He evidently had a very guilty feeling about them—despite the fact that it was no fault of his that I had stowed away aboard the moth that brought us here. A million and one things filled his mind these days, of course; but whenever there was a letdown, a gap, in the stream of his scientific inquiry, he would come back to the subject.

"Stubbins," he'd say, "you shouldn't have come. . . . Yes, yes, I know, you did it for me. But Jacob, your father—and your mother too—they must be fretting themselves sick about your disappearance. And I am responsible. . . . Well, we can't do anything about that now, I suppose. Let's get on with the work."

And then he'd plunge ahead into some new subject and the matter would be dropped—till it bothered him again.

Throughout all our investigations of the moon's vegetable kingdom we could not get away from the idea that the animal life was still, for some unknown reason, steering clear of us. By night, when we were settling down to sleep, we'd often get the impression that huge moths, butterflies, or beetles were flying or crawling near us.

We made quite sure of this once or twice by jumping out of our beds and seeing a giant shadow disappear into the gloom. Yet never could we get near enough to distinguish what the creatures were before they escaped beyond the range of sight. But that they had come—whatever they were—to keep an eye on us seemed quite certain. Also that all of them were winged. The Doctor had a theory that the lighter gravity of the moon had encouraged the development of wings to a much greater extent than it had on the earth.

HUGH LOFTING

"Seeing a giant shadow disappear into the gloom"

And again those tracks of the strange Giant Man. They were always turning up in the most unexpected places; I believe that if the Doctor had allowed Polynesia and Chee-Chee complete liberty to follow them, that the enormous human would have been run down in a very short time. But John Dolittle seemed still anxious to keep his family together. I imagine that with his curiously good instinctive judgment he feared an attempt to separate us. And in any case of course both Chee-Chee and Polynesia were quite invaluable in a tight place. They were neither of them heavyweight fighters, it is true; but their usefulness as scouts and guides was enormous. I have often heard John Dolittle say that he would sooner have that monkey or the parrot Polynesia with him in savage countries than he would the escort of a dozen regiments.

With some of our experimental work we wandered off long distances into the heath lands to see what we could do with the gorgeous flowering shrubs that thronged the rolling downs; and often we followed the streams many miles to study the gigantic lilies that swayed their stately heads over the sedgy banks.

And little by little our very arduous labors began to be repaid.

I was quite astonished when I came to realize how well the Doctor had prepared for this expedition. Shortly after he decided that he would set to work on the investigation of this supposed language of the plants, he told me we would have to go back and fetch the remainder of our baggage, which we had left at the point of our first arrival.

So the following morning, bright and early, he, Chee-Chee, and I set out to retrace our steps. Polynesia was left behind. The Doctor told none of us why he did this, but we decided afterward that, as usual, he knew what he was doing.

It was a long and hard trip. It took us a day and a half going there and two days coming back with the load of baggage. At our original landing-place we again found many tracks of the Giant Human, and other strange marks on the sands about our baggage-dump, which told us that here, too, curious eyes had been trying to find out things without being seen.

A closer examination of the tracks made by the Giant Human in these parts where they were especially clear told the Doctor that his right leg stride was considerably longer than his left. The mysterious Moon Man evidently walked with a limp. But with such a stride, he would clearly be a very formidable creature anyway.

When we got back and started unpacking the bundles and boxes that had been left behind, I saw, as I have already said, how well the Doctor had prepared for his voyage. He seemed to have brought everything that he could possibly need for the trip: hatchets, wire, nails, files, a handsaw, all the things we couldn't get on the moon. It was so different from his ordinary preparations for a voyage—which hardly ever consisted of more than the little black bag and the clothes he stood in.

"He seemed to have brought everything he could need."

As usual he rested only long enough to get a few mouthfuls of food before he set to work. There seemed to be a dozen different apparatuses he wanted to set up at once, some for the testing of sound, others for vibrations, etc., etc. With the aid of a saw and an ax and a few other tools, half a dozen small huts had sprung up in an hour around our camp.

The Magellan of the Moon

LAYING ASIDE FOR THE PRESENT ALL WORRY on the score of why he had been summoned to the moon—of why the animal kingdom continued to treat us with suspicion, of why the Giant Human so carefully kept out of our way, the Doctor now plunged into the study of plant languages heart and soul.

He was always happy so, working like a demon, snatching his meals and his sleep here and there when he thought of such earthly matters. It was a most exhausting time for the rest of us, keeping pace with this firebrand of energy when he got on an interesting scent. And yet it was well worthwhile too. In one and a half days he had established the fact that the trees *did* converse with one another by means of branch gestures. But that was only the first step. Copying and practicing, he rigged himself up like a tree and talked in the glade—after a fashion—with these centuries-old denizens of the jungle.

From that he learned still more—that language, of a kind, was carried on by using other means—by scents given out, in a definite way—short or long perfumes, like a regular Morse code; by the tones of wind-song when branches were set to the right angle to produce certain notes; and many other odd strange means.

Every night, by bedtime, I was nearly dead from the strain and effort of taking notes in those everlasting books, of which he seemed to have brought an utterly inexhaustible supply.

Chee-Chee looked after the feeding of us—Thank goodness!—or I fear we would easily have starved to death, if overwork itself hadn't killed us. Every three hours the faithful little monkey would

*"The faithful monkey would come to us every three hours
with his strange vegetables."*

come to us wherever we were at the moment with his messes of strange vegetables and fruits and a supply of good clean drinking water.

As official recorder of the expedition (a job of which I was very proud even if it was hard work), I had to book all the Doctor's calculations as well as his natural history notes. I have already told you something of temperature, air pressure, time, and whatnot. A further list of them would have included the calculation of distance traveled. This was quite difficult. The Doctor had brought with him a pedometer (that is a little instrument which, when carried in the pocket, tells you from the number of strides made the miles walked). But in the moon, with the changed gravity, a pace was quite different from that usual on the earth. And what is more, it never stayed the same. When the ground sloped downward it was natural to spring a step that quite possibly measured six or seven feet—this with no out-of-the-way effort at all. And even on the up grade one quite frequently used a stride that was far greater than in ordinary walking.

It was about this time that the Doctor first spoke of making a tour of the moon. Magellan, you will remember, was the first to sail around our world. And it was a very great feat. The earth contains more water area than land. The moon, on the contrary, we soon saw, had more dry land than water. There were no big oceans. Lakes and chains of lakes were all the water area we saw. To complete a round trip of this world would therefore be harder, even though it was shorter, than the voyage that Magellan made.

It was on this account that the Doctor was so particular about my booking a strict record of the miles we traveled. As to direction, we had not as yet been so careful about maintaining a perfectly

HUGH LOFTING

"It was natural to spring a step that measured six or seven feet."

straight line. Because it was by no means easy, for one thing; and for another, the subjects we wished to study, such as tree music, tracks, water supply, rock formation, etc., often led us off toward every quarter of the compass. When I say the *compass,* I mean something a little different from the use of that word in earthly geography. As I have told you, the magnetic compass that John Dolittle had brought with him from Puddleby did not behave in a helpful manner at all. Something else must be found to take its place.

John Dolittle, as usual, went after that problem, too, with much energy. He was a very excellent mathematician, was the Doctor. And one afternoon he sat down with a notebook and the Nautical

Almanac and worked out tables that should tell him from the stars where he was and in what direction he was going. It was curious, that strange sense of comfort we drew from the stars. They, the heavenly bodies that from the earth seemed the remotest, most distant, unattainable, and strangest of objects, here suddenly became friendly; because, I suppose, they were the only things that really stayed the same. The stars, as we saw them from the moon, were precisely as the stars we had seen from the earth. The fact that they were nearly all countless billions of miles away made no difference. For us they were something that we had seen before and knew.

It was while we were at work on devising some contrivance to

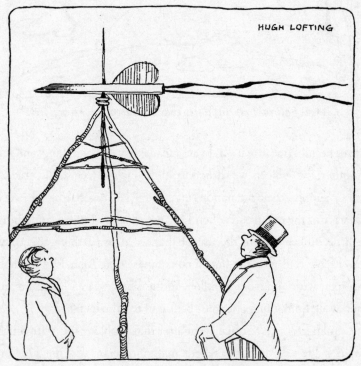

"We rigged up weather vanes."

take the place of the compass that we made the discovery of the explosive wood. The Doctor, after trying many things by which he hoped to keep a definite direction, had suddenly said one day:

"Why, Stubbins, I have it. The wind! It always blows steady—and probably from precisely the same quarter—or at all events with a regular calculable change most likely. Let us test it and see."

So right away we set to work to make various wind-testing devices. We rigged up weather vanes from long streamers of light bark. And then John Dolittle hit upon the idea of smoke.

"That is something," said he, "if we only place it properly, which will warn us by smell if the wind changes. And in the meantime we can carry on our studies of the animal kingdom and its languages."

So without further ado we set to work to build fires—or rather large smoke smudges—which would tell us how reliable our wind would be if depended on for a source of direction.

We Prepare to Circle the Moon

WE WENT TO A LOT OF TROUBLE WORKing out how we could best place these fires so that they should give us the most satisfactory results. First of all we decided with much care on the exact position where we would build them. Mostly they were on bare knolls or shoulders, where they couldn't spread to the underbrush and start a bushfire. Then came the question of fuel: What would be the best wood to build them of?

There were practically no dead trees, as I have said. The only thing to do then was to cut some timber down and let it dry.

This we proceeded to do but did not get very far with it before the Doctor suddenly had qualms of conscience. Trees that could talk could, one would suppose, also *feel*. The thought was dreadful. We hadn't even the courage to ask the trees about it—yet. So we fell back upon gathering fallen twigs and small branches. This made the work heavier still because, of course, we

HUGH LOFTING

"Mostly they were on bare knolls."

needed a great deal of fuel to have fires big enough to see and smell for any distance.

After a good deal of discussion we decided that this was a thing that couldn't be hurried. A great deal depended on its success. It was a nuisance, truly, but we had to be patient. So we went back into the jungle lands and set to work on getting out various samples of woods to try.

It took a longish time, for the Doctor and myself were the only ones who could do this work. Chee-Chee tried to help by gathering twigs; but the material we most needed was wood large enough to last a fair time.

Well, we harvested several different kinds. Some wouldn't burn at all when we tried them. Others, we found, were pretty fair burners, but not smoky enough.

With about the fifth kind of wood, I think it was that we tested out, we nearly had a serious accident. Fire seemed to be (outside of the traces we had found of the smoke signal apparatus) a thing quite unusual in the moon. There were no traces of forest burnings anywhere, so far as we had explored. It was therefore with a good deal of fear and caution that we struck matches to test out our fuel.

About dusk one evening the Doctor set a match to a sort of fern wood (something like a bamboo) and he narrowly escaped a bad burning. The stuff flared up like gunpowder.

Chee-Chee and I examined him. We found he had suffered no serious injuries, though he had had a very close shave. His hands were somewhat blistered and he told us what to get out of the little black bag to relieve the inflammation.

We had all noticed that as the wood flared up it sent off dense masses of white smoke. And for hours after the explosion, clouds of heavy fumes were still rolling round the hills near us.

When we had the Doctor patched up he told us he was sure that we had stumbled by accident on the fuel that had been used for making the smoke signals we had seen from Puddleby.

"But my goodness, Doctor," said I, "what an immense bonfire it must have been to be visible all that distance! Thousands of tons of the stuff, surely, must have been piled together to make a smudge that could be seen that far."

"And who could have made it?" put in Chee-Chee.

For a moment there was silence. Then Polynesia spoke the thought that was in my mind—and I imagine in the Doctor's, too.

"The man who made those torches," she said quietly, "could move an awful lot of timber in one day, I'll warrant."

"You mean you think it was *he* who sent the signals?" asked Chee-Chee, his funny little eyes staring wide open with astonishment.

"Why not?" said Polynesia. Then she lapsed into silent contemplation and no further questioning from Chee-Chee could get a word out of her.

"Well," said the monkey at last, "if he *did* send it, that would look as though he were responsible for the whole thing. It must have been he who sent the moth down to us—who needed the Doctor's assistance and presence here."

HUGH LOFTING

"You mean you think it was he who sent the signals?"

He looked toward John Dolittle for an answer to this suggestion. But the Doctor, like Polynesia, didn't seem to have anything to say.

Well, in spite of our little mishap, our wood tests with smoke were extremely successful. We found that the wind as a direction-pointer could certainly be relied on for three or four days at a time.

"Of course, Stubbins," said the Doctor, "we will have to test again before we set off on our round trip. It may be that the breeze, while blowing in one prevailing direction now, may change after a week or so. Also we will have to watch it that the mountain ranges don't deflect the wind's course and so lead us astray. But from what we have seen so far, I feel pretty sure that we have here something to take the place of the compass."

I made one or two attempts later, when Polynesia and Chee-Chee were out of earshot, to discover what John Dolittle thought about this idea that it had really been the Moon Man who had brought us here and not the animal kingdom. I felt that possibly he might talk more freely to me alone on the subject than he had been willing to with all of us listening. But he was strangely untalkative.

"I don't know, Stubbins," said he, frowning, "I really don't know. To tell the truth, my mind is not occupied with that problem now—at all events, not as a matter for immediate decision. This field of the lunar vegetable kingdom is something that could take up the attention of a hundred naturalists for a year or two. I feel we have only scratched the surface. As we go forward into the unknown areas of the moon's farther side, we are liable to make discoveries of—well, er—who can tell? When the Moon Man and the animal kingdom make up their minds that they want to get in touch with us, I suppose we shall hear from them. In the meantime we have our work to do—more than we can do.... Gracious, I wish I had a whole staff with me!—surveyors, cartographers, geologists, and the rest. Think of it! Here we are, messing our way along across a new world—and we don't even know where we are! I think I have a vague idea of the line we have followed. And I've tried to keep a sort of chart of our march. But I should be making maps, Stubbins, real maps, showing all the peaks, valleys, streams, lakes, plateaus, and everything. Dear, dear! Well, we must do the best we can."

"'I don't know, Stubbins,' said he, frowning."

THE TWELFTH CHAPTER

The Vanity Lilies

O F COURSE, ON A GLOBE LARGER THAN THAT
of the moon, we could never have done as well as we
did. When you come to think of it, one man, a boy, a
monkey and a parrot, as a staff for the exploration of a
whole world, makes the expedition sound, to say the least, absurd.

We did not realize, any of us, when we started out from our first
landing that we were going to make a circular trip of the moon's
globe. It just worked out that way. To begin with, we were expecting
every hour that some part of the animal kingdom would come forward into the open. But it didn't. And still we went on. Then this
language of the trees and flowers came up and got the Doctor going
on one of his fever-heat investigations. That carried us still farther.
We always took great care when departing from one district for
an excursion of any length to leave landmarks behind us, camps or
dumps, so that we could find our way back to food and shelter if we
should get caught in a tight place.

In this sort of feeling our way forward Polynesia was most

"We always took care to leave landmarks behind us."

helpful. The Doctor used to let her off regularly now to fly ahead of us and bring back reports. That gave us some sort of idea of what we should prepare for. Then in addition to that, the Doctor had brought with him several small pocket surveying instruments with which he marked on his chart roughly the points at which we changed course to any considerable extent.

In the earlier stages of our trip we had felt we must keep in touch with the first fruit section we had met with, in order to have a supply of vegetables and fruits to rely on for food. But we soon discovered from Polynesia's scouting reports, that other wooded sections lay ahead of us. To these we sent Chee-Chee, the expert, to investigate. And when he returned and told us that they contained even a better diet than those farther back, we had no hesitation in leaving her old haunts and venturing still farther into the mysteries of the moon's farther side.

The Doctor's progress with the language of the trees and plants seemed to improve with our penetration into the interior. Many times we stopped and pitched camp for four or five days, while he set up some new apparatus and struggled with fresh problems in plant language. It seemed to grow easier and easier for him all the time. Certainly the plant life became more elaborate and lively. By this time we were all grown more accustomed to strange things in the vegetable kingdom. And even to my unscientific eyes it was quite evident that here the flowers and bushes were communicating with one another with great freedom and in many different ways.

I shall never forget our first meeting with the Vanity Lilies, as the Doctor later came to call them. Great gaudy blooms they were, on long slender stems that swayed and moved in groups like people whispering and gossiping at a party. When we came in sight of them for the first time, they were more or less motionless. But as we approached, the movement among them increased as though they were disturbed by, or interested in, our coming.

I think they were beyond all question the most beautiful flowers I have ever seen. The wind, regular as ever, had not changed. But the heads of these great masses of plants got so agitated as we drew near, that the Doctor decided he would halt the expedition and investigate,

We pitched camp as we called it—a very simple business in the moon, because we did not have to raise tents or build a fire. It was

"Certainly the plant life became more elaborate and lively."

really only a matter of unpacking, getting out the food to eat and the bedding to sleep in.

We were pretty weary after a full day's march. Beyond the lily beds (which lay in a sort of marsh) we could see a new jungle district with more strange trees and flowering creepers.

After a short and silent supper, we lay down and pulled the covers over us. The music of the forest grew louder as darkness increased. It seemed almost as though the whole vegetable world was remarking on these visitors who had invaded their home.

And then above the music of the woods we'd hear the drone of flying, while we dropped off to sleep. Some of the giant insects were hovering near, as usual, to keep an eye on these creatures from another world.

I think that of all our experiences with the plant life of the moon, that with the Vanity Lilies was perhaps the most peculiar and the most thrilling. In about two days the Doctor had made extraordinary strides in his study of this language. That, he explained to me, was due more to the unusual intelligence of this species and its willingness to help than to his own efforts. But of course if he had not already done considerable work with the trees and bushes, it is doubtful if the lilies could have gotten in touch with him as quickly as they did.

By the end of the third day Chee-Chee, Polynesia, and I were all astonished to find that John Dolittle was actually able to carry on conversation with these flowers. And this with the aid of very little apparatus. He had now discovered that the Vanity Lilies spoke among themselves largely by the movement of their blossoms. They used different means of communication with species of plants and trees other than their own—and also (we heard later) in talking with birds and insects; but among themselves the swaying of the flower heads was the common method of speech.

The lilies, when seen in great banks, presented a very gorgeous and wonderful appearance. The flowers would be, I should judge, about eighteen inches across, trumpet-shaped and brilliantly colored. The background was a soft cream tone and on this great blotches of violet and orange were grouped around a jet-black tongue in the center. The leaves were a deep olive green.

But it was that extraordinary look of alive intelligence that was the most uncanny thing about them. No one, no matter how little he knew of natural history in general or of the moon's vegetable

HUGH LOFTING

"The flowers would be about eighteen inches across."

kingdom, could see those wonderful flowers without immediately being arrested by this peculiar character. You felt at once that you were in the presence of people rather than plants; and to talk with them, or to try to, seemed the most natural thing in the world.

I filled up two of those numerous notebooks of the Doctor's on his conversations with the Vanity Lilies. Often he came back to these flowers later, when he wanted further information about the moon's vegetable kingdom. For as he explained to us, it was in this species that plant life—so far as it was known on either the moon or the earth—had reached its highest point of development.

THE THIRTEENTH CHAPTER

The Flower of Many Scents

ANOTHER PECULIAR THING THAT BAFFLED US completely, when we first came into the marshy regions of the Vanity Lily's home, was the variety of scents that assailed our noses. For a mile or so around the locality there was no other flower visible; the whole of the marsh seemed to have been taken up by the lilies and nothing else intruded on their domain. Yet at least half a dozen perfumes were distinct and clear. At first we thought that perhaps the wind might be bringing us scents from other plants either in the jungle or the flowering heath lands. But the direction of the breeze was such that it could only come over the sandy desert areas and was not likely to bring perfumes as strong as this.

It was the Doctor who first hit upon the idea that possibly the lily could give off more than one scent at will. He set to work to find out right away. And it took no more than a couple of minutes to convince him that it could. He said he was sorry he did not have Jip with him. Jip's expert sense of smell would have been very useful here. But for ordinary purposes it required nothing more delicate than an average human's nose to tell that this flower, when John Dolittle had communicated the idea to it, was clearly able to give out at least half a dozen different smells as it wished.

The majority of these perfumes were extremely agreeable. But there were one or two that nearly knocked you down. It was only after the Doctor had asked the lilies about this gift of theirs that they sent forth obnoxious ones in demonstrating all the scents that they could give out. Chee-Chee just fainted away at the first sample. It was like some deadly gas. It got into your eyes and made them run. The Doctor and I only escaped suffocation by flight—carrying the body of the unconscious monkey along with us.

The Vanity Lilies, seeing what distress they had caused,

"Chee-Chee just fainted away at the first sample."

immediately threw out the most soothing, lovely scent I have ever smelled. Clearly they were anxious to please us and cultivate our acquaintance. Indeed, it turned out later from their conversation with the Doctor (which I took down word for word) that in spite of being a stationary part of the moon's landscape, they had heard of John Dolittle, the great naturalist, and had been watching for his arrival many days. They were in fact the first creatures in our experience of the moon that made us feel we were among friends.

I think I could not do better, in trying to give you an idea of the Doctor's communication with the vegetable kingdom of the moon, than to set down from my diary, word for word, some parts of the conversation between him and the Vanity Lilies as he translated them to me for dictation at the time. Even so, there are many, I am sure, who will doubt the truth of the whole idea: that a man could talk with the flowers. But with them I am not so concerned. Anyone who had followed John Dolittle through the various stages of animal, fish, and insect languages would not, I feel certain, find it very strange, when the great man did at last come in touch with plant life of unusual intelligence, that he should be able to converse with it.

On looking over my diary of those eventful days, the scene of that occasion comes up visibly before my eyes. It was about an hour before dusk—that is the slight dimming of the pale daylight which proceeded a half darkness, the nearest thing to real night we ever saw on the moon. The Doctor, as we left the camp, called back over his shoulder to me to bring an extra notebook along, as he expected to make a good deal of progress tonight. I armed myself, therefore, with three extra books and followed him out.

Halting about twenty paces in front of the lily beds (we had camped back several hundred yards from them after they had nearly suffocated Chee-Chee), the Doctor squatted on the ground and began swaying his head from side to side. Immediately the lilies began moving their heads in answer, swinging, nodding, waving, and dipping.

"Are you ready, Stubbins?" asked John Dolittle.

"Yes, Doctor," said I, making sure my pencil point would last a while.

"Good," said he. "Put it down":

The Doctor—"Do you like this stationary life—I mean, living in the same place all the time, unable to move?"

The Lilies—(Several of them seemed to answer in chorus)— "Why, yes—of course. Being stationary doesn't bother us. We hear about all that is going on."

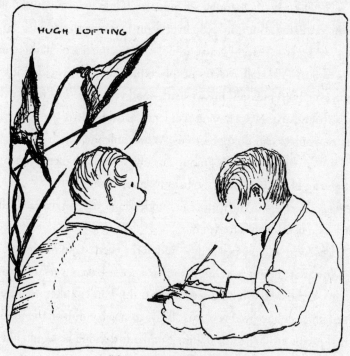

"Are you ready, Stubbins?"

The Doctor—"From whom, what, do you hear it?"

The Lilies—"Well, the other plants, the bees, the birds, bring us news of what is happening."

The Doctor—"Oh, do you communicate with the bees and the birds?"

The Lilies—"Why, certainly, of course!"

The Doctor—"Yet the bees and the birds are races different from your own."

The Lilies—"Quite true, but the bees come to us for honey. And the birds come to sit among our leaves—especially the warblers—and they sing and talk and tell us of what is happening in the world. What more would you want?"

The Doctor—"Oh, quite so, quite so. I didn't mean you should be discontented. But don't you ever want to move, to travel?"

The Lilies—"Good gracious, no! What's the use of all this running about? After all, there's no place like home—provided it's a good one. It's a pleasant life we lead—and very safe. The folks who rush around are always having accidents, breaking legs and so forth. Those troubles can't happen to us. We sit still and watch the world go by. We chat sometimes among ourselves and then there is always the gossip of the birds and the bees to entertain us."

The Doctor—"And you really understand the language of the birds and bees! You astonish me."

The Lilies—"Oh, perfectly—and of the beetles and moths, too."

It was at about this point in our first recorded conversation that we made the astonishing discovery that the Vanity Lilies could *see*. The light, as I have told you, was always somewhat dim on the moon. The Doctor, while he was talking, suddenly decided he would like a smoke. He asked the lilies if they objected to the fumes of tobacco.

They said they did not know because they had never had any experience of it. So the Doctor said he would light his pipe and if they did not like it he would stop.

So taking a box of matches from his pocket he struck a light. We had not fully realized before how soft and gentle was the light of the moon until that match flared up. It is true that in testing our woods for smoke fuel we had made much larger blazes. But then, I suppose we had been more intent on the results of our experiments than on anything else. Now, as we noticed the lilies suddenly draw back their heads and turn aside from the flare, we saw that the extra illumination of a mere match had made a big difference to the ordinary daylight they were accustomed to.

HUGH LOFTING

"He struck a light."

THE FOURTEENTH CHAPTER

Mirrors for Flowers

WHEN THE DOCTOR NOTICED HOW THE lilies shrank away from the glow of the matches, he became greatly interested in this curious unexpected effect that the extra light had had on them.

"Why, Stubbins," he whispered, "they could not have felt the heat. We were too far away. If it is the glare that made them draw back, it must be that they have some organs so sensitive to light that quite possibly *they can see!* I must find out about this."

Thereupon he began questioning the lilies again to discover how much they could tell him of their sense of vision. He shot his hand out and asked them if they knew what movement he had made. Every time (though they had no idea what he was trying to find out) they told him precisely what he had done. Then, going close to one large flower, he passed his hand all round it; and the blossom turned its head and faced the moving hand all the way round the circle.

There was no doubt in our minds whatever, when we had fin-

HUGH LOFTING

"He passed his hand all round it."

ished our experiments, that the Vanity Lilies could in their own way see—though where the machinery called eyes was placed in their anatomy we could not as yet discover.

The Doctor spent hours and days trying to solve this problem. But, he told me, he met with very little success. For a while he was forced to the conclusion (since he could not find in the flowers any eyes such as we knew) that what he had taken for a sense of vision was only some other sense, highly developed, which produced the same results as seeing.

"After all, Stubbins," said he, "just because we ourselves only have five senses, it doesn't follow that other creatures can't have more. It has long been supposed that certain birds had a sixth sense. Still, the way those flowers feel light, can tell colors, movement, and form, makes it look very much as though they had found a way of seeing—even if they haven't got eyes. . . . Humph! Yes, one might quite possibly see with other things besides eyes."

Going through his baggage that night after our day's work was done, the Doctor discovered among his papers an illustrated catalog that had somehow got packed by accident. John Dolittle, always a devoted gardener, had catalogs sent to him from nearly every seed merchant and nurseryman in England.

"Why, Stubbins!" he cried, turning over the pages of gorgeous annuals in high glee. "Here's a chance; if those lilies can see, we can test them with this. Pictures of flowers in color!"

The next day he interviewed the Vanity Lilies with the catalog and his work was rewarded with very good results. Taking the brightly colored pictures of petunias, chrysanthemums and hollyhocks, he held them in a good light before the faces of the lilies. Even Chee-Chee and I could see at once that this caused quite a sensation. The great trumpet-shaped blossoms swayed downward and forward on their slender stems to get a closer view of the pages. Then they turned to one another as though in critical conversation.

Later the Doctor interpreted to me the comments they had made, and I booked them among the notes. They seemed most curious to know *who* these flowers were. They spoke of them (or rather of their species) in a peculiarly personal way. This was one of the first occasions when we got some idea or glimpses of lunar *Vegetable Society*, as the Doctor later came to call it. It almost seemed as though these beautiful creatures were surprised, like human ladies,

"He held them before the lilies."

at the portraits displayed and wanted to know all about these foreign beauties and the lives they led.

This interest in personal appearance on the part of the lilies
was, as a matter of fact, what originally led the Doctor to call their
species the Vanity Lily. In their own strange tongue they questioned
him for hours and hours about these outlandish flowers whose pictures he had shown them. They seemed very disappointed when he
told them the actual size of most earthly flowers. But they seemed
a little pleased that their sisters of the other world could not at least
compete with them in that. They were also much mystified when
John Dolittle explained to them that with us no flowers or plants

(so far as was known) had communicated with man, birds, or any other members of the animal kingdom.

Questioning them further on this point of personal appearance, the Doctor was quite astonished to find to what an extent it occupied their attention. He found that they always tried to get nearer water so that they could see their own reflections in the surface. They got terribly upset if some bee or bird came along and disturbed the pollen powder on their gorgeous petals or set awry the angle of their pistils.

The Doctor talked to various groups and individuals; and in the course of his investigations he came across several plants who, while they had begun their peaceful lives close to a nice pool or stream that they could use as a mirror, had sadly watched while the water had dried up and left nothing but sun-baked clay for them to look into.

So then and there John Dolittle halted his questioning of the Vanity Lilies for a spell while he set to work to provide these unfortunates, whose natural mirrors had dried up, with something in which they could see themselves.

We had no regular looking-glasses of course, beyond the Doctor's own shaving mirror, which he could not very well part with. But from the provisions we dug out various caps and bottoms of preserved fruits and sardine tins. These we polished with clay and rigged up on sticks so that the lilies could see themselves in them.

"It is a fact, Stubbins," said the Doctor, "that the natural tendency is always to grow the way you want to grow. These flowers have a definite conscious idea of what they consider beautiful and what they consider ugly. These contrivances we have given them, poor though they are, will therefore have a decided effect on their evolution."

"These we rigged up on sticks."

That is one of the pictures from our adventures in the moon that always stands out in my memory: the Vanity Lilies, happy in the possession of their new mirrors, turning their heads this way and that to see how their pollen-covered petals glowed in the soft light, swaying with the wind, comparing, whispering, and gossiping.

I truly believe that if other events had not interfered, the Doctor would have been occupied quite contentedly with his study of these very advanced plants for months. And there was certainly a great deal to be learned from them. They told him, for instance, of another species of lily that he later came to call the *Poison Lily* or *Vampire Lily*. This flower liked to have plenty of room and it obtained it by sending out deadly scents (much more serious in their effects than those unpleasant ones that the Vanities used) and nothing round about it could exist for long.

Following the directions given by the Vanity Lilies, we finally ran some of these plants down and actually conversed with them—though we were in continual fear that they would be displeased with us and might any moment send out their poisonous gases to destroy us.

From still other plants that the Vanities directed us to, the Doctor learned a great deal about what he called "methods of propagating." Certain bushes, for example, could crowd out weeds and other shrubs by increasing the speed of their growth at will and by spreading their seed abroad several times a year.

In our wanderings, looking for these latter plants, we came across great fields of Moon Bells flourishing and growing under natural conditions. And very gorgeous indeed they looked, acres and acres of brilliant orange. The air was full of their invigorating perfume. The Doctor wondered if we would see anything of our giant moth near these parts. But though we hung about for several hours, we saw very few signs of insect life.

Making New Clothes

I DON'T UNDERSTAND IT AT ALL," JOHN DOLITTLE muttered. "What reason at least can the moth who brought us here have for keeping out of our way?"

"His reasons may not be his own," murmured Polynesia.

"What do you mean?" asked the Doctor.

"Well," said she, "others may be keeping him—and the rest, away from us."

"You mean the Moon Man?" said John Dolittle.

But to this Polynesia made no reply and the subject was dropped.

"That isn't the thing that's bothering me so much," said Chee-Chee.

There was a pause. And before he went on I know that all of us were quite sure what was in his mind.

"It's our getting back home," he said at last. "Getting here was done for us by these moon folks—for whatever reason they had. But we'd stand a mighty poor chance of ever reaching the earth again if they're going to stand off and leave us to ourselves to get back."

Another short spell of silence—during which we all did a little serious and gloomy thinking.

"Oh well," said the Doctor, "come, come! Don't let's bother about the stiles till we reach them. After all, we don't know for certain that these—er—whoever it is—are definitely unfriendly to us. They may have reasons of their own for working slowly. You must remember that we are just as strange and outlandish to them as they and their whole world are to us. We mustn't let any idea of that kind become a nightmare. We have only been here, let's see, not much over two weeks. It is a pleasant land and there is lots to be learned. The vegetable kingdom is clearly well disposed toward us. And if we give them time, I'm sure that the—er—others will be too, in the end."

Another matter that came up about this time was the effect of moon food on ourselves. Polynesia was the first to remark upon it.

"Tommy," said she one day, "you seem to be getting enormously tall—and fat, aren't you?"

"Er—am I?" said I. "Well, I *had* noticed my belt seemed a bit tight. But I thought it was just ordinary growing."

"And the Doctor, too," the parrot went on. "I'll swear he's bigger—unless my eyesight is getting bad."

"Well, we can soon prove that," said John Dolittle. "I know my height exactly—five feet two and a half. I have a two-foot rule in the baggage. I'll measure myself against a tree right away."

When the Doctor had accomplished this he was astonished to find that his height had increased some three inches since he had been on the moon. Of what my own had been before I landed, I was not so sure; but measurement made it a good deal more than I had thought it. And as to my waistline, there was no doubt that it

"His height had increased some three inches."

had grown enormously. Even Chee-Chee, when we came to look at him, seemed larger and heavier. Polynesia was of course so small that it would need an enormous increase in her figure to make difference enough to see.

But there was no question at all that the rest of us had grown considerably since we had been here.

"Well," said the Doctor, "I suppose it is reasonable enough. All the vegetable and insect world here is tremendously much larger than corresponding species in our own world. Whatever helped them to grow—climate, food, atmosphere, air pressure, etc.— should make us do the same. There is a great deal in this for the investigation of biologists and physiologists. I suppose the long seasons—or almost no seasons at all, you might say—and the other things which contribute to the long life of the animal and vegetable species would lengthen our lives to hundreds of years, if we lived here continually. You know, when I was talking to the Vampire Lilies the other day, they told me that even cut flowers—which with them would mean of course only blossoms that were broken off by the wind or accident—live perfectly fresh for weeks and even months—provided they get a little moisture. That accounts for the Moon Bells that the moth brought down with him lasting so well in Puddleby. No, we've got to regard this climate as something entirely different from the earth's. There is no end to the surprises it may spring on us yet. Oh well, I suppose we will shrink back to our ordinary size when we return home. Still, I hope we don't grow too gigantic. My waistcoat feels most uncomfortably tight already. It's funny we didn't notice it earlier. But, goodness knows, we have had enough to keep our attention occupied."

It had been indeed this absorbing interest in all the new things that the moon presented to our eyes that had prevented us from noticing our own changed condition. The following few days, however, our growth went forward at such an amazing pace that I began seriously to worry about it. My clothes were literally splitting and the Doctor's also. Finally, taking counsel on the matter, we proceeded to look into what means this world offered of making new ones.

Luckily the Doctor, while he knew nothing about tailoring, did know something about the natural history of those plants and materials that supply clothes and textile fabrics for man.

"Let me see," he said one afternoon when we had decided that almost everything we wore had become too small to be kept any longer: "Cotton is out of the question. The spinning would take too long, even if we had any, to say nothing of the weaving. Linen? No, likewise. I haven't seen anything that looked like a flax plant. About all that remains is root fiber, though heaven help us if we have to wear that kind of material next to our skins! Well, we must investigate and see what we can find."

With the aid of Chee-Chee we searched the woods. It took us several days to discover anything suitable, but finally we did. It was an odd-looking swamp tree whose leaves were wide and soft. We found that when these were dried in the proper way they kept a certain pliability without becoming stiff or brittle. And yet they were tough enough to be sewn without tearing. Chee-Chee and Polynesia supplied us with the thread we needed. This they obtained from certain vine tendrils—very fine—which they shredded and twisted into yarn. Then one evening we set to work and cut out our new suits.

"Better make them large enough," said the Doctor, waving a pair of scissors over our rock worktable, "Goodness only knows how soon we'll outgrow them."

We had a lot of fun at one another's expense when at length the suits were completed and we tried them on.

"We look like a family of Robinson Crusoes," said John Dolittle. "No matter: they will serve our purpose. Any port in a storm."

For underwear we cut up all we had and made one garment out of two or three. We were afraid as yet to try our new tailoring next to the skin. Luckily, we only had to provide for a very mild climate.

"Now what about footwear?" I said when I had my coat and trousers on. "My shoes are all split across the top."

"We look like a family of Robinson Crusoes."

"That part is easy," said Chee-Chee. "I know a tree in the jungle, which I found when hunting for fruits. The bark strips off easily and you can cut it into sandals that will last quite a while. The only hard part will be plaiting thongs strong enough to keep them in place on your feet."

He guided us to the tree he had spoken of and we soon had outfitted ourselves with footgear that would last us at least a week.

"Good!" said the Doctor. "Now we need not worry about clothes for a while, anyway, and can give our attention to more serious matters."

THE SIXTEENTH CHAPTER

Monkey Memories of the Moon

I T WAS WHEN WE WERE ON OUR WAY TO VISIT still another new kind of plant that the subject of the moon's early history came up again in conversation. The Doctor had heard of a "whispering vine" which used, as a method of conversation, the rattling or whispering of its leaves.

"Do you remember, Chee-Chee," the Doctor asked, "if your grandmother ever spoke, in her stories of very ancient times, of any peculiar or extraordinary plants or trees?"

"I don't think so, Doctor," he replied. "My grandmother in her talks of the Days Before There Was a Moon kept pretty much to animals and people. She hardly ever mentioned the trees or vegetable world, except to say of this country or that, that it was heavily wooded, or bare and desert. Why?"

"Well, of course in my mind there is no doubt that the moon was once a part of the earth, as many scientists believe. And if so, I am wondering why we do not see more plants and trees of our own home kinds here."

"Well, but we have, Doctor," said Polynesia. "How about the Asparagus Forests?"

"Quite so," said the Doctor. "There have been many that reminded one of earthly species in their shapes, even if they have grown into giants here. But this speech among plants and trees—and other evidences of social advance and development in the vegetable kingdom—is something so established and accepted here that I am all the time wondering if something like it had not started on the earth long ago—say in the Days Before There Was a Moon. And it was merely because our naturalists were not quick enough to—er—catch on to it, that we supposed there was no means of communication among flowers and trees."

"Let me think," said Chee-Chee, and he held his forehead tightly with both hands.

"No," he said after a while, "I don't recall my grandmother's speaking of things like that at all. I remember in her story of Otho Bludge, the prehistoric artist, that she told us about certain woods he used to make handles for his flint chisels and other tools and household implements. She described the wood, for instance, that he used to make bowls out of for carrying water in. But she never spoke of trees and plants that could talk."

It was about midday and we had halted for lunch on our excursion in search of the Whispering Vines we had been told of. We were not more than two or three hours' walk from our old base camp. But that, with the speed so easy in moon marching, means a much greater distance than it does on the earth. From this camp where the Doctor had set up his apparatus for his special botanical studies, we had now for nearly a week been making daily expeditions in search of the various new species that the Vanity Lilies had

"'Let me think,' said Chee-Chee."

described for us. But we always got back before nightfall. Well, this noon the Doctor was leaning back, munching a large piece of yellow yam—a vegetable we got from the edges of the jungle and that we had found so nourishing we had made it almost our chief article of diet.

"Tell me, Chee-Chee," said he, "what was the end of that story about Otho Bludge the prehistoric artist? It was a most fascinating tale."

"Well, I think I have told you," said Chee-Chee, "pretty nearly all there was to tell. In the Days Before There Was a Moon, as Grandmother always began, Otho Bludge was a man alone, a

HUGH LOFTING

"Leaning back, munching a piece of yellow yam"

man apart. Making pictures on horn and bone with a stone knife, that was his hobby. His great ambition was to make a picture of man. But there was no one to draw from, for Otho Bludge was a man alone. One day, when he wished aloud for someone to make a picture from, he saw this beautiful young woman—Pippiteepa was her name—kneeling on a rock, waiting for him to make a portrait of her. He made it—the best work he ever did, carved into the flat of a reindeer's antler. About her right ankle she wore a string of blue stone beads. When the picture was finished, she started to disappear again into the mountains' evening mist, as mysteriously as she had come. Otho called to her to stay. She was the only human being he had ever seen besides his own image in the pools. He wanted her company, poor Otho Bludge, the carver of horn, the man apart. But even as she passed into the twilight forever, she cried out to him that she could not stay—for she was of the Fairy Folk and not of his kin. He rushed to the rock where she had knelt; but all he found was the string of blue stone beads that she had worn about her ankle. Otho, brokenhearted, took them and bound them on his own wrist, where he wore them night and day, hoping always that she would come back.

"There is nothing more. We youngsters used to pester my grandmother for a continuance of the tale. It seemed so sad, so unsatisfying, an ending. But the old lady insisted that that *was* the end. Not long after apparently, Otho Bludge, the carver of horn and the man apart, just disappeared completely, as though the earth had swallowed him up."

"Humph!" muttered the Doctor. "Have you any idea when?"

"No," said the monkey. "You see, even my grandmother's ideas of time and place in these stories she told us were very hazy. She had only had them handed down to her by her parents and grandparents, just as she passed them on to us. But I am pretty sure it was around the time of the Great Flood. Grandmother used to divide her stories into two periods: those belonging to the Days Before There Was a Moon and those that happened after. The name of Otho Bludge the artist only came into those before."

"I see," said the Doctor thoughtfully. "But tell me: Can you recall anything your grandmother said about the time of the change—I mean, when the one period left off and the other began?"

"Not a very great deal," said Chee-Chee. "It was the same when we questioned her about the Flood. That that event had taken place, there was no doubt; but, except for a few details, very little seemed to have been handed down as to how it came about, or of what was going on on the earth at the time, or immediately after it. I imagine they were both great catastrophes—perhaps both came together—and such confusion fell upon all creatures that they were far too busy to take notes, and too scattered afterward to keep a very clear picture in their minds. But I do remember that my grandmother said the first night when the moon appeared in the sky, some of our monkey ancestors saw a group of men kneeling on a mountaintop worshiping it. They had always been sun worshipers and were now offering up prayers to the moon also, saying it must be the Sun's Wife."

"But," asked the Doctor, "did not man know that the moon must have flown off from the earth?"

"That is not very clear," said Chee-Chee. "We often questioned my grandmother on this point. But there were certainly some awful big gaps in her information. It was like a history put together from odd bits that had been seen from different sides of the earth and filled in by gossip and hearsay generations after. It seems that to begin with the confusion was terrible. Darkness covered the earth, the noise of a terrible explosion followed and there was great loss of life. Then the sea rushed into the hole that had been made, causing more havoc and destruction still. Man and beast slunk into caves for shelter or ran wild across the mountains, or just lay down and covered their eyes to shut out the dreadful vision. From what Monkey History has to relate, none lived who had actually seen the thing take place. But that I have always doubted. And much later there was a regular war among mankind when human society had pulled itself together again sufficiently to get back to something like the old order."

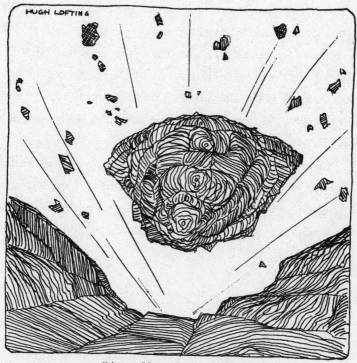

"A terrible explosion followed."

"What was the war about?" asked the Doctor.

"Well, by that time," said Chee-Chee, "man had multiplied considerably and there were big cities everywhere. The war was over the question: Was the moon a goddess, or was she not? The old sun worshipers said she was the wife or daughter of the sun and was therefore entitled to adoration. Those who said the moon had flown off from the flanks of the earth had given up worshiping the sun. They held that if the earth had the power to shoot off another world like that, that *it* should be adored, as the Mother Earth from which we got everything, and not the sun. They said it showed the earth was the center of all things, since the sun had never shot off children. Then there were others who said that the sun and the new earth should be adored as gods—and yet others that wanted all three, sun and earth and moon, to form a great triangle of Almighty Power. The war was a terrible one, men killing one another in thousands—greatly to the astonishment of the Monkey People. For to us it did not seem that any of the various parties really *knew* anything for certain about the whole business."

"Dear, dear," the Doctor muttered as Chee-Chee ended. "The first religious strife—the first of so many. What a pity! Just as though it mattered to anyone what his neighbor believed, so long as he himself led a sincere and useful life and was happy!"

THE SEVENTEENTH CHAPTER

We Hear of "The Council"

THIS EXPEDITION ON THE TRAIL OF THE WHISpering Vines proved to be one of the most fruitful and satisfactory of all our excursions.

When we finally arrived at the home of this species, we found it a very beautiful place. It was a rocky gulch hard by the jungle, where a dense curtain of creepers hung down into a sort of pocket precipice with a spring-fed pool at the bottom. In such a place you could imagine fairies dancing in the dusk, wild beasts of the forest sheltering, or outlaws making their headquarters.

With a squawk Polynesia flew up and settled in the hanging tendrils that draped the rock wall. Instantly we saw a general wave of movement go through the vines, and a whispering noise broke out that could be plainly heard by any ears. Evidently the vines were somewhat disturbed at this invasion by a bird they did not know. Polynesia, a little upset herself, flew back to us at once.

"Shiver my timbers!" she said in a disgruntled mutter. "This

"It was a rocky gulch."

country would give a body the creeps. Those vines actually moved and squirmed like snakes when I took a hold of them."

"They are not used to you, Polynesia," laughed the Doctor. "You probably scared them to death. Let us see if we can get into conversation with them."

Here the Doctor's experience with the Singing Trees came in very helpfully. I noticed as I watched him go to work with what small apparatus he had brought with him that he now seemed much surer of how to begin. And it was indeed a surprisingly short time before he was actually in conversation with them, as though he had almost been talking with them all his life.

Presently he turned to me and spoke almost the thought that was in my mind.

"Stubbins," he said, "the ease with which these plants answer me would almost make me think *they have spoken with a man before!* Look, I can actually make responses with the lips, like ordinary human speech."

He dropped the little contrivance he held in his hands, and hissing softly through his teeth, he gave out a sort of whispered cadence. It was a curious combination between someone humming a tune and hissing a conversational sentence.

Usually it had taken John Dolittle some hours, occasionally some days, to establish a communication with these strange, almost human moon trees good enough to exchange ideas with them. But both Chee-Chee and I grunted with astonishment at the way they instantly responded to his whispered speech. Swinging their leafy tendrils around to meet the breeze at a certain angle, they instantly gave back a humming, hissing message that might have been a repetition of that made by the Doctor himself.

"They say they are glad to see us, Stubbins," he jerked out over his shoulder.

"Why, Doctor," I said, "this is marvelous! You got results right away. I never saw anything like it."

"They have spoken with a man before," he repeated. "Not a doubt of it. I can tell by the way they—Good gracious, what's this?"

He turned and found Chee-Chee tugging at his left sleeve. I have never seen the poor monkey so overcome with fright. He stuttered and jibbered but no intelligible sounds came through his chattering teeth.

"Why, Chee-Chee!" said the Doctor. "What is it? What's wrong?"

"Look!" was all he finally managed to gulp.

He pointed down to the margin of the pond lying at the foot of the cliff. We had scaled up to a shelf of rock to get nearer to the vines for convenience. Where the monkey now pointed there was clearly visible in the yellow sand of the pool's beach two enormous footprints such as we had seen by the shores of the lake.

"The Moon Man!" the Doctor whispered. "Well, I was sure of it—that these vines had spoken with a man before. I wonder—"

"Sh!" Polynesia interrupted. "Don't let them see you looking. But when you get a chance, glance up toward the left-hand shoulder of the gulch."

Both the Doctor and I behaved as though we were proceeding with our business of conversing with the vines. Then, pretending I was scratching my ear, I looked up in the direction the parrot had indicated. There I saw several birds. They were trying to keep themselves hidden among the leaves. But there was no doubt that they were there on the watch.

As we turned back to our work an enormous shadow passed over us, shutting off the light of the sun. We looked up, fearing as anyone would, some attack or danger from the air. Slowly a giant moth of the same kind that had brought us to this mysterious world sailed across the heavens and disappeared.

A general silence fell over us all that must have lasted a good three minutes.

"Well," said the Doctor at length, "if this means that the animal kingdom has decided finally to make our acquaintance, so much the better. Those are the first birds we have seen—and that

"There was no doubt that they were on the watch."

was the first insect—since our moth left us. Curious, to find the bird life so much smaller than the insect. However, I suppose they will let us know more when they are ready. Meantime we have plenty to do here. Have you a notebook, Stubbins?"

"Yes, Doctor," said I. "I'm quite prepared whenever you are."

Thereupon the Doctor proceeded with his conversation with the Whispering Vines and fired off questions and answers so fast that I was kept more than busy booking what he said.

It was indeed, as I have told you, by far the most satisfactory inquiry we had made into the life of the moon, animal or vegetable, up to that time. Because while these vines had

"Proceeded with his conversation with the vines"

not the almost human appearance of the Vanity Lilies, they did seem to be in far closer touch with the general life of the moon. The Doctor asked them about this warfare that we had heard of from the last plants we had visited—the struggle that occurred when one species of plant wished for more room and had to push away its intruding neighbors. And it was then for the first time we heard about the Council.

"Oh," said they, "you mustn't get the idea that one species of plant is allowed to make war for its own benefit regardless of the lives or rights of others. Oh dear, no! We folk of the moon have long since got past that. There was a day when we had constant strife, species against species, plants against plants, birds against insects, and so on. But not anymore."

"Well, how do you manage?" asked the Doctor, "when two different species want the same thing?"

"It's all arranged by the Council," said the vines.

"Er—excuse me," said the Doctor. "I don't quite understand. What council?"

"Well, you see," said the vines, "some hundreds of years ago— that is, of course, well within the memory of most of us, we—"

"Excuse me again," the Doctor interrupted. "Do you mean that most of the plants and insects and birds here have been living several centuries already?"

"Why, certainly," said the Whispering Vines. "Some, of course, are older than others. But here on the moon we consider a plant or a bird or a moth quite young if he has seen no more than two hundred years. And there are several trees, and a few members of the animal kingdom, too, whose memories go back to over a thousand years."

"You don't say!" murmured the Doctor. "I realized, of course, that your lives were much longer than ours on the earth. But I had no idea you went as far back as that. Goodness me! Well, please go on."

"In the old days, then, before we instituted the Council," the vines continued, "there was a terrible lot of waste and slaughter. They tell of one time when a species of big lizard overran the whole moon. They grew so enormous that they ate up almost all the green stuff there was. No tree or bush or plant got a chance to bring itself to seeding-time because as soon as it put out a leaf it was gobbled up by those hungry brutes. Then the rest of us got together to see what we could do."

"A species of big lizard overran the moon."

"Er—pardon," said the Doctor. "But how do you mean, got together? You plants could not move, could you?"

"Oh no," said the vines. "We couldn't move. But we could communicate with the rest—take part in conferences, as it were, by means of messengers—birds and insects, you know."

"How long ago was that?" asked the Doctor. "I mean, for how long has the animal and vegetable world here been able to communicate with one another?"

"Precisely," said the vines, "we can't tell you. Of course, some sort of communication goes back a perfectly enormous long way, some hundreds of thousands of years. But it was not always as good as it is now. It has been improving all the time. Nowadays it would be impossible for anything of any importance at all to happen in our corner of the moon without its being passed along through plants and trees and insects and birds to every other corner of our globe within a few moments. For instance, we have known almost every movement you and your party have made since you landed in our world."

"Dear me!" muttered the Doctor. "I had no idea. However, please proceed."

"Of course," they went on, "it was not always so. But after the institution of the Council, communication and cooperation became much better and continued to grow until it reached its present stage."

The President

THE WHISPERING VINES THEN WENT ON TO tell the Doctor in greater detail of that institution which they had vaguely spoken of already, "the Council." This was apparently a committee or general government made up of members from both the animal and vegetable kingdoms. Its main purpose was to regulate life on the moon in such a way that there should be no more warfare. For example, if a certain kind of shrub wanted more room for expansion, and the territory it wished to take over was already occupied by, we'll say, bullrushes, it was not allowed to thrust out its neighbor without first submitting the case to the Council. Or if a certain kind of butterfly wished to feed upon the honey of some flower and was interfered with by a species of bee or beetle, again the argument had to be put to the vote of this all-powerful committee before any action could be taken.

This information explained a great deal that had heretofore puzzled us.

"You see, Stubbins," said the Doctor, "the great size of almost all life here, the development of intelligence in plant forms, and much more besides, could not possibly have come about if this regulation had not been in force. Our world could learn a lot from the moon, Stubbins—the moon, its own child whom it presumes to despise! We have no balancing or real protection of life. With us it is, and has always been, 'dog eat dog.'"

The Doctor shook his head and gazed off into space to where the globe of our Mother Earth glowed dimly. Just so had I often seen the moon from Puddleby by daylight.

"Yes," he repeated, his manner becoming all of a sudden deeply

"Where the globe of the earth glowed dimly"

serious, "our world that thinks itself so far advanced has not the wisdom, the foresight, Stubbins, which we have seen here. Fighting, fighting, fighting, always fighting! So it goes on down there with us. . . . The 'survival of the fittest'! . . . I've spent my whole life trying to help the animal, the so-called lower, forms of life. I don't mean I am complaining. Far from it. I've had a very good time getting in touch with the beasts and winning their friendship. If I had my life over again I'd do just the same thing. But often, so often, I have felt that in the end it was bound to be a losing game. It is this thing here, this Council of Life—of life adjustment—that could have saved the day and brought happiness to all."

"Yes, Doctor," said I, "but listen: compared with our world, they have no animal life here at all, so far as we've seen. Only insets and birds. They've no lions or tigers who have to hunt for deer and wild goats to get a living, have they?"

"True, Stubbins—probably true," said he. "But don't forget that that same warfare of species against species goes on in the insect kingdom as well as among the larger carnivora. In another million years from now some scientist may show that the war going on between man and the housefly today is the most important thing in current history. And besides, who shall say what kind of a creature the tiger was before he took to a diet of meat?"

John Dolittle then turned back to the vines and asked some further questions. These were mostly about the Council; how it worked; of what it was composed; how often it met, etc. And the answers that they gave filled out a picture that we had already half guessed and half seen of life on the moon.

When I come to describe it I find myself wishing that I were a great poet, or at all events a great writer. For this moon-world was indeed a land of wondrous rest. Trees that sang; flowers that could see; butterflies and bees that conversed with one another and with the plants on which they fed, watched over by a parent council that guarded the interests of great and small, strong and weak, alike—the whole community presented a world of peace, goodwill, and happiness that no words of mine could convey a fair idea of.

"One thing I don't quite understand," said the Doctor to the vines, "is how you manage about seeding. Don't some of the plants throw down too much seed and bring forth a larger crop than is desirable?"

"That," said the Whispering Vines, "is taken care of by the birds. They have orders to eat up all the seed except a certain quantity for each species of plant."

"Humph!" said the Doctor. "I hope I have not upset things for the Council. I did a little experimental planting myself when I first arrived here. I had brought several kinds of seed with me from the earth and I wanted to see how they would do in this climate. So far, however, the seeds have not come up at all."

The vines swayed slightly with a rustling sound that might easily have been a titter of amusement.

"You have forgotten, Doctor," said they, "that news travels fast in the moon. Your gardening experiments were seen and immediately reported to the Council. And after you had gone back to your camp, every single seed that you had planted was carefully dug up by long-billed birds and destroyed. The Council is awfully particular about seeds. It has to be. If we got overrun by any plant, weed or shrub, all of our peaceful balance would be upset and goodness knows what might happen. Why, the president—"

"Every single seed was carefully dug up by long-billed birds."

The particular vines that were doing the talking were three large ones that hung close by the Doctor's shoulder. In a very sudden and curious manner they had broken off in the middle of what they were saying like a person who had let something slip out in conversation which had been better left unsaid. Instantly a tremendous excitement was visible throughout all the creepers that hung around the gulch. You never saw such swaying, writhing, twisting, and agitation. With squawks of alarm a number of brightly colored birds fluttered out of the curtain of leaves and flew away over the rocky shoulders above our heads.

"What's the matter? What has happened, Doctor?" I asked,

as still more birds left the concealment of the creepers and disappeared in the distance.

"I've no idea, Stubbins," said he. "Someone has said a little too much, I fancy. Tell me," he asked, turning to the vines again: "Who is the president?"

"The president of the Council," they replied after a pause.

"Yes, that I understand," said the Doctor. "But what, who, is he?"

For a little there was no answer, while the excitement and agitation broke out with renewed confusion among the long tendrils that draped the rocky alcove. Evidently some warnings and remarks were being exchanged that we were not to understand.

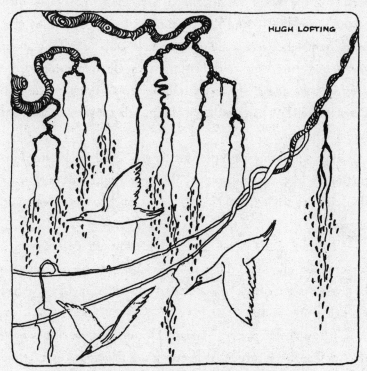

"Still more birds left the concealment of the creepers."

At last the original vines that had acted as spokesmen in the conversation addressed John Dolittle again.

"We are sorry," they said, "but we have our orders. Certain things we have been forbidden to tell you."

"Who forbade you?" asked the Doctor.

But from then on not a single word would they answer. The Doctor made several attempts to get them talking again but without success. Finally we were compelled to give it up and return to camp—which we reached very late.

"I think," said Polynesia, as the Doctor, Chee-Chee, and I set about preparing the vegetarian supper, "that we sort of upset society in the moon this afternoon. Gracious, I never saw such a land in my life!—And I've seen a few. I suppose that by now every bumblebee and weed on the whole globe is talking about the Whispering Vines and the slip they made in mentioning the president. *President!* Shiver my timbers! You'd think he were St. Peter himself! What are they making such a mystery about, I'd like to know?"

"We'll probably learn pretty soon now," said the Doctor, cutting into a huge melonlike fruit. "I have a feeling that they won't think it worthwhile to hold aloof from us much longer. I hope not, anyway."

"Me too," said Chee-Chee. "Frankly, this secrecy is beginning to get under my skin. I'd like to feel assured that we are going to be given a passage back to Puddleby. For a while, anyway, I've had enough of adventure."

"Oh, well, don't worry," said the Doctor. "I still feel convinced that we'll be taken care of. Whoever it was that got us up here did so with some good intention. When I have done what it is that's wanted of me, arrangements will be made for putting us back on the earth, never fear."

"Humph!" grunted Polynesia, who was cracking nuts on a limb above our heads. "I hope you're right. I'm none too sure, myself— No, none too sure."

The Moon Man

THAT NIGHT WAS, I THINK, THE MOST DIS-
turbed one that we spent in the whole course of our
stay on the moon. Not one of us slept soundly or
continuously. For one thing, our growth had proceeded at an alarming and prodigious rate; and what bedding
we had (we slept in that mild climate with the blankets under us
instead of over us) had become absurdly short and insufficient
for our new figures. Knees and elbows spilled over the sides
and got dreadfully sore on the hard earth. But besides that dis-
comfort, we were again conscious throughout the whole night
of mysterious noises and presences. Every one of us seemed
to be uneasy in his mind. I remember waking up one time and
hearing the Doctor, Chee-Chee, and Polynesia all talking in
their sleep at the same time.

Hollow-eyed and unrested, we finally, at daybreak, crawled out
of our various roosts and turned silently to the business of getting
breakfast. That veteran campaigner Polynesia was the first to pull

herself together. She came back from examining the ground about the camp with a very serious look on her old face.

"Well," said she, "if there's anyone in the moon who *hasn't* been messing round our bunks while we slept, I'd like to know who it is."

"Why?" asked the Doctor. "Anything unusual?"

"Come and see," said the parrot, and led the way out into the clearing that surrounded our bunks and baggage.

Well, we were accustomed to finding tracks around our home, but this which Polynesia showed us was certainly something quite out of the ordinary. For a belt of a hundred yards or more about

HUGH LOFTING

"With a very serious look on her old face"

our headquarters the dirt and sand and mud was a mass of foot-prints. Strange insect tracks, the marks of enormous birds, and—most evident of all—numberless prints of that gigantic human foot that we had seen before.

"Tut-tut!" said the Doctor peevishly. "They don't do us any harm anyway. What does it matter if they come and look at us in our sleep? I'm not greatly interested, Polynesia. Let us take break-fast. A few extra tracks don't make much difference."

We sat down and started the meal.

But John Dolittle's prophecy that the animal kingdom would not delay much longer in getting in touch with us was surprisingly and suddenly fulfilled. I had a piece of yam smeared with honey halfway to my mouth when I became conscious of an enormous shadow soaring over me. I looked up and there was the giant moth who had brought us from Puddleby; I could hardly believe my eyes. With a graceful sweep of his gigantic wings he settled down beside me—a battleship beside a mouse—as though such exact and accu-rate landings were no more than a part of the ordinary day's work.

We had no time to remark on the moth's arrival before two or three more of the same kind suddenly swept up from nowhere, fanned the dust all over us with their giant wings, and settled down beside their brother.

Next, various birds appeared. Some species among these we had already seen in the vines. But there were many we had not: enormous storks, geese, swans, and several others. Half of them seemed little bigger than their own kind on the earth. But others were unbelievably large and were colored and shaped somewhat differently—though you could nearly always tell to what family they belonged.

Again more than one of us opened his mouth to say some-

"Others were unbelievably large."

thing and then closed it as some new and stranger arrival made its appearance and joined the gathering. The bees were the next. I remembered then seeing different kinds on the earth, though I had never made a study of them. Here they all came trooping, magnified into great terrible-looking monsters out of a dream: the big black bumblebee, the little yellow bumblebee, the common honey bee, the bright green, fast-flying, slender bee. And with them came all their cousins and relatives, though there never seemed to be more than two or three specimens of each kind.

I could see that poor Chee-Chee was simply scared out of his wits. And little wonder! Insects of this size gathering silently about one were surely enough to appal the stoutest heart. Yet to me they were not entirely terrible. Perhaps I was merely taking my cue from the Doctor who was clearly more interested than alarmed. But besides that, the manner of the creatures did not appear unfriendly. Serious and orderly, they seemed to be gathering according to a set plan; and I felt sure that very soon something was going to happen that would explain it all.

And sure enough, a few moments later, when the ground about our camp was literally one solid mass of giant insects and birds, we heard a tread. Usually a footfall in the open air makes little or no sound at all—though it must not be forgotten that we had found that sound of any kind traveled much more readily on the moon than on the earth. But this was something quite peculiar. Actually, it shook the ground under us in a way that might have meant a moonquake. Yet somehow one *knew* it was a tread.

Chee-Chee ran to the Doctor and hid under his coat. Polynesia never moved, just sat there on her tree branch, looking rather peeved and impatient but evidently interested. I followed the direction of her gaze with my own eyes, for I knew that her instinct was always a good guide. I found that she was watching the woods that surrounded the clearing where we had established our camp. Her beady little eyes were fixed immovably on a V-shaped cleft in the horizon of trees away to my left.

It is curious how in those important moments I always seemed to keep an eye on old Polynesia. I don't mean to say that I did not follow the Doctor and stand ready to take his orders. But whenever anything unusual or puzzling like this came up, especially a case where animals were concerned, it was my impulse to keep an eye on the old parrot to see how she was taking it.

Now I saw her cocking her head on one side—in a quite characteristic pose—looking upward toward the cleft in the forest wall. She was muttering something beneath her breath (probably in Swedish, her favorite swearing language), but I could not make out more than a low peevish murmur. Presently, watching with her, I thought I saw the trees sway. Then something large and round seemed to come into view above them in the cleft.

It was now growing dusk. It had taken, we suddenly realized, a whole day for the creatures to gather; and in our absorbed interest we had not missed our meals. One could not be certain of his vision, I noticed the Doctor suddenly half rise, spilling poor old Chee-Chee out upon the ground. The big round thing above the treetops grew bigger and higher; it swayed gently as it came forward, and with it the forest swayed also, as grass moves when a cat stalks through it.

Any minute I was expecting the Doctor to say something. The creature approaching, whatever—whoever—it was, must clearly be so monstrous that everything we had met with on the moon so far would dwindle into insignificance in comparison.

And still old Polynesia sat motionless on her limb, muttering and spluttering like a firecracker on a damp night.

Very soon we could hear other sounds from the oncoming creature besides his earth-shaking footfall. Giant trees snapped and crackled beneath his tread like twigs under a mortal's foot. I confess that an ominous terror clutched at my heart, too, now. I could sympathize with poor Chee-Chee's timidity. Oddly enough though, at this, the most terrifying moment in all our experience on the moon, the monkey did not try to conceal himself. He was standing beside the Doctor fascinatedly watching the great shadow towering above the trees.

Onward, nearer, came the lumbering figure. Soon there was no mistaking its shape. It had cleared the woods now. The gathered insects and waiting birds were making way for it. Suddenly we realized that it was towering over us, quite near, its long arms hanging at its sides. *It was human.*

We had seen the Moon Man at last!

"Well, for pity's sake!" squawked Polynesia, breaking the awed silence. "You may be a frightfully important person here. But my goodness! It has taken you an awfully long time to come and call on us!"

Serious as the occasion was in all conscience, Polynesia's remarks, continued in an uninterrupted stream of annoyed criticism, finally

"It was human!"

gave me the giggles. And after I once got started, I couldn't have kept a straight face if I had been promised a fortune.

The dusk had now settled down over the strange assembly. Starlight glowed weirdly in the eyes of the moths and birds that stood about us, like a lamp's flame reflected in the eyes of a cat. As I made another effort to stifle my silly titters, I saw John Dolittle, the size of his figure looking perfectly absurd in comparison with the Moon Man's, rise to meet the giant who had come to visit us.

"I am glad to meet you—at last," he said in dignified well-bred English. A curious grunt of incomprehension was all that met his civility.

Then seeing that the Moon Man evidently did not follow his language, John Dolittle set to work to find some tongue that would be understandable to him. I suppose there never was, and probably never will be, anyone who had the command of languages that the Doctor had. One by one he ran through most of the earthly human tongues that are used today or have been preserved from the past. None of them had the slightest effect upon the Moon Man. Turning to animal languages, however, the Doctor met with slightly better results. A word here and there seemed to be understood.

But it was when John Dolittle fell back on the languages of the insect and vegetable kingdoms that the Moon Man at last began to wake up and show interest. With fixed gaze Chee-Chee, Polynesia, and I watched the two figures as they wrestled with the problems of common speech. Minute after minute went by, hour after hour. Finally the Doctor made a signal to me behind his back, and I knew that now he was really ready. I picked up my notebook and pencil from the ground.

As I laid back a page in preparation for dictation, there came a strange cry from Chee-Chee.

"Look!—*The right wrist!*—Look!"

We peered through the twilight. . . . Yes, there *was* something around the giant's wrist, but so tight that it was almost buried in the flesh. The Doctor touched it gently. But before he could say anything, Chee-Chee's voice broke out again, his words cutting the stillness in a curious, hoarse, sharp whisper.

"*The blue stone beads!*—Don't you see them? . . . They don't fit him anymore since he's grown a giant. But he's Otho Bludge the artist. That's the bracelet he got from Pippiteepa, the grandmother of the Fairies! It is he, Doctor, Otho Bludge, who was blown off the earth in the Days Before There Was a Moon!"

"'*Look!*—The right wrist—*Look!*'"

The Doctor and
the Giant

ALL RIGHT, CHEE-CHEE, ALL RIGHT," SAID the Doctor hurriedly. "Wait now. We'll see what we can find out. Don't get excited."

In spite of the Doctor's reassuring words, I could see that he himself was by this time quite a little agitated. And for that no one could blame him. After weeks in this weird world where naught but extraordinary things came up day after day, we had been constantly wondering when we'd see the strange human whose traces and influence were everywhere so evident. Now at last he had appeared.

I gazed up at the gigantic figure rearing away into the skies above our heads. With one of his feet he could easily have crushed the lot of us like so many cockroaches. Yet he, with the rest of the gathering, seemed not unfriendly to us, if a bit puzzled by our size. As for John Dolittle, he may have been a little upset by Chee-Chee's announcement, but he certainly wasn't scared. He at once set to work to get in touch with this strange creature who had called on us. And, as was usual with his experiments of this kind, the other side seemed more than willing to help.

The giant wore very little clothes. A garment somewhat similar to our own, made from the flexible bark and leaves we had discovered in the forest, covered his middle from the armpits down to the lower thighs. His hair was long and shaggy, falling almost to his shoulders. The Doctor measured up to a line somewhere near his anklebone. Apparently realizing that it was difficult for John Dolittle to talk with him at that range, the giant made a movement with his hand, and at once the insects nearest to us rose and crawled away. In the space thus cleared, the man-monster sat down to converse with his visitors from the earth.

It was curious that after this I, too, no longer feared the enormous creature who looked like something from a fairy tale or a nightmare. Stretching down a tremendous hand, he lifted the Doctor, as though he had been a doll, and set him upon his bare knee. From this height—at least thirty feet above my head—John Dolittle clambered still farther up the giant's frame till he stood upon his shoulder.

Here he apparently had much greater success in making himself understood than he had had lower down. By standing on tiptoe he could just reach the Moon Man's ear. Presently descending to the knee again, he began calling to me.

"Stubbins—I say, Stubbins! Have you got a notebook handy?"

"Yes, Doctor. In my pocket. Do you want me to take dictation?"

"Please," he shouted back—for all the world like a foreman yelling orders from a high building. "Get this down. I have hardly established communication yet, but I want you to book some preliminary notes. Are you ready?"

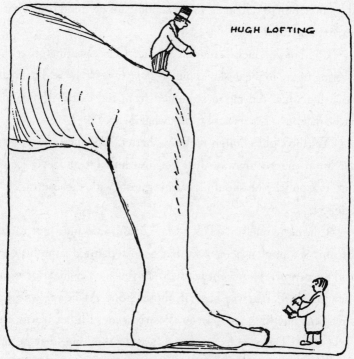

HUGH LOFTING

"'Stubbins—I say, Stubbins!'"

As a matter of fact, the Doctor, in his enthusiasm, had misjudged how easy he'd find it to converse with the Moon Man. For a good hour I stood waiting with my pencil poised, and no words for dictation were handed down. Finally the Doctor called to me that he would have to delay matters a little till he got in close touch with our giant visitor.

"Humph!" grunted Polynesia. "I don't see why he bothers. I never saw such an unattractive, enormous brute. Doesn't look as though he had the wits of a caterpillar anyway. And to think that it was this great lump of unintelligent mutton that has kept the Doctor—John Dolittle, MD—and the rest of us, hanging about till it suited him to call on us! After sending for us, mind you! That's the part that rattles me!"

"Oh, but goodness!" muttered Chee-Chee, peering up at the towering figure in the dusk. "Think—*think* how old he is! That man was living when the moon separated from the earth—thousands, maybe millions, of years ago! Golly, what an age!"

"Yes, he's old enough to know better," snapped the parrot. "Better manners, anyway. Just because he's fat and overgrown is no reason why he should treat his guests with such outrageous rudeness."

"Oh, but come now, Polynesia," I said, "we must not forget that this is a human being who has been separated from his own kind for centuries and centuries. And even such civilization as he knew on the earth, way back in those Stone Age days, was not, I imagine, anything to boast of. Pretty crude, I'll bet it was, the world then. The wonder is, to my way of thinking, that he has any mind at all—with no other humans to mingle with through all that countless time. I'm not surprised that John Dolittle finds it difficult to talk with him."

"Oh, well now, Tommy Stubbins," said she, "that may sound all very scientific and highfalutin. But, just the same, there's no denying that this overgrown booby was the one who got us up here. And the least he could have done was to see that we were properly received and cared for—instead of letting us fish for ourselves with no one to guide us or to put us onto the ropes. Very poor hospitality, I call it."

"You seem to forget, Polynesia," I said mildly, "that in spite of our small size, we may have seemed—as the Doctor said—quite as fearful to him and his world as he and his have been to us—even if he did arrange to get us here. Did you notice that he limped?"

HUGH LOFTING

"Very poor hospitality, I call it."

"I did," said she, tossing her head. "He dragged his left foot after him with an odd gait. Pshaw! I'll bet that's what he got the Doctor up here for—rheumatism or a splinter in his toe. Still, what I *don't* understand is how he heard of John Dolittle, famous though he is, with no communication between his world and ours."

It was very interesting to me to watch the Doctor trying to talk with the Moon Man. I could not make the wildest guess at what sort of language it could be that they would finally hit upon. After all that time of separation from his fellows, how much could this strange creature remember of a mother tongue?

As a matter of fact, I did not find out that evening at all. The

Doctor kept at his experiments, in his usual way, entirely forgetful of time or anything else. After I had watched for a while Chee-Chee's head nodding sleepily, I finally dozed off myself.

When I awoke it was daylight. The Doctor was still engaged with the giant in his struggles to understand and be understood. However, I could see at once that he was encouraged. I shouted up to him that it was breakfast time. He heard, nodded back to me, and then apparently asked the giant to join us at our meal. I was surprised and delighted to see with what ease he managed to convey this idea to our big friend. For the Moon Man at once sat him down upon the ground near our tarpaulin, which served as a table-

"I had watched Chee-Chee's head nodding sleepily."

cloth and gazed critically over the foodstuffs laid out. We offered him some of our famous yellow yam. At this he shook his head vigorously. Then, with signs and grunts, he proceeded to explain something to John Dolittle.

"He tells me, Stubbins," said the Doctor presently, "that the yellow yam is the principal cause of rapid growth. Everything in this world, it seems, tends toward size; but this particular food is the worst. He advises us to drop it—unless we want to grow as big as he is. He has been trying to get back to our size, apparently, for ever so long."

"Try him with some of the melon, Doctor," said Chee-Chee.

This, when offered to the Moon Man, was accepted gladly; and for a little while we all munched in silence.

"How are you getting on with his language, Doctor?" I asked presently.

"Oh, so-so," he grumbled. "It's odd—awfully strange. At first I supposed it would be something like most human languages, a variation of vocal sounds. And I tried for hours to get in touch with him along those lines. But it was only a few vague far-off memories that I could bring out. I was, of course, particularly interested to link up a connection with some earthly language. Finally I went on to the languages of the insects and the plants and found that he spoke all dialects, in both, perfectly. On the whole I am awfully pleased with my experiments. Even if I cannot link him up with some of our own dead languages, at least his superior knowledge of the insect and vegetable tongues will be of great value to me."

"Has he said anything so far about why he got you up here?" asked Polynesia.

"Not as yet," said the Doctor. "But we've only just begun, you know. All in good time, Polynesia, all in good time."

How Otho Bludge
Came to the Moon

THE DOCTOR'S WARNING TO THE PARROT that perhaps we were just as terrifying to the Moon Man (in spite of his size) as he and his world were to us, proved to be quite true. After breakfast was over and I got out the usual notebook for dictation, it soon appeared that this giant, the dread president of the Council, was the mildest creature living. He let us crawl all over him and seemed quite pleased that we took so much interest in him. This did not appear to surprise the Doctor, who from the start had regarded him as a friend. But to Chee-Chee and myself, who had thought that he might gobble us up at any moment, it was, to say the least, a great relief.

I will not set down here in detail that first talk between the Moon Man and the Doctor. It was very long and went into a great many matters of languages and natural history that might not be of great interest to the general reader. But here and there in my report of that conversation I may dictate it word for word, where such a course may seem necessary to give a clear picture of the ideas exchanged. For it was certainly an interview of great importance.

The Doctor began by questioning the giant on the history that Chee-Chee had told us as it had been handed down to him by his grandmother. Here the Moon Man's memory seemed very vague; but when prompted with details from the monkeys' history, he occasionally responded and more than once agreed with the Doctor's statements or corrected them with a good deal of certainty and firmness.

I think I ought perhaps to say something here about the Moon Man's face. In the pale daylight of a lunar dawn it looked clever and intelligent enough, but not nearly so old as one would have expected. It is indeed hard to describe that face. It wasn't brutish and yet it had in it something quite foreign to the average human countenance as seen on the earth. I imagine that his being separated from humankind for so long may have accounted for this. Beyond question it was an animal-like countenance, and yet it was entirely free from anything like ferocity. If one could imagine a kindly animal who had used all his faculties in the furtherance of helpful and charitable ends, one would have the nearest possible idea of the face of the Moon Man, as I saw it clearly for the first time when he took breakfast with us that morning.

In the strange tongues of insects and plants, John Dolittle fired off question after question at our giant guest. Yes, he admitted, he probably was Otho Bludge, the prehistoric artist. This bracelet? Yes, he wore it because someone . . . And then his memory failed him. . . . What someone? . . . Well, anyway, he remembered that it had first been worn by a woman before he had it. What matter, after all? It was long ago, terribly long. Was there anything else that we would like to know?

There was a question I myself wanted to ask. The night before, in my wanderings with Chee-Chee over the giant's huge body, I had discovered a disc or plate hanging to his belt. In the dusk then I had not been able to make out what it was. But this morning I got a better view of it: the most exquisite picture of a girl kneeling with a bow and arrow in her hands, carved upon a plate of reindeer horn. I asked the Doctor, did he not want to question the Moon Man about it? We all guessed, of course, from Chee-Chee's story, what it was. But I thought it might prompt the giant's memory to things out of the past that would be of value to the Doctor. I even whispered to John Dolittle that the giant might be persuaded to give it to us or barter it for something. Even I knew enough about museum relics to realize its tremendous value.

The Doctor indeed did speak of it to him. The giant raised it from his belt, where it hung by a slender thong of bark, and gazed at it a while. A spark of recollection lit up his eyes for a moment Then, with a pathetic fumbling sort of gesture, he pressed it to his heart a moment while that odd, fuddled look came over his countenance once more. The Doctor and I, I think, both felt we had been rather tactless and did not touch upon the subject again.

I have often been since—though I certainly was not at the time—amused at the way the Doctor took charge of the situation and raced all over this enormous creature as though he were some new kind of specimen to be labeled and docketed for a natural history museum. Yet he did it in such a way as not to give the slightest offense.

"Yes. Very good," said he. "We have now established you as Otho Bludge, the Stone Age artist, who was blown off the earth when the moon set herself up in the sky. But how about this Council? I understand you are president of it and can control its workings. Is that so?"

The great giant swung his enormous head round and regarded for a moment the pigmy figure of the Doctor standing, just then, on his forearm.

"The Council?" he said dreamily. "Oh, ah yes, to be sure, the Council. . . . Well, we had to establish that, you know. At one time it was nothing but war—war, war all the time. We saw that if we did not arrange a balance we would have an awful mess. Too many seeds. Plants spread like everything. Birds laid too many eggs. Bees swarmed too often. Terrible! You've seen that down there on the earth, I imagine, have you not?"

"Yes, yes, to be sure," said the Doctor. "Go on, please."

"Well, there isn't much more to that. We just made sure, by means of the Council, that there should be *no more warfare.*"

"Humph!" the Doctor grunted. "But tell me: How is it you yourself have lived so long? No one knows how many years ago it is that the moon broke away from the earth. And your age, compared with the life of man in our world, must be something staggering."

"Well, of course," said the Moon Man, "just how I got here is something that I have never been able to explain completely, even to myself. But why bother? Here I am. What recollections I have of that time are awfully hazy. Let me see: when I came to myself I could hardly breathe. I remember that. The air—everything—was so different. But I was determined to survive. That, I think, is what must have saved me. I was *determined* to survive. This piece of land,

I recollect, when it stopped swirling, was pretty barren. But it had the remnants of trees and plants that it had brought with it from the earth. I lived on roots and all manner of stuff to begin with. Many a time I thought that I would have to perish. But I didn't—*because I was determined to survive.* And in the end I did. After a while plants began to grow; insects, which had come with the plants, flourished. Birds the same way—they, like me, were determined to survive. A new world was formed. Years after, I realized that I was the one to steer and guide its destiny since I had—at that time, anyway—more intelligence than the other forms of life. I saw what this fighting of kind against kind must lead to. So I formed the Council. Since then—oh dear, how long ago!—vegetable and animal species have come to—Well, you see it here. . . . That's all. It's quite simple."

"Yes, yes," said the Doctor hurriedly. "I quite understand that—the necessities that led you to establish the Council. And an exceedingly fine thing it is, in my opinion. We will come back to that later. In the meantime, I am greatly puzzled as to how you came to hear of me—with no communication between your world and ours. Your moth came to Puddleby and asked me to accompany him back here. It was you who sent him, I presume?"

"Well, it was I and the Council who sent him," the Moon Man corrected. "As for the ways in which your reputation reached us, communication is, as you say, very rare between the two worlds. But it does occur once in a long while. Some disturbance takes place in your globe that throws particles so high that they get beyond the influence of earth gravity and come under the influence of our gravity. Then they are drawn to the moon and stay here. I remember, many centuries ago, a great whirlwind or some other form of rumpus in your world occurred, which tossed shrubs and stones to such

"I lived on roots."

a height that they lost touch with the earth altogether and finally landed here. And a great nuisance they were, too. The shrubs seeded and spread like wildfire before we realized they had arrived and we had a terrible time getting them under control."

"That is most interesting," said the Doctor, glancing in my direction as he translated, to make sure I got the notes down in my book. "But please tell me of the occasion by which you first learned of me and decided you wanted me up here."

"That," said the Moon Man, "came about through something which was, I imagine, a volcanic eruption. From what I can make out, one of your big mountains down there suddenly blew its head off, after remaining quiet and peaceful for many years. It was an enormous and terribly powerful explosion, and tons of earth and trees and stuff were fired off into space. Some of this material that started away in the direction of the moon finally came within the influence of our attraction and was drawn to us. And, as you doubtless know, when earth or plants are shot away, some animal life nearly always goes with it. In this case a bird, a kingfisher, in fact, who was building her nest on the banks of a mountain lake, was carried off. Several pieces of the earth landed on the moon. Some, striking land, were smashed to dust, and any animal life they carried—mostly insect of course—was destroyed. But the

"The piece fell into one of our lakes."

piece on which the kingfisher traveled fell into one of our lakes."

It was an astounding story and yet I believe it true. For how else could the Doctor's fame have reached the moon? Of course any but a water bird would have been drowned because apparently the mass plunged down fifty feet below the surface, but the kingfisher at once came up and flew off for the shore. It was a marvel that she was alive. I imagine her trip through the dead belt had been made at such tremendous speed that she managed to escape suffocation without the artificial breathing devices that we had been compelled to use.

How the Moon Folk Heard of Doctor Dolittle

THE BIRD THE MOON MAN HAD SPOKEN OF (it seems he had since been elected to the Council) was presently brought forward and introduced to the Doctor. He gave us some valuable information about his trip to the moon and how he had since adapted himself to new conditions.

He admitted it was he who had told the Moon Folk about John Dolittle and his wonderful skill in treating sicknesses, of his great reputation among the birds, beasts, and fishes of the earth.

It was through this introduction also that we learned that the gathering about us was nothing less than a full assembly of the Council itself—with the exception, of course, of the vegetable kingdom, who could not come. That community was, however, represented by different creatures from the insect and bird worlds, who were there to see to it that their interests were properly looked after.

This was evidently a big day for the Moon People. After our interview with the kingfisher, we could see that arguments were

"The bird was introduced to the Doctor."

going on between different groups and parties all over the place. At times it looked like a political meeting of the rowdiest kind. These discussions the Doctor finally put down quite firmly by demanding of the Moon Man in a loud voice the reason for his being summoned here.

"After all," said he, when some measure of quiet had been restored, "you must realize that I am a very busy man. I appreciate it as a great honor that I have been asked to come here. But I have duties and obligations to perform on the earth which I have left. I presume that you asked me here for some special purpose. Won't you please let me know what it is?"

A silent pause spread over the chattering assembly. I glanced round the unique audience of birds and bugs who squatted, listening. The Doctor, quite apart from his demand for attention, had evidently touched upon a ticklish subject. Even the Moon Man himself seemed somewhat ill at ease.

"Well," he said at last, "the truth is we were sorely in need of a good physician. I myself have been plagued by a bad pain in the foot. And then many of the bigger insects—the grasshoppers especially—have been in very poor health now for some time. From what the kingfisher told me, I felt you were the only one who could help us—that you—er—perhaps wouldn't mind if we got you up here where your skill was so sorely needed. Tell me now: You were not put out by the confidence we placed in you? We had no one in our own world who could help us. Therefore we agreed, in a special meeting of the Council, to send down someone and try to get you."

The Doctor made no reply.

"You must realize," the Moon Man went on, his voice dropping to a still more apologetic tone, "that this moth we sent took his life in his hand. We cast lots among the larger birds, moths, butterflies, and other insects. It had to be one of our larger kinds. It was a long trip, requiring enormous staying power. . . ."

The Moon Man spread out his giant hands in protest—a gesture very suggestive of the other world from which he originally came. The Doctor hastened to reassure him.

"Why, of course, of course," said he. "I—we—were most glad to come. In spite of the fact that I am always terribly busy down there, this was something so new and promising in natural history, I laid every interest aside in my eagerness to get here. With the moth you sent, the difficulty of language did not permit me to make the preparations I would have liked. But pray do not think that I have regretted coming. I would not have missed this experience for worlds. It is true I could have wished that you had seen your way to getting in touch with us sooner. But there—I imagine you, too, have your difficulties. I suppose you must be kept pretty busy."

"Busy?" said the Moon Man blankly. "Oh no. I'm not busy. Life is very quiet and pleasant here. Sometimes too quiet, we think. A session with the Council every now and then and a general inspection of the globe every so often: that is all I have to bother with. The reason I didn't come and see you sooner, to be quite honest, was because I was a bit scared. It was something so new, having human folks visit you from another world. There was no telling what you might turn out to be—what you might do. For another thing, I expected you to be alone. For weeks past I have had the birds and insects—and the plants, too—send me reports of your movements and character. You see, I had relied solely on the statements of a kingfisher. No matter how kind and helpful you had been to the creatures of your own world, it did not follow that you would be the same way inclined toward the Moon Folk. I am sorry if I did not appear properly hospitable. But you must make allowances. It—it was all so—so new."

"Oh, quite, quite," said the Doctor, again most anxious to make his host feel at ease. "Say no more, please, of that. I understand perfectly. There are a few points, however, on which I would like to have some light thrown. For one thing, we thought we saw smoke on the moon, from Puddleby, shortly after your moth arrived. Can you tell us anything about that?"

"Why, of course," said the Moon Man quickly. "I did that. We were quite worried about the moth. As I told you, we felt kind

"I had the birds bring me reports of your movements."

of guilty about the risky job we had given him. It was Jamaro who finally drew the marked card in the lottery."

"Jamaro!" muttered the Doctor, slightly bewildered. "Lottery? I—er—"

"The lottery to decide who should go," the Moon Man explained. "I told you: we drew lots. Jamaro Bumblelily was the moth who drew the ticket which gave the task to him."

"Oh, I see," said the Doctor. "Jamaro. Yes, yes. You give your insects names in this land. Very natural and proper of course, where they are so large and take such an important part in the life and government of the community. You can no doubt tell all these insects one from another, even when they belong to the same species?"

"Certainly," said the Moon Man. "We have, I suppose, several hundreds of thousands of bees in the moon. But I know each one by his first name, as well as his swarm, or family, name. Anyhow, to continue: it was then Jamaro Bumblelily who drew the ticket that gave him the job of going to the earth after you. He was very sportsmanlike and never grumbled a bit. But we were naturally anxious. It is true that creatures had come, at rare intervals, from the earth to our world. But so far none had gone from us to the earth. We had only the vaguest idea of what your world would be like—from the descriptions of the kingfisher. And even in getting those, we had been greatly handicapped by language. It had only been after days and weeks of work that we had been able to understand one another in the roughest way. So we had arranged with Jamaro Bumblelily that as soon as he landed he was to try and find some way to signal us to let us know he was all right. And we were to signal back to him. It seems he made a bad landing and lay helpless in your garden for some days. For a long while we waited in great anxiety. We feared he must have perished in his heroic exploit. Then we thought that maybe if we signaled to him he would be encouraged and know that we were still expecting his return. So we set off the smoke smudge."

"Yes," said the Doctor. "I saw it, even if Jamaro didn't. But tell me: How did you manage to raise such an enormous smudge? It must have been as big as a mountain."

"True," said the Moon Man. "For twenty days before Jamaro's departure, I and most of the larger birds and insects had gathered the Jing-Jing bark from the forest."

"Gathered the *what*?" asked the Doctor.

"The Jing-Jing bark," the Moon Man repeated. "It is a highly explosive bark from a certain tree we have here."

"But how did you light it?" asked the Doctor.

"By friction," said the Moon Man. "Drilling a hardwood stick into a soft-wood log. We had tons and tons of the bark piled in a barren rocky valley where it would be safe from firing the bush or jungle. We are always terrified of bushfires here—our world is not large, you know. I set the pile off with a live ember that I carried on a slate. Then I sprang back behind a rock bluff to defend my eyes. The explosion was terrific, and the smoke kept us all coughing for days before it finally cleared away."

HUGH LOFTING

"I set the pile off with a live ember."

The Man Who Made Himself a King

WE WERE FREQUENTLY REMINDED during this long conversation (it lasted over a full day and a half) that the strange crowd about us was the great Council itself. Questions every now and then were hurled at the Moon Man from the dimness of the rear. He was continually turning his head as messages and inquiries were carried across to him from mouth to mouth. Sometimes without consulting the Doctor further he would answer them himself in odd sounds and signs. It was quite evident that the Council was determined to keep in touch with any negotiations that were going on.

As for John Dolittle, there was so much that he wanted to find out it looked—in spite of his hurry to get back to the earth—as though his queries would never end—which, in a first meeting between two worlds, is not after all to be wondered at.

"Can you remember," he asked, "when you first felt the moon steadying herself, how you got accustomed to the new conditions? We had on our arrival a perfectly terrible time, you know. Different air, different gravity, different hearing and the rest. Tell me: How did you manage?"

Frowning, the Moon Man passed his gigantic hand across his brow.

"Really—it's so long ago," he muttered. "As I told you, I nearly died, many times. Getting enough food to stay alive on kept me busy the first few months. Then when I was sure that that problem was solved, I began to watch. Soon I saw that the birds and insects were faced with the same difficulties as I was. I searched the moon globe from end to end. There were no others of my own kind here. I was the only man. I needed company badly. 'All right,' I said, 'I'll study the insect and bird kingdoms.' The birds adapted themselves much quicker than I did to the new conditions. I soon found that they, being in the same boat as myself, were only too glad to cooperate with me in anything that would contribute to our common good. Of course I was careful to kill nothing. For one thing, I had no desire to; and for another, I realized that if, on such a little globe, I started to make enemies, I could not last long. From the beginning I had done my best to live and let live. With no other human to talk with, I can't tell you how terribly, desperately lonely I felt. Then I decided I'd try to learn the language of the birds. Clearly they had a language. No one could listen to their warblings and not see that. For years I worked at it—often terribly discouraged at my poor progress. Finally—don't ask me when—I got to the point where I could whistle short conversations with them. Then came the insects—the birds helped me in that, too. Then the plant languages. The bees started me. They knew all the dialects. And . . . well . . ."

"Go on," said the Doctor. The tone of his voice was calm and quiet, but I could see that he was deeply, intensely interested.

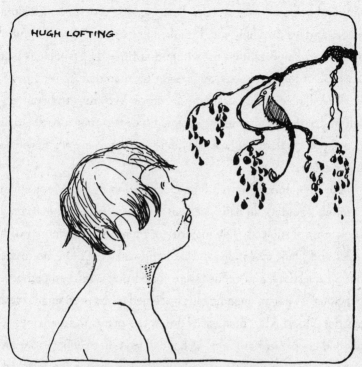

"I could whistle short conversations."

"Oh, dear me," sighed the Moon Man, almost petulantly, "my memory, you know, for dates as far back as that, is awfully poor. Today it seems as though I had talked Heron and Geranium all my life. But just when it was, actually, that I reached the point where I could converse freely with the insects and plants, I couldn't give you the vaguest idea. I do know that it took me far, far longer to get in touch with the vegetable forms of life than it did with either the insects or the birds. I am afraid that our keeping count of time throughout has been pretty sketchy—certainly in our earlier history, anyway. But then you must remember we were occupied with a great number of far more serious tasks. Recently—the last thousand years or so—we have been making an effort to keep a history and we can show you, I think, a pretty good record of most of the more important events within that time. The trouble is that nearly all of the dates you want are earlier than that."

"Well, never mind," said the Doctor. "We are getting on very well under the circumstances. I would like very much to see that record you speak of and will ask you to show it to me, if you will be so good, later."

He then entered into a long examination of the Moon Man (carefully avoiding all dates, periods, and references to time) on a whole host of subjects. The majority of them were concerned with insect and plant evolution, and he kept a strict eye on me to see that all questions and replies were jotted down in the notebook. Gracious! What an unending list it seemed to my tired mind! How had the Moon Man first realized that the plants were anxious to talk and cooperate with him? What had led him to believe that the bees were in communication with the flowers they fed on? Which fruits and vegetables had he found were good for human food and how had he discovered their nutritious qualities without poisoning himself? etc., etc., etc. It went on for hours. I got most of it down, with very few mistakes, I think. But I know I was more than half asleep during the last hours of the interview.

The only trouble with most of it was this same old bugbear of time. After all these ages of living without human company, the poor giant's mind had gotten to the point where it simply didn't *use* time. Even in this record of the last thousand years, which he had proudly told us was properly dated, we found, when he showed it to us, that an error of a century more or less meant very little.

This history had been carved in pictures and signs on the face of a wide flat rock. The workmanship of Otho the prehistoric artist showed up here to great advantage. While the carvings were not by any means to be compared with his masterpiece of the kneeling girl, they nevertheless had a dash and beauty of design that would arrest the attention of almost anyone.

Nevertheless, despite the errors of time, both in his recollections and his graven history, we got down the best booking that we could in the circumstances. And with all its slips and gaps it was a most thrilling and exciting document. It was the story of a new world's evolution; of how a man, suddenly transported into space with nothing but what his two hands held at the moment of the catastrophe,

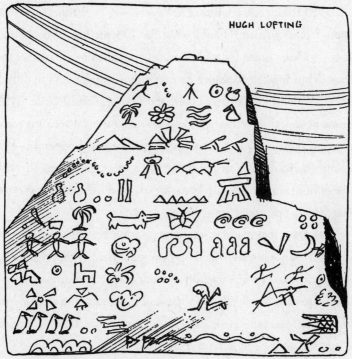

HUGH LOFTING

"This history had been carved in pictures on the face of a rock."

had made himself the kindly monarch of a kingdom—a kingdom more wondrous than the wildest imaginings of the mortals he had left behind. For he was indeed a king, even if he called himself no more than the president of the Council. And what hardships and terrible difficulties he had overcome in doing it, only we could realize—we, who had come here with advantages and aids that he had never known.

Finally a lull did come in this long, long conversation between the Doctor and the Moon Man. And while I lay back and stretched my right hand, cramped from constant writing, Polynesia gave vent to a great deal that she had evidently had on her mind for some time.

"Well," she grunted, lifting her eyebrows, "what did I tell you, Tommy? Rheumatism! That's what the Doctor has come all this way for—*rheumatism!* I wouldn't mind it so much in the case of the Moon Man himself. Because he certainly is a man in a hundred. But *grasshoppers!* Think of it! Think of bringing John Dolittle, MD, billions of miles" (Polynesia's ideas on geographical measurement were a bit sketchy) "just to wait on a bunch of grasshoppers! I—"

But the remainder of her indignant speech got mixed up with some of her favorite Swedish swear words, and the result was something that no one could make head or tail of.

Very soon this pause in the conversation between the Doctor and the Moon Man was filled up by a great deal of talking among the Council. Every member of that important parliament apparently wanted to know exactly what had been said and decided on and what new measures—if any—were to be put in force. We could see that the poor president was being kept very busy.

At length the Doctor turned once more to the giant and said:

"But grasshoppers!"

"Well now, when would it be convenient for you and the insect patients to be examined? I shall be most happy to do everything possible for you all, but you must realize that I would like to get back to the earth as soon as I conveniently can."

Before answering, the Moon Man proceeded to consult his Council behind him. And, to judge from the length of the discussions that followed, he was meeting with quite a little criticism in whatever plans he was proposing. But finally he managed to quiet them; and addressing John Dolittle once more, he said:

"Thank you. If it will not inconvenience you, we will come tomorrow and have you minister to us. You have been very kind to come at all. I hope we will not seem too large an undertaking for you. At least, since you have approved of our system and government here, you will have the satisfaction of knowing that you are assisting us in a time of great need."

"Why, of course, of course," said the Doctor at once. "I shall be only too glad. That is what I am for, after all. I am a doctor, you know, a physician—even if I have become a naturalist in my later years. At what hour will you be ready for me?"

"At dawn," said the Moon Man. Even in these modern days, ideas of time on the moon seemed strangely simple. "We will wait on you at sunrise. Till then, pleasant dreams and good rest!"

Doctor Dolittle Opens His Surgery on the Moon

EVEN THE GARRULOUS POLYNESIA WAS TOO tired to talk much more that night. For all of us it had been a long and steady session, that interview, tense with excitement. The Moon Man and his Council had barely departed before every one of us was dozing off without a change of clothes or a bite to eat. I am sure that nothing on earth—or moon—could have disturbed our slumbers.

The daylight was just beginning to show when we were awakened. I am not certain who was the first to arouse himself (probably John Dolittle), but I do know that I was the first to get up.

What a strange sight! In the dim light hundreds, perhaps thousands, of gigantic insects, all invalids, stood about our camp staring at the tiny human physician who had come so far to cure their ailments. Some of these creatures we had not so far seen and never even suspected their presence on the moon: caterpillars as long as a village street with gout in a dozen feet; immense beetles suffering from an affliction of the eyes; grasshoppers as tall as a three-story house with crude bandages on their gawky joints; enormous birds with a wing held painfully in an odd position. The Doctor's home had become once more a clinic; and all the halt and lame Moon Folk had gathered at his door.

The great man, when I finally roused him, swallowed two or three gulps of melon, washed them down with a draft of honey and water, took off his coat, and set to work.

Of course the poor little black bag, which had done such yeoman service for many years in many lands, was not equal to a demand like this. The first thing to run out was the supply of bandages. Chee-Chee and I tore up blankets and shirts to make more.

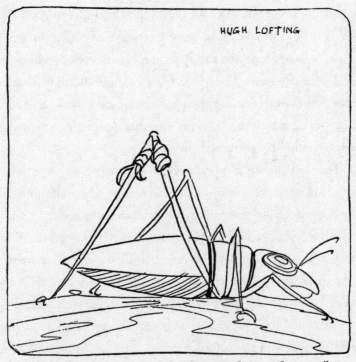

HUGH LOFTING

"Grasshoppers with crude bandages on their gawky joints"

Then the embrocation became exhausted; next the iodine and the rest of the antiseptics. But in his botanical studies of the trees and plants of this world the Doctor had observed and experimented with several things that he had found helpful in rheumatic conditions and other medical uses. Chee-Chee and Polynesia were dispatched at once to find the herbs and roots and leaves that he wanted.

For hours and hours he worked like a slave. It seemed as though the end of the line of patients would never be reached. But finally he did get the last of them fixed up and dispatched. It was only then he realized that the Moon Man had let all the other sufferers come forward ahead of himself. Dusk was coming on. The Doctor peered round the great space about our camp. It was empty, save for a giant figure that squatted silent, motionless and alone, by the forest's edge.

"My goodness!" muttered the Doctor. "I had entirely forgotten him. And he never uttered a word. Well, no one can say he is selfish. That, I fancy, is why he rules here. I must see what is the matter with him at once."

John Dolittle hurried across the open space and questioned the giant. An enormous left leg was stretched out for his examination. Like a fly, the Doctor traveled rapidly up and down it, pinching and squeezing and testing here and there.

"More gout," he said at last with definite decision. "A bad enough case too. Now listen, Otho Bludge."

Then he lectured his big friend for a long time. Mostly it seemed about diet, but there was a great deal concerning anatomy, exercise, dropsy, and *starch* in it too.

At the end of it the Moon Man seemed quite a little impressed, much happier in his mind, and a great deal more

HUGH LOFTING

"Then he lectured his big friend."

lively and hopeful. Finally, after thanking the Doctor at great
length, he departed, while the ground shook again beneath his
limping tread.

Once more we were all worn out and desperately sleepy.

"Well," said the Doctor as he arranged his one remaining blanket on his bed, "I think that's about all we can do. Tomorrow—or
maybe the next day—we will, if all goes well, start back for Puddleby."

"*Sh!*" whispered Polynesia. "There's someone listening. I'm
sure—over there behind those trees."

"Oh, pshaw!" said the Doctor. "No one could hear us at
that range."

"Don't forget how sound travels on the moon," warned the parrot.

"But my goodness!" said the Doctor. "They *know* we've got to go some time. We can't stay here forever. Didn't I tell the president himself I had jobs to attend to on the earth? If I felt they needed me badly enough, I wouldn't mind staying quite a while yet. But there's Stubbins here. He came without even telling his parents where he was going or how long it might be before he returned. I don't know what Jacob Stubbins may be thinking, or his good wife. Probably worried to death. I—"

"Sh!—*Sh!*—Will you be quiet?" whispered Polynesia again. "Didn't you hear that? I tell you, there's someone listening—or I'm a Double Dutchman. Pipe down, for pity's sake. There are ears all round us. Go to sleep!"

We all took the old parrot's advice—only too willingly. And very soon every one of us was snoring.

This time we did not awaken early. We had no jobs to attend to and we took advantage of a chance to snooze away as long as we wished.

It was nearly midday again when we finally got stirring. We were in need of water for breakfast. Getting the water had always been Chee-Chee's job. This morning, however, the Doctor wanted him to hunt up a further supply of medicinal plants for his surgical work. I volunteered therefore to act as water carrier.

With several vessels that we had made from gourds, I started out for the forests.

I had once or twice performed this same office of emergency water carrier before. I was therefore able, on reaching the edge of the jungle, to make straight for the place where we usually got our supplies.

I hadn't gone very far before Polynesia overtook me.

"Watch out, Tommy!" she said in a mysterious whisper as she settled on my shoulder.

"Why?" I asked. "Is anything amiss?"

"I don't quite know," said she. "But I'm uneasy and I wanted to warn you. Listen: that whole crowd that came to be doctored yesterday, you know? Well, not one of them has shown up again since. Why?"

There was a pause.

"Watch out, Tommy!"

"Well," I said presently, "I don't see any particular reason why they should. They got their medicine, their treatment. Why should they pester the Doctor further? It's a jolly good thing that some patients leave him alone after they are treated, isn't it?"

"True, true," said she. "Just the same, their all staying away the next day looks fishy to me. They didn't *all* get treated. There's something in it. I feel it in my bones. And besides, I can't find the Moon Man himself. I've been hunting everywhere for him. He, too, has gone into hiding again, just the same as they all did when we first arrived here. . . . Well, look out! That's all. I must go back now. But keep your eyes open, Tommy. Good luck!"

I couldn't make head or tail of the parrot's warning and, greatly puzzled, I proceeded on my way to the pool to fill my water pots.

There I found the Moon Man. It was a strange and sudden meeting. I had no warning of his presence till I was actually standing in the water filling the gourds. Then a movement of one of his feet revealed his immense form squatting in the concealment of the dense jungle. He rose to his feet as soon as he saw that I perceived him.

His expression was not unfriendly—just as usual, a kindly, calm half smile. Yet I felt at once uneasy and a little terrified. Lame as he was, his speed and size made escape by running out of the question. He did not understand my language, nor I his. It was a lonely spot, deep in the woods. No cry for help would be likely to reach the Doctor's ears.

I was not left long in doubt as to his intentions. Stretching out his immense right hand, he lifted me out of the water as though I were a specimen of some flower he wanted for a collection. Then with enormous strides he carried me away through the forest. One step of his was half-an-hour's journey for me. And yet it seemed as though he put his feet down very softly, presumably in order that his usual thunderous tread should not be heard—or felt—by others.

At length he stopped. He had reached a wide clearing. Jamaro Bumblelily, the same moth that had brought us from the earth, was waiting. The Moon Man set me down upon the giant insect's back. I heard the low rumble of his voice as he gave some final orders. I had been kidnapped.

Puddleby Once More

NEVER HAVE I FELT SO UTTERLY HELPLESS IN my life. While he spoke with the moth, the giant held me down with his huge hand upon the insect's back. A cry, I thought, might still be worth attempting. I opened my mouth and bawled as hard as I could. Instantly the Moon Man's thumb came round and covered my face. He ceased speaking.

Soon I could feel from the stirring of the insect's legs that he was getting ready to fly. The Doctor could not reach me now in time even if he had heard my cry. The giant removed his hand and left me free as the moth broke into a run. On either side of me the great wings spread out, acres-wide, to breast the air. In one last mad effort I raced over the left wing and took a flying leap. I landed at the giant's waistline and clung for all I was worth, still yelling lustily for the Doctor. The Moon Man picked me off and set me back upon the moth. But as my hold at his waist was wrenched loose, something ripped and came away in my hand. It was the masterpiece, the horn picture of Pippiteepa. In his anxiety to put me aboard Jamaro again, who was now racing over the ground at a terrible speed, he never noticed that I carried his treasure with me.

Nor indeed was I vastly concerned with it at the moment. My mind only contained one thought: I was being taken away from the Doctor. Apparently I was to be carried off alone and set back upon the earth. As the moth's speed increased still further, I heard a fluttering near my right ear. I turned my head. And there, thank goodness, was Polynesia flying along like a swallow! In a torrent of words she poured out her message. For once in her life she was too pressed for time to swear.

"Tommy! They know the Doctor is worried about your staying away from your parents. I told him to be careful last night. They heard. They're afraid if you stay he'll want to leave too, to get you back. And—"

The moth's feet had left the ground and his nose was tilted upward to clear the tops of the trees that bordered the open space. The powerful rush of air, so familiar to me from my first voyage of this kind, was already beginning—and growing all the time. Flapping and beating, Polynesia put on her best speed and for a while longer managed to stay level with my giant airship.

"Don't worry, Tommy," she screeched. "I had an inkling of what the Moon Man had up his sleeve, though I couldn't find out where he was hiding. And I warned the Doctor. He gave me this last message for you in case they should try to ship you out: Look after the old lame horse in the stable. Give an eyes to the fruit trees. *And don't worry!* He'll find a way down all right, he says. Watch out for the second smoke signal." (Polynesia's voice was growing faint and she was already dropping behind.) "Good-bye and good luck!"

I tried to shout an answer, but the rushing air stopped my

breath and made me gasp. "Good-bye and good luck!" It was the last I heard from the moon.

I lowered myself down among the deep fur to avoid the pressure of the tearing wind. My groping hands touched something strange. It was the Moon Bells. The giant, in sending me down to the earth, had thought of the needs of the human. I grabbed one of the big flowers and held it handy to plunge my face in. Bad times were coming, I knew when we must cross the Dead Belt. There was nothing more I could do for the present. I would lie still and take it easy till I reached Puddleby and the little house with the big garden.

Well, for the most part my journey back was not very different from our first voyage. If it was lonelier for me than had been the trip with the Doctor, I, at all events, had the comfort this time of knowing from experience that the journey *could* be performed by a human with safety.

But dear me, what a sad trip it was! In addition to my loneliness, I had a terrible feeling of guilt. I was leaving the Doctor behind—the Doctor who had never abandoned me nor any friend in need. True, it was not my fault, as I assured myself over and over again. Yet I couldn't quite get rid of the idea that if I had only been a little more resourceful or quicker-witted this would not have happened. And how, *how* was I going to face Dab-Dab, Jip, and the rest of them with the news that John Dolittle had been left in the moon?

The journey seemed endlessly long. Some fruit also had been provided, I found, by the Moon Man; but as soon as we approached the Dead Belt I felt too seasick to eat and remained so for the rest of the voyage.

At last the motion abated enough to let me sit up and take observations. We were quite close to the earth. I could see it shining cheerfully in the sun and the sight of it warmed my heart. I had not realized till then how homesick I had been for weeks past.

The moth landed me on Salisbury Plain. While not familiar with the district, I knew the spire of Salisbury Cathedral from pictures. And the sight of it across this flat, characteristic country told me where I was. Apparently it was very early morning, though I had no idea of the exact hour.

The heavier air and gravity of the earth took a good deal of getting used to after the very different conditions of the moon. Feeling like nothing so much as a ton-weight of misery, I clambered down from the moth's back and took stock of my surroundings.

Morning mists were rolling and breaking over this flat piece of my native earth. From higher up it had seemed so sunny and homelike and friendly. Down here on closer acquaintance it didn't seem attractive at all.

Presently when the mists broke a little, I saw, not far off, a road. A man was walking along it. A farm laborer, no doubt, going to his work. How small he seemed! Perhaps he was a dwarf. With a sudden longing for human company, I decided to speak to him. I lunged heavily forward (the trial of the disturbing journey and the unfamiliar balance of earth gravity together made me reel like a drunken man) and when I had come within twenty paces I hailed him. The results were astonishing to say the least. He turned at the sound of my voice. His face went white as a sheet. Then he bolted like a rabbit and was gone into the mist.

I stood in the road down which he had disappeared. And suddenly it came over me what I was and how I must have looked. I had not measured myself recently on the moon, but I did so soon after my return to the earth. My height was nine feet nine inches and my waist measurement fifty-one inches and a half. I was dressed in a homemade suit of bark and leaves. My shoes and leggings were made of root fiber, and my hair was long enough to touch my shoulders.

No wonder the poor farm hand suddenly confronted by such an apparition on the wilds of Salisbury Plain had bolted! Suddenly I thought of Jamaro Bumblelily again. I would try to give him a message for the Doctor. If the moth could not understand me, I'd write something for him to carry back. I set out in search. But I never saw him again. Whether the mists misled me in direction or whether he had already departed moonward again, I never found out.

So, here I was, a giant dressed like a scarecrow, no money in my pockets—no earthly possessions beyond a piece of reindeer horn with a prehistoric picture carved on it. And then I realized, of course, that the farm laborer's reception of me would be what I would meet with everywhere. It was a long way from Salisbury to Puddleby, that I knew. I must have coach-fare; I must have food.

I tramped along the road awhile thinking. I came in sight of a farmhouse. The appetizing smell of frying bacon reached me. I was terribly hungry. It was worth trying. I strode up to the door and knocked gently. A woman opened it. She gave one scream at sight of me and slammed the door in my face. A moment later a man threw open a window and leveled a shotgun at me.

"Get off the place," he snarled. "Quick! Or I'll blow your ugly head off."

More miserable than ever, I wandered on down the road. What was to become of me? There was no one to whom I could tell the truth. For who would believe my story? But I must get to Puddleby. I admitted I was not particularly keen to do that—to face the Dolittle household with the news. And yet I must. Even without the Doctor's last message about the old horse and the fruit trees, and the rest, it was my job—to do my best to take his place while he was away. And then my parents—poor folk! I fear I had forgotten them in my misery. And would even they recognize me now?

Then of a sudden I came upon a caravan of gypsies. They were camped in a thicket of gorse by the side of the road and I had not seen them as I approached.

They, too, were cooking breakfast and more savory smells tantalized my empty stomach. It is rather ironic that the gypsies were the only people I met who were not afraid of me. They all came out of the wagons and gathered about me, gaping; but they were interested, not scared. Soon I was invited to sit down and eat. The head of the party, an old man, told me they were going on to a county fair and would be glad to have me come with them.

I agreed with thanks. Any sort of friendship that would save me from an outcast lot was something to be jumped at. I found out later that the old gypsy's idea was to hire me off (at a commission) to a circus as a giant.

But as a matter of fact, that lot also I was glad to accept when the time came. I had to have money. I could not appear in Puddleby like a scarecrow. I needed clothes, I needed coach-fare, and I needed food to live on.

The circus proprietor—when I was introduced by my friend the gypsy—turned out to be quite a decent fellow. He wanted to book me up for a year's engagement. But I, of course, refused. He suggested six months. Still I shook my head. My own idea was the shortest possible length of time that would earn me enough money to get back to Puddleby looking decent. I guessed from the circus man's eagerness that he wanted me in his show at almost any cost and for almost any length of time. Finally, after much argument, we agreed upon a month.

Then came the question of clothes. At this point I was very cautious. He at first wanted me to keep my hair long and wear little more than a loincloth. I was to be a "Missing Link from Mars" or something of the sort. I told him I didn't want to be anything of the kind (though his notion was much nearer to the truth than he knew). His next idea for me was "The Giant Cowboy from the Pampas." For this I was to wear an enormous sun-hat, woolly trousers, pistols galore, and spurs with rowels like saucers. That didn't appeal to me either very much as a Sunday suit to show to Puddleby.

Finally, as I realized more fully how keen the showman was to have me, I thought I would try to arrange my own terms.

"Look here, sir," I said, "I have no desire to appear something I am not. I am a scientist, an explorer, returned from foreign parts. My great growth is a result of the climates I have been through and the diet I have had to live on. I will not deceive the public by masquerading as a Missing Link or Western Cowboy. Give me a decent suit of black such as a man of learning would wear. And I will guarantee to tell your audiences tales of travel—true tales—such as they have never imagined in their wildest dreams. But I will not sign on for more than a month. That is my last word. Is it a bargain?"

Well, it was. He finally agreed to all my terms. My wages were to be three shillings a day. My clothes were to be my own property when I had concluded my engagement. I was to have a bed and a wagon to myself. My hours for public appearance were strictly laid down and the rest of my time was to be my own.

It was not hard work. I went on show from ten to twelve in

the morning, from three to five in the afternoon, and from eight to
ten at night. A tailor was produced who fitted my enormous frame
with a decent-looking suit. A barber was summoned to cut my
hair. During my show hours I signed my autograph to pictures of
myself, which the circus proprietor had printed in great numbers.
They were sold at threepence apiece. Twice a day I told the gaping
crowds of holiday folk the story of my travels. But I never spoke
of the moon. I called it just a "foreign land"—which indeed was
true enough.

At last the day of my release came. My contract was ended, and
with three pounds fifteen shillings in my pocket, and a good suit of
clothes upon my back, I was free to go where I wished. I took the
first coach in the direction of Puddleby. Of course many changes
had to be made and I was compelled to stop the night at one point
before I could make connections for my native town.

On the way, because of my great size, I was stared and gaped at
by all who saw me. But I did not mind it so much now. I knew that
at least I was not a terrifying sight.

On reaching Puddleby at last, I decided I would call on my parents first, before I went to the Doctor's house. This may have been
just a putting off of the evil hour. But anyway, I had the good excuse
that I should put an end to my parents' anxiety.

I found them just the same as they had always been—very glad
to see me, eager for news of where I had gone and what I had done.
I was astonished, however, that they had taken my unannounced
departure so calmly—that is, I *was* astonished until it came out that,
having heard that the Doctor also had mysteriously disappeared,
they had not been nearly so worried as they might have been. Such
was their faith in the great man, like the confidence that all placed

in him. If *he* had gone and taken me with him, then everything was surely all right.

I was glad, too, that they recognized me despite my unnatural size. Indeed, I think they took a sort of pride in that I had, like Caesar, "grown so great." We sat in front of the fire and I told them all of our adventures as well as I could remember them.

It seemed ironic that they, simple people though they were, accepted my preposterous story of a journey to the moon with no vestige of doubt or disbelief. I feared there were no other humans in the world—outside of Matthew Mugg, who would so receive my statement. They asked me when I expected the Doctor's return. I told them what Polynesia had said of the second smoke signal by which John Dolittle planned to notify me of his departure from the moon. But I had to admit I felt none too sure of his escape from a land where his services were so urgently demanded. Then when I almost broke down, accusing myself of abandoning the Doctor, they both comforted me with assurances that I could not have done more than I had.

Finally my mother insisted that I stay the night at their house and not attempt to notify the Dolittle household until the morrow. I was clearly overtired and worn out, she said. So, still willing to put off the evil hour, I persuaded myself that I *was* tired and turned in.

The next day I sought out Matthew Mugg, the Cat's-Meat-Man. I merely wanted his support when I should present myself at "the little house with the big garden." But it took me two hours to answer all the questions he fired at me about the moon and our voyage.

At last I did get to the Doctor's house. My hand had hardly touched the gate latch before I was surrounded by them all.

Too-Too the vigilant sentinel had probably been on duty ever since we left, and one hoot from him brought the whole family into the front garden like a fire alarm. A thousand exclamations and remarks about my increased growth and changed appearance filled the air. But there never was a doubt in their minds as to who I was.

And then suddenly a strange silence fell over them all when they saw that I had returned alone. Surrounded by them I entered the house and went to the kitchen. And there by the fireside, where the great man himself has so often sat and told us tales, I related the whole story of our visit to the moon.

At the end they were nearly all in tears, Gub-Gub howling out loud.

"We'll never see him again!" he wailed. "They'll never let him go. Oh, Tommy, how *could* you have left him?"

"Oh, be quiet!" snapped Jip. "He couldn't help it. He was kidnapped. Didn't he tell you? Don't worry. We'll watch for the smoke signal. John Dolittle will come back to us, never fear. Remember he has Polynesia with him."

"Aye!" squeaked the white mouse. "She'll find a way."

"*I* am not worried," sniffed Dab-Dab, brushing away her tears with one wing, and swatting some flies off the breadboard with the other. "But it's sort of lonely here without him."

"Tut-tut!" grunted Too-Too. "Of course he'll come back!"

There was a tapping at the window.

"Cheapside," said Dab-Dab. "Let him in, Tommy."

I lifted the sash and the cockney sparrow fluttered in and took his place upon the kitchen table, where he fell to picking up what bread crumbs had been left after the housekeeper's careful "clearing away." Too-Too told him the situation in a couple of sentences.

"Why, bless my heart!" said the sparrow. "Why all these long faces? John Dolittle stuck in the moon! Preposterous notion! *Pre*-posterous, I tell you. You couldn't get that man stuck nowhere. My word, Dab-Dab! When you clear away you don't leave much fodder behind, do you? Any mice what live in your 'ouse shouldn't 'ave no difficulty keepin' their figures."

Well, it was done. And I was glad to be back in the old house. I knew it was only a question of time before I would regain a normal size on a normal diet. Meanwhile here I would not have to see anyone I did not want to.

"Don't worry, Tommy, he'll come back."

And so I settled down to pruning the fruit trees, caring for the comfort of the old horse in the stable, and generally trying to take the Doctor's place as best I could. And night after night as the year wore on Jip, Too-Too, and I would sit out, two at a time, while the moon was visible, to watch for the smoke signal. Often when we returned to the house with the daylight, discouraged and unhappy, Jip would rub his head against my leg and say:

"Don't worry, Tommy. He'll come back. Remember he has Polynesia with him. Between them they will find a way."

The End

DOCTOR DOLITTLE'S

RETURN

by HUGH LOFTING

Illustrated by the Author

Contents

PART ONE

THE FIRST CHAPTER

Waiting!

DOCTOR DOLITTLE HAD NOW BEEN IN THE moon for a little over a year. During that time I, as his secretary, had been in charge of his household at Puddleby-on-the-Marsh. Of course a boy of my age could not take the great man's place—nobody could, for that matter. But I did my best.

At the beginning for a few weeks it was not easy. We were all so anxious and worried about John Dolittle. We did not seem to be able to keep our minds on anything but that he was still on the moon and what might be happening to him. So it was in our talking, too: no matter what we started to discuss or chat about, our conversation always ended on the same question.

Yet I do not know what I would have done if it had not been for the animals. Ah, those animals of John Dolittle's! Dab-Dab the duck, the careful housekeeper who spent her life looking after others—even if she did it scolding them most of the time; Jip the dog, brave, generous, happy-go-lucky sportsman, always ready for a good scrap, a good story, a good country walk, or a good sleep; Too-Too the owl, silent and mysterious, with ears that could hear a pin drop in the snow, a lightning calculator—you never knew what he was thinking about—but he seemed to guess things, to *feel* them, witchlike, before they happened; dear, old, clumsy Gub-Gub the pig, always in hot water, taking himself very seriously, forever treading on somebody's toes but providing the world with lots of fun; Whitey the white mouse, a gossip, very well behaved, very clean and neat, inquisitive, taking in life every moment and finding it full of interest. What a family! No one, unable to talk the language of birds and beasts, will ever understand how thoughtful and helpful they could be.

Of course, it must not be forgotten that they were very experienced. Never before, I suppose, has a group of animals been gathered under one roof that had seen so much, gone so many places, and done so many things with human beings. This made it possible for them to understand the feelings of people, just as knowing their language made it possible for John Dolittle and myself to understand them and their troubles.

Although I tried hard not to show it, they all knew how miserable I felt about having left the Doctor in the moon, and they did their best to cheer me up. Dab-Dab formed a regular school program for me for what she called an "advanced course in animal languages." Each night, when there was no moon to be watched— or when it was cloudy—she told off one of the household to play the part of teacher for me. And in this way I was not only able to keep up my Piggish, Owlish, Duckish, Mouser languages and the rest, but I improved a great deal upon what I already knew. I came to understand and use a great many tricky little niceties of meaning that I had never known before.

Of this Gub-Gub the pig, Too-Too the owl, the white mouse, and the others of the Doctor's household were very proud. They said that if I kept on at that rate it would not be long before I could talk their different tongues as well as John Dolittle, the greatest naturalist of all time. Of course I could never quite believe that; but it encouraged me a lot just the same.

One who did a great deal to cheer us up in those long days and nights was Cheapside, the London sparrow. Born and brought up in the struggle and strife of a big city, he would not, could not, be beaten by any misfortune. It was not that he did not know and feel the danger the Doctor was in, as much as any of us. But it was part of his character always to look on the bright side of things. He was not with us all the time. He had to pop over (as he called it) to London every once in a while to see his wife, Becky, and his hundreds of children, cousins, and aunts who picked up a living around the cab-ranks near St. Paul's Cathedral and the Royal Exchange.

From these relations he would bring us back all the gossip of the big city, such as, the queen had a cold in her head (one of Cheapside's nieces had a nest behind a shutter in Buckingham Palace); there was a dog show on at the Agricultural Hall; the prime minister had tripped over his own gown, going up the steps at the opening of Parliament, and fallen on his nose; a ship had arrived at the East India Docks with three real live pirates on board, captured in the China Sea, etc., etc.

I could always tell when he had arrived at the Doctor's house by the great commotion raised. Gub-Gub or Jip the dog could be heard yelling in the garden that the little Londoner had come. And no matter how low our spirits were, Cheapside would not be in the house two minutes, chattering and twittering and giggling over his own silly little Cockney jokes, before everybody would be roaring with laughter or listening with great attention to the news he had to tell. He always brought us also the latest comic songs from the city. Some of these that staid old housekeeper,

HUGH LOFTING

"He always brought the latest comic songs from the city."

Dab-Dab, said were very vulgar; but I noticed she often had much difficulty to keep from laughing with the rest of us, nevertheless.

And then that very extraordinary character, Matthew Mugg, the Cat's-Meat-Man, was a comfort to me too. I did not go off the Doctor's place much, and there were days when I was lonely for human company. At such times, now and then, Matthew would drop in for a cup of tea, and I was always glad to see him. We would sit and chat over old times, about the Doctor and our adventures, and make guesses as to what he might be doing there, now, up in the moon.

It was a good thing for me that I had plenty to keep me busy, I suppose. Looking after ordinary needs of the house, the garden, and the animals was not all I had to attend to. There were the Doctor's instruments—microscopes and all sorts of delicate scientific apparatus that he used in his experiments; these I kept dusted and oiled and in apple-pie order.

Then there were his notes—shelves and shelves full of them. They were very valuable. John Dolittle himself had never been very orderly or careful about his notes, although he would not have had a single page of them lost for anything in the world. He had always said to me, "Stubbins, if ever the house catches fire, remember, save the animals and the notes first and take care of the house afterward."

I therefore felt a great responsibility about those notes. Their safekeeping was my first duty. And thinking about the possibility of fire, I decided to move them away from the house altogether.

So I built a sort of underground library outside. With the help of Jip and Gub-Gub I dug out a place at the end of the garden, tunneling into the side of a small hill near the old zoo.

It was a lovely spot. The wide lawn sloped gently up to a rise of about twenty feet, on the top of which a beautiful grove of weeping willows swept the grass with their graceful trailing branches. It was a part of the Doctor's big garden of which I was particularly fond. After we had burrowed out a big hole, the size of a large room, we took stones and timbers and built them into the sides to keep the earth from falling in. We floored it with some more stones; and after we had roofed it over, we covered the roof with earth two feet deep. A door was set on hinges in the front. Then we sowed grass all over the top and the sides, so it looked like the rest of the lawn. Nothing could be seen but the entrance. It was entirely fireproof.

Into this chamber we carried down all the notes which I, as the Doctor's secretary, had made of our travels and doings. From those notes I had written many books about John Dolittle; but there was much more, of course, that I had not put into books—purely scientific stuff which the ordinary readers would not be interested in.

Gub-Gub called it the *Underground Dolittle Library,* and he was very proud of having helped in the building of it. Not only that, but he was still more proud that his name was so often mentioned in those stacks and stacks of writing that we piled against the walls inside. Winter nights the animals often asked me to read aloud to them by the big kitchen fire, the same as the Doctor had done. And Gub-Gub always wanted me to read those parts from the books that spoke about him. He liked particularly to hear about himself and his great performances in the days of *The Puddleby Pantomime.* The other animals were not always pleased at this.

"Oh, gosh, Gub-Gub!" said Jip. "I should think you'd get tired of hearing about yourself *all* the time."

"But why?" said Gub-Gub. "Am I not the most important pig in history?"

"Poof!" growled Jip in disgust. "Most important pig on the garbage heap, you mean!"

But the day came when, as general manager of the Doctor's home, I found myself in difficulties. You cannot keep a family of animals and yourself on nothing at all. What money I had made shortly after my own return from the moon was all used up. True, a good deal of food could be raised on the place. Wild ducks (friends of Dab-Dab's) brought us eggs. With the animals' help I kept the garden in very good condition. I pruned the apple trees as the Doctor had told me; and the kitchen garden was always well planted with vegetables.

Gub-Gub the pig was the one most interested in this. Although his habit of digging with his nose instead of a spade was somewhat untidy, he was a great help in keeping watch over everything as it grew. A pig was much better for this—in many ways—than a gardener. "Tommy," he would say, "the cutworms are getting at the celery roots." Or, "Tommy, the caterpillars are spoiling the cabbages—and the new spinach needs watering."

Some of the vegetables I exchanged with neighbors, who had farms, for milk; and after I had learned how to make cheese from milk, I could supply the white mouse with his favorite food.

But money in cash I needed for a lot of other household things like candles, matches, and soap. And some of the animals, although they were not meat-eaters, could not be fed from the garden. For instance, there was the old lame horse in the stable whom the Doctor had told me especially to look after. The hay and the oats in his stable were all gone. What grass he could eat from the lawns was already cropped down to the roots. He must have oats to keep his strength up. No, there was nothing for it: I must make some money, earn some money. But how?

The Cat's-Meat-Man's Advice

I WENT OUT INTO THE GARDEN TO THINK. I always seemed to be able to think better in that great garden of the Doctor's than anywhere else. I wandered down toward the new library and from there into the zoo. This quiet spot, enclosed by high walls on which the peach trees grew, had once been a very busy place. Here we had kept the Rat and Mouse Club, the Home for Crossbred Dogs, and all the other institutions for animals' comfort and happiness. They were all deserted now, with nothing but a few early swallows skimming over the grass that the old lame horse had nibbled short and neat and trim.

I felt very sad. Nothing seemed the same without the Doctor. I began pacing to and fro, thinking about my problem. I heard the latch in the garden door click. I turned. There stood Matthew Mugg, the Cat's-Meat-Man.

"Oh, hulloa, Matthew!" I cried. "I'm glad to see you."

"My, Tommy!" said he. "You do look serious. Anything the matter?"

"Yes, Matthew," I said. "I've got to get a job—must make some money. Need it for housekeeping."

"Well, what kind of a job do you want?" he asked.

"Any kind, Matthew," said I, "any kind that I can get."

"'Ave you been to your father about it? Why can't you 'elp 'im in 'is business and earn money that way?"

He started walking back and forth at my side.

"Yes, I've been to see my parents. But it wasn't much use. Father's business is too small for him to need an assistant—even if I were any good at shoemaking, which I'm not."

"Humph!" said the Cat's-Meat-Man. "Let me think."

"You see," I said, "it can't be a job that will take me away from here. There is too much that I must attend to—the garden and the rest. And besides, there's the Doctor's return. I wouldn't be away from here at the moment he gets home for anything in the world. You haven't told anyone about our trip to the moon, have you, Matthew?"

He tapped his pipe out against the heel of his boot.

"Not a word, Tommy, not a word."

"That's right, Matthew. It must be kept an absolute secret. We have no idea what he will be like to look at when he arrives. We don't want newspapermen coming around and writing up reports."

"No," said Matthew. "That would bring the whole world clattering at the gates. Everybody would want to 'ave a look at the man from the moon."

"Quite so, Matthew; that's another reason why I have to have a job. I don't know what the Doctor may need when he gets here. He may be sick; he may need special kinds of food. And I haven't a penny in the house."

"I know, I know," said Matthew, shaking his head. "Money, money, money, what a curse it is!—as the good man said himself. Can't seem to do nothing without it, though. But look 'ere, Tommy, you shouldn't 'ave no trouble findin' a job. 'Cause you got eddication, see?"

"Well, I've *some* education, Matthew. But what good does it do me here in Puddleby? If I was able to get away and go to London, now, that would be different."

"Oh, listen," said the Cat's-Meat-Man. "You boys all think you 'ave to go to London to make yer fortunes—same as Dick Whittington. But young men what 'as eddication can make a good livin' 'ere in Puddleby. You can read and write and do 'rithmetic. Why can't you be a clerk in the Puddleby Bank, or a secketary, or somethin' like that?"

"But, Matthew," I cried, "don't you see? I'd have to stay at work in the town after it was dark—in the winter months, anyhow. And as you know the Doctor told me to watch the moon for signals of his coming down. Of course it is true the animals take their turns, too, watching for the smoke signals. But I would have to be there even if I'm sleeping, so that I could be called at once if—er—if—"

I don't exactly know why I broke off without finishing what I had to say. But I suppose my voice must have sounded uncertain, puzzled, and upset; because Matthew suddenly looked up from refilling his pipe and said:

"But, Tommy, you ain't worried, are yer?—I mean, about the Doctor's returnin'. You feel sure 'e *is* comin' back from the moon?"

"Oh yes," I said. "I suppose so."

"*Suppose* so!" cried Matthew. "Why, of course 'e will, Tommy!

John Dolittle's one of them men what never comes to 'arm. 'E'll get back all right. Don't you worry."

"But supposing the Moon Man won't let him come?" I said.

"It'll take a good deal more than a bloomin' Moon Man to stop John Dolittle from gettin' away if 'e wants to."

"Well, but—er—Matthew," I said, "I sometimes wonder if he does *want to come back.*"

Matthew's eyebrows went up higher than ever.

"*Want* to come back!" he gasped. "What d'yer mean?"

"Matthew Mugg," I said, "you know the Doctor cannot be judged the same as other folk. I mean, you never can tell what he'll do next. We found a very curious state of affairs in the moon. It is a year now since he has been gone. I haven't said anything about it to the animals in the house here, but the last few weeks I've begun to wonder if John Dolittle has not perhaps decided to stay on the moon—for good."

"Oh, what an idea, Tommy!" said he. "Why would 'e want to do that? From what you told me about the moon, it didn't sound like a pleasant place at all."

"It was not an unpleasant place, Matthew. It was very strange and creepy at first. But when you got used to it—no, you could not call it unpleasant. Dreadfully lonely, but the most peaceful place either the Doctor or I had ever seen."

"Well, but, Tommy, you don't mean to tell me that a busy man like John Dolittle would throw up all the things 'e's interested in 'ere on the earth and settle down on the moon, just for the sake of peace and quiet?"

"He might, Matthew," I answered sadly. "I've often remembered, since I left him, something he said when we first learned about the moon's Council of Life, from the Whispering Vines up there. 'Our world,' he said, 'down on the earth is dog eat dog. Fighting, fighting all the time. Here in the moon they manage things better. Life is arranged and balanced. Even the plants and trees are not allowed to crowd one another out. The birds, instead of eating up the bees and insects, eat up the extra seed of the plants and flowers so they will not spread too fast.' You see, Matthew, the Council planned and watched over everything so that peace reigned—in an almost perfect world. You can understand how such a state of things would appeal to a man like John Dolittle. Don't you see what I mean?"

"Er—yes, partly," muttered Matthew. "Go on."

"What I'm afraid of is this," I said. "We had the same difficulty with him on Spidermonkey Island. When he found that he was doing fine work there, getting the natives to give up war—in a very special way, without money and all that—he wanted to stay there. Said that no work he had ever done in Puddleby or anywhere else could compare with what he was doing in Spidermonkey. All of us—Prince Bumpo, Long Arrow the naturalist, and myself—begged him to leave. And I'm sure he never would have left if it hadn't been for me. He felt it was his duty to get me back to my parents. . . . Well, if I had stayed on the moon with him he would have come back here for the same reason. But since I got kidnapped by the Moon Man and shipped out on the giant moth, he won't have to worry about me. And there is nothing to stop him from staying as long as he likes—if he thinks he's doing more good up there than he can down here. Now do you see?"

"Yes, but what I don't see is, 'ow 'e can be doing any good up there."

"Why, by looking after the Moon Man, Matthew. The Doctor has often told me that Otho Bludge, the only man in the moon and the president of the Council, was the greatest human being that ever lived. He might be ignorant according to the ideas of a country bumpkin or a nine-year-old schoolboy down here—he could hardly be otherwise, born in the Stone Age as he was; but his was the brain that worked out the Council and all that it did. And his was the hand that held it together and kept it working. His great trouble, as I've told you, was rheumatism. 'Stubbins,' the Doctor said to me, 'if anything ever happens to Otho Bludge, I fear it will be the end of the Council. And the end of the Council must mean that all this great work they have built up for happy, peaceful living will fall apart and crumble away.'"

Matthew frowned.

"Well, but still I can't imagine, Tommy," said he, "that the Doctor would chuck up all 'is connections down 'ere just for the sake of plants and insects and birds on the moon. After all, this is the world what 'e was born in."

"Oh, I don't mean that he would forget us all down here, thoughtlessly, or anything like that. You know how utterly unselfish he is. That's just the point. Any other man would think of himself and his home and his own comforts first; and would hurry down to the earth as quick as he could and spend the rest of his life boasting about his great adventures. But not so John Dolittle. If he thinks it is necessary to act as doctor for the Moon Man, he might stay on and on and on. He has for many years now been dreadfully disappointed in human beings and their stupid, unfair treatment of animals. And another thing: we discovered that life seemed to go on to tremendous lengths up there. Some of the talking plants told us that they were thousands of years old—the bees and birds, too. And the age of the Moon Man himself is so great that not even the Doctor could calculate it."

"Humph!" said Matthew thoughtfully. "Strange place, the moon."

"I've sometimes wondered," I added, "if the Doctor had some ideas about everlasting life."

"What do you mean, Tommy? Living forever?"

"Yes, for the Moon Man—and perhaps for himself, for John Dolittle, as well. That vegetable diet, you know. A world where nobody, nothing dies! Maybe that's what he sees. If the Moon Man is wearing out a little now—but only after thousands of years—and the Doctor thinks it just requires the help of our science and medicine to keep him living right along, I'm afraid, Matthew, terribly afraid, that he would be greatly tempted to stay."

"Oh, come, come, Tommy," said the Cat's-Meat-Man. "Meself, I think it's much more likely, if 'e 'as discovered the secret of everlastin' life, that 'e'll be wantin' to bring it down to old Mother Earth to try it on the folks 'ere. You mark my words, one of these fine nights 'e'll come tumblin' in on top of you, all full of mooney ideas what 'e wants to try out on the poor British public. You mark my words."

"I hope you're right, Matthew," I said.

"O' course I'm right, Tommy," said he. "We ain't seen the last of our old friend yet—not by a long chalk. And even if 'e 'asn't got no other 'umans to persuade 'im to come back, don't forget 'e 'as Polynesia, 'is parrot, and Chee-Chee the monkey with 'im. They're somethin' to be reckoned with. Why, that parrot, by 'erself, would talk down the whole House o' Lords in any argument! 'E'll come."

"But it is a whole year, Matthew, that he's been gone."

"Well, maybe 'e wanted to see what the spring and summer was like up there."

"Yes, he did say something once about wishing to see the difference in the seasons on the moon."

"There you are!" Matthew spread out his hands in triumph. "'E's been gone a twelve-month—seen the spring, summer, autumn, and winter on the moon. You can expect 'im back any day now, you mark my words. Cheer up, young man. Don't be down-'earted. Now let's get back to this job you was a' thinkin' of."

"Yes, Matthew. We have strayed away from what we started to talk of, haven't we? You must forgive me if I sounded sort of blue and dumpy. But I have been dreadfully worried."

"O' course you 'ave, Tommy—with everything to look after and all. Very nacheral, very nacheral! Now you said you wanted some sort of a job what you could do at 'ome, didn't yer—so as you could keep one eye on the moon like?"

"That's it, Matthew."

"Humph!" grunted the Cat's-Meat-Man. "Now let me see ... Yes, I 'ave it! You remember that butcher what I buys my meat from to feed the cats and dogs with?"

"Oh, that round fat man with the little button of a nose?"

"Yes, that's 'im. Old Simpson. Now listen: Simpson couldn't never do figures, see? Always gettin' 'is books mixed up, sendin' wrong bills to people, and 'avin' no end of rows with 'is customers. 'E's very sensitive about it. 'Is missus could do 'is figurin' for 'im but 'e won't let 'er, see? Doesn't like to admit that 'e can't add up straight. Now maybe I can persuade 'im to let me bring you 'is books twice a week; and you can put 'em right and make out 'is bills proper for 'im, see?"

"Oh, Matthew," I cried, "that would be splendid if you could!"

"Well, Tommy," said he, "I'll see what can be done. I'll go 'ave a chat with old Simpson in the mornin' and I'll let you know. Now I got to be off. Don't worry, Tommy, everything's goin' to be all right."

Cheapside Calls on Us

THE CAT'S-MEAT-MAN WAS QUITE SUCCESSFUL. Obadiah Simpson, the butcher, was only too glad to hear of someone who would do his bookkeeping for him without telling anybody about it. Matthew Mugg brought me two large brand-new ledgers, as they were called, heavy, red-bound, blank books with *OBADIAH SIMPSON & SONS— BUTCHERS: PUDDLEBY-ON-THE-MARSH* stamped in gold on their covers. With these, twice every week, he brought also an envelope full of greasy slips of paper on which were written the butcher's sales of meat to his customers.

The writing was awful and very hard to make out. Most of the customers' names were spelled wrong—often many different ways in one batch of bills. But after I had asked Matthew to get the proper spelling of the names for me, I entered up each customer in the big elegant red books. I used a bold round hand-writing, very elegant, I thought. It was in fact a boyish copy of Doctor Dolittle's. But anyhow, alongside of poor Simpson's dreadful-looking pothooks of letters and figures it did look very clear, grown-up, and businesslike.

The butcher was delighted with my work. I learned afterward that he told his family that the bookkeeping and the bold round handwriting were his own and that he had taken a special course in mathematics from a professor!

He paid me three shillings and sixpence a week. It does not sound much, I know. But in those days money went a great deal further than it does now. By economizing I was able to buy the things I needed for the house and the animals and I even managed to save a little out of it for a rainy day. And it was a good thing, too, that I did, as I will explain later on.

Spring was now turning into summer and the days were getting long again. One late afternoon we were sitting down to tea, and although daylight still lasted, a beautiful, pale full moon hung in the sky. The animals were gathered around the table in the kitchen.

"Who is on duty watching the moon tonight, Tommy?" asked Jip, looking up at the sky through the window.

"Too-Too," I said. "He will be there till midnight, then I will go up, Jip."

"Listen, Tommy," said the dog, "I see some cloud banks over in the west there. What will happen if the clouds spread over the moon just at the moment when the Doctor wants to set off the smoke signals?"

"You can see the earth from the moon just as plainly as you can see the moon from here," I said, "only the earth looks much larger. You remember I told you the earthlight on the moon was much stronger than the moonlight is on the earth. If the Doctor sees clouds around the side of the earth that is facing toward the moon, he will put off signaling till they clear away."

"Yes, but suppose," said Jip, "that he is trying to get away secretly, without letting the Moon Man know; he might miss a chance that way which he would never get again."

"I am afraid, Jip," I answered, "that getting off the moon without Otho Bludge knowing it would be impossible for the Doctor—or anybody else."

"It doesn't seem to me," squeaked the white mouse, "from what Tommy has told us about that horrid old Moon Man—that John Dolittle will stand any chance at all of leaving without his permission *and* his help. Isn't that so, Tommy?"

"Er—yes, I'm afraid it is, pretty much," I answered. "You see, gathering together enough of that special wood I told you about is a big job. To make a smoke explosion big enough to be seen from here you need to have a regular mountain of the stuff."

"Is there any other way for him to get down," asked Jip, "except by using the giant moth who took you both up there?"

"Well, Jip," I said, "that's the only means that *I* know he could use. Still, you must remember, that I was only on the moon for a short time. And although we went partway into the farther side of the moon—the side you never see from here—we had not explored it all when I left, by any means. The Doctor may have discovered new animals since—flying insects and birds, you know—which I never saw. He might get help from them."

"But look here," said Gub-Gub, "didn't you say that all the creatures and plants on the moon obeyed the orders of Otho Bludge because he was president of the Council? Well, how could they help—"

"Oh, do be quiet!" snapped Dab-Dab. "Enough of your ever-lasting questions. The Doctor will get down in his own time and his own way."

I was glad of the old housekeeper's interruption. For months now I had had to answer a never-ending stream of inquiries about the Doctor and his chances of getting off the moon. With her clever motherly sense, Dab-Dab had seen that my heart was sinking lower and lower as the months went by, while I still tried to keep up a cheer-ful front. Yet no one was more uneasy about the Doctor's safety—though she did not show it—than Dab-Dab herself. I had found her more than once of late secretly dusting his room, brushing his clothes, and putting his shaving things in order with tears in her eyes. She con-fessed to me, years afterward, that she had given up all hope of seeing her dear old friend again when the tenth month had passed.

"Yes, but what I don't understand," said the white mouse, "is how the—"

"There are a lot of things you don't understand," Dab-Dab put in. "Who wants a piece of hot toast?"

"I do," said Gub-Gub.

I took a large plate full of toast from the hearth and set it on the table. And for a while we all munched away and drank tea in silence.

"What are you thinking about, Gub-Gub?" asked the white mouse presently.

"I was thinking of the kitchen garden of Eden—if you must know," grunted Gub-Gub with his mouth full.

"The *kitchen* garden of Eden! Tee, hee, hee!" tittered the white mouse. "What an idea!"

"Well, they had apples in the garden of Eden, didn't they?" said Gub-Gub. "And if they had orchards, they must have had a kitchen garden. I do wish the Bible had said more about it. I could have used it very nicely in my *Encyclopedia of Food*."

"What would you have called it?" tittered the white mouse. "'Chapter on Biblical Eating'?"

HUGH LOFTING

"Well, they had apples in the garden of Eden, didn't they?"

"I don't know," said Gub-Gub seriously. "But listen: I did know a biblical family once."

"You did!" cried the white mouse. "A biblical family!"

"Certainly," said Gub-Gub. "Very biblical. They all wore bibs—the children, the parents, and even the grandfather. But I do wish I knew what Adam and Eve ate besides apples."

"Oh well, why bother?" sighed Jip. "Just make it up out of your fat head as you go along. Who will know the difference? Nobody was ever there."

"Why not call it 'Heavenly Vegetables'?" said the white mouse, carefully brushing the toast crumbs out of his silky whiskers.

"Yes, I was thinking of that," said Gub-Gub. "After all, what would heaven be without vegetables?"

"Just heaven," said Jip with a sigh.

"Sh!" said Dab-Dab. "What's that noise?"

"Why, it's Cheapside! Look!" cried the white mouse. "At the window."

We all glanced up and there, sure enough, was the Cockney sparrow tapping on the glass with his stubby bill. I ran and pushed the window up. He hopped inside.

"What ho, me 'earties!" he chirped. "'Ere we are again! The old firm—what, 'avin' tea? Good, I'm just in time. I always makes an 'abit of arrivin' places just in time for tea."

He flew onto the table and began helping me to eat my piece of toast.

"Well," said he, "what's new in Puddleby?"

"Nothing much, Cheapside," I said. "I have a small job that brings in a little money—enough to keep us going. But we always expect *you* to bring the news, you know. How is Becky?"

"Oh, the wife," said he. "She's all right. Yer know the old sayin', 'naught can never come to 'arm.' Ha, ha! We're busy buildin' the new spring nest now—Yes, same old place, St. Edmund's left ear, south side of the cathedral. But we got a new architect in charge of St. Paul's now. And what d'yer think was the first thing 'e did? Why, 'e gave orders to 'ave all the saints *washed!* It's a fact. Sacrilegious, I calls it. And ain't we sparrows got no rights neither? Mussin' up our nests with dirty water! Why, me and Becky 'ave built our nest in St. Edmund's left ear for six years now. Thought we was goin' to 'ave to move over to the Bank of England *this* spring— straight, we did. But at last them bloomin' masons got finished with their moppin' and sloppin' and we're back at the old address for another year. Any word of the Doctor?"

A little silence fell over us all.

"No, Cheapside," I said at last. "No signals as yet. But tell me, what is the news from London?"

"Well," said Cheapside, "they're all talkin' about this 'ere eclipse of the moon."

"What are 'clips of the moon'?" asked Gub-Gub.

"An eclipse, Gub-Gub," I said, "is when the earth gets between the sun and the moon—exactly in between. The earth's shadow is then thrown upon the moon and its light is put out—for us. When is this eclipse, Cheapside?"

"It's tonight, Tommy," said the sparrow. "It's the first full eclipse in I don't know how many years. And everybody up in London is getting out their telescopes and opery-glasses so as to be ready to see it. That's why I come 'ere tonight. 'Becky,' I says to the missus, 'I believe I'll take a run down to Puddleby this evenin'.' 'What d'yer want to do that for?' she says. 'What about the nest buildin'?' she says. 'Ain't you interested in yer children no more?' 'Ho no!' I says to 'er, I says. 'It ain't that, old girl. But when a feller's 'ad as many families as I've 'ad, yer can't expect—well, the newness of the idea gets worn off a bit, you know. There's an eclipse tonight, Becky,' I says, 'and this 'ere city air is so foggy. I'd like to run down to the Doctor's place and see it from the country. You can finish the nest by yerself. It's nearly done already.' 'Oh, very well,' she says. 'You and your eclipses! It's a fine father you are! Run along.' And 'ere I am, the old firm. Let's 'ave another piece of toast, Dab-Dab."

"Do you know what time the eclipse is supposed to be, Cheapside?" I asked.

"A few minutes after eleven o'clock, Tommy," said he. "I'm going to go up and watch it from the roof, I am."

The Eclipse of the Moon

AT CHEAPSIDE'S WORDS A GREAT CHATTER-ing broke out among the animals. Every one of them decided he wanted to stay up and see the eclipse. Usually our household was a very free one, quite different in that way—as well as many others—from a household of people. Everybody went to bed at whatever hour he wished—though if we did not want a scolding from Dab-Dab, we all had to be pretty much on time for meals. The last few months, however (even while we carefully took turns watching the moon for the smoke signals), we had been going to bed pretty early in order to save candles.

Gub-Gub was dreadfully afraid that he would miss the eclipse by falling asleep. This was something he did very easily at any hour at all. He made us promise to wake him if he should doze off before eleven o'clock. Cheapside's coming had cheered us all up. We certainly needed it. I thought something should be done to celebrate.

And so, as it turned out, that particular eclipse of the moon was made a very special occasion and a sort of a party.

Immediately after tea I ran down to the town and spent a little of the money I had saved up on some things for a special supper. I got the right time, too, while I was shopping and corrected the grandfather clock in the hall when I got back to the house.

We had a very happy meal, everybody chattering and laughing over the sparrow's ridiculous jokes and songs. As usual, I was asked no end of questions—this time about eclipses and what they were like. I found some of them very difficult to answer, because, though I had seen an eclipse of the sun once, I had never seen one of the moon.

All the animals wanted to make sure of a good place to watch from, where they could see the show properly. This was not easy. There were several high trees near the house; and at half past ten the moon looked as though it might very soon be hidden by their top branches—that is, if one tried to watch the eclipse from the garden. So Gub-Gub said he wanted to see it from the roof, the same as Cheapside. I explained to him that it was easy for the birds, like Too-Too, Dab-Dab, and the sparrow—and even for the white mouse, because they could cling to the ridge and keep their balance, but that it would be much more difficult for him and Jip and myself.

However, there was a trapdoor in the roof which let you out from the attic onto the tiles, close to the big chimney. In the attic I managed to rig up two stepladders with a sort of platform, made out of boards and packing cases on the top. By standing on this we were able to stick our heads out of the trapdoor.

It was a fine place for a view. I could see the town of Puddleby, three miles away, even the buildings and everything—the church tower, the town hall, the winding river, all bathed in the light of the moon.

On the platform Jip, Gub-Gub, and I stationed ourselves to wait. The white mouse I had brought up in my pocket. I let him go on the tiles where, with squeals of joy, he ran along the ridge or capered up and down the steep slopes of the roof, absolutely fearless, just as though he were on solid ground.

"Can't I get out onto the tiles too, Tommy?" asked Gub-Gub. "Whitey is going to get a much better view than we can here—with just our noses poking out of this hole."

"No," I said, "better not. You can see the moon quite well from where you are. Whitey can cling on to steep places where none of us could."

However, while my back was turned, Gub-Gub did scramble out onto the roof—with sad consequences. I heard a terrible squawk, and turning around I saw him lose his balance and go rolling down the slope of the roof like a ball.

"Great heavens!" I said to Jip. "He'll be killed—or badly hurt, anyway."

"Don't worry," said Jip. "He's well padded. Most likely he'll just bounce when he hits the ground. You can't hurt that pig."

With a dreadful shriek Gub-Gub disappeared into the darkness over the edge of the slope, and for a second we listened in silence. But instead of the thud of his falling on the garden path, the sound of a big splash came up to us. The white mouse ran down the slope and looked over the edge of the rain gutter.

"It's all right, Tommy," he called back to me. "He's fallen into the rainwater barrel."

I jumped to the attic floor, ran down the stairs, and out into the garden.

In those days all country houses had rainwater barrels. They were set close to the walls to catch rainwater from the roof. Into one of these poor Gub-Gub had fallen—luckily for him. When I came up he was swimming and gasping in the water, quite unable to get out, but not hurt in the least. I fished him up to the top, carried him into the kitchen, and rubbed him with a towel. He was a wetter but a wiser pig.

When I had gotten him dry I heard the hall clock strike eleven and we hurried back to the trapdoor.

As we started to get up onto the platform, Jip called to me:

"Hurry, Tommy, hurry! It's beginning!"

Then I heard Too-Too calling from the other end of the roof:

"Here it is. The shadow! Look! The shadow creeping over the moon."

I sprang out of the trapdoor and stood on the ridge, steadying myself with one hand on the chimney.

It was indeed a remarkable sight. There was not a cloud in the sky. A great round shadow, like a tea tray, was creeping slowly across the face of the moon. The country about us had been all flooded with light, almost like day. But now the world slowly began to darken as the moon's light went out, shut off by the giant shadow of the earth. Even Puddleby River, which had shone so clearly, was gone in the darkness. Little by little the shadow crept on until the moon was hidden altogether; only a faint, pale, glowing ring—like a will-o'-the-wisp—was left standing in the sky where it had been. It was the blackest night.

"My goodness, Tommy!" whispered Gub-Gub, "isn't it exciting? Will it stay this way?"

"Not for long, Gub-Gub," I said. "In a few seconds you will see the moon again, just the edge of it at first, when our shadow passes off it."

"But I don't see myself there," said Gub-Gub. "We're sitting up on top of the house, as plain as a pikestaff. There ought to be the shadow of a pig and a dog and a boy there."

"Tee, hee, hee!" tittered the white mouse out of the darkness at my elbow.

"No, Gub-Gub," I said. "Our bodies can throw a shadow on the ground, or a wall, both by sunlight or moonlight. But we are too small—as far away from it as this—to throw a shadow on the moon."

"Humph! I'm very disappointed," grunted Gub-Gub. "I would have liked to see my shadow on the moon."

"You are a kind of a comical scientist, you are, Piggy," chirped Cheapside from the chimney top above our heads, "An eclipse of the bacon, ha!"

"But listen, Tommy," said Jip. "You said the moon's light is only the light of the sun reflected back to us here, the same as a mirror, didn't you? Very well, then: if the earth on which we stand is now in between the sun and the moon—throwing a shadow over it—then anyone in the moon at this moment will have the light of the sun cut off, won't he?"

"Yes, Jip," I said. "That's quite right. The moon is now having an eclipse of the sun while we are having an eclipse of the moon. . . . There you are, Gub-Gub, the shadow is passing off now. You can just see a thin line of the moon beginning to show on the—My goodness, what was that?"

"Tommy! Tommy!" screamed Dab-Dab. "Did you see that? A puff of smoke—just at the end of the white line of the moon!"

"Yes, I saw it!" I shouted back. "Yes, look—there it goes again!"

"White smoke!" said Jip solemnly.

"The signal, the signal at last!" cried Too-Too.

"It's the Doctor!" said the white mouse.

"Yes, it's the Doctor, all right," chirped Cheapside. "'E's comin' back to us. Gawd bless 'im!"

THE FIFTH CHAPTER

I Send for Help

THE DOCTOR'S LITTLE HOUSE ON THE Oxenthorpe Road had in its time seen many days and nights of excitement and thrill. But I don't believe that it ever saw anything quite as uproarious and crazy as it did now. All the animals asked me a question at once, and, without waiting for an answer, asked me another. When they were not asking questions they were chattering and cheering or giving advice, or just singing for sheer joy. And I must admit I was pretty well excited myself.

"Cheapside," I said, "fly over to Matthew Mugg's house, will you? He'll be in bed, but tap on his window and wake him up. Point to the moon. He'll understand. Get him to come here right away. Bring him in his nightshirt if necessary, but get him here. I may need his help."

"Okay!" chirped the sparrow, and with a flirt of his wings he was underway.

"How long do you think it will be before the Doctor gets

here?" asked Gub-Gub. "What will he do if a storm comes up? Will he be hungry? Yes, of course he will. I'll go and dig up some of the spring onions at once."

"Listen, Tommy," said the white mouse. "What will he be wearing? Most likely his clothes will be all in rags after this long time, won't they? I'll go and thread some needles for him right away."

Dab-Dab was a changed duck. Instead of carrying her usual look of seriousness, care, and responsibility, she was now weeping and smiling at the same time.

"Just to think of it!" she kept muttering. "The dear man! On his way back at last! Which room shall we put him in, Tommy—his old one? It's the only large bedroom facing east—and he always did like to wake up with the morning sun on the windows, you know. You've got it full of dried plants and specimens. But no matter, we'll soon clear it. I'll go and make his bed up."

"There is no hurry about that, Dab-Dab," I said. "He can't get down to the earth for many hours yet."

The eclipse was nearly over now. We waited a few minutes—just to make sure we did not miss any further signals. Then, after the shadow had cleared away entirely and the moon sailed the sky again in all her glory, we went down into the house.

"Listen, everybody," I said when we were gathered in the kitchen, "you know we agreed to keep the Doctor's visit to the moon a secret. And we have. That is one of the reasons why I have hardly left the house since I came back to you—I did not want to be asked questions by people I might meet. Now it is more import-ant than ever that we say nothing—nothing to any living thing, you understand—of John Dolittle's return. Do not speak of it even to your animal friends or we shall have a string of cows and dogs and horses a mile long waiting at the gate to greet him. That will attract the attention of people, and the Doctor will get no peace day or night. He may be very much in need of rest and sleep when he arrives. So remember: not a word."

"Tommy," Jip whispered, "you're not fearing he'll be sick when he gets here, are you?"

"I'm not fearing anything, Jip," I answered. "But on the other hand, I don't know what to expect. The journey down here is a very trying and hard one, as I told you. The changes of air and gravity and climate are awfully sudden and disturbing. John Dolittle has been more than a year on the moon. I was only up there a short time. It may be much more difficult for him to get used to the earth again than it was for me. I would feel happier if I had another doctor here in case he needs medical care. But Matthew will be along presently. I'll be able to send him into the town if we need anything."

"But everything will be all shut up now, Tommy," said he. "It's nearly midnight."

"I doubt if we shall see the Doctor before tomorrow night, Jip," I said. "Even at the tremendous speed that the giant moth travels, it takes a long time. Then again, he may not leave immediately after signaling. He may wait awhile. I have an idea he chose the time of the eclipse for some special reason. Too-Too, would you please see how much money I have?"

"Yes, Tommy," said the owl, "right away."

In those days we only had metal money—copper, silver, and gold—except for large amounts. What I had saved I kept in the same old money box the Doctor used. It stood in the same place, too—on the dresser shelf in the kitchen. Too-Too, who had always been a wizard at mathematics, now emptied the money box into a flat dish and began to count up the coins.

"If he arrives in the daylight," said Jip, "what will we do then? I mean about people seeing him land. How are we going to keep it a secret?"

"I imagine the Doctor will think of that himself," I said. "Most likely he will time his departure from the moon so as to land here in the dark. I think, Jip, we had better have someone stay on watch at the trapdoor till the moon sets. Will you go?"

"Certainly," said Jip, and he made for the stairs.

"Tommy," called Too-Too from the dresser, "you have here exactly seven shillings and fourpence ha'penny. Let's see: you've had your job five weeks now. That means you've saved eighteen pence a week. Not bad, Tommy, not bad."

"No," I said. "I didn't think I had so much. Well, we'll need it—and maybe a good deal more."

There came a familiar *tap-tap* at the windowpane.

"Cheapside!" said the white mouse.

I let him in.

"You didn't take long," I said. "Did you find Matthew?"

"Yes," said the sparrow. "'E's comin' right along be'ind me. I can fly much quicker, see? So I come on ahead."

It was not many minutes after Cheapside's return that Gub-Gub came in from the kitchen garden. He had a beautiful bunch of spring onions that he had gathered.

"I do love digging up onions by moonlight," said he. "There's something so poetic about it. Listen, Tommy, I saw Matthew's figure from the gate, way down the road, coming here on the run."

At that moment Matthew burst into the room.

"Tommy!" he cried, all out of breath. "You don't mean to say you got the signal!"

"That's it, Matthew," I said. "We all saw it—twice—two distinct puffs of smoke. Isn't it grand?"

"'You don't mean to say you got the signal!'"

"Why, I should say it is!" said the Cat's-Meat-Man, sinking into a chair. "I run all the way 'ere. Ain't done such a thing since I was a boy. I *thought* it was Cheapside, but then I couldn't be sure, because all sparrers look alike to me. Me and Theodosia 'ad gone to bed; but that blinkin' little bird woke us up—kept peckin' at the glass and pointin' to the moon. My, I wish I could talk these bird languages, the same as you can! But at last I tumbled to the idea and I jumps into me clothes like a fireman and 'ere I am. 'Ow soon do yer expect the Doctor?"

"I can't tell, Matthew. My guess is some time tomorrow night. But I wanted to have you here right away to help me if necessary. You don't mind, do you?"

"I'm *dee*lighted, Tommy, *dee*lighted! I wouldn't miss being 'ere to welcome the Doctor, not for nothin' in the world."

All the animals were far too excited to go to bed that night. They kept skipping in and out of the house, peering at the moon. Matthew Mugg sat up with me in the kitchen, where we talked till the dawn showed in the east windows.

THE SIXTH CHAPTER

The Sound in
the Sky

EVEN THEN, WHEN DAYLIGHT CAME, THE CAT'S-
Meat-Man and I only took short sleeps in our chairs,
setting Too-Too on watch with orders to rouse us if anything happened.

About noon Dab-Dab woke us and said breakfast was ready.
We were hungry and ate a hearty meal.

"We ought to get some things in from the town, Tommy," said
the housekeeper as she waited on us. "The larder is pretty low in
provisions."

"All right, Dab-Dab," I said. "Tell me what you need."

"I'm short of milk," she said. "The Doctor always drank a lot
of milk. And I'm low on sugar, too. And—let me see—yes, tapioca,
macaroni, and three loaves of bread. I think that's all."

I made out a list, gave it to Matthew with some money, and
asked him to do the shopping for us. The Cat's-Meat-Man was
very proud of being a friend of John Dolittle's; so, fearing he
might be tempted to talk, I reminded him once more as he set

out for Puddleby to keep a closed mouth about the great event we were waiting for.

"Don't you worry, Tommy," he said. "I won't talk. But listen, would you mind if I was to tell my wife Theodosia? She was at me last night to tell 'er why I was rushin' off in such an 'urry. She always thinks I'm goin' poachin' when I stays out nights. But she knows 'ow to keep a secret. And, while Dab-Dab is a pretty good cook and housekeeper, we might be glad of 'er 'elp when the Doctor arrives. Theodosia would be right pleased to do anything she can for John Dolittle."

"Why—er, yes, Matthew," I said. "I see no reason why you shouldn't tell Mrs. Mugg."

Not long after the Cat's-Meat-Man had gone, the old lame horse came round to the kitchen door.

"Tommy," said he, "I see the woodshed is nearly empty. Maybe the Doctor will need a fire when he gets down. The nights are still pretty cool. Don't you think we ought to go and gather some wood?"

"Yes," I said. "I think we should. But how is your hoof?"

"Oh," said he, "not too bad. I have to limp a bit. But if you put those two wood baskets on my back I can manage them easy."

So I got an ax and we went off into the small forest that bordered the Doctor's garden at the bottom. Here I chopped enough wood for three or four good fires. I loaded it into the baskets and the old horse carried it up to the shed.

It was about half past four in the afternoon when Matthew got back. Besides the stores I had sent him for, he brought Theodosia Mugg, his wife. I was glad to see her big motherly figure coming up the garden path. She was a very clever and capable woman, was

Theodosia. This she had shown when she traveled with the Doctor in the circus, years ago, and had acted as wardrobe woman in the famous *Canary Opera* that John Dolittle had put on in London.

Dab-Dab did not quite care for the idea of having anyone share her duties as housekeeper. But she had always liked Theodosia; and very soon she saw that the good woman could get a lot more done in one hour than a duck could in three.

A few minutes after she arrived, Mrs. Mugg had all the carpets out on the lawn to be beaten; she had the lace curtains in the wash-tub to be cleaned; the kitchen floor was scrubbed; every dish in the house was spick-and-span. You never saw a house change so quickly.

"Oh, Master Tommy," said she (I could never understand why I was just plain "Tommy" to Matthew, but always "Master Tommy" to his wife), "ain't it wonderful to think of the Doctor's comin' back? It threw me all of a twitter—the news did, when Matthew told me. Oh, would yer mind chasin' that pig out into the garden? 'E's muddin' up the clean floor."

Gub-Gub, much to his disgust, was asked to leave.

"Yes," she went on, "Matthew told me, too, what you said about keepin' the Doctor's comin' a secret. Never fear, I don't want to be laughed at. People wouldn't believe you—not if you told 'em one quarter of what's true about the Doctor. Why, when I was workin' with 'im in the circus and 'e put on *The Canary Opera*, it was plain to everyone in London that 'e could talk the languages of all them birds—just as if 'e come of a canary family 'isself. But even then, with it right under their noses, would people believe it? No. 'Talk canary language!' says they. 'Impossible! It's just trainin' tricks.' No, you needn't think I'd speak to anyone about the Doctor's bein' in the moon. I don't want to be laughed at. That's the way folks are: tell 'em anything new and they think you're cracked."

Theodosia shook her head sadly and went on dusting the pantry closet.

"Yes," I said. "And I fancy that is partly why John Dolittle has kept so much to himself of late years. For one thing, many of the scientific discoveries he has made in natural history are far too extraordinary for people to believe; and for another, he does not want to be bothered with people fussing at him and admiring him and hindering him from working. Why, Jip told me that while he was running the opera in London it took him an hour each day to sign the autograph albums that were sent to him for his signature."

"It was worse than that, Master Tommy," said Theodosia, "sometimes. Indeed, we 'ad to get the 'elp of the police to keep the crowds away when they discovered what 'ouse 'e was livin' in in London. Well, now look 'ere! This won't do. I mustn't stand gossipin'. I want to get this 'ouse finished before 'e comes."

It began to get dark about a quarter past seven. By that time the animals had all had sleep of some sort, even if it was only a few minutes. They now began to fuss around again, chatting in the garden in twos and threes, determined not to be caught napping at the last moment. I noticed some blackbirds and robins watching this moonlight garden party from the trees. So I sent out Dab-Dab to call the animals in.

When the moon rose at a quarter past eight, Matthew and I stationed ourselves at one of the bedroom windows. We left this window open.

"You feel sure 'e'll come tonight, Tommy, don't you?" asked the Cat's-Meat-Man.

"Pretty certain, Matthew," I said. "I only hope he arrives in darkness. That's the one thing I'm afraid about now."

"Well, the Doctor don't often go wrong on calculations," said he.

"No," I said, "that's very true. But you see I'm by no means certain he'll come on the moth. If he does, he could be sure of his timing, because on our way up his watch never stopped. After we'd landed it went all wrong, on account of the gravity and different climate. But he noted down the exact number of hours it took us to get up there. However, Jamaro Bumblelily was the only specimen of the giant moth we saw in the moon. It is possible she may not be able to bring the Doctor on this trip."

"What will 'e do then?"

"I've no idea, Matthew," I said. "Perhaps he'll come on some other insect—which may take a longer or may take a shorter time."

At that moment there was a scratching on the door.

"Tommy, Tommy!" called Jip through the door. "Too-Too says he hears something—in the sky, a long way off. Listen and see if you can catch it!"

The Great Locust

BOTH MATTHEW AND I PUT OUR HEADS OUT the window.

"Do you hear anything?" I asked.

"Not a thing, Tommy," said the Cat's-Meat-Man.

"Humph!" I said. "Neither do I. But that's not surprising. That owl Too-Too can hear things that no human ear can ever catch. Why, once when we were—"

"Sh!—Listen!" whispered Matthew. "Do you get that? A low humming noise."

Then came another knocking on the door. This time it was Dab-Dab.

"Tommy," she called. "Come out into the garden—the back garden—quick!"

Matthew and I dashed for the door and down the stairs.

Behind the house, on the big lawn, we found all the animals with Theodosia, gazing skyward. And now I heard it: a deep, soft, purring kind of noise, still a long, long way off.

"Well, if that's a moth," said Matthew, "it's as big as a young town."

"It isn't the moth," I said. "Jamaro Bumblelily made an entirely different sound. The Doctor's coming down on something else. We must get the lawn clear. Let's run that wheelbarrow into the shed, Matthew."

"All right. I'll do it," said the Cat's-Meat-Man.

This fine sweep of turf had always been known as the Long Lawn. It was one part of that grand old garden of which the Doctor was very proud. Bordered by great elm trees on one side and by a long, tall yew hedge on the other, it ran in one unbroken sweep of a hundred and fifty yards, from the house at one end toward the fish pond and the zoo at the other. At the bottom there was an old card house, a pavilion made like a small Greek temple out of gleaming white stone. On this lawn, the history of the place told us, a duel had been fought by fine gentlemen in brocade and lace ruffles, after they had quarreled over their card game in the pavilion.

It was a romantic spot. And just to look at it by moonlight carried you back hundreds of years. I could not help wondering as I gazed upon it now whether, with all its memories of the past, it had ever seen anything as strange as it would see tonight.

It is curious that from the time when the hum in the sky could be first plainly heard, none of us spoke. We had all drawn away, close to the house, so as to leave the Long Lawn clear for the Doctor's landing. Silent, Matthew presently joined us. And there we all stood, faces upturned toward the moon, too breathless with excitement to speak, while the booming drone of great wings grew louder and louder.

How long we waited I cannot tell. It may have been a minute;

it may have been an hour. I know I had intended to note down the exact time the Doctor landed. He had so often reminded me of the importance, in keeping scientific or natural-history notes, of putting down the date and the time of day. For this reason I had brought out with me one of his old watches, which I had carefully set by the grand-father clock in the hall. But I forgot to look at it. I forgot everything. All I thought of was that he was there—somewhere in the sky, with that tremendous growing sound—coming, coming back to us at last!

But though I lost all count of time that night, everything that actually happened I remember as sharply now as though it were drawn in pictures before my eyes at this moment. Somewhere in that space of time while we stood gazing, a great shadow swept sud-denly between us and the moon. For a little while it stood, hovering and humming, high up above the lawn. I could not yet make out much as to its shape. Then, like some roaring machine turned off sharply, the noise ceased. The air rested in a big dead silence.

I guessed that whatever creature it might be, it was prob-ably now sailing with outspread wings, looking for a place to land. Next the shadow passed from off the smooth grass. Was it circling—circling downward? Yes, because once more its great body shut off the light like a cloud.

And at last—*whish!*—it came skimming over the treetops in plain view. The air whistled like a fierce gust of wind as it banked around in a graceful curve and dropped on the turf before us.

It filled the whole of the Long Lawn!

It was clear to me now that it was some member of the grass-hopper family. (Later I learned that it was a locust.) But for the present I was not so concerned with the nature of the insect as I was with what it carried.

Alone, I moved out into the moonlight toward it. On tiptoe, trying to see the top of its back, I peered upward. But the highest part of it was hidden by the curve of the body. The great locust, apparently exhausted by the long journey, lay absolutely still. Nothing moved anywhere.

A terrible fear came over me. Where was the Doctor? Had the hard journey proved too much for him? Or could it be that he had not come at all? Perhaps this great thing from the moon's animal kingdom had only brought a message to us—maybe a message to say that John Dolittle had decided to stay on that other world after all.

Frantic at the thought, I started to scramble up the locust's wings, which were now folded at his sides. Beautiful, transparent wings they were, smooth and opal-colored—with great hard veins running through them, standing out from the glassy surface like gnarled roots.

But suddenly I heard a voice, a harsh, grating, but well-remembered, well-loved voice. A parrot's! "Chee-Chee, Chee-Chee! Wake up! We're here—in Puddleby. Shiver my timbers! You're not as sick as you think you are. Wake up!"

And then for the first time, the earth spoke back to the people from the moon.

"Polynesia!" I shouted. "Is that you? Where is the Doctor? Is he with you?"

"Yes, he's here all right," called the parrot. "But he's unconscious still. We've got to go easy with him. Had an awful time getting through the dead belt. Gosh, what a journey! I wonder if I can fly straight anymore in this gravity? Look out! I'm coming down."

I saw something shoot out off the top of the locust's back. It looked like a bundle of rags, turning over and over in the air. Then it landed on the grass at my feet with a distinct thud. Polynesia, ruffled and disgruntled, broke out into a long string of Swedish swear words.

HUGH LOFTING

"Like a bundle of rags turning over and over"

"Ouch!" she ended. "Did you see that? Landed right on my nose, like a pudding! I've got to learn to fly all over again—at my time of life! All unbalanced and fluffed up! Just because that stupid old moon doesn't keep the right kind of air. You haven't got a cracker in your pocket, I suppose? I'm as hungry as a bear."

I called to Dab-Dab to go and fetch me some from the pantry.

"But, Polynesia," I said, "what about the Doctor? You say he's unconscious?"

"Yes," she said, "but he's all right. Difficulty with his breathing, you know. Leave him to rest a little while. We'll get him down presently. Poor old Chee-Chee's seasick, or air sick, or whatever it is. The last few hours of the trip, I was the only one on deck, the only one left to guide that blessed grasshopper to the garden here. That comes of my years of seafaring, Tommy. Hard as nails, hard as nails. So would you be if you had lived a hundred and eighty years on sunflower seeds and cracker crumbs! Trouble with humans is they eat too many different kinds of foods. Parrots have more sense!"

She strutted a few paces with her funny, straddling, sailorlike gait. Then she fell down on her side.

"Drat it!" she muttered. "This air is heavy! Can't even walk straight."

"But listen," I said. "The Doctor—can't we—"

"Sh!" she whispered. "He's woken up. Look!"

I glanced toward the locust's back. An enormous foot was sliding down toward us. It was followed by a still more enormous leg. Finally the body came in sight. Polynesia and I moved back a little. Then, with a run, the whole mass of an unbelievably big human figure came slithering down the locust's wings and slumped into a heap on the lawn.

I rushed forward and gazed into the motionless face. The eyes were closed. The skin was tanned to a deep brown color by sun and wind. But, for me, there was no mistaking the mouth, the nose, the chin.

It was John Dolittle.

The Doctor's Voice

I RAN INTO THE HOUSE FOR THE BRANDY FLASK that was always kept in the dispensary. But when I got back the Doctor was standing up. He was eighteen feet and three and a half inches high. (This I am sure of because I measured him the next day while he was lying asleep.)

It is difficult to describe his appearance. His sun hat was home-made out of materials he had evidently gathered in the moon and so were his clothes—all but his trousers. These were fashioned out of the blankets we had taken up with us.

"Doctor, Doctor!" I cried. "Oh, I'm so glad to see you back!"

To my surprise he did not answer at once.

I noticed that Chee-Chee the monkey had gotten over his sickness enough to come down into one of the willows nearby, where Polynesia had joined him. Dab-Dab also had come forward and was now gazing at the Doctor with an odd expression, a mixture of motherly affection, worry, great joy, and a little fear. But no one uttered a word. We were all waiting in silence for this strange figure before us to speak.

Presently the Doctor stretched down his hand and took a couple of tottering, unsteady steps toward me. He seemed dreadfully weak and sort of dazed. Once, he lifted up his left hand and brushed it across his eyes, as though his sight, as well as his legs, was uncertain. Then his enormous right hand grasped mine so that it disappeared entirely.

At last in a curious hesitating way he said:

"Why—why, it's Stubbins! Good old . . . good old . . . S-s-s-stubbins. Er—er—how are you?"

The voice was the only part of him that had not changed. If he had grown horns in the moon no one, in any doubt before, could be uncertain now of who it was that spoke. That voice did something to his friends over by the house, who still waited with almost bated breath. For suddenly all of them—Jip, Gub-Gub, the white mouse, Cheapside, Too-Too, Matthew, and Theodosia—broke out into resounding cheers and came flocking across the lawn on the run.

They formed a ring around him, all talking at once.

He smiled and tried to say something to each of them. But in a moment he stopped short, swaying.

"Stubbins," he muttered. "I must sit down."

He sank heavily to the grass and propped his back against a tree.

"Can I get you anything, Doctor," I asked. "Brandy? I have it here."

"No, I'll be—be all right soon, Stubbins. It's my er—er—breathing, you know. Funny how I've forgotten the language—partly. Haven't talked it in so long. Have to—er—stop to remember words."

"Well, don't try to talk now, Doctor," I said. "Just rest here."

"The change of air pressure . . . c-c-catches my breath," he murmured, closing his eyes. "And the stronger gravity—with my weight. Never dreamed the change would be so great. Just take my pulse, will you?"

I took out the watch and held his wrist.

"It's all right, Doctor," I said after a while. "It's a little fast, but strong and regular."

I turned to Theodosia and asked her to get some mattresses and bedding from the house. She was not sure where to look for them, so I went with her.

"Mercy, Master Tommy!" she whispered when we were inside. "The Lord be praised 'e's back! But did you *ever* see such a size?"

"It's terrific, Theodosia," I said. "I was over nine feet when I returned. But he's twice that height."

"But where are we going to put him?" she asked. "None of these bedrooms is big enough—even if 'e could get through the door."

"Well," I said, "we'll think up some way to manage. Let's get him comfortable where he is for the present."

"Don't you think you ought to 'ave a doctor look at 'im, Master Tommy? I 'ad a sister once who came down with dropsy. Like an elephant she swelled up. But a doctor gave 'er some pills and she got all right."

"Yes, Theodosia," I said. "I *would* feel happier if I had a doctor to keep an eye on him. And if I have to, I will. But so long as John Dolittle is conscious, I know he would rather I didn't."

"Doctor Pinchbeck, over to Oxenthorpe, is very good, they tell me," said she. "Now where are them blankets, Master Tommy?"

"In these three closets here," I said. "Look, I'll load you up and then you send Matthew back to help me get these mattresses out. We're going to need three at least—maybe four."

"All right," she called, running down the stairs under a pile of bed covers.

"And listen, Mrs. Mugg," I called after her. "Don't let those animals be fussing the Doctor with questions. Let him rest."

Well, we got the poor man comfortably settled after a while. By placing four double-bed mattresses end to end we made a bed big enough for him, right there on the lawn beneath the elms. Then we got all the bolsters in the house, made them into a pile at one end, and covered them with a sheet. That was his pillow. I got him to roll over a couple of turns from where he sat; and there he was, safe in bed.

"It's pretty cool out here, Doctor," I said. "How much cover do you think you'll need?"

He said he thought two thicknesses would be enough. So Theodosia got some carpet thread and by stitching four blankets into one piece, twice, she had two covers big enough to spread over him.

"But listen, Tommy," said Dab-Dab, "what if it should rain? There are clouds over there to the southwest."

"You're right," I said. "So there are. Let me see, I wonder what—"

"How about the circus tent?" said Gub-Gub. "That's big enough to keep the rain off him."

"Splendid!" I cried. "Let's go and get it." And off we all went toward the stable.

The big tent, a perfectly tremendous affair, was all that the Doctor had kept from his circus days. He had thought it might come in handy some time for housing larger animals in the zoo. It was stored in the hayloft over the stable. It weighed I don't know how much. But I do know that it took all of our strength to drag it down out of the loft. But once we got it down, the old horse told us to hitch him on to one end of it with a rope and collar. Then he trailed it across the grass to where the Doctor lay.

We found that some of the poles were missing. But after we had sent Chee-Chee aloft in the trees to tie the ridge-ends to branches, we finally managed to get it strung up and pegged down somehow so that it would serve as a shelter over the bed.

"This is splendid, Tommy," said Dab-Dab when we had finished. "Because, you see, the tent is hidden here from the road by the house and trees. No one will suspect anything."

"Yes," I said, "the Doctor can make this his bedroom till he has grown small again—the same as I did—and can live in the house. We'll have to get some furniture out for him later. But he won't need it yet. Now comes the question of food, Dab-Dab. Have we plenty of milk?"

"About three quarts," said the housekeeper.

I asked Matthew to get me some oil lamps. And after we had them lighted we went inside the tent.

For the present the Doctor seemed very comfortable. His breathing sounded a little better already. He drank up the three quarts of milk as if it had been no more than a glassful. I guessed that, as usual, he had been too busy getting ready to travel to bother about eating and had probably gone without food for many hours. I rigged up a place for myself to sleep beside him and told the others they could go to bed.

Presently he began to doze off again. But just before he fell asleep he murmured:

"Stubbins, see the locust has a good feed of lettuce. He will be leaving again before daylight."

"All right, Doctor," I said. "I'll attend to it."

"And don't forget to unload all the baggage off him—some very important specimens, Stubbins, and a lot of notes—very important."

"Yes," I said, "I'll get them unloaded and stored away safe."

I took his pulse again, and while I was doing it he dropped off into a peaceful sleep.

The Moon Cat

SEVERAL TIMES DURING WHAT WAS LEFT OF that night I heard John Dolittle stir. By the light of the turned-down lamp I went and looked at him quietly. It was when the first gray of dawn was showing through the canvas of the tent that he called to me. And as I bent over him, I heard the great locust outside whirr up off the lawn and start its return journey to the moon.

"Listen, Stubbins," he said weakly. "In the baggage you'll find a package done up in large orange-colored leaves."

"Yes, Doctor," I said. "I saw it. I have it stored safely away with the other things."

He beckoned me to come nearer. Then he whispered in my ear:

"There's a cat inside it."

I tried not to show my surprise. But I must say it was a shock. The Dolittle household had kept almost every kind of animal on earth in its time, but never a cat. The Doctor always feared that it wouldn't get on happily with the birds and the others. But I only answered:

"Yes, Doctor."

"I had to bring it, Stubbins," he went on, "simply had to. I found it on the far side of the moon, in the twilight zone. There was a whole colony of them there. They were the one kind of animal that refused to join in the Council's work for balancing life and stamping out the everlasting warfare of one species against another. You know they're very independent, cats. Consequently they had had to live by themselves. But when I visited them they did not seem very happy just the same."

"But how did cats come to be on the moon in the first place?" I asked.

"Oh, I imagine there must have been a pair of cats on that piece of the earth which shot away into the sky and became the moon, thousands of years ago. The same thing that happened to the Moon Man himself. I made a lot of other discoveries, too, in the animal kingdom up there after you left. I'll tell you all about them when I'm feeling stronger."

I was simply crazy to ask him a thousand questions concerning these discoveries. But for his sake I held my patience.

"All right, Doctor," I said, "there's no hurry."

"No, but listen," he said, dropping his voice to a whisper again. "Keep it quiet—about the cat. Don't say anything to our own animals for the present. It would just upset them. I'll speak to them myself later on. She's a nice cat—quite a character. You know most people think cats are just stay-at-homes. They are not. They're very adventurous. This one astonished me. Said that Otho Bludge, the only man up there, didn't understand cats. And she wanted to travel to see the world—the earth down here where her ancestors came from. Could she come with me? Well, what was I to do? She promised she would kill no birds, eat no mice, and live on nothing but milk—if I'd only take her. You see, Stubbins, I just had to bring her. Polynesia raised an awful row, but there was nothing else for it."

"Very good, Doctor," I said. "I'll see she is fed regularly."

But while I said the words I foresaw a revolution in the Dolittle household ahead of us.

"Now run and get breakfast," said the Doctor. "Look, it's daylight outside."

Weary from the effort of talking, he sank back upon the pillow. It made me terribly unhappy to see him lying there so weak and weary. I had never known John Dolittle to have a single day's sickness in his life. He had always been so up-and-doing, cheerful, strong and active.

"Tell me," I said, "don't you think it would be a good idea if I got a doctor in to see you?"

"Oh no, Stubbins," he smiled. "I'll be all right. You just keep note of my pulse. We don't want any medical men coming here. It might bring those newspaper fellows around."

"Can I get you anything to eat?" I asked.

"Bring me a half dozen eggs beaten up—with a little pepper and salt. But there's no hurry. Get your own breakfast first, Stubbins. I'll take another little sleep now. And don't forget the cat, will you?"

"No, Doctor," I said, "I won't forget."

"By the way," he added as I pulled aside the tent flap to leave, "you will find her difficult to talk to. Took me quite a while to get on to the language. Quite different from anything we've tried so far in animal languages. A curious tongue—very subtle, precise and exact. Sounds as though whoever invented it was more anxious to keep things to himself than to hand them over to others. Not chatty at all. There's no word for *gossip* in it. Not much use for people who want to be chummy. Good language for lawyers, though."

When I got indoors I found everyone sitting down to a good breakfast that Dab-Dab and Theodosia had prepared. I was glad to be able to tell them that the Doctor could breathe and speak better this morning, though he still seemed very weak and easily tired.

"The first thing," I said, "is to make him really strong and well. After that we'll have to get his weight and size down to what it was. But that must be done gradually, without letting him lose strength. I'll get him to lay out a diet for himself—then we'll know just what things to give him and what not to give him."

"Then you ain't goin' to get another doctor to see 'im, Master Tommy?" asked Theodosia.

"No," I said, "not for the present, anyhow."

"What would he want with a doctor?" Gub-Gub asked, raising his eyebrows. "John Dolittle knows all there is to be known, himself, about doctoring, doesn't he?"

"Well," I explained, "you see, when doctors get sick, they sometimes have to get other doctors to doctor them."

"Humph!" grunted Gub-Gub. "How extraordinary! Seems a dreadful waste of money."

"Now," I said, "the main thing for the present—you must forgive me if I repeat it—is that all of you (you Gub-Gub, Jip, Whitey, Too-Too), everybody, must leave him in peace. Don't visit the tent unless you're sent there specially. He has a lot to tell us and I am just as anxious to hear it as you are. But we have got to wait till he is well enough to tell us in his own way and in his own time. Is that clear?"

They all promised that they would do as I asked. And I must

say that they were very good about it. Anyone knowing the way they loved the Doctor can imagine how hard it was for them to keep away from him at this time, when they had not seen or talked with him for so long.

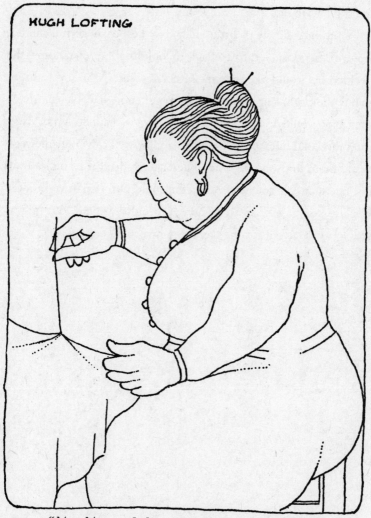

"Mrs. Mugg took three suits and made them into one."

Matthew and Theodosia I allowed into the tent—and, once in a while, Polynesia and Chee-Chee. But I never let any of them stay long. It is true that I was a very worried boy those first few days. And if the Doctor's pulse had acted in any way strangely I would have gotten another doctor in, no matter what my patient himself had to say.

But, very slowly, a little each day, he began getting better. Before Theodosia left to go back to look after her own home, she decided she would like to make him a new suit. Matthew was sent to buy the cloth. But he found that to get enough woolen cloth for such a job would cost far more money than we had. So Mrs. Mugg took three old suits of the Doctor's and by very clever needlework made them into one big one. Then she re-dyed it to make it all of one color. Of course the Doctor could not wear it right away because he was not yet well enough to move around. But he was very glad to have it for the day when he could get up.

The Dolittle Household Revolution

I FOUND THAT THE DOCTOR HAD GIVEN ME A hard job when he told me not to let the other animals know about the cat. That same night I sneaked off quietly by myself and opened up the crate to feed her. I suppose I had expected to find an ordinary cat. But there was nothing ordinary about her. She had a long, thin, snaky sort of body and long thin legs—something like the Indian cheetah. And she was the wildest creature I had ever seen.

Most likely she had thought it was the Doctor coming to see her when I started to undo the wrapping on her cage. But when she saw a strange human looking in at her she bounded away from me and cowered, snarling, in a corner. I saw it was no use trying to coax her in that state of fear. I would have to let her get used to me gradually. So I put the bowl of milk down inside and closed up her crate. Soon I heard her lapping up the food hungrily and I tiptoed quietly away.

I thought it best to consult with Polynesia. I took her aside where we could talk without being heard.

"Listen, Polynesia," I said, "you know about this cat?"

She jumped as though I had stuck a pin in her.

"Young man," she said severely, "if you wish to remain a friend of mine don't ever speak of that animal by the usual word. Those *creatures*—well, just call it *It!*"

"Very well, Polynesia," I said, "we'll call her It—No, let's call her Itty, shall we?"

"Itty?" muttered the parrot with a frown—"Itty? Kitty?—*Pity* would be better. Oh well, have it your own way."

And from that time on the cat was called Itty.

"You see, Polynesia," I said, "this cat—"

"Don't use that word!" she screamed. "It gets me all fluffed up."

"Excuse me," I went on. "But Itty has to be fed on the quiet for the present. The Doctor doesn't want the other animals to know about her until he can tell them himself. But you can understand it isn't going to be easy for me to get meals to her. Now what I was going to ask you to do is this: when I want to go and give—er—Itty food, I'll make a sign to you. Then you lead the other animals off somewhere or keep them busy till I get back, see?"

The parrot agreed she would do this. And for a while the plan worked all right. Every day when I wanted to take milk to the cat, Polynesia would suggest to the animals that they all go with her to see how the lettuce was coming up in the kitchen garden, or something like that. And the coast would be left clear for me to attend to Itty.

The cat began gradually to get used to my visits, and when she saw that I meant to do her no more harm than to bring her milk, she actually became friendly in a strange, awkward way.

However, the household finally got suspicious. Maybe

Polynesia's excuses for getting them out of the way began to grow stale. Anyway, Gub-Gub asked me one evening what was the reason for my disappearing so mysteriously at the same hour every day. Then Too-Too, that bird with the keenest ears in the world, remarked that she had heard strange, unearthly noises in the attic. (The attic was where I had stored the Doctor's moon baggage.) And finally Jip—who had been decorated with a golden dog collar for his cleverness in smelling—said he had sniffed a new strange scent on the upper stairs.

I began to get uncomfortable. I glanced across at Polynesia to see if I would get any help from her. But the old rascal was gazing up at the ceiling, humming a Danish sea song to herself, pretending not to hear a word of the conversation. Chee-Chee, the only other one in on the secret, was frightfully busy clearing up the hearth, in hopes, no doubt, that he wouldn't be asked any questions. The white mouse was watching, silent, from the mantelpiece, his big pink eyes wide open with curiosity. I heard Dab-Dab through the open door to the pantry, drying dishes at the sink. I got more uncomfortable still.

"Tell me, Tommy," said Jip, "what's in all that baggage the Doctor brought down from the moon?"

"Oh—er—plants," I said, "moon plants, and seeds—no end of seeds, Jip, things the Doctor wants to try out down here on the earth to see how they'll do."

"But this wasn't any plant smell that I caught," said Jip. "It was something quite different."

"What was it like?" asked Too-Too.

"Seemed like an animal," said the dog.

"What kind of an animal?" asked the white mouse.

"I couldn't quite make out," said Jip. "It was very strange. It set the hair on my back all tingling. And I couldn't understand why. Is there nothing else but plants in that baggage, Tommy?"

For a long minute I remained silent while all the animals watched me, waiting for an answer. At last Polynesia said:

"Oh, you might as well tell them, Tommy. They're bound to know sooner or later."

"Very well, then," I said. "The Doctor had asked me not to say anything for the present. But I see it can't be helped. There's a cat in the baggage."

Polynesia squawked at the hated word. Jip jumped as though he'd been shot. Too-Too let out a long, low whistle. Dab-Dab in the pantry dropped a plate on the floor, where it broke with a loud crash—the first time she had ever done such a thing in her life. Gub-Gub grunted with disgust. As for the white mouse, he uttered one piercing squeal and fainted dead away on the mantelpiece. I jumped up and dashed a teaspoonful of water in his face. He came to immediately.

"Gracious!" he gasped. "Such a shock!"

"What," I asked, "the water?"

"No," said he, "the cat. Oh, how could he? How *could* the Doctor have done it?"

"The place will never be the same again," groaned Too-Too.

"Oh me, oh my!" wailed Gub-Gub, shaking his head sadly. "How awful!"

Dab-Dab stood in the pantry doorway, shaking with sobs. "It can't be true," she kept saying. "It just can't be true."

"A cat!" muttered Jip. "I should have known! Nothing else could have made my spine tingle like that but the smell of a cat. Gosh! I'll chase her off the place."

Then they all broke out together in a general uproar. Some

were for going away at once, leaving the beloved home they had enjoyed so long. Some begged that they be allowed to see the Doctor and ask him to send the animal away. Others, like Jip, swore they would drive her out. Panic, pandemonium, and bedlam broke loose in the kitchen.

"Stop it!" I cried at last. "Stop it! Now listen to me, all of you. You're just making a lot of fuss without knowing what you're talking about. You ought to know the Doctor well enough by now to be sure he would not bring anything here that would make any of you unhappy. I admit I'm not fond of cats in a general way myself— neither is Polynesia. But this cat is different. It's a moon cat. It may have all sorts of new ideas on cat behavior. It may have messages for us. The Doctor is fond of it. He wants to study it."

"But, Tommy," squeaked the white mouse, "our lives won't be safe for a moment."

"Please be quiet, Whitey," I said sharply. "How many times have you heard John Dolittle say, 'Man, as a race, is the most selfish of all creatures'?"

"There's nothing as selfish as a cat," put in Jip with a growl.

"How often," I went on, "have you heard him railing against people who are forever spouting about glorious freedom while they deny it to animals? Are you going to be like that? You haven't met *this* cat. You know nothing about her. And yet you all start squawking like a lot of day-old chicks as soon as I mention her."

"She'll have to wear a bell—she'll *have* to!" cried Dab-Dab. "Cats when they come sneaking up in the dark just give me the heebeejeebees. I couldn't stand it. I'd have to leave home—after all these years!"

She began to weep again.

"Calm yourself, Dab-Dab," I said, "*please*! At least I expected some sense from you." I turned to the others. "This cat is a sportsman, everyone must give her that credit. She trusted the Doctor enough to ask to be brought down to the earth. Which of you would have the courage, if a strange man came down from the moon, to ask to be taken away from this world and planted on another you had never seen? Answer me that."

Rather to my surprise, my long, high-sounding speech seemed to have quite an effect on them. When I ended there was a thoughtful silence. Presently Jip said quietly:

"Humph! You're right, Tommy. That certainly was nerve. She took a big gamble."

"Now I'm going to ask you all," I said, "for the Doctor's sake, to treat this cat with kindness and consideration. You don't have to like her if you can't. But at least let us be polite and fair to her."

"Well," said Dab-Dab with a sigh, "I hope it will work out all right. But if she goes and has kittens in my linen closet, I'll fly south with the first flock of wild ducks that passes over the garden, as sure as shooting!"

"Don't worry," I said. "Leave her to the Doctor. He'll know how to manage her. I can't even talk her language yet. She is still very shy and wild. But she'll fit in all right, once she gets used to us all."

Little Chee-Chee the monkey, squatting by the hearth, spoke up for the first time.

"She's smart," he said, "a bit mysterious and odd—and independent as the dickens, too—but mighty clever. Polynesia wouldn't bother to learn her funny language. But I picked up a few words of it."

"And another thing," I said, "you need have no fears about her slaughtering other creatures. She has promised the Doctor not to kill birds and"—I glanced up at Whitey on the mantelpiece—"*not to eat mice.*"

"What's her name?" asked Gub-Gub.

"Her name is Itty," I said.

"Humph!" murmured the white mouse thoughtfully. "Itty, eh? Itty—Pretty!"

"Are you trying to make up poetry, Whitey?" asked Gub-Gub.

"Oh no," said the white mouse, airily twirling his whiskers. "That's just called doggerel."

"*Whatterel?*" barked Jip in disgust.

"Doggerel," said the white mouse.

"Cat-and-doggerel, I'd call it," grunted Gub-Gub.

And they all giggled and went off to bed in a much better mood than I had hoped for.

The Doctor's Accident

B Y THE END OF THE WEEK THE DOCTOR WAS showing a great improvement in health. So far he had lived almost entirely on milk, eggs, and lettuce. These three foods seemed to strengthen him better than anything else. And it was a good thing that they did. Because we could not have afforded a more expensive diet. The lettuce, of course, cost practically nothing while we could grow it in the garden. (Gub-Gub and I planted several new beds of it.) Just the same, I was gladder than ever that I had my bookkeeping job. I saved every penny I could out of the three shillings and sixpence a week, in case anything unexpected should turn up that might require a special lot of money.

I still slept in the Doctor's tent in case he should need anything during the night. Early one morning he called me to him and said:

"Stubbins, I'm feeling pretty well. I think I'll try to get up today."

"But, Doctor," I said, "are you sure you'll be strong enough?"

"No, I'm not sure," he said. "But the only way to find out is to try. Help me into that suit that Theodosia made for me, will you?"

I was very anxious. At the same time I was very glad. I helped him on with his clothes; but when it came to helping him to stand up and walk, I found I wasn't much use. Though I measured then something over five feet and a quarter, he had to bend down to reach my shoulder. And he was terribly afraid he might fall on me.

However, after I had cut a long walking stick for him out of the forest, he managed to hobble around the tent pretty well. Then he got more adventurous still and wanted to go out into the garden. I did my best to persuade him not to, but he tried it anyway. He actually got halfway across the lawn before he sank down from weariness.

The next day he did better still. It was strange to see his towering form walking about the turf, his head occasionally disappearing among the leaves of the high elm trees. This time after a few rests he said he would like to go as far as the zoo enclosure. And when he got to it he actually stepped over the ten-foot wall instead of bothering with the door.

After that he was impatient to get into the house. There was one door to the old building that was never used by us. Closed up for years now, its faded green paint and tarnished brass knocker faced toward the Long Lawn, the same as did the back door. But it was always known for some reason or other as the side door. The Doctor was sitting against one of the elms, staring at it while taking a rest.

"You know, Stubbins," said he, "I believe I could get through that door."

"Oh, Doctor," I said, "why, it isn't half your height!"

"I didn't mean to try it standing up," he said. "But by lying down and sort of worming my way in I think I might manage it. You see, it's a double door. A very long time ago, before the days of my great grandfather, they used to use that door for garden parties—in fact, it was the main door. There was a driveway running up to it too, close to the house, where the peony beds are now. Just open it and take a few measurements for me, will you? It is my hips that will be the difficulty. If they'll go through, the rest of me will."

So I got the long garden tape and measured the width of the Doctor's hips. Then, after hunting with Dab-Dab through all the drawers in the house, I found the key to the side door. Its hinges creaked with age and rust as we swung both halves of it open.

I went back to the Doctor.

"It looks to me as if it should be all right," I said. "That is, as far as the width of the door frame is concerned. But what are you going to do when you get inside?"

"Oh, the headroom of the hall there is extra high," he said. "Let's try it, Stubbins."

Well, that was when we had our accident. By wriggling and squirming the Doctor got in—halfway. There he stuck. Dab-Dab was in a terrible state of mind. I pushed him to see if I could get him all the way in. Then I pulled at him to see if I could get him out. But I couldn't budge him either way. I had made a mistake of six inches in my measurements.

"We had better get some carpenters and workmen in, Tommy," said Dab-Dab. "We certainly can't leave him like this."

"No, don't do that," said the Doctor. "You'll have the whole town here gaping at me. Get Matthew to come."

So I sent off Too-Too to bring the Cat's-Meat-Man to the rescue.

Matthew scratched his head when he saw the Doctor's legs sticking out into the garden, and the other half of him inside the house.

"Well, now wait a minute, Tommy," said he. "Yer see that fanlight window over the door? If you give me a saw and a ladder I can maybe cut away the head of the door frame."

"But won't the bricks come tumbling down, then?" I asked.

"No, I don't think so," said Matthew. "The frame of the window-arch will hold the wall up. Give me a saw. D'yer mind if I stand on top of you, Doctor?"

"Not a bit," said John Dolittle. "Only get me either in or out. Don't leave me the way I am."

I got a saw; and Matthew—who was a very handy man with tools—climbed up on top of the Doctor and sawed away the doorhead. This gave us, after we had taken the glass out of the window, another foot-and-a-half clearance. The Doctor squirmed and wriggled some more.

"Ah!" he said presently. "I think I can manage now. But I'll have to go in, not out."

We next drove a stake into the ground to give him something to push against with his feet. The rest of the animals stood around while, with much grunting and puffing, he finally pried the whole of his big body into the hall. He lay down with a sigh.

"Splendid," he said, "splendid!"

"But you can't sit up where you are, Doctor, can you?" I asked.

"Half a mo', Doctor," said Matthew. "Wait till I cut a hole in the ceiling. We can put the boards back afterward so no one would know the difference. Wait while I run upstairs. I'll 'ave you comfortable."

The Cat's-Meat-Man ran round by the kitchen stairs and soon we heard him sawing away at the floor above. Bits of plaster began falling on the Doctor; but Chee-Chee and the white mouse cleared them off him as fast as they fell.

Before long a hole appeared in the hall ceiling big enough even for the Doctor's head to go through.

"Thank you, Matthew," said John Dolittle. "What would I do without you?"

He hoisted himself into a sitting position, and his head disappeared from my sight into the opening.

"Ah!" I heard him say with a sigh. "Here I am, home at last! Upstairs and downstairs at the same time. Splendid!"

After he had taken a rest he managed to turn himself right around inside the hall. Then, facing the door once more, he tried to get *out* into the garden. It was a hard job. He got stuck again halfway.

"Listen, Doctor," said the white mouse, "and I'll tell you what we mice do when we want to get through a specially small hole."

"I wish you would!" said the Doctor, puffing.

"First you breathe in, deep," said Whitey. "Then you breathe out, long. Then you hold your breath. Then you shut your eyes and think that the hole is only half as big as it is. Of course if you're a mouse, you think that a cat is coming after you as well. But you needn't bother about that. Try it. You'll see. You'll slide through like silk. Now, a deep breath—in, out—and don't forget to shut your eyes. Do it by feeling. Just imagine you're a mouse."

"All right," said the Doctor. "I'll try. It's hard on the imagination, but it should be awfully good for my figure."

Whether there was anything in Whitey's advice or not, I don't know. But, anyway, at the second attempt the Doctor got through all right and scrambled out on the lawn, laughing like a schoolboy.

We were all very happy now that he could get both in and out of the house. Right away we brought in the mattresses from the tent under the trees and turned the big hall into a bedroom for him. He said he found it very comfortable, even if he did have to pull his knees up a bit when he wanted to sleep.

Before long, finding himself so much better, John Dolittle gave all his attention to bringing his size down to a natural one. First he tried exercise. We rigged up a heavy sweater for him made out of a couple of eiderdown quilts. And in this he ran up and down the Long Lawn before breakfast. His thundering tread shook the whole garden till the dishes rattled on the pantry shelves and the pictures began falling from the walls in the parlor.

But this did not thin him down fast enough to satisfy him. Someone suggested massage. So we laid him out on the lawn where Matthew, Chee-Chee, and I pummeled and pounded him for hours. He said it reminded him of the time when the elephant fell sick in the circus and he and all the crew had climbed aboard the animal with ladders to rub the pains out of it, till everybody had to lay off with stiff muscles.

Gub-Gub asked why we didn't use the lawn roller on him. But we decided this would be a little too drastic.

"Why don't you try it on yourself, Gubby?" Jip said. "Your figure could do with a little taking down, too."

"What's the matter with my figure?" said Gub-Gub, gazing down at his ample curves. "Why, I wouldn't change it for anything!"

It proved to be a slow business for the poor Doctor, this

getting back to ordinary size. But he certainly kept at it with a will. And soon with the diet, the exercise, and the massage (besides, of course, the change of climate and gravity), he began to look more like himself.

HUGH LOFTING

"*He ran up and down the Long Lawn before breakfast.*"

The Moon Museum

B UT ALL OF US, INCLUDING JOHN DOLITTLE, saw that it was still probably a matter of some weeks before he would be able to carry on a usual life the same as other people. He could not yet pass through an ordinary door without going down on all fours; he could not sit in the biggest armchair without having the arms break off; he could not grasp a common pencil or pen in his huge fingers and make it write properly.

This annoyed him greatly. He was so eager to get at his notes. He planned to write a new book, a book about the moon.

"It will be the greatest thing I have ever done, Stubbins," he said. "That is, of course, if I make a good job of it. And even if I don't, it will at least contain information of great value for future writers on natural history. The general public will probably begin by thinking I'm a great humbug or a splendid liar. But the day will come when they'll believe me."

I, too, of course was very keen to have him get at those notes.

Being his secretary, I would have to help him and would so get a glimpse of what studies and experiments he had made. But Dab-Dab was of quite another mind about it.

"Tommy," she said, "there's no hurry about that book he wants to write. I don't mean to say it isn't important—though, for my part, I can't see much sense in mixing up the moon and the earth, as though life weren't mixed up enough as it is for simple country folk. But the main thing is this: you know how he is— once he gets started on a new line of work he goes at it like a crazy man, night and day; doesn't stop for meals; doesn't stop for sleep; nothing but work. He isn't strong enough yet for that sort of thing. For pity's sake, keep him away from those notes—at least till he is perfectly well."

As a matter of fact, there was no urgent need at present for the housekeeper's fears. The Doctor himself saw that there was not much sense in his attempting to write a long book until he could move around his study without upsetting things, or smashing delicate laboratory apparatus with clumsy experiments.

By daytime he contented himself with exercising and with some gardening. He had brought many different sorts of seeds with him from the moon, also roots of plants. He wanted to see if these could be grown in our world, and what differences they would show in new climate and conditions. Some were vegetables and fruits, good to eat. In these, of course, Gub-Gub was especially interested; and he immediately started to keep notes on his own account, planning to make a new volume for his famous *Encyclopedia of Food*. This volume was to be called *Moon Meals*.

With the pig's assistance, the Doctor and I planted rows and rows of new and strange-shaped seeds. All the rows were carefully marked with wooden labels giving the date of planting and the kind of soil. The temperature, the air pressure, the amount of rainfall, etc., were noted down from day to day in a book we called the *Garden Diary*. With one kind of these seeds the Doctor told me to be particularly careful.

"This plant," said he, "if it comes up, Stubbins—may prove exceedingly useful. From it I got the leaves I made my clothes out of—you know, the coat I was wearing when I arrived. Extraordinarily tough and pliable. I found a way of tanning them like leather. Every bit as good as real cloth."

In that great bulk of baggage that he had brought down with him were also the eggs and grubs of insects: ants, bees, water flies, moths, and whatnot. These had to have special hatching-boxes made for them, so they could be kept warm against cool nights; while others had to be planted in proper places in the garden, among grasses or trees, where they would be likely to find food and conditions to their liking.

Then again, he had brought sacks full of geological specimens; that is, rocks, pieces of marble, something that looked like coal, and all manner of samples out of the handmade mines he had dug in the mountains of the moon. Among them were pieces that had precious stones in them—or what looked like precious stones—pebbles and crystals that could have been opals, sapphires, amethysts, and rubies. And fossils he had too—shells of curious snails, fishes, lizards, and strange frogs that no longer lived either on earth or moon—all turned now to stone as hard as flint.

To take care of these we added another department to the Doctor's many-sided establishment. We called it the Moon Museum. In a disused harness room of the big stable, I set up shelves around the walls and even showcases with glass tops. And here were placed all the fossils and geological specimens along with some very beautiful pressed flowers and leaves that had also come down in the baggage.

Jip suggested that I put the cat there, in a glass case too—so she wouldn't get hurt.

I was very proud of my job when it was done. I must say it did look like a regular museum; and the Doctor was no end pleased with its workmanlike, scientific appearance.

"You have a real gift for order and neatness in these things, Stubbins," he said. "That's the trouble with me—never could be orderly or neat. My sister Sarah—she used to be housekeeper for me, you know—she was always at me about my untidiness. In fact, that's why she left me to go and get married. Poor dear Sarah, I wonder how she's getting on. An excellent woman—in many ways. But this, Stubbins, this is splendid! And you've done it all yourself. What would I do without you?"

But though with one thing and another the Doctor managed to keep quite busy during the daylight hours, it was not so with the evenings and nights. Usually in times past he had filled this part of the day writing in his study, doing experiments in his laboratory and, once in a while, reading aloud in the kitchen when the animals of his household could persuade him to leave his work and amuse them.

It had never been his habit to take much sleep. In fact I would often, after I had left him late at night, find him again the next morning working away with his lamp still burning, apparently quite unaware that the morning sun was shining in his window.

But now it was very different. He retired to his bedroom in the big hall regularly after supper; and I, knowing that he would not sleep for hours, would sit up and read the newspapers to him or just chat with him of this and that.

As I have said, I had been careful not to ask him questions about the moon until he wished to speak of it himself. I am proud of my own patience in this; for anyone can imagine how keen I was to learn how he had at last got away from the Moon Man—and a thousand other things besides.

So far he had said little or nothing of his last months in that other world. But it was natural that in our talks after supper he would sooner or later get started. And at last one evening he did.

"By the way, Stubbins," said he, "what became of Bumpo? He was here with you when I left. Where is he now?"

"He was gone before I got down from the moon, Doctor," I said. "He left messages for us with Matthew. It seems he wanted to go back to Oxford to visit some of his old friends and perhaps to take up some new studies there too. He couldn't tell just how long he would be gone. But he said he would surely come and visit you again before he went back to Africa."

"Well, I'm glad of that," said the Doctor. "Fine fellow, Prince Bumpo, one of the best. . . . Yes, yes. There have been many times when I don't know what I would have done without him. But tell me, Stubbins, do you remember how long it took the giant moth to bring you down?"

"Not exactly, Doctor," I answered. "Passing through the dead belt, I got awfully sick, dazed, and mixed up. And then my mind was so full of worry about having left you up there alone, I don't know that I would have remembered anyway."

"Humph!" said he thoughtfully. "It's too bad you can't remember. I wanted to make a little calculation between the speed of your moth and that of my locust—that is for the downward journey. But you have no cause to blame yourself for leaving me. You never had a chance to do anything else. You see, the Moon Man, Otho Bludge, wanted to get rid of you: but he wanted to keep me. I had quite a time with him when I wished to get back here. That is after—"

I interrupted him. I knew something interesting was coming—that at last he was going to speak of how he got away. Many more ears besides mine wanted to hear that story.

"Pardon me, Doctor," I said. "But would you mind if I got the animals in so they can listen? I know they are all crazy to hear what happened after I left you."

"Why yes, certainly," he said. "Bring them in, by all means. As a matter of fact, I meant to have told you all, before this, about my last days up there. But I have been talking those moon languages for such a long time, I found I had grown sort of rusty and hesitating in speaking the languages of my own world. But they are coming back to me now and I think I can manage all right—that is, if you don't mind my speaking slowly."

"Of course, Doctor," I said as I got up, "we understand that. But you will promise not to overtire yourself, won't you? Send us all away the first minute you feel weary."

He said he would. And I ran out into the garden to go around to the kitchen. In the dusk on the lawn I bumped into Matthew Mugg, who had just arrived to pay John Dolittle a visit.

"The Doctor's going to tell us how he got off the moon, Matthew," I said. "Would you like to come and listen?"

"You bet I would, Tommy," said he. "But of course if he talks in them animal lingos I won't understand the same as what you will.

Never mind, you can explain to me afterward. But I wouldn't miss it for anything. No, you bet I'll come!"

Then I ran on and found the animals gathered round the big fireplace in the kitchen. Here I spied another visitor, Cheapside. The sparrow had "popped over" from London to hear the latest news of his old friend. They all let out a whoop of joy when I told them that at last they were going to hear the tale they had waited for so long.

And so, with two guests added to our own company, it was quite a circle that gathered round the Doctor that night. I had brought pencil and notebooks with me. For some months back I had been studying shorthand. And I was anxious to see if I could take down his words as fast as he spoke them.

"Ah!" whispered the white mouse, tittering with eager excitement as he settled down to listen. "Tommy, this is like old times!"

PART TWO

Why John Dolittle Stayed
So Long on the Moon

W ELL," THE DOCTOR BEGAN, "BEFORE you came in I was telling Stubbins here that I had quite a difficult time getting away from Otho Bludge, the Moon Man. But since you all want to listen to the story I had better begin at the beginning— that is, from where Stubbins was carried off by the moth and taken away. You know of course why that was. The Moon Man, who had bird spies in every corner of that world up there, heard that I was uneasy about Stubbins—or rather about his mother and father. The young rascal hadn't even told his parents he was going—just stowed away aboard the moth without even my knowing it. Of course I feared his parents would be terribly worried when he no longer came to visit them.

"These bird spies overheard us talking about this one night in our camp and they told Otho Bludge. Now I had been treating him for rheumatism, and he didn't want to lose me, it seemed. He thought if he got Stubbins back to the earth I would no longer worry about him and would be willing to stay. So he kidnapped the boy and shipped him off before I had a chance to say a word about it one way or the other.

"At first it was a great load off my mind. I knew the trip could be made in safety—although, to be sure, it was a hard and trying one. When the moth got back and reported that he had landed Stubbins on the earth I was very happy. I admit I was terribly sorry to lose him. And, no doubt, I would have felt awfully lonely up there if I had not been so busy.

"I have never known any one single year in my whole life when so many interesting things for study were presented to me at once. The days never seemed long enough. There were great portions of the moon that Stubbins and I had not yet even explored. I found new lakes with all sorts of strange life in the waters. High in the mountains, among the old craters of dead volcanoes, I found fossil remains of different animals that had thrived on the moon long, long ago and since died out—become extinct, as we call it. Then there were the rocks at lower levels. Comparing these with what I knew of our own rocks down here, I was able to calculate the exact age of the moon, that is, I could tell within a few thousand years, just when it was that the great explosion occurred—the explosion that shot the moon off from the earth and made it into a separate little world, revolving around us in the heavens."

The Doctor paused a moment and turned to Chee-Chee.

"By the way, Chee-Chee," said he, "now that we're back, don't forget to have me alter that chapter in my book on Monkey History."

"You mean the part about the story my grandmother told when I was little?" asked the monkey.

"Oh, I remember that," cried the white mouse. "It was called 'The Days Before There Was a Moon.'"

"That's right," said the Doctor. "The legend of how a man, a prehistoric artist, was shot away from the earth the day before the

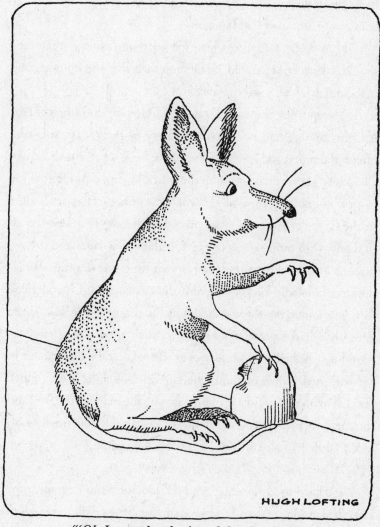

HUGH LOFTING

"'Oh, I remember that,' cried the white mouse."

moon appeared in the sky for the first time. I put it into my book, even if it was only a story. But it now appears that it was all practically true—the Legend of Pippiteepa, the beautiful young woman with whom poor Otho Bludge was in love. And by examining the rocks up there we now know that the monkey race is much older than most naturalists had thought."

"How sad," said the white mouse thoughtfully, "that they should have been separated, one left on the earth and one stuck up in the moon. A very sad romance."

"Yes, but just the same," said the Doctor, "don't forget that if Otho Bludge had not been shot away by the great explosion, life on the moon today could never have been what it is. It was he who saved the animal world up there from dying out. He told me it took him a long time to see what was going to happen. Some of the larger creatures—great prehistoric beasts that went off so suddenly with him—some in egg-form like dinosaurs and such—began eating up the plant life so fast that the entire vegetable kingdom could hardly keep up against the destruction. Of course all this, you understand, took thousands of years. But at last, when Otho had had enough time to get himself used to his new surroundings, he began to ponder over what should be done about it. He had then grown immensely big. And though he wasn't much good at arithmetic and astronomy he saw the planets, the sun, and the earth revolving around him in the heavens and he finally realized that he had already lived a terribly long while."

"About how long?" asked Gub-Gub.

"It's hard to say exactly," said the Doctor. "But certainly dozens of times longer than he knew man usually lived on the earth. It must have been something in the vegetable diet, and of course the climate, lighter gravity and other things peculiar to that new world. It looked to him, he told me, as if life could go on up there pretty nearly forever—*provided it was properly taken care of.*"

I whispered a word of explanation in Matthew's ear at this point. He nodded and winked back at me understandingly.

"And so," the Doctor went on, "Otho Bludge made up his mind that *he* would see to it that life *was* properly taken care of— life of both kinds, animal and plant. First he went round the whole of the moon, exploring it many times, so that there was hardly a square yard of it that he hadn't examined. In a crude, rough way he made a list of all the different forms of animals, insects, trees, shrubs, and plants that he found. Knowing how long he had lived and how long he was likely still to live, he felt there was no need for hurry and he made a very complete job of it."

"Humph! Must 'ave been quite a naturalist 'imself," Cheapside put in.

"Yes, he most certainly was," said the Doctor. "A very great naturalist, rather the way that Long Arrow was, the man that we found in Spidermonkey Island. He didn't use science such as we use. But he gathered a tremendous lot of information and showed a remarkable common sense in what he did with it. Well, having listed all his animals and plants—or, I should say, all that were still living at the time—he began upon the work. He next found out just what each of them lived on and about how much food each required."

"He told you all this himself, Doctor?" Too-Too asked.

"Yes," said the Doctor, "but you must remember that conversation between him and myself was not exactly the same thing as Matthew and I talking in English together. No, no. Not nearly so—er—exact. Whatever language Otho Bludge had used in talking with his fellow men on the earth of prehistoric days, he had, when I met him, almost entirely forgotten. After all, how could he have remembered it—not having another human to speak with for thousands of years?"

"Well, how did you manage to talk with him at all?" asked Jip.

"In animal languages, mostly," said the Doctor. "For, you see, in his years and years of observing, counting, watching, and examining the other forms of life up there, the Moon Man saw that the animals could communicate with one another. And presently he began, little by little, to catch on to the different ways in which they spoke—signs, noises, movements, and so forth. How long this took him, I couldn't find out. That was one of the great difficulties I always had in questioning him—he was so vague, hazy, about lengths of time, quantities, numbers—in fact, anything that had to do with figures. It was curious, because the cleverness of the man was in all matters most astonishing."

"Well, but, Doctor," said Too-Too, "wouldn't that be because he had lived so long?"

"Exactly," said John Dolittle. "He had lived many hundreds of our lifetimes. So, in some ways, his mind, his experience, was—well, he was like hundreds of men rolled into one, if you know what I mean. Then again, he had kept his attention on just a few subjects. Life in the moon is a very simple matter—as it would be anywhere else where there were no human beings to make it complicated— er—you know, fussy, hard, and mixed up."

"Were the animals' languages on the moon anything like the animal languages down here?" asked Gub-Gub.

"They were and they weren't," said the Doctor. "Of course they had all sprung from the languages of the earth creatures. But after so long up there, the birds and the rest of them spoke quite differently. Of course my own knowledge of animal languages helped me greatly in talking with them. But I found it dreadfully difficult at first. The words and phrases had nearly all changed. Only the manner, the way, of speaking remained.

"But this will show you how hard Otho Bludge himself must have worked: he discovered, without any education in natural history at all, the great part that the insects, like bees, play in the life of the plants. He knew all about it. I found that his knowledge of insect languages, even down to the water beetles, was tremendous—far and away better than my own. And from that he went on to learn the languages of the vegetable world."

"The language of vegetables!" cried Gub-Gub.

"Well," said the Doctor, "not exactly the languages of potatoes and carrots. We hadn't any up there. The expression 'vegetable world' takes in anything that grows in the ground—trees, flowers, vines. Otho Bludge was the first naturalist to make any discoveries in this field of study. I had often wondered, years ago, if our plants down here had any way of talking to one another. I am still wondering.

"But up there, with a very much smaller animal kingdom, and entirely different conditions, certain kinds of trees and plants had worked out and developed languages of their own. You see, in this world, we are always mixing up breeds—crossing different sorts of dahlias to make new kinds, grafting fruit trees, and even sticking rosebuds onto raspberry canes to make roses grow in a raspberry root. That's called a hybrid. How could we expect such a mixture to know what language to talk. Poor thing doesn't even know whether he's a raspberry or a rose!"

"Yes, most confusin', I should say," Cheapside put in.

"But in the moon," said the Doctor, "left to themselves for thousands of years, with no human hands to get them mixed up, the plants were much freer to work out things for themselves. Well, Otho Bludge thought out his plan and started off to try it. He did not want to interfere in the freedom of anything, but only to stop them all from interfering with the freedom of one another—to keep them from fighting and getting killed off. And that, when I got there, he had very thoroughly succeeded in doing. It must have been a terrifically hard thing—but then we must remember that *he* was not interfered with by any of his own kind, either. I doubt very much if it could ever have happened in our world. But, remember again, his was a far smaller world—easier to manage. At the beginning, when he explained his plan to the animals, the insects and the plants, he found that not all of them were pleased with the idea."

"Why, did they go on fighting and eating one another up?" asked Gub-Gub.

"Yes," said the Doctor. "But all parts of a world, no matter what its size or kind, have to work together. And those that would not help the safety of others very soon found themselves in a bad way—crowded out or starved out. Later Bludge told them he wanted to form what he called the Council. It was like a parliament or congress. Members of both the animal and the vegetable kingdoms came to it. They arranged everything that affected life on the moon. Anybody could get up and say his say in this council or give his advice or make his complaint. Otho Bludge, the Moon Man, was president. And after a while they practically all saw that Bludge was right. It was clear to them that he had brains and they accepted him as the leader, as the guide, in forming a new and properly balanced world where everything could live happily—more happily—without fighting."

THE SECOND CHAPTER

The Naturalists'
Paradise

AND SO YOU SEE," THE DOCTOR WENT ON, "for quite a while after Stubbins left I was kept very busy learning more and more about this strange new state. It fascinated me. I had never seen anything like it before. I saw at once that while the Moon Man had done so much, there was a lot left for me to do too. I assure you I had no conceit about that. Beside this other human, as old and experienced as the moon herself, I felt like a very humble little creature. But I had something of science which he had not; my mind was trained to make deductions, to reason—from my own experiences and those of others—as well as from history, human history, geological history, natural history.

"And besides wishing to help Otho Bludge—which I think I did do with scientific and medical advice—I began to wonder more and more how much of this new way of living could be brought about in my own home world, the earth. I will speak of that again later. But the first thing I gave my attention to in this connection was the foods of the moon."

"Ah!" said Gub-Gub, sitting up.

"There were many members of the pumpkin family—melons, calabashes, squashes, luffas, marrows, cucumbers, and whatnot. Most of them were good to eat. But anyone who picked a ripe fruit had to keep one of its seeds after he had eaten it. That was a law made by the Council.

"Well, again by questioning Otho and, later, by talking with the moon creatures directly, I learned that certain members of the moon pumpkin family were terribly fattening. Not only just flesh-making, but they made your whole figure—bones and all—taller, wider, and deeper. You became a giant if you didn't watch out. It was quite clear that only a few living things on the moon had stayed the same size as they are on the earth. It was almost impossible to avoid growth to some extent up there. The poor Moon Man himself had become a giant and he remained a giant. But he told me that at one time he was much bigger than he was when I met him. Some of the foods were much more fattening than others. Stubbins and I sprouted up like beanstalks the first few weeks we were there. Otho, however, was able to give me lists of certain foods that he had found the best for keeping your size down as much as possible.

"Next I turned my attention to the length of life on the moon. This was most interesting, but often I was very puzzled when it came to getting any definite information about ages. From weeks and weeks of study I came to the conclusion that nearly all kinds of life as I saw them up there had stayed the same for many thousands of years. Certain kinds, like the Whispering Vines and the Singing Trees, were much older than the rest.

"For quite a spell after that I just had an awfully good time. I asked myself, 'Why bother about returning to the earth? This is a naturalists' paradise. Adding your scientific knowledge to what Otho Bludge has done here will keep you busy all your days. And what better work could you be employed in? Keep the Moon Man in good health; fix up his rheumatism for him whenever he falls sick; and just go on this way. Why worry? Maybe you, John Dolittle, will yourself live forever—or anyhow as long as the moon lives, which will probably be many thousands of years yet.' That's what I said to myself.

"But after a while I began to wonder—to wonder and wonder about something. And about this something I started to take notes. By the way, Stubbins, on the note-taking I missed you badly. You had done it for me so long, you know. But Polynesia here was my salvation."

"But how? She can't keep notes," snorted Gub-Gub.

"No," laughed the Doctor, "but she has a memory that is often better than any notebook. It's almost like a mailbox you drop things into. You tell her to remember something when you're experimenting and she will always be able to fish it up out of her old head when you ask for it again later. I don't know what I would have done without her."

Polynesia cocked one eye at the ceiling, twisted her head a couple of times and tried hard not to look pleased by the Doctor's flattery. Then she said, sighing:

"Ah, well, that's the difference between people and parrots. Men when they get old say they can remember things in their childhood quite plainly—the things far off. But those that happened only yesterday, the things near to now, they can hardly remember at all. You talk about long life in the moon, Doctor: What about me? I'm a hundred and eighty years old—and how much more, I'm not telling. How much longer I'll live, I don't know. Maybe I'm only a child yet myself, and that's why I'm as good as a notebook for remembering. Anyway, when I met King Charles hiding in the oak tree in England, he was trying to remember how many soldiers he had seen chasing him—awful scared he was, talking to himself, you know. And I—Oh well, it doesn't matter. I mustn't interrupt you, Doctor. Go on with the story."

"The thing for which I now started to keep notes," said the Doctor, "was how much of this well-regulated, smoothly-running world could be copied down here among us. The thought kept coming back to me, stronger and stronger each time. Always, even when I was an ordinary doctor and took care of people, natural history—animals, insects, plants, trees, fossils, rocks—had been my hobby. That hobby had become my life. And yet anyone who studies natural history must come to fear sooner or later that all life faces a losing game down here with us."

"Excuse me, Doctor," said the white mouse, "but I don't quite understand what you mean."

"Life keeps on killing life," said the Doctor. "Don't you see? The fly is swallowed by the fish; the fish is eaten by the duck; the duck is devoured by the fox; the fox is slaughtered by the wolf; the wolf is shot by the man. And then men—the only ones on top in our world—turn round and kill one another in war."

There was a short silence. Dab-Dab had brought a pile of linen with her (the housekeeper always kept busy, even while listening to a story). She was turning over a stack of table napkins, looking for tears and holes.

"I told you that, Doctor," she said quietly, "long ago, when you wanted to start your Country House for Houseflies."

"Yes, yes," said the Doctor, frowning thoughtfully. "My idea with that was that if I gave the houseflies a house for themselves—full of sugar, you know, and all that—maybe they would leave people's houses alone. It didn't work. They ate up all the sugar and came back to my house. But there you are, Whitey: that's what I mean. It's a losing game. Any naturalist who tries to save one kind of creature in our world finds out sooner or later that he is taking away the food from some other blessed creature—or making life impossible for himself. I had never had anything against the houseflies, except that they would tickle the back of my neck when I was trying to write. And, as a medical man, I knew that they carry germs of disease. But they don't mean to. They're merely going about their own business like the rest of us."

"They're a pest," said Dab-Dab, laying aside a napkin that needed mending.

"Oh, quite, quite," said the Doctor. "But I'm sure they have some good in them somewhere—though I confess it's pretty hard to find. But you can all very well see, can't you, that when I found a world which was run along sensible lines, where no kind of life trod on the toes of any other kind of life, I began to wonder if something of those ideas could not be brought home and started here. That accounts for the note-taking, those bundles and bundles of palmleaf paper that made up such a large part of my baggage, Stubbins. It is out of those notes that I will write my book."

"There's plenty of time for that, Doctor," sighed Dab-Dab. She spread out a woolen antimacassar eaten full of holes. "Moths!" she hissed in disgust and threw it aside.

THE THIRD CHAPTER

Otho Bludge's Prisoner

"NOW, ALL THIS TIME," THE DOCTOR CONTINued, "the Moon Man was calling me in every so often to treat him for his rheumatism. I had fitted up a sort of makeshift laboratory for myself. Of course I had not many chemicals. All the medicines I had with me were what I had brought in the little black bag. But I had found a whole lot of useful drugs and things in the trees and rocks—such as quinine, zinc for making zinc ointment, and a whole lot more.

"Well, although my laboratory was a very rough and poor one, I was soon able to find out how to deal with his trouble. He was eating too much starch, for one thing. I changed his diet. I compounded some medicines for him. So long as he did what I told him, he got along very well. In fact, in the end I fancy I knew more about moon foods and what they did to the human body than he did.

"There was one special kind of melon he was very fond of. It was called goy-goy. This I had found was very bad for him. I had told him not to eat it. But, like a child—he was very childlike in many ways—he just wouldn't leave it alone. Finally I got quite severe with him. I ordered him not to touch it. He promised he wouldn't. But the next time he called me in about his rheumatism I saw, by the peelings that lay around him, that he had been eating goy-goy again.

"Well, this was when I was wondering if I could carry down to the earth some of those sensible ideas about diet, long life, and peaceful living which had panned out so well in the moon. I saw no reason why they shouldn't work with us—partly, at all events. I was a little homesick too, I imagine. Anyway, I was anxious to get down here and start experimenting with those ideas.

"So when, for the sixth or seventh time, Otho sent for me to attend to him—and again I found that he had been eating the forbidden goy-goy—I began to wonder if my staying on the moon any longer would be of much use. I especially felt this way now, because I had nearly completed my observations of the moon's seasons. The moon, you see, revolves in a small circle round the earth once a month; while the earth, carrying the moon with it, swings in a much bigger ring around the sun, once a year. The moon, hanging on to the earth, as it were, in this long journey would be bound to show effects and differences, not only with her own changing seasons, but with ours, too. I particularly wanted to make some observations at the earth's equinoxes—that is, in our spring and autumn. This of course meant staying up there a whole year. That year was now nearly over.

"Very well, then: this time Otho Bludge was a pretty sick Moon Man. And I realized that no matter how much medicine I gave him, sooner or later it would have no effect on him whatever—as long as he would go on eating goy-goy.

"So I got still more severe with him. I gave him a terrific

lecturing. 'I can do nothing with you,' I said, 'if you won't obey my orders. And anyway, very soon now I must go back to the earth. I have promised my people that I will set off a smoke signal—the same as you did when you sent the moth for me—to let them know that I am coming. I shall expect you, when the time comes for me to leave, to help me in every way you can. After all, it was you who wanted me to come up to the moon. And this, I feel, is the least you can do.'

"He said nothing in answer. But I could see that he was not pleased with the idea at all. I left a small bottle of medicine with him and went away to go on with my studies and note-taking. Polynesia told me that the bird spies were watching me again—though I can't see why Otho Bludge bothered with that. There was no possible chance of my getting off the moon unless I had his permission and his help. However Polynesia—clever bird, I really don't know what I would have done without her—Polynesia started spying on the spies. And with her help I was kept just as well informed about Otho's doings as he was about what I was doing. However I was too busy with my observations on the moon's seasons to attend to much else for the time being.

"At last the year was over and my notes were complete. I felt very glad. No one had ever seen the moon's seasons, from the moon, before. I had stacks and stacks of notes on temperatures, sunlight and earthlight, with their effects on the animal and vegetable kingdoms, air pressures, rainfall, and goodness knows how much more. I was packing up the last of these when word came to me that the Moon Man was not feeling so well and would I come to see him.

"This time I decided I would be more than severe. The moment had come for me to put my foot down. I gave him some medicine. And I stayed with him several nights until I had him in good health again. Then I said, 'Listen, Otho Bludge, I want to go back to the earth. I want to go now. I feel I have done all I can here. Will you please help me to set off the signal and return home?' Again he did not answer at once—he often thought a long while before he spoke. At last he said, 'No, John Dolittle, I will not let you go. I need you here!'

"I was dumbfounded. The thought had never occurred to me that he would refuse my request—yet I don't know why it shouldn't have done. First I tried to argue with him. I explained how unfair this was. I reminded him again that it was he who had brought me up there—for his own purposes. This made no effect on him. Then I got angry. But it was no use. He was determined to keep me. I left him and went away very puzzled.

"Then for some weeks I wandered and wandered around the moon, wondering what I should do. But the more I thought it over the more difficult the situation seemed. It looked now as though I was going to become a citizen of the moon for good, whether I liked it or not. And, with all the plans I had in mind, I must confess I was very much annoyed.

"Then Polynesia one day had an idea. She said it was quite possible of course for Otho Bludge to keep me—as well as herself and Chee-Chee—prisoners on the moon; but it was *not* possible for him to make me doctor him if I didn't want to. This sounded like good sense. And the next time the Moon Man sent word to me that he was suffering from rheumatism I refused to go to him.

"Again he sent me a message. He was very sick, he said. And again I sent back word that I would not come to help him until he was willing to help me. But it seemed he could be just as stubborn as I. No further message came to me.

"Then, I confess, I began to get worried. What if Otho Bludge should die? It was not that I was afraid that that would ruin my chances of getting away. I had done a lot for many of the birds and insects up there, curing them of different sicknesses from which they suffered occasionally. And Polynesia said she was sure that they would do anything they could for me, even flying me back to the earth, once the Moon Man was out of the way and they need no longer be afraid of disobeying his orders. But—well, once a doctor, always a doctor, I suppose. No physician, if he feels that his services may save a man's life—and there is no one else there—can stand aside and refuse to help.

"Maybe if the Moon Man had sent more messages I would have acted differently. But he didn't. That was the worst of it. Not another word came from him. We—Polynesia, Chee-Chee, and I—had moved our camp over to the far side of the moon, the side you never see from the earth; and I was trying to study the music of the Singing Trees. This had presented some problems in harmony that I was anxious to get to the bottom of.

"But suddenly the trees refused to sing anymore. I could understand their language by then and I asked them why. They would tell me nothing. They remained silent. The same with the Whispering Vines. The birds, who did most of the spying for Otho, had disappeared. I tried talking with the insects—bees and the like. They wouldn't tell me anything either. I got more and more worried. It seemed as though the whole of the moon life was determined to be silent. It gave me a creepy sort of feeling. I began to wonder if they were all waiting for Otho Bludge to die—expecting it every minute.

"At last I couldn't bear it anymore. I knew that if Otho—the man who had done something no human has ever done before—if

Otho were to die, I would never forgive myself. I was lying in bed, tossing and turning, trying to sleep. I jumped up. 'Polynesia,' I said, 'I am going to him—I've got to!' She just swore in Swedish but did not try to stop me. I packed the black bag and left camp alone.

HUGH LOFTING

"'Polynesia,' I said, 'I am going to him—I've got to!'"

"I had a long way to go. I started off in darkness. But I knew that soon I would see the earth rise and would have light from it to travel by. I never hurried so in all my life. How many hours the journey took me I don't know. My great fear was that I might be too late. When at last I began to get round onto the near side—the side of the moon you see from here—the going was easier and I broke into a run. Soon I saw Otho's hut in the distance. I call it a hut, but it was really a very big house made of leaves. Gathered about it there was a great crowd of birds, insects, and some animals—all waiting in silence in the gray of the earthlight. I pushed my way in. Otho Bludge was lying on a cot with his eyes closed."

THE FOURTH CHAPTER

The Gentleman in the Moon

I RUSHED TO HIS BEDSIDE.

"'Otho, Otho!' I cried. He did not stir. He was unconscious. I felt his pulse. It was fast and jumpy. I got a thermometer out of the bag. His temperature was high—far too high. His rheumatism had run into complications—probably some form of rheumatic fever.

"I worked over him for hours. I knew if I did not bring the temperature down soon, this by itself could kill him. I got cold water and soaked big leaves in it. I plastered these all over his body and, by fanning him, I did manage to get the temperature lower by several degrees. I realized I had only got there just in time to save his life.

"It seems funny, when I look back on it now. There I was working like a slave to save the life of the man who meant to hold me a prisoner! Yet I did not think of it then. The only idea that filled my mind was that I, as a physician, must leave no stone unturned to keep him from dying.

"At last, after I had given him a heart stimulant with the

hypodermic needle, he became conscious. Weakly he opened his eyes and looked at me. He said nothing. There came a curious, ashamed sort of expression into his face as he recognized who I was—that it was I who was working to save him. Presently he fell off into a peaceful sleep. I took his pulse again. While it was still fast, it was ever so much better and quite steady. I knew that the worst was over. I told one of the birds to call me as soon as he woke up. Then I curled up on the floor of his hut to get some sleep myself. As I dozed off I felt more at peace in my mind than I had done for many hours.

"I stayed with him I don't know how long—maybe four or five days. During all that time he never spoke. At the end, when I was about to leave him, he was quite well again, but still weak. I gave him the usual instructions as to what he should do. It was hardly necessary, for he had heard them many times before. I fastened up my medicine bag and turned toward the open door of his hut.

"The sun was shining on the beautiful moonscape. You know how it looked, Stubbins—sort of dreamlike and mysterious—rows and rows of mountains, dead volcanoes with that strange greenish light on them. I paused a moment to gaze on it before I stepped out of the hut. 'So, John Dolittle,' I said to myself, 'I suppose you are a big fool. But you chose to be a doctor when you were a youngster and this is the price you pay. You are a prisoner of this world for life. This landscape is what you will see for the remainder of your days. Well, what else could you do? So be it.'

"I stepped over the doorsill into the open air. Then I heard a cry from within the hut. The Moon Man, for the first time in days, was speaking to me. I turned and went back to his bedside.

"He was trying to sit up. 'There, there,' I said, 'settle down and rest. I will come again tomorrow to see how you are.' He sank back looking awfully feeble and I wondered whether I really ought to leave him. I felt his pulse again. It was good. Then suddenly he broke forth, speaking in a mixture of all sorts of languages, so that I had hard work keeping up with what he was trying to say.

"'My mind is sort of fuzzy,' he whispered. 'But I wanted to tell you that I know you have saved my life—without gaining anything for yourself. . . . While I was sleeping just now I seemed to remember something of the Days Before There Was a Moon. I have not dealt with men in so long. . . . But I remember—yes, I remember those times when I was on the earth, ages and ages ago. I remember how men acted toward one another. . . . You are what was called—er—a very true friend. Isn't that it, John Dolittle? . . . So I just wanted to tell you that any time you wish to return to your world I will help you in any way I can. . . . You are free to go—whenever you wish.'"

The Doctor paused a moment.

"Well, you can imagine my astonishment. A moment before I had seen myself a prisoner on the moon for life—giving up all hope of ever seeing the earth, Puddleby, my friends, home, again. Now I was free. Suddenly all the unkind thoughts I had felt against this man fell away. I was bound to admit that he was greater, bigger, even than I had guessed. Something in his recollections of the earth had made up his mind to this determination. And my coming to his assistance, the very thing that should have ruined my chances of ever getting home, had acted for me just the other way. I was free!

"And then all at once I realized that, child as he was, the Moon Man had wanted my company as well as my help as a doctor. For some moments I did not answer him. I was thinking—thinking how much it meant to him to say those words, 'You are free to go.' He was giving up the only human friendship he had known in thousands of years. And that is why, for a little, I did not speak.

"At last I said, 'No man can know how long you will live—probably for many thousands of years yet, if you do as I tell you. When I return to the earth I mean to write a book, a book about the moon—and it's about you too, a great part of it. People on the earth, you know, have always spoken of the *Man in the Moon,* but I hope that when my book is written—and read—they will come to speak of the *Gentleman in the Moon.* Certainly I shall do my best to show them that what I found in you, Otho Bludge, was not only a great man, but one of the realest gentlemen I have ever known.'

"Then I left him and went back to my camp.

"There is little more to tell. The next time I visited him he was able to get up and move around. He was as good as his word. He wasted no time in preparing the bonfire for my smoke signal. For this he got thousands and thousands of birds to help him. They all brought a stick or twig of that explosive wood that he had used for his own signal. It reminded me of the time when I got the birds in Africa to build the island in the lake out of stones. But, for these creatures in the moon to gather together a bonfire whose smoke would be large enough to be seen from the earth, was a tremendous undertaking.

"Just about the time it was finished I happened to discover—in some astronomical almanacs I had with me—that we were due to have an eclipse in about ten days from then. This interested me very much. For one thing, I was most keen to see an eclipse from the moon and to find out what the other planets looked like when they came out in daylight hours. And, for another thing, I felt sure that my signals would show better when the moon was partly in shadow.

"So I asked Otho to put off firing the bonfire till the eclipse was underway. He became very interested in the matter himself. He wanted to know just how I had calculated that it would come at a certain hour on a certain date. He suggested that we have two bonfires ready and set them off separately—to make sure that at least one of them would be seen. I found out, Stubbins, also that when he tried to get a signal down to us here, to tell us of the coming of the moth, he had set off several before we happened to be looking at the moon and saw one.

"Then came the question of what sort of creature I should have to fly me down. I had grown so big by then; and there was considerable weight, too, in the baggage that I wanted to bring with me. The giant moth when we tried out a practice flight could hardly rise from the ground under the load. So something else had to be found to make the trip.

"Birds were out of the question. Here we always think of birds as being larger than insects; but up there they were smaller—difference in diet again, I suppose. And then birds need more air—they have a different sort of breathing apparatus. The trip between the moon and the earth requires a tremendous amount of effort—very hard work. Getting through the dead belt, where there is practically no air at all, is easier for the insect fliers than any other. I doubt if a bird, no matter what his wingspread, could manage it.

"Well, after a few experiments Otho and I decided to try the Mammoth Locust. You all saw what a tremendous creature he is. His way of flying is quite extraordinary—not at all the same as his cousins, the grasshopper, the cicada, and the mantis. The locust flies both like a bird *and* an insect. The number of wingbeats per second is sort of betwixt and between. I have notes on that too.

"Anyway, we got the baggage and ourselves aboard this Mammoth Locust and made a trial flight. He could lift the load quite easily—that is, he could in that gravity. Whether he could have done the same with the earth's gravity, I cannot say. But that didn't matter so much. When he got near to this world he would be coming *down;* and going back he would have no load to carry, beyond the weight of his own body."

THE FIFTH CHAPTER

The Farewell

HEN THE TIME WAS AT HAND FOR THE eclipse to begin, there was quite a gathering to see the show. I had calculated the exact point on the moon—pretty exact, anyhow—from which it could best be seen. As I gazed over the great crowd it seemed as though every creature in the moon had collected there. Of course this was not true. But it looked like it. I have never seen such a tremendous herd—not even when we called the animals together on the Island of No Man's Land off the coast of Africa to set up the post office and the classes in animal writing.

"But the crowd had not only come to see the eclipse; they had come to see me off. Many—some of them grateful patients whom I had cured of sicknesses—brought presents. Foodstuffs and the like. They wanted to show their gratitude. It was very touching. I thanked them as best I could, bade them good-bye, and wished them luck. The Moon Man himself had said he would set off the bonfire signals. It was a ticklish business, this lighting of so much

HUGH LOFTING

"'The baby's down there,' said the mother. 'Please hurry!'"

explosive stuff; and he was the only one—with his big strides and speed of running—who could do it without getting hurt.

"Exactly at the time I had foretold, the big shadow began to creep across the earth and the light on the moon grew dim. The crowd watching was greatly impressed. I believe many of them thought I had had a hand in it myself and was deliberately darkening the earth to suit my own purposes.

"The bonfires were set off, a few minutes apart, and great enormous columns of smoke shot up into the air. The fumes of that explosive wood rolled all about us, making everyone splutter and cough. Finally it cleared away. I hoped that at least one of the signals had been sighted on the earth.

"It was a very impressive scene. We were standing in a wide plain between two ranges of mountains. The watching crowd of moon creatures had drawn away a little, leaving plenty of space for the Mammoth Locust to take off on his long journey. The baggage was on board, strapped down securely by ropes of vine bark. Chee-Chee, Polynesia, and I stood at the locust's side ready to go.

"Suddenly one solitary figure separated itself from that ring of watchers and stalked out into the open toward me. It was a cat."

Polynesia jumped as usual, and Jip snorted something between a growl and a grunt.

"I think Stubbins has told you," the Doctor went on, "that I had already met with a colony of cats in my wanderings over the moon. I had great difficulty in learning their language. They were so reticent—didn't seem inclined to talk, I mean—even when it looked as if they had something on their minds to say. Well, you know, without being told, that all animals of the same kind are not the same. Each one is different. And certainly this cat was different. Usually cats are fond of places rather than people. Well, this goes to show. This particular cat did *not* think more of places than she did of people. As it happened, I had cured her of a bad attack of bronchitis. She did not like the moon. But, apparently, she liked me.

"She came stalking across the wide open space all alone. When she got to me she said, 'Doctor Dolittle, I want to go with you.' That was all. I had never been fond of cats. And yet I knew of no exact reason why I should feel less friendly toward her kind than I did toward any other sort of animal. On the other hand, I knew of course that if I took her into my household down here many of you would object.

"I argued with her. I told her cats had many enemies in the world where I was going. She said, 'Don't bother about my enemies, Doctor. I'll take care of them.' Then—still hoping to discourage her, I said, 'But you understand that if I take you, there is to be no killing—birds, mice, and so forth. We can't have any of that, you know.' All she answered was, 'John Dolittle, I'm a moon cat. For thousands of years we have not killed birds—or any living creature. We have learned here to live on other things. We hunt no more. I want to see the earth, where my people came from. Take me with you.'

"Well—there you are—there was no answering her argument. She was running a big risk. And she knew it.

"'Very well,' I said at last. 'Get aboard the locust.' And without another word she climbed up onto the insect's back. There Chee-Chee stowed her in a crate and secured her for the big journey.

"But the worst part of the whole business for me was saying good-bye to Otho Bludge. It was not easy. As I told you, I had realized of a sudden how terribly lonely the poor fellow was going to be. Perhaps he would never have felt so if I had not come to the moon. It is true this was his own doing—yet, so far as his losing my company was concerned, it made no matter. He had said very little to me after he had told me I could go. But now when he came striding over toward us, as we stood by the locust's side, I wondered what was going on inside his mind. He was about to say good-bye to the first human being he had talked with in thousands of years.

"He held out his hand. I remember asking myself how it was he had not forgotten that this was the fashion in which the people of the earth bade one another farewell. I did not know what to say. At last it was he who spoke.

"'Good-bye,' he said in an awkward kind of way. 'Do you think that—someday—you may come back?'"

"Oh," quacked Dab-Dab, "I do hope you didn't promise him you would, Doctor!"

"No," said John Dolittle, "I didn't promise anything. Although I must admit the moon was a most interesting place to visit. No—I just said, 'Well, Otho, keep off the goy-goy and you'll live longer than any of us. I have left a dozen bottles of the medicine in your hut. But you won't need them if you will only follow the diet I have told you to.'

"It was a terrible moment. I was anxious to get it over with. He turned and moved away. Evidently at the very last he would sooner not see our going. I climbed aboard the locust. My size, you must remember, was terrific. But even when I lay down flat on a creature's back—over his thorax, his shoulders—there still seemed to be lots of room to spare. We had on board many of those oxygen Moon Bells, Stubbins, which we used on the other trip. I pulled one up, handy to dip my nose in. The locust scrabbled his feet into the sand of the valley so he could make a good takeoff. 'Good-bye!' yelled the crowd. 'Good-bye!' we called back. With a terrific kick of his hind legs the insect shot up into the air and spread his wings.

"The trip was terrible. I suppose having stayed on the moon

so long my lungs had got sort of accustomed to the air up there and unaccustomed to the air of the earth—to say nothing of the dreadful dead belt. Anyway, when we did reach that terrible part of the journey, I honestly thought it was all over with me. The locust had got instructions about the navigation from Jamaro Bumblelily, the giant moth, before he set off. But it was terrible anyhow. I grabbed one of the oxygen flowers and stuck my face in it. Nevertheless I went unconscious—and stayed so till after we landed. When I came to at last I heard you, Stubbins, talking with Polynesia. Everything was still. I looked up at the moon, steady in the sky. Last time I had seen it it was swinging around the heavens like a crazy thing.

"Well, that's all. Here I am, none the worse for the trip—the most interesting journey I have ever made in my life."

Quite clearly the Doctor felt that his tale had rather saddened us toward the end. As a matter of fact, all the animals were certainly very serious when he finished.

"Tell me, Doctor," said Jip at last, "do you think the Moon Man will be able to manage by himself—now?"

"Of course he will," Dab-Dab broke in. "How did he manage before the Doctor went there?"

"I wasn't asking you, Dab-Dab," said Jip quietly. "I was asking the Doctor."

"Oh, I think he'll be all right," said John Dolittle after a pause.

"He'll miss you, won't he?" said Jip. "Mighty sporting of him to let you go, wasn't it? Humph! The 'Gentleman in the Moon.' Good luck to him!"

"Poor man!" said Whitey—always sentimental and romantic. "Left all alone!"

"Hum! Hum!" said Gub-Gub. "It must be kind of hard to be the only one of your kind in a world."

"But you won't go back, Doctor, will you?" said Dab-Dab anxiously. "After all, you've seen the moon now—spring, summer, autumn, and winter. There's no sense in your fooling with it anymore, is there? You know what I mean?"

"Yes, I understand, Dab-Dab," said the Doctor. "But"—his voice trailed off in a sleepy tone—"it was—er—well, it *was* a very interesting place."

I saw that he was getting tired. I made a signal to the animals and Matthew. They understood.

"All right, Doctor," I said. "Thank you. We will now leave you in peace to sleep. Good night!"

I folded up my notebooks. John Dolittle's head was nodding on his chest. We all crept out on tiptoe and closed the door behind us.

THE SIXTH CHAPTER

Setting the Zoo
to Rights

IT WAS NOT UNTIL ALMOST THE END OF THE summer that the Doctor got back to his ordinary size. He was now no longer afraid of being seen; and he moved about the house without upsetting things or smashing furniture; and he was very happy about it.

First of all he went over the whole garden from end to end. Though I had done the best I could to keep it up in good condition for him, there was much of course that his eye fell on which mine had overlooked. John Dolittle was a very good gardener himself and very particular. (Dab-Dab always used to say he never seemed to mind how untidy his house was, as long as the garden was spick-and-span—"Just like a man!" she would add.) Gub-Gub and I— and sometimes Matthew when he was around—helped him with the work; dividing up the iris roots; pegging down the raspberry canes; digging up and reseeding some of the turf patches that had grown bare and brown.

"The coming of autumn, Stubbins," said he, "is always the most important season for a sensible gardener. That's the time when we put the earth to bed, as it were. If you get the ground and your plants and trees in good condition for their long winter sleep, you will have something to show in the spring."

When we came to look over the big enclosure that we had called the zoo, the emptiness of it seemed to sadden him. He gazed over the long walled-in lawn some moments without speaking; but I knew what was in his mind. So did Jip.

"Humph!" muttered the Doctor after a while, "those dog-houses down at the bottom look pretty sad, don't they? The roofs all full of holes and rotten. We must do something to clean up this mess, Stubbins. A year seems such a short time, and yet what a lot can happen in it!"

"Look here, Doctor," said Jip, "why can't we repair them and start the Home for Crossbred Dogs over again? There's a half-breed setter down in the town. His name is Flip. He has no home at all. He gets his meals any old place—off garbage heaps mostly. And there are a lot of other dogs too. Couldn't we take them in, the same as we used to when you kept open house for stray dogs?"

"Well, Jip, I'd love to," said the Doctor. "They surely were jolly times when we had the dogs' home running full blast. You remember that little rascal, Quetch, the Scotty who used to run the dogs' gymnasium for us—and bossed you all over the place when we had the jumping contests? And wasn't that a wonderful yarn—when he told us the story of his life? My, what a character he was! But you see, Jip, I don't know about the money side of it. A lot of dogs need a lot of food. It seems to me I've got to live on Stubbins' salary here—of three shillings and sixpence a week—till I begin to make something from my new book."

"Well, but, Doctor," said Jip. "Why can't we take in just Flip for the present—till you're feeling richer? I'm afraid he'll get shot one of these days for stealing people's chickens or something. No one takes care of him. He's just a tramp. He comes round to the front gate twice a week to see if I have any old bones to give him. Most of the time he's practically starving."

"Humph! Starving, eh?" said the Doctor seriously. He looked at me. "Can we manage it, do you think, Stubbins?"

"Oh, surely, Doctor," said I. "We'll manage somehow. We always seem to have milk and vegetables anyway."

"Good!" said the Doctor. "Milk and vegetables are much better for a dog than too much meat. All right, Jip, bring your friend in next time he calls and we'll fix up one of the doghouses for him here."

The white mouse, always inquisitive, had been following us around on the inspection of the garden. He now piped up in his funny, squeaky, little voice,

"Oh, and, Doctor, wouldn't it be a good idea if we set up the Rat and Mouse Club again too? There's a new family of mice up in the attic. And you know Dab-Dab would much sooner have them out of the house, down here instead. It won't be any trouble. I can fix up our old Rat Town the way it was. I know how they like it, you see. And they'll be no expense. A few crusts of bread and rinds of cheese. It would be lots of fun to have them here once more, don't you think? Then we could have them telling us stories over the kitchen fire after supper—just like old times. Do let's start the Rat and Mouse Club again!"

"Humph!" said the Doctor thoughtfully. "I don't see why not. It would make the place more homelike. I certainly hate to see the zoo enclosure all empty and deserted like this. Yes, let's set up the Rat and Mouse Club. I'll leave the matter in your hands, Whitey. At least we can afford that."

And then the old lame horse who had been helping us weed the garden with a cultivator put in his say.

"Doctor," he said, "how about the Retired Cab and Wagon Horses' Association—you know, the farm you bought for them about two miles away?"

"Ah yes," said the Doctor, "to be sure, to be sure. I'd forgotten all about them. Tell me, how are they getting on?"

"Well," said the old fellow, swishing the flies off with his tail, "I hear there have not been any new members joined of late. But the fences need repairing. Dogs getting in and yapping and snapping about the place—in spite of all the signs we put up, 'Trespassers Will Be Prosecuted—Dogs Will Be Kicked,' you remember?"

"Yes, yes, of course," said the Doctor.

"And the scratching post you set for them—it got pushed down. And they would like another."

"Dear me, dear me," said John Dolittle. "Yes, I remember how they used to like to scratch their necks—on the top of the hill there, where they could see the view as the sun went down. Well, I'll certainly have to attend to that. I'll go over with you in the morning and see about it."

And so it was that before very long most of the old institutions that the Doctor had set up for the comfort and happiness of animals got put back into running order after his long stay on the moon. All of his own animal household were very happy about this—and, I was surprised to find, Dab-Dab in particular.

"Tommy," she said to me one evening, "this is a good thing.

It will keep John Dolittle out of mischief—I mean keep him away from his book for a while more anyhow. Why shouldn't he have a good time giving the animals a good time?—so long as he doesn't start any of those crazy charitable ideas for pests, like the Country House for Houseflies. Poof!" (She shrugged up her wings in disgust.) "Don't let him start *that* again. He'll have a Wardrobe for Clothes Moths or a Bedroom for Bedbugs first thing you know."

Squib the Cocker Spaniel

BUT THESE DEPARTMENTS OF HIS BIG ESTABlishment were not the only things that began leading John Dolittle back into his old ways of living. In former days the most important concern in "the little house with the big garden" had been the dispensary, where animals and creatures of all sorts came to him for the treatment of their sicknesses and injuries. Of course anyone can understand that as soon as he began to move around and let himself be seen word would get abroad to the animals outside that the famous man was back in Puddleby once more.

And, sure enough, it was only a few weeks later that our patients began to call—first a pair of rabbits, very scared and timid. I found them on the doorstep at the crack of dawn one morning. Could they see the Doctor, please? I asked them what was the matter. They said they had a sick baby—didn't know what was the trouble with it. I told them the Doctor was still in bed and I didn't like to wake him because he was very tired. Where was the baby?

"Oh," said the mother rabbit, almost bursting into tears, "it's not far away. If you'll come with us we'll show you and maybe if you bring it back here the Doctor will be awake by then. But we must make haste. It's very sick."

"All right," I said, "I'll come with you. Lead the way."

Well, the mother rabbit was in a hurry. She and her mate shot out the garden gate and went bolting down the road like a streak of lightning. Time and again I had to call to them to wait and let me catch up. After they had gone about a mile toward Oxenthorpe they left the highway and started off across country. Over ditches, plowed fields, and swamps they led me—under hedges, through copses, over hill and dale. At last they came to a stop before a hole in a bank beside a wood.

"The baby's down there," said the mother. "Please hurry up and get it out. It's terribly sick."

Of course there was no earthly chance of my getting down a hole that size. But there was a farm nearby. I ran over to it. It was still very early in the morning and no one was about. I found a garden spade in a turnip field. I borrowed it and ran back to the rabbits. Then I got the father to show me about how far his hole ran into the bank. I dug down in that spot and got the young one out. He certainly looked pretty ill—breathing very hard. Some sort of asthma, I suspected. I picked him up, left the spade where the farmer would find it, and started off, on the run, back to the Doctor's house with both the parents at my heels.

John Dolittle was up and shaving by the time we got there. He gave one look at the baby rabbit, dropped his razor, took the patient out of my hands, and ran down the stairs with it to the dispensary. There he swabbed its throat out with some kind of disinfectant and laid it in a shoebox on a bed of hay.

HUGH LOFTING

"'The baby's down there,' said the mother. 'Please hurry!'"

"You only just caught it in time, Stubbins," he said. "I think it will be all right. But we'll have to keep an eye on it for a few days. Put it up in my bedroom—under the bed. Tell the parents they can live there, too, for a few days. Give them some apples.

Hah, it's a fine youngster! We'll fix it up all right."

At breakfast I told Dab-Dab about it. She rolled her eyes toward the ceiling with a sigh.

"We'll have to take the carpet up," she said. "There will be apple cores all over the room. Ah well! We might have expected it. That's the way it always begins—after he's been away. Now we'll have every kind of animal in the countryside calling on him with their toothaches and bruises and blisters!"

And, sure enough, she was right. From that time on, the animal patients began to arrive thick and fast, all hours of the day and night. Foxes, badgers, otters, squirrels, weasels, hedgehogs, moles, rats, mice and every kind of bird, formed a line outside the dispensary door—a line which seemed to grow forever longer and longer. The wild animals' world had learned that the great doctor was back.

And so the little house suddenly became a very busy place. The Doctor was here, there, and everywhere. Jip's friend Flip came and was given a comfortable home in one of the doghouses in the zoo enclosure. In fact, he found it so comfortable, and enjoyed being a guest of the Doctor's so much, that next time he visited the town he told all his friends about it. And as soon as it got abroad in dog society that the famous Home for Crossbred Dogs was open once more, we had all descriptions of waifs and strays and mongrels for miles around wagging their tails at the gates and asking to be taken in as members. The Doctor never could resist a hard-luck story from animals. And we soon had a wonderful collection down there in the zoo enclosure. Never had I seen such mixtures—crosses between greyhounds and dachshunds, between airedales and mastiffs, Irish terriers and foxhounds. But the more mixed they were, the better the Doctor seemed to like them.

"They're always more intelligent and interesting, these cross-breds, Stubbins," he said, "than the pedigreed dogs. This is splendid. I always like to have lots of dogs around."

He *did* have them; there was no question about that. The real trouble came when not only the stray dogs of the neighborhood—those who had no owners or places to go, nights—but the regular dogs, many of them purebreds, heard of the home in the Doctor's garden and just ran away and came to us.

This, as can be easily understood, caused a lot of trouble for John Dolittle. (It had done the same before, as a matter of fact.) Angry owners of pet poodles, dogs who had won prizes and blue ribbons in shows, came round to see the Doctor. Furiously they accused him of luring away their precious darlings from their proper homes. And the Doctor had hard work pacifying them. One case I remember that amused me very much. It was a cocker spaniel. When she arrived at the house she told the Doctor she was annoyed with her owner because she would treat her as a lapdog.

"And you know, Doctor," she said very haughtily, "we cockers are *not* lapdogs, like the King Charles or Pekinese spaniels—those piffling fleabags who do nothing but sit on cushions. *We* are not that kind. We are sporting dogs. I can't stand my owner. I wish to live my own life. We're descended from the water spaniels—a very old and respected breed."

"Of course, of course," said the Doctor. "I quite understand."

"I don't want to sit on sofas," the dog went on. "I want to run in the woods—to smell the deer. I love going after deer. I've never caught one and I don't suppose I'd know what to do with it if I did. But it's the fun of the thing, don't you see? My mistress says I mustn't get myself wet, running through the long grass and all that. But I just hate the life of drawing rooms and afternoon teas! I want to come and live with you and all those jolly mongrels down in your zoo."

"I see, I see," said the Doctor. "And I understand your point of view. Quite, quite. But what am I to say to your owner when she traces you back here and comes to tell me I've stolen her dog?"

"Oh, let her go and buy herself a toy one," said the spaniel, "one of those made out of rags. It would do just as well for her. She doesn't know anything about real dogs."

Well, that was the kind of thing the Doctor found himself faced with all the time. And it certainly kept him busy. This particular spaniel did actually stay with us. We called her Squib; but, as the Doctor had prophesied, her owner, a very elegant lady of one of the country's best families, called and raised a rumpus. However, Squib was so rude and unfriendly to her former mistress and made such a fuss about being taken away, that the lady, after the Doctor had explained things to her, finally went off and left her with us. And the spaniel, to her great delight, was allowed to join the Home for Crossbred Dogs.

Although she was frightfully well-bred, a champion in her class and all that, she never boasted about her pedigree to the other dogs. Squib's one great ambition was to trail a deer and run him down in the woods. She never succeeded—with the short legs she had. But it didn't matter anyway. In fact, it was just as well she never did. Always she had still something to look forward to. As she had explained to the Doctor, the fun of the game was the thing that counted. She was a true sportswoman; and all the other dogs were crazy about her.

THE EIGHTH CHAPTER

How to Get into Jail?

O F COURSE AS TIME WENT ON THE DOCTOR became more and more anxious to get at his notes and the writing of his book about the moon. One evening, after all our work for the day had been attended to, we were sitting in the kitchen. Matthew Mugg, the Cat's-Meat-Man, was with us. It was nearly midnight and I had packed all the animals off to bed because both John Dolittle and myself were pretty tired.

The Doctor was filling his pipe from the big tobacco jar, and when he got it lighted and going well he said to me:

"You know, Stubbins, I can't see how I'll ever get that book started, the way things are going at present."

"Yes, Doctor," I said, "I know what you mean."

"It isn't that I begrudge the time I give to the animals here, you understand," he went on. "It's just that there *are* only twenty-four hours to the day. And no matter how I try to arrange it, I don't—I simply don't—seem to find any time for writing. You see, I always feel that these animals that call upon me with their troubles, well, that is a living, an immediate, thing. The book should be able to wait. Maybe nobody will take any notice of it, anyway, when it comes out. But I do want to get it written. I *hope* it's going to be a very important work."

"You ought to go away somewhere, Doctor," said the Cat's-Meat-Man, "so you could 'ave peace and quiet. From what Tommy tells me, you ain't likely to get none 'ere."

"That's an idea," cried John Dolittle. "To go away—but where?"

"Take a seaside 'oliday, Doctor," said Matthew. "Go down to Margate. Lovely place! I got a cousin down there in the lobster-fishin' business. Nobody would bother you in Margate. It's far enough off from Puddleby so not even the animals 'ere-abouts would know where you'd gone."

The Doctor frowned slightly as he looked into the bowl of his pipe.

"Yes," he said, "but you see, Matthew, there's always that wretched question of money. Where can a man go without money?"

Matthew drummed a moment on the table with his fingers.

"Now, Doctor," he said presently, "the main thing you're lookin' for is peace and quiet, ain't it?"

"That's it," said John Dolittle. "A place where I can write my book undisturbed."

"Well," said Matthew. "There's only one place I know where a man can get all the peace and quiet 'e wants and it don't cost 'im nothin'."

"Where's that?" asked the Doctor.

"In jail," said Matthew.

"Oh," said the Doctor, a little surprised. "Ah yes, I see. I hadn't thought of that. Yet—er—after all, it *is* an idea. Quite an idea. But tell me—er—how does one go about getting into jail?"

"That's a fine thing for you to be askin' *me*, John Dolittle! My trouble wasn't never 'ow to get into jail; it was always 'ow to stay out of it."

Both the Doctor and I knew Matthew's occasional troubles with the police. His great weakness was poaching, that is, snaring rabbits and pheasants on other people's property. Nothing on earth could ever persuade him this was wrong. And whenever he was missing and suddenly turned up again after several weeks' absence, the Doctor never asked him where he had been. For he guessed he most likely had had one of his "little run-ins with the police" as he called them. But tonight neither of us could keep from laughing outright.

"Now listen," said Matthew, leaning forward, "let's go into committee on this. First thing we got to decide is which jail we got to get you into, see? There's lots o' difference in 'em. I wouldn't recommend you Puddleby jail. No—too drafty. I got an awful nooralgy in me face last time I was there. Well, then there's Oxenthorpe jail. No—come to think of it—I wouldn't pick that one neither. It's a nice jail, you understand. But the old justice of the peace what sits on the bench up there is a snooty old bloke and 'e's liable to give you 'ard."

"Hard?" said the Doctor. "I don't quite understand."

"'Ard labor," said Matthew. "You know, work. You 'ave to work all the time you're in there—makin' ropes and that kind o' thing. You wouldn't want that. You want peace and quiet so you can write a book. No, Oxenthorpe is out. But then there's Gilesborough. Ah, now that's the place you—"

"But excuse me," the Doctor put in. "One has to do something to get into jail, doesn't one? I mean, you must commit some sort of an offense, break the law. Right?"

"Oh, that's easy, Doctor," said the Cat's-Meat-Man. "Listen, all you got to do is go up to a policeman and push 'im in the face. You'll get into jail all right."

"But, my dear Matthew," cried the Doctor, "how can I possibly go up to a policeman, a perfect stranger, a man who never did me any harm, and—er—push him in the face?"

"Doctor," said Matthew, "don't let your conscience worry you none. It's a worthy deed—a werry worthy deed—that's what it is. All policemen had oughter be pushed in the face. Look, if you don't think you can do it, I'll come and 'elp yer!"

"Er—er—well, now wait a minute," said the Doctor. "I'm not what's called conventional, as you know, Matthew. In fact, I too have been in prison. I was thrown into a dungeon in Africa by Prince Bumpo's father, the king of the Jolliginki. But I didn't have to do anything for that. The king just didn't like white men. And I can't say that I blame him—seeing what his experience with them had been. But, to come back: I think that your idea sounds good in many ways. A prison, with high stone walls, should be a splendid place to write."

"The grub's rotten—that's the only thing," said Matthew, reaching for the tobacco jar.

"Well, that won't bother me," said John Dolittle. "I'm eating as little as possible now, you know, on account of my weight. But the way to get into jail is the thing that may prove difficult. Listen, Matthew: don't you think I could do something less violent? I mean, instead of pushing a policeman's face, couldn't I just—er—break a window or something?"

"Oh, positively," said Matthew. "There's lots of ways of getting into jail. But, you see, just for bustin' a window you'd only get a sentence of a few days. 'Ow long was you thinkin' you'd want to stay?"

"Er—I don't just know, Matthew," said the Doctor. "But certainly until I get most of my book finished."

"Well," said the Cat's-Meat-Man, "there's no need to worry about that yet a while. If the judge only gives you fourteen days and you want to stay longer, all you got to do is tear up your bed or something like that. Or, if they puts you out, you can just break another window and come right back in again, see? That part's easy. Now I got to be goin'. Theodosia always gets kind of fussy if I'm out late, nights. But you think it over, Doctor. If you wants peace and quiet, there's no place like a prison cell. But when you starts your window breakin' you better let me come and 'elp you—No, don't thank me, Doctor, it'll be a pleasure, I assure you! 'Twould never do to 'ave no bunglin'. The job's got to be done right. Yer might get into trouble! And choose Gilesborough. Trust me. It's a nice jail. Good night!"

THE NINTH CHAPTER

Gilesborough

FTER MATTHEW HAD LEFT, THE DOCTOR and I sat chatting for a while longer. It was quite plain, as John Dolittle talked, that he was becoming more and more taken up with the idea of jail as his one best place to go for finishing his book. The work at his house interested him no end; but there was clearly no possible chance of his getting at his writing while he stayed at home. He felt that this book was a greater thing than he had done, or ever would do. At the same time, he hated to leave his patients. He put these matters before me now for consideration; and I was very flattered that he wanted my opinion.

"Well, Doctor," I said, "it seems to me that it is a question of which is the most important, the book or the patients."

"Quite so, Stubbins," said he. "That's just it. And it's hard for me to make up my mind. You see, as I told you, so many of these sick animals have come to rely on me—and me alone—to help them in their troubles."

"Yes, but just the same," I said, "how did they get along while you were away before? I can't see why you feel you must take care of everybody and everything in the world, Doctor. That's more than anyone could do. It won't take you forever to write your book. Why can't the patients manage without your help for that length of time, the same as they did while you were away in the moon?"

He shrugged his shoulders but did not answer.

The next day I talked the matter over with Dab-Dab.

"Tommy," said she, "that man Matthew Mugg is a scallywag, but he's got brains. Jail may not be the pleasantest place in the world. But don't you see what's going to happen if John Dolittle doesn't go away somewhere?"

"What?" I asked.

"He'll try and do both things," said Dab-Dab. "He'll try to look after all these blessed animals—many of them aren't really sick, you know, they just want to get a look at the great man and then go back and brag about it to their friends—*and* he'll try to write the book. Both at the same time. He'll get sick from over-work. No, the more I think of it, the surer I feel. Matthew's right. The place for John Dolittle is jail. He'll be safe there."

Well, it was toward the end of that week that the Doctor came to a decision. We had a very long line of patients calling on him—worse than usual. The cases were not serious ones, but they kept him on the go from the time he got out of bed till the time he went back to it—long after midnight. To make matters crazier still, four new dogs arrived who wished to become members of the home. And the same afternoon Whitey discovered two new families of wild mice who said they'd like to join the Rat and Mouse Club. When I went with the Doctor up to his bedroom that night he was all worn out.

"Stubbins," he said as he sank into a chair, "it's no use my staying here any longer. I've just got to go away."

"Yes, Doctor," I said, "I think you're right."

"Tomorrow, Stubbins," said he, "we'll go over to Gilesborough. You get hold of Matthew for me. I am a little bit afraid of what he may do. But, on the other hand, I am not—er—as experienced as he is in these matters. So I think it would be a good idea if we had him with us, don't you?"

"Yes," I said, "I do."

"Anyway," he went on, "call me early, won't you? We must get those notes arranged. I fancy one is not allowed to take much baggage when one goes to jail. We'll have to copy the notes out onto ordinary paper, you know—much less bulky than those palm-leaf sheets I brought down from the moon."

"Very good," said I. "We can manage that all right. Now get some sleep, Doctor. It's a quarter to one."

I was down very early the next morning; and, thinking I was up ahead of everybody, I was tiptoeing through the house on my way out to visit Matthew when I found the whole family sitting at breakfast round the kitchen table.

"Well, Dab-Dab," I said, "he's going!"

"Who's going?" asked Gub-Gub.

"The Doctor," I said.

"Where is he going?" asked the white mouse.

"To jail," I answered.

"Why is he going?" asked Jip.

"Because he has to," said I, as patiently as I could.

"When is he going?" asked Too-Too.

"As soon as he can," I said.

It was the usual bombardment of questions that I got regularly whenever I broke any news of the Doctor.

"Now look here," said Dab-Dab, addressing the rest of them. "Stop bothering Tommy with your chatter. The Doctor has decided to go to jail so he can be free."

"Free—in jail!" cried the white mouse.

"Just that," said Dab-Dab. "He needs quiet. And you must all understand that where he is going is to be kept a secret."

"Dear me!" sighed the white mouse. "We always seem to be having to keep secrets round here."

"Well, there's to be no *seeming* about this," snorted Dab-Dab. "No one is to know where John Dolittle is going. Is that clear to all of you? For a while the Doctor has just got to disappear from the world—the world of animals as well as of people. All of us must see to it that no one, absolutely no one, gets to hear of where he has gone."

After a glass of milk I hurried away to see Matthew. The Cat's-Meat-Man agreed to meet us, the Doctor and myself, in Gilesborough that afternoon.

On my return I got the notes arranged as the Doctor wanted. We did not plan to take them all with us at once. We felt sure I could bring him more later, as he needed them. And so it was only with a satchel for baggage that we set out together to walk to Gilesborough—a distance of some seven miles from Puddleby.

I must confess that I had to smile to myself as we set off. John Dolittle, the great traveler who had undertaken such adventurous voyages, was starting off on the strangest journey of all: to go to jail! And for the first time in his life he was worried that he might not get there.

Gilesborough was quite a place—in many ways more important than Puddleby. It was a Saxon town, the center of a "hundred," as it was called in the old days. Its square-towered little church sat up among its surrounding oak trees and could be seen from a long way off. What is more, it was a market-town. Every Friday, fine cattle were driven in—blooded Jersey cows, sheep and Berkshire hogs—by the farmers of the neighborhood. And then once a year, just before Michaelmas, there was the Goose Fair. This was attended by visitors from many miles around and was a countywide affair of great importance.

I had visited the town before; and I had enjoyed seeing those jolly farmers with their apple-cheeked wives gathering in the White Hart Inn or the FitzHugh Arms Hotel to talk over the fine points of the sheep shown in the market pens, or neighbors' calves sold at new high prices. They always had splendid horses for their gigs, these men, in which they drove to town—even if the gigs were in sad need of repairs, painting, and washing. Taken all in all, Gilesborough was one of the spots of old England anyone would love to visit.

The Doctor and I arrived there on a late Friday afternoon. The market was over and the farmers had retired to take their last mug of cider at the taverns before going home. We found the Cat's-Meat-Man at our meeting place, waiting for us.

"Now look here, Matthew," said the Doctor, "about this window-breaking business: you understand I wouldn't want to break the windows of any poor people—those who couldn't afford it, you know."

"A worthy thought," said Matthew, "a werry worthy thought. I take it you'd like better to break the windows of the wealthy. So would I. Well, 'ow about the bank—the Gilesborough Investment Corporation? They've got lots of money and they'd be sure to prosecute, too, mind yer. That's important. They just loves to prosecute people. Yes, Doctor, that's the idea. Let's bust the bank's winders. They're made of plate glass—lovely! They'll be closed to customers now, but the clerks and cashiers will still be there. We'll go and take a whack at the bank—helegant! Now, let me see—where are some good stones? Yes—'ere we are! You take a couple in your pockets and I'll take a few too. Wouldn't never do to 'ave no bunglin'!"

Matthew picked up a handful of large pebbles from the roadway. He handed some to the Doctor and put some more in his own pockets.

"Now," said he, "we just go and stroll down the street—saunterin' like. Then when we gets in front of the bank we—"

"Just a minute," said the Doctor. "Are you going to throw the stone to break the window or am I?"

"It just depends, Doctor," said Matthew, "on how much of a crowd we finds in front of the bank and the distribution of the population, as you might say, see?"

"No, I can't say that I see—quite," said the Doctor.

"Well," said the Cat's-Meat-Man, "you got to use judgment in these things—tactics, yer know. You might find a whole lot of people in between you and the bank front, and you wouldn't be able to let fly proper, while me—I might get a chance when you wouldn't, see? It won't do to 'ave no bunglin'! You take your cue from me, Doctor. I'll get you into jail all right!"

Matthew went ahead of us a little. The Doctor, with me following behind, was clearly worried.

"I don't quite like this, Stubbins," he whispered. "But I suppose Matthew knows what he's doing."

"I hope so, Doctor," I said.

We arrived in front of the bank. It was in a wide square known as the Bargate. Many people were on the sidewalk. The Doctor was craning his neck here and there, dodging about, trying to see over their heads. Suddenly there was a crash, followed by the noise of falling glass.

"It sounds to me," said the Doctor, "as though Matthew has been helping us."

Before I had time to answer him I heard cries from the people around us: "Stop him! Stop thief!—He tried to break into the bank—Stop him! Catch him!"

"Dear me!" said the Doctor. "Is it Matthew they're after?"

We saw a scuffle going on ahead of us.

"Yes—Yes!" cried the Doctor. "That's he. Matthew's broken the bank window. Follow me, Stubbins."

We shouldered our way into the crowd that was now gathering thick and fast. In the center of it, sure enough, we found Matthew struggling in the grasp of a policeman.

"Pardon me," said the Doctor politely, touching the policeman on the shoulder, "but it was I who threw the stone—er—thereby breaking the window."

"I might believe you, sir," said the policeman, "being as how you *looks* an honest gent. But I seen him with my own eyes. Took a stone out of his pocket—with me right behind him, and threw it through the bank's front window. Besides, I know this cove. He's a poacher over from Puddleby way. A bad lot, he is. Come along o' me, young feller. And it's my duty to warn you that anything you say may be held agin you in court!"

And poor Matthew was marched away toward the jail.

"But, Constable," said the Doctor to the policeman, "you must listen to me. I—"

"Never mind," whispered Matthew. "Don't you come to the court, Doctor. You don't want to be known there—not yet. No cause to worry about me. I'll be out of that jail almost afore they puts me in there. I know all the locks, see. . . . Yes, I'm a-comin', old

HUGH LOFTING

"Matthew struggling in the grasp of a policeman"

funny face. Stop pullin'. Gimme a chance to talk to me friend before
I goes to the scaffold, can't yer? I'm surprised at you!" (Matthew
dropped his voice to a whisper again.) "I'll be seein' yer, Doctor.
Just a little mistake, see? If at first yer don't succeed, try, try—Yer
know the old sayin'. Better wait till I can 'elp yer. Wouldn't do to
'ave no bunglin', you know. I'll get yer into jail all right, never fear!"

THE TENTH CHAPTER

Lady Matilda Beamish

JOHN DOLITTLE WAS ALL FOR FOLLOWING our unlucky friend, but I persuaded him not to.

"I think he'll be all right, Doctor," I said. "And certainly, as he told you, you don't want to get known at the courthouse yet—for fear they think there is something funny about us."

"They'll think that in any case if we go on this way," said the Doctor gloomily. "But, Stubbins, I can't bear to feel I have got Matthew into jail. For years I've been trying to persuade him to keep out of it. I almost wish I hadn't started out on this crazy idea."

"Oh, Doctor," said I. "As far as Matthew is concerned, I'm sure you have nothing to worry about. He's so—well—he's so experienced in these matters."

"Yes," said the Doctor thoughtfully, "that is true. But still, if I'm going into Gilesborough jail, I don't think I should wait for his assistance any further. I'd better leave the bank alone, don't you think?"

"Yes, Doctor," said I. "I think I would."

We went on strolling down the main street till presently we came to the outskirts of the town, where there were no shops anymore, just private houses.

"This looks like a prosperous place," said the Doctor, stopping before a large house with a very elegant front. "I should think the folks here could easily afford a broken window, what? Well, here goes! Now listen, Stubbins, you better keep out of the way. We don't want the wrong man arrested a second time."

The Doctor drew a stone from his pocket and let fly at a big window on the ground floor. Another crash, and more sounds of falling glass. We waited, watching the front door for someone to come out. No one came. Presently an urchin stepped up behind us.

"Mister," said he, "there ain't no use in breaking the windows in that house."

"Why?" asked the Doctor.

"The people's gone away," said the boy. "Yes, gone abroad for the winter. I broke all the windows in the back yesterday and no one even chased me off the place!"

"Good gracious!" murmured the Doctor. "Have I got to spoil every house in this town before I get stopped? Come, Stubbins, let us go on."

Once more we sauntered, looking for points of attack.

"I don't seem to be doing very well," said the Doctor dismally. "I had no idea how difficult it was to get into jail."

"Well, Doctor," I said, "I suppose there's a good deal in looking the part, as they say. Matthew didn't seem to find it difficult to get into jail."

"Look," said the Doctor, pointing down the street. "There's

another big house—with lots of carriages driving up to the door. I wonder what's going on there."

"Most likely they're giving a tea party, or something of the kind," I said. "See, there's a policeman there regulating the traffic."

"A policeman!" cried the Doctor. "Why, so there is! This is splendid, Stubbins. I can't go wrong this time. Important people with plenty of money; a party going on; crowds of witnesses, *and* a policeman. He'll just be bound to arrest me.—I'll report him for neglect of duty if he doesn't!"

When we came up to the house we saw there was quite a gathering of townspeople watching the guests driving up in their carriages. It certainly seemed to be quite a large and elegant affair that was going on. The Doctor told me to hang back; and he elbowed his way into the crowd till he was near enough to make sure of his aim. By standing on tiptoe, from where I was I could see him and his tall hat plainly. Again he took a stone from his pocket and scored a bull's-eye on the largest of the ground-floor windows.

Another crash—and once more the clatter of falling glass. This noise was instantly followed by indignant cries from the crowd. Everybody drew away from the Doctor as though they feared he was dangerous. Suddenly, as it were, he was left all by himself in the center of a small ring, blushing ridiculously but looking quite happy and triumphant. The policeman came through the crowd and looked at him. He was clearly very puzzled by the respectable appearance of the stone-thrower. His eye roamed over the Doctor's satchel, his top hat, and his kind, genial face.

"Pardon me, sir," said he, "but was it you who threw that stone?"

"Yes," said the Doctor, "I threw the stone. My pockets are full of them, look!"

He pulled a handful out of his pocket and showed them.

"'E's an anarchist," I heard someone in the crowd whisper. "I'll bet yer 'e makes bombs in 'is bathroom!"

"Maybe 'e's crazy," said a woman near me. "'E's got an awful odd look in his eye—Come back there, Willie! You keep away from 'im! 'E might bite yer, or something!"

But the constable seemed more puzzled than ever.

"Did you throw it—er—*on purpose,* sir?" he asked in a disbelieving voice.

"Oh yes, indeed!" said the Doctor brightly. "Let me show you."

He took another stone from his pocket and drew back his arm.

"No, no," said the policeman quickly. "You needn't break any more. You can explain to the magistrate. You must come with me. And it's my duty to warn you that anything you say now may be used in evidence against you."

"Well, just tell me what to say and I'll say it," said the Doctor eagerly as he moved away at the policeman's side.

"Yes, 'e's crazy all right," murmured the woman near me. "Come along, Willie. Time to go home."

"Maybe he was annoyed because he didn't get asked to the party, Ma," said Willie.

The commotion inside the house was now greater than that outside. Maids and footmen were flying around, pulling down blinds. The front door was shut and bolted. It looked as though they feared a bombardment of stones from the crowd.

As soon as the Doctor and the policeman had gotten to the outskirts of the mob I began following them, keeping a hundred yards or so behind. This was not difficult because the helmet of the tall constable could be easily seen at quite a distance. It was clearly the policeman's intention to avoid people following; because he took side streets instead of main ones.

After a little while I decided it was no longer necessary for me to keep back out of the way. The deed was done now and the Doctor need no longer fear that I would be accused of having a hand in it. So presently, when the pair were going through a quiet little alley, I overtook them.

The constable asked me who I was and what I wanted. I explained that I was a friend of the man he had arrested and I wished to go with them to the police station. To this he made no objection, and the three of us marched on together.

"Stubbins," said the Doctor, "can't *you* think of something I could say which will be used in evidence against me?"

"I don't imagine there will be any need for that," I said.

The constable just raised his eyebrows, looking more mystified than ever. He probably thought he ought to be taking us before a doctor instead of a magistrate.

Presently we arrived at the courthouse and were taken inside. At a tall desk, like a pulpit, an elderly man was writing in a book. He looked very dignified and severe.

"What's the charge?" he said without looking up.

"Breaking windows, Your Honor," said the constable.

The magistrate put down his pen and gazed at the three of us through shaggy gray eyebrows.

"Who, the boy?" he asked, jerking his head toward me.

"No, Your Honor," said the constable. "The old gentleman here."

The magistrate put on his glasses and peered, scowling, at John Dolittle.

"Do you plead guilty or not guilty?" he asked.

"Guilty, Your Honor," said the Doctor firmly.

"I don't understand," murmured the magistrate. "You—at *your* time of life! Breaking windows! What did you do it for?"

The Doctor was suddenly overcome with embarrassment. He blushed again; shuffled his feet; coughed.

"Come, come!" said the magistrate. "You must have had some reason. Do you hold any grudge against the owner of the house?"

"Oh no," said the Doctor. "None whatever. I didn't even know whose place it was."

"Are you a glazier? Do you repair windows? I mean, were you looking for a job?"

"Oh no," said the Doctor, more uncomfortable than ever.

"Then why did you do it?"

"I—er—did it—er—just for a lark, Your Honor!" said the Doctor, smiling blandly.

His Honor sat up as though someone had stuck a pin in him.

"For a *lark!*" he thundered. "And do you think the people of this town consider it a lark to have their houses damaged in this ruffianly manner? A lark! Well, if you are trying to be funny at the expense of the law, we will have to teach you a lesson. What is your calling—I mean what do you do—when you're not breaking windows?"

At this question poor John Dolittle looked as though he was about to sink into the floor.

"I am a doctor," he said in a very low voice.

"A doctor! Ah!" cried the magistrate. "Perhaps you hoped to get some patients—bombarding a house with stones! You ought to be ashamed of yourself. Well, you have admitted the charge. So far as I know it's a first offense. But I shall inflict the severest penalty that the law allows me. You are fined five pounds and costs!"

"But I haven't any money," said the Doctor, brightening up.

"Humph!" snorted His Honor. "Can't you borrow funds? Have you no friends?"

"No friends with money," said the Doctor, glancing at me with a hopeful smile.

"I see," said the magistrate, taking up his pen. "In that case, the law gives me no choice. The court regrets the necessity of imposing this sentence on a man of your years and profession. But you have brought it on yourself and you certainly deserve a lesson. In default of the fine you must go to jail for thirty days."

The Doctor gave a big sigh of relief. He shook me warmly by the hand. "Splendid! We've done it, Stubbins!" he whispered as he picked up his satchel.

There was a knocking on the door. Another policeman entered. Behind him was a large flouncy sort of woman wearing many pearls. With her was a coachman, also a footman. The magistrate got up at once and came down out of his pulpit to greet her.

"Ah, Lady Matilda Beamish!" he cried. "Come in. What can we do for you?"

"Oh, good heavens!" I heard the Doctor groan behind me.

"I do hope, Your Honor," said the lady, "that I'm not too late. I came as fast as I could. It was in my house that the window was broken. Is the trial over? I thought you would need me as a witness."

"The case has been already dealt with," said the magistrate. "The accused pleaded guilty—so there was no need of witnesses beyond the constable who made the arrest."

"Oh, I was so upset!" said the woman, fluttering a lace handkerchief before her face. "We were holding the monthly meeting of the County Chapter of the Society for the Prevention of Cruelty to Animals. Refreshments had been served and we were just about to call the meeting to business when a large stone came flying through the drawing-room window and dropped right into the punch bowl. Oh, it was terrible! Sir Willoughby Wiffle was splashed all over! As for myself, I positively swooned away."

She sank down into a seat and the coachman and footman stood about her, fanning her. The magistrate sent one of the policemen to get a glass of water.

"Dear Lady Matilda," he said, "I cannot tell you how sorry I am this outrage should have occurred at your home. However, the prisoner has defaulted on his fine and he is being sent to jail. It will teach him a lesson. I just have to book some particulars. I will be with you in a moment."

Up to this point the woman had been so busy, gasping and fluttering and talking, she had not even looked at the Doctor or myself. Now, when the magistrate left her to go back to his pulpit, she saw us for the first time. The Doctor turned quickly away from her gaze. But she sprang up and cried out:

"Your Honor, is *that* the man who broke my window?"

"Yes," said the magistrate, "that is he. Why? Do you know him?"

"*Know* him!" cried Lady Matilda Beamish, bursting into smiles and gurgles of joy. "Why, I *dote* on him! My *dear* Doctor Dolittle, I am delighted to see you again! But tell me, why didn't you come in to the meeting instead of throwing a stone at the window?"

"I didn't know it was your house," said the Doctor sheepishly.

The woman turned gushingly to the magistrate.

"Oh, Your Honor," she cried, "this is the most wonderful man in the world. A doctor—that is, he was a doctor, but he turned to animals instead. Well, five years ago Topsy, my prize French poodle, had puppies. And she was dreadfully sick—so were the puppies, all of them. The cutest little things you ever saw—but, oh, so sick! I sent for all the vets in the county. It was no use. Topsy and her children got worse and worse. I wept over them for nights on end. Then I heard about Doctor Dolittle and sent for him. He cured them completely, the whole family. All the puppies won prizes in the show. Oh, I'm so happy to see you again, Doctor! Tell me, where are you living now?"

"In jail," said John Dolittle, "or, that is, I expect to be, for a while."

"In jail!" cried the lady. "Oh, the window—of course. I had forgotten about that. But let me see"—she turned to the magistrate again—"wasn't there something said about a fine?"

"Yes," said His Honor. "Five pounds. The prisoner was unable to pay it. He was sentenced to thirty days in jail instead."

"Oh, good gracious!" cried the lady. "We can't have that. I'll pay the fine for him. Atkins, go and bring me my purse. I left it in the carriage."

The footman bowed and went out.

The Doctor came forward quickly.

"It's awfully good of you, Lady Matilda," he began, "but I—"

"Now, Doctor, Doctor," said she, shaking a fat finger at him, "don't thank me. We can't possibly let you go to jail. It will be a pleasure for me to pay it. In fact, I'm not sure I wouldn't have considered it a privilege to have my window broken, if I had only known it was you who had done it. A very great man," she whispered aside to the magistrate, "a little odd and—er—eccentric, but a very great man. I'm so glad I got here in time."

The purse was brought by the footman and the money was counted out. The Doctor made several more attempts to interfere but he stood no chance of getting himself heard against the voice of the grateful, talkative lady who was determined to rescue him from jail.

"Very well," said the magistrate finally, "the fine is paid and the prisoner is released from custody—with a caution. This was a particularly flagrant breach of the law and it is to be hoped that the prisoner will take the lesson to heart. The court wishes to express the opinion that the lady against whose premises and property the offense was committed has acted in more than a generous manner in paying the fine imposed."

The policeman beckoned to the Doctor and me. He led us down a passage, opened a door, and showed us out—into the street.

THE ELEVENTH CHAPTER

In Jail at Last

IT WAS ALMOST TWILIGHT NOW AND BOTH THE Doctor and I were hungry. Feeling that nothing more could be done that day, we set off to tramp the seven miles back to Puddleby and supper. For quite a while neither of us spoke. At last, when we were nearly home, the Doctor said:

"You know, Stubbins, I almost wish I had followed Matthew's advice and—er—pushed a policeman in the face. It would have been so much—er—so much safer. Did you hear what that woman said—almost a privilege to have her window broken by me? Good heavens! And you know, it was the simplest case, her Topsy and the pups. All I did was give them some digestive pills—an invention of my own—and get their precious mistress to stop fussing over them and leave them in peace. Topsy told me that Lady Matilda was just driving them all crazy, buzzing around them like a bee and giving them the stupidest things to eat. I forbade her to go near the dogs for a week and they got all right—on milk. Ah, well!"

There was great excitement when we reached the house and stepped in at the kitchen door.

"Why, Doctor!" squeaked the white mouse. "Didn't you go to jail, then?"

"No," said the Doctor, sinking miserably into a chair, "but Matthew did. I feel perfectly terrible about it. I must go over and see his wife Theodosia in the morning. I don't suppose she'll ever be able to forgive me."

"Matthew! In jail!" said Too-Too. "Why, I saw him out in the scullery just now, washing his hands."

"You must be mistaken," said the Doctor. "The last we saw of him was in Gilesborough. He was being marched off to prison. He threw a stone into the window of the bank, hoping that the people would think it was me. But they didn't. He was arrested."

At that moment the door into the pantry opened and Matthew entered, smiling.

"'Ulloa, Doctor," said he cheerily. "So they wouldn't take you in up at Gilesborough jail, eh? Too bad! Most in'ospitable of 'em, I calls it—most in'ospitable!"

"But, look here, Matthew," said the Doctor, "what about yourself? Do you mean to say they turned you away too?"

"Hoh, no!" grinned the Cat's-Meat-Man. "They never turns me away—not from jails. But you see, on the way to the police station I 'appened to remember that I 'adn't got me skeleton key with me. And though I could, most likely, 'ave got myself out of that jail without hartificial means, I thought maybe it would be best to be on the safe side and escape *before* I got to jail. So I sizes up the copper what was takin' me along, see? And I notices 'e was a kind of 'eavy-built bloke, no good for runnin' at all. So with great foresight and hindsight—still goin' along peaceful with 'im like—I picks out a spot to shake 'im. You know that fountain on the green with the big marble pool around it?"

"Yes," said the Doctor, "I remember it."

"Well, just as we comes alongside o' that pool I says to 'im, I says, 'Why, sergeant!'—I knew 'e was only a constable, but they all likes to be called sergeant—'Why, sergeant,' I says, 'look, yer boot-lace is untied.' 'E bends down to look—and, bein' very fat, 'e 'ad to bend away down to see 'is feet. Then I gives 'im a gentle shove from the rear and in 'e goes, 'eadfirst, into the marble pool. Ha! Just as neat as a divin' walrus. Then I dashes off across the green and down an alley. I took to the open country as soon as I got a chance. And, well—'ere I am!"

"Humph!" said the Doctor. "Good gracious me! Anyway, I'm glad you're safe and sound, Matthew. I was very worried about you. What have we got for supper, Dab-Dab?"

"Fried eggs, cheese, tomatoes, and cocoa," said the housekeeper.

"A-a-a-h!" said Gub-Gub coming up to the table. "Tomatoes!"

"Um-m-m-m, cocoa!" said Chee-Chee. "Good idea!"

"And cheese, hooray!" squeaked the white mouse, scrambling down from the mantelpiece.

"You know, Matthew," said the Doctor when we were seated at the meal, "I think we had better leave Gilesborough alone. What with you giving a policeman in uniform a bath, and my fine being paid by the most prominent lady in the town, I feel we better stay away from there. In fact, I'm very discouraged about the whole business. As I told Stubbins, I had no idea it was so hard to get into jail."

"Well, yer see, Doctor," Matthew said, buttering large slabs of bread, "that's the way it is: when yer wants to get into jail they won't 'ave yer, and when you don't want to get into jail, they takes yer and puts yer there. The whole law, I might say, is a very himperfect hinstrument. But don't you be down-'earted, Doctor. Keep up

"*The whole law, I might say, is a very himperfect hinstrument.*"

the good work! After all, yer did get arrested this last shot, and yer didn't even get that far the first time. You see, you got the beginnings of a reputation now. It's easy to get into jail when you got the right reputation."

Polynesia, sitting on the window sill, let out a short "Huh!"

"Yes, but just the same," said the Doctor, "I don't think we should use Gilesborough anymore for our—er—experiments."

"That's all right, Doctor," said Matthew, reaching for the cheese. "There's lots of other places. Your reputation will spread. Wonderful 'ow a good jail reputation gets around. Now listen: there's Goresby-St. Clements, pretty little town—and a good jail, too! And I was thinkin'—should 'ave thought of it before—the best thing for you to do is not to bother with banks and charity meetin's this time. Just go and bust the window of the police station itself— or the court 'ouse, whichever yer fancy. They'll be bound to lock you up then!"

"Humph!" said the Doctor. "Er—yes, that sounds like a good idea."

"I'll come along with yer, Doctor," said Matthew. "Yer might not be able to—"

"No, Matthew," said the Doctor firmly. "I am afraid you may get arrested again by mistake. In fact, I don't believe I'll even take Stubbins with me this time. I'll go alone. It will be safer."

"All right, Doctor," said Matthew, "any way what makes you most comfortable. But you will see there ain't no bunglin', won't yer? And don't forget, choose the police station, or the court 'ouse, when the judge is there. Use a good big stone, too. My, but I'd love to see it! When will we be hearin' from yer?"

"You *won't* be hearing from me—if I get into jail," said the Doctor. "But you will if I don't."

The next morning John Dolittle set out for Goresby-St. Clements. This was another long walk from Puddleby, and for that reason he made an early start. Dab-Dab had provided him with a large packet of sandwiches and a bottle of milk. He also took with him a good supply of writing paper and lots of pencils—and of course his notes.

I went down the road a little way with him to see him off. He seemed very happy and hopeful as he bade me good-bye. The last thing he said was:

"Stubbins, if I'm not back here by midnight you'll know I've succeeded. Don't bother about visiting me for a good while. And on no account let Matthew come at all. I'll be all right. Look after the old lame horse. And keep an eye on those moon plants for me. So long!"

Well, that time he did succeed—as we heard later. All the animals insisted on sitting up with me that night to see if John Dolittle would return. When the old clock in the hall struck midnight we knew that he was in jail at last. Then I sent them off to bed.

The Twelfth Chapter

Itty

FOR THE NEXT FEW DAYS I WAS KEPT VERY BUSY. Without the Doctor in the house I felt entirely responsible that everything should go well. And there was much more to attend to now than when I had been in charge before.

For one thing, there were the animal patients. Although the number of these calling at the house daily fell off as soon as it was known that the Doctor was away from home, the sick animals did not by any means stop coming. They all wanted to know where the Doctor had gone. I refused to tell them. Then some of them asked me to give them more of this medicine, or that ointment, which they had been getting before from the Doctor. Next thing, a few who had cuts or bruises asked if I would treat their troubles, since the Doctor was no longer there. Of course in my years of helping John Dolittle in this sort of work I had learned a lot. I bandaged them up and even set a broken bone or two.

I got very interested in the work. I felt proud that I could handle sick cases all by myself. Then I began to notice that the line waiting outside the dispensary door wasn't getting any less each morning, as it had at the start. Once in a while a more difficult case would come in, needing pretty ticklish surgery. I wished the Doctor was there to help me. But he wasn't. Some of these were urgent cases that needed attention at once. There was no one else to handle the work, so I did it.

I began to study John Dolittle's books, volumes he had written on animal medicine and animal surgery. I took on more and more difficult tricks of doctoring—sometimes with my heart in my mouth, scared to death the poor creatures might die under my hands. But none of them did—thank goodness!

Without doubt I was very lucky in this. But also it must not be forgotten that I was greatly helped by knowing animal languages—I was the only one (at that time) besides the great man himself who did. I noticed that more and more the animal patients seemed to have confidence in me. Even when I had to put a stitch in a bad cut they lay wonderfully still, apparently knowing that I would save them all the pain I possibly could.

I began to ask myself where all this might lead me to. My reputation among the animals was growing—the same as the Doctor's had done when he first left the profession of human medicine and took to the care of the animal world. I don't mean to say that I dreamed for one moment that I could take the great man's place. No one living could ever have done that. But as I got busier and busier with the work of the dispensary I did begin to wonder—if the Doctor should stay long enough in prison—whether I too might some day have to run away and hide to get peace and quiet. Anyhow, it can be easily understood how a young boy would be tremendously thrilled to find he was doing even as much as I was to carry on the work of so important a person.

But besides my duties as assistant doctor there were plenty of other things to keep me on the go. There were the animal clubs down in the zoo. I had to keep an eye on Jip and Flip so that they didn't bring in too many new members for the home. Feeding them properly these days was the big problem. It required money to do that. (My job as bookkeeper for the butcher had to be kept going too, or there wouldn't have been any money at all.)

And then that blessed little Whitey! In spite of his small size he was all over the place at the same time, poking his cheeky pink nose into everything. He seemed to discover a new family of wild mice or rats every day. He would come to me with a long sad story of their troubles and ask if they could join the Rat and Mouse Club—which I usually found they had done already, before I had given permission.

And I had to take care of the moon plants. This was a big job—keeping notes on weather conditions, rate of growth, and goodness knows what more. But this was one of the departments of our establishment that could not be neglected on any account. Not only had the Doctor on leaving instructed me to give it special attention, but I knew that the raising of these foodstuffs from the moon would be necessary for his book. He felt that the very secret of everlasting life itself might be contained in these seeds of vegetables and fruits which he had brought down from that other world. If I let the plants die while he was away, he would never be able to try them out on the creatures of the earth.

And then there was Itty, the moon cat—strangest and most puzzling of animals. True, she did not demand any of my time; but I became very interested in her. She had not yet taken her place as part of the household (for which the rest of the animals were not sorry). But she was now at least willing to leave her cage. And she used to wander around the garden on silent feet, examining everything with great care and curiosity. She seemed particularly interested in the birds and watched them by the hour. This frightened the birds a good deal, especially those who were late nesters and still had young ones to raise. But Itty seemed to remember her promise to the Doctor; for I never saw her kill, or even try to catch, one.

Occasionally at night I would see her looking up at the moon wistfully—as though she was wondering what was going on there, in that home world of hers from which she had cut herself off with so much courage. The other animals, when she first came out and began to move around, left her severely alone. They sneaked into corners when they saw her coming, and kept out of her way. Her answer to this was to keep out of *their* way—but in a superior, far grander manner. It seemed almost as though, having lived so many thousands of years longer than these upstart earth animals, she felt she should meet their rude unfriendliness with dignity instead of anger—rather the way one might leave impertinent, naughty children to grow older and learn better manners.

Just the same, whenever I saw her gazing at the moon in that strange dreaming way, she seemed to me like a very sad and forlorn soul, one who perhaps carried the secrets and mysteries of all the ages in her heart and had not so far found anyone worthy to share them. And I wondered if the Doctor, in bringing her down, had not had at the back of his mind some wish to keep with him this one last animal link between the world of the moon and the world of the earth. Had he not perhaps felt after twelve months on the moon that a year is but a little time in the life of the universe, and that the moon cat—if and when she would—could still tell him much he did not know?

Certainly I have never known an animal who had such complete confidence in herself. She always seemed to be mistress of the situation, whatever happened. Her eyes! This world of ours has never seen anything like them. In the dark they didn't just glow, they burned and smoldered with a light of their own—sometimes with the sudden white flash of diamonds; sometimes like the green glimmer of emeralds, a sleeping southern sea at twilight, a cool forest at daybreak; sometimes like rubies, flaming, dangerous, red; sometimes like the opal—all colors, mingling, changing, fading, and gleaming again. . . . What eyes! When they looked into your own, steadily, for minutes on end, they seemed to be reading your thoughts, searching you and your whole life—all the lives that lay behind you, your father's, your grandfather's, back to the beginning of time. Itty, often uncomfortable company perhaps, was for me always fascinating.

Quite a while before this I had learned something of her language. She talked very little—gave no opinions. She appeared to be feeling her way around this new world, so to speak, before she would say what she thought of it. When I told her that the Doctor had gone away she seemed quite upset. But I assured her at once that he would be back before very long.

From then on she tried in her funny stiff way to show me that she liked me. This I am sure was not just because I fed her, but because I always treated her in the way she liked to be treated. Of her own accord she would often follow me around the place and watch with great interest whatever I was doing. But she had never as yet gone into the house.

One evening when I was returning from some of my gardening work I found her sitting on the Long Lawn gazing at the moon. I asked her if she would not like to come inside and join the animals round the kitchen fire. Rather to my surprise, she came in with me right away without saying a word.

In the kitchen they were all there: Gub-Gub, Chee-Chee, Dab-Dab, Polynesia, Jip, Too-Too, and Whitey. They greeted me with friendly shouts; but when poor Itty stalked in behind me, they all bristled like a lot of porcupines and a dead silence fell over the room.

The cat went over everything in the kitchen with her usual careful inspection. On the bottom shelf of the dresser there was a sort of deck for pots and pans. She peered into all the pots and smelled each of the pans. She moved silently over to the fireplace and examined the poker and tongs as though wondering what they were for. The fire itself she stared at for a long while and I wondered if it was the first time she had seen one burning inside a house.

During all this the rest of the animals never uttered a sound or a word, but followed her around the room with seven pairs of suspicious eyes as though she were a bomb that might blow up, or a creeping, deadly snake. I felt so angry I could have slapped them.

I nudged Jip with my knee and whispered:

"Can't you say something, you duffer? Start a little conversation. I never saw such hospitality. Make her feel at home!"

Jip coughed and spluttered and grunted like someone coming out of a trance.

"Oh, ah yes," he said. "Er—ahem—er—splendid weather we're having, eh?"

I made signs to the rest of them to wake up and show some life. Gub-Gub came to the conversational rescue.

"Yes, indeed," said he, "though I did think it might rain in the early part of the morning. But who cares? There will be lots more weather tomorrow."

I glanced for help toward Polynesia on the windowsill. She looked as sour as a pickle, but she understood I wanted entertainment. She broke into a dismal Russian sea song about a shipwreck.

Then Whitey started to tell jokes, particularly dull ones which no one apparently heard—and even he himself forgot to laugh at them. Everybody's eyes and attention were still on the cat, who continued to stalk around the room. She looked as though she were taking no notice whatever of anything but her tour of inspection. Yet I felt certain she was listening to every word that was being said, and, quite possibly, understanding a good deal of it.

Finally she disappeared under the table. Then all the company became more uncomfortable and awkward than ever. When they couldn't see her they seemed to feel their very lives were in danger from a hidden enemy. They reminded me of a lot of old maids at a tea party, scared that a mouse was going to run up their skirts. I truly believe that if I had not been there they would have broken and run off in a panic. I was furious with them, knowing how much John Dolittle wanted the moon cat to feel at home in his house. Things were going from bad to worse. I did some chattering myself, talking about anything that came into my head. It was hard, uphill work. But I did manage to bully them at least into making a noise. It was the most ridiculous kind of conversation, but it was better than nothing.

After several minutes of it, Dab-Dab said:

"Sh! What's that noise?"

We all listened. It *was* a strange sound.

"It's almost like a strong wind in the trees," whispered Gub-Gub.

"More like the sea breaking on a beach," said Jip.

"No—an engine, I'd say," murmured Dab-Dab. "Or a band playing in the distance—Extraordinary!"

"I wonder where it's coming from," squeaked the white mouse, who had, as usual, retired to the mantelpiece.

I looked under the table.

It was Itty. Although her eyes were half closed, I thought I saw the shadow of a smile on her face.

She was purring!

In the Doctor's Cell

UT IN SPITE OF ALL THERE WAS TO DO, THE old place was not the same without John Dolittle. I missed him terribly—so did the animals. The chats around the kitchen fire after supper were not the same. Somebody would start a story and we would all begin by listening attentively. Yet sooner or later the interest would wear off, the thoughts of the listeners would stray away, and we would end by talking about the Doctor and wondering how he was getting on.

Dab-Dab, Too-Too, Jip, and Chee-Chee—although they missed him as keenly as any—did not seem to worry about him so much. They were old and experienced friends of John Dolittle. They felt that he could take care of himself and would send us news of how he was getting on as soon as it was convenient for him to do so. But Gub-Gub and the white mouse began to get very upset as day after day went by and no news came from Goresby-St. Clements. They took me aside one morning when I was attending to the moon plants. (Polynesia was with me at the time.) They both looked very serious.

HUGH LOFTING

"They took me aside one morning."

"Tell me, Tommy," said Gub-Gub, "when are you planning to visit the Doctor?"

"Oh," said I, "I hadn't set any exact date. But he especially asked me to leave him alone for a good while. He's afraid that the police may find out that he got in jail on purpose. He wants to get sort of settled down before he has any visitors."

"Settled down!" cried the white mouse. "That sounds as though he might be there a terribly long time."

"We don't even know," said Gub-Gub with a very worried look, "how long they sent him to prison for. Maybe they sent him to jail for life!"

"Oh no, Gub-Gub," I said, laughing. "They don't send people to prison for life—except for terribly serious crimes."

"But we haven't *heard*," squeaked the white mouse. "Maybe he did do something serious. He wasn't very successful with the window-breaking business. Perhaps he got desperate and killed a policeman—or a judge—just by accident I mean. Who knows?"

"No, no," I said, "that's not at all likely. If he got a sentence of a month in jail, that would be the most. And he would consider himself lucky to get that."

"But we don't *know*, Tommy, do we?" said the white mouse. "This—er—uncertainty is very wearing. We've heard nothing since he left. I can hardly sleep worrying about it, and ordinarily I'm a very good sleeper—at least I was until you brought that terrible cat into the house. But I do wish we had some word of how he is."

"What is he getting to eat?" asked Gub-Gub.

"I've no idea," I said, "but enough, anyhow, I'm sure."

"When we were thrown into jail by the king of the Jolliginki in Africa," said Gub-Gub, "we weren't given anything to eat at all!"

"Fiddlesticks!" snorted Polynesia, who was sitting on a tree nearby. "We got put in prison after lunch and we escaped again before suppertime. What do you expect in jail—*four* meals a day?"

"Well, we didn't get anything to eat while we were in prison," said Whitey. "Gub-Gub's right. I was there, too, and I know. Something should be done about the Doctor. I'm worried."

"Oh, mind your own business!" said Polynesia. "The Doctor will take care of himself. You're a fussbudget."

"A which budget?" asked the white mouse.

"A fussbudget," squawked the parrot. "Mind your own business."

As a matter of fact, I was beginning to be a little bit disturbed about the Doctor myself. Although he had told me he would "be all right" I was anxious to hear how he was getting on. But that same afternoon Cheapside, the London sparrow, came to pay a visit. He was of course very interested to hear what had happened to his friend. When I told him that the Doctor had gone to jail to write a book, he chuckled with delight.

"Well, if that ain't like 'im!" said he. "Jail!"

"Listen, Cheapside," said I, "if you're not busy, perhaps you'd fly over to Goresby and see what you can find out."

"You bet," said Cheapside. "I'll go over right away."

The sparrow disappeared without another word.

He was back again about teatime—as was usual with him. And I was mighty glad to see him. I took him into the study where we could talk privately. He had seen the Doctor, he told me—got through the bars of his prison window and had a long chat with him.

"How did he look, Cheapside?" I asked eagerly.

"Oh, pretty good," said the sparrow. "You know John Dolittle—'e always keeps up. But 'e said 'e'd like ter see yer, Tommy. 'E wants some more of his notes. And 'e's used up all the pencils 'e took with 'im. 'Tell Stubbins,' 'e said, 'there ain't no special 'urry but I would like to see 'im. Ask 'im to come over about the end of the week—say Sunday.'"

"How is he otherwise?" I asked. "Is he getting enough to eat and all that?"

"Well," said Cheapside, "I can't say as 'ow 'is board and lodgin' is any too elegant. 'E 'ad a kind of thing to sleep on—sort of a cot, you'd call it, I suppose. But it looked to me more like an iro-nin' board. Grub? Well, there again, o' course 'e didn't complain. 'E wouldn't. You know John Dolittle—the really important things o' life never did seem to hinterest 'im. I 'ad a peek in the bowl what was left from 'is supper. And it looked to me like it was 'ash."

"Hash?" I asked.

"Yus, 'ash," said Cheapside, "or maybe oatmeal gruel, I wouldn't be sure which. But it wouldn't make no difference to the Doctor. 'E'd eat what was given 'im and ask no questions. You know 'ow 'e is!"

At this moment I heard a scuttling among the bookshelves.

"What was that noise, Cheapside?" I asked.

"Sounded to me like a mouse," said he.

It was hard for me to wait until the end of the week. But I did not want to visit the Doctor earlier than he had asked me to; so in spite of the animals clamoring at me to go right away, I had to con-tain my soul in patience.

Starting out early on Sunday morning I reached Goresby jail about eleven o'clock. I noticed as I entered the building that many laborers were digging at the side of one wall, as if they were at work on the foundations.

Inside, a policeman booked my name at the desk and made out a pass for me as a visitor. As he gave it to me he said:

"Young man, I think you're maybe just in time."

"Pardon me," I said. "Just in time? I don't quite understand."

"The superintendent," he said. "He's awful mad. He wants to have the prisoner Dolittle removed."

I was about to ask him why the superintendent wished to get rid of the Doctor. But at that moment another policeman led me away to my friend's cell.

It was a strange room. The high walls were made of stone. There was a window near the ceiling. Seated on the bed which was littered with papers, John Dolittle was writing fast and furiously. He was so taken up with his work that he did not seem even to notice our coming in. The policeman went out again right away and, locking the door behind him, left us together.

Still the Doctor did not look up. It was only when I started to make my way across to where he sat that I noticed the condition of the floor. It was paved with cobblestones—or rather, I should say, it had been. Now it looked like a street which had been taken up by workmen. The whole floor was broken into big holes and all the cobblestones lay around higgledy-piggledy. Littered among these were scraps of food, pieces of cheese, hunks of bread, radishes— even chop bones, looking the worse for wear.

"Why, Doctor," I asked, touching him gently on the shoulder, "what's happened here?"

"Oh, hulloa, Stubbins," said he. "Well, I hardly know—er— that is, not exactly. You see I've been so busy. But it seems that I'm going to have to leave very soon."

"Why, Doctor?" I asked. "Why? What has happened?"

"Well," said he, "everything went fine until three days ago. I had done my best. I broke all the windows in the front of the police station. I was arrested at once. They gave me a sentence of thirty days in jail, and I thought everything was all right. I set to work on the book and I got a good deal done. Everything was going splendidly. And then, Wednesday—I believe it was Wednesday—a mouse came in and visited me. Yes, I know you'd think it was impossible, with all these stone walls. But he got in somehow. Then more came, rats too. They seemed to burrow under the corners, everywhere. They brought me food. They said they had come to set me free."

"But how did they know you were here?" I cried. "It has been kept a dead secret."

"I've no idea," he said. "I asked them, but they wouldn't tell me. Then after the mice had fetched up a lot of rats, the rats went off and fetched a whole lot of badgers. They brought me food, too—all sorts of stuff. Apparently they did not think I was getting enough to eat. The badgers began digging a tunnel under the prison wall to let me out by. I begged them to leave the place alone, but they wouldn't listen. Their minds were made up that it wasn't good for me to stay in jail. And there you are. . . . Sit down, Stubbins, sit down!"

I moved some of the papers aside on the bed and made room for myself.

"When the police discovered what a mess had been made," he went on, "they moved me into another cell, this one here. But the same thing happened again. The rats and badgers came tunneling in at night under the walls."

"But, Doctor," said I, "outside, as I came in, they told me something about the superintendent. What does it mean?"

"It means, I fear," he said, "that I'm going to get put out of the prison altogether. After all my work in getting in here! And my book isn't one quarter done yet!"

As the Doctor finished speaking we heard the rattling of a key in the lock. Two policemen entered. One I could see from his uniform was a superior officer of some kind. He held a paper in his hand.

"John Dolittle," he said, "I have here an order for your release."

"But, Superintendent," said the Doctor, "I was sentenced to thirty days. I've hardly been here half that time."

"I can't help it," said the superintendent. "The whole building is falling down. A new crack has just shown up in the guardroom wall—all the way from floor to ceiling. We've called the architect in and he says the whole jail is going to be wrecked if something isn't done. So we've got a special order from the court withdrawing the charge against you."

"But look here," said the Doctor, "you must admit I was a very well-behaved prisoner. All this disturbance was not my fault."

"I don't know anything about that," said the superintendent. "Whether these were your own trained circus animals that did the mischief is not the point. I've been in charge here for seven years now and nothing like this ever happened before. We've got to save the jail. The charge is withdrawn and out you've got to go."

"Dear, dear!" sighed the Doctor, "and just when I was getting so comfortably settled and everything. I don't know what I'll do now, really I don't."

He looked again at the superintendent as if he hoped he might relent and change his mind. But all that gentleman said was:

"Get your things packed up now. We've got to let the workmen in here to fix this floor up."

Miserably the Doctor put his papers together and I helped him pack them into the satchel. When we were ready the police once again showed us, very politely, to the door and freedom.

The Little Villain

WE GOT BACK HOME ABOUT THREE IN the afternoon.

Once again the whole household wanted to know what had happened—all of them, that is, except Whitey. I noticed that he was not among the welcoming committee who met us in the garden.

When the Doctor was inside the house he explained why he had come back so soon.

"Did you say your first visitor was a mouse, Doctor?" asked Dab-Dab suspiciously.

"Yes," said the Doctor. "First one and then hundreds—then rats and then badgers. They turned the whole jail upside down. It will cost the police hundreds of pounds to put the building right again. I really can't blame them for wanting to get rid of me. But just the same it was very provoking, most annoying—just when I was getting into a nice swing with my book and everything was going splendidly. You see, I had planned, after they would turn me loose at the end of my thirty days, to break another window and come right in again for a new sentence. But there wouldn't have been much use in trying to do any more harm to *that* police station. The mice and rats and badgers had positively wrecked the place already."

"Humph! Mice, eh?" said Polynesia. "I smell a mouse myself now—a white mouse. Where's Whitey?"

I suddenly remembered the noise I had heard behind the books when I had been talking to Cheapside.

"Yes," I said, "where *is* Whitey?"

A general search for that inquisitive little animal was made at once. Too-Too discovered him hiding behind an egg cup in the china closet. He was brought out looking very ashamed of himself and quite scared. Dab-Dab seemed to be the one he was most afraid of. He immediately scrambled up onto the mantelpiece to get out of her reach. Dab-Dab positively bristled with anger as she came forward to talk to him.

"Now," she said, "tell us: Did you have anything to do with this?"

"With what?" asked the white mouse, trying very hard to look innocent but making a poor job of it.

"With all these mice and rats and badgers going to the prison to set the Doctor free?" snapped the duck. "Come on, now—out with it. What do you know?"

The housekeeper stretched up her neck toward the small culprit with such blazing anger in her eyes that for a moment it looked as though she was going to gobble him up. Poor Whitey was absolutely terrified.

"Well," he gasped, "you see, Gub-Gub and I—"

"Oh, so Gub-Gub was in it too, was he?" said Dab-Dab. "Where's that pig?"

But Gub-Gub had apparently thought it wiser to go off gardening. At any rate, he could not be found in the house.

"Go on then, go on," said Dab-Dab. "What did you and that precious Gub-Gub do?"

"We didn't really do anything," said Whitey. "But—er—well, you see—er—we couldn't find out how the Doctor was getting on over there at Goresby-St. Clements. No one could tell us even whether he was getting enough to eat or not. We knew that the food in prisons isn't usually very good. So we—er—well, I—"

"Yes, go on!" Dab-Dab hissed.

"I thought it would be a good idea to talk it over with the members of the Rat and Mouse Club," said Whitey.

Dab-Dab looked as though she was going to have a fit.

"So!" she snorted. "You knew perfectly well it was to be kept a secret—where the Doctor had gone and everything—and yet you went down and gabbled your silly little head off at the Rat and Mouse Club!"

"But don't you see," wailed Whitey, real tears coming into his pink eyes, "don't you see we didn't know what had happened to him? For all we knew, he might have been put in jail for life. When we had talked it over at the club, the old Prison Rat—you remember, the one who told us that story years ago—he said, 'John Dolittle should be set free right away.' He didn't tell us then how he was going to do it. But he is a very old and cunning rat—frightfully experienced where prisons are concerned. And we trusted him."

"Oh," said Dab-Dab. "Well, will you be good enough to tell us what happened next?"

Then Whitey explained how the old Prison Rat (who in his day had set free an innocent man from jail by carrying a file in to him so he could cut his window bars) had taken charge of the situation and acted as commander-in-chief in this plot to set the Doctor free.

Rats and mice are curious folk. They live in the houses and homes of people although they are not wanted there—and they know it. But they listen behind the paneling or under the floors, and they hear everything and know what is going on. They know what time a man goes to bed; what time the cook closes the pantry; at what time the lady of the house wakes up; whether she takes tea or coffee for breakfast; and whether she takes it in bed or at the dining room table. They know when the cat comes home at night and when the dog goes to sleep in front of the fire; they know all the plans of the whole family. They know everything, because they are always listening.

And so the Prison Rat, that old gray-haired veteran of many adventures, had engineered the whole thing. Directly Whitey had spoken at the club about his fears, this general had laid his plans without asking further questions. All the underground machinery of the world of rats and mice was set in motion. Word was sent out that the beloved John Dolittle, the man who had cured the sicknesses of all the animal world, was locked up in a town called Goresby-St. Clements.

The troops were mustered immediately—at first only mice and rats. The message was sent from house to house. Then the field mice were called on and the news flew across country from town to town. John Dolittle was in danger! The message reached Goresby. Larger burrowing animals, like badgers, were needed to pry up the stones of the prison floor. Food was needed! All right. Every larder for miles around was robbed of slices of cheese, pieces of bread, apples, bananas—anything. The great man must have food. At night, when only a few policemen were on guard, the army set to work and drilled tunnels under the prison walls. And that was how Goresby jail had been wrecked.

When Whitey finished his story there was a short silence. Suddenly I heard something outside. I could see from the Doctor's face that he heard it too. It came from the bottom of the garden. It was a most peculiar noise. To any ordinary ears it was just a lot of squeaks— loud squeaks. But to us who knew animal languages it meant something more. It was coming from the Rat and Mouse Club down in the zoo. A party—a very noisy party—was going on, to celebrate the Doctor's homecoming. We listened. Speeches were being made. There was a lot of applause as one speaker ended and another began. Cheers—and more cheers. Now we could even make out the words in the distance: "Hooray! Hooray! The Doctor's back home again! Hear, hear! Hooray! . . . Who brought him back? Who set him free? The Prison Rat! . . . Three cheers for the Doctor! Three cheers for the Prison Rat! . . . Hooray, hooray, hooray!"

The voices trailed off and faded away. Dab-Dab turned again to scold Whitey.

"You little villain!" she began. "I could—"

"Oh, never mind, never mind," said the Doctor. "Leave him alone, Dab-Dab. The harm is done now. And, anyway, it was the Prison Rat who was probably responsible for most of it. Whitey thought he was acting for the best, no doubt. Let bygones be bygones."

HUGH LOFTING

"You little villain!"

THE FIFTEENTH CHAPTER

A Grand Party

AT THIS MOMENT THE DOCTOR WAS CALLED away to see a patient in the dispensary. I went with him. It was a weasel with a sprained back—not an easy matter to put right at all. I helped the Doctor with the case.

After hours of working on it we got the small creature into a sort of jacket made of twigs, like a tube, so that he couldn't bend his spine in any direction. It looked as though it was very uncomfortable for the weasel. They are naturally squirmy, wriggly things. But this one soon found, when the Doctor had laid him down in one of his little box beds that he kept for cases of this kind, that the pain in his back was greatly eased as long as he did what the Doctor told him to—which was to keep perfectly still. We moved him into the small-animal hospital in the attic.

As we started to go downstairs Chee-Chee met us with the news that a heron was waiting to see him with severe gout trouble in the leg joints.

"There you are, Stubbins," said John Dolittle, "you see?

What chance is there for me to get this book finished—with all the experiments that have to be made—while I have to look after these patients? I can't neglect them, can I? What am I to do?"

"Look here, Doctor," said I. "I have an idea. While you were away, many cases came to the house. I told them that you were not here—wouldn't be back for some time. Well, some of them needed attention right away. They asked me to fix them up. I was awfully scared at first, afraid I wouldn't do the right thing. But you see, being your assistant so long, I had learned a good deal."

At this point I noticed Polynesia hopping up the stairs to meet us.

"Some of the cases, Doctor," I said, "were quite tricky. But you were not here and I had to take them on. I actually set a wren's broken wing. What do you think of that?"

"Why, Stubbins!" he cried, "that's splendid! Setting a wing on a bird as small as that is about as delicate a job as I know of. Splendid, splendid! And it came out all right?"

"It certainly did, Doctor," said Polynesia. "I was there and I know. Remember, I gave Tommy his first lessons in bird languages, the same as I did to you. I always knew he'd turn out a good naturalist."

"Now you see, Doctor," I said, "there's no reason why you should not turn over the dispensary to me. If any particularly difficult job should come along I can always call you in. But you need not bother with the ordinary work of the patients. Go ahead and write your book in peace here, in your own home. Why not?"

"Er—yes, Stubbins," he said slowly. "After all, why not? An excellent idea! Anyhow, we can see how it works."

And so the plan was actually tried out. Dab-Dab and Polynesia gave orders to everybody in the household that as soon as a patient

appeared at the gate I should be sent for and not the Doctor. I was
a little bit scared at first, fearing still that I might make some serious
mistakes with the more ticklish cases; and while I was better off than
when the Doctor had been away, I did not want to call upon him for
help too often.

But on the whole, things went very well. I made Chee-Chee
and Polynesia my assistants. The monkey was a wonderful help with
his small hands. For all such work as rolling narrow bandages (some
of them no wider than a shoelace), his slender fingers were just the
thing. He was, too, a naturally kindly soul and the animal patients
liked him. I taught him how to count a pulse with the watch and
take temperatures with the thermometer.

Polynesia I used mostly as a special interpreter when difficulties
in animal languages cropped up. We often had new and rare animals coming to the dispensary, like bats and voles and bitterns and
choughs. And without the old parrot's help it would have been very
hard for me to talk with them.

As soon as I had the whole thing running smoothly, I must
admit I felt very proud—especially when the Doctor came and visited us and said he thought we were doing exceedingly well.

And of course all the members of the household were more
than delighted. They saw now a chance of keeping the beloved
Doctor under his own roof for a long time, since he was busy on a
book and his experiments in moon vegetables.

One evening, just as I was closing up the dispensary, they all
came to me in a body and asked me to do them a special favor. Naturally I asked them what it was before I made any promises.

"Well, Tommy, it's like this," said Gub-Gub. "While we are
no end pleased that the Doctor is staying with us for a spell, we

don't see as much of him as we used to. He sticks at that book all
the time. We think he ought to give himself a holiday once in a
while. And then again, we miss him awful much at our evening chats
over the kitchen fire. You know what splendid stories and disgust-
ings" (*"Discussions, you booby, discussions!"* snapped Jip in his ear).
"Yes—er—discussions is what I mean," Gub-Gub went on. "And
it isn't the same anymore now."

"Yes, I understand that," I said.

"So we all thought," said Gub-Gub, "that it would be a
good way to celebrate the Doctor's returning home to ask him
to come to one of our after-supper parties in the kitchen—the
way he used to."

"And you see, Tommy," said the white mouse, "it will be specially nice now because we're well into autumn and we can have a
roaring fire."

"Exactly," said Gub-Gub. "Only yesterday I was thinking
of covering my spinach." (Gub-Gub always spoke of everything
in the garden as "my"—"my rhubarb," "my parsley," "my tomatoes," etc.) "We may have frost any day now," he went on. "And,
after all, a fire is a real fire only when there's frost in the air. What
do you say, Tommy?"

"Well, Gub-Gub," said I, "I think it would do the Doctor
good to get away from his work for one evening. I'll go and talk
with him and see what he says."

As a matter of fact, it was not easy for me to persuade the
Doctor. I found him in his study, writing busily as usual. Sheets
of papers with notes on them lay all over the floor; more pieces
of paper were pinned on the walls around his desk; plates full of
sandwiches (which the devoted Dab-Dab brought him three times

a day) were scattered round the room, many of them untouched. I explained to him what the animals had asked of me.

"Well, Stubbins," he said. "I would most willingly come down to the kitchen after supper—I used to regularly at one time, you know. But—er—well—just now it's different. I'm behindhand with the book. Thought I would have been much further along with it by this time. And then there are the experiments with the plants waiting for me. You see, I'm dividing the book into two parts. The first part is concerned with my discoveries *on* the moon; animal, vegetable and mineral, you know. I haven't got halfway through that yet. The second part is about my trying to grow certain moon things down here on the earth—mostly vegetable, but some insect forms. And it is in that, Stubbins, that I hope to discover some of the really big secrets—such as the great length of life up there, almost everlasting life. Yes, perhaps even that itself—with scientific guidance—everlasting life!"

"But listen, Doctor," I said. "It will do you good to leave your desk for one evening. The animals have set their hearts on it. They want to celebrate your coming back to your own home—to them. You know, whether you like it or not, they do feel you belong to them."

He smiled. Then he laughed. Then he threw his pencil down on the desk.

"All right, Stubbins," he said. "It probably will do me no harm to get away for a while."

He rose from his chair and we left the study.

It was indeed a very successful evening. Everybody was there: Jip, Too-Too, Polynesia, Chee-Chee, Gub-Gub, Whitey, Dab-Dab, and Cheapside. Matthew Mugg had dropped in again, so we had him, too. And the old lame horse, when he heard that the Doctor was going to be present, said he would like to be there. We got him into the house through the big double doors we had used for the Doctor when he was still a giant. And though Dab-Dab was terribly scared he would knock the dresser over, we finally managed to bed him down under the windows where he could see and hear everything that went on.

And then there was Itty. The moon cat now came and went about the house without anyone's being afraid of her. I had been amused to notice that the two who had raised the biggest rumpus about her at first, Whitey and Jip, had become the best friends she had in the whole family circle.

Piles and piles of wood had been gathered in the kitchen and stacked near the hearth. The air was cold and brisk, and a splendid fire was roaring up the chimney. Dab-Dab had prepared plates of sandwiches, hard-boiled eggs, toasted cheese on crackers, radishes, and glasses of milk. Gub-Gub had brought for himself a large heap of rosy autumn apples. (He said he always listened best on apples.) The big kitchen table looked like a grand picnic.

When the Doctor came in he was greeted by a noisy chorus of cheers.

"Ah!" the white mouse whispered to me as he climbed to his place on the mantelpiece. "This, Tommy, is *really* like old times. Hand me up one of those cheese-crackers, will you?"

Well, stories were told by everybody: new stories, old stories, true stories, and stories that might have been true. Jip told one; Too-Too told one; Chee-Chee told one; the Doctor told four, and I told two. The white mouse told the latest jokes from the Rat and Mouse Club. Cheapside gave us all the up-to-date news from

London. Gub-Gub recited one of his salad poems and another romantic piece of his own (which we had heard before) called, "Meet Me on the Garbage Heap When the Moon Is Hanging Low." And old Polynesia sang us sea songs in five different languages. I have never heard so much laughing, gaiety, and chattering in all my life. The kitchen floor was simply covered with the shells of hard-boiled eggs, radish tops, and sandwich crumbs. It was a grand party.

I was beginning to think it never would break up, when at last, somewhere about two o'clock in the morning, Matthew said he ought to be getting back home. This gave Dab-Dab, who wanted to get the kitchen cleaned up before breakfast time, a chance to shoo the family off to bed. The Doctor, Matthew, and I went into the study.

"'Ow are you gettin' on with the book, Doctor?" asked the Cat's-Meat-Man.

"Well, Matthew," said John Dolittle, "not as fast as I would like. But I'll be all right now that Stubbins is taking over the patients for me. You heard about that? Isn't it splendid? What would I have done without him?"

"But listen, Doctor," I said. "You won't sit up too late, will you? You'll have plenty of time to work in the morning now, you know."

"Time, Stubbins?" said he, a strange dreamy look coming into his eyes. "Time! If I'm successful with my book and my experiments, I'm going to make time for everybody—for all the world!"

"I'm afraid I don't quite understand, Doctor," I said.

"Why—er—life," said he, "long life; perhaps everlasting life. Think of it, Stubbins, to live as long as your own world lives! That's what they're doing up there in the moon, or they will do it—some of them—I'm sure. If I can only find the secret!"

He sat down at his big desk and turned up the wick of the whale-oil reading lamp. There was a slight frown on his face.

"That's it—" he muttered, "if I can only *find* it. All my life I've never had time enough. It's getting to be the same with most people now. Life seems to grow crazier every day. We are always rushing, afraid we won't have time enough—to do all the things we want to—before we die. And the older we grow the more worried we get. Worried! Worried that we won't get what we want done."

He suddenly turned around in his chair and faced us both.

"But if we never grow old?" he asked. "What then? Always young. All the time we want—for everything. Never to have to worry again about time. History tells us that philosophers, scientists before me, have always been seeking this thing. They called it 'The Fountain of Youth,' or some such name. Whenever an explorer found a new world he always heard some legend among the natives, some story of a wonderful spring or something whose waters would keep men forever young. But they were all just—just stories and nothing more. But there in the moon I have seen it. Creatures living on and on—in good health. That's the thing I'm working for—to bring everlasting life down to the earth. To bring back peace to mankind, so we shall never have to worry again—about Time."

He turned back to his desk as though he had a new thought he wanted to make a note of.

"I'm just going to see Matthew down to the gate, Doctor," I said. "Now *please* don't work too late."

The Cat's-Meat-Man and I stepped out into the garden. On our way round the house to the front, we had to pass the study window. We both stopped and gazed in a moment. John Dolittle was already writing away furiously. The little reading lamp with its green glass shade threw a soft light on his serious, kindly face.

"There 'e is," whispered Matthew, "workin' away. Ain't it like 'im? Tryin' to set the world to rights? Well, it takes all kinds. . . . You know, Tommy, me, I never seemed to 'ave time to bother about settin' the world to rights. The world was always tryin' to set me to rights—if yer know what I mean. . . . Everlastin' life! Ain't it like 'im? D'yer think 'e'll ever find it, Tommy?"

"Yes, Matthew," I whispered back, "I believe he will. He has always succeeded in anything he's set his heart on, you know."

"Humph!" muttered the Cat's-Meat-Man. "Yus, I wouldn't wonder but what you're right, Tommy."

And silently we walked away through the darkness toward the garden gate.

The End

DOCTOR DOLITTLE
and
THE SECRET LAKE

ILLUSTRATED BY THE AUTHOR

BY HUGH LOFTING

Contents

PART ONE

The Seeds from the Moon

I WAS WRITING AT MY OFFICE TABLE, IN DOCTOR Dolittle's house; and it was about nine o'clock in the morning.

Polynesia the parrot sat at the window, looking out into the garden. She was humming a sailor song to herself as she watched the tree boughs sway in the wind. Suddenly, with a squawk, the song stopped.

"Tommy," said she, "there's that good-for-nothing Matthew Mugg coming in at the gate."

"Oh, splendid!" I cried, getting up from my desk. "I'll go and let him in. The Cat's-Meat-Man hasn't been around to see us in ages."

"Oh, he's been in jail again, I suppose—as usual," muttered the parrot. "Been *borrowing* a few rabbits or pheasants from Squire Jenkins' place. The lazy poacher! I'm going out into the pantry to get a drink."

I hurried to open the big front door. Matthew Mugg stood, smiling, on the steps.

*"'Tommy,' said she, 'there's that good-for-nothing
Matthew Mugg coming in at the gate.'"*

"Why, Tommy Stubbins!" he cried. "I declare you grow a foot
taller every time I meet you."

"You shouldn't stay away so long, Matthew," said I. "Come in.
It's good to see you."

"Thank you, Tommy. Hope I ain't interruptin' your work."

"No, Matthew. The Doctor will be glad you've come too. Let's
go into my study. And then I'll find him and tell him you're here."

"*Your* study!" said Matthew, following me down the passage.
"You mean to say you got an office of your own now?"

"Well," I said, "it's really the Doctor's old waiting room. But he lets me use it as an office—gives him more peace to write alone. Here it is: What do you think of it?"

I opened the door off the hall and let him in. The Cat's-Meat-Man gasped.

"My word, Tommy, but it's helegant! What a lovely office! And all to yourself, too. This must make you feel awful grown-up. My, but you're a lucky boy!"

"Yes," I said, "very lucky, Matthew."

"I'll bet your ma and pa are proud. At your age, to be secretary to the great Doctor John Dolittle! Getting all your schooling pleasant-like. No teacher running after you with a stick. And here's your office; with a desk, and inkpots, and books and microscope and—everything! I suppose you can talk the animal languages as good as the Doctor now."

"Ah, no," I laughed, "not as well as the Doctor. I don't think anyone will ever do that. But let me go and tell him you're here, Matthew. I know he wants to see you."

"No, hold on a minute, Tommy. Don't bother him just yet. I want to have a word with you first—just you and me—if you don't mind."

"Why, certainly, Matthew," said I. "Sit down, won't you?"

I closed the door while the Cat's-Meat-Man settled himself in an armchair.

"Now," I said, "we won't be disturbed here—for a while at least. What was it, Matthew?"

He leaned forward, glancing over his shoulder as though afraid someone else would hear.

"Well—" he began. Then he laughed. "Funny, ain't it? I just can't seem to help talkin' in whispers when I get speakin' of your voyage to the moon with the Doctor. Sort of habit I got into—when we was so afraid of them newspapermen comin' around, trying to find out things."

"Yes," I said, "I don't wonder at that."

"You remember last time I saw you, Tommy? The Doctor was busy on them melon seeds he brought back from the moon. Trying to grow vegetables, he was, to keep a man alive forever. You remember?"

"Yes, Matthew, he was."

"And that's what I wanted to talk to you about. How's he getting on with that everlasting-life business? Seemed a kind of a balmy notion to me."

"It's hard to say, Matthew. Although I help him all I can, you know, I believe the Doctor is beginning to get a bit discouraged. This climate here in England is very different from the climate we found in the moon. And while we have used the conservatory and the hothouses in the garden trying to copy the moon climate, we have not had any great success so far. You know the Doctor, Matthew; he never grumbles or complains; but I'm afraid he's growing discouraged just the same. Polynesia thinks so too."

The Cat's-Meat-Man shook his head.

"Well, Tommy, if that parrot thinks that John Dolittle is downhearted, you can be sure he is. What do you suppose the Doctor is going to do now?"

"I'm not sure, Matthew, I never pester him. He hates to be hustled. That's what interested him about lengthening life—the way it is on the moon. He wanted to feel that he had all the time in the world for all the things he wants to do—without this hustling and bustling, as he calls it."

"Do you think, maybe, he'll be going on a voyage, Tommy?"

"I don't know, Matthew. He'll tell us when he's ready to. That at least is sure."

"It's a long time since he went on one. Let's see—how long is it?"

"Quite a while," I answered. "But let me go and try to find him. You wait here. I'll be back in a minute."

I was pretty certain that the Doctor would be in his study—at that hour of the morning he usually was. But today he wasn't. Then I started to hunt for Polynesia the parrot; for I felt sure she could tell me where the Doctor was. But I could not find Polynesia either. So I supposed the Doctor must have gone for a walk.

When I came back and told Matthew, the Cat's-Meat-Man said he would not wait now for John Dolittle's return. He had some business to attend to in Puddleby; but, he would try to come in again later in the day.

So I bade him good-bye for the present and went back to the work in my office.

Funny old Matthew! He was always hoping that John Dolittle (of whose friendship he was so proud) would take him along on one of his voyages. He wanted to see the world and have adventures in foreign lands. But Polynesia said she was sure that all he really wanted was to keep away from the police—when he had done something he shouldn't.

Prince, the Irish Setter

ITHIN THE DOCTOR'S HOUSE AND garden there were a tremendous lot of things for me to do these days. But Matthew had been right when he said I was lucky. No youngster could have been busier—or happier. And certainly no one can look back upon his years of learning with more pleasure than can I, Tommy Stubbins of Puddleby-on-the-Marsh.

The schooling I got from Doctor Dolittle, through being his secretary, was not only good schooling; it was wonderful fun, thrilling and exciting for a boy, as well. I dipped into so many things that most people do not study till they are quite grown-up. Astronomy; navigation; geology, or the history of rocks and fossils; the science of medicine; kitchen gardening—for both the sick and the well; all these—and a hundred more—interested me tremendously.

But one thing above all made my education most different from that of other young people: animal languages. Through this I was able to learn so much that I could not have done in any other way.

The same thing had been true for the Doctor himself. Many times he had said to me: "Stubbins, if it had not been for Polynesia—and the lessons she gave me in parrot talk years ago—I never could have learned a quarter of what I have about natural history."

And to this I answered: "Yes, sir. But let's not forget that the animals are grateful to you, too. Before you came along, how much was known about animal doctoring?"

There were times, though, when even I was bound to wonder whether knowing the languages of animals was *always* a good thing for us. The creatures that came to the Doctor's door with their troubles (everything from plow horses to field mice) took up a terrible lot of our time. But the Doctor would not turn a single one of them away.

And then, besides the doctoring work, there were many other things we did for the animals—sometimes quite peculiar things. For instance, when I got back to my office that morning, I found the Doctor's dog, Jip, waiting for me. And Jip had brought a friend with him.

This friend was an Irish setter called Prince. And he had been well named; for he was, I think, the most princely, gentlemanly dog I have ever known. Many months ago Jip had brought him to us to try and get him into the Doctor's "Home for Crossbred Dogs." Not that he was a crossbred, a mongrel—indeed, no! He had in his day been a prizewinner, a blue-ribbon champion, at the shows. And though the Doctor suspected that he had run away from some rich home, Jip and Prince never told anyone where he came from. And they begged very hard that he should be made a member of the Doctor's dog club, which was inside the zoo enclosure at the bottom of the garden.

John Dolittle was quite willing, of course. But, by the club rules, Prince couldn't be a member unless the other dogs (the club committee) said they wanted him. Well, to my great surprise, at first the committee did not want poor Prince.

You see, they were all mongrels and crossbreds themselves; and they did not want any purebreds joining *their* club. Jip got so angry with the committee he took the whole lot of them on in a free-for-all fight; and I had to get up in the middle of the night and stop the battle.

But before morning the committee gave in; and the beautiful Irish setter was made a club member and allowed to stay with us.

Well, this morning, as I looked at the two dogs waiting in my office, I knew at once that something was wrong. In Prince's proud but friendly face there was a great sadness; while Jip just looked very disgruntled and upset. It was Jip who started the talk.

Now when I speak of "talk" between animals and myself, you who read this must understand that I do not always mean the usual kind of talk between persons. Animal "talk" is very different. For instance, you don't only use the mouth for speaking. Dogs use the tail, twitchings of the nose, movements of the ears, heavy breathing—all sorts of things—to make one another understand what they want. Of course the Doctor and I had no tails of our own to swing around. So we used the tails of our coats instead. Dogs are very clever; they quickly caught on to what a man meant to say when he wagged his coattail.

Doctor Dolittle had started learning dog talk long before I had; and I never got to be as good at it as he was. But I managed all right. After getting lessons from old Jip (and from Polynesia the parrot—who spoke English, too, very well), I could make myself understood by any dog—even the German dachshund.

"Well, Tommy," Jip began, "Prince here doesn't want to stay with us any longer. He wants to leave."

"Wants to leave!" I asked. "Why? Isn't he comfortable at the dogs' club?"

Poor Jip seemed almost too unhappy to go on talking. He fidgetted uneasily with his front feet. At last he said:

"No, Tommy, it's not that. But—er—he—well—er he—" Then suddenly he turned almost savagely to the other dog.

"*You* tell him, Prince," he snapped. "Why do you leave it to me to do all the talking for you?"

Prince had been looking out of the window into the garden. Now he started to squirm and fidget too. Presently he said:

"Well, Tommy, I—er—we brought this to you—I mean, we didn't go to the Doctor about it—because we didn't want to hurt the Doctor's feelings. I have been very happy at the dogs' club— happier than I have ever been in my life—anywhere. But—"

The setter stopped and looked out of the window again. And I began to wonder if I would ever get to hear what the trouble was. The morning was almost gone and I had a lot of work to do.

"Come, come!" said I. "Tell me: you say you like living at the club. Then why do you want to go away?"

Again there was a short silence. At last Prince looked straight at me and said in a low voice:

"It's the rabbits, Tommy."

"The rabbits?" I gasped. "You don't mean to say *they* are driving you away!"

"Yes, I do," said the dog. "They have made my life just unbearable."

"But how?" I asked. "I don't understand."

Then suddenly speaking fast, he said:

"They're so cheeky—those wretched rabbits. You know, Tommy, that the Doctor won't allow Jip or me to *touch* them—not even to chase them. He says that every animal who lives here, in his house or his garden, is to be allowed to live in peace—even the rats in the toolshed. The Doctor's so kindhearted. But you should just *see* those rabbits! They've dug their holes right in his lawn, all over the place—ruined it. But that isn't enough. Just because John Dolittle protects them from us dogs, they try to poke fun at us. It gets worse and worse all the time. They don't even pop into their holes when I walk over the lawn now. I have to shut my eyes, so I won't see them. And the other day, as I crossed the garden with my eyes closed, I ran smack into a tree and gave my head a terrible crack. They thought that was a great joke and burst out laughing. One of them—his name's Floppy, I think—he's made up a song about me. Something like this:

> *'Mincie, mincie, mincie!*
> *Look at silly Princie!*
> *Always walking on his toes*
> *While rabbits run right by his nose.*
> *You can't catch ME!'*

"It's more than any dog could stand, Tommy. Those horrible, little underground, lop-eared vermin! I believe if they had hands they would thumb their noses at me, *me* the grandson of 'Will o' the Mist,' the greatest gun dog, the most famous prizewinning Irish setter of all time. . . . I—I'm sorry, but I've *got* to go."

If you can imagine a dog just about to break down crying, real tears and all, then you have a picture of Prince at that moment—and of Jip, too, for that matter. I myself was a little bit inclined to laugh at the story of the cheeky rabbits; but seeing how serious a matter it was to the well-bred setter who had told it, I kept a very straight face as I said:

"Well, but Prince, why not let the Doctor speak to this silly Floppy—or whatever his name is? Maybe that's all that is needed to make him behave—and the rest of the rabbits too."

"No, Tommy," said Prince sadly. "I don't want to cause trouble between the Doctor and his friends. Besides, my nose—for a good gun dog—is getting spoiled entirely. If I stay here much longer I won't be able to smell the difference between a rabbit and a cat on a damp wind. The only thing for me to do is to leave."

"But where will you go when you leave us?"

"Well, Tommy," said Prince, "that's part of what I came to talk to you about. When people have lost their dogs, don't they sometimes put a piece in the newspaper about it?"

"Oh," said I, "you mean an advertisement—for lost and found property, eh?"

"Yes," said the setter, "I suppose that's what you call it. Only this wouldn't be an advertisement for a lost dog; just for a new home for a dog. Couldn't you put a piece in the newspaper saying a purebred Irish setter can be had for nothing?"

"Why, certainly, Prince, I should think so. But there's no telling what kind of a home you'll get—that way. It might not be as good as what you have here."

"Well," said the dog, "can't we say in the advertisement just what kind of a home I'd like?"

"Humph!" I muttered. "It's a new idea: a dog advertising in the newspaper for the kind of home and people *he* wants, instead of the people going round picking and choosing the dog *they* want."

"They'll want me all right, Tommy," said Prince. "I'm not conceited, you know that. But after all, I do know more about the business of being a good gun dog than anyone else. And you could put this in the paper too: say that I'll be willing to teach young puppies to be good gun dogs. You know those little tykes: how they're always running in front of the guns just as the men fire—and getting their tails shot off. Yes, put that in: I'll give classes for setter pups—so long, of course, as I am given the kind of home and treatment *I* want. Oh, I almost forgot: I don't want any children, either, around the place—that is, not real young children."

"Why, Prince?" I asked. "Don't you like children?"

"Oh yes," said he. "But not the very young ones—under, say, six years old. Those little boys and girls always want to play with dogs on the nursery floor. They haven't much sense—can't tell the difference between us, the live dogs, and those stuffed, woolly dogs they get for Christmas. They're always trying to pull our eyes out and change them over. And their mothers raise no end of fuss if we even growl at the brats for it. . . . Oh, and another thing: no flea soap—please! I don't want anyone washing me with flea soap."

It was hard for me not to smile at the serious look on Prince's face as he spoke. Jip, too, showed by a nod and a deep growl that he agreed with what his friend said. While Jip had never won prizes as a gun dog, as Prince had, he was, in his own way, a better, more clever smeller even than this purebred setter. He still wore around his neck the solid-gold dog-collar (with his name on it) that had been given to him years ago for saving a sailor's life at sea, by tracing him to a desert island just by smell.

So, to keep them both from seeing that I was trying not to laugh, I reached for paper and a pencil on my desk and began taking notes of what Prince was telling me.

"No, Tommy," he went on, "most of those flea soaps smell of carbolic—or tar. It may be very healthy and all that. But it's an awful whiff! Besides, no gun dog could tell if he's following a pheasant or a quail or a beer barrel, so long as his own coat smells like a chemist's shop."

"All right, Prince," I said. "I'll put that down too. Now is there anything else? How about cats? Do you mind if your new home has any cats?"

I was surprised when he told me no—he had no objection to cats. As a matter of fact, I had noticed that the setter was the only dog in the Doctor's club who seemed really friendly with Itty, the cat that John Dolittle had brought back with him from the moon. All the other animals in the Doctor's household still kept away from her. But the gentle Prince could often be seen walking and talking with the moon cat in the garden. I sometimes wondered if he was, in his own way, a little sorry for this strange and lonely creature who had been willing and brave enough to come down to earth with the Doctor.

So, I wrote out the advertisement to be put in the newspaper, *The Puddleby Press*. I am very sure that nothing like it ever appeared, before or since, in the whole history of advertising. It ran like this:

WANTED a good home for pedigreed Irish setter, grandson of Champion "Will o' the Mist." No money required. Dog must be free at all times, never chained up or fenced in. Good manners. Three-time winner of the West Counties Trophy for the Best Sporting Dog of the Year. Willing to teach purebred puppies to be good gun dogs for all kinds of game. No baths with flea soap. Will come on trial. Strictly no small children. Home and family must be the very best. Only those with good-natured gamekeepers need apply. Write to "Prince," care of Puddleby Press.

THE THIRD CHAPTER

A Visit from Cheapside

NOT LONG AFTER PRINCE'S ADVERTISEMENT was put in the newspaper, he found a good home and left us. But he made an arrangement that he would be given one weekend of holiday every month, so that he would be free to visit the Doctor, Jip, and all his old friends of the club.

On the day he left to go to his new home, he came into my office to thank me.

"It was very kind of you, Tommy," he said. "It made it much easier for me—like that. I would have hated to go straight to the Doctor saying I wanted to leave his club."

That was the way it always was: if the animals wanted anything done, which they were afraid might hurt the Doctor's feelings, they asked me to do it for them. That same morning when I wrote the advertisement a bird, a mother chaffinch, came to see me. Would I, please, she asked, speak to the Doctor for her? With a sigh I put away the notebook I was working on. I asked the chaffinch what was the trouble.

"It's the Doctor, Tommy," she said. "He *will* keep feeding my children—with birdseed—close to the nest."

"Well," I asked, "what's wrong with that?"

"What's *wrong*, young man!" said the mother bird almost angrily. "Why, my children aren't learning to fly! Oh yes, they'll flutter a few feet, off a bush, down to the ground to eat the seed and then back to the nest again. Their father and I just don't know what to do. *Our* children have always been such good fliers. But this lot! They could barely fly over a barn. They're as fat as turkeys. Stuffing their faces, instead of hunting their food. . . . Between meals they sleep all day . . . waiting for the Doctor to—"

The mother chaffinch was on the edge of tears, I could see. So before she started weeping, I quickly interrupted her.

"Why didn't you speak to the Doctor?" I asked.

"Oh, I couldn't," she said quickly. "The Doctor has always been so kind. I'd be afraid—"

"Ah yes," I said hurriedly. "I'd forgotten. Well, I wish some of you, *once* in a while, would be afraid you might overwork me too. . . . All right, I'll speak to him. I'll go and do it right away."

But of course, while it was sometimes a nuisance, when I was especially busy, it was a thing I was very proud of: that the creatures so often brought their troubles to me—because I was the only one, besides the Doctor, who could speak their languages.

I went back to the Doctor's study. I did not find him there—but I did find, to my great surprise, Cheapside the London sparrow. He was looking at a book that lay open on the Doctor's desk. At the same time he was eating cake crumbs from a plate the Doctor had used last night.

"Why, hulloa, Cheapside!" I cried. "I had no idea you were in the house. How long have you been here?"

"Only just come," he mumbled with his mouth full. "Was awful hungry. Good cake, that. Tell me, Tommy, this book the Doc's been reading, what's it about?"

I looked at the top of the open page.

"It seems to be—er—a sort of very ancient history—long, long ago, you know, when people lived in caves and all that."

"Yer don't say!" murmured the sparrow as I turned over the leaves. "Oh, look, there's a pitcher! Ain't 'e a rummy-looking bloke? What's 'is name?"

"It doesn't say, Cheapside. It's just a picture of a caveman."

"Well, 'e should 'ave 'ad 'is air cut afore 'e 'ad 'is likeness took. But tell me, Tommy: What's the Doctor studying all this stuff for? I thought you said 'e was working on them moon plants and hever-lastin' life."

"Yes," I said, "he was. But lately I've noticed he is doing a lot of reading on what they call *prehistoric times*. That's one of the reasons I fear he is getting discouraged over the work he has been busy on ever since we got back from the moon."

"Humph!" muttered Cheapside thoughtfully. "Pre-'istoric times, eh? John Dolittle's got one friend, anyway, what could tell 'im a lot about them days."

"Oh, who's that?" I asked.

"Why, old Mudface the turtle," said the sparrow. "'E could tell 'im plenty. Claims 'e was one of the animals on the Ark with Old Man Noah. Meself, I don't believe a word of the yarn."

"Oh, of course!" said I. "You were on that trip to the Secret Lake to visit Mudface with the Doctor, weren't you, Cheapside?"

"You bet I was, Tommy. The muddiest, messiest journey I ever made. The trouble with old Mudface was 'e talked too much. But if the Doc is takin' up early 'istory, Mudface could tell 'im more than any books could."

"Yes," I said. "He brought back many notebooks that he had filled with things that Mudface told him. They're all carefully stored away in the underground library, you know, Cheapside—the one I made in the garden while we were waiting for the Doctor to get back from the moon?"

"That's right, Tommy. There must 'ave been a good twenty of them notebooks. And when the turtle was finished, the Doctor got all of us birds to build 'im a new home—a sort of island we made by dropping stones into the lake where the old Mudface lived."

"My, but that must have taken a long time, Cheapside! Even the biggest birds could not carry a very large load of stone. How deep was the lake?"

"I've no idea, Tommy. But deep enough, I can tell you. Days and days the job took us. Of course big birds—eagles and the likes of them—they could bring stones as big as bricks. Little blokes, in my class, we fetched pebbles."

"Goodness, Cheapside, I'd have thought it would take years instead of days!"

"No. You see there was millions of us on the job. That was when the Doctor had his post-office service—you know, the Swallow Mail, as 'e called it. It seems the old turtle got a message to him, somehow, through the mail. 'E was 'avin rheumatics in 'is legs."

"I see, Cheapside. The usual thing: the animals bringing their ailments to John Dolittle to cure."

"That's it, Tommy. Only this time the Doctor was brought to the patient, instead of the other way around. My, what a trip it was to get to that Secret Lake! Right into the heart of darkest Africa."

"How big was the island you made?" I asked.

"As big around as St. James's Park," said the sparrow, "bigger, if anything. Yes, we done a nice job, if I do say it meself. Nice and high—and flat on the top. That was to keep old Mudface dry when he wasn't swimming. Seemed to me a lot of that fancy business was wasted on a turtle. But the Doc said nothin' was too good for an animal what had sailed on the Ark with Noah."

"Well," I said thoughtfully, "it does seem kind of wonderful, when you come to think of it."

"Maybe," grunted Cheapside. "But gettin' back to dear old London seemed a lot more wonderful to me. I don't know what the Doctor wrote down in all them notebooks 'e filled about the Flood. The story part of it we all understood; but there was some skyentific stuff we didn't."

"As a matter of fact, Cheapside," said I, "I haven't looked into those notebooks, myself. I've been too busy. . . . But—I'm not sure yet—I think you have given me an idea. Let us go and hunt up Polynesia. I can't find the Doctor anywhere—maybe she can tell us where he is."

THE FOURTH CHAPTER

The Doctor Disappears

I WENT TO THE KITCHEN FIRST. AND HERE I found most of the Doctor's regular animal family. Dab-Dab the duck was there; also Jip, Too-Too the owl, Chee-Chee the monkey, Gub-Gub the pig, and Whitey the white mouse. There was perfect silence in the kitchen when I came in. But somehow I was sure that they had only just stopped talking before I opened the door—most likely when Too-Too's keen ears had heard my step coming along the passage.

Then I noticed that Polynesia was not among them. I asked Dab-Dab if she knew where the parrot was. And that seemed to break the spell, as it were; they all started talking at once. But I begged them to be quiet so that I could hear the duck's answer to my question. Then Dab-Dab poured out a long story.

The Doctor had disappeared! No one had seen him since he went to bed last night. I would not ordinarily have been upset by this news; but I had, myself, been wondering that morning what had become of him. It was now nearly noon; and usually by that hour I had seen the Doctor several times.

But, as I had told Matthew, the ever-cheerful Doctor had lately seemed discouraged about his work. I was not, however, going to let Dab-Dab or any of the others see I was upset.

I said that, after all, there was no reason why John Dolittle couldn't go for a walk by himself without having to tell everyone in his house. He might have wanted to go shopping in the town, I said—or half a dozen other things.

But Dab-Dab interrupted me by telling me something else that sounded serious. Polynesia had sent off some thrushes who lived in the garden and told them to ask all the wild birds in the country if they had seen the Doctor. The sparrows in the marketplace of Puddleby had also been told to let her know if the Doctor had been seen shopping. These birds had come back (Dab-Dab was almost in tears as she told me) and they had brought no word of the Doctor—no news, either from the town or from the country round about.

It was difficult for me, after that, to think of anything to say to comfort Dab-Dab. She was openly weeping when she ended by telling me that in all the years she had been housekeeper for the Doctor, he had never done such a thing before.

Luckily, a message was brought to me at that moment that there was a mother weasel in the surgery with a sick young one. So I whispered to Cheapside to do his best to cheer up Dab-Dab and the rest of them in the kitchen; and I hurried off to do my job as the Doctor's assistant.

Once I got to the surgery, I was kept there—very busy. There were plenty of other animal patients, besides the baby weasel. And before I had finished, the whole afternoon was gone, and the long shadows of evening already stretched across the Doctor's lawn. And still John Dolittle had not shown up!

I began to wonder what I should do if this went on for some days. Ought I to go to the police in Puddleby, so they could arrange a search for him? Then I thought how foolish that sounded: set the police to hunt for John Dolittle when the birds themselves couldn't find him! And what would he say, or think, of my fussing like an old woman? He hated fuss. . . . But still, just because he had always seemed to us so calm and safe against danger, that did not mean that no harm could come to him. . . . And it was true, what Dab-Dab had said: the Doctor had never done such a thing before. Although he mixed so little with the world of people, we, the members of his household, always knew where he was—and usually what he was doing. . . . Where, and why, had he hidden himself?

While these upsetting thoughts ran through my mind, I was walking across the big lawn at the back of the house. As I passed under an apple tree I heard a voice I knew well.

"*Psst!*—Tommy!"

I looked up. And there on a bough above my head was Polynesia the parrot.

"He's coming, Tommy," she whispered. "Down the road. He looks awful weary—as though he'd been for a long walk. Though how those stupid thrushes and larks couldn't spot him for me is more than I can tell you."

"Anyway, thank goodness he's back," I said. "He had got me really worried."

"Me too, Tommy," said the parrot, "me too. But don't let on. Just pretend we never had any idea he could have been in trouble."

"'He's coming, Tommy,' she whispered."

But news travels fast in the animal world. John Dolittle's high hat had no sooner appeared at the gate than there were squawks and squeals from the house; and all his animal family spilled out of the doors and windows to greet him.

I could see at once that Polynesia was right: he did indeed look weary. Just the same, his cheerful, kindly smile spread over his face as his pets gathered about him, all chattering at once.

"Where on earth have you been, Doctor?" asked Dab-Dab.

"I was out walking on Eastmoor Heath," he answered innocently.

"For twelve hours!" cried the housekeeper.

"Well, most of that time," said he. "I wasn't actually walking every moment of course. Anyway, I admit I'm pretty tired now."

"Come into the kitchen and let me give you some tea," said Dab-Dab. "Gub-Gub, Jip—and the rest of you—stop pestering the Doctor. Get out of his way so that he can walk, will you!"

"Ah, tea!" said the Doctor. "That sounds like a wonderful idea. What would I do without you, Dab-Dab?—Oh, hulloa, Stubbins! How is everything?"

"Quite all right, Doctor," said I. "There is only one really urgent case in the surgery—a fox with a broken leg."

"Oh, then I'll look at it right away," said he, "while Dab-Dab gets the kettle boiling."

But the motherly housekeeper would not allow any of the household to question the Doctor anymore that night—much to Gub-Gub's and the white mouse's disgust. And it was not until after supper, when most of the family were in bed, that I myself learned what had happened. We were in his study, he and I. The only others with us were Cheapside and Polynesia. The Doctor was filling his pipe carefully and thoughtfully from the tobacco jar upon his desk. In silence, the three of us waited for him to speak—quite sure that something important was coming.

The End of a Dream

WHEN THE DOCTOR HAD HIS PIPE lighted he sat back in his chair, sent a puff of smoke toward the ceiling and said:

"Today I had to make quite an important decision. I made up my mind to stop my work not only on—er—making everlasting life possible for man through the vegetable seeds we brought down from the moon, but—"

Here the Doctor stopped suddenly and stared at the flame of his reading lamp; while a smile, a sad smile of bitterness, came into his eyes for a moment. Then he went on:

"But—for the present at least—*even of lengthening* human life . . . I'm dropping it."

And then there was a silence. I suppose it only lasted a part of a minute. But to me it seemed endless. I glanced in turn at Polynesia and Cheapside the London sparrow. The look on their faces was very solemn. For they knew, as well as I did, what a serious thing it was that John Dolittle had just said to us. Ever since he had come back from the moon he had worked untiringly on this, and only this: to get the moon seeds to grow properly in the climate of the earth. It was to leave his time free for this that he had taught me surgery and animal medicine, so I could look after the patients who came daily to his door.

The dream he had had was a truly great one. It was to make human life in this world last practically forever, the same as we had seen it in the moon. He was certain that the secret was in the food they ate up there—vegetables and fruits. As the Doctor explained to me, the trouble with our world down here was *time*. People were in such a hurry. If, said he, man knew he could live as long as he wanted, then we would stop all this crazy rushing around; this fear—which even he, the easygoing John Dolittle had felt—would be taken from us. . . . Yes, it was a great dream.

And now, here in his quiet study, he had just told us he was giving up that dream—saying that he knew he was beaten! I had never felt so sorry for anyone in my whole life. His body, slumped in the chair, looked desperately tired. As his eyes went on staring at the lamp, I wondered if he remembered we were in the room. I noticed that the pipe he had lit had gone out again. I rose quietly from my chair, struck a match, and held it over his pipe bowl.

"Oh, thank you, Stubbins, thank you!" he said, sitting up with a start.

"Tell me, Doctor," I said, as he puffed the tobacco into life again: "What made you make up your mind to this now—I mean, why today, particularly?"

"Well, Stubbins," he said, "I got some news today. I told you I had been hoping to get Long Arrow, the naturalist, to help me grow these moon seeds we brought back. Wonderful fellow on plants and trees, you know, Long Arrow."

"Oh yes, Doctor, of course. And I remember very well that years ago he got lost; and you tried to find out exactly whereabouts he was at that time. It was Miranda, the purple bird-of-paradise, who brought you the message. None of the birds could tell where he was."

"That's right, Stubbins. I got another message from Miranda. And—well—history has repeated itself, as they say. Long Arrow once more is—is missing."

"But you went and found him anyway before, Doctor. Maybe you could do the same again."

The Doctor shook his head.

"That was just a freak chance, Stubbins. We couldn't expect such luck as that to happen a second time. No, I'm afraid my one last great hope—of getting his help—has faded out."

"Did the bird-of-paradise think an accident had happened to him?" I asked fearfully.

"Well, Stubbins, who can say? Long Arrow used to take such awful chances with his life. A most extraordinary man: I was always nervous about him. He would take such fearful risks."

If I had not been in such a serious mood, I would have been amused at that. John Dolittle and Long Arrow made a good pair. Both of them took the most hair-raising chances with their safety, without so much as batting an eyelid.

"But, Doctor," I asked, "did Miranda tell you nothing that would give you any hope?"

"It wasn't Miranda who brought me the news," he answered. "She sent her daughter, Esmeralda. That is why I did not have her come here to the house. Esmeralda's a bit young—terribly shy and all that sort of thing."

Then, Polynesia, sitting atop the bookcase, spoke for the first time.

"How did you know she was arriving this morning, Doctor?"

"Her mother, Miranda, told a seabird—a gull, who was coming this way anyhow—to let me know."

"Huh!" grunted Polynesia. "But how was it that the wild birds around here didn't see you out walking, Doctor?"

"Well, of course I knew it might be a long job, waiting. I couldn't tell the exact time Esmeralda would arrive. And birds-of-paradise can't pop up suddenly in the English countryside without a lot of finches or sparrows crowding around and gaping. So I just gave instructions to a pair of thrushes in my garden to go out and tell all the wild birds exactly where my meeting place with Esmeralda was to be—and ask them all to keep away."

"Good heavens!" groaned Polynesia. "The mystery is solved! I should have known."

"Is there no one else, Doctor," I asked, "whom you could get to help you, besides Long Arrow?"

"Oh yes," he said wearily. "There are several great scientists—botanists, they're called—who have made a special study of just this thing. *Acclimatization* is the proper name for it; making seeds and trees, taken from foreign countries, grow in other lands and other climates, you know. But, my goodness, Stubbins, there would be no sense in my going to them! . . . They would only say I was cracked—crazy."

Again a short silence fell upon the room. Then the Doctor knocked out his pipe and refilled it before he went on:

"I gave a lot of time to this—before I made up my mind. Well, it can't be helped. That time's been wasted. . . . Time, time! But something tells me to stop right now—for the present, at all events. There are other things I want to work on. We'll keep the moon seeds we have left—especially that of the long-life melon—with the greatest care. But we'll do no more work on acclimatization. From today on" (the Doctor made a little movement with his hand, like sweeping something away) "from today on, Stubbins, I am done with it. It is finished."

THE SIXTH CHAPTER

Cheapside and I Agree
upon a Plan

IT WAS NOT OFTEN THAT THE DOCTOR WENT TO bed early. He got along with very little sleep. But that night (it could not have been later than half past nine, I believe), even while I was trying to think of some comforting answer to his last words, he got up from his desk, bade us all good night, and left his study.

"Golly!" muttered Cheapside the sparrow as the door closed behind him. "I never saw the good old Doc so down-'earted. Swap me if I did! It takes a lot to lick 'im. Anyone can guess 'ow 'e feels, though—years' work throw'd away! Poor old Doc! Gone to bed without 'is supper."

"Oh, we should get him away on a voyage," said Polynesia impatiently. "He's gone stale: that's what's mostly wrong with him. I've never known him to stick to anything the way he has to this blessed everlasting-life business. He needs a change from this beastly English climate. And so do I. We've only had two hours of sunshine this whole month. Fog, rain, mist, and drizzle. Only fit for frogs and ducks. Now, in Africa—"

"But, Polynesia," I interrupted, knowing that the old parrot was starting off on one of her long lectures about the weather of the British Isles, "where are we going to get him to go?"

"Yes, Polly, me old chicken," chirped Cheapside hopping across the Doctor's table to see if he had missed any cake crumbs, "for me, you can 'ave your blinkin' Hafrican climate— and welcome. Too 'ot—much too 'ot. Just the same, I agree with you that the old gentleman needs a change—needs it bad."

The sparrow, while he was speaking, skipped about the table till he was in front of the open book, the book which he and I were talking of that morning. And suddenly he looked up at me and said:

"By Jove, Tommy, this might do it!"

"How do you mean?" I asked.

"Well," chirped the sparrow, "you wanted something that would take the Doctor on a sea voyage to foreign lands, didn't yer?"

"Yes," I said, "that's true."

"And 'is mind is still on this long-life business, ain't it? Anyone can see that, in spite of 'is sayin' he's done and finished with it, eh?"

"Yes."

"Well, like I told you this morning, Tommy, when we was lookin' at the picture of Mr. Caveman 'ere. Mudface the turtle was on the Ark with Noah—or, leastways 'e says 'e was. And *that's* ancient 'istory, ain't it?"

"Certainly, Cheapside," I said. "Go on."

"Old Man Noah was supposed to be 'undreds and 'undreds of years old. See? So it's my idea that you get the Doc interested in making another visit to the Secret Lake and our good friend, Mudface the turtle."

"Oh, splendid, Cheapside!" I cried. "Of course! Everybody lived to a great age, they tell us, in those days before the Flood. And there is at least a chance Mudface could tell the Doctor something about how they did it—what they ate and how they lived and so on. At the same time, your plan would get the Doctor on a voyage—a change of scene and all that—which is what he needs *now*, above all."

"Erzackerly, young man," said the sparrow in a very grand tone. "You catches on real quick—for a youngster."

"What do *you* think of the idea, Polynesia?" I asked, turning to the parrot.

"Not bad, not bad at all—for a Cockney sparrow," said she.

"All right, all right, you stuffed pincushion," snorted Cheapside, as the feathers on his neck rose in anger. "Don't get puttin' on airs—just because you're a couple of 'undred years old yourself. I notice some birds never get no sense, no matter 'ow long they live."

"Now, now," said I. "We must get together peaceably and work this thing out."

I looked across at the parrot again to see if she had any ideas.

"Well," said Polynesia after thinking a moment, "I believe that now, for once in his life, John Dolittle has money enough to take a voyage."

"Yes," I said, "I think that is so."

"Then," the parrot went on, "he has a whole lot of notebooks

HUGH LOFTING

*"'Now, now,' said I. 'We must get together peaceably
and work this thing out.'"*

that he filled on his last voyage to the Secret Lake—when he wrote
down the turtle's story of the Flood. I wasn't with him on that trip,
but Cheapside was."

"That's right," said the sparrow. "And you didn't miss much on
that picnic, old girl. Mud, mud, mud! But the Doc wrote all day and
all night. 'E said our Mr. Mudface—as far as 'e could make out—
was surely the last of the passengers left what sailed on the Ark. 'E
said it was 'ighly skyentific stuff. 'E told us 'e never expected to write
all of it in a regular book for ordinary folks to read, 'cause they
wouldn't believe it. And, meself, I wouldn't blame 'em neither. But
the Doc, 'e says it was all waluable hinformation, werry waluable.

And some day 'e might make use of it. He took it all down: what Noah said; what Mrs. Noah said; and what all the little Noahs said. And when the Doc ran out of notebooks, he got dried palm leaves, and wrote on them instead. We 'ad that blinkin' canoe so 'eavy-loaded comin' back, I thought we was goin' to sink."

"Tommy," said Polynesia, "you'd better hunt out those note-books in the morning. I don't know what work the Doctor has in mind to go after next. You know he always has millions of things that he intends to take up—to study. He was certainly blue and miserable enough tonight. But that won't last long, you may be sure. In a day or so he'll be off on something new. You better tackle him about a second visit to Mudface before he thinks up something out of his own head. Because that something may not mean a voyage. It *may* mean his staying right here at home."

"Very true, Polynesia," I agreed. "Those notebooks are import-ant. I'd better get after them without wasting any time, first thing, tomorrow. That is, after I've spoken to the Doctor, you know—said good morning and sort of sounded him out a bit on the *idea* of a new voyage."

"*That's* the plan, young feller," said the parrot. "I won't come in on the business unless he gets difficult. You try him out by your-self first. Let me know how you get on. And—good luck to you, Tommy."

"Same 'ere, young man," sighed Cheapside sleepily. "We got to pull the old Doc out of this some'ow. Never saw 'im in such a spell of the dumps."

And with that, our little committee meeting broke up and we all went to bed.

The Seventh Chapter

Memories of Mudface
and the Secret Lake

THE NEXT MORNING, WHEN I CAME INTO THE Doctor's study, I found him working at his desk. He glanced over his shoulder as I opened the door.

"Oh, good morning, Stubbins, good morning!" he said cheerfully enough. "You're up earlier than usual, aren't you?" (It did my heart good to see him smile like that—after last night.)

"Good morning, Doctor," said I. "Yes, I suppose I am a little earlier than usual. I've—er—I've been thinking over what you said last night. And I wanted to ask you something."

"Well?" he said, seeing me hesitate.

"Tell me, Doctor: What is the oldest creature you ever met? I don't mean in the moon, but the oldest earthly creature—in this world?"

"Oh, Mudface the turtle, of course," said he, arranging the papers on his desk. "He was on the Ark, you know, with Noah. Why did you want—?"

He broke off suddenly. His hands became quite still among the papers. Then he looked up at me slowly.

"*Mudface!*" he murmured. "Noah . . . All of them . . . They lived to a great age. Or so we are told. But there couldn't be any doubt about that turtle—the structure of his shell. . . . I examined it myself. Thousands and thousands of years old it must have been. . . . Why, the carapace—oh, but I'm finished with all that long-life business. I told you last night I've wasted too much time on it already. . . . Yet—"

Again he fell silent. He looked away from me to the ceiling. For a moment he stared up with a puzzled frown, while his lips moved as though he were talking to himself. But I managed to catch a word or two.

"It . . . all so long ago. I know I took down a tremendous lot of notes. But only zoology—some history—and archaeology. I wrote it very fast. Haven't looked at it since. . . . I wonder—"

And then of a sudden he looked back to me and spoke out loud.

"What made you ask me about all this now—today, Stubbins?"

"Well, Doctor," I said, "of course I had heard about your visit to Mudface and the Secret Lake; your building an island for him and all that—although I wasn't with you on that voyage. And I know you will not think it cheeky of me, sir, to—er—well, to make a suggestion—give an idea?"

"Oh my goodness, no!" said he. "Fire away. I'd like to hear it."

"You have spent years, Doctor, on trying to bring everlasting life to the people of this world by growing the melons and foodstuffs of the moon for them. But have you yet given much time to the people in the earth's history who lived to a far greater age than folk do nowadays?"

"Er—no," he answered slowly. "In a general way that's true, Stubbins."

"Then, another thing," said I, "if you'll allow me to say so, sir, you have not been well. Oh, I don't mean real sick, Doctor—thank goodness, you are never that. But you have seemed discouraged and—er—out of sorts. That's not like you."

"Yes, Stubbins," he muttered, "I'm afraid you're certainly right there. I should have chucked up the business a long while back. But, you know, I hated to throw away the time I'd already given to it. . . . Time—always time! . . . And then, besides, you never can tell. The whole history of discovery is full of cases where men have worked and slaved for years—with their families begging them to give up, take their meals regularly and live like human beings. And then!—Then, just as they are about to quit, success comes to them at last! No, Stubbins, that's the trouble in this *research* game, as they call it: you never know. But go on with what you were saying."

"I think you need a change, Doctor. It isn't how hard you've been working. You always work hard. But you've been on this one thing too long—without a real change."

He made no answer to that—just nodded thoughtfully to show that he partly agreed with what I had said.

"How about taking a voyage, Doctor?" I asked, trying hard to steady my voice so it would not show my excitement. "It's a long while since you took one. And I was wondering if you would perhaps make a second visit to Mudface and the Secret Lake. At least there would be a chance that you could learn something from the turtle about long life, wouldn't there?"

"It would all depend, Stubbins, on—er—well, on two things. First, whether we could find Mudface again. I've had no news from him, you know, in some time. And second, I'm by no means sure that he would have noticed the sort of things that made people live to such ages as they did then—supposing of course that what we are told about their enormously long lives is true."

"But, Doctor," said I, "there can be no question about the great age of the turtle himself, can there? Didn't he remember things that actually happened before the Flood?"

"True, quite true," he said. "But while Mudface was a very intelligent creature, it was only the history of the Flood itself I asked him to tell me. I doubt if he could give me much information—scientific information I mean—about what it was in the foods they ate, or in the way they lived, which caused their long lives."

"Well, Doctor," said I, "that first trip of yours to the lake was a good long while back, wasn't it? All your notebooks about it have been kept, as I told you, in the underground library I made—to protect them against fire. Suppose I get those notebooks out, Doctor, and let us see if some of what you wrote won't be helpful to you in this study of how to live a long time. What do you say?"

"I can't see any harm in that, Stubbins," he murmured after a moment's thought. . . . "No, as you say, there isn't any reason why you shouldn't get those notebooks out and let us take a look at them."

"Very good, Doctor," I said, and quietly left the room.

Never in my whole life had I found it so hard to pretend I wasn't in a hurry! But as I walked those few steps from his desk to the door, I reminded myself of something Polynesia had said the night before. "Remember, Tommy," she had whispered as I went upstairs to bed, "whatever you do, don't hustle the Doctor."

So I even stopped halfway to the door and went back to fetch the sandwich plate off his desk to take to the pantry sink. And I closed the door of his study *very* softly behind me. But the moment it was latched, I raced down the passage on tiptoe, like the wind, to find Polynesia—to tell her what the Doctor had said.

The Mystery of the Notebooks

AFTER SOME HUNTING, I FOUND POLYNESIA in the pantry, perched on a dripping faucet over the sink. She was trying to get a drink upside down—while she gargled Swedish swear words through the water.

"Listen, Polynesia," I said in a low voice. "I've just come from the Doctor—and I spoke to him *about a voyage!*"

"Oh, you did, eh? Well, we can't talk here. Lift me out of this rats' shower-bath, will you? Onto your shoulder, please. . . . So . . . Now let's go into your office—while we still have a chance to chat, without the rest of the household joining in."

In my office I quickly told the parrot what the Doctor had said. When I had finished, the old bird muttered:

"Humph! Sounds good to me, young feller. Quite good. At least he didn't say he had work that would keep him here in Puddleby. It will all depend on what's in those notebooks. He's forgotten, you see? And no wonder, when you think of all the things he makes notes on."

"Yes," I said. "If there is anything in the books about the food they ate in those days before the Flood, then I think the Doctor might be persuaded to go back to the turtle again—to ask a few more questions."

"Exactly," said she. "You go and dig out those notebooks right away. But try not to let the others know—at least as long as possible. That silly pig, Gub-Gub, and the rest of them will only be pestering the poor man with questions—asking can they come on the voyage too."

"All right, Polynesia," I said. "I'll keep it as quiet as I can.

"And remember, Tommy, there's no time to lose. You know

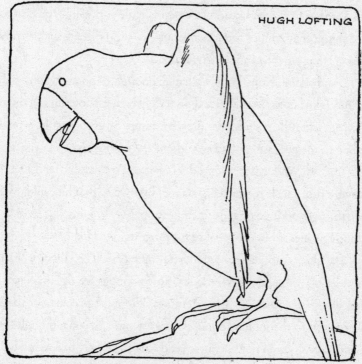

HUGH LOFTING

"You go and dig out those notebooks right away."

John Dolittle. He hates to be idle for a minute. If we don't watch out, he'll be off on some new tack in natural history before you can turn around. And then we'll never get him away."

So, being careful not to run into any of the other house pets, I went and got the key to the underground library. I hardly ever came to this library alone; almost always I took Whitey the white mouse with me. That was because Whitey, quite a long time ago, had been made our chief librarian. Of course such a small animal as a mouse was not strong enough to move the books around by himself. He always got me to help him with the heavier work.

But the Doctor had discovered that a mouse has one thing that is very useful in taking care of books: he has *microscopic eyes*. That means that his special kind of eyesight made it possible for him to see things that neither the Doctor nor I could see at all, such as tiny insects that eat into and destroy books.

And then his tiny body was small enough to go anywhere—all around the books, as they stood on the shelves, without taking them down. And if he found any mites, or damp, or even dust he would come to me about it and we would put the matter right.

He was indeed a splendid librarian. And after the Doctor bought him a little magnifying glass of his own so that he could even see the eggs of these tiny insects that eat paper, Whitey was tremendously proud of his job—*and* of his magnifying glass!

Whitey also had a wonderful memory. The Doctor had, besides all his precious notebooks, an enormous lot of books written by other naturalists and scientists. The most precious of these were kept in the underground library for safety. And although the white mouse could not of course read English, I only had to tell him what a book was about, when I put it into the library for the first time, and forever after he could immediately tell me where to look for it. Some years later he told me that his very keen sense of smell helped him a lot in this. If he could not tell one book from another by its title printed on the back, he could often tell it by its color or by the way it smelled.

Today, as I put the key into the heavy lock of the library door, I glanced back over my shoulder, wondering where he was. Little Whitey always had a trick of turning up in the most unexpected way—and the most unexpected places. He had a most enormous curiosity—just couldn't bear having anything happen without his knowing all about it.

But this morning I felt sure I had given him the slip. In the garden behind me there was no one in sight, except Polynesia in a willow tree. Her sharp old eyes were darting about in every direction, keeping watch for me. I swung the heavy door open, stepped inside, and locked it behind me.

I struck a match. On the big table in the center of the room we always kept oil lamps and candles. I lit the largest of the lamps. As the light glowed up, I noticed there was dust on the table—a lot of it. This, I thought, was strange because the white mouse was usually most particular about keeping the library furniture and floor—as well as the books—neat and clean.

I remembered exactly where those notebooks were kept—the ones about Mudface the turtle, and the Secret Lake. It is true I had never read them, though I had always planned to. But that was not surprising. I did not get time to read much now. I lit a candle and carried it at once to the northwest corner of the room, where the notebooks I wanted had always been kept.

When they had first been put in here I had, myself, wrapped

and tied them in careful packages, to keep them from the damp; and these parcels had, I remembered, been put on the second shelf from the bottom, right in the corner—almost against the north wall. There had been four packages of them; and together they had taken up quite a little space.

By the light of the candle I now saw that this space on the second shelf was empty!

I knelt down on the floor and peered in so I could see right to the back of the shelf. There was not a single notebook there. I swept the shelf with my left hand. Some crumbs of chewed-up paper fell silently onto the floor at my knees.

I didn't stop to look anywhere else in the library. I knew at once that something had happened—something serious.

I rushed to the door, turned the key and swung it open. Outside, in the brilliant sunlight, the old parrot was still perched in the willow tree.

"Polynesia!" I cried. "The notebooks have disappeared. They're—they're *gone!*"

The Ninth Chapter

The White Mouse Librarian

NEITHER DID THE PARROT BOTHER ABOUT searching the library further after I showed her those crumbs of paper on the floor. She let fly a few swear words and then muttered to me:

"Tommy, we've got to find him—Whitey. He's the only one who can tell us about this. Come on, boy—let's hunt him down."

She climbed up onto my shoulder again (where she usually traveled when she was with me). I blew out the lamp and candle, locked up the library and together we started for the house.

"You know, Polynesia," I said, as we were crossing the lawn, "I've just remembered; it has been a long time—weeks and weeks—since our chief librarian has come to me about the books back there. Usually it was every few days—and nearly always about something that didn't matter a bit—just wanted to show off his importance as librarian. But now—my goodness, I can't remember—but it's simply ages since he came and asked for my help with the books."

"Huh!" grunted the parrot. "Didn't you smell a rat, then—or a mouse?"

"Yes, I should have done, it's true," I said. "But I've been so busy—especially with the surgery and the dispensary. You know how it is in early summer, when the birds have new broods that are learning to fly; and the squirrels and foxes and the rest have young ones who are always falling and getting themselves hurt?"

"Heigh-ho! Don't I know?" sighed the parrot. "Sometimes I wonder how John Dolittle is alive today, when I think how he worked alone at the doctoring business before he had you to help him."

"Oh, I'm glad to do it, Polynesia," I said quickly. "Don't think I'm not. And it's very interesting—most of it. But, after all, there are only twenty-four hours in the day, you know. The trouble is—"

"The trouble is *time*," the parrot interrupted. "That's what the Doctor himself said: 'Time! If we only had the time to do all the things we want to do. . . .' Poor man! That's what fascinated him most, I think, about the life on the moon. Well, here we are at the house. We had better separate now. You go in by the front door and I'll fly round to the kitchen door. Watch it now! Don't let our librarian escape—that is, *if* he's in the house."

We found out afterward that our precious librarian had overheard the talk between the Doctor and me about the notebooks; and the mouse knew of course that he would be in for trouble as soon as I found them missing and came to look for him.

Well, no one would think it, but it took us the rest of the day to find Whitey—or, I should say, to catch him. When a mouse (even a *white* mouse) really wants to hide himself in an old-fashioned, English country house, it is surprising how many places he can use for dodging into, or behind, to keep out of sight. What a chase he led us! He would get in the china closet and hide behind an egg cup. Then, after I had moved every single piece of china separately, there would suddenly be a white flash and Polynesia would yell: "There he is!"

But he *wasn't*. He would dive through a knothole in the back of the closet; and two seconds later he would be in the next room, hiding under a corner of the carpet—or upstairs in my bedroom, behind the clock on the dressing-table.

By this time, of course, the whole household had joined in the

"... behind the clock on the dressing table"

hunt—though we had not told them yet why we were going after the little villain (nor why he was running away from us).

Gub-Gub thought the whole thing was some kind of a new game; and while he tried very hard to be helpful, all he succeeded in doing was getting in the way. I think I must have tripped over that pig a good dozen times—once on the stairs (when I almost had the mouse by the tail) and I somersaulted all the way down from the attic to the first floor—where I landed with a bruised elbow, two barked shins, and a crack on the head that all but stunned me.

After that we called a council of war.

"Listen, Tommy," whispered Dab-Dab: "we have got two of the best mouse-catchers in the business right here with us—a dog and an owl."

"Why, of course!" said I. "Jip and Too-Too."

"Suppose the rest of us go out for a walk in the garden," said the duck quietly. "I fancy Jip's nose and Too-Too's ears will very soon find out where that little devil is hiding. But be careful, you two," she added, turning to them, "how you do it. The Doctor would never forgive us if the mouse got hurt. You'll have to corner him someway in a place where he can't get out. Then talk to him. Talk him into surrendering."

"That's the idea," I said. "Tell him that he will only be questioned in front of the Doctor. John Dolittle will see that he isn't hurt—no matter *what* he has done. He will trust John Dolittle to look after him, even if he won't trust me. We'll be out on the front lawn, Jip. When you've cornered him, bark gently, to signal us. We won't come back till we hear you."

So we left the two of them at it and went out into the garden. Jip told me afterward that it was really Too-Too who ran Whitey down. He said his own sense of smell wasn't much good for that job; because the Doctor's house smelled so strong of mice anyway (from all Whitey's friends who used to visit him). Jip told me that no dog living could tell where one mouse's scent left off and another's began.

But Too-Too, with his marvelous sense of hearing, just listened at the paneling and the flooring. And Whitey couldn't even scratch his ear or polish his whiskers without the owl's knowing it—much less move from place to place. Too-Too had the patience of a mountain. And he waited, motionless—just waited.

At last Whitey, hearing no sound in the house at all, made up his mind we must have *all* gone outside. He felt hungry. Then he remembered he had left half a walnut in the coal scuttle, beside the fireplace. On tiptoe he went to get it. But Too-Too's ears could hear a mouse walking tiptoe as easily as you or I can hear a horse trotting on a cobblestoned street. The owl made a sign to Jip to stand ready. The mouse's white body crept down into the deep scuttle. And then, suddenly, they jumped. With the two of them barring the only escape for the mouse—the only way out—Whitey was cornered at last.

The Tenth Chapter

How the Story of the Flood Was Lost

WHEN I CAME BACK INTO THE HOUSE, IN answer to Jip's bark, I took Whitey in my coat-pocket and went to see the Doctor. Polynesia, Jip, and Cheapside came with me.

"Well, well, what's all this, Stubbins?" asked the Doctor as the dog and I, with the parrot on my shoulder, came to a stop in front of him.

I fished the white mouse out of my pocket and set him down on the desk before the Doctor.

"Whitey will have to explain to you, sir," said I. "Your note-books about the Flood are missing from the library. Every single one of them is gone."

"Good gracious!" cried the Doctor. "From the underground library! Is it possible? How did this happen, Whitey? You always took such good care of the books."

"Well—er—" Whitey began. Then as he looked up at the eyes of Polynesia blazing down at him with anger, his voice trailed off and he stopped.

"Tell the truth, now," snapped the parrot, "you—you monstrous cheese-pirate! Or I'll swallow you alive."

"Gently, gently!" said the Doctor. "Let him answer my question, Polynesia, *please*. What happened to the books, Whitey?"

"Well, it was about a month and a half ago," the mouse began in a trembly sort of voice, "when those Ship's Rats—you remember them, Doctor? They asked could they become members of your Rat and Mouse Club. And you said, yes, it was all right if the other members were willing. Well, soon after that, they wanted to set up housekeeping, because Mrs. Ship's Rat was going to have a whole lot of babies and they wished to make a nest."

"And where did they want to make the nest, Whitey?" asked the Doctor quietly.

"In your potting shed, where you keep the lawn mower," said the white mouse. "But, you see, they were foreigners—from some hot country—and they always used palm leaves—shredded out, you know—for building their nests with."

"Oh, lumme!—I think I know what's coming," I heard Cheapside whisper.

"Yes, yes, go on, please, Whitey," said John Dolittle.

"So they came to me," said the librarian, "and asked if I knew where you had any old palm leaves that were not being used. At first I said, no, I didn't. But then suddenly I thought of something. You remember, Doctor, when you were taking notes on Mudface's story of the Flood, you ran out of ordinary notebooks; and you took dried palm leaves and finished the story on them?"

"Yes," said the Doctor seriously, "I remember."

"Well," said the white mouse, "I had been in charge of the library almost since it was built. And I knew that you had never once looked at those notebooks you brought back from the Secret Lake. The packages had stayed in the same place on the shelves, just as Tommy had wrapped them up and put them away."

Once more the chief librarian stopped while his frightened eyes glanced at the angry face of the parrot.

"So," said Whitey in a small, scared voice, "I thought there couldn't be any great harm if the Ship's Rats borrowed—"

"Shiver my timbers, you salty pantry-robber!" roared Polynesia from my shoulder. "Do you mean to say that you took the Doctor's notebooks—notes that he had gone halfway across Africa to get— and gave them to a couple of bilge rats to line their nest with?"

"But I didn't tell them they could take *all* the notebooks," said Whitey, almost in tears. "It was only a week later—after I had shown them how to get into the library through a hole I had dug for myself under the wall—that I found they had taken, not only the palm-leaf covers, but all the other notebooks too, for their friends' nests, as well as their own. I hoped, even then, that some part of what the Doctor had written could be saved. But it was too late. Every single notebook had been chewed up into little tiny pieces and carried away."

"But why didn't you come and tell me, Whitey?" I asked.

"I—I was too scared," stuttered the mouse, "of Polynesia."

Then there was a silence. And I knew that everyone in the room was, like myself, waiting to hear what the Doctor would say. For a moment his fingers drummed upon the desk; and at last he murmured as though he were speaking to himself:

"It's sort of strange that we should have been talking about those notes only last night. . . . Losing them would not have mattered so much, if I were sure that Mudface is still alive and I could see him again. . . . But—lately—I have begun to doubt if he *can* still be living. I asked several seabirds to call at his home and find out how he is getting on. They have all brought me the same message: no news of the giant turtle. . . . Poor old Mudface—a wonderful character. And what things he had seen! . . . I should have attended to those notebooks long ago—got them written up in proper form so they could be published anytime I wanted. . . . Now it can never be written: the history of the Flood! There is no one left who saw it happen with his own eyes from the decks of Noah's Ark—so far as we know. . . . Well, it's no use crying over spilt milk, as they say."

Poor Whitey was weeping out loud now; and the rest of us felt pretty miserable. The Doctor seemed lost in thought. It was getting late, I knew. So I made a sign to the rest of them and we all went quietly out of the study and left John Dolittle alone.

Cheapside Goes Back to London

IN THE KITCHEN, DAB-DAB PREPARED A SUPPER for us and fixed up a tray to be taken in to the Doctor. You may be sure our talk was not very cheerful. Our plans and hopes for a voyage had been badly dampened, to say the least.

However, after we had had hot cocoa and something to eat, we gradually grew more cheerful. And presently Cheapside the London sparrow, said:

"Well, Tommy me lad, what are you goin' to do now? I mean, about gettin' the Doctor off on a trip?"

"I'm afraid I really don't know, Cheapside—with those notebooks gone. It is strange; but I have never known the Doctor to forget anything so important, so completely. He tells me he hardly remembers a single word he wrote in those notes."

"Huh! No wonder, at the speed *he* was writing," grunted the sparrow. "I never saw nobody write that fast, never in all me life. What's more, *I* don't remember what the turtle told us, myself— though I was right alongside the Doctor all the time."

HUGH LOFTING

"In the kitchen, Dab-Dab prepared a supper for us."

"It's a terrible pity," I said, "that none of you who were with John Dolittle can remember any of it. If Mudface is dead, as the Doctor fears he may be, the story of the Flood will never be known now."

"Yes, I s'pose so, Tommy," said Cheapside thoughtfully. "But, you know, this destroyin' the notebooks *might* work just the other way."

"How do you mean?" I asked.

"Well," said Cheapside, putting his foot on a slice of toast while he broke a corner off it with his beak, "we ain't got no proof yet that old Mudface *is* dead, 'ave we? And *if* it should turn out that 'e's still alive—or even that there's a fair chance of 'is bein' alive—the Doc will be all the keener to go and have another talk with him—so 'e can spend three more weeks sittin' in the mud, listenin' to the family troubles of Mr. and Mrs. Noah. Tell me, Tommy, when was the last time the Doc had news of our friend Mudface?"

"I'm not exactly sure," I said. "As you know, the Doctor gets messages and news by bird carriers, at all times of the year, from all over the world. Let me see: I think the last news of Mudface was brought—er—about three months back."

"Humph!" muttered Cheapside. "Then that would be somewhere in March, wouldn't it?"

"Er—yes," I said. "I think that would be right."

"What sort of birds was they what brought these reports to the Doctor?" asked Cheapside.

"Oh," said I, "usually they were gulls, I think—or some of the heavier kinds of seabirds who used to make a special trip inland to the Secret Lake, as a favor to the Doctor. And once in a while they would be waders—like the herons or the storks. But why did you want to know, Cheapside?"

The sparrow didn't answer my question; instead, he murmured:

"None of them birds you speak of is what I'd call very hintelligent, Tommy. *Storks!* All they're good for is standin' on one leg and fishin' in a puddle, like schoolboys. . . . Humph! I got an idea, young feller. Nothin' may come of it. And then again, a whole lot might come. But, first of all, I want to 'ear what Becky, my wife, thinks of it. I'm goin' back to the city right now—tonight. We're raisin' the last brood of the season, you know—cutest little youngsters you ever saw! Two of 'em can talk already. Becky says they're the best-lookin' family we ever raised. But then—you know mothers—she's said the same about every family we ever 'ad. Only don't never tell 'er I told you. And if I don't get back tonight to help her with the feeding, I'll be in trouble."

"All right, Cheapside," I said, opening the kitchen window for him. "I'm sorry you can't stay with us longer now. The Doctor has hardly seen you on this visit. And you know how he enjoys hearing the news of London. You always manage to cheer him up—and goodness knows he needs it just now!"

"Yes, Tommy, you're right. But I shan't be gone long this time—or, that is, I hadn't oughter be, if things pan out the way I 'ope they does. But I really oughter get back to poor Becky tonight, to 'elp the old girl."

"Yes, I understand that of course," I said. "You are still building your nest in the same place—outside St. Paul's Cathedral?"

"That's right, Tommy," said the sparrow. "Same old spot: in Saint Edmund's left ear. 'Ave you got any of that cake left—the same as I was eatin' the crumbs of, off the Doctor's plate the other night?"

"Yes," said Dab-Dab, "I think I've got a little piece in the larder. Wait a moment and I'll see."

"It don't 'ave to be a big piece," said the sparrow. "I'm flyin' against the wind gettin' back to London, you know. So I can't carry much. Ah, good old Dab-Dab! That's just the very ticket—the right size."

As Cheapside took the little ball of cake that Dab-Dab laid on the table before him, he glanced up at me with a twinkle in his eye.

"This'll be a treat for the kids," he said. "Kind of a surprise, you know. *Cake from John Dolittle's table!* My word! Becky will be boastin' about this for a week to all the other sparrow mothers round St. Paul's. You never saw such happetites as this last family of ours has! They keep poor Becky and me fair worn out, fetchin' and carryin' grub for 'em all day. But they'll be ready to fly next week. Then we'll get a rest."

"Good-bye, Cheapside," I said. "Don't forget to give Becky our very best regards."

"You bet, Tommy. And don't let the Doc get down-'earted. I got an idea. And *maybe* it'll work out. You'll be seein' me again in a few days. So long, everybody!"

Then, taking a firm grip on the cake between his claws, Cheapside gave a flirt of his wings and was gone through the open window, out into the night.

The Work of a Naturalist's Assistant

F OR MOST OF THE NEXT WEEK THE DOCTOR'S
house settled down into a regular, humdrum program—
or perhaps I should say it came as near as possible to
settling down in such a way. John Dolittle's household
never stayed very regular for long, I fear. Perhaps that was one of
the things that made it so interesting.

But if life went along more quietly than usual for those few
days, I was not sorry—and neither was Polynesia. The night
that Cheapside flew back to London the old parrot came into
my office where I was working late. As soon as she appeared I
could tell from her manner she had something unusual on her
mind. She flew up on my desk and silently nodded toward the
open door. I knew what she meant. I got up and very quietly
closed it.

I smiled as I came back and sat down.

"I don't think," I said, "that you need be afraid of poor Whitey
trying to listen now. You certainly gave him a terrible scare."

"Maybe," said she. "But I wouldn't trust that little long-nosed snooper farther than I could throw him. The trouble with him is he *has* to know everything. He has already been gabbing around, trying to find out what idea Cheapside had in mind tonight when he left us. Luckily, there isn't much chance of his learning *that*."

"No," I agreed, "there isn't. The London sparrow was a bit mysterious though, wasn't he, Polynesia? Have you any notion, yourself, of what he had in mind?"

"That's what I came to talk to you about," said the parrot. "No, I don't know what it was he was hinting at. But I do know this: Cheapside may be a quarrelsome, vulgar, little guttersnipe. Yet there is one thing about him no one can deny. When he makes up his mind to a thing, he generally sees it through—gets it done. There's a streak of Cockney stubbornness in that bird. And I like it."

"He said he was going to talk over his idea with his wife, Becky. Do you suppose it is something about a voyage, Polynesia?"

"I couldn't say," she murmured, shrugging up her wings. "But I'll bet you shillings to cracker crumbs that Becky won't make him change—if Cheapside has made up his own mind first, *before* he gets to London."

"No," I said. "I think that's a pretty safe bet. . . . He's a funny character, that Cheapside."

"Well," said Polynesia, "all the others of the Doctor's family—besides our wonderful librarian—are trying to guess what plan or idea the sparrow had. That silly pig, Gub-Gub, has asked me a half a dozen times tonight. And he won't believe me when I tell him *I don't know!*"

The old parrot stopped a moment with her head turned to one side. I could see that she wasn't sure, even here, that someone might not come and interrupt us—or be listening outside the door to our talk. But no sound reached us from the rest of the house; and presently she went on again:

"What I wanted to tell you, Tommy, was this: it may be that Cheapside has some plan to get the Doctor to go back to Africa— to the Secret Lake. He was with John Dolittle on the first trip, you know. And you remember he said we would see him back here in a few days' time. Now, what I want you to do is to try your best to sidetrack the Doctor from getting started on any new important work before Cheapside pays us another visit."

"Well, I'll certainly try, Polynesia," I said. "But, as you know very well yourself, it isn't always so easy to—er—sidetrack the Doctor away from any plans he may make. He is worse than Cheapside in that—once his mind is made up."

"But that is just what I mean, Tommy," said the parrot in a low, earnest voice. "I want you to keep him busy, so he won't be thinking out any new, big plans—just for a few days, I mean, till we hear from Cheapside again. For months now, John Dolittle has left the running of the whole place to you—practically every-thing except the tricky surgical jobs on the animals that come to his door."

"Er—yes," said I. "It is true, he has."

"Very well, then," said the parrot. "There must be lots and lots of things that you want to ask him about—to get him to decide on. Just keep him busy, that's the main thing. And stick close to him all day long."

"As a matter of fact," I said, "there *are* a whole heap of things

I want to talk over with him—things I've put off because I knew he was busy and didn't want to be interrupted."

"*That's* the idea, Tommy," said she. "Just keep him busy, deciding this and that. Cheapside will keep his word, you may be sure. He said he'd be down again in a few days. And I'll make you any bet he will."

The After-Supper
Story Hour

AS A MATTER OF FACT, I WAS SURPRISED myself at what a lot of things there were for which I needed the Doctor's help and advice, now that he had some free time to give me.

There were the moon seeds; and, although the Doctor was closing that chapter of natural history for the present, they were the only ones in the world. He might someday want to try again. He handed them over to Polynesia (a seed-eating bird), sure that she would store them away so they would keep in good condition.

And there was the garden. You never saw such a jungle of weeds in your life! Only those beds where we had tried so patiently to make the moon seeds grow—and the hothouses—had been looked after at all.

And this time, I think, John Dolittle really saw (after Polynesia and I had taken him round to the worst spots on purpose) that if he didn't give the garden his attention right away, there soon would be nothing of it left. While his back was turned a moment, and he examined some raspberry canes, the parrot nodded meaningly to me; and I knew that the same thought had passed through her mind. However, I did what she had told me: I stuck close to the Doctor all day and every day.

No, Polynesia and I had no difficulty keeping the Doctor busy during the *daylight* hours. It was the evening-time, when he usually went into his study (sometimes to sit at his desk until very, very late) that worried the old parrot and me. For it was then we feared he might think up some new and important work which—once he got started on it—we could not possibly get him to leave.

However, it was Gub-Gub the pig who gave me an idea that was very helpful in this.

"My word, Tommy," he said to me one evening as he was gathering some rhubarb to take into the house (Gub-Gub still took very good care of the vegetables). "It is really wonderful to see the Doctor around again! It had got so we hardly saw him at all, while he was working on that old everlasting-life business—with him taking his meals and everything in his study."

"Yes, Gub-Gub," said I. "It's much better this way. He was working far too hard—at his desk."

"He paid me quite a compliment," said Gub-Gub, rooting out a large weed with his nose, "over the way I'd kept the tomatoes. But, you know, Tommy, there is one thing I still miss—about the Doctor and his ways."

"Oh?" I said. "What's that?"

"It's the stories he used to tell us around the kitchen fire after supper," said Gub-Gub, his little eyes twinkling with memories as he looked up at me over his muddy nose. "Ah!" he sighed. "Those were the days, Tommy, those were the days!"

"Yes," I agreed. "You're right."

But I fear I was hardly thinking of what I said. My mind was turning over the words Gub-Gub had just spoken.

"Do you realize, Tommy," said the pig, "the Doctor has not told us a single fireside story since he got back from the moon? We were talking about it only yesterday, Chee-Chee, Too-Too, and I. And you remember there was a time when he told us a story every single night?"

"Well," said I, "listen, Gub-Gub: Why don't you ask him to do the same now—now that he has more time? And take Chee-Chee and Too-Too with you when you go and ask him."

This the pig did. And not only Chee-Chee and Too-Too went to the Doctor, but the whole of the Dolittle household: Whitey, Jip, Dab-Dab, and—of course Polynesia. Even the old lame horse in the stable came clumping across the lawn and told the Doctor (through the window of his study) that the long summer evenings in his stall were very dull, and that *if* the Doctor should be telling stories to the crowd after supper, he would like very much to listen outside the kitchen window, the same as the Doctor had let him do in times gone by.

Well, of course in the end the Doctor gave in. Myself, I think he was rather glad to. And so that nice old habit, which all the animals enjoyed so much, was started over again: the after-supper storytelling round the kitchen fire.

As soon as the dishes were cleared away and washed, there would be the same old scramble for seats or places. Gub-Gub (who took up more room than the rest) always made the most fuss getting seated and settled. Again the white mouse climbed to his favorite listening spot—the corner of the mantelpiece,

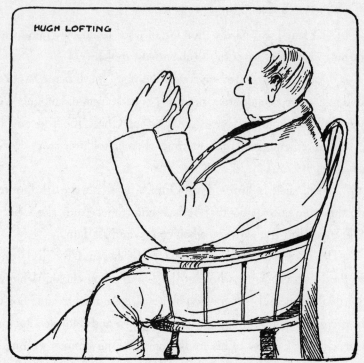

HUGH LOFTING

"Well, of course in the end the Doctor gave in."

where he could see and hear everything. And I noticed that
Itty, the moon cat, was now always in the audience too—though
often you wouldn't know it; because she would choose places
where she wouldn't be seen—and, as usual, she never spoke
and never moved.

THE FOURTEENTH CHAPTER

The Storm

I CANNOT SAY THAT JOHN DOLITTLE LOOKED better, all at once, from these changes in his way of living. But he was much cheerier; more active in body and mind; more interested in everything going on in, and around, his home.

And the days passed quickly, as they always do when people are busy and happy.

But one wet and stormy night the old parrot again came into my office. The evening story was over; and the Doctor and his family had gone to bed. I remember how the wind and rain beat furiously against the windowpanes, as Polynesia strutted toward me across the floor. Then with her claws and beak she climbed up the heavy curtain, like a sailor, hand over hand. When she reached the level of the desk, where I was writing, she stepped across onto it. There she fluffed out her feathers, looked me in the eye, and said:

"Tommy, I'm worried—about Cheapside. We should have heard from him by now!"

"Why, how long is it," I asked, laying down my pen, "since he was here last?"

"It's ten days tonight," the parrot grunted.

"Is it really!" I cried. "I had no idea it was as long ago as that."

"With any other bird I don't think I'd be anxious," she said. "But—I told you—I've been noticing little Cheapside lately. He's very reliable. If he says he'll do a thing, he'll do it. . . . I hope to goodness nothing has happened to him."

"Oh, well, come now, Polynesia," said I, smiling at her worried frown, "what could happen to him? There never was a bird in all the world better able to take care of himself than that London sparrow."

"Accidents can happen to anybody," the parrot muttered.

Suddenly with a sharp gust the wind and rain burst against the side of the old house, rattling the windows in their frames.

"Perhaps this storm has got you fidgety," I said. "I wouldn't start to worry yet."

"I tell you, young man, accidents can happen to anybody," she repeated slowly and clearly.

"But listen," I argued: "Cheapside didn't say *exactly* how long—how many days—it would be before he visited us again, did he?"

"He said 'a few days,' Tommy. That means, in my seven languages, less than a week—or, not more than a week, anyhow. And besides, if he was delayed, why couldn't he have let us know? Cheapside has plenty of sparrow friends, who would have flown down here for him, to bring us a message. There are London sparrows in every corner of the world. And a pesky nuisance they are too—sometimes."

It took a good deal to get Polynesia upset. Although she often squabbled and argued with Cheapside, I knew she was very fond of him. What she had just said was true. And having no answer to it, I said nothing. The silence in the room was broken only by the noise of rain outside and the old Dutch clock upon the wall, ticking away the seconds, the minutes, the hours—the lifetimes of sparrows and men.

Presently I saw Too-Too the owl appear from behind a pile of books on the top shelf of my bookcase. He looked sleepy, as he always did at this hour—which was his time for getting up. Polynesia's back was turned and she did not see him. No one could move more silently than Too-Too—just as no creature could hear as well as he, or see better in the dark. And suddenly, without even opening his wings, he dropped down on the desk beside the parrot, like a pudding falling out of a dish.

Poor Polynesia! With a frightened squawk, she jumped as though stuck with a pin. A string of terrible seafaring swear words, in three foreign languages, broke out; and for a moment I thought she was going to bite the little owl's head off.

"Don't *do* that!" she screamed. "Let a body know you're coming, if you *must* fall off the ceiling like a spider."

"I'm very sorry, Polynesia, really I am," said Too-Too, blinking the sleep out of his eyes. "Something woke me up—all of a sudden."

"Huh! Me and Tommy talking, I suppose," snapped the parrot, still in a very bad humor from the fright she had had. "You're no better than that snooping little cheese thief, Whitey. You were just trying to listen in on what we were saying."

"Not at all, Polynesia, you are mistaken," said Too-Too quietly. "I slept right through your chatter. The noise that woke me up came from the garden—or, at least, from outside."

"What nonsense!" snorted the parrot. "There is a strong wind

"I'm very sorry, Polynesia, really I am."

blowing outside—and rain. You couldn't have heard anything over
that noise. Why, it's almost a gale!"

"Pardon me," said Too-Too wearily, "but you are forgetting
that we owls, for thousands of years, have trained ourselves to hear
the sounds that other creatures make at night—the creatures we
hunt for food."

"Oh, fiddlesticks!" growled Polynesia. "What did you hear,
then?"

"The noise that woke me," said Too-Too, "was birds flying—
battling with the wind. Even on a fairly stormy night I can tell you

what kind of a bird it is by the noise his wings make, beating the air. That is, of course, if there aren't a whole lot of different sorts mixed up together."

I could see that Polynesia was really interested now. So, indeed, was I. I opened my mouth to ask the owl a question. But he held up a claw to me to keep silent.

Both the parrot and I stayed still, holding our breath, while Too-Too, the great Night Listener, used those wonderful ears of his.

"They're small birds," he whispered presently. "And not many of them. . . . Ah, now they've made it! They were trying to fly across the big lawn to the house, I guess. Saw your light, I suppose. But they were driven back three times. Now they've reached the windowsill. . . . If I'm right, you'll hear from them yourself now, Tommy."

And, sure enough, as the little owl stopped speaking, there came a signal I had often heard before: it was the tapping of a bird's bill on the glass of the windowpane.

I didn't wait then, you may be sure. I leapt to the window and pulled it open at the bottom. The papers on my desk went swirling everywhere, as wind and rain and dead leaves tore into the room. But I took no notice of my papers, nor the wet, nor my guttering lamp, which was all but blown out. For I had seen two other things that the wind had swept into the house with the leaves: the bodies of two little rain-drenched birds that now lay panting on the floor. In a second I had slammed the window shut again and was kneeling on the wet carpet beside them.

They were Cheapside and his wife, Becky.

First Aid for Sparrows

THE TWO SPARROWS WERE CERTAINLY IN A very bad state. You could hardly tell them from dead birds, so still they lay there, with the water trickling across the floor from under them. The eyes of both had now closed entirely. Only the slightest moving of Cheapside's feathers showed me that he, at least, was alive. Poor Becky, his wife, was so completely still I feared she was already gone. Very gently Polynesia lifted up Cheapside's bill with her own, softly calling him by name. But the sparrow's eyes did not open; and his head fell back, sideways, as she let it go.

"Quick, Tommy," said the parrot. "Wake the Doctor up and bring him down here. This will be a close shave. Too-Too, you rouse up Dab-Dab and Chee-Chee. Tell 'em to build up the kitchen fire—hot. And get some flannels warmed in front of it. I'll stay with them here. Hustle now, both of you. This bird's breathing is slowing down."

I found the Doctor reading in bed. But I only got halfway

through my message before he sprang up, shot past me, and was running down the stairs. Over his shoulder he called back:

"Take my bedside lamp, Stubbins, and fetch the little black bag from the surgery, please."

It was in cases of this kind that always I most admired John Dolittle as an animals' doctor—when I felt that I myself, compared with him, would never be much better than a slow and ordinary bungler. By the time I had gotten his bag, he had already carried the unconscious bodies of the sparrows to the warmer air of the kitchen and laid them upon the table. Chee-Chee had piled wood upon the fire; and Dab-Dab had some flannels hung before it on chairbacks.

Then, taking them in turn, the Doctor made me hold the birds with their beaks pointing straight upward. Next, his flying fingers took a tiny teaspoon and filled it with some reddish medicine out of a bottle in the black bag. He sharpened a matchstick to a chisel-point with his penknife. And with this, very, very gently, he pried each bird's beak apart, held it so with the fingers of his left hand while he took the spoon filled with medicine in the other. Then (I noticed his hand was as steady as a rock) he dropped three drops into the throat of each sparrow. After that he laid the tiny bodies down again—upon their backs; and swiftly but carefully his fingers massaged the legs, the wings, and the ribs for a moment. From the bag he now yanked out a stethoscope—a special one that he had invented for small patients; and for a second or two he listened to the heartbeats.

All of us—Polynesia, Chee-Chee, Dab-Dab, Too-Too, and myself—silently watched the Doctor's face, waiting for an answer to the question we were afraid to ask. Meanwhile the storm outside—

growing worse now—buffeted and slapped against the old house with a noise like cannon firing far away.

"Give me the hot flannels, please," the Doctor said to me.

Then the little travelers were rolled up till they looked like tiny mummies. Only their heads poked out of the coverings. A chair was put upside down before the fire; and on its sloping back, with a couple of heavy bath-towels under them, Mr. and Mrs. Cheapside were set to dry.

"Cheapside has a good chance," he muttered. "But I'm by no means sure about poor Becky. We'll change the flannels every ten minutes. Must get the bodies dried out. I've never seen feathers so saturated. Usually they resist the water, you know, have a sort of oil in them. Almost any bird can fly in ordinary rain for hours and come to no harm. But against a storm, that's different. Goodness! These little fellows, they're almost like a case of drowning. Even their stomachs are all filled with water. I'd like to know why on earth they flew through this weather to reach me tonight. They should have taken shelter someplace—and come on in the morning. Didn't either of them say anything at all, Stubbins, when you let them in?"

"Not a word, Doctor. Of course the roaring of the gale, when I opened the window, made it hard to hear anything—short of a shout. And by the time I got it closed again, they had both passed out, fainted away on the floor."

"Very peculiar," muttered the Doctor, "very! Give me some more hot flannels, please. It's time to change their coverings now. We must get them dry, Stubbins, we *must* get them dry."

Well, I couldn't tell you how often we unwrapped and rewrapped those soaked little birds. From time to time the Doctor would give them one or two drops more of the medicine, while all of us around him looked on, hoping for some sign of returning life. But still the eyelids did not open; and the sparrows' heads swayed and rolled on their necks, in a way that really frightened me.

I am quite sure that John Dolittle was afraid, too, that we would not be able to save them. No one, who did not know him as well as I, would have guessed this, just from watching him. As a rule, the more serious a case was, the calmer the way he treated it (except of course where tremendous speed was necessary; and then, even while he hurried, he never got anybody nervous—least of all himself).

But this long, long waiting between the many changes and so on was hard on the Doctor and on us who idly watched. Yes, waiting and *doing nothing*—because there was nothing more to be done; that was the most difficult thing of all for the Doctor and all of us.

What time it was I do not know. I had grown afraid that perhaps my own anxiety might interfere with the Doctor's tremendous calm. Anyway, I had moved away from the table, feeling worse than useless. I was looking miserably out of the window. The force of the wind and rain had not dropped. The gray of the morning was, however, showing behind the darker gray of the overcast eastern sky. I realized that the Doctor had been working on Cheapside and Becky through the whole night.

He and I had not spoken to each other for an hour.

I started thinking over what it could have been that these sparrows had flown through such a storm and danger to tell us. . . . Perhaps, now, neither we nor anyone else would ever know why they had so bravely given up their lives to reach us. . . . I, as well as Polynesia and the Doctor, had become very fond of that rowdy little

Cheapside the London sparrow. Perhaps, too, I was more tired than I realized. Anyway, I felt terribly like crying.

And maybe I would have done so; but at that moment I heard John Dolittle call me by name. I swung around from the window and was back at his side like a flash.

The End of a Long Night

THE DOCTOR STILL HAD THE TUBES OF THE stethoscope in his ears and the fingers of his right hand lightly pressed the cone over Cheapside's heart when I came to the table. I peered up anxiously into John Dolittle's face; and at once—before anything was said—I was greatly comforted. For the expression in the Doctor's eyes was now a very different one.

"Stubbins," he whispered, "I do believe it's getting firmer— the heart-action, I mean—and more regular, too. Move your head aside, please. I want to see the watch."

I shifted the watch that lay upon the table, closer to him, turning it round so he could read the dial more easily.

"Yes," he repeated, "it's firmer. With luck we're going to pull this little fellow round all right."

"Thank heaven for that!" I sighed. I did not dare to ask him about poor Becky.

"Get me some warm milk—quickly, please, Stubbins. Not

hot, you know, just warm—and another teaspoon."

Chee-Chee the monkey had a pile of light wood handy beside the hearth. He and I—both of us glad to have something useful to do—went to work on the fire, which had been allowed to die down because the kitchen had grown over-warm. We soon blew up the dying embers into a brisk blaze. Over this I warmed some milk in a long-handled saucepan.

"Ah! That's what we want," said the Doctor when I brought it to him at the table, "nourishment. These birds are weak from hunger, as well as nearly drowned. Hold him for me now, Stubbins, the same as you did before."

Then Cheapside was given three teaspoonfuls of warm milk. And both the Doctor and I noticed that, with the last one, the sparrow's throat actually made the movement of swallowing. This was the first sign of life the bird had shown; and we who stood around smiled at one another.

Next, we took poor little Becky and treated her the same way. She, however, made no movement of any kind.

But, on coming back to Cheapside again, we noticed that his eyes were opening slightly. We fed him more of the warm milk, as much as he could hold.

Soon we could see he was looking at the Doctor in a puzzled sort of way, as though he were trying to remember who he was. And at last in a very weak voice he murmured: "Oh, it's you, Doc. What a night, what a night!"

Then his head rolled feebly on his shoulders again and it looked for a moment as though his eyes were going to close once more. But suddenly they opened wide, he struggled weakly as if to get up and look around.

"Where—" he gasped. "Where's Becky?"

"Cheapside, please—" the Doctor began. Then he stopped; for another voice, a sparrow's voice, was speaking at his elbow. Both of us turned sharply toward the sound. *It was Becky talking!*

"Here I am, Cheapside," said she. "I'm all right. How are you?" Cheapside's head fell back wearily.

"Ain't that the limit, Doc?" he murmured faintly. "The old girl wants to know 'ow *I* am—when I thought she was a goner for sure."

And with that Cheapside went fast asleep again. Becky did the same a couple of minutes later.

"Who would have thought it?" said the Doctor in a whisper, as he put the things back in his bag. "But Becky, to pull out of a battering such as that storm gave her! I assure you, Stubbins, that throughout the last hour it was impossible for me to hear her heart-action at all. . . . It's a wonderful thing, the will to live. . . . Well, well, thank goodness that's over!"

"They certainly looked done for, Doctor," I said, "when that storm blew them into the room."

"What we must do now," said he, "is to let them rest and sleep. Your office will be the best place—where they won't be disturbed. We'll get a fire made up there and when the room's warm we'll move them in. Then you must go and get some rest yourself, Stubbins. It's been a long night for you. We will put Too-Too on watch and he will come and wake us as soon as we are needed. For the present there's nothing more we can do for them but to keep them warm and let them sleep."

When at last I got upstairs to my bedroom, I think I must have fallen asleep before lying down; because I certainly don't remember undressing and getting into bed.

It was around teatime, between four and five o'clock in the afternoon, when Polynesia awakened me (by biting me gently on the nose, as she usually did when she wished to rouse me out of sleep).

"Oh—er—Hulloa!" I said drowsily, sitting up and rubbing my eyes. "How are they, the sparrows?"

"Doing nicely, very nicely," said she. "They've had a good long sleep and they've eaten a big meal. The Doctor has not let them talk so far—although he has been awake for a couple of hours. He didn't want them tiring themselves out, you know. But soon, I think, he is going to let them tell their story. And I just came up to see if you wanted to come and listen."

"You bet I do, Polynesia," I cried, jumping out of bed. "Do me a favor, will you? Ask the Doctor not to let them start till I'm there."

"All right," said the parrot, making for the door. "But you better hurry down. Dab-Dab is giving him breakfast now in your office."

"Tell them I won't be but a minute," said I, struggling into my clothes. "And ask Dab-Dab to let me have some buttered toast and a cup of cocoa."

The Travels of Mr. and Mrs. Cheapside

HEN I GOT DOWN TO MY OFFICE I SAW at once that the sparrows' story had already begun—but only just. Cheapside and Becky were standing on my big desk. The Doctor was seated in the chair where I usually wrote.

As I slipped quietly into the room, John Dolittle was speaking.

"But, Cheapside," he was saying, "honestly I don't believe I ever heard of anything so utterly crazy! Just the two of you to make such a trip—about four thousand miles! You know what the migrating birds do when they make a journey as long as that: great flocks string out in sight of one another—in a line ten or twenty miles long—so they can keep in touch with the leaders. The day, in fact the exact hour, they leave for those oversea hops are set by the best weather-prophets they've got. Yet you, a couple of city birds, just flip off for *Africa* as though you were hopping across a London street. Such madness! Why, at this time of year you were liable to run into an equinoctial gale!"

"'But, Cheapside,' he was saying."

"Quite right, Doc," murmured Cheapside, "we did run into one—on the way back. Goin' down there we stayed in sight of land all the way. But flying home to England we found a wind against us. And we came by way of the Canary Islands, thinkin' we'd get out of the worst of the weather. We took a four-hour rest on the islands. But it was the last part, gettin' from there to Cornwall—Jimminy! That was the worstest. We hit a northeaster what pretty near blew us inside out. Lucky for us, we picked up an old freight ship comin' our way. We sneaked onto the stern of her, when nobody was lookin', and hid in a ventilator. And did she roll, that ship? Crikey, I come near to gettin' seasick!"

"And will you please tell me," asked John Dolittle in a very severe voice, "what in the name of goodness made you take this journey at all?"

"Well, Doc," said Cheapside, shifting his feet, "you remember last time I was 'ere you discovered that your notebooks about Mudface 'ad all got chewed up by some kind friends of Whitey's."

"Ah!" said the Doctor. And suddenly a sparkle of new excitement was shining in his eyes as he leaned forward in his chair. (I glanced at Polynesia who nodded her head and winked at me.) "Yes, yes," said the Doctor, "I remember, Cheapside—the notebooks. Go on, please."

"Well," said the sparrow, "I seed as how you was pretty bad upset. You was afraid the turtle might be dead. I asked a few questions of Tommy, 'ere. 'E told me it 'adn't never been proved that Mudface *was* dead. And me, I always says, no news is good news—especially when you use storks to get it. They ain't the same as London sparrows, Doc."

"Oh, stop boasting, and get on with it!" snapped Becky.

"Anyway," said Cheapside, "an idea comes into me 'ead. And when I gets back to London that night, I asks Becky 'ow she'd like a trip down to Africa, as soon as our new family could fly and take care of theirselves. And—would you believe it?—the Missus, most unladylike, asks me straight out if I've gone nutty."

"Yes, and I can't blame her," murmured the Doctor. "Go on, please."

"So I says to 'er, I says, the Doc's done a lot for you and me, old gal. Remember the time when 'e come all the way up to London to look at one of our youngsters what was sick?"

"Oh yes," muttered the Doctor. "Long ago. I'd forgotten all about it."

"Well," Cheapside went on, "Becky 'adn't. You saved our little Ernie's life that time, Doc. And pretty soon I persuades the Missus. I knew the way down to Fantippo all right, 'cause I'd made the trip that time you sent for me—to 'elp you with the mail deliveries in old King Koko's country—you remember?"

"Indeed I do," said the Doctor. "But you made that journey at a very different time of year from this."

"You bet, Doc—very different. Anyway, it was that same week we got the new family managin' for theirselves. Then we hops across the Channel near Dover and starts flyin' south, down the coast of France. Good weather stayed with us all the way; and in a few days we reaches Fantipsy harbor. And so—"

Then Becky broke in again.

"For pity's sake, Cheapside!" she scolded. "The Doctor is dying to hear what happened to Mudface the turtle. You can tell him all this stuff about our trip afterward. Give him the news, give him the news—such as it is."

"Oh—er—humph!" said Cheapside in a disgruntled sort of way. "Well now, 'old yer 'orses, old gal. It all 'angs together. You—"

And this time the Doctor interrupted (I knew he was afraid that a family row was going to break out between Mr. and Mrs. Cheapside). He said:

"To tell you the truth, Cheapside, I *am* terribly anxious to hear what has become of Mudface. Were you able to find out anything?"

"Er—yes and no," said Cheapside. "Becky and me went off as

fast as we could for the Secret Lake; but we 'ad to lose some time o' course, huntin' for food—seeds, you know. Regular birdseed don't grow in the jungle; but we found a kind of wild rice that would do."

"Good!" said the Doctor.

"But suddenly, when we was gettin' near the lake—within about a hundred miles, I'd guess—I says to the Missus, I says, 'Something's wrong here, Becky. I reckernize the country—general-like. But this river right below us: look 'ow it is!' I says. 'The stream out of the Secret Lake used to be just a little brook.' You remember, Doc?"

The Doctor nodded.

"But this river we was flyin' over now was miles wide. And I says to Becky, 'There's somethin' strange about this. I'd swear we're on the right track. *But the landscape's changed.* And if I'm right, this could explain a whole lot—maybe—about what's 'appened to the Doc's friend, Mr. Mudface. Let's drop down to the bank and look for some birds, Becky. I want to ask a few questions about this.'"

Finding the Secret Lake

I WAS SO INTERESTED IN WHAT THE LONDON sparrow had to say that I had hardly taken my eyes off him since I came into the room. Now, as Chee-Chee the monkey quietly brought me some buttered toast and a cup of cocoa, I noticed the whole family was gathered there in my office. They had all stowed themselves in different places round the room, silently listening.

"And so," Cheapside went on, "down we drops a good many thousand feet, out of the cool air we'd been flyin' in, to the steamy heat of the jungle. We goes pokin' along the riverbank till we meet up with a couple of birds—some sort of a snipe, I think they was. And I asks 'em, I says: 'Are we on the right road to Lake Junganyika, the Secret Lake?' 'Yes,' they says. 'Follow the river. You'll come right to it.' 'But look 'ere,' I says: 'I traveled over this stretch years ago—with Doctor Dolittle, MD, no less. And the blinkin' country don't seem the same now. The stream we followed in our canoe was narrow. This river's four or five miles wide in places. Who's been monkeyin' with the landscape?'

"'Hoh,' says one of the snipe, 'hadn't you heard? We 'ad a big shake-up here—sort of an earthquake. The ground began trembling something terrible and big floods of water started coming down; and the river's been wide like this ever since. You'll find the Secret Lake changed quite a bit too.'

"'You better ask the storks,' they says. 'They live right on the shore of the lake. We ain't seen Mudface in a long while.'

"'Storks!' I says. 'They ain't no good.'

"'Oh,' says the snipe, 'there's a couple of old ones up at the lake what we thinks very 'ighly of around 'ere.'

"'Listen,' I says, 'I'd just as soon ask the bulrushes for hinformation. Storks ain't got no sense. Why, they build their nests on people's chimney pots! That shows 'ow bright *they* are. Don't talk to me about storks. 'Ave you seen anythin' of the Great Water Snake?'

"No, they said, they 'adn't. So me and Becky left Mr. and Mrs. Snipe and we goes on up toward the lake. And the nearer we comes to it, the more I sees the landscape 'ad changed. There was the same mangrove swamps around, like we'd seen when you was there, Doc. But when we flies over the lake proper, it was plain to see that the open water was ever so much bigger—makin' it very 'ard for me to get me bearings and be sure just where I was."

"I can indeed believe it," said the Doctor. "But tell me: Could you find the island that we built for Mudface?"

"Yes," said Cheapside, "we found that all right. But it didn't look the same. You understand we was now flyin' 'igh up again—so we could get a better view. At first I hardly reckernized it, Doc, as the island we 'ad built accordin' to your orders. It seemed a different shape. On the west side it looked pretty much as we 'ad left it—

though of course palms and such was growin' there now. But you remember the shape you told us to make it, Doc—good and high, and flat on the top?"

"Yes, I remember that very clearly," said the Doctor.

"Well, it was like that still on the west side, toward the sea. And all lovely and green it looked too. But when we went around on the *farther* side, I saw at once what 'ad 'appened. Half of the island wasn't there no more."

"Great heavens!" I heard the Doctor mutter beneath his breath.

"You never saw anything like it, Doc. It looked just like a big loaf of bread what had been cut in 'alf with a knife. That earthquake sure done a neat job. It hadn't been so very long ago neither, 'cause there was a high cliff of bare gravel, where the land 'ad been cut off."

"Yes, I understand," said the Doctor.

"Then," Cheapside went on, "we flew over what was left of the island and searched it from end to end. But no trace of old Mudface could we find. 'Owever, we met some wild ducks. They was kind of snooty at first. But when we told 'em we was friends of yours, they changed their tune and got real chummy. They was there, nest building. Then we asks 'em about Mudface—and when they 'ad seen 'im last. And they told us they'd seen 'im on the morning of the very day when the island got cut in two."

"And whereabouts on the island *was* the turtle—I mean at the time of the earthquake?" asked the Doctor in a voice which, to me, plainly showed his excitement.

"He was at that same end of the island," said Cheapside, shaking his head sadly. "He was on the half that broke off and disappeared. The ducks was certain of it. Mudface had found a kind of a warm spring, what was good for 'is rheumatism, down by the water's edge on the east side of the island. The ducks said that as soon as the earth began to tremble they was scared and took to the air. But, as they flew off, they saw tons and tons of sand and gravel and mud pour down on top of the old turtle, who was wading in the warm spring with only his head out of the water. The ducks said they was afraid to come back for three days—till everything was quiet again. And when they did, half the island was gone, they said, disappeared beneath the water. And they reckoned old Mudface 'ad gone with it. . . . And—well, I reckon that's all, Doc."

As Cheapside stopped speaking, a gloomy, short silence hung over the room. I knew that all of the listeners to the sparrow's story were—like myself—just bursting to ask questions. But no one said a word. For a moment the Doctor, with a worried frown, stared down thoughtfully at the floor. At last he looked up at Cheapside and said quietly:

"I want to thank both of you, Cheapside and Becky, for making this dangerous journey—especially at such a time of year—for my sake—and for Mudface's. Just the same, please don't do such a thing again without telling me. Imagine how I would have felt if you had lost your lives and never come back. Because, sooner or later, I would have heard of your trip, you may be sure, from your children, from the snipe, or from the ducks."

"Yes, I suppose so," said Cheapside. "But—well, me and Becky thought we'd take a chance. Nothin' venture, nothin' gain: that's what I says. We're—we're awful sorry, Doc. I reckon we didn't do no good."

"Oh, I'm by no means sure of that yet," said the Doctor quickly (and I noticed how all the animals around the room leaned forward suddenly, with a new interest, to hear his words). "Tell me, Cheapside," he went on, "would you say the level of the water in the Secret Lake itself is higher now, or lower, than when you and I saw it the first time?"

"Well," said the sparrow, "me and Becky explored along the lakeshore quite a way. It seemed as though the earthquake, or whatever it was, had heaved the land up some places and let it down in others. I ain't no skyentist; but even I could see how the great rush of water—and the new wide river—had been made. Like fillin' a soup plate, made of rubber, and then bending and twisting it: of course the soup would run out on the table and all over the place."

Then Becky spoke.

"Yes, but the level of the water *now* is what the Doctor wants to know about."

Cheapside thought a moment before going on. Then he said:

"There ain't no doubt the water *did* rise a lot higher than what it was when you saw it, Doc. But I think that was only while the earthquake was going on. . . . It seems to me—" Again he stopped a moment in thought.

"Yes," he cried suddenly, "I remember now. The water *must* have fallen back to near its old level. Because, when we had built the island, somebody asked me how high I reckoned it would be from the water to the top. And I said it was about the same as St. Paul's Cathedral. And this time, when we went round to the far side where half the island had been cut away, the cliff was just about the same height. That's right, Doc: the water level *is* about the same now as when you was there."

"Good!" said the Doctor. "That's the first thing. Now, did

you find any birds—any living creatures, in fact—who could say they were sure that Mudface was dead?"

"Er—no, Doc," said Cheapside in a hesitating, slow sort of voice. "But—but them ducks, Doc?—Like I told you: they *saw* the old feller get buried under tons and tons of stuff! And, natural-like, after we'd been told the turtle had half the island on top of 'im, we—we reckoned 'e was finished."

The Doctor's next words made even me sit up. I forgot all about the breakfast I was eating.

"No, not necessarily, Cheapside," said John Dolittle. "You see, most of the amphibian creatures—that is, those who live on the land *and* in the water, like turtles, frogs, crocodiles, and so on—can stay a long time underwater, if they want to."

"But, Doc," cried the sparrow, "wouldn't he get crushed? Think what would happen to you or me if St. Paul's Cathedral was to fall on us!"

"But we are not turtles, Cheapside," said the Doctor, smiling. "If Mudface's island had been solid rock, and the earthquake cut it in two, that would have been very different. But you remember: when we built that island, we made it out of earth and sand and stones—which the birds brought up from the seashore. The very biggest of those stones was only as large as an apple. Mudface's back is covered with a shell enormously strong and thick. Even that great load of gravel and stuff would not crush him, I feel fairly sure. More likely, it would just press him down into the mud floor of the lake."

The look of surprise on Cheapside's face would have been comical enough to make us laugh, if the talk had not been so serious.

"Well, swap me pink!" he said with a gasp. "Do you mean to say, Doc, you think old Mudlark's still alive down there?"

"I think there's certainly a good chance he is," said the Doctor.

"But if he's still living," cried Cheapside, "why don't 'e crawl out, back to 'is home on the island?"

"Ah, no," said John Dolittle. "That's something very different. He would have pulled his head and legs and tail inside his shell at once, as soon as the gravel began to rattle on it. But after half the island had slid on top of him, the weight, as you said, would be tremendous. He could not have moved after that—probably couldn't even poke his head out of his shell, much less walk around."

"But what about food, Doctor?" asked the sparrow. "It's quite a while since that earthquake, and 'e ain't 'ad a thing to eat."

"That's true," said the Doctor. "But amphibian reptiles can, if necessary, go without food for a long, long time. Did you ever hear of hibernating, Cheapside?"

"Er—ain't that what the bears does, sort of holing up for the winter?"

"That's right," said the Doctor. "But the turtles, when they want to hibernate, bore their way down into the mud and gravel, underwater, at the bottom of a river or lake. I hope that is what has happened to our old friend—only in his case of course, he didn't go into hibernation on purpose. But, from what you tell me, it is just the same as if he had."

"But, Doctor," asked the sparrow, "how is the old feller ever goin' to get out of there?"

The Doctor rose from his chair and, standing, gazed out a moment through the window into the garden.

"Cheapside," he said presently, "I don't think there's any chance of his ever getting out, unless someone goes to help him."

Again a quiet spell fell over the room. It came into my head to ask the Doctor a question myself. But I glanced over at Polynesia first. And I could see that that strange bird already knew what was in my mind; for she shook her head at me and raised her right claw to her beak, like a person motioning you to keep quiet. And soon the Doctor was speaking again.

"I wonder, Cheapside," he said, "if you would mind making that journey to Africa again—to Lake Junganyika—quite soon, would you?"

"Why, of course," said the sparrow, "of course I'd be glad to. But I'd stick to the coastline this time, you bet. What did you want me to find out for you, Doc?"

"Oh, I didn't mean to have you go alone this trip," said John Dolittle. "I was thinking of going down there myself, by ship, and taking you with me. You might be very helpful as a guide and all that, you know—having found your way into the Secret Lake, after it's changed so much. I would have to borrow a canoe from King Koko of Fantippo. I don't know of course whether I can be of any real help to my old friend Mudface. But I feel that at least I ought to go down there and see what I can do."

And then Polynesia said:

"I quite agree with you, Doctor. You remember when Long Arrow was trapped in the cave in the mountain? That looked hopeless enough. And yet you got him out. Of course we ought to go back to the Secret Lake—not only on the turtle's account, but to get the story of the Flood again, to put in your notebooks."

And then, after the parrot had joined in the talk, it seemed as though pandemonium broke loose in my office. All the animals had been bursting to say something for a long time. And now, after Polynesia had spoken, suddenly they all started asking questions, giving advice and talking at once. You never heard such a racket.

Seeing that it was impossible for me to talk to the Doctor in an uproar like that, I made a signal to Jip to clear them out of the room. And that he did very quickly, leaving only the parrot and the sparrows. But even then the noise did not entirely stop. Arguments and discussions could be heard through the closed door, going on in the passage, on the stairs—everywhere in the house.

When at last these had somewhat died down, I started to ask a question of the Doctor. But at that moment a terrible mixture of squeals and barks went rushing by under the windows. I looked out. It was Jip chasing Gub-Gub, who was galloping down the garden to carry the news to the animals in the zoo. The white mouse was clinging to the pig's neck like a jockey on a racehorse.

"Hey!" yelled Gub-Gub. "Hey! The Doctor's going on a voyage—to Africa. Hooray! . . . Hooray!"

PART TWO

The First Chapter

Our Ship, The Albatross

AFTER THE NEWS WAS OUT, THAT THE DOC-
tor was going on a voyage, it seemed to me no time at
all before we were actually there, in Africa.

But, despite the need to be on our way as quickly
as possible, there was of course a tremendous lot which had to be
done before we could leave. First of all, we had to get a ship. This,
Polynesia took charge of. The parrot was an old sailor. When she
looked at a ship, right away she could tell you a whole lot about the
craft without even getting onto it. The Doctor knew he could trust
her to find the boat he wanted—one which was not too large for us
to handle; one which could go into shallow harbors like Fantippo.

In this we had good luck (indeed, good luck stayed with us on
this voyage, not only on the trip itself, but even in the preparations
we made for it). We went and saw my old friend, Joe, the mussel
man, at his little hut on the riverbank near King's Bridge. And Joe
had just what we wanted. He took us a short way down the river
where he showed us a boat tied up to a wharf.

"Here she be, Mr. Tom," said he. "I don't reckon I could have found a better ship no where for what the Doctor wants."

She was indeed a lovely little craft. Joe had, only ten days ago, finished repainting her from stem to stern. She was named *The Albatross*. Joe took Polynesia and me aboard her. I could see the old parrot's seafaring eyes noticing everything; and, although she did not ask any questions, I could tell that she was as pleased as I was with the good ship *Albatross*.

"She's a sloop, as you see, Mr. Tom," said Joe, "but cutter-rigged. Easy to handle in any weather. Nice, roomy cabin with bunks for six. And complete, too: lamps, dinghy, dishes—she's got everything, even to her charts, nautical almanac, and the rest."

So I told the mussel man I would bring the Doctor down to see the boat later that day or tomorrow; and we left.

"We've got to think about victualling her, next," said Polynesia from my shoulder, as I walked toward the marketplace. "Have you got a pencil and paper on you, Tommy?"

I had; and as we went along, the old parrot gave me lists and lists of things which, she said, we must take along on a trip like this.

"And mind you, young man," she added, "these are just provisions—things to eat and wear and so on, for ourselves. But besides all this, there is the stuff which the ship herself may need: oil for the lamps, extra rope, and so on. But we'll take care of all that later. Old Joe says she's got everything—and maybe she has. But no good ship's master puts to sea without making sure, for himself, that his craft isn't short of anything he really needs.

Once more poor old Matthew was told that he would have to be left behind when the Doctor went abroad. He complained bitterly.

His wife, Theodosia, had come secretly to the house and begged John Dolittle not to take her husband. She was sure, she said, Africa wouldn't agree with him.

"You see, Matthew," the Doctor explained to the cat's-meat-man, "I'm counting on you to look after so many things while I am gone. Not only the things you have taken care of for me before, but now there's the garden, as well. I haven't half finished getting it back in proper order. And if I were to leave it to run wild any longer, it would be just ruined by next spring. You know the way I like it kept. And you're the only man I'd put in charge of the work. In fact, I don't know what I'd do without you—really, I don't."

And so Matthew agreed to stay behind and act as general caretaker, gardener, and zookeeper. It relieved the Doctor's mind tremendously.

The day after we had seen the *Albatross*, Polynesia and I took the Doctor down to look over her. He was very pleased with the ship; and the same night he and I were in his study after dinner, "armchair-traveling," as he used to call it.

"Who else had you planned to take with you, Doctor?" I asked.

"Oh, I think all of my regular household, Stubbins; that is, if they want to come along. Too-Too, Jip, Dab-Dab, the white mouse—and then of course Chee-Chee. You remember how valuable he is in the jungle at finding foods and all that? And besides, he's very handy aboard ship, too. Quite a good little sailor. And then there's Cheapside and his wife."

"How about Gub-Gub the pig, Doctor? I know he is expecting you to take him. He says he hopes to add a new chapter to his

Encyclopedia of Food. He claims he is now the best pig scientist living, as well as the most famous pig comedian."

"Maybe so," said the Doctor thoughtfully. "He discovered some new kinds of wild sugarcane on our last trip."

"But he weighs an awful lot," I remarked, remembering that a sloop is not a very big ship.

"Quite, quite," said John Dolittle. "Well, don't worry about Gub-Gub. We'll take him if we can. But better not make any promises till we see just how much space we have."

He reached for the tobacco jar and started to fill his pipe.

"You know, Stubbins," said he, "I'm quite pleased with the way this trip has fallen out—just happened, as you might say. If those rats hadn't chewed up my notebooks to make their nests, we wouldn't be going on this journey, would we? Of course . . . Mudface, poor old fellow! . . . Even when I get there, I may find I can't do anything for him. But somehow I feel we're going to be lucky on this voyage."

He struck a match and held it to the bowl of his pipe. Then he leaned forward in his chair. I had never seen his manner show greater, keener, interest.

"And if our luck stays with us," he went on, "and we are able to get the turtle's story of the Flood again, it will be tremendously important to science."

"How long before the Flood was Mudface born, Doctor?" I asked.

"Ah!" said John Dolittle. "That I can't say. Maybe he told me; maybe not. My memory isn't clear on any details, any particulars. I wrote so fast. But if I'm right about his speaking of the other animals in the world at that time, as well as the trees, the plants, the rocks, and so on—you see how important it will be? Perhaps there were books written on natural history before Noah's time. But, anyhow, they were all swept away—lost. Don't you see how important this trip of ours may be?"

"I certainly do," I said solemnly. "With all the books before the Deluge destroyed, only one man can bring back the knowledge that was drowned: he who speaks the language of the animals—John Dolittle."

At once (as he always did when someone said anything complimentary to him) he looked uncomfortable.

"Oh, goodness, Stubbins!" said he. "We mustn't forget that there are many big *ifs* between us and success. And the biggest of them is: everything will depend on *if* I can get poor old Mudface out of the lake from under that mountain of gravel."

"Yes, Doctor. But also, don't forget that you said you thought we'd be lucky this trip."

"Ah, to be sure, to be sure!" he answered, breaking into a smile. "And I meant it. . . . It's a funny thing: sometimes a man feels that way and sometimes he doesn't. Sounds like a lot of superstitious nonsense, doesn't it? And yet, you know, I don't think it really is. . . . Well, anyway, Stubbins, I *do* feel we're going to be lucky on this voyage."

"How soon do you think we'll be ready to sail, Doctor?" I asked.

"Oh—er—let me see: This is Tuesday, isn't it?" he murmured. "Well, I think Saturday would be all right, Stubbins. And by the way, you won't forget to go and say good-bye to your mother and father, will you? They have both been awfully good about letting you stay here and help me. I'm afraid they haven't been seeing very much of you lately, eh?"

"No, Doctor," I said. "I'll attend to that. I'll go over and see them tomorrow night."

"Good," he said. "We'll set our sailing date for next Saturday, then. But don't tell anyone the exact day, Stubbins, please. It might leak out and—you know—newspapermen and all that sort of thing . . . ?"

"No, Doctor," I repeated. "Not a word to anyone."

<small>THE SECOND CHAPTER</small>

Good-bye to Puddleby

OUTGOING SHIPS ALWAYS LEAVE WHEN THE tide in the river has just turned to ebb—that is, running out toward the sea. And when we had looked up the hour of the ebb tide for that Saturday, we found it was five o'clock in the morning. Of course, as early in the day as that, practically no one was up and about. So we were able to slip away down the river, without the newspapermen (or, indeed, anybody else) seeing us or knowing we had left.

Joe the mussel man and Matthew Mugg were the only ones at the wharf to bid us good-bye. (I always asked my parents *not* to see me off on voyages. I was afraid my mother would cry.)

The morning air was cold; and full daylight had not yet lit up the sky, as the Doctor gave the keys of the house and stable to Matthew. Then the mooring ropes were let go and hauled aboard. The good ship *Albatross* was poled out into the current and headed downstream toward the sea. Joe stayed aboard for a short while (with his little mussel boat trailing behind on a towrope). He helped the Doctor and me set one of the smaller sails. And in the misty half-light, the ghostly tall shapes of warehouses on the riverbanks began to slip astern of us faster and faster.

At last Joe shook the Doctor and me by the hand, got into his mussel boat and shouted to the Doctor to cast off. John Dolittle told me to take the wheel while he undid the towrope.

"Good-bye!" called Joe. "Good-bye and good luck to yer voyage!"

I had not realized how fast we were moving. Even as we called our answering farewells to him, Joe disappeared into the mist astern of us. The Doctor took the wheel from me and asked

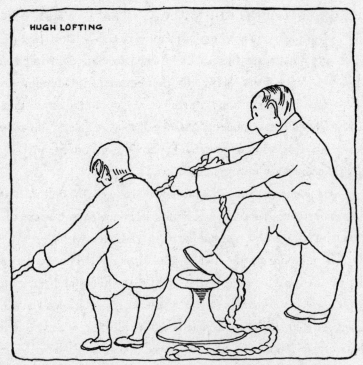

HUGH LOFTING

"Then the mooring ropes were let go and hauled aboard."

me to find Polynesia because he wished to speak with her.

I discovered the old parrot up forward, humming a sailor song to herself as she looked over the baggage piled on the deck.

"Look at that, my lad, look at that!" said she in her severest, most seamanlike manner. "All that gear will have to be stowed below before we get out of the river into open water. The first sea that comes over her bow will wash the whole lot overboard. What's that? The Doctor wants to see me? All right. But get Chee-Chee to help you stow this stuff belowdecks. And hop to it, my lad! You haven't got much time, the way this tide is running."

John Dolittle set Polynesia as a forward lookout, up in the fo'c'sle. Here, being right in the front or foremost part of the boat, she was able to see things ahead sooner than the Doctor at the wheel. And very helpful she was, too. There were ships and barges anchored in Puddleby River—as well as buoys marking the channel of the stream. Often we would hear the old seafaring parrot roar out: "Hard-a-port, Doctor! Schooner off the starboard bow. Hard-a-port!"

Then the Doctor would spin the wheel to swing us over—but not too far, lest he run the *Albatross* out of the channel, onto the mud of the riverbank. And suddenly, in the mist ahead of us, the hull of a big ship at anchor would rear up high; and it would look as though we must surely crash into her. But Polynesia's keen old eyes had seen her in time to warn the Doctor; and we would skid silently by, under her towering shadow—with only six feet of room to spare.

Speaking of the Doctor as a sea captain, the parrot had often said: "Yes, John Dolittle almost always does things wrong at sea— and most skippers would go gray-haired in one voyage with him. But you know, when he's managing his own boat, it doesn't seem to matter. He always gets there—where he means to go—just the same. Remember that, Tommy: you're always safe with John Dolittle."

For the next half hour Chee-Chee and I were kept busy carrying baggage belowdecks and stowing it in safe places, where it would not slam around when the sloop should start to pitch and roll. This, we knew, would begin as soon as we got out of Puddleby River into the open sea.

It was a strange collection of stuff we had brought with us. There was not much of what you would call ordinary baggage, such as trunks and the like; but there was plenty that was not ordinary. There were butterfly nets, collecting-boxes for birds' eggs, hatching-cages for caterpillars, and all sorts and kinds of other things that naturalists and explorers take with them on their travels.

All the packages were carefully labeled, telling what they had inside them. I think a stranger, reading some of these labels would have been quite puzzled. For instance, one label read: MOON SEEDS—STORE IN A DRY PLACE. The Doctor, just before we left, had said: "We are going to West Africa, but Long Arrow might turn up anywhere. Let's take a few of those seeds along—just in case. They won't need much room."

And there was another box, much larger, marked: LIVE TURTLES. KEEP THIS SIDE UP—WITH CARE! John Dolittle knew that I did not understand turtle language at all well. And, as I was going to act as secretary this time and write down all that Mudface should tell us (*if,* of course, we succeeded in rescuing him from under the lake), the Doctor thought I ought to practice up on the language as much as I could before we got there. So he had sent Matthew Mugg up to London to buy a few turtles at a pet shop: and I spent a couple of hours each day learning turtle talk (with the help of the Doctor himself).

The Doctor also bought me a book on shorthand writing; and I studied that, too. Because, he said, Mudface was a fast talker—though not always. The Doctor thought it would be far easier and less tiring for me to use shorthand.

Most of the rest of the baggage was of course food supply; you have to buy many things for even a few people who are going to be cut off from all shopping for several weeks at a time. And you have no idea how easy it is to forget the most important. However, with the help of Dab-Dab and Polynesia (both of whom had sailed with John Dolittle before), I can proudly say there was very little I had missed.

I did have one dreadful moment, though, as I now carried the packing cases and barrels and parcels belowdeck. Cheapside and his wife Becky had been hopping around the baggage, as if hunting for something. Myself, I was too busy to talk; but presently I heard the Cockney sparrow say to his wife:

"No, Becky. It ain't 'ere. They've been and forgot it."

"What were you looking for, Cheapside?" I asked as I heaved a small but heavy case of prunes up onto my shoulder.

"The birdseed, of course!" said Cheapside. "What d'yer think we'd be looking for—cigars?"

"Oh my goodness," I cried, "don't tell me I forgot the *birdseed*!"

"That's just what I am tellin' yer," shouted the sparrow in his most fighting manner. "Now me and my old lady has got to live on biscuit crumbs for three or four thousand miles. Nice kind of a first mate you are! And what 'appened to that wonderful old ship's master, Polynesia? She 'elped you make out the lists. Listen: if she 'ad you bring sunflower seeds for parrots, and no birdseed for sparrows, I'll pull 'er tail out for 'er. Swap me pink if I don't!"

Cheapside's angry voice had now become so loud that it clearly reached the ears of the Doctor at the wheel. For suddenly he called out:

"It's all right, Cheapside. We have plenty of birdseed aboard. I happened to think of it, myself, on my way to the post office the last time. It's in my overcoat pocket hanging on the back of the cabin door."

"Oh—er—excuse me, Doc," said the sparrow. "I just wanted to make sure—kind of checking up on the ship's stores, like."

And as Cheapside went below, followed by his wife, I could hear Becky scolding him.

"Of all the bad-mannered birds," she was saying, "you're the worst! Anyone would think you were home, the way you behave."

The Dolittle Family at Sea

WHEN WE AT LAST REACHED THE mouth of the river the sun had risen upon a fair and beautiful day. The long arm of the dike (a sort of high earth bank that marked the end of the stream) had a lighthouse on the seaward tip of it. The keeper was an old friend of ours. He waved to us from the lantern-railing, as our ship took her first plunging pitch in the swell of the open sea.

Poor Gub-Gub was lapping up a drink of water from a bucket when the pitch came; and our ship's stern reared up so steeply and unexpectedly, the pig scientist suddenly found himself standing on his head in the pail, instead of on the deck.

Of course our sloop was small. The weather was only what regular sailors would call a swell. But I liked the way our boat handled it, the way she rode over the crests of the waves and down into the troughs between. There was something about the brave little *Albatross* (buried out of sight, she was, half the time) which gave you confidence and trust in her. The morning sun glistened on her bright new paint; she moved like something truly alive; and the tang of the salt spray on your lips made you glad to be alive with her, in this wide world of water where she seemed so much at home.

I was glad, though, that I had obeyed Polynesia and got the baggage stowed below before we passed the lighthouse. Because the ship's motion now made work on the deck pretty hard. Indeed there was plenty to keep me busy. The Doctor called to me to get Gub-Gub down below. He was afraid the pig (who was very round in shape) might get rolled right overboard. So I took him downstairs and put him to helping Dab-Dab and Chee-Chee tidy up the cabin.

Then I arranged our animal family: the sleeping quarters for each, and so on—in the way the Doctor and I had agreed upon beforehand.

Gub-Gub was not the only one who had difficulty with the rolling and pitching of the ship. Mice, when they sleep, have a habit of drawing their legs in, so they look like a ball. Whitey, to begin with, wanted to sleep in the cabin with the rest of us—mostly, I think, because he was afraid that anywhere else he couldn't hear us talking and so might miss something that was being planned. Well, the first night or two he would go to sleep under my bunk; but before morning, the roll of the ship would trundle him across the cabin floor and wake him up by banging his head against the door.

So in the galley (which is what you call the kitchen aboard ship) I found an old teacup with the handle broken off. I gave it to Whitey for a nest. He lined it with ends of twine and shreds of newspaper, so it was very snug and comfortable. Then I set the cup back in the china rack (that is where you keep your dishes at sea, so they won't slide on the floor). And for the rest of the voyage Whitey slept in peace—but Dab-Dab was very annoyed. "What next, I'd like to know?" she snorted. "Mice in *my* china rack!"

"Fussy old party, ain't she?" said Cheapside, who had overheard her scolding me. "By the way, I heard the Doctor calling for you just now, Tommy."

I found the Doctor. He wanted me to go forward with him and look at some maps in the chart-room, as it was called. This was, to me, one of the most interesting parts of the ship. It had windows or portholes all around it. Here the charts, or maps, were kept—also the instruments that are used for finding your way at sea: the sextant, the chronometer, and many more. In this little room the course of the ship was worked out: that is, the direction she should go in.

My boyish imagination could always conjure up smugglers—and even pirates—who might have been captains of this ship in days gone by. And in fancy I could see them bending over the broad desk, with pistols in their belts, plotting the sloop's course to some little, uninhabited island, where they meant to bury treasure they'd stolen from other ships.

"We will hold her sou'sou'-east, Stubbins, for the present—till we pick up Cape Finisterre," said the Doctor as he spread out one of the maps. "I want to check with the chart. This following wind is grand. We're making good headway. Hope it keeps up. We'll try more canvas—more sail—on her soon."

After we had cleared Cape Finisterre, the weather got warmer and warmer as we made our way south. At times it got a little too warm for the Doctor and myself; but Polynesia and Chee-Chee just reveled in it.

"Ah!" gurgled the old parrot, fluffing out her feathers. "Wonderful to see the sun again! I declare if you lived in England long enough, you'd forget what sunshine looked like."

"You got a cheek, you stuffed stocking!" snorted Cheapside. "Always grousing about the Henglish climate. We *like* it kind of moist there. That's what keeps our brains from dryin' up—the way yours is. *Phew!* This deck is 'ot. I'm goin' down to the cabin—before I turns into fried chicken."

The weather certainly stayed wonderfully good and—what was still better—our northerly winds blew steadily the whole voyage. In fact, everything seemed to go pleasantly and well. I do not remember any other sea trip with the Doctor where we had better or easier sailing. Even the after-supper story hour was kept up aboard ship, the same as it had been in the old house at Puddleby.

It was strange that aboard the *Albatross* the animals always asked the Doctor to tell them sea stories. And by the end of the first week, John Dolittle said he had told them all he knew. But the next day Whitey the librarian, hunting through the lockers in the chart-room, came upon a nice thick book called *Tales of the Seven Seas.* And for the rest of that peaceful journey the Doctor's family got him to read them a chapter aloud out of this every night, translating it into animal language as he went along.

The Stormy Petrel

THE ONLY INTERRUPTION—IF INDEED I COULD call it that—to the smooth sailing and our happy voyage came toward its end. For a whole morning the Doctor had been looking at the barometer (that is the instrument for telling the weather) every ten or fifteen minutes; and I noticed he usually frowned over it. However, I was too busy to pay much attention at the time.

But presently, when the Doctor had gone down to the cabin, I noticed a bird skimming low down over the sea on the starboard side. Of course I had to watch the compass carefully (I was handling the wheel just then). But I managed to glance, every once in a while, at the bird. It was a *stormy petrel*.

In bygone days this kind of bird was supposed to be a sign of bad weather. As a matter of fact it isn't—though to be sure, it is often seen when the sky is gloomy or overcast. I have always admired the petrel (sometimes called Mother Carey's Chicken) because, hunting alone or in pairs, it seemed so safe and really at home in mid-ocean, no matter what the weather or the sea might do.

Well, to my surprise, presently this petrel came and perched upon the rail quite close to me.

"Is this Doctor Dolittle's ship?" he asked. And then, at the same moment, we both recognized each other.

"Why, it's Tommy!" he cried. "Grown so big no one could recognize you."

"And you're the petrel that came and found me after the shipwreck—on our trip to Spidermonkey Island," I said. "I know you by that gray feather in your right wing. I'm awfully glad to see you again."

"Thank you," he said politely. "Ever since daybreak I've been hunting all over the ocean for the Doctor's ship. What I have to tell him is important. Is he awake?"

"Yes, I think so," I said. "I'll call him for you." I snatched out my bosun's whistle, which I wore on a cord round my neck, and blew a quick, sharp blast. In a moment the Doctor came trundling up on deck and ran to my side.

"Doctor," said the petrel, "you're sailing right into a tornado, a real bad one—ninety-mile-an-hour-wind and a heavy sea. It's blowing right across your path, the way you are sailing now. You're too close to the land. Head farther out to sea and you can get behind it—but you've got to hurry, or it will pile your ship up on the coast."

"All right," said the Doctor. "We're sailing due south now, with one point to westward. If I—"

"Swing her due west," the bird interrupted quickly. "Due west, Doctor, hurry!"

John Dolittle took the wheel from my hands. Then, with his eyes shifting from the compass to the sails to watch their behavior, he carefully pulled the ship's bow over till we were heading straight out into mid-ocean.

"How's that?" he said at last.

"That's fine," said the bird. "Hold her to that until I tell you to change. You're now running alongside the storm—coming in the opposite direction—and you're about thirty miles this side of the hurricane—but nothing to hurt you. If you had gone on and cut right across its path, I don't know what would have happened. I'm surely glad I found you in time."

"So am I," said the Doctor, laughing. "And I am very grateful for your warning. I thought my barometer was dropping awfully fast. And I knew there must be bad weather brewing somewhere close to us. But I couldn't make out in what direction it was. By the way, you said you had been searching for me. How did you know I was at sea?"

"Oh, very simple, Doctor," said the petrel. "Most of the sea-birds know you by sight—at least, along these coasts. I was talking with some gulls I met; and they told me they'd seen you on a small sailing ship. But the duffers had not noticed what course you were on—just that your sloop was heading generally southward. And that *wasn't* so simple—I mean, finding you. I didn't know whether you were making for the Canary Islands or following the African coast, closer inshore. I had just flown out of the path of that same storm myself. Well, I searched the sea for a long time. And I was on my way to get some more petrels to help me hunt for you when—only by pure luck—I spied your little ship right below me."

"Yes," said the Doctor, suddenly serious, "good luck has

certainly been with us on this voyage—so far. Let's hope it stays. You have been most helpful. Wouldn't you like something to eat? We have some excellent sardines in the larder—real Portuguese."

Well, in the end, the petrel stayed with us a whole day and night—and very good company he was, too. He was an entirely different sort of bird from Polynesia, Too-Too, Cheapside, or the rest of our friends. The stormy petrel is a citizen of the sea. And he looked it, with his sleek, long wings (indeed, when he was flying, he seemed to be all wings—with just a little hinge for a body between them, pointed at both ends). I never got tired of watching the beautiful, easy way he flew into the teeth of a high wind.

He was different, too, in other things: in his likes and dislikes, in his thinking—in fact, in almost everything. He was very fond of John Dolittle, who had mended one of those long wings years ago—when he had broken it flying round the rigging of an old wrecked ship, stranded on the rocks. At our after-supper story-time in the cabin, the Doctor got him to tell us pieces out of his own life; and they were more thrilling than any stories of the sea that I have ever heard or read. Yet he never boasted, but spoke of the most hair-raising adventures as though they were nothing more than what a petrel must expect any day in the year.

It was quite clear that he knew a tremendous lot about sea-weather in general and of winds in particular. John Dolittle asked him many questions about winds and what caused them; and he got me to write down the petrel's answers in a notebook.

Good luck again? Who can say? Anyway, I thought, as I scribbled down the questions and answers, for me it was a mighty comfortable feeling, right now, that a stormy petrel would pop up out of nowhere and make us change our course to miss a terrible storm.

After we had sailed due west for about six hours, the petrel told the Doctor the danger was passed and we could go back on our old course.

"What port are you making for, Doctor?" he asked.

"Fantippo," said John Dolittle.

"Oh well, you're not far off it now," said the bird. "Head your ship straight in for the land. No, no, a little more east. That's good. Hold it," he added, when the Doctor had pulled the helm over a little farther. "In a short while you'll come in sight of the island of No Man's Land and the entrance to Fantippo Bay. I'll be leaving you now. I must get back up north. I'm meeting a brother of mine. Is there nothing more I can do?"

"No, indeed, thank you," said the Doctor. "You have been most kind. I'm sorry I delayed your meeting with your brother."

"Oh, that's all right," said the bird. "He'll just loaf around, fishing, till I come. We sea-folk don't bother too much about time, you know."

The Doctor had given the wheel back to me, as soon as his eyes had noted the new course for Fantippo on the compass card. The petrel took a little jump off the rail and spread those beautiful long wings upon the air. With no flapping or slapping, he just soared around the sloop, making the wind lift him as he wished, till at last he skimmed over the tip of the mainmast. Then he lunged off toward the north.

"Good-bye, John Dolittle," he called down. "Good-bye and good luck!"

"Good-bye, old friend," the Doctor shouted back. "And the best of luck to you!"

"The Doctor had given the wheel back to me."

He stood quite still at my side, his eyes watching the bird swoop over the white-capped waves till it was out of sight.

"You know, Stubbins," he murmured at last, "I've never wished to be anything but what I am, a doctor. Yet I believe if I *had* to change into something else, that's what I would choose to be, out of all other creatures in the world: a stormy petrel."

Late that afternoon Too-Too, who was on lookout duty atop the mast, suddenly shouted, "Land ahead! Land on the starboard bow, sir!"

And so our lucky voyage came to an end.

THE FIFTH CHAPTER

Our Welcome at Fantippo

MOST OF THE DOCTOR'S ANIMAL FAMILY had been to Fantippo before. But for me this was my first visit to that kingdom. So, as you can easily understand, I was a little excited and very interested to see what it would be like.

We had taken down the big mainsail from the sloop's mast and left only enough canvas to move us at the speed of a walk. Polynesia was now on lookout duty up in the peak of the forecastle; and the Doctor, who knew these waters to be full of rocks and sandbars, had taken the wheel himself. I stood at his side with the telescope to my eye, watching the land grow nearer and clearer in the slanting light of the evening sun. Presently he pointed to a round lump ahead of us, on the north side of the opening to Fantippo Bay.

"That's where I had my post office, Stubbins," said he. "On a big houseboat, moored to the shore of that island."

"I see it," I said. "And the houseboat is still there. This *is* a good telescope. Why, I can even see the geraniums growing in the window boxes."

"You can!" he cried. "Well, that's my old friend King Koko's doing. The swallows told me that he had always kept the houseboat spick-and-span after I left—hoping, I believe, that someday I'd come back and run the Swallow Mail for him again. What's the matter? What are you seeing now?"

"I don't know, Doctor. Strange! Seems like crowds and crowds of canoes or something. You have a look. I'll take the wheel a moment."

The Doctor took the telescope from me and peered toward the land.

"You're right, Stubbins. Hundreds of canoes waiting, just inside the reef. I can see the king's canoe among them too, with the flag at the stern, the royal standard. . . . Why, it almost looks as though they were waiting to welcome us. But how on earth did they know we were coming? . . . Oh, for heaven's sake!—I know what's happened: there are great flocks of gulls around the post office. Most likely they heard, through the petrel, that we were sailing in these waters and they gathered at my old houseboat to give us a welcome. The king must have seen them; and he probably thinks I am coming to run his mail for him again. I'm afraid he'll be disappointed. Well, anyway—from birds or kings—it *is* nice to get a welcome when you come to foreign shores. Don't you think so, Stubbins?"

"It certainly is, Doctor," I answered. "Just *look* at those gulls! You don't need any telescope now. See them rising over the island—like white clouds! I don't wonder the king thought there was something happening."

"My goodness!" laughed the Doctor. "I fancy they have

sighted our ship. . . . Yes, sure enough. Here they come, flying out to meet us."

It was indeed a sight to be remembered for a lifetime. We were still a good mile from the shore. But the air and the heavens between us and the island seemed to be filled with white wings flashing in the sun. Soon we could hear the peculiar high-pitched voices of the gulls. "Welcome!" they called. "Welcome, John Dolittle, welcome back to Fantippo!"

The noise they made grew into a deafening roar, as the first flights of them reached our ship and circled round the masts. The air was so thick with them that, gazing up, I wondered how they managed to keep from jostling and colliding in that densely crowded space, big as it was. For I now saw, when they were closer, that this enormous army on wings had spread itself out at least a mile wide. They did not settle on the ship itself; but, like a guard of honor, formed themselves up on either side of us—leaving a wide path ahead of the *Albatross* empty and clear. They seemed to understand that they must not fly directly in front of us toward the harbor—for if they had, of course, it would have been impossible for anyone to steer his way through that fog of feathers.

It was no new thing, Polynesia told me, for the Doctor to receive welcomes by birds. But that evening I felt this was surely something that no man could ever get used to. I glanced at his smiling face behind the wheel. And I felt glad indeed that the old parrot and Cheapside had made him come; and that I, in my own way, had helped.

Any more talk was impossible for the present, with the noise that the gulls made. So John Dolittle, watching for signals from the lookouts, steered the sloop carefully through the dangerous shallows till he at last brought her within the safety of the harbor. Chee-Chee and I were waiting, with our hands upon the anchor cable, for him to signal us. And when at last he waved his hand, we let go. The big bow-anchor splashed into the water; the coils of rope at our feet ran out through the hawse-pipe and then suddenly went slack. We made fast to a cleat. The good ship *Albatross* swung slowly round, down-wind, and then came to rest—anchored in Fantippo Bay.

As I walked toward the stern to speak to the Doctor, I noticed that the roaring chorus of seabirds had stopped. But now another sound—though not so great—had taken its place. It was the chatter of human voices. And it came from the waiting canoes.

This crowd of little craft had stood off some distance from us, so as not to interfere with our handling of the sloop. These small boats were simply packed with people, all dressed in bright-colored clothes—all, that is, except the paddlers. As soon as our anchor splashed into the water a shout went up; and the whole fleet started across the bay toward us at a most surprising speed.

But though they came fast, it was no higgledy-piggledy rush. The leading paddler in one of the canoes started a song; and then all crews in all the canoes sang along with him. I now saw that this was to keep them in line, so that all the paddles should plunge into the water together. The paddles, and the canoes too, were curiously carved and painted. There seemed to be ten men or so working in each boat; and, as there were easily two hundred canoes, that made a lot of singers.

The sun had now dropped down to the sea's edge; and its red light flashed back from all the wet paddle blades together, as the men shouted their strange but pleasing song. And the whole canoe fleet seemed to leap forward at each powerful stroke. It was a wondrous, fascinating sight to watch.

In the center of this crowd of canoes there was one much larger than the rest. It was more like a wide barge, with a purple awning over it to keep off the sun. Under the awning sat an enormously fat man with a crown on his head and a green lollipop in his hand. Sometimes he put the lollipop in his mouth to suck upon; and at others he held it up to his eye, to gaze through it like a quizzing-glass.

On my way to the wheel I had stopped amidships to watch the show. Now as I leaned upon the rail the Doctor came up and joined me. Cheapside was with him.

"Oh, look," cried the sparrow. "There's old King Coconut.— Criminy giblets! 'E's fatter than ever."

"Yes," said the Doctor. "And he's not likely to get any thinner, so long as he eats lollipops morning, noon and night. They were always his great weakness."

"You're right, Doc," said the sparrow. "Old King Lollipop! Eatin' candy, couldn't stop.—Lumme, Doc, that's poetry, that is! Maybe I should 'ave been a writer, same as you."

"Oh, there are plenty of writers," said John Dolittle. "But," he added, smiling at the sparrow, "there's only one Cheapside."

"Huh!—Thank goodness for that," said a voice behind us. And, turning around, we found that Polynesia had joined us.

"Why, you heathen, Hafrican hedgehog!" snapped Cheapside. "For two pins I'd wring—"

But the Doctor stopped the squabble before it got really started.

"Listen, *please*," he said. "We will let down the rope-ladder— on this side. The canoes are making way, see—so the king's barge can come through. It looks to me as though we are going to get an official visit from His Majesty. Lend me a hand, please, with the ladder, Stubbins."

The Dinner Party on the Houseboat

KING KOKO'S VISIT OF WELCOME TO OUR ship turned out to be a very grand business indeed. For not only did His Majesty himself come aboard to pay his compliments, but all the important men in his kingdom came—with all their wives and all their children. I thought that our able seaman, Polynesia, was going to have a fit. She and I were sitting up in the rigging. We had climbed there to get away from the crowd. Looking down, we could see that our visitors actually covered the deck from stem to stern.

"We must get the Doctor to stop them, Tommy," the parrot sputtered. "We've only got six inches of freeboard left; and they're still climbing up the ladder—and more yet coming out from the shore. This sloop may turn turtle and go down any minute. Shiver my timbers! I thought I'd seen everything a sailor can. But, by cracky, it seems I'm yet going to see a ship sunk by kindness! *I* can't even make the Doctor hear me. Can't *you* do so something to get his attention, Tommy? The water will be over the main deck any moment."

I cupped my hands and yelled down to John Dolittle as hard as I could. No use. He didn't even look up. Then an idea came to me (I can't tell why it hadn't before). I snatched my bosun's whistle from my pocket and blew on it hard and long.

That did the trick. It was a new kind of sound to the Fantippans, I suppose. Anyway, there was a sudden, complete silence. John Dolittle looked up and saw me in the rigging.

"Doctor," I cried. "Stop the crowd. Get them off the ship. We've only six inches of freeboard left. We're top-heavy. We're going to sink if—"

But the Doctor didn't wait to hear more. He said something quickly to the king at his side. His Majesty raised the sacred lollipop on high; and everyone respectfully paid attention to the royal command. He only said five or six words in a strange, clicking kind of language. But it was enough. The crowd scrambled for the canoes.

By good luck, all the portholes down below were shut; otherwise the cabin and the hold would have been swamped. As it was, the scuppers of the main deck were underwater; and now the poor little *Albatross* leaned and listed with the rush of the visitors to one side or the other, looking for canoes with space left to take them off. In the confusion a few children fell into the sea; but they were fished out again. Nobody was hurt.

The sun had now set and it was growing dark. The king had not left the Doctor's side. As soon as Polynesia and I had climbed down out of the rigging John Dolittle introduced us. Koko had a nice merry face; and despite some odd habits (like his everlasting lollipop and his always wearing his crown, even in a canoe), there *was* something kingly and commanding about his great enormous figure, which even my young eyes took notice of. I liked him right away. I was surprised to find that he talked English—and well, too.

"I am *deelighted* to meet you, Mr. Stubbins," said the king, bowing with difficulty from his very thick waist. "I have just been inviting Doctor Dolittle to take dinner with me tonight, with all of his ship's company. May I trust you will honor me with your presence also?"

"Thank you, sir—I mean, Your Majesty," I stammered. "If the Doctor is coming, I would like to, too."

"Where is the dinner to be, King Koko," the Doctor asked, "in your palace on the edge of the town?"

"No," said the king. "This is a special banquet, Doctor. It will be in your old houseboat, the post office. Look behind you across the bay, please."

We all turned. Then both the Doctor and I gasped at the same moment. Nearly all daylight had gone now. Only to seaward was there a faint crimson glow where the sun had set. The far shore of the bay was just a black line. Faint starlight shimmered on the silvery water; but where the sky met the shore against the island of No Man's Land, the houseboat was all lit up with strings of Chinese paper lanterns—red, green, yellow, and violet. There seemed to be no end to the beautiful surprises of this strange country of Fantippo.

The king turned to me and said:

"When John Dolittle ran my post office for me, he always had tea served to the public at four o'clock. English visitors have told me that mine was the only post office in the world where they got a cup of tea given to them with a penny stamp. So it is only fitting and right that I should give my reception-dinner for him in the post-office houseboat. We shall expect you at seven o'clock, Doctor. It will be a grand feast."

And gently patting his enormous stomach in happy expectation, the king walked to the ladder and went down it onto the royal barge.

Well, the dinner was a great success. A little before seven we all piled into our ship's dinghy and rowed across the bay to the gaily lighted houseboat. Here Koko himself met us and led us to our places at a big table that was all set and ready under an awning at the stern of the boat.

Perhaps no other king in the whole world would have treated the Doctor and his strange animal family with such polite kindness and hospitality. Of course the king of Fantippo had met nearly all these animals already. And he had special foods for them that he knew they liked; and special places at the table—including a highchair for the white mouse, with tiny dishes of many sorts of cheese set before it.

Gub-Gub, who was seated next to me with a wonderful collection of vegetables and fruits in front of him, was a little nervous about his table manners.

"You know, Tommy," he whispered, "I had dinner with a marchioness once. That was in London—when the Doctor was putting on *The Canary Opera*. But this is the first time I've eaten at the table of a real king. Thank goodness the servants haven't put any spoons and forks at my place! That's what bothers me at these grand dinners: the silverware. I always use the fish fork for the salad and the dessert spoon for the soup. But here, look, no table tools at all. The king has remembered I like best to pick my food up and eat it. Very thoughtful of him. Ah, ripe mangoes! Um-m-m!"

I must say that the animals behaved very well indeed. The only difficulty was the great number of dishes or courses. For, from the soup at the beginning to the nuts at the end, there were forty altogether! Truly King Koko was a mighty eater. The Doctor, who in the old days had often had dinner with him, had warned us all to take only a taste of each dish, so that we would have some room left inside us for the rest. His Majesty, it seemed, always got most unhappy if any of his guests stopped eating before the dinner was over. But even with the Doctor's warning, I could see that many round the table were having hard work to stay with it. And as for myself, by the time I had reached dish number twenty-four, I felt I'd surely crack down the middle if I ate another crumb.

The Jungle-Scouts

THE NEXT DAY THE DOCTOR ONCE MORE started to hurry things along. Those easygoing weeks while we had been at sea had given him a good change and rest; and he was now full of "ginger and gumption"—as Polynesia called it. In the cabin at an early breakfast he said to me:

"I am anxious to lose no time in rushing on to Lake Junganyika. Mudface's life may depend on how soon we get there."

"But I thought," said I, "you felt he should be safe where he is, in a sort of—er—state of hibernation."

"True, Stubbins, quite true. And if he were a younger turtle I wouldn't worry about him. But he's old—unbelievably old. He has been sick. Everything depends on how strong he was when that earthquake happened. But he is helpless now—with those tons of gravel on top of him."

"Have you any plan," I asked, "for getting him out?"

"No, Stubbins, I haven't any notion at all. I'm just hoping some idea will come to me after I look over the scene. That's another reason why I want to get there as soon as we possibly can."

"Yes," said I, "I can well understand you don't want to loaf around here. Did the king say anything last night about your running his post office for him again?"

"No, not a word."

"What will you do, then, Doctor, when the king does ask you?"

"I'm not going to wait for him to ask me!" said John Dolittle. "I'm going to ask *him* to do something for *me*, first. We have reason to return his call anyway—that's etiquette business, you know. As soon as we have finished breakfast, we will go over to his palace and get him to lend us a good canoe. And I shall want him to give us a man to stay on the sloop here while we're gone. You understand, to take care of things, to set up her riding lights at night, so other boats won't run into her—and all that."

Just as we were about to leave the table, Polynesia and Cheapside came into the cabin. It seemed they had been having one of their arguments. The sparrow was still talking.

"And listen to me, my old Pollywog," he ended, "the next time you call me *Mr. Cockney* I'll put you on the end of a stick and mop the decks with you. You—flyin' dishrag!"

"One of these days," said the parrot thoughtfully, as she took a place on the table's edge beside me, "I'm going to forget I'm a lady and bite that guttersnipe's head off."

"Oh dear," sighed the Doctor, "squabbling again! You know, to listen to you two, anyone would think you had never been shipmates before on a voyage. Now settle down quietly and have your breakfast, please. We have a lot to do today."

Dab-Dab, with Chee-Chee to help her, came in bringing

breakfast for the newcomers. "And please don't crack your seeds all over the cabin," she said to the birds. "Chee-Chee and I are tired of sweeping up seed shells off the floor. Crack 'em onto the table; and then they'll be cleared away with the crumbs."

"Right you are, right you are," said Cheapside, starting to eat. "But it's old Pollysnoot over there what makes all the mess." As soon as the duck and monkey had started back for the galley, he added, "Why is it that 'ousekeepers always 'as to be so fussy? That Dab-Dab really is a wonder—when you think of all the jobs she gets done in a day. Only a short time back I was sayin' to Tommy 'ere: old Dab-Dab's more pernickety, in some ways, than your sister, Sarah Dolittle, was. Do you remember how upset she got about that crocodile you kept?"

"Ah yes, indeed!" murmured the Doctor dreamily. "Poor, dear Sarah! I wonder how she's getting on. A splendid woman. But she would let the little things of life annoy her. . . . That crocodile—he came to me from a traveling circus, with a toothache. Then he wanted to stay with me. So I let him. . . . Sarah said he ate the linoleum. Can you imagine it?"

"Sounds 'orrible to me," said Cheapside with his mouth full of food. "*Linoleum*—why, even parrots wouldn't eat that!"

Polynesia pretended not to hear this last insult, but went on noisily cracking her sunflower seeds.

"You know," said the Doctor in the same sort of faraway, remembering voice, "Sarah simply wouldn't believe me when I told her the poor creature had promised me not to bite anyone—not even the goldfish in my garden pond. She thought that crocodiles, when they see an arm or a leg, they just *have* to bite it—even if it is the leg of a table. . . . As a matter of fact, crocodile . . . crocodiles . . ."

The Doctor's words died away in a murmur. I had been watching him as he spoke. The look on his face had changed; and I knew, before he ended, that he was no longer thinking of what he was saying. Polynesia, too, stopped eating and watched him. He was now staring down at the tablecloth, his thoughts a thousand miles away.

Suddenly he looked up, all smiles.

"That's it!" he cried. "Why didn't I think of it before? Cheapside, you're a wonder. I don't know what I'd do without you."

Cheapside looked puzzled.

"'Scuse me, Doc," said the sparrow, "but what might you be talking about?"

"Why, crocodiles, of course!" the Doctor cried. "Here I've been badgering my brain for weeks—in fact, ever since you brought me the news of that earthquake—for some way I could get Mudface up from under the floor of the lake. And then you spoke of it just now: *crocodiles*! Polynesia, would you please find Chee-Chee and bring him down here?"

The parrot fetched the monkey; and when he was seated at the table the Doctor said:

"Now please listen carefully. You two, Chee-Chee and Polynesia, are the best jungle-scouts anyone could ask for. This country is your native land. And often in my travels you have gone ahead of me to find the way, to hunt fruits to keep us fed—and to warn us of dangers. The River Niger is not very far from us here. And on the Niger there lives a crocodile, who was once a pet of mine in Puddleby-on-the-Marsh. I brought him back to this country and left him here. He told me he was going on to the Niger, which, he says, is the finest stream for crocodiles in all of Africa. Do you think you could find him for me now?"

Solemnly little Chee-Chee nodded. But Polynesia put her head on one side and said:

"*Well,* I *think* I'd recognize him—I surely ought to: I was with him enough at your home, Doctor. Let me see: he had a sort of a scar across his back—where the tail joins on. But those messy brutes are always so caked up with mud you couldn't tell one from the rest, if he was wearing a coat and pants. Besides, remember, Doctor, there's an awful lot of crocodiles in the Niger River."

"Oh, please, Polynesia," said John Dolittle quickly, "do not think I don't know I am giving you a hard job. I am asking you to search a stream, which is thousands of miles long, for *one* animal. Of course I hope that you will be helped by asking the other crocodiles where to look for him, on what stretch of the river he was seen last—and so on."

"Well," said the parrot, "can't say I was ever very good at their language—though I can talk it a little. I hate the messy creatures, myself."

"But Chee-Chee speaks it well," said the Doctor. "And if you succeed—well, I can't tell you how important it may be for me— and for natural history as well."

It was plain the parrot did not like the idea very much. She frowned and scowled a moment before she said:

"And what do you want me to do with him when—and if—we find him," she asked, "wrap him up in a palm leaf and fly down here with him?"

"No, listen," said the Doctor patiently. "This particular croc-odile has thousands and thousands of relatives living on the Niger. I want him to bring as many friends with him as he can and to meet me at the Secret Lake. I think he will be willing, on account of my fixing up his toothache long ago. Crocodiles will be the best animals of all to dig down into that mud and gravel and set the turtle free—in fact, I believe they're the only ones who could do it. But we will need a lot of them. Underwater digging is hard work."

"But will he know the way," asked Polynesia, "across from the Niger country to the Secret Lake?"

"Perhaps," said the Doctor. "The landscape has changed somewhat since the earthquake, it's true. But to be on the safe side, I am going to ask Cheapside to go with you. He has been there only a short while back."

That of course started another squabbling argument between the parrot and the sparrow. But I knew all along that both of them would end up by doing what the Doctor wanted.

Nor was there any time wasted in their going. That same afternoon we rowed the dinghy over to the mainland and watched them start their journey into the jungle. Of course Chee-Chee's speed of travel was slower than the birds'; but it was surprisingly fast, just the same. He did not touch the ground at all, but leapt from tree to tree in the dense, tangled forest. He reminded me of a squirrel, the way he would run out to the tip of a limb and shoot himself off the end of it to the next tree, like an arrow.

The parrot and the sparrow always waited for the monkey to catch up to them; so they had plenty of time to argue and quarrel. And even after the jungle had hidden them from our view, we could still hear them calling names at one another, back and forth, within its leafy shade.

"Ah!" said the Doctor as we turned away to go on to the king's palace. "That's a great team. I am lucky to have such friends. What *would* I do without them?"

On the Little Fantippo River

IT WAS AGREED THAT CHEAPSIDE'S WIFE, BECKY, was to travel with us because the Doctor felt we could save time on the long water-trip from Fantippo to the Secret Lake if we had a guide with us who had flown over this same stretch of country since the earthquake had happened. Also, he might wish to use Becky as a messenger between himself and the "advance party," as he called it—that is, Chee-Chee, Polynesia, and Cheapside.

So the little hen-sparrow was with us when we called at the king's palace—as were Too-Too, Jip, and the white mouse. Dab-Dab and Gub-Gub had been left on the ship to wash up the breakfast dishes.

I must say that Koko behaved very well indeed when John Dolittle told him he was in a great hurry to go "up-country" on special business. I could see from the king's face that he was very disappointed to lose his friend again so soon. The post office was not even spoken of at all. And as soon as the Doctor said he would need a good canoe, His Majesty sent for a man he called

"Admiral"—so we supposed this was the commander-in-chief of the Royal Navy of Fantippo.

After we had thanked the king for the dinner and told him we would call on him again on our return journey, we left the palace and went back with the admiral to the harbor.

Here we were shown a great many canoes. Most of them were beautifully carved and painted. At last the Doctor chose one of middling length, which would float in very shallow water.

"It can't be too heavy, Stubbins," he explained. "I remember places on the way to Junganyika where the river runs over rapids and waterfalls. We have got to be able, once in a while, to lift everything and carry it around, on the banks, to the smooth water farther up. This canoe should do very nicely. Now we'll want three extra paddles—and we must arrange for a man to take care of the sloop while we're gone. Then, I think, we'll be all ready to go."

We paddled the canoe out to the ship. The admiral came with us. And when the Doctor had shown him over the *Albatross*, he was so pleased with her that he told the Doctor he would be glad to live aboard her, himself, while we were away and to take good care of her.

When we had gathered all the stuff together in a pile on the ship's main deck, it certainly looked like a great deal of baggage; and we began to wonder if, after we got it into the canoe, we would have any room left for ourselves.

In this the admiral was especially useful, and he set to work having the baggage stowed away for us. When the job was finished, there was comfortable space for the Doctor and myself to kneel, or sit, where we could paddle properly—as well as room for Gub-Gub, Jip, and the others.

It was late afternoon before we had finished getting ready. But the Doctor said he would start today anyway. And so we bade the admiral good-bye and set out.

The Doctor explained to me that the river we were going to follow was not the big one that flowed out through the reef into the ocean. A smaller stream, called the Little Fantippo River, he said, flowed into the bay on its southern side.

Besides that, the mouth of the Little Fantippo was not easy to find, where it crept out through the heavily wooded coast to join the bay.

However, Becky and Dab-Dab did some scouting ahead. And presently they found it all right and led us into it.

The mouth of the Little Fantippo was peculiar. It was so narrow and grown over you could pass it by a hundred times without guessing there was a river there at all. But once inside the mouth, we saw there was nothing "little" about the Little Fantippo. A wide lagoon (a sort of lake) spread out before us, hidden from the bay and the ocean—calm and smooth as a mirror. We crossed this, going northward now; and soon I could see we were coming into a regular broad river. And then, little by little, it became narrower again.

It was very interesting to me to watch the jungle-covered banks of this stream draw in closer together as we paddled inland. Presently the shores were near enough for me to catch glimpses of brightly colored birds, parrots, macaws and others, flitting from branch to branch. Here and there beautiful orchids hung from the tree-forks. And once in a while, the chatter of monkeys reached our ears from the depths of the forest, reminding me of Chee-Chee, of Polynesia, of Cheapside and the errand the Doctor had sent them on.

The stream ahead of us was now winding and turning much more, as we followed it ever onward. Just before the last of the daylight had gone, we rounded a bend and came upon a riverside village. A cleared space lay between it and the edge of the stream.

"I think, Stubbins," said the Doctor, "this will be a good place for us to spend the night."

We drew in to the shore and landed. Then while we were getting some of our baggage out of the canoe, we saw the Chief himself and other important men of the place coming down to the landing to greet us. It seemed he had recognized our canoe as one coming from Fantippo—whose king he greatly liked. The Chief made quite a speech to the Doctor, bidding him welcome to the village and inviting him to use one of the houses as his home for as long as he wished.

As a matter of fact, all of us were only too glad to sleep ashore for a change. And when we had thanked him, the Chief sent for some porters, and our baggage was quickly carried up to one of the larger houses. Here we were invited to dinner, too. But the Doctor was afraid of more long speeches and feasts. So he explained that our whole party was very, very tired from much traveling and work, and that, since we wanted to make an early start tomorrow morning, it would be best for us to prepare our own simple meal and get to bed as soon as possible.

All the villagers were disappointed (as was Gub-Gub, who had looked forward to another grand feed with forty different courses). However, the Chief bade us good night, saying he would be happy if the Doctor visited him again on his return journey.

And after we had brewed a cup of tea and eaten a very light supper, John Dolittle and I climbed into our hammocks and pulled our mosquito nets over us. In a very few moments we were lulled to sleep by the croaking of frogs and that strange and restful chorus of insects, birds, and other creatures that makes African river-nights something to remember.

The Mystery of the Crocodiles

THE NEXT MORNING WE WERE UP EARLY— even a little ahead of the sun; and again it was only a quick meal we took for breakfast. A half hour later we had repacked the canoe and were back on the water once more, paddling northward.

"In this country, Stubbins," said the Doctor, "it is a good thing to start the day early—before the sun gets high and hot. You can always take a good rest around noon, when the heat is at its worst. . . . My! This paddling is hard. What a current! That's the ebb tide—flowing out—and still strong. It will be easier for us once we get above the first rapids."

After that we didn't talk much, saving our breath for the work. But about ten o'clock in the morning I asked: "When do you think we'll hear from the advance party, Doctor?"

"It's hard to say," he answered. "My old crocodile friend, Jim, lives on the Niger, you know. And that river is over there, about fifty miles to the east—according to the maps. But it may be much farther;

no maps have yet been made that we can trust very exactly."

"Well, why don't we go up the Niger River ourselves, Doctor," I asked, "instead of bothering with this one?"

"The Niger would not bring us to the Secret Lake," he said. "There is only one stream flowing out of the lake: and that's the one we're following now, the Little Fantippo. Besides, it is more important that I should get to Mudface's island—or what's left of it—without losing any time. Our advance party can do the searching work much better than you or I could. . . . Oh, look! Up ahead. There's the first rapids. And a waterfall just beyond."

While we had been talking, and I had my head turned sideways to listen to the Doctor in the stern, we had rounded another bend in the stream. Now, in front of us, I saw a straight stretch. Along this the river was so shallow that the stony bottom it raced over could be plainly seen. There were low sandbars, too, here and there. A little farther upstream I saw a white ribbon of a waterfall. The spray rose above it like a thin mist; and faintly the distant roar of the tumbling river reached our ears.

"There should be some crocodiles on those sandbars," said the Doctor. "That's where they love to bask in the sun. If we see any, maybe they can tell us something of the advance party."

The sun was indeed well up in the heavens by now, and the heat was considerable. Presently I felt the Doctor steering us over toward the east shore.

"Take it easy now, Stubbins," said he. "And keep an eye open for sudden shallows—especially for boulders and rocks."

Paddling in the bow of that canoe, where I was, it was of course easier to watch the depths of the water for stones—and for crocodiles.

We met with no accidents—nor any sight or trace of crocodiles.

"Humph! That's strange," the Doctor muttered. "I felt almost certain we would have seen at least a few at such a place as this."

Then Becky said.

"There were plenty of crocodiles here when Cheapside and I flew over, Doctor. I remember this place well. We came down at the foot of the falls up there, for a drink and a shower-bath in the spray. And I remember Cheapside pointing the creatures out to me. *I* thought they were logs, they kept so still. But there were simply hundreds of them—all over these sandbars—then."

"Well, quite possibly," said John Dolittle, "they're still back in the deeper water, waiting for the sun to get hotter or something. See if you can find the landing for a portage trail over there, Dab-Dab, please. We have to go ashore now and carry everything around the falls."

Dab-Dab had been over this same journey with the Doctor years ago; and she did not take long now to discover the landing-place he spoke of. But when we nosed the canoe's bow into the bank where she stood calling to us, it was so tangled and overgrown with thick bushes I was surprised she had been able to find it at all. Behind these bushes and vines there was a little cleared space. And a trail, running alongside the stream northward, could be seen.

We tied the canoe by her painter rope to a palm tree and unloaded the baggage onto the riverbank. Then the Doctor and I each took a load and started up the trail. Jip took one of the smaller packages in his mouth and said he would go ahead of us.

The upper end of the portage trail came out on the rivershore above the falls, where the water was calm and deep. Here the landing's clearing was much bigger. You could see that, in spite of the heavy jungle, this trail was in use all the year round. For, although we met no one on it today, the earth of this narrow path through the forest was worn and patted smooth by the bare feet of many native travelers who had carried their loads around the falls.

It took four trips to get all our stuff over the portage. The canoe was sort of tricky to carry. We took it upside down on our shoulders—which made it hard for the Doctor and myself to see where we were going, with our heads inside it. But Jip and the others helped guide us; and we got it safely above the falls at last.

"I think we've earned a rest, Stubbins," said the Doctor. "Let us have a bite to eat and then hang the hammocks between these trees in the clearing here. A couple of hours' nap, what? But first of all: a nice cold bath in the stream?"

"That sounds the best of all to me, Doctor," I said. "I don't believe I *ever* felt so hot."

In a moment we were undressed and swimming in the river— Jip and Dab-Dab with us. (Gub-Gub decided *not* to risk the crocodiles.) We kept upriver and near the shore, though; because the Doctor feared the drag of the falls might still be strong enough to pull us over them, even here.

"You know, Stubbins," said he, "it's funny about those crocodiles—none of them being around. I can't make it out. Ah, this cold water feels grand! Refreshing, eh?"

"Wonderful," I panted. "Too bad we can't swim all the way to the lake, instead of paddling."

"Yes, quite so," he said. "I'm satisfied, Stubbins," the Doctor went on, "that there are no crocodiles near these sandbars—not now at least. But I confess I am completely puzzled."

"I wish," said Dab-Dab, who was paddling close behind the Doctor like a toy steamboat, "that you'd stop talking about crocodiles while I am swimming. You make me feel that one of the brutes is going to come up right underneath me any moment and swallow me whole."

The Doctor laughed.

"Never fear, Dab-Dab," he said. "You'd see him first."

THE TENTH CHAPTER

The Advance Party

AS THE DOCTOR HAD FORETOLD, WE FOUND the work of paddling far easier after we had passed the first rapids. Indeed we made very good time, seeing that we were going against the current—and how many waterfalls we had to portage around. At each of these we looked for crocodiles in the shallows and sandbars that lay below; but as before, we found none. However, at last we did come upon a few tracks which, the Doctor said, were certainly made by crocodiles' feet.

At one of our midday rests we were looking at a map. It showed the Little Fantippo—and the Niger, too, the third largest river in all of Africa. According to this map, the two rivers flowed down from the north, staying pretty much the same distance apart. But at a certain point, about three hundred miles from the sea, the course of the Niger River changed; above that point it was shown flowing from the west. This place was marked on the map as the Great South Bend.

"You see that, Stubbins?" asked the Doctor. "And then this other point here, where the Little Fantippo comes nearest to the Niger? I am holding my pencil on it. Do you see it?"

I said I did.

"Well, that will be the shortcut," said he. "The shortcut for anyone who wishes to come across from one river to the other. I wish I knew what kind of country lies between the rivers. But of course this doesn't show that."

"You mean that is where our advance party will come over from the Niger into this stream we're traveling on?" I asked.

"I wasn't thinking of that so much," he said. "Birds and monkeys can travel through almost any kind of country: it makes little difference to them. It was something else I had in mind. Anyway, we ought to be almost there by now—I mean, at that point nearest the Great South Bend. Let's see: today is Wednesday, isn't it?"

He took an old envelope out of his pocket and made a calculation in pencil on it.

"I should say we have been doing thirty miles a day," he muttered. "Er—that will come to, er—" For a moment I could not hear his words as he mumbled a little arithmetic.

"Why, yes," he said at last, in a puzzled kind of way, "we should have reached the shortcut yesterday—that is, of course, unless the distances on this map are utterly crazy. . . . Too-Too, just check over my calculation here, will you please? I may have made a mistake. Stubbins, will you glance through it too?"

I took the envelope from the Doctor; and Too-Too, the mathematical wizard, looked over my shoulder as I ran through the Doctor's reckoning. I was only halfway through the multiplication, when the owl snapped out: "Right, Doctor—correct."

"Humph!" said John Dolittle thoughtfully. "Well, I wonder why we haven't seen it yet."

"But what would there be to see, Doctor?" I asked. "The Great Bend itself is over on the other river, the Niger, isn't it?"

"Quite so," said he. "But there would certainly be a path, across from one river to the other, at the shortest distance between them. Such a path is also called a portage trail—like the short ones round the waterfalls. The trail to the Great South Bend has probably been used for hundreds of years by native traders, bringing their stuff down to the coast from up-country. . . . This *is* strange! . . . I wonder, could we have paddled past it without noticing it? The jungle is still awfully thick on the banks. Where is Becky?"

"She's just down below, at the third rapids, Doctor," said Too-Too. "I'll go and fetch her for you."

But when the little hen-sparrow was brought, she said that she and Cheapside had flown over this stretch of the river at a great height. And so it would have been impossible for them to see small things on the riverbank—even a trail through the jungle. They were trying then, she told us, to spy out the Secret Lake itself.

"But listen, Doctor," Becky added, "why not let me and Dab-Dab fly ahead, scouting for you, while you take your midday rest? If the Great South Bend trail is even another day's paddle farther on, we can come back and let you know before you've got the canoe repacked. There's no wind against us."

So the Doctor let Becky and the duck go forward while we strung up our hammocks to the trees to take a rest. As we climbed into them the Doctor said:

"Dear me! What would I do without them? I mean Becky

and Dab-Dab. But you know, Stubbins, having a guide with you is sometimes not altogether a good thing."

"Well," I said, "you've done so much exploring in outlandish countries, it is not surprising to me that you can't remember every river and trail you've been over."

"Ah, but I should," said he. "That's one of the most important things any good explorer must do: take note of everything he passes, so he'll be able to find his way back. But the trouble was that I had too good a guide on that first trip."

"What do you mean, Doctor?" I asked.

"The Great Water Snake," said he.

"Oh yes," I answered. "I remember now: Cheapside told me about him."

"He was perfectly marvelous," said John Dolittle.

"Yes," said Jip. "Do you remember the way he used to get our canoe off the mudbanks, when we got stuck, Doctor? Take a turn around the bow-post with his tail and yank us into deep water, as though we weighed no more than a feather."

The Doctor nodded, smiling to the old dog, and then went on:

"So of course, Stubbins, seeing the snake knew the streams and the swamps hereabouts so well, I'm afraid I didn't bother noticing the *way* he was taking us. There was such a lot of other things I was looking out for—birds, animals, trees, and so on. Very interesting country—never been explored. That's why the animals call it the Secret Lake. They claim that its water is the actual water of the Flood—which never dried up from its swamps. You may have noticed that the map does not show the Little Fantippo River as flowing *out* of it at all. According to the map, that river begins only about a hundred miles *this* side of the lake—which is surrounded by wide swamplands. Mud, mud, mud—miles and miles of it—with shallow water in pools and narrow streams running all through it; and the mangroves, ten feet high, sprouting and sprawling out of every square yard. Lake Junganyika, Mudface the turtle calls it. Strangest country I've ever seen; I don't wonder that it's stayed a secret lake. Why, when I was once on the shores of the Black Sea, the—"

Never before do I remember falling asleep while the Doctor was telling me of his travels; but I confess I did that day. We had been paddling hard all morning; and we had made an extra early start; so maybe I was particularly tired. Anyway, I heard no more of what he was saying. Without any break at all, his deep, restful voice changed right into a dream.

I was in a sea of mud somewhere, after traveling on foot, by coach, sailing ship, and canoe for months—through oceans of more mud. I was lying on my back, all tangled up with jungle vines—and a big snake was trying to yank me free by the neck. Then immediately a tremendous crocodile appeared from nowhere, grabbed hold of my boots, and started to pull me the other way. At that, Cheapside popped up onto a tree limb above me and started to laugh his silly head off.

When I opened my eyes the Doctor was standing over my hammock gently shaking me by the shoulder; and my sleepy ears heard him say:

"Stubbins, *please* wake up! Becky's back. Listen: Becky's back. And Cheapside's with her—and *all the advance party* too. Wake up, Stubbins! They've brought great news!"

THE ELEVENTH CHAPTER

The Trail to the Great South Bend

WHEN AT LAST I SHOOK MYSELF FREE of the dream and sat up, everybody was gathered around me—and all of them talking at once. Besides the Doctor, there were Polynesia, Chee-Chee, Jip, Cheapside, Becky, Dab-Dab, Gub-Gub, Too-Too, and the white mouse. After a moment I got myself really awake.

The Doctor and I went down to the water's edge to freshen up in the cool river; but John Dolittle also wished to get me alone so we could talk in peace.

"Stubbins," said he, as we knelt down upon a flat rock and began scooping up the water, "our luck is holding. Polynesia tells me everything went wonderfully well. In almost the first lot of crocodiles they met, over on the Niger, there was one who knew all about me. Had known my old pet, Jim, from the circus—was a sort of relative of his. What do you think of that—speaking of luck?"

"Oh well," I sputtered through the water I was throwing over my face, "nothing very extraordinary, Doctor. The birds and the monkeys know you—throughout the whole of Africa."

"Well, but Stubbins," said he, "these are reptiles. It's different. Imagine it: just because I cured a simple toothache for that poor beast, years afterward I come here and find I have friends—and cold-blooded, amphibian friends at that—in an African swamp! Positively astonishing! What makes this water so muddy here?"

"*I* was wondering about that too," I said.

At the place where we were kneeling there was a sort of natural basin for washing. No mud lay anywhere near; and the clean rock bottom of the river could be plainly seen—when we had first come to it. But now, as we both stared down into the water, we saw it had grown muddy. Then it cleared again; and a moment later it was muddy once more.

"How very strange!" the Doctor murmured. "Well, let's get the canoe packed, Stubbins, and be on our way. Becky says the trail to the Great South Bend is only about ten miles farther up the river; so we should be able to get there before nightfall."

There was now a feeling of excitement among all of us, as the hammocks were taken down and stowed in the canoe. Yet, after the first greeting, there was little talk—very little, seeing that we had now been joined by our advance party.

I remember that this struck me as a bit curious at the time. After all, these three—Chee-Chee, Polynesia, and Cheapside—had traveled many hundreds of miles since we last saw them; and anyone would suppose they would have a lot to chat over. I noticed a rather strange look in Cheapside's eyes: as though he were trying a little too hard to make us think that a trip like that was nothing out of the ordinary for *him*. The thought went through my mind that perhaps

"'How very strange,' the Doctor murmured."

he and Polynesia, in spite of all their arguments and squabbles, had agreed together to keep something a secret from us—a surprise.

However, I was too busy loading the canoe to attend to anything else just now.

We found the flow of the river much stronger in this stretch than it had been anywhere throughout the whole trip. One of the few times that the Doctor spoke, he told me the extra-hard current we were fighting was caused by the river being narrower and shallower here. This was one of the stretches where the trees formed a solid roof over us.

Both the Doctor and I, without knowing it, had caught some

fever of hurry and were paddling harder than we had ever done in our lives. All the animals were silent—even Gub-Gub and the white mouse. In the green tunnel of that jungled-shaded river, no sound broke the silence but the regular *plash plash* of our paddles.

I was sure now that, for all our hard work, we were not making as good a speed against this swift current as we had done most days. But, just the same, I also had a strange feeling (it sent a sort of tingle up my spine) that something very important was going to happen—and soon.

I think it was about four in the afternoon when we came around a wide curve and headed up a long straight stretch. Here the banks lay back on either side and let the full sunlight in upon our heads once more. And it went on like that all the way up the straight stretch, which must have been over a mile in length. At the far end of it some sort of commotion seemed to be going on, a tremendous splashing—whose low white line, like a bar across the river, could be plainly seen from where we were. Yet even I could tell that *this* was not made by any waterfall or rapids.

From the sudden easing of the canoe's speed, I knew that the Doctor behind me had stopped paddling. I rested too.

"What in the name of goodness is *that*?" John Dolittle gasped.

And then old Polynesia's grating voice answered:

"Crocodiles, Doctor—just crocodiles."

She said it in a quiet, offhandish sort of way, as though telling us she thought it might rain.

"But—but," the Doctor stammered, "how *many*!"

"Ha!" giggled Cheapside with a cheeky chirp. "'Ow many, Doc? Well, I don't reckon old Too-Too, the mathematooter, could count *them* for yer, John Dolittle. Up there is where the land trail comes across from the Niger River's Great South Bend. And when we left it, I calculated—by dead reckonin' and pigonometry—that the crocs was pouring across into the Little Fantippy here at the rate of two million an hour—this is, o'course, roughly speakin'—in round numbers."

A second passed without anyone moving or talking. Our canoe lay perfectly still. The eyes of all of us were fixed on that strange white line across the river a mile ahead of us. Then, when the breeze changed a moment and blew into our faces, the distant sound of a mighty, hissing roar come down to us.

"Great heavens!" the Doctor murmured at last. "No wonder the water was muddy above the last falls!"

Then suddenly he shouted like a schoolboy in a football match: "*Let's get on*! Run her up!"

Our paddles dug into the river together; and the canoe almost left the water as it leapt forward, heading for the South Bend trail.

General Jim

WE WERE NEARLY THERE WHEN WE saw one large crocodile swimming all alone toward us.

"Here comes your old circus friend to welcome you, Doc," cried Cheapside. "Good old Jim!"

It was a great and important meeting; and when Jim came alongside our canoe, many questions were asked and answered. Myself, I could only understand, so far, a few words of the language.

Once or twice the Doctor explained to me what was being said. But, as he was in great haste, he asked old Jim to turn around and swim beside our canoe as we went on upstream.

In the books of the life of Doctor Dolittle there are a few places where I have written of certain happenings which I shall never be able to forget: scenes that are pictured so lastingly in my memory that today, years afterward, I can see them all over again, exactly as they took place. And this, as we paddled up close to the trail-landing of the Great South Bend, was one of those pictures that was to stay in my memory for life, clear and unforgettable.

The right bank of the river rose here to quite a height. And down this slope the crocodiles from the Niger were pouring—in a solid procession—into the Little Fantippo River. The jungle, whose heavy tangle covered all the land on either bank, had here been torn up and cleaned off by millions of clawed feet, making a wide, crowded road.

You could barely see the ground they walked on—only the creatures' backs, as close together as stitches in a carpet. But once in a while a free spot in the parade would open up; and then you saw that the earth had been trodden as smooth as pavement.

As they reached the water's edge, this great army did not stop or hesitate a moment. They flopped into the river a hundred abreast, and headed upstream. The water all around looked as though it were boiling. I wondered how none of them got hurt, with those heavy tails slapping right and left.

Old Jim now left us and swam out to a low flat rock in mid-stream. Onto this he crawled and began directing the traffic—exactly like a policeman at a busy street-crossing. The noise of all that splashing made it hard to hear anything. We had stopped paddling; and the canoe rose and fell gently where the Doctor halted it, a hundred yards or so downstream from the trail-landing.

But as I chanced to look back a moment, I saw him signal to Cheapside. And the sparrow flew onto his shoulder where he could speak right into the Doctor's ear. Then I saw John Dolittle get out a piece of paper and a pencil. I guessed what calculation he was making this time. Cheapside would be telling how many days ago this living flood had begun flowing over the trail. I saw him take his watch from his pocket and hold it in his hand while he kept an eye on the crocodiles who, row after row, came down to the edge and splashed into the water. He was trying to reckon how many of the creatures had already passed up the Little Fantippo on their way to the Secret Lake.

I glanced up the river myself, and I saw that this, too, seemed to have changed into a solid mass of reptiles. Dry-shod you could have walked from bank to bank. After about another half hour, John Dolittle sent Polynesia over to the rock in midstream with some message for old Jim.

And it was now that a strange thing happened. Jim began swinging his tail wildly from side to side. Clearly the Doctor's message was: "Enough!" For very soon I could see the swarm of beasts pouring over the trail begin to thin out—to grow less crowded. I suppose Jim's message was sent back from mouth to mouth all the way to the Niger River.

Anyway, it was almost twilight when it stopped altogether. In the sudden quiet I realized that it was now possible again for us to talk. For General Jim had commanded his army to halt.

But it was Cheapside's cheeky voice that first broke that silence.

"You know, Doc," he chirped, "I'm beginnin' to understand your sister Sarah's notions about them crocs. You can't call 'em 'ouse pets—really you can't. Just look what they've gone and done to that there poor jungle! Made it look like a racetrack after a ten-day rain. It's a good thing for you that old Jim didn't 'ave to bring 'is friends through your garden to get 'em to the Secret Lake."

"Yes, indeed!" murmured Gub-Gub in a hushed, scared sort of voice. "What *would* they have done to my tomato plants?"

"Yes—and to you, too, Mr. Bacon," said Cheapside, "if they

took a fancy for a little fresh ham while Jim and the Doctor was lookin' the other way."

As the light was now fading fast, the Doctor was anxious to pitch camp. A place was found, this time on the left bank. As soon as we had the hammocks set up and a nice fire burning, the Doctor had a talk with Jim. This time either John Dolittle or Chee-Chee translated everything for me.

I had been anxious to get a good, close-up look at this famous reptile who had, quite unintentionally, so upset the Doctor's household years ago on account of Sarah, the Doctor's sister. Well, it may be hard for you to imagine a crocodile looking friendly and quite un-dangerous, but this one did.

We gathered around the fire on which our supper was being cooked. The Doctor's own animals all knew Jim of course already; and none was in the least afraid of him. Not even the white mouse was scared—indeed, he kept running up and down the great beast's knobbly back, from nose to tail. Whitey's only worry was that he might miss something that was being said. And he never seemed to be certain whether it was Jim's head or Jim's tail that was doing the talking.

Meanwhile, our visitor, for his part, seemed to be greatly enjoying the attention he received at this meeting with his old friend the Doctor—answering his questions, and suggesting ideas as to how the work of setting Mudface free could best be carried out. Just the same, I could not help thinking that if any of the good people of Puddleby were to come upon us now and see John Dolittle, MD, sitting over a fire in the African jungle and talking to a crocodile, his reputation as a crazy man would surely be more firmly fixed on him than ever.

Jim told the Doctor that he had already been up to the Secret

"Not even the white mouse was scared."

Lake himself, as soon as Polynesia had told him what the Doctor wanted. He had taken two of his brothers with him. They had gone all around the turtle's island to make sure where to start the underwater digging. He had left his two brothers up there to wait for the coming of a big herd of crocodiles. These would set to work, under the brothers' leadership, as soon as they arrived.

"I am very hopeful, Doctor," said he, "from what we saw of the lake bottom at the north end of the island, that we shall be able to dig your friend Mudface out all right. Only it may take us a couple of days, possibly longer."

"I am happy indeed to hear that," the Doctor answered. "And

I find it difficult to thank you enough—not only you, but all the others who came this distance to help."

"Oh, we were only too glad to do it," said Jim.

"You certainly brought an awful big crowd across from the Niger," said the Doctor, smiling.

"You know, Doctor," said Jim, "when you brought me back here to my homeland years ago, the story of how you had cured my toothache and got me away from that wretched circus, soon spread up and down the Niger—even as far as Timbuktu. Your monkey here, Chee-Chee, told me that the same thing happened when you stamped out that sickness that was killing off his people. You don't realize, John Dolittle, how widely known you are among the wild animals of the world."

"Well," said the Doctor, "with birds and monkeys, that's something else. They travel more freely—and news, I suppose, travels with them."

Old Jim shook the mouse—who was tickling him—off his nose (much to Whitey's astonishment) and then he said:

"You'd be surprised, Doctor, how fast we can pass messages along a river—underwater. It was only half a day after I sent out word that *you* needed *our* help that they began arriving. And an hour later the Great South Bend was packed so solid with crocodiles, the open water of the Niger River had disappeared. Handling the traffic back there was a job, I can tell you—even when I got six big cousins of mine to help me. The overland trail was rubbed right out in no time. But your advance party went ahead of us—they could travel on land much faster than we, of course—and so the mob kept going in the right direction. But the crush was something awful, just the same."

"My goodness!" said the Doctor. "I had no idea you could collect so many crocodiles in so short a time."

"The main reason for *that*, Doctor," said Jim, "was because every single one of them was just crazy to see you."

"Humph!" said John Dolittle thoughtfully. "That is really a great compliment."

"I'm afraid the others must have been terribly disappointed, Doctor," Jim said. "I mean those I had to send back to the Niger, when you told me that enough had gone up to the lake."

"I'm sorry," said the Doctor, "very sorry that so many took the long journey for nothing."

"Oh well," said Jim, "it was a change for them anyway. Life on the Niger River gets a bit dull sometimes."

"How far," asked the Doctor, "do you calculate we are from the Secret Lake here?"

"Not a great distance," said the crocodile. "The edge of the swamps that surround it are just around the second bend. I think we should easily reach Mudface's island tomorrow afternoon."

By this time our supper had been prepared and eaten. And so, with the comforting picture of our journey's end at last so near, we turned in and went to sleep.

The Last Lap

EXT DAY THE DOCTOR PUT ON ANOTHER OF those bursts of speed of which I have spoken before. As we passed by the trail-landing this morning, it looked very different from what it had yesterday. There was not a single crocodile in sight—except old Jim, who, swimming a few yards ahead of us, acted as guide. The great wide avenue on the right bank, over which the thousands had come swarming down last evening, was now empty and deserted. It looked strange indeed, in the bright light of morning, clear and clean, cutting through the green jungle, up the low hill, till it disappeared from sight. I wondered how many ridges and valleys it climbed up and down before it joined the Niger so many miles away.

And now, following Jim's lead, we did not have to be watching out for those dangerous rocks and shallows. We could give all our attention to steady powerful paddling. And I knew, by the way the banks slipped by us, that we were making a far better pace than we had done before.

As our guide had told us last night, we saw, at the end of the second curve in the stream, that we were entering on the wide swamplands that surrounded Lake Junganyika. This was country such as I had never seen before. I could guess how easy it would be for a traveler to get lost here.

Gradually the Little Fantippo seemed to disappear as an easy-to-follow waterway. And soon we found ourselves in a flat, flat world stretching out in all directions as far as the eye could see. Most of it was water. What patches of land were here never stood up more than a foot or two above the muddy slush. They were nowhere larger than a barnyard and often as small as a footstool.

"And soon we found ourselves in a flat, flat world."

There seemed to be very little animal life: a few wading birds were all we saw.

As for the water, wherever you looked it lay in pools and ponds of every size and shape, joined together by a network of narrow channels and creeks. These did not seem to be coming *from*, or going *to*, anywhere—in fact, it was hard to believe they flowed at all, so still was the water. Once in a while we would reach a spot where we could see down these unmoving streams for a fair distance. But to get a longer view in this deserted swampland did not cheer you up at all: instead, it made you wonder how far the useless country went on—or if this was (as some had said) the end of the world.

But old Jim was certainly not bothered by any such notions. This puzzle of brooks and ditches never stopped our guide for a moment. He would shoot across one of these pools and disappear into a tangle of mangroves. We would follow as fast as possible. And behind a clump of bushes on the farther shore we would always find him waiting for us with a new way to get through.

Today we did not take our regular sleep at noon. We just halted by a clump of mangroves and ate our luncheon, which we had made and packed at breakfast-time. When we had finished, the Doctor asked me if I was tired from the paddling. I said no: and on we went again.

Presently I saw that the surface of the water was no longer quite smooth. Waves, very tiny but very wide, were washing toward us. With these wavelets came a breath of gentle wind that sometimes carried a thin mist. Soon the waves grew a little bigger, rocking the canoe; while the fog kept parting. One moment you saw quite a distance ahead; and the next, little indeed could be seen—even nearby.

I looked over my shoulder at the Doctor. He smiled, nodding, as though he knew the question in my mind; then he pointed ahead.

Peering forward once more, I found the fog now billowing over us so thick I could see absolutely nothing at all. The next moment, magiclike, the soft wind swept it away.

But before it had time to shut down again, I knew we were in the Secret Lake at last!

I have already spoken of some stretches on the Little Fantippo where that stream had flooded out so that you could not see across them. But this was different. I am sure anyone, waking up to look on this for the first time, would have sworn he was at sea.

In every direction the water stretched out to meet the dim, straight line of bleak gray sky. I had the feeling now so strongly of being on a body of water that had no shores at all, that I got uneasy about our heavy-laden canoe if a storm should come up.

The clear spell lasted only a moment. But, as my eye swept around the empty circle in front of us, it stopped at one point. Almost dead ahead of us there seemed to be something sticking up above the water. I couldn't be sure. It was very far away. Perhaps it was only an odd-shaped cloud touching the lake there. . . . And then, down came more fog, blotting everything out.

But the Doctor's eyes had been as sharp as mine. "Did you see that, Stubbins?" he cried.

"I *thought* I saw something," I called back. "It was away off on the horizon—right where we are headed now."

"Well, that's it!" he shouted happily. "That was Mudface's island. Take it easy now. Don't tire yourself out. We've had a long pull. But this is the last lap, Stubbins—the last lap!"

The City of Mystery

AS JOHN DOLITTLE AND I SETTLED DOWN TO an even, steady paddle-stroke to finish this open run across the lake, all the animals began to cheer up and talk. (They had barely said a word that day, so far.)

"Ah well," sighed Gub-Gub comfortably, "it's a long road that has no turnip—as the saying goes."

"You've got that wrong," grunted Jip. "It's a long road that has no *turning*."

"Yes, of course," said Gub-Gub. "But I changed it. After all, it's far more important that a road should have a turnip in it than a turning."

"Tee, hee, hee!" tittered the white mouse. "Gubby always carried a turnip with him on his travels—in case of sickness, you know."

"Good Lord!" groaned Jip. "I might have known. Golly but this fog is wet!"

"Yes," said Cheapside, who sat with hunched-up wings on the

gunwale of the canoe, "a *very* pretty climate! Gray sky, gray water, gray fog, gray mud, gray parrots, gray everything. Kind of colorful, ain't it? This is merry old Africa, me hearties. I'm just tellin' yer, for fear yer might think we'd lost our way and wandered into a public steambath."

"Huh!" squawked Polynesia. "And I suppose you're going to say you don't have any fog in London! Last time the Doctor and I were there the streetlamps were lit, night and day, for a whole week. And at that, we did nothing but bump into people if we dared go outside the house. It isn't like this *all* over Africa, you ninny! This is flat swamp country; but, just the same, it is very, very high here. So high, you practically have your head in the clouds."

"Lumme!" muttered Cheapside, as a drop of water fell from the tip of his beak. "'Your 'ead in the clouds!' says you. 'Ow you do run on, old sweet'eart! Seems to me more like I got my 'ead stuck in a drainpipe. Listen: London, at its worstest, never 'ad a climate as wet, as 'ot or as gummy as this. Go stick your 'ead back in the clouds, old Polly-sponge: you're welcome to it. Gimme London any day."

"An awful city," said Polynesia, closing her eyes in painful memory, "just awful! Never in my life was I so glad to get away from a place."

"Not 'alf as glad as what the Londoners was to see you go, I'll bet," Cheapside muttered.

As for me, I hardly heard what they were saying. My attention was given to trying to see ahead through the mist. Africa was never more mysterious than it was here. Behind that fog you could imagine anything rising up on the horizon. You felt like an explorer crossing a sea that had never been traveled before—and that, as you went forward, even enchanted countries might appear. But the curtain of mist had not lifted again, after it had given us that one glimpse of the turtle's island.

It was almost a rule with the Doctor not to chatter while we were paddling—to save breath and strength for the work. So I was surprised to hear him join the general talk.

"You remember, Cheapside," said he, "that Mudface told us something about an old, old city lying beneath this lake?"

"Oh yes, Doc," said Cheapside, "the most wonderful city ever built—accordin' to 'im: palaces, racetracks, zoos, and everything—belongin' to a big king. But, you know, I never believed 'is story meself. Who would ever pick a place with a climate like this 'ere to build a city?"

"Ah, but don't forget," said the Doctor, "the climate here may have been quite different when the city was built, from what it is now. In fact, many people believe that the Deluge, the Flood, was caused by the North and the South Poles shifting their positions. That would change climates all over the world."

Cheapside shook the wet out of his feathers before he answered.

"Well," said he, "*this* neck-o'-the-woods sure got a dirty deal."

We had now been traveling on for quite a while, unable to see much—but chatting, to make up for it, of this and that. How old Jim, our guide, was keeping the right direction we had no idea.

And then suddenly (the Doctor told me afterward it was about three o'clock in the afternoon) the fog lifted and the sun actually shone! We could hardly believe our eyes. The steamy lake was clear in every direction. The high hump of Mudface's island was now much clearer to us, though I reckoned we were still a good five miles from it. It was wonderful how cheered up I found myself, just by the sun's coming out and warming my back.

I could feel the canoe was moving faster now; and I guessed that our complete change of weather had done the same to John Dolittle as it had to me—that he was working harder on that long stern-paddle of his. And then, just as suddenly, our speed slacked off and I knew that his powerful strokes had stopped altogether. His voice sounded hushed almost to a whisper when he spoke; but I heard what he said quite plainly in that wide, silent desolation of water.

"Look, Stubbins, over to starboard!"

At the Doctor's words, I shipped paddle, turning my head quickly to the right.

What I saw did not stand high out of the lake; but there could be no mistaking what it was. *It was a row of buildings!* Perhaps it would be better to say it was what was left—the ruins—of a row of buildings. It was only a short distance from us—a hundred yards, I'd judge. And as our canoe, which was still moving forward, ran silently and slowly by it, you had the feeling you were passing the waterfront, the shops and houses, of some riverside harbor.

The buildings were all of stone or brickwork. Their fronts were lined up, as though they bordered, or faced, upon a street. Yet they were not all alike by any means, either in size or style. There was no land to be seen on which they stood. They rose straight out of the lake like ghosts of the past. The wet of the fog, which had wrapped them from our sight, still glistened on their walls where the sunlight fell; and this added to their ghostly appearance. It was easy to imagine that some magician had waved a wand, only a moment before, and made this city rise out of the depths of the lake.

HUGH LOFTING

"It was a row of buildings."

Some of the lower houses showed only their roofs; others, with no roof at all on them, showed a story and a half—and the level of the water lapped gently in and out of the second-floor windows. Here and there, behind the front line, we could see pillars and pieces of wall belonging to a second row of houses.

"My goodness!" said Whitey softly. "Why, it's a *town*! What's it doing here?"

Indeed, that seemed a fair enough question to ask at the time. To find ourselves, in the middle of the Secret Lake, where mankind never came, suddenly facing a row of buildings—as though we were on a London street—was something hard to explain.

"Cheapside," said the Doctor, "did you see these houses when you were here a few weeks ago?"

"Yes, Doc," said the sparrow. "Though when *you* was here last there was nothing of the kind to be seen. Sort of a dismal sight, ain't they? Becky and me didn't pay much attention to 'em, being anxious to get news to you of your friend Mudface. And so we forgot to speak of 'em. Dear, dear! In a shockin' state of repair: just look at them cracks runnin' down the walls!"

"That's not surprising, Cheapside," the Doctor murmured, "when you think how long ago those stones were set together and carved—before the Flood, before Noah launched his Ark! . . . My goodness! If, instead of becoming a naturalist, I had gone in for archaeology, what a find *this* would be!"

"What's archaeology, Doctor?" asked Gub-Gub.

"Oh—er—archaeology?" said John Dolittle. "Well, an archaeologist is a man who studies ruins—such as these we see now."

"Huh!" grunted Cheapside. "Archaeologist or naturalist? I'd call you a bit of both, Doc; a sort of a *Noah's-arkeeologist.* 'Ad you a notion to go over and take a look around them ruins?"

"No, no, not now," said the Doctor quickly, "although I'd like to. Maybe later, Cheapside. We must get on and see about Mudface. Ah, there's another crocodile, see, talking to Jim. Perhaps he has brought some news."

It turned out that this newcomer was one of Jim's brothers. He had been left at the island to take charge of the digging till John Dolittle himself should arrive. The brother and Jim now swam down to the stern of the canoe to give the Doctor a report.

At the Turtle's Island

P OLYNESIA GUESSED THE DOCTOR WOULD try, without losing any time, to get down underwater and take a look at the old turtle. So she volunteered to go up to the island ahead of us all and find out what she could.

In about twenty minutes she was back. She had asked all the crocodiles to quit working till the Doctor should arrive; to leave the water and scramble out onto the land. This she had done, the parrot explained, so that the mud stirred up by the diggers would settle and leave the water clear.

John Dolittle was glad; but he wanted to hurry more than ever now. Until the island at last came in sight, I had had no idea how large it was. And it was hard to believe that birds alone had (at the Doctor's orders, years ago) built this great body of land, stone by stone.

Now, as we stopped in the shadow of it—our long journey ended at last—I gazed at it with great curiosity and respect. Here John Dolittle had, through his friendship with the animal kingdom, actually changed geography in a small way.

Jip had told me that none of the great things he had done (except, perhaps, setting up his post office and the Swallow Mail) had made him so popular with the creatures of all the world. This island was a monument to the Doctor's memory, Jip said, such as no kings had ever left behind them. It had taken an earthquake to disturb it; still it remained a work that men must wonder at!

As I stared up, kneeling in the canoe, at the steeply sloping sides of the island, I could well understand that what the old dog had told me was true. All animal life was important to the Doctor; but Mudface, who had known Noah, who had come through the Flood and still lived, *he* was different. When John Dolittle found him dying in the swamps of Lake Junganyika, he had made up his mind that the old turtle should have the finest home possible, on high ground.

From where I knelt I could not see the flat top of the island. Many trees had grown to a great height. Midway up the slopes, flowers bloomed in a few open places. But mostly (except upon the side where the land had broken off) the whole island was draped up to the top with heavy jungle such as we had seen on the river-shores nearer the coast.

And everywhere I looked I saw the little beady eyes of the crocodiles, who had now all crawled ashore and were resting in the undergrowth. The water was very still and clear and calm.

A sudden splash made me turn my head. The Doctor had taken off his clothes and dived overboard. For a moment I thought he was going to swim down right away to the turtle. I had no idea how deep he would have to go; and I admit I was afraid for his safety. But in a moment he bobbed up again, with his head quite close to my paddle blade.

"Stubbins," he said, "you'll find a short coil of rope—

underneath the grub box, I think. Get it out and tie it in a loop for
me, will you? Jim's brother is going to tow me down to Mudface.
It's deep where he is—but getting towed will save my strength for
looking around after I reach him."

In a moment I got the rope out and tied it the way he said. By
that time the Doctor's crocodile guide was beside him in the water.
He opened his great jaws and took the loop in his mouth like a
horse's bit and reins. John Dolittle grabbed the free end. Then his
tow-horse plunged downward underwater. I could see the Doctor's
white skin go glimmering deeper and deeper, dimmer and dimmer,
as it was hauled into the lower depths of the lake. Then it disappeared altogether.

I called at once to Too-Too to get the Doctor's watch out of his
waistcoat and bring it to me. John Dolittle, I knew, was a sturdy
swimmer; but I also knew that the length of time the best swimmer
can stay underwater has to be measured in minutes and seconds. I
was taking no chances. As the little owl gave me the watch, I noted
the exact time, jotting it on a package nearby.

"Huh!" grunted Cheapside. "Just like the good old Doc, that.
'E no sooner harrives on the spot, after a trip of three or four thousand miles, then 'e jumps out of 'is clothes, jumps out of 'is canoe,
jumps on an alligator, and continues 'is journey on 'orseback underwater, as you might say. 'E don't waste no time. There ain't many
doctors would do that for their patients—specially if they knew
they wasn't goin' to get paid nothing for the visit."

But I was too anxious to listen to the sparrow's chatter. My
eyes were on the second hand of the watch. I had now asked
Polynesia to have Jim stay close to the canoe; for I intended, as
soon as a minute and a half had gone by, to send him down after

the Doctor. . . . One minute and ten seconds—the tiny hand went jumping round the dial . . . One minute and twenty seconds . . . One minute and twenty-five seconds—my right arm rose straight up to give Jim the signal I had arranged. And then suddenly there was a swirl in the water at the canoe's other end. The Doctor's head appeared. He was gasping for breath. He still had hold of the towing-rope. But now there were three or four crocodiles around him who seemed to be bearing him up. However, I could tell at once that he was all right, even if badly exhausted.

Polynesia called to me to come forward and make the rope fast, so that if the Doctor went unconscious he could not slip back underwater. Then the crocodile nosed the canoe across to the shore of the island. This took only a few minutes. And soon we had the canoe alongside a gravel landing where we could unload. I spread a tarpaulin and got John Dolittle to lie down and rest; meanwhile Chee-Chee slung up a hammock; and Jip scurried around and collected wood for a fire.

Presently, John Dolittle crouched over a cheerful blaze. Polynesia, Cheapside, and I waited close to him till he should have breath enough to speak.

At last, with a deep sigh, he straightened his shoulders, then turned and looked at me, smiling,

"By George, Stubbins!" said he in a low voice. "Kind of—kind of out of training—for that sort of thing. . . . My goodness, I'm winded!"

"It's not surprising, Doctor," I answered. "You gave me a real scare. One minute and thirty-one seconds."

"Hah, good old Stubbins!" he puffed. "So you kept track of me with the watch, eh? What *would* I do without you?"

"How did you find things, Doctor? Is the turtle still alive?"

"I'm pretty sure he is," said John Dolittle. "It's hard to tell, though. We can't wake him up. He's fast asleep."

"Asleep!" I cried. "I don't understand."

"Conditions," said the Doctor. "Just hibernation conditions. The earthquake that buried Mudface came at the exact month of the year which is the regular time for turtles to start their hibernation—their winter sleep."

"But, Doctor," I said, "do you mean he never even knew he was in any danger at all?"

"Well, Stubbins, perhaps no danger of getting killed or seriously injured, no. They are naturally a very calm race, turtles. He has buried himself before, of course, every year. But not so deep. Goodness knows how he would have got out, after his hibernation was over—if Cheapside and Becky had not come to Africa."

There was a moment's silence. It was broken by Cheapside, who had been listening thoughtfully.

"Asleep, 'is 'e? Well, swap me pink, Doc! After we makes a record trip to rescue 'im, we finds the old boy takin' 'is after-dinner nap!—Criminy! That's what I'll do next time Becky starts one of 'er lectures on the duties of a good father. 'Hush, my dear!' I'll say. 'I feels my 'iberation comin' on.'" (Cheapside closed his eyes, sighing noisily.) "'*Sh!* Can't you see I'm gettin' drowsy? Bye, bye! You may call me in April—if the weather's good.'"

THE SIXTEENTH CHAPTER

The Voice of Thunder

THE DOCTOR TOLD JIM HE FEARED THAT, even if Mudface was awake—and trying to help lift himself—it would still be unlikely that he could be freed from the grip of that terrible mud-suction. Only after the turtle was able to use his legs to swim with, the Doctor added, would it be possible to get him to the top.

The three crocodiles had already gathered together all the other leaders and heads of families to listen to the Doctor's instructions. And a strange-looking council of war they made, crowding around Big Chief Dolittle (still wrapped in his red blanket).

"Listen, Jim," said the Doctor, "now that you have cleared the gravel off the *top* of the turtle, why not set a big gang to work prying *under* his lower shell—at one point only? I mean, don't let the crocodiles waste their strength working all around him at once. He's much too heavy to lift that way—tons and tons."

"I understand, Doctor," said Jim. "You want us to let the water leak in under him at one place to break the mud-suction?"

"That's it exactly," cried the Doctor. "But for pity's sake, be careful you don't crack his shell. You had better pry him up by the shoulder—a turtle's lower shell is thicker there."

"All right," said Jim. "But in digging down to him, we had to make a deep hole in the floor of the lake. Now it's the same as if he were lying at the bottom of a basin—very little room for us. So I was just thinking that while I have one gang prying him up close to his head, I could set another to work behind his tail—you know, to cut away the wall of the basin."

"A splendid idea, Jim!" cried the Doctor. "You mean you would make a sort of downslope ready behind him. Then, once you get his shoulders free of the suction, he would slide down backward into the deeper water and be able to swim. For he will surely wake up as soon as he feels himself moved. Good! Jim, you should have been an engineer—marvelous!"

I found that, as the Doctor's hopes rose higher, I was becoming strangely thrilled at the thought of actually seeing Mudface, the only living passenger left who had trod the decks of the Ark, the one link in all the animal kingdom between history and the days before history. After all, it was for this that we had come so far. But I never dreamed, as the Doctor finished speaking and started to put his clothes on again, that he meant to try and get the turtle free *that night*!

There was, I suppose, about two hours of daylight left. As soon as the meeting was finished, Jim gave out orders to all the leaders. Then many things seemed to start happening at once. Even with Chee-Chee's help as a translator, I couldn't keep track of it all. But later on I managed to put things together and write them into my notebook.

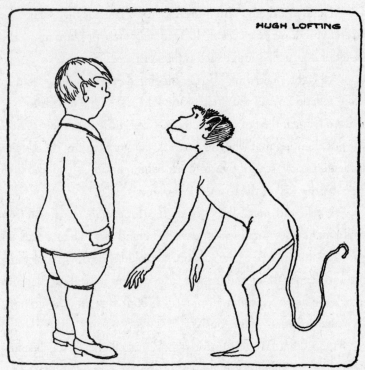

"Even with Chee-Chee's help as a translator, I couldn't keep track of it all."

First of all, a strange noise struck my ears. This was the *plop, plop—splash, splash,* as all those great beasts, in sixes and sevens, threw themselves off the land into the lake. The leaders had been ordered by Jim to divide the diggers into regular work-teams. As the Doctor had told me, it was very exhausting. So, as soon as one lot was tired out, the order would be given to change over: the weary gang would come back to rest; and a fresh lot would *plop, plop* into the water and disappear.

What was going on below, of course, I did not know till afterward. But every once in a while Jim would come and tell the Doctor something; and I hoped it was good news.

After about an hour Jim and his two brothers—all three of them together—brought up some specially important information. (I knew this, because the Doctor clearly became tremendously interested; and he gave them very careful instructions to take back to the workers underwater.)

It turned out that the diggers had scooped out the slope behind the turtle and were now ready to finish prying up in front to let the water under him. John Dolittle told me this was the one part of the whole job where he was afraid that the noses of all those crocodiles, heaving together, might crack or break the turtle's shell—in spite of its thickness.

The way they went about it was very clever, I thought. A dozen crocodiles, set close side by side, thrust their flat, chisel-like noses under the shoulder of the shell, as deep into the mud as they could go. Then a dozen more got up onto the tails of the first lot and bore down with all their weight.

At the first try nothing happened. And Jim's brother was all for sending word up to the Doctor for new instructions. But Jim, it seems, said no: he didn't believe in giving up so easily. Then he sorted out the crocodiles by size; and, taking only the very largest and heaviest, he lined up another two dozen and tried again.

This time they had better success. From the way the water started to flow in under Mudface's body, Jim felt sure that the suction must soon let go. He got two more gangs of heavyweights and lined them up on the turtle's other shoulder, the right one. Then, by heaving first on one side and then on the other, he got the whole of Mudface's front part levered up a good foot out of the mud. And at last, as the water rushed in under the whole length of the turtle from head to tail, the great beast's body slid slowly down the slope prepared for it and rolled over on its back, free!

I cannot say what picture as to Mudface's size I had ever had. Cheapside had spoken of him airily as being "as big as a house"— but then I knew that the sparrow often exaggerated. I had heard the Doctor tell of the turtle's size as "unbelievably large" or "perfectly huge"—which could mean anything.

But when at last I saw him with my own eyes—though really I only saw parts of him that night—I thought I must be having another nightmare (like the one I'd had about the giant snake, back in the swamplands).

Twilight was coming on now. But you could still see pretty well—except where the setting sun threw the island's long shadow on the calm water. John Dolittle had finished dressing and was standing on the shore by our campfire, staring out into wide and silent Junganyika.

Presently, in this darker, shaded part of the lake, I thought I saw something come to the surface, gently breaking the calm of the water—something round and flat, like a ball just afloat. At first it seemed no bigger than a tea tray. But as it rose, it slowly grew—larger and larger and larger still.

Close behind me I heard the Doctor give a long sigh of relief.

"Thank goodness I . . . They've managed it. . . . Here he comes!"

Too-Too, the night-seer, made some clicking noises with his tongue; while little Chee-Chee, always so brave in real danger, whimpered fearfully somewhere in the gloom.

It was getting harder to make things out in the fading daylight. But I could tell that this great mass out there had stopped rising and was slowly moving toward us. And, from the smoothness of its motion, I guessed it must be swimming.

"Well, well, the lucky voyage, Stubbins!" the Doctor whispered over my shoulder. "The lucky voyage!"

John Dolittle was never one to make a show of his feelings. (This, Polynesia had often said, was the most English thing about him.) But as the strong fingers of his right hand suddenly gripped my shoulder, they told me, better than any words, how much this successful ending to our voyage meant for him.

"He's crawling now," I heard him say. "You can tell his feet have touched bottom by the way he moves. You see that? Good! Then his legs—his rheumatism, you know—can't be too bad, or he couldn't even walk that much."

Our campfire gave only a dim light. But I was glad we had built it well back from the water's edge; for if Mudface was coming ashore right here, we did not want it to be in his way. Nearly all of the Doctor's animals had moved inland, too, for fear of being stepped on in the half-dark.

Exactly when I first saw the turtle's head I don't know. My eyes were busy staring down into the water, watching for what might come out of it. There was a single large palm tree quite close to me. I had noticed Chee-Chee the monkey look up at the top of this palm from time to time; and I suppose my own gaze followed his. Anyway, I suddenly saw that, besides the head of the palm tree up there, there was something else, swaying against the sky. It was the same height as the top of the palm—and about the same size. Then, before the Doctor told me, I, too, moved back; I suddenly knew what it was. *It was Mudface's head!*

And, in the way we often get reminded in great moments of things unimportant and far away, I thought of a picture in the

Doctor's library back home. It showed big lizards who roamed the earth thousands of years ago, nibbling the leaves from the tops of the forest.

But my dreaming thoughts were suddenly brought back. The ground beneath my feet seemed to be trembling. Was this another earthquake, I wondered? . . . No. This monster, towering over us, was *speaking* to the Doctor.

How thrilled I was to find I could understand what this thunderous voice was saying! Later, when I was writing out his story of the Flood, I was to miss a word or sentence here and there; and I had to fill them in later. But this evening, when Mudface spoke his first greeting to his old friend, I caught every word of it—perfectly. My hours of study with the little turtles had not been wasted. I felt very proud, I can tell you, as I wrote down the great animal's first rumbling words in my notebook:

"Again, John Dolittle, you come in time of danger, in time of trouble—as you have always done. For this, the creatures of the land, the water, and the air shall remember your name when other men, called *great*, shall be forgotten. Welcome, good friend! Welcome once more to Lake Junganyika!"

PART THREE

THE FIRST CHAPTER

The Hippopotamus Ferryboats

AND NOW, IN A VERY SHORT TIME, THE island was changed in many ways.

For one thing, before General Jim and his great army of the Niger left us, they cleared out a wide space on the high flat top. This was for the camp. They dug a good ditch around it, so that all rainwater would be drained down into the lake. Mudface's old path up to the top had disappeared with the earthquake; and the crocodiles also put that right for us. They made a new fine road from the canoe-landing at the water's edge to the camping ground where it was always dry underfoot.

Here, so much higher than the lake, the sun was often shining; and we could look down upon the tops of colored clouds partly hiding the wide waters of Junganyika.

"Humph!" grunted Cheapside, one day as all of us were gazing down at this strange sight. "Looks like a sea of rollin' rosy pillows, don't it? Makes me feel I ought to be flyin' around over 'em in me nightshirt, blowin' a trumpet."

"Tee, hee, hee!" tittered the white mouse. "Fancy Cheapside as an angel—in a *nightshirt*!"

"And why not, pray?" stormed the London sparrow. "Angels always wears nightshirts—in pictures. It's sort of a uniform with 'em—for flyin'. I suppose you think I ain't good enough to be an angel, eh? Well, let me tell *you* some-think: I want no more sauce from you, Whitey-me-lad. Or you'll suddenly find that smart young mice are wearing their tails shorter this season, see?"

The Doctor and I set up a tent. And the change to sleeping inside, in regular beds of dried, sweet-smelling grass—after several weeks of hammocks—was very pleasant.

And then there was the need for more food to keep us going while we listened to the story of the Flood from Mudface. We had brought only enough from the *Albatross* to last us for our trip up here, being afraid of overloading the canoe. So Polynesia and Chee-Chee set out on foraging expeditions. The parrot and monkey, native Africans, knew how, and where, to look for wild nuts, fruit, honey, and roots which were good to eat.

One sort of food we did *not* have to fetch and carry. A hippopotamus and his wife called upon the Doctor, and wanted to know could they be of any help to him and his party. When they had been told about our need for food, the father hippo asked if we liked rice. The Doctor said, yes, rice was very nourishing. (It turned out that John Dolittle had treated the father, when he was a baby, years ago at his post office, for some trouble.)

Then the hippos said they would see that we got all the wild rice we wanted. And they went off and fetched us enough to last an army for a month.

"That's done it!" grumbled Cheapside to me. "Now old lady

Dab-Dab will serve us rice-puddin' every meal for the rest of the trip. Of all the dull mush! I can stand it once or twice a year. But— oh, what's the use? Sometimes, Tommy, I think the animals are a bit *too* kind to the Doc."

John Dolittle's main concern at first was Mudface's health. He gave him a thorough medical examination. At the end of it he told me that, all in all, he was pleased to find the great beast as well as he was.

"You know, Stubbins," said he, "in a way, I'm back where I was: on the study of long life. Very different from the humankind, of course. Just the same, I could write a book about Mudface's case that would make a whole lot of doctors in London open their eyes."

"I'm sure you could," I agreed, exchanging glances with Polynesia, who was listening to our talk. "But you want to get the story of the Flood from him again, don't you, first?"

"Quite so, quite so," said he. "I was only telling you about my examination of him. I feared it might be weeks and weeks before I could let him tell his story to us. But now," the Doctor went on, "after looking him over, I think it will be only a matter of days, instead of weeks."

"Oh, that's splendid, Doctor," said I.

"In spite of his enormous age—so great we can only guess at it—I find nothing we would call radically wrong. The rheumatic condition is worse of course, I expected that. I've written out a prescription for him. Our difficulty will be to make up enough, you know. The medicine must be taken, not in teaspoonfuls, but in barrelfuls! We can get everything I'll need for this tonic in the jungle. But how to get enough. That's my problem."

I asked why he did not speak to our hippo friends about this, and he said he intended to.

Those strange and gentle beasts (they lived almost entirely on wild rice; and Cheapside said, of course, that accounted for their having no character at all) turned out to be most helpful. Mr. Hippo took the Doctor on his back and swam off with him in search of medicinal herbs. He looked a strange sight, with his high hat and all, astride that wide back, crossing the lake. Cheapside roared with laughter; and even the Doctor realized how comical he looked.

"Hippopotamus means *river horse*," he laughed back at us. "They're very comfortable, plump and well padded. Too bad the Puddleby newspapermen aren't here now! Good-bye!—I'll see you later."

And thus, as old Mudface himself had said, the creatures of the wild remembered John Dolittle and his kind deeds; they tried in every way to repay him.

All sorts of animals came to welcome him to Africa. They were all very respectful, staring at him in wonder—as though he were something magical. A good few of them, I suspected, came just out of curiosity, or to be able to boast to their children that they had actually seen the great man himself. But there were others who turned out to be very useful to us in setting up our camp and making our work lighter in many ways.

A large band of monkeys (most of them were cousins of Chee-Chee's) traveled two or three hundred miles to visit us. When they reached the shores of the lake they could get no farther. So they called across to us in a loud chorus of howls and shrieks. Chee-Chee heard them and told the Doctor what it was. Then John

Dolittle asked Mr. and Mrs. Hippo if they would kindly swim over and ferry the monkeys across to the island.

This was done. And I believe there must have been a good thousand of them. Every single monkey had brought a couple of bananas with him—which they knew the Doctor was especially fond of. We had not tasted any since we left Fantippo; so we had a grand feast that night. And Gub-Gub enjoyed it no end because we saved all the banana skins for him—which he preferred to the fruit itself.

Turtletown

WHAT THE DOCTOR SAID CAME TRUE: as soon as he mixed enough of the medicine and Mudface started taking it regularly, we could almost see the giant turtle getting better by the hour. John Dolittle was a great doctor—as well as a great naturalist.

This large band of monkeys who came to visit him stayed with us till we left; and it was almost unbelievable how helpful they turned out to be.

They were a bit scared of Mudface at first, of his truly tremendous size. But they quickly got over that. And as soon as they learned what the Doctor wanted, they built huts around our camping ground. I never saw such fast and clever workmen. They dug holes, using their paws to scoop out the sand. And in these holes they set posts, about as thick as your arm. Then they covered the roofs of the huts with palm leaves—and the walls the same. They left spaces for just a door and a window.

In no time at all, it seemed, our camp (which before had been one single tent) had a cookhouse; a comfortable, roomy bunk-house where the Doctor and I slept; a storage hut in a cool place for keeping food; a surgery where the Doctor made up medicines and attended to any animals who were sick; and a big roofed shelter for Mudface himself. Altogether, it looked like a little village.

Cheapside, who was perched on my shoulder as I watched the monkeys cleaning up around the new buildings, remarked:

"Pretty nifty, eh, Tommy? Look, we got a street-cleaning department and all. We gotter give them monks credit. They're smart. It ain't everybody could put a town up for you in only a day. All we needs now is a few lampposts and a copper walking up and down. Yes, pretty nifty village. What'll we call it? . . . Why, *I* know! *Turtletown*, o' course!"

And still another hut was called the office. This was set well away from any of the others, so that I could write my notes without the noise of monkeys chattering nearby. Also, I had made up my mind that *this time* the notebooks about the story of the Flood should be kept from harm, so far as I could prevent it.

Many notebooks I had already filled with things the Doctor wanted taken down on our journey here from Puddleby; and these I carefully brought from the canoe-landing and stored in a dry hole in the floor of the office. Jip and Polynesia took it in turns to mount guard over this hut for me, night and day. And later, as each new notebook was finished, it was put away safely in the hole. I found a few large stones to cover the hole—so the notebooks would be protected in case the hut should take fire.

The day after the monkeys finished Turtletown, the Doctor said that Mudface should be well enough by tomorrow to tell us his History of the Deluge.

"But we must go easy with him, to begin with, Stubbins—say, half an hour or so a day—and see how it goes. Remember there are those monkey carpenters who want to listen. So, with them all, poor Mudface is going to have a large audience to talk to. I'll give you my watch. Keep an eye on it, will you? Don't let him talk more than three-quarters of an hour the first day, eh?"

"Very good, Doctor," I said. "I'll signal you at forty minutes. . . . I only hope I can understand him."

"Ah, don't worry about that," he said with a smile. "You can always ask us afterward—if you get stuck, Stubbins."

"When will we begin, Doctor?" I asked.

"Tomorrow evening, Stubbins. Mudface is always in better form at night. We'll start after supper—an early supper."

And so, the following evening we gathered at the turtle's shelter. All the Doctor's family came: Jip the dog; Too-Too, the owl mathematician of marvelous memory; Dab-Dab the duck; Chee-Chee, proudly at the head of all the visiting monkeys; Whitey, the inquisitive mouse who wouldn't have missed the show for anything; and Gub-Gub the pig, who was also present. Then there was Cheapside the London sparrow, and Polynesia the African parrot. These two famous quarrelers, while pretending to be bored by the turtle's story, were, I knew, far more interested than they would admit. And Becky, Cheapside's wife, she came along too.

The big crowd found places—somehow—around Mudface within the shed. (It was not much more than a roof supported by poles.)

From this high ground you could see out in all directions.

The view of lake Junganyika was extremely lovely as the big stars came out over the quiet water and spangled it with their silvery light.

And so I started the hardest—and perhaps the most important—job of note-taking that I had ever done in all my experience as the Doctor's secretary.

The Third Chapter

Days of the Deluge

VERY WELL, THEN, DOCTOR," SAID THE
giant turtle, "I will tell you the story of the Flood just
as though I had never told you any of it before. It is a
good thing that we have this second chance—since all
your writings have been lost.

"When I was a young turtle, I was captured with five others
and put in a menagerie. It was a sort of zoological gardens—owned
by the great King Mashtu. May his bones rot in the mud! Would
that all memory of him might be wiped out forever!"

As the turtle stopped a moment and glared savagely out across
the gloomy lake, the Doctor asked:

"You sound bitter, Mudface. King Mashtu did you harm?"

"I should say he did," growled the enormous beast, "to the
whole world!"

The look in the turtle's eyes changed—though he still stared
out across the waters—a look of memories: sad, fond, thrilling, all
changing and mixed up.

"Out there, John Dolittle," said he after a moment, "in the middle of the lake, beneath hundreds of feet of water, lie the ruins of the city of Shalba, King Mashtu's capital. Once it was the proudest, most beautiful city in the world. It had everything: a grand, royal palace for the king; lovely buildings of white marble; shops that sold anything you could wish; theaters; great libraries filled with books brought from every country on earth; an enormous circus; a race-track; parks of flowering trees—and a zoo where wild animals were kept. And it was there, to the zoo, that I was brought when I was captured.

"The head-keeper of the zoo was a very old man. He too had been captured—taken prisoner in the wars by King Mashtu's gener-als. This man, in his own country, had been what is called a patriarch. And all of his family were also brought to the city of Shalba and made to work in King Mashtu's service. But the patriarch himself, for a special reason, was made head-keeper of the zoo. He was very old— for a man—six hundred years of age. His name was Noah."

"Ah!" said the Doctor. "I had guessed it would be Noah. But for what reason, Mudface, was he made zookeeper?"

"Because," the turtle answered, "he spoke animal languages. He was the first and only man, besides yourself, John Dolittle, who could understand animal talk. Having lived six hundred years, you see, he had plenty of time to learn."

"Of course, of course," said the Doctor. "And how wonder-fully well he must have learned to speak in that time!"

"No, there you're mistaken, Doctor. He could make him-self understood, it is true. But he could not chat in turtle talk, for example, half as well as you can—nor even as well as Tommy, here. And as for writing down things, he *never* learned. He was not as wise and clever as he was cracked up to be. In fact, often he was downright stupid—as you will see later."

I was pleased by the turtle's praise; and I looked up to smile. But Mudface was going on with his story—this time much faster. And I had to hurry on, scribbling away like mad.

"Although," said Mudface, "I was much smaller in those days than I am now, still I was by far the biggest and oldest of the six turtles who had been captured. And you may remember, Doctor, my kind is both sea turtle and fresh-water turtle."

"Yes, I remember that," said John Dolittle. "You are the only one of your sort left in the world today. But please go on."

"Well, they prepared a pond for us in the zoo gardens. It had no mud in it, only clean bright gravel—which we didn't like at all. We loved mud. The king and his people would come to look at us through the strong iron fence surrounding the pool. And sometimes I, the Giant Turtle as I was called, gave the visitors rides on my back—though it was as much as your life was worth if the keeper didn't watch me all the time. Because I used to spill the people off into a puddle, when I could find one, pretending it was an accident.

"We were fed by Noah. The other five turtles, even if they were unhappy, ate their food regularly. But I did not. I was separated from my wife."

"Er, Mudface," the Doctor interrupted. "How is it your wife wasn't captured with you?"

"Well, you see, Doctor," said Mudface, "Belinda was in another part of the country visiting her relatives. Of course, I was glad for her sake she was still free, but I was dreadfully lonely for her. . . . " Mudface stopped a moment, sighing in memory.

"Oh dear," said the Doctor, "then that is the reason Belinda is not with you now—you never saw her again?"

"Yes, indeed," said the turtle, "I did see her soon after my capture. I'll tell you about that as my story progresses."

Mudface paused, wrinkling his brows. "But her absence *now* puzzles me. She left quite suddenly a few months ago—just before the earthquake—and I haven't heard from her since. I'm worried."

"Ain't that just like a woman, Doc?" said Cheapside. "Galavantin' off when 'er 'usband needs 'er most."

"Quiet, Cheapside," said John Dolittle. "I'm sure Belinda will be back immediately when she hears about Mudface's trouble."

The giant turtle raised his head and smiled at the Doctor. "Thank you, John Dolittle," he said. "Perhaps I shouldn't worry. Belinda has always been able to take care of herself." He settled his shell comfortably and went on.

"I was pretty unhappy. I moped and ate no food at all. Noah told this to the king and asked to be allowed to let me go. But Mashtu said I was the finest and the biggest of the collection; and that I would soon settle down and eat my food. But I didn't. I hated the life of the zoo. Still, as you know, turtles can go a long time without eating. And I did not die.

"All six of us spent most of the time trying to work out some plan of escape. The fence around our pond was not very high, but it was too much for a turtle to climb over. I was the oldest and strongest; and the others looked to me to find them a way to liberty and freedom. And one night I thought of a clever idea for undermining the low wall, on which the iron fencing was set, and getting out underneath the fence—instead of over it. For three whole nights I worked, burrowing and scratching. At last I got one of the big square stones loose enough to pull out. Freedom was in sight!

"But we agreed to wait till the following night, so as to have plenty of darkness to get away in. The zoological gardens were large; and turtles are slow on land.

"Well, the next night came; and my five companions waited breathlessly while I pulled the stone down into the pond and then made the hole large enough to climb through. All went well. We got out under the fence and started to cross the park in the dim light of a rising moon. But we had scarcely gone twenty steps when the park gates opened to a blare of trumpets. The king himself entered with a party of friends to show them his collection of animals! With him came hundreds of guards and torchbearers. Mashtu especially wished to show the visitors his new turtles. He made straight for our pool.

"Escape then, for such slow creatures as we, was of course impossible. We were caught at once and put back. The fencing, with its wall, was made stronger than ever, so that we shouldn't get out again.

"We were all terribly downhearted. My grand plan had only made things worse than they were before.

"However, Noah had an assistant-keeper, little more than a boy—and he had been, like Noah, captured in the wars and brought here from some foreign land. He took pity on us turtles—out of sympathy, I suppose, for fellow prisoners. He was our one comfort. His name was Eber. And I shall speak of him again, often.

"He had begun as a gardener—at which work he was very skillful. But later he was put under Noah, in the menagerie, as assistant-keeper.

"Eber had a kind heart; and he did his best to make our lives happier: bringing us special foods; spraying us with fresh cold water when the weather was unbearably hot; and doing anything else he could for our well-being.

"Eber had fallen in love with a beautiful young girl called Gaza. She, too, was a slave. To foreign travelers, Shalba—always boasting of her freedom—must have seemed full of slaves. Gaza, who had a truly lovely voice, used to sing for Mashtu's chief wife, who lived in a smaller palace of her own—called the Queen's Pavilion—close by the zoological gardens.

"And often in the twilight I listened to her songs of far-off lands, which reached us on the evening wind in our wretched prison-pond. Mashtu's spies discovered that Eber was meeting her secretly in the park. As a punishment, Eber was beaten most unmercifully. He could not walk for days after. King Mashtu was a cruel-hearted man.

"After a month or two had rolled by, life for me was suddenly made much brighter. Belinda, that clever wife of mine, found out where I had been taken. And she used to come at night and talk to me through the bars of the fence. You can have no idea how much this meant to me. I had begun to give up all hope—to look forward to nothing but this stupid life of prison for the rest of my days. Belinda's visits made me fearful that she might be caught; but just seeing and talking with her every night put new heart into me. She was so cheerful and so certain that we would yet escape some way, if only we'd be patient.

"Now, I had always given a good deal of study to the weather, even as a youngster. And by this time I had become quite well known among all the water-creatures as a good weather-prophet.

I used to foretell the rain-showers for the other turtles in our pond. You see, we looked forward to them. We like rain. It is pleasant to feel it trickling down your shell and running off the tip of your nose—exceedingly refreshing in hot climates. And on account of my being able to tell when it was going to rain, the weather became the favorite thing for us to talk about. It is hard to find much to chat over when you are fenced in a pond only fifty feet across. And Noah himself, who often used to listen to us, got in the habit of talking of the weather, too. And so it was handed down, as the favorite thing to talk about, for thousands of years.

"Well, one day a gale sprang up toward evening. The trees of the park bent down before it like lily stalks; and big gravel stones blew along the walks just as if they were dust. The other turtles gathered around me, asking what I thought of it. I looked up at the sky and saw a whirlpool of angry black clouds spinning, twisting and crossing, the heavens. It was different from anything I had ever seen.

"'Cousins,' I said, turning to the other turtles, 'it will rain before night.'

"'Good!' said they. 'It is uncomfortably hot.'

"Suddenly a terrific crash of thunder seemed to split the air; and the clouds came right down low, wrapping themselves about the trees.

"'My friends,' said I, 'it will be a great, great rain.'

"'Good!' they said. 'The water in our pond needs changing badly.'

"Then, with a roar, the heavens seemed to open; and a great flash of lightning spat earthward, ripping a stout oak tree, which stood near our fence, clean in two, from fork to roots. Suddenly I wondered if Eber was in safety.

"'Turtles,' I said, 'somehow I'm sure the time of our escape is close at hand. This will be the greatest of great rains. These men are but weak creatures in some things. Many will be killed. They can stand only so much rain, while we turtles love it. In ten days from tonight the water in this pool will rise above the fence, freeing us to swim where we will.'

"'Good!' said they. 'Long have we suffered in slavery. Welcome, rain! How sweet will be the mudbanks of liberty!'

"Now, *that* rain began falling in a peculiar way. It started on a Friday—no, it was a Monday—no, now wait a second. . . . Let me see, it was—"

The listening Cheapside (I had thought he was asleep) opened one eye and muttered:

"Let's hope it wasn't an Easter Monday—spoil the holiday. There ain't nothin' worse than a wet Bank Holiday. Come on, old Muddypuss, make up yer mind. It's past bedtime."

"Anyway," whispered Dab-Dab the duck, "there's no one can argue with him. That's one thing sure."

"Well," the turtle went on, "whatever day of the week it was, the rain began in the forenoon; and it began very gently. At first my friends were very disappointed. And they thought I must be mistaken as a weather-prophet—that it was going to be only an ordinary shower.

"'Wait!' I said to them angrily. 'Have I ever foretold the weather wrong for you? This rain will last for forty days, beginning light but growing heavy. After the first ten days, as I have promised, you will be free. But at the end of the forty days, King Mashtu the proud, and his city of Shalba, shall be no more. The earth will be covered in water. For this, brother turtles, *this is the Deluge.*'

"'Good!' said they again. 'What could be more delightful than a deluge? A lovely flood! It is high time these men who have enslaved us should be washed away. In a world of water, we, the slow walkers and swift swimmers, will be the great ones of the earth.'

"To this for a moment I said nothing. My mind had strayed away from them and their chatter.

"At last, my voice sounding strangely serious even to my own ears, I answered:

"'Perhaps . . . perhaps.'

"I was thinking—of Eber. . . ."

THE FOURTH CHAPTER

The Elephants' March

REMEMBERING SUDDENLY WHAT THE DOC-tor had told me about keeping an eye on the time, I grabbed his watch out of my pocket, as Mudface stopped a moment. My goodness! The turtle had been talking a whole half hour longer than John Dolittle had said he should—to begin with. I made a signal to the Doctor that, for tonight, our time was up. He rose from his seat at once.

"Thank you, Mudface," said he. "There are a million questions already I would like to ask you about those times. But you must take a dose of your medicine now and get to bed. We will look forward—if you will be so kind—to hearing more of your story tomorrow night."

"You can bet on that," said Cheapside sleepily. "We're going to be listenin' to *that* old chap's yarn for months yet."

As the Doctor and I prepared to leave for our bunkhouse a few doors farther up the main street of Turtletown, Mudface started humming a tune. The sound—though not unpleasant to the ear—

was so unbelievably powerful that the earth shook beneath us. The Doctor paused at the door.

"Pardon me," said he. "But what is that tune?"

"It is the 'Elephants' March,'" said the turtle. "It was always played in Shalba, on circus days, for the elephants' procession on their way to the show. I learned it by heart; it's become a habit for me to hum it as I'm going to bed."

"Very interesting indeed," said John Dolittle. "I've always been keen about music myself. But never in my wildest dreams did I expect to hear a march that was written before the Flood. You must teach it to me sometime. We will write it out—the score, I mean. Good night, Mudface."

As we started off down the street, the pavement still trembled with the humming from the big shelter we had left.

"As I believe I remarked before," said Cheapside, who was perched on the Doctor's shoulder, "a voice like old Mudpan's is kind of wasted in this gawd-forsaken swamp. He ought to get a job as foghorn on an ocean rock somewhere. Ships could hear 'im twenty miles away."

"Tee, hee, hee!" tittered the white mouse from my left pocket.

"What an experience, what a story!" muttered the Doctor, his mind still full of the Deluge.

Once in our snug bunkhouse—terribly tired—I was soon asleep. Never had I written so fast. My right hand was so cramped I wondered if I'd ever be able to straighten it again. And all night long, though I never woke once, dreams kept flitting through my mind—and always about the same person. . . . In my sleep, like Mudface, I was thinking of Eber.

THE FIFTH CHAPTER

Fireworks for the King's Birthday

THE NEXT EVENING MUDFACE SEEMED TO BE feeling better still. Waiting for us to settle down, he looked fresher. And his voice sounded keener and less tired when he spoke.

"Then," said he, "we turtles for the present, just sat behind our prison bars and waited as before. But our mood was different. For instead of thinking dreary thoughts, we were dreaming great dreams. Where would we go when, for the first time in so long, big voyagings were made easy? Each of us of course had a different plan in his heart as to what he would do first with his new freedom.

"How clearly I remember it! It was King Mashtu's birthday, that Friday—or whatever day it was—and a public holiday. There had been shows going on at the circus ever since midday; and the royal elephants had paraded to that march I hummed last night. Though the music sounded very sour, with the band's instruments all wet.

"The day's celebrations were to end with a display of fireworks in the Royal Zoological Park. Through the fencing around our pond we watched them getting ready for this grand finish. The wind had now eased off, though the rain still fell evenly. A deathly calm hung over the twilit park, the sort of calm that can turn a steady rain into a cyclone.

"With a most unmusical blare from wet trumpets, the king entered the park and gave orders for the fireworks to begin. The darkness, with the overcast sky, was now almost complete; and lanterns of colored paper had been lit and hung in the trees. But they did not stay lit long.

"Oh, how we chuckled in our prison-pond as the rain suddenly grew heavier! The last of the lanterns flickered out. And when the men tried to light the fireworks, not a single one of them would go off. *How* we chuckled!"

Mudface leaned down to moisten his throat from a calabash nearby filled with muddy lake water. (He always liked his drinking water muddy.) And while he was at this, I scribbled away in the notebook more furiously than ever; for he was talking fast again and I had fallen behind.

"The magicians," he went on presently, "and the astrologers of the court looked up at the black, starless sky; and said the rain was a bad omen. They did not recommend that His Majesty go on with the celebrations tonight. The king, trying to take the matter lightly, then gave orders to put off the fireworks and merrymaking till tomorrow. He turned and left by the same gate through which he had entered. But I noticed that on passing through it he signaled to the trumpeters to stop their blowing. This could be easily understood; for the poor drenched men were now blowing nothing but water out of their trumpets instead of music. We could just see the dim forms of Mashtu and his family as they entered the lighted palace in the distance.

"The astrologers looked up at the sky."

"'Cousins,' said I to my fellow prisoners, 'King Mashtu enters his palace for the last time. Never again will he leave dry-shod.'

"Beneath the now heavier rain the crowd which had gathered for the fireworks scattered to their homes; and the park was soon left empty. In our pond we frisked and frolicked and splashed water at one another, like kittens at tag. Even I so far forgot my dignity and age as to join in the fun. Throughout the whole night it rained, heavier and heavier; and all night we played on, celebrating Mashtu's wettest birthday.

"Well, after that date we did not see the sun again for forty days. Next morning, when dawn came, it was merely a murky light, little better than twilight—and it was still raining. A few brave citizens came out with umbrellas, to see if the jollifications were going on as the king had promised. But all they found was mud. The royal palace was closed. The people hurried back home again.

"Late that afternoon my wife came to see me, walking carefully across the park behind the cover of the trees, lest she be seen. When she was within hearing I shouted to her:

"'There's no need to keep yourself hidden now. No one will bother you anymore. This is the Deluge!'

"'As soon as the park is flooded deep enough,' I said, 'we are going to swim out over the top of this fencing. See, the water of our pond has already risen two inches in the night.'

"My poor wife, who had already suffered much worry through our separation, was very happy. But she could not believe that our prison days were really over.

"'Are you quite sure, my dear,' she said, 'that enough rain will fall to float you out?'

"'Am I sure!' I cried, astonished. 'Listen, Belinda: Have I, as a weather-prophet, ever led you wrong? In nine days I will join you on the other side of this wretched fence, or my name's not Mudface.'

"I could see I had taken a load off her mind. Her mood changed. And suddenly all seven of us, out of sheer recklessness, turned and shouted toward the king's palace as hard as we could:

"'Hooray!—Happy Birthday, Mashtu!'

"But no one came out to bid us be still.

"Now, when I had foretold our freedom in ten days' time, I had calculated on a growing fall of rain each day. And I was right. The next morning the level of the water in our pool had risen another three inches. And we could see that many parts of the park now lay wholly underwater. The day after that—it was a Sunday—or I think it was. No, maybe—"

"Oh, never mind the day of the week!" Dab-Dab snapped. "Just tell us what happened; don't bother about what day it was."

"I don't believe he *knows* the days of the week," muttered Too-Too.

"Well, you can't never tell," said Cheapside, as the turtle still tried to remember. "Maybe in those days they had two Sundays every week, one at each end, like. You can't never tell. They was a churchgoing lot, them antedelvulians."

"The next day," said the turtle presently, "Belinda, who had gone into the city to find out how things were getting along, came back to us in a great state of excitement.

"'What do you think, Mudface?' she said. 'Just outside the town, where the old racetrack was, there's a man trying to build an enormous boat. And all sorts of animals, hundreds of them, are standing around watching him!'

"'What does the man look like?' I asked.

"'He seems terribly old,' said she. 'But—listen: he can *speak to the animals in their own languages*!'

"'Why, that's Noah,' I said, 'our head zookeeper. I suppose he guesses this is no ordinary rain—that a flood is coming—and he's making a ship to save himself in.'

"Well," (old Mudface looked out over the lake, and something like a smile played around his grim mouth) "the great hour arrived at last—on the tenth day, as I had said it would. The water level in our pool had kept on creeping up and up till at last I could put my front claws on the top of the railing. Then with a mighty heave I pulled myself over the fence into freedom! Belinda and

I embraced each other; and both of us wept tears of joy into the flooded park.

"I knew the other turtles would be all right now; so, partly swimming and partly walking, I led Belinda toward the main gate. I wanted to see the sights—and especially Noah's ship. Of course by this time water covered most of the park. Only the heads of the trees stood up out of it. As we passed the king's palace we saw people leaving by the windows in beds or rafts or anything that would float. Farther on we saw that the river that ran through Shalba was now a mad, roaring torrent. The stone bridge near the Silk Market had been swept away like a piece of paper. Indeed, only the higher ground in the city could be seen at all—thus it was not easy to tell whereabouts in the town you were. And the people were leaving even these higher places and making off for the mountains.

"These mountains stood about two miles from the city. And everyone thought that if he could only reach them he would be safe.

"Everyone, I ought to say, except the patriarch Noah. My wife, after we had swum and scrabbled around sightseeing, guided me to where she had seen Noah building a ship. This was on a high flat piece of land at the western end of the city. It had been a racetrack. It was now used as a timber yard.

"I have often thought that many more people would have been saved from the Flood if they had only realized, at the start of the forty days' rain, that they must take to strong boats, prepared to live in them a long time. But everyone thought that any minute the rain would stop. So all they did, when the ground floors of their homes became flooded, was to go upstairs and wait at the top windows. And by the time they saw that the water was going to rise right over their roofs, it was too late to build boats of any kind.

"But Noah must have known somehow—or guessed—what was going to happen. Perhaps he heard me promising the forty days' rain.

"Anyway, reaching the old racetrack, we found him with a tape and rule in his hands, measuring beams of timber. His thumb, which he had hit with a hammer, was done up in a dirty rag. He looked very wet, unhappy, and upset. He hadn't done much boat-building yet; all he seemed to be doing for the present was measuring—just measuring miserably in the rain. I heard him mutter to himself over and over again the same thing: 'A hundred cubits by fifty by thirty.' And every time he said it he looked more puzzled than ever.

"...just measuring miserably in the rain"

"He had his three sons Ham, Shem, and Japheth with him, the sons' wives—and his own wife. But none of them seemed to be helping him much. The men were quarreling about who had lost the hammer; and the women were arguing over who should have the best room on the boat when it was finished.

"And all the while the water kept rising around them. The flat island, on which they worked, kept growing smaller. And Noah kept on measuring—and muttering—in the rain."

Noah's Ark and the Great Wave

ISTEN, MUDFACE," SAID THE DOCTOR, THE following evening, "before you begin tonight, may I ask you something?"

"Of course, John Dolittle," said the turtle. "I'll be glad to answer your questions anytime—if I can."

"Well," said the Doctor, "couldn't you tell us a few things about what the world was like *before* the Flood?"

"What sort of things, Doctor?"

"Well," said John Dolittle, "for instance, how did King Mashtu become so great that his palaces had foreign slaves brought from every corner of the earth? How were these slaves transported? What was the most important trade or business of the people who lived in King Mashtu's kingdom; and—er— oh, a thousand things about the music and art of that strange civilization."

In silence Mudface thought a moment before he answered.

"Suppose, Doctor, you first let me get further on with the story of the Deluge and what followed it. I'm sure you will find many of your questions answered as I go along."

"Certainly," said the Doctor. "Please begin."

"Now, at either end of this old racetrack," Mudface went on, "two crowds of different animals stood around waiting. They were waiting, we guessed, for the ship to be finished and ready. It was, we learned later, called the *Ark*. Just as well, because it couldn't be called a ship: the *Stable* would have been a better name. These waiting creatures were wet, but patient and quiet. All except the cats—you know, Doctor—tigers, leopards, panthers, and beasts like that. Their behavior was *not* good—cats don't like getting wet. They were snapping at the other animals and pushing everyone out of the way—so as to be ready to rush for the driest places on the Ark as soon as Noah gave the word.

"As soon as the patriarch Noah caught sight of my wife and myself, he said: 'Ah, turtles!' Then he read down a long damp paper that he brought out from a pocket of his gown, containing instructions about the Ark. I've no idea where he got it from. Presently he ticked off a name in the list. 'Go and stand over there,' he ordered us. 'I have no turtles as yet.'"

"Pardon me, Mudface," said the Doctor. "But did they have regular paper then—in Shalba?"

"Oh yes, indeed," said the turtle. "They had everything—or so it seemed to me."

"Make a note of that, Stubbins, please—*paper*."

"Very good, Doctor," said I, jotting it down.

"Excuse the interruption," said John Dolittle. "Go on, Mudface—if you will, please."

"'We don't want to go into your Ark,' I said to Noah. 'We turtles can swim. We *like* deluges.'

"'Don't argue with me,' he said angrily, going back to his measuring. 'You're down on the passenger list and you'll have to come. . . . Let me see: a hundred cubits by fifty by thirty. It's that window that . . .'"

"Shiver my timbers!" muttered Polynesia, the sailor. "'A hundred by fifty by thirty'; sounds like a barrel to me."

"Yes," groaned Cheapside, "and mark you, only *one* window is mentioned—for all them people and animals. *Phew*! Ain't you glad you wasn't at sea then, old Pollypatriarch?"

"So," said Mudface, "Belinda and I started walking toward the north end of the racetrack to join the crowd of waiting animals.

"'No, not there,' Noah shouted after us. 'That's the end for the clean beasts. It says I'm to keep them separate. You creep. You belong to the *unclean* beasts. Up this other end. Hurry along!'

"I was furious. 'What do you mean: *unclean beasts*?' I asked the old man. 'I'm as clean as you are.'

"As a matter of fact, the patriarch did look frightfully bedraggled and messy after ten days of measuring in the rain.

"'Oh, don't argue with him,' Belinda whispered. 'Let him get on building the ship—or all these animals who can't swim will be drowned before he has it finished.'

"I did as she said. But as I moved off, I couldn't help firing a last shot at Noah over my shoulder.

"'Listen,' I called, 'we turtles *live* in water, washing all the time. You're a fine one to talk! *Your* beard has mashed potatoes in it—yes, and prune stones as well!'

"I was never so angry in my life."

Mudface hesitated a second, as though to calm himself down before going on with his story.

"Now, the citizens of Shalba—or what was left of the poor wretches—had all by this time gone off to the mountains. We could see them from the racetrack, herding like sheep here and there on the slopes, gradually being driven higher and higher. It was lucky for Noah that they forgot about the high flat land of the racetrack or he would have certainly been mobbed by folk, clamoring for a place on the Ark. And of course the citizens, once they were on the mountains, could not come back. Because now, between us and them, there was a lake ten miles long.

"Well, for days and days my wife and I stood among the other waiting animals at the south end of the racetrack—wondering why, if we were unclean animals, anyone was bothering to save us at all. Every hour the rain grew fiercer—so fierce that if there ever was any difference between *clean* and *unclean* beasts, nobody could tell it after a wash like that.

"The middle of the racetrack—where the ship-building gave room—was piled high with bales of hay, sacks of corn, peanuts and suchlike, to feed the animals. No cover had been spread over this fodder; and of course most of it was already soaked and waterlogged.

"The workers at last realized that something should be done about this—that the ship's main deck must be finished in a hurry to protect all that food from being spoiled. They stopped quarreling about the tools and set to ship-building with a will. By the end of the thirtieth day, the Ark began to look like a real boat.

"And a very good thing it was, too. For the downpour had been getting worse and worse—so that Noah's family could scarcely see one another through the curtain of rain. Although the ground was not yet underwater, the mud was terrific. Then, to add to the mess, Noah said the Ark had to be tarred—inside and out—before it put to sea. It was in his instructions, he said, and must be done.

"The old man was awfully particular about those instructions. And when he wasn't getting in the men's way, measuring, he was studying that piece of paper.

"Then they got barrels of tar and started messing up the Ark inside and out. Before long they had the tar all mixed up in the mud under their feet; they had it on the tools; they had it all over their hands and faces. And the wives couldn't tell one husband from another.

"At last, on the night of the thirty-eighth day of rain, everything was in readiness. And after Noah had read his instructions for the last time, he folded the paper up and put it in his pocket. There was a long, heavy gangplank leading up to a door in the ship's side. And standing at the head of this plank, Noah faced the animals gathered in the race-track and shouted (the falling rain was real noisy now): 'All aboard! Unclean beasts for'ard; clean beasts aft; and my family amidships.'

"Then all the animals rushed to get into the Ark. And Noah was knocked right off the gangplank into the mud by two big deer who got there first. Some time was lost before things were straightened out. And Noah and his sons made the animals walk in, two by two, in a proper orderly manner. It took hours and hours to get them all in this way. And just as the last tail was disappearing through the Ark's door, Noah remembered the fodder!

"Then a terrible argument broke out among the sons, Ham, Shem, and Japheth. It seems Noah had told them to be sure and remind him about the fodder before the animal passengers were let into the Ark; and now each one of his sons was saying it wasn't *his* fault. And it came out in the argument that every one of those

"Then all the animals rushed to get into the Ark."

young men had passed on the reminding job to one of the others.
Then of course each had proceeded to forget all about the fodder,
which was still out there in the wet.

"The argument among the sons got so nasty that at last their
parents had to interfere.

"There were many tons of stuff that had to be brought in. The
only thing Noah could do now was to fetch out all the animals again
(that is the beasts of burden, like horses and donkeys and camels),
load them up with the hay and corn, and bring it aboard.

"Belinda and I began to grow nervous over this last delay,

because the storm had really become terrible by this time. However, unbelievable though it may seem, they did get the big job done.

"Now, ever since that first clap of thunder, when the oak tree was lightning-struck, the heavens had been quiet. True, they'd been darkly, gloomily threatening of course; but the droning hiss of the rain as it beat into the puddly earth—as if indeed it never meant to let up—was the only sound the storm made.

"However, on the morning of the thirty-ninth day—after our first dry sleep since the Deluge started—we awoke to hear strange, rumbly noises beneath us, over our heads and all around us. I opened my eyes and for a moment wondered where I was—till I remembered that we had just spent a night aboard the Ark. I could tell the ship still rested in the mud, because she was not rocking like a ship at sea. But what was all this rumbling racket? I at once left our quarters down below and hurried up on deck to see what was happening.

"Well, the whole racetrack had almost entirely disappeared underwater. You could see only the earth—or mud—just close around the Ark. Far away to the eastward I could see the upper parts of the mountains. Here the townsfolk yet clung and clustered—though they were fewer than before.

"Our ship's gangplank had been drawn up. But old Noah was still standing outside on the last strip of ground that wasn't flooded. He was watching, like me, those miserable people on the mountaintops. Tears were trickling down the patriarch's dirty face. His tremendous work was finished; and all he had to do now was to wait till the waters lifted the Ark up and floated her away.

"One of his sons' wives stuck her head out of the door, scolding him. She asked, didn't he know enough to come in out of the rain? He was old enough in all conscience, she added. But Noah, weeping

"She asked, didn't he know enough to come in out of the rain?"

and watching the last of the folk on the mountains, did not even seem to hear her.

"Again I began to think of Eber, the slave who had been so kind to us. And Gaza: What of her? I had not seen her in months and months.

"As for the other people of Shalba, to tell you the truth, I did not worry very much. *They* had certainly never bothered themselves about me. To them, wild animals were just something to eat; to be made to work; or looked at in menageries. Why should I—like the weeping Noah—care, now that they were being swept away to make room for other creatures? But Eber!—I had been really fond of that boy. And, as I watched those wretched folk huddling on their last mountain refuge, I wondered only how Eber had fared. Had he been saved?. . . And, as I watched, a strange thing happened.

"Suddenly behind the mountain, a long way off, the waters—which now stretched out in nearly every direction to the skyline, like a sea—seemed to rise up as a wall and rush toward us. It was a huge wave, as wide as the world—and growing higher and higher as it came nearer.

"At that, Noah cried out to his daughter-in-law:

"'Heaven help King Mashtu's people now! See, the ocean herself has broken bounds and is running abroad like a wild thing.'

"Then the rumbling noise that had been rising steadily since it first woke me, grew into a terrible roar. I sometimes wonder if the spilling over of the seas did something inside the mountains—made the volcanoes' fires explode, maybe—and earthquakes under the water. Anyway, the next thing I knew, the whole earth was heaving and rolling about in the most terrifying way. I glanced again toward the mountains.

"And they were gone! The sea stretched flat and unbroken now, right around the world. Not a spot of land was in sight. What had happened to them I did not know. They had disappeared like magic. For Eber, my heart went sick.

"But the great wave of the ocean was now roaring on toward the racetrack and ourselves—quite near. Noah's wife came and joined the other women. They all screamed to the old man to come in and fasten up the door.

"'So be it,' he said. And he stepped into the Ark."

The Floating Tree

O N THE MORROW WE GATHERED AGAIN IN the twilit shed. The turtle went on:

"Even while Ham, Shem, and all of them were frantically barring up the door inside with strong beams, the walls of the ocean struck us. It lifted our clumsy boat high in the air, like a cork. And then down, down a great hill of water—which seemed to have no end—we were swept along, spinning and turning—down, down, down. It looked as though the ocean were shifting—as indeed it was, I believe—from one side of the world to the other. For hours we sped on down this rushing cataract of water. And I began to wonder if, and where, we'd ever stop.

"It was the last floundering agony of our Mother Earth in the grip of the Deluge. After that—when calm came—the world was water so far as we could see or know."

In a solemn silence Mudface hesitated. Then he moved slowly to the edge of his shelter and craned his neck outside, as though to see better over the misty lake far below.

"You see that stump, John Dolittle," he asked, pointing with a muddy claw, "the one jutting out from the shore, where the mangroves make a sort of cape? Well, that is the very spot where Noah stood, his hand still upon the doorsill of the Ark, watching the great sea-wave sweep toward us. That is where we started from—started upon a long and wearisome voyage.

"For then began long days of idleness for us, the animal passengers. We all felt dizzy in the head from the spinning and pitching; and I even heard that Noah's wife had been a trifle seasick. However, the sun *did* come out—a sort of a sun, and the sea eventually calmed—to a sort of a calm. The coming of this calm was taken as a good sign by all—and Mrs. Noah sat up and drank a cup of beef-tea.

"But oh, time hung heavy on our hands. To amuse ourselves the best we could do was guessing—guessing how long it would take the water to dry up off the land.

"As for the course we followed, I don't believe Noah himself had much idea of where we were or where we were going. We were just drifting. Nevertheless, a weak wind began presently to blow; and the Ark moved slowly before it under some makeshift sails that Shem rigged up on the main deck.

"However, if we were bored, for Noah and his family it was a very busy time. Feeding all those animals and keeping the ship clean was an enormous job. The three sons were hard at it all day, carrying and sweeping. Some of the animals got ill with the rolling of the ship, and Noah had to doctor them.

"Of Noah's sons, Shem seemed the most sensible; so he was worked hardest. Ham was very lazy; and most of the day he spent playing tunes on a whistle down in the hold. One day he played the

'Elephants' March.' And the two elephants thought that the circus was beginning. They started parading up and down the main deck, upsetting and smashing things in all directions. After that, Ham's mother took the whistle from him and threw it overboard.

"The elephants gave a lot of trouble—though they didn't mean to at all. They were so enormously big; and they ate such a lot. The Ark was a big boat, it's true; but when you have elephants for passengers—even just a pair—you need room for them, for their fodder and for their drinking water. Quite early in the voyage their food supply ran low; and the amount they were given at each meal had to be cut down. One day the bull-elephant fainted from hunger. He fell against his stable-partition and smashed it flat. And it took all of Noah's family, with Mrs. Elephant and two hippos, to get him up on his feet again.

"On the first Thursday after we started, I was looking over the side of the ship. Suddenly I noticed something a little distance away. The waters, smooth enough, moved gently under a firm wind.

"Presently this thing I was watching rolled in the swell of the sea; and I saw it was a large uprooted tree. On it there was a man's body. The breeze brought it closer to the Ark's side. And then I could see there were two bodies on it: a man and a girl. Their eyes were closed. But something told me they were not just sleeping. They were dead or unconscious. The man had an ugly cut across the back of his neck. And the only thing that kept them at all upon that floating tree was that their arms and legs were so tangled up in the roots they just couldn't slip off.

"I was about to move away and go down to dinner, when the tree pitched and turned again. With the motion, the man's head rolled backward on his shoulders. And then, for the first time, I

"One day the bull-elephant fainted from hunger."

could see his face. It was Eber, the slave who had been so kind to us during our imprisonment!

"At first, thinking he was dead, I was very sad. He was the only man in the whole world that I had wanted saved from the Deluge. And now he had been drowned! . . . It seemed so unfair.

"But, while I still watched the little waves gently lapping across his body, I saw his eyelids move—only a flutter; and his lips parted, though no sound came from them. Still, that was enough to tell me that at least he was yet alive.

"With a whoop of joy I bolted down below to find Noah, upsetting a pair of guinea pigs who were playing some game on the stairs. On my way, I met Belinda; and I told her in a few hurried words what I had seen. Then the two of us started to run through the ship in search of Noah.

"We found the patriarch at dinner with his family.

"'Listen, Noah!' I cried, rushing up to him, breathless. 'There's a man out there—in the water—floating on a tree. He's drowning—only half-conscious. It's Eber! You remember? Your helper in the zoo. Come upstairs and save him—quick!'

"But, to our great surprise, Noah did not jump up and rush to the rescue. Instead, he chewed away till his mouth was empty—he was eating potatoes. Then he turned to me and said:

"'I've no authority to save him.' Then he got that old paper out of his pocket. 'What name did you say?' he asked.

"'Eber,' I said impatiently. 'Eber, your assistant.'

"'I'm sorry,' said he, reading the list on the paper. 'But his name is not down here. There's nothing I can do.'

"And he handed his plate to his wife for a second helping of potatoes.

"Then I think I went a little mad.

"'Look here!' I almost screamed at him. 'Do you mean to tell me you're going to let that boy drown just because it isn't in your instructions to save him?'

"'I can do nothing,' he repeated. 'That's what it says: *Only the righteous shall be saved.*' I must obey the orders given me. Ham, take your elbows off the table.'

"I thought I would choke, I was so angry.

"'And is it your idea,' I spluttered, 'that you and your stuffy old family are the only righteous people on the earth—the only ones worth saving? If that's how you've read your orders, then you've read them wrong, Noah. You've read them cross-eyed with stupid conceit. That boy Eber is just as righteous as you and all your family. If you will not save him, then I and my wife will leave the Ark this minute. For we would be ashamed to stay on it while such a man as Eber is dying out there.'

"In answer, the old man said nothing—just went on munching potatoes.

"Then I turned to my wife.

"'Come,' I said. 'Let us leave the Ark to this self-righteous family and try to rescue that boy by ourselves. And if heaven is on our side we'll win, Belinda. For Gaza, too, is out there upon the floating tree. Gaza, the queen's singing-girl. Eber snatched her from the Flood—even while it threatened his own life. Come! Who knows? If they're both alive, that boy who was kind to us in our captivity may someday start a world and a people of his own.'"

THE EIGHTH CHAPTER

In Mid-Ocean Mudface Leaves the Ark

THEN, OUR NOSES IN THE AIR, BELINDA AND I walked out of Noah's dining saloon and up the stairs to the main deck. With no hesitation we scrambled up the rail and dived straight into the sea. A crazy thing perhaps. But I have never been sorry for it—though we paid dearly enough later for our boldness. It took one hundred and fifty days—five whole months—for the earth to show again after the Deluge.

"Eber himself was made of wonderful stuff. And it was he in the end—rather than Belinda and I—who saved Gaza. Any ordinary man would have died in the first week from exhaustion. But that boy, in his life as a slave, had grown hard and wiry.

"When we reached those two upon the floating tree, they were in terrible shape. Their lips and tongues were swollen from sunburn and thirst. They lay upon that log like dead folk. Things didn't look hopeful at all. We saw at once that the tree was dreadfully low in the water and could not float much longer.

"So, first of all, Belinda and I untangled them from among the roots. Then each of us took one of them on our backs; and we swam off looking for something better to put them on. There was plenty of stuff still floating around—all manner of things, the wreckage of a lost world.

"After about an hour of hard swimming—you have no idea what a job it is for a turtle to keep his shell above water with the weight of a man on his back—we found something that would do. It was the roof of a small house, floating complete—just as it had been lifted off its walls by the Flood. And it was big enough to carry us all.

"Belinda and I climbed right up onto it."

"Indeed, it turned out to be almost as good as a ship. The slope of the roof was gentle and flattish. Belinda and I climbed right up onto it with our burdens.

"There we laid the boy and girl down side by side. My, but they looked terrible! Eber's eyelids had not even moved again since that first flutter. Both he and Gaza were unconscious the whole time.

"When we had got our breath, we two turtles talked over what we'd better do with these almost-dead humans. Neither of us had much idea of how to set about such a job—with people, that is; with turtles we could have been far more helpful. Anyway, we patted them and rubbed them gently with wet seaweed. But nothing seemed any use.

"We were both dreadfuly discouraged. For it began to look as though we'd failed in our task; and these two poor youngsters were going to die before our eyes after all. My wife stood watching them gloomily a moment; and then she said:

"'Husband, I reckon it's food they want. This is the tenth day that they've been drifting on the ocean. It's not likely they've had a single thing to eat in all that time—except the bark or roots of that tree. See, Mudface, how thin and pinched the girl's cheeks are. It's food they need. I'm certain.'

"'Ah, food!' said I. 'That's easier said than found.' And I gazed miserably all around the flat ocean, trying to spy a single thing afloat that could be eaten by a man. . . . Nothing but driftwood and the wreckage of houses.

"'We haven't even fresh water,' I said, almost weeping, 'to let them drink.'

"Then, suddenly, an idea came to me.

"'Listen, Belinda,' I said. 'It is no use our trying to find men's food in water. Men are land-creatures, remember. Fish would be our only chance—and all fish have run from the anger of the Flood and taken refuge in the deepest oceans. We've only one hope of getting food or drink for them.'

"'And what is that?' she asked.

"'To swim down *under* the water,' I answered, 'till we come upon a city or town; and there to search among the houses of men till we find men's food.'

"'I think you're crazy,' said she. 'Cities don't grow like pebbles on the beach. How do you think you'll find a town under this sea that covers the earth? Why, we don't even know what side of the world we're on! We may be a thousand miles from any of the drowned lands where men ever lived.'

"'Perhaps, Belinda,' said I. 'Yet I'm going to try.'

"I went to the edge of the raft to dive off.

"'Wait a minute,' my wife called out. 'I don't think there is any hope at all. But if you *should* find houses of men, go down into the lowest room, the one underneath the ground—and bring wine. It is kept in bottles or jars; and it's always stored *below* the house. Wine is what men use in case of sickness. When the Flood was first getting bad in Shalba, I saw many families trying to rescue their wine from beneath the ground. Of course, Mudface, bring any other food you can find. But be sure and bring that: *wine*. It is red in color; and it grows in bottles, remember. And listen: don't go off too far and get lost. If a storm should come up it may be more than I can manage, alone, to keep these two people from rolling off the raft.'

"'All right, Belinda,' I said. 'And in the meantime you can

busy yourself rigging up some sort of tent over Eber and the girl—there are still plenty of leafy boughs floating around. That girl's skin is all cracking open from the sun. Good-bye, my dear!'

"Then I dived into the water and disappeared."

Belinda's Brother

WELL, TO BEGIN WITH, I SWAM STRAIGHT downward for nearly an hour. And at the end of that time I seemed no nearer the bottom than I was when I started. I was surely over low land or the bed of an old ocean.

"So I stopped swimming downward and took a new direction by the sun—which I could still dimly see far, far above me. Then I started off in a straight line westward: hunting for mountains; looking for a town; searching for a bottle of wine beneath the waters of the Flood—for Eber, my friend.

"For another hour I kept on, swimming level. I began to fear perhaps Belinda had been right—and I was on a fool's errand—when I met another turtle. I spied him long before he saw me. He was paddling away in a southerly direction, at the same level as I was. What good luck—I said to myself—that the first living creature I meet in this puzzling, underwater world turns out to be one of my own people, a turtle! I hastened to overtake him.

"I swam downward."

"On coming nearer—would you believe it?—I recognized an old friend: it was a relative of my wife's—her favorite brother, in fact—a splendid fellow.

"As soon as we had exchanged greetings, I told him what I was after.

"'Well,' said he, 'if it's mountainous country you want, you had better take me along. I've just left some quite high hills to the north of here. Not what you'd call mountains exactly, but perhaps farther behind them we'll find a real range. . . . Isn't it splendid weather we're having—just the stuff for turtles? Quite new, all this water. I haven't had such a splendid swim in weeks. No traffic at all. I hope it keeps up. Was on my way to the Turtles' Meeting—a sort of convention, you know. I heard it's being held about a hundred miles from here. Our people are going to talk over what's to be done by all the water-folk, now that there's so little land anywhere. Important business! But I'll gladly turn back and lead you to the hilly ground I left—though it's still covered over, you understand. . . . How's Belinda?'

"He always had been a cheerful sort. And you've no idea how his chatty company cheered me up. My wife called him Wag—sort of a nickname.

"So off we went together. And, sure enough, after we'd traveled about half an hour we ran right into the face of a steep cliff. We crawled up this; and found ourselves on the top of a sort of rolling plain. We swam on farther; and soon we noticed that the ground was growing steeper. We were sure we were coming to real mountains.

"It was very strange to see, around these parts, land trees still growing underwater—and wide meadowy slopes where deer had once fed. Of course in the riverbeds much damage had been done—great holes in the banks, big enough to put a large house in. Here, in the first fury of the Flood, the streams had torn out trees by the roots and swirled them down the hillsides, before beginnings of a calm had come to the tormented earth.

"Soon I saw the tops of the mountains whose foothills we'd been exploring. I clambered up one of these to the peak. And there, standing with my feet on a rock pinnacle (from which eagles had looked out in past times, no doubt), I found that by stretching up my neck I could just poke my nose out into the air. Only six feet of water covered the top of that mountain! It was a strange feeling to look over a flooded world with my feet on *land*.

"'Within a few days,' I said to Wag, 'this mountaintop will show above the Deluge.'

"'What a pity!' said he.

"'Oh, I don't know,' I answered. 'It's sort of dreary, all this wet desolation. I know it's grand for us water-animals. But somehow I'll be glad to see the land-creatures around again. Besides, the scenery was better the way it was, too.'

"Now of course, where the water was so shallow the light was much brighter.

"'Listen, Wag,' said I. "We mustn't waste any time in hunting up a town or a village where we can find food. I'm awfully worried about that boy. Suppose we separate and search in two directions at once. You go east and I'll go west. And let's meet here again in half an hour.'

"Well, on that first trip we had no luck. We met again as planned; and because night was not far off we agreed to give up the hunt till the next day. We lay down where we were on the mountaintop to sleep."

"Pardon me," the Doctor interrupted. "You slept on the rock, eh? But you have often spoken of how much you like mud. Tell me: Can turtles see in the mud?"

"No," said the great creature, "at least very little. While moving or traveling in mud you find your way by bumping instead of seeing. When you meet anything, and you want to be sure what it is, you bump it. Then you know."

"Ha!" murmured Cheapside. "There you 'ave the sixth sense, Doc, what you naturalists is always talking about: hearing, tasting, touching, smelling, seeing—and bumping. Glad I don't have to travel under the mud. . . . I wonder how you tell the time."

"One of the senses *you* haven't got, Cheapside," snapped his wife, Becky, "is *common* sense. For pity's sake, hold your tongue and let the turtle get along with his story!"

"Thank you, Mudface," said the Doctor. "Please go on."

"I ain't worried about his *going* on," whispered Cheapside. "Question is: When is 'e goin' to *stop*? Old Mud-pie has been drooling longer than usual tonight, seems like."

"Well of course, John Dolittle," said the turtle, "our eyes are always very good and far-seeing. But in exploring a whole country for houses, when we had to work in a hurry, we needed the best light we could get. That's why I had come to the high mountain levels, where the shallower water would let more of the sunshine through.

"Early next morning Wag said to me, 'Let's go off to the other end of this mountain range. I fear we're not going to have much luck around here.'

"I agreed. And together we set off, keeping along the top of the ridge, so we could find our way back. We had gone about ten miles when suddenly we came to a deep gap in the mountains—a sort of saddle. Across on the other side of this we could dimly see the ridge and the line of peaks going on into the distance.

"Wag wanted to swim across this gap at the level we now stood at—to save distance and time. But I said: 'No. It will take us longer, I agree, to go down into this saddle and crawl up the other side. But I have a feeling that if we swim over it we may miss something. Let's explore it on foot.'

"And it was lucky we did—or Eber might have died before I got back to him; and the later history of the world would have been different."

THE TENTH CHAPTER

Wine Beneath the Sea

AFTER WE HAD GONE DOWN THE SLOPE OF this gap a little distance, I spied something whitish in the gloom below. It looked tremendously long and snaky; and, as far as I could make out, it wound its way still lower, toward the very foot of the mountains—where it faded into the dark of the deeper water. When we had climbed down to it we found it flat and hard. It was about twelve feet wide.

"'What on earth is this?' asked Wag.

"'This,' I said, 'is called a road—sort of a trail. Men, when they travel, don't go straight across country, like we do—through swamps and everything. They have to have a track prepared for them, along which they drive in carts, or walk.'

"By the edge of the road there stood a square, chiseled stone with some letters on it.

"'And this stone,' I said, 'is a milestone. I wish I could read those letters—then I could tell how far we have to go. We will follow this road; and it will lead us to a town. This highway has been made to cross the mountain range at the lowest point—through this saddle, see? My, but I'm glad we came down into this gap on foot, instead of swimming across it! How stupid of us! We could have saved ourselves the trouble of looking for towns on the top of the ridge. Let us hurry, Wag. Eber and the girl are starving for food.'

"So off we tramped, side by side, along the broad road leading downward, toward a valley. And as it took us lower and lower, the light grew dimmer and dimmer. Presently the country began to flatten out into what looked more like real farming land. By counting the milestones, we knew how far we had come—but, alas, not how far we had to go!

"'And this stone,' I said, 'is a milestone.'"

"Just as we were passing out of sight of the mountains we'd left, we came upon something strange. It was an outpost or a sentry station. This was to mark the line between one kingdom and another. We had no idea what kingdoms they had been: but clearly the lands of one king had run up to the foot of the mountains. And there, before the Flood, soldiers had been posted to guard the borders of his kingdom. The men's spears and helmets, reddening with rust, were stacked against the little shelter-hut beside the road. Near the hut there was a well. And its wooden bucket, tied at the end of a rope, now stood straight upright, floating at anchor a hundred feet above our heads. Wag laughed outright at the sight of it.

"And its wooden bucket stood straight upright, floating at anchor."

"'The big rain certainly turned things upside down all right,' said he. And he was all for biting the rope in two, just for the fun of seeing the bucket shoot up to the surface of the ocean. But I made him leave it and hurry on. I had no idea what time it was—being unable down here to see the sun. I was afraid night might come on and force us to rest again till the following day. So on we went.

"After we passed the fifth milestone, we suddenly stumbled upon an ax lying in the middle of the road.

"'That's a good sign,' I said. 'A town or a village is probably not far off now.'

"And I was right. Near the sixth milestone we came to the outskirts of a town—at first no more than a few houses, set wide apart, here and there on either side of the road. Heavens! You could scarcely call them houses anymore. Roofless they were, most of them; while some had had their walls undermined by rushing water and were now just piles of bricks and mortar.

"However, we pried and searched each one of them in turn, hunting for that precious bottle of wine. Such rubbish and wreckage we dug through! The first building was a blacksmith's shop; and the smith's tools lay around the anvil, where he had dropped them to flee for his life. There was no food here.

"Of course, getting into the cellars of some of the houses in our hunt for wine was often impossible, on account of the big stones that blocked the cellar stairs. But the homes became more plentiful as we went on; and I was tremendously excited and hopeful. I hustled Wag along at such a pace from door to door, the poor fellow had to swim half the time to keep up with my longer legs.

"At last, when we had reached a sort of town square or market, we saw a large brick house, complete and almost undamaged. Over the door hung a sign with a picture of a bottle on it.

"'If I'm not mistaken,' I said to my brother-in-law, 'this is a wine shop. And if we can make our way into it, I believe our search is ended.'

"We found the doors and all the windows locked. How to get in? That was going to be a problem. But at last Wag thought of the chimney. He was no fool. By swimming up onto the roof, we were able to scramble our way down a dirty, sooty chimney; and we came out, by the fireplace, into the large main room of the house. Here we found bottles in plenty. But they had all been opened and the wine washed out of them long ago.

"Then we went down into the cellar, where, to our great delight, we saw rows and rows of more bottles stacked up neatly against the walls. These had their corks still firmly fastened in them. Down here the light was awfully bad—the cellar having only one small window, high up in the west wall. So, to make sure these bottles were not empty too, we smashed one against the stone floor. And Wag whooped with joy as the ruby wine flowed out and mingled with the water all about us. It got in our noses and made us awful dizzy—so that for a while we could barely make our way around.

"'Ah, at last, at last!' I hiccuped to Wag. 'Now let's each of us take two bottles and get out of here—while we can still stand up.'

"Just as we were about to leave—by the chimney again—I remembered that, besides the wine, I ought to take something for my friends to eat. So once more we hunted through the flooded rooms looking for food of a solid kind.

"In a cupboard we came upon some loaves of bread. But these were ruined by the water and fell to pieces as soon as we touched them. However, in the same closet, on the top shelf, Wag found a basket of apples, three unopened coconuts, and a whole cheese. There were some old sacks lying in a corner of the cellar. We put some of the fruit, the cheese, and two bottles of wine into a couple of these bags.

"It wasn't easy, scrabbling back up the chimney, dragging those loads clutched in our mouths. But at last we managed it; and came out onto the roof. I mumbled to Wag through a mouth full of sacking:

"'Your sister said I'd never do it. Won't *she* be surprised? Let's go! It's quite a while since I left her—and we might yet be too late to save that brave boy's life. Swim your best now, Wag—*swim!*'"

Eber Saves
Gaza's Life

THE JOURNEY BACK TO THE RAFT, IN SPITE OF the loads we dragged, did not take as long as the outward trip. I had been careful to watch and remember every change of direction I'd made since I left Belinda. And when Wag and I bobbed up to the surface of the water, I at once looked at the sun. It was still fairly high; so there would be some hours yet before darkness. I took a bearing on it and led my brother-in-law off in a straight line for where I reckoned the raft to be.

"Up here, on the top, it was a great change to feel the comforting hot sun on our shells, instead of the numbing cold that had chilled us in the lower depths. Putting our best foot forward, we churned along merrily to make good time.

"At last, far off on the rim of the sea, we spied a black speck which I felt sure must be the raft. We sighted it at this long range because Belinda, while I'd been gone, had built a fine roof of leaves and boughs to shade the girl from the sun; and this, upstanding like the mast of a ship, could be seen from quite a distance.

"As soon as I'd come within hearing, I called to my wife, 'Have they opened their eyes yet?'

"'No,' she answered.

"'Are they still breathing?' I yelled.

"'Yes. But that's about all.'

"Indeed it was a close thing. When Wag and I dragged our burdens up onto that raft, those two people were as near dead as anyone could be. I immediately got a bottle of wine out of my sack. And then we found the cork so tight in the neck that we couldn't budge it. Both Belinda and I were almost weeping from rage and impatience as we struggled with it. Why on earth had these silly men-creatures invented such a crazy way to seal their wine?

"But the good Wag again came to the rescue. 'Give it to me,' he said sharply.

"I handed it over. And in a flash he'd bitten the head right off the bottle and was spitting the broken glass out into the sea. Then, while my wife gently pried open Eber's clenched teeth with her front claws, I poured the gurgling wine into the boy's throat.

"It acted like magic. In a moment his hands began to open and shut. Then his head started rolling slowly from side to side. And presently he opened his eyes. They were blue in color—like the sea when the sun is shining. But a great fear showed in them, as he gazed round into the faces of us who had rescued him from death.

"I was puzzled by this—at the time. Yet I suppose it was natural enough. We were not of his kind. And awakening from a long wet sleep to find three giant turtles bending over him (Wag, who had a trickle of blood running from his mouth, where the broken glass had cut him a little, looked especially tough), Eber must, no doubt, have gotten something of a shock. And remember, the boy had already been through all the terrors of the Deluge.

"But presently I could see, from a changing expression in the lad's eyes, that he half recognized me. For, ever so slightly, he smiled up into my face. And, though you may hardly believe it, John Dolittle, that smile brought me one of the greatest thrills I'd felt since before I'd lost my freedom in King Mashtu's zoo.

"I had paid back a debt.

"Presently the boy closed his eyes and seemed to sleep again.

"'Let him rest now, Husband,' said Belinda. 'We have the girl, too, to look after. Bring the bottle over here and I'll see if I can open her mouth without hurting these cracked lips.'

"'Wait!' cried my brother-in-law. 'Don't you two realize what you're doing? Eber was your friend, Mudface. That's different. But who is this woman? If you save her, too, she'll marry the boy and raise a family. We'll have the earth overrun with men again. Zoos for animals and all that; while now the earth belongs to us, the water-creatures—as it should. Why bother with the girl?'

"'Brother,' I answered, 'the boy would be lonely in a world all to himself, with no others of his own kind—just as you or I would be. I doubt if he would want to live, if we let her die. For Eber—for my friend's sake—she *must* be saved.'

"And, bending over Gaza, Belinda and I set to work.

"Bringing the woman to her senses was a much harder job than reviving the man. We found that on her the wine didn't seem to do any good at all. After we had worked over her for a full half hour—and she still lay like a lifeless thing—Belinda and I became very discouraged.

"'I'm afraid,' said my wife, frowning, 'that with her, Mudface, we are too late.'

"'You think she is already dead?' I asked fearfully.

"'Yes,' whispered Belinda. 'Her flesh is growing cold. She is not as strong as the man. It is no use pouring more wine into her. See, she does not swallow it.'

"'Alas,' I said, 'that it should be so! I feel sorrier for Eber than I do for her. . . . Well if she is dead, then let us roll her quietly into the ocean—before the boy wakes up again and sees us do it.'

"So, with heavy hearts, my wife and I began to push her toward the edge of the raft.

"But just as we were about to thrust her body into the water, I felt something clutch the shoulder of my shell from behind. With a guilty start, I turned my head. It was Eber. His eyes were staring wildly from his exhausted, haggard face; his left hand gripped me; while his arm reached out over my back toward the girl.

"'What is it?' I asked Belinda. 'What does he want?'

"'He's trying to stop us from burying her in the sea,' said my wife. 'Maybe he thinks she is not dead yet. Stand aside and let us see what he will do.'

"We drew Gaza's body back from the roof's edge and laid it at his feet. Over it Eber knelt; and, while big tears welled up in his bloodshot eyes, he bent and listened at her heart. Then suddenly with frantic efforts he tried to roll her over, face-downward. The task was too much for his weakened strength—and we helped him. Next, he pressed her back and sides, then he worked her arms up and down.

"He seemed to know a lot more about what to do with half-drowned humans than we did; for when, in answer to his signals, we

"I felt something clutch my shell."

turned her face-upward again, we could see that she was now plainly breathing—though with a gurgling sound in her throat.

"Presently Eber pointed to the bottle. And this time after we trickled the wine into her mouth, she gulped and swallowed it.

"And then—thank goodness!—she, too, opened her eyes.

"At that the lad gave a great cry of joy. Suddenly he fainted from exhaustion, fell down beside the woman and lay still."

THE TWELFTH CHAPTER

The Sign in the Sky

AND, A MOMENT LATER, WE KNEW THAT
Eber and the girl were sound asleep. Belinda and I
breathed a sigh of thankfulness.

"'They will both live,' said my wife, turning away.
'Let us get out the fruit and cheese you brought and prepare it for
the time when they awake.'

"'Well,' muttered my brother-in-law, opening the second sack,
'it seems all wrong to me. However—just as you say, Belinda. But
remember, if you're sorry for this later, don't say I didn't warn you.
Don't say I didn't warn you!'

"'And where,' my wife asked of him, 'did you pop up from,
Wag? I've been too busy with this job even to give you a single
word of greeting. Gracious, what a home to welcome you to!
But it's good to have you with us, Brother. For we're in need of
cheerful company. Tell me: How is it you and Mudface returned
together?'

"'Oh,' said Wag airily, 'we ran into one another—by chance,

— 635 —

you know. Your husband was hunting for mountains; and he took me along—just for the trip.'

"Wag was never one to boast.

"'Don't you believe him, Belinda,' said I. 'He was tremendously useful to me. It was he who led me to the country where we found the wine. I don't know what I could have done without him.'"

"Hah!" whispered Cheapside the sparrow. "That's what the Doctor's always sayin': 'What *would* I do without you?' . . . Funny, how people is always wondering what they'd do without you—when you're useful; and when you ain't, they're wonderin' what they'll do *with* you."

"That's not surprising—in your case," murmured Becky wearily.

"Cockney chatterbox!" snapped Polynesia the parrot. "I'd hate to tell you what *I* would like to do with you—if you don't keep quiet."

"Tee, hee, hee!" tittered the white mouse.

"Ho, indeed!" said Cheapside, turning upon Polynesia and bristling up for a fight. "Becky was talkin' to *me*. But of course *you* have to shove yer hooked nose in, interfering between 'usband and wife. Breakin' up 'omes and the like—you—you flyin' carpet, you! Why, for two pins I'd—"

"Now, now!" said the Doctor quickly. "Stop the squabbling, *please*! Isn't it bad enough to have me interrupting with questions all the time, without you birds starting a fight? Settle down, settle down, for pity's sake, and let's hear the rest of Mudface's story."

"Okay, Doc," said Cheapside wearily. "But I do wish old Fuddymuddy would lay off for the night. I'm gettin' sleepy."

"By the way, Mudface," said the Doctor. "Some time back

you spoke of Noah eating potatoes on the Ark. In our histories, potatoes were not known on this side of the world till long after the Flood. Sir Walter Raleigh is said to have brought them back with him from the Americas. I meant to ask you about it, when you told us of Noah eating them, but I forgot. I won't stop your story for that question at this time. But remind me to ask you later on. Please go ahead now—whenever you are ready."

"And so," the turtle went on, "I moved down to the other end of the raft to help Wag get out the food which Belinda had asked for. But I had hardly turned my back when she suddenly cried out, 'Look, *look*!'

"I swung round and found her pointing at the western skyline. And there, just peeping out of the waters, was a mountaintop!

"A drowned world was at last arising from the Flood!

"That mountain peak was a long way off and very little of it showed as yet; but the setting sun behind made it stand out sharp and clear. I turned once more to help Wag—facing eastward now. And in that quarter, where a slight shower was falling, I saw a rainbow. Two great, gaily colored arches, one within the other, curved across the sky, dazzlingly bright.

"The gorgeous beauty of that double rainbow fairly took your breath away; and I could not take my eyes off it. I felt my wife move up close to me, her shell touching mine. And together, in solemn silence, we gazed at this glory of the heavens—till it began to grow dim in the twilight of coming night.

"'It is a sign, Husband,' whispered Belinda, 'a sign of better things and brighter days to come—with this first showing of the drying land.'

"'Maybe so,' said I. 'Anyway, my dear, I'm glad we saved those youngsters. For, come what may, at least we've made a good start—in whatever new world is being born tonight.'

"Then the rainbow faded out, as the sun behind us slipped gently into the sea."

A New Language
Is Born

WHEN, NEXT DAY, DAWN BROKE OVER a sunlit sea, the tip of the mountain, which Belinda had sighted, showed much plainer—and larger. My wife and I took to the water and pulled the raft close to it. Then Eber and Gaza got out onto the land at last.

"They were both, of course, still very weak and exhausted. The mountaintop had nothing on it whatever to eat. It was all bare rock. But firm land of any kind was better for them than the raft, which had often pitched and swung terribly in the swell of the ocean.

"In a day or so the fruit and cheese that we had got for them was nearly gone—since the two, as soon as their appetites came back, needed more food. So I made many trips again to the village of the wine shop, away down in the drowned valley, to get more supplies. And besides food, I brought up blankets for them which, when dried, kept off the cold night winds. I got tools, too, to make things with—axes and the like."

"Excuse me," the Doctor interrupted again. "But how did you communicate with Eber? What I mean is: He couldn't talk your language, could he? How did you manage about that?"

"No," said the turtle. "At first it was very difficult. Belinda and I had to do a lot of guessing over what things he needed. Besides, Eber could not even talk the girl's language. This surprised us; for we had supposed that all men used the same talk—the way we turtles do, all over the world. But, you will remember that these two young people, although they had met in Shalba, were not born there. They were both slaves; they had been brought to Mashtu's court from different lands, as prisoners of war: Eber, the clever gardener and Gaza, the beautiful singer. And neither one spoke the other's language.

"Now, as I have said, everything in Shalba was very grand—away ahead of all other countries—for the free people, that is: the Shalbians themselves. Especially education. After paper was invented—instead of that old clumsy business of writing on bricks—all who were free people learned to read and write.

"Besides the main library in the Square of Victory, there were many smaller branch libraries all about the city; and bookstores and magazine stands on every street corner. Millions of books were printed every year. Myself, I think there were far too many books. Everyone spent his time loafing around, reading. And—still worse—if they weren't *reading* books, they were *writing* them. Everybody seemed to think he just had to write a book. Goodness only knows why! So you see the Shalbians had plenty to read; and if anyone wasn't well educated, it was his own fault.

"But now, with the drowning of the world, all this printed stuff was swept away, every bit of it—except a few storybooks that were taken onto the Ark by Ham, the lazy one. But even these were later eaten up by the goats, when their regular food ran low. You know, Doctor, goats don't seem to care *what* they eat.

"Sometimes I think that was perhaps the only good thing the Deluge did: sweeping away all the books. Because if it hadn't, the authors, who made their living by writing books, would surely have had to go out of business—into plowing or something—since there would have been nothing left to write about when the Flood was over.

"But for those who were slaves, it was very different, of course. They had to do honest, real work—and plenty of it.

For them there was no time to learn reading and writing. All they had was the spoken language they were born with.

"And when Eber and Gaza found themselves rescued together on our raft, a new language was made. Up to that time, just making love as they had done in the Royal Park, well, *that* of course has always been something that needed no *real* language at all. Folks in love get along simply with '*Goo, goo!*' and such stuff; but now these two had to talk really—sensibly.

"At first it was a puzzle for them. They began by picking up things and saying a sound. And that sound would be whatever their mothers had taught them when they were little. Eber would pick up, for instance, an apple; and say to the girl, '*Boo-boo?*' Then Gaza would shake her head and say, '*Bah-bah.* So in the end they would mix the two sounds and call it a *boobah*. And in that way *boobah* became the word for apple in their new language.

"By this time dear old Wag had gone off and left us—because he suddenly remembered he had a wife and family of his own some-where, who probably needed looking after. So then there were only Belinda and I to listen to this new language that Eber and Gaza were building up together, word by word. We were tremendously interested. And of course we could not help but learn it too—after a fashion. I mean, to *understand* what was being said: of course we never learned to *speak* it—turtle talk being so different.

"But I'm sure if there had been other kinds of animals on our raft, some of them at least would have learned to talk it, as well as to understand it. And then you might have had animal-folk and human-folk talking to one another like friends everywhere—which of course is the way it should have been in the new-born world.

"Soon after the first mountaintop appeared and showed that the earth was drying again, a visitor turned up. It was a raven. He had been sent out by Noah from the Ark to look for land. He stayed with us for quite a while. He said the Ark smelled like everything; and he wasn't going back to it for the patriarch Noah or anybody else—not to stay.

"He was good company—even if he was an everlasting chatterbox. And he learned the new language of Eber and Gaza better than any of us. But I heard that later—when his mating season came around and he went off and left us for a while—he soon forgot almost every word of man talk that he'd learned. That's the way with ravens, you know: easy come, easy go. But he was very useful to Belinda and me while he was with us.

"Our mountaintop, of course, kept growing bigger and bigger with the lowering of the water. But still we could find no food fit to eat. Soon other peaks of mountains began to show here and there, like a chain of islands. I swam over to some of them and hunted for food. But scarcely a thing could I find. And I came back to the raft very discouraged, because I knew how starved that boy and girl were.

HUGH LOFTING

"It was a raven."

"Belinda, the raven and I all agreed that Eber and Gaza were getting into poor health for want of something decent to eat; and, although they complained hardly at all, we knew that human-folk couldn't live long without regular meals. Suddenly the raven said:

"'Look here, you two: it's quite likely I can find my way back to the smelly old Ark. There, too, everyone was desperately hungry. But when I left, Old Man Noah had put everybody on strict rations—only so much to a meal, you know—to make the grub last longer. What do you say I go and look for him?'

"My wife and I both agreed readily.

"'When I saw him last,' the raven went on, 'Noah was just

batting around, looking for land. Since I didn't go back to him he's probably still waiting for me. There won't be a lot to eat on the Ark; but your boy and girl will certainly be no worse off than they are on this boulder of bare rock—and perhaps much better. I might be able to pinch a few things from the larder for them meanwhile—if Mrs. Noah isn't looking. Anyway, it's worth trying, don't you think?'

"We said we were sure it was. And right away the raven took wing—flying up to a great height so he could look over a good wide stretch of the sea. Then off he went toward the southwest.

"To our great delight he was back again in three hours. And he was all out of breath from excitement.

"'What *do* you think?' he gasped as he landed on the raft. 'Noah and his Ark—I tracked 'em down more by smell than anything else—have found land on their own account! Or rather the land found *them*, I should say. The ship ran ashore on another mountaintop that lay just beneath the level of the water. Very proud, the Noah family is. You'd think they'd found the land by mathematics—when really they only escaped a shipwreck by good luck.'

"'Oh, how splendid!' cried Belinda.

"'That was about a week ago—when they ran ashore, I mean. And now there's quite a wide piece of land showing on the mountain—with that smelly old Ark sitting up in the middle on top of it. Looks like an island wearing a cock-eyed hat. Mrs. Pigeon told me the mountain is called Ararat—though how they're sure of that, goodness only knows. Myself, I don't think Old Man Noah has any better idea of where in the world he is than you have here.

"'I didn't stop to explore,' said the raven. 'As soon as I'd made sure of their position, I flew straight back here. Thought you and Belinda would want to hear the news as soon as possible. There's a full moon tonight. Soon as I've got my breath I'll lead you over there. Gather up those young people and get them on the raft. Hitch on those vine towing-ropes you used before; and let's get started, if you want to come.'

"'Don't worry, Raven,' said I. 'We'll waste no time.'

"'And listen,' said he, 'I'll fly ahead of you—but slow enough so you won't lose me against the night sky. I can see the moonlight flashing on your wet shells as you swim. The two of you, harnessed to that light raft, can make a fair speed. I'll keep an eye on you. And bring what's left of that fresh rainwater you caught in the last shower we had. The direction we'll travel will be a little south of southwest. If all goes well, we ought to sight the Ark by daybreak—and if we don't see it, we'll smell it, believe me.'

"My wife and I were very grateful to the raven and we began getting ready at once. We rounded up Eber and Gaza who had gone off exploring somewhere on our island hilltop. We made them understand by signs that we were leaving for a new part of the ocean. And the raven was very proud that he could squawk, '*Ark! Ark!*' Because they understood then where we were going."

THE FOURTEENTH CHAPTER

The Tigress

THE JOURNEY WENT OFF VERY SMOOTHLY. A nice steady wind followed behind us and made our job much easier and faster than we'd hoped for.

"As the sun rose next morning it showed another island ahead of us. The raven was right: Noah's ship, which had been so much trouble to build, was perched, all lopsided, on a high peak in the middle of this island. From far off it did look like a crazy hat.

"As we pulled the raft in closer, we saw animals of different kinds standing around it on the rock—and Noah's family in twos and threes also. Nobody seemed to be doing anything. And as we drew closer yet, we saw why: there was nothing whatever growing on this island, either. All the trees had been killed by the salt water, and seeds of the grasses and plants had been rotted and spoiled.

"The starving animals, as soon as they saw our raft coming, rushed down to us at the shore, hoping, poor things, that we'd brought food for them. The raven whispered to me, 'Look out

HUGH LOFTING

"Noah's ship was perched on a high peak in the middle of this island."

for that big cat in the front of the gang, the tigress. It's good-bye to Eber and Gaza, once she gets her claws on them. She's a meat-eater—and a fiend.'

"'Yes, she looks big and savage enough to eat anything,' said Belinda.

"'You bet,' said the raven. 'Mrs. Pigeon told me that the mother pig had a family of babies while the Ark was at sea—and she wasn't the only one. The mother animals kept Noah busy, with the food running short and all. Well, that tigress, when the old man wasn't looking, ate up three of the baby pigs. Of course there were plenty left in the litter. But Mrs. Pig made no end of fuss. Can't blame her altogether. After that, Noah, who is the only one the tigress is afraid of, made her promise—with a pitchfork—to leave the piglets alone. But I wouldn't trust her farther than I could carry her in my beak. Keep an eye on her, Mudface. You and your wife are safe against her—with your hard shells. But Eber and Gaza; they're juicy. Remember, a hungry tigress is about the most dangerous beast in the world.'

"Belinda and I *did* remember it. We took no chances—for the boy and girl—with Mrs. Tiger.

"For the present I left the raft floating a quarter-mile away from the island; only so, I knew, would Eber and Gaza be safe—because the tigress couldn't swim. But, to make double-sure, I asked the raven to stay with them on the raft and bring me word if anything went wrong. Then Belinda and I swam ashore to look for Noah.

"We found the patriarch in an even greater state of puzzlement than he was when building the Ark. Food, food, *food* was his trouble now. All the supplies of hay and such stuff were pretty nearly eaten up; and the animals that lived on meat hadn't had a meal for days. Things looked awful bad. After we had talked to the old man awhile, we swam back to the raft. And I said to the raven:

"'It's no use our staying around here. There isn't a bite of food to spare—except the fish that the seals are catching; and that's barely enough to feed themselves and their pups.'

"'Humph!' said the raven. 'If you'll mount guard over the raft here, I'll fly across the Ark presently and see if I can swipe a piece of bacon for you. But I can't carry much, you know.'

"'Listen,' said Belinda, 'do you know what I think we should do? Try to find our way back to Shalba. I've no idea how far Africa is from here. But you remember Mashtu's Royal Botanical Gardens.

Every fruit tree—oranges, olives, bananas, grapes, pineapples—everything was grown there. Surely some of them must be left.'"

"Pardon," said the Doctor. "But are you sure about the pine-apples? Christopher Columbus, you know, was supposed to be the discoverer who first brought them to this side of the world—long after the Deluge."

"If you'll allow me, Doctor," said the turtle, "I'll answer that question, too, later on? For the present, it may interest you to know that, in the days of Shalba, not only did we have nearly every fruit you can find today, but many more besides. You see, the Flood killed off many delicious fruits and vegetables—with their seeds—so that they never grew in our earth again."

"Oh quite, quite," said John Dolittle, "most interesting. Certainly put off all that till you're ready to tell it. I am most keen now to hear what luck you had in trying to get back to Shalba from the Ark. Excuse my breaking in, please. What did Belinda say next?"

"'Well,' she said, 'we've *got* to do something, Mudface. Eber and Gaza are going to starve to death if we stay here.'

"That raven was a clever and adventurous bird. (He had already slipped across to the Ark and got a piece of bacon for us.)

"'You're right,' he said after thinking a minute. 'I'm willing—though I have only a foggy notion which way to go to reach Africa. But I've always trusted my good luck. Maybe we'll fall in with other animals on the way—water-creatures—or whatnot—who are still alive. For myself, I can probably pick up a thing or two to eat. If it hadn't been for the floating plants, which use no roots—like the water hyacinth—those two elephants over there would have been dead long ago. Water hyacinth is all right for vegetable-feeders—if they can find nothing better. But it carries air-balls to keep it floating. And Mrs. Pigeon told me the bull-elephant nearly died of colic—gas in the stomach, you know. And when an elephant has gas, he has an awful lot. Like a balloon—very uncomfortable. But he stayed alive.'

"'It's those youngsters I'm worried about,' said Belinda. 'They're just skin and bone. . . . Shalba! It's a long trip ahead of us.'

"'Well, now,' said the raven, 'perhaps we can pick up a cormorant—or some other fishing bird—and take him along. If we can, we'll be all right, you know. We'll manage on shrimps, flying fish, and such food. You turtles are too slow for that kind of diving and catching. Myself, being a land bird, I'd be even less use. But a cormorant or a kingfisher could keep us supplied.'

"And so it was agreed that all five of us would set out on a very daring journey. I was afraid to keep those youngsters near that fiendish tigress.

"No doubt it's natural that meat-eating animals should kill others, to get food. But Eber and Gaza were now the same to Belinda and me as our own children. I am sure that neither Belinda nor I would have hesitated one second to give our own lives, if it would have saved those youngsters from destruction.

"The animals around the Ark were sorry to have us go. They had seen how I had come through the Flood—leaving the Ark and going off on my own; and how Belinda and I had now returned after rescuing two human beings from drowning. They had hoped I would stay with them for a while to help them with my cunning and wisdom. Seeing their food growing less and less each day, they were losing their faith in Noah as a leader—and they, too, were afraid of that tigress.

"The deer, giraffes and the rest gathered around, begging us to stay or to take them with us. I felt sorry for them. But the mysterious thought that I might yet be more useful in saving one man and one woman—the very creatures whose kind had imprisoned me and enslaved the world—that thought kept coming back to me: Eber and Gaza must live at all costs. To the hungry animals that clustered around me as I crawled back ashore, I found my heart grow suddenly, strangely hard. All I said was:

"'I must go. I've only returned for a barrel of fresh water to take on the raft. But no one, except my wife, the boy and girl and the raven, come with me on this voyage.'"

The Raven Meets with Adventures

FTER WE HAD LEFT THE ARK THIS SECOND time, the clumsy old ship seemed to drop out of sight below the skyline strangely fast. And then only wide empty seas spread all around us again—which gave us a feeling of great loneliness.

"Now an odd thing I'd noticed as we had pulled away from those islands was that some storks and seabirds seemed to be following us—just drifting here and there, in twos and threes, as if on no particular business.

"Belinda, too, was uneasy about them. 'It looks to me, Mudface,' she said, 'as if those birds might be trailing us. Yet why? They're a lot better off, on the Ark back there, than we are—with only a pound of bacon between us. Whatever are they up to? . . . I don't like it. Wish they'd mind their own business.'

"I said nothing in answer. But I well knew of what—or of whom—my wife was thinking.

"As for the raven, he gave them only one glance, frowned,

and then went on with his calculations for the voyage.

"'Let me see,' said he. 'We are starting about the second hour after sunrise'—though I myself was by no means certain of the time, because—"

"I wish he'd stop trying to remember what time it was," whispered Polynesia to me in her squawky voice. "All I want to know is, what *happened*."

"The raven seemed a little puzzled in his reckoning. 'Look here,' he said presently, 'suppose you keep pulling the raft along this line, changing your course gradually for the position of the sun. I will go ahead of you, flying high, and maybe I'll see something. If I do, I'll come back over this same course and meet you. But remember: if it gets cloudy and there's no sun to guide you, stop dead where you are and leave it to *me* to find *you*.'

"So the raven went off. And we plowed along through the seas at an easy pace. After about a couple of hours the sun did cloud over; and remembering our instructions, Belinda and I at once stopped swimming, so as to stay more or less in the same place.

"My wife got sort of anxious. 'What would happen,' she asked, 'if the raven was unable to pick us up again?' A heavy mist lay on the breast of the waters and you couldn't see more than ten feet ahead of you.

"'Don't worry,' said I. 'That raven, though he's no seabird, is clever. He'll get in touch with us again—never fear, if the mist lasts for three days. We've got a whole keg of fresh water, remember— and that piece of bacon he took from Mrs. Noah's larder. There's no need to get nervous about the youngsters yet.'

"But night settled down upon the ocean with still no sign of the raven. And next morning, I confess, I was very uneasy when I awoke to find the sea mist as thick as ever. Belinda was of course full of worries: What if the mist should last a whole week? The piece of bacon would keep Eber and the girl for only a couple of days. Suppose the raven himself was lost, having no sun to go by? And a whole lot more.

"But I kept on telling her that I had faith in that chatterbox; and I was quite sure he would turn up any minute, so long as we did as we were told and didn't drag the raft all over the ocean looking for *him*.

"Well, I got the poor old lady quieted down at last—though I never let her know how unhappy I felt myself.

"Somewhere around half past five in the evening—no, maybe later—six or half past, as near as I could judge by the growing dark—"

"Oh, gracious," sighed Too-Too. "Now he's worrying about the time again."

"Well, anyhow, the light was very dim, I remember," the turtle went on, "when I thought I heard a sound away off over the stillness of the misty sea.

"'Belinda,' I whispered, 'did you hear that?'

"'No,' she grumbled. 'I heard nothing.'

"'It's coming from behind you,' I said. 'Listen again.'

"We both strained our ears. And, sure enough, a long way off we could both hear a faint, hoarse sort of cry: '*C-r-a-r-k! . . . C-r-a-r-k!*'

"'The *raven!*' I whispered to my wife, nearly falling into the water in my excitement. 'I told you he'd never get lost. He's hunting for us somewhere. Let's answer him!'

"Then the two of us let out the most awful noises you ever heard. We waited. A moment passed. And at last we were answered. This time the grating voice came closer still—though the fog was terrible.

Soon we felt, rather than saw, dark shapes that swept and circled in the air about us.

"Then, *plop! plop!*—two somethings—the light was too bad to tell what they were yet—landed on the raft between Belinda and myself.

"'Is that you, Raven?' I asked the smaller one.

"'Who do you think it was?' growled the scrapy voice. 'Gosh! What a night!'

"'And who's that, the dumpy thing over there, you've brought with you?' asked Belinda.

"'Sh!' hissed the raven. 'Not so loud! That's a pelican, the diving bird I said I'd look for. Marvelous to see him work—brings up a pailful of herring in one swoop. But they're very touchy about their looks, pelicans. Reminds you of a cross between a coal shovel and a coffeepot. Stop staring at him, will you? *He* can't help his shape.'

'Oh, Raven!' sighed Belinda. 'What *would* we have done without you?'"

Cheapside woke up with a snap.

"There you are! See what I mean?" he asked.

"Oh, go to sleep!" muttered Becky. "Wonderful how you can always pick the wrong time for wakin' up—and the wrong one for goin' to sleep!"

"Now, now!" said the Doctor gently. "Let Mudface get on."

"The next day," said the turtle, "we were glad to find the fog cleared away and the sun shining brightly. There was no land in sight. But over breakfast the raven told us of his adventures since he had seen us last.

"'I kept straight on, like I told you,' said he, 'but I couldn't seem to find a piece of land big enough for a *canary* to perch on.

It was getting dark; so knowing I was going to have to spend the night at sea, I flew around as best I could in circles. I was aiming to stay in the same place till sunrise. But Jiminy! In the morning the fog was worse than ever.

"'Well, after slapping around a while longer, I spied what might be a barrel, floating a ways off. I was tired from flying all night. And I needed some place to rest. On my way to the barrel I picked up an orange. It was pretty rotten; but I reckoned that if I could get it to the barrel, I might be able to make a breakfast off what good seeds were left inside it. When I got close I saw there was another bird sitting on the barrel. I recognized him at once—the last kind of bird in the world you'd expect to find in a place like that. I know neither of you will believe me; but it was a *dove*—not stuffed, mind you—a real one.

"'"Hulloa!" says I. "You're a long way from home. How did you get here?"'

"'"Noah sent me," says he.

"'"*Noah* sent you," I says. "What for?"

"'"He said I was to bring back an olive branch," sniffed the dove, water dropping off his nose. His bill chattered so you could hear it a mile off. Altogether he looked like something they'd used for washing out bottles.

"'"Noah," he went on, "said that the dove was the bird of peace. And the olive branch I'd bring back would be a sign—a sign of the end of the Deluge."

"'"Ho, ho!" I says, snickering. "A *sign*, did he say? Of the end of the Deluge, eh? Sounds more to me like a sign of softening of the brain. True, the rain's stopped. But look at the mess it's left! Now I tell you what you do, old lovey-dovey: you fly straight back to Old Man Noah before you get your death of cold and tell him there aren't any olive trees growing round these parts yet.

"'"He ought to be ashamed of himself, sending a *dove* out to catch olives—in a wind blowing forty miles an hour! I wonder he didn't tell you to bring in a gallon of vinegar along with the bottle of olive oil. Look, here's a couple of good orange seeds. Toss them down the crop. They'll last you till you reach Noah's ship. And you tell the old man from me that as far you bein' a 'bird of peace,' he's lucky he ain't getting you back *in pieces*."

"'Well,' added the raven thoughtfully, 'poor old Dovey was awful glad to be let off duty. And, with his crop full of orange seeds, he wasted no time flying off to try and sight the Ark from the higher levels. Myself, after tearing what was left of that smelly orange in pieces, I began to work out a plan. The sun was warming up now; and I decided I'd fly as high as the limit and see what I could see.

"'After climbing for more than an hour, I ran into a couple of vultures. They were huge, hungry beasts and had made up their minds I'd be a slick sandwich. But while their speed was better than mine, they were no good at dodging. Still, I knew they could get me in the end because they had longer wind.

"'But suddenly I remembered the wonderful gift for smelling dead meat at long distances, which vultures are supposed to have. I'll try a bluff, I told myself. Maybe it will work. Then as I looped and ducked around their tails, I said to them, "What good will a little snack like me do to the hungry stomachs of great creatures like you? You'll be starving again in ten minutes. But listen: not far off from here I've found great lands—not little rocky islands—but huge countries where men once farmed. And there, teams of drowned oxen, flocks of sheep, and trains of camels lie dead and rotting in the sun. If you will but leave me alone, I will lead you there and you may eat your fill on the long-dead meat you love so well. Your scent is no good over the sea—*you* know that. Should you kill me now, brothers, you will lose your guide—and likely starve—all for the sake of a little raven."

"'I could see I'd got them thinking. Myself, I hadn't an idea of where these great lands lay. But my bluff worked. I saw the vultures start talking to one another in argument. At last they gave in to me.

"'"So be it, Brother Raven," said they. "Lead on—to the big lands where the carcasses of camels lie rotting in the sun." I could see that rotten meat stuff had done the business. "But listen: fulfill your promise—and no monkey business—or we will snap you up like a field mouse."

"'Well, my luck was with me. At the end of the first day, when I thought I was going to drop into the water from weariness, I saw a long land line stretching out ahead of me. It looked like a continent. As soon as the vultures saw it too, I noticed their beaks open and their tongues smear round their dirty faces. They could smell dead camel meat, the brutes.

"'That did it. They at once forgot all about me. By sheer accident I had led them to an enormous continent with enough rotten camel meat on it to poison an army. They raced ahead of me at twice my speed and never even looked back.'

"My wife, Belinda, sighed heavily as the raven ended the story of his adventures. 'My goodness, Raven,' she said at last, 'I think you're wonderful!'"

"What *would* you have done without him?" said Cheapside, mimicking the Doctor, with a yawn. "Come on, folks—bedtime! I was in the middle of a nice nap; but the smell of them rotten camels woke me up."

The Seabirds
over the Garden

WHAT LAND, MUDFACE, WAS THIS CON-
tinent," the Doctor asked the following night,
"I mean, where the raven escaped from the
vultures?"

"I am pretty sure it was Asia Minor," said the turtle. "But I
will come back to that, too, in just a minute, John Dolittle, if you
don't mind. It was at first frightfully confusing to turtles of our
kind, who often travel great distances by both sea and land. Only
a long time after the earth dried completely were we able to get a
true picture of what the new world looked like—and even then we
often had to go by guesswork."

"I can quite understand that," said the Doctor. "Excuse my
impatience. I am very keen to learn how much the world was
changed by the Deluge. But tell me in your own time. We are all
ready—when you are—to go on."

"Well," said the turtle, "after we had finished up our piece of bacon, the raven called to the pelican whom he had brought back with him last night.

"'Take a dive, Pel,' says he. 'We're going to need some grub before we sight the land.'

"The pelican grunted and took off. Marvelous it was to see the difference, in that dumpy bird, between his walking and his flying. In the air, he soared most gracefully. He scouted round the raft quite a while before he suddenly shut his wings and dropped like a stone toward the water. His keen eyes had seen fish swimming near the top. What a splash he made! Reminded me of pitching an anchor into the sea.

"But he knew his business. Disappearing under the water for five minutes, he suddenly pops up again, only a yard away from the raft. We helped him aboard. Then he opens that great shovel-mouth of his and spilled out a load that looked like a fish market. There were two fine haddock, a mackerel, and a lot of little fish besides.

"'Will that do—as a starter?' says the pelican in a gentle grunt. 'Light wasn't so good—and many got away from me underwater.'

"'Brother,' says the raven, 'that will do elegant. Enough food to hold us all for quite a while. Boy, you may not hit the water pretty; but you're surely a great fisherman. Oh, watch that mackerel! He's trying to flip overboard.'

"Indeed Belinda, Eber, Gaza, and myself had to get busy keeping the jumping, live fish from hopping back into the sea. Eber had a sharp stone knife he had made. He chopped the heads off the fish, slit them open, and—after washing them—set them outside the roof shelter to dry in the sun. Then the raven says:

"'Now, my hearties, as soon as you're ready, let's go. Your pace—swimming and dragging this crazy raft—will not be fast.'

"He spoke the truth. I can only guess how far it really was—close to five or six hundred miles, I'd say. Luckily the wind helped us most of the way. But oh, how sick we got of fish, the only food we had. Yet we never could have made the trip without it.

"At last, on the fifth day, however, we sighted a low line of land ahead of us; and hopes of a new home, on dry earth, put heart into us. We found a nice harbor or bay, where we anchored the raft. How wonderful it felt to step out onto something dry—which kept still under your feet!

"But oh, the country was desolate! There was nothing growing yet of course—even here. And, although the water had dropped much lower in these parts, the shore was cut by many large rivers. You see, a great deal of water lay on the high plains, many miles inland from the sea; and this was still rushing down to get to the ocean, cutting riverbeds on its way.

"We set about making a home at once—just a hut—out of driftwood, planks, and old wreckage we found along the beaches. Our good friend, the raven, went off searching for seeds of fruits and vegetables. He brought back many kinds that seemed still in good condition. Eber, you will remember, was a very clever gardener, having been chief assistant to King Mashtu's park-keeper—till he was changed over to help Noah in the menagerie. Well, he dug a garden behind the hut and planted seed. But not a single one of them sprouted.

"This puzzled him for some time. But in the end (being a good gardener) he found out the reason. Down here, close to the shore, the salt water of the ocean—when it had been higher—had so poisoned all the soil, that for years it would be useless for plant growth. After that we moved farther inland, hunting for hilly country where the ground might not be as salty. We found what we were looking

"He dug a garden behind the hut."

for only a few miles away. There we built another home, dug a garden, and planted more seed.

"This time our luck was better. In a few weeks many of the seeds took root and came up. They grew very slowly and were not much to be proud of, but you've no idea how happy it made us to see anything green sprout out of that bare earth.

"By now, too, the waters at the shore were beginning to settle down; and when rains came we noticed that, in the rivers, it was almost drinkable—though we still did not use it for drinking. We did what we had all along: caught the fresh rainwater in anything we could, and stored it away for drinking and cooking. Off the rocks at the shore, the fishing too was better, as the currents grew calmer. Eber rigged up a kind of spear, or harpoon, and killed sea otters and the like. So at last we had some fresh meat, instead of that everlasting fish-food that poor Gaza was dreadfully tired of.

"From time to time, when we were working on our garden, we noticed many large seabirds in the sky above, soaring around in circles. But at the time we did not pay much attention to them. We supposed they were just interested to see green plants of any kind coming up for the first time in so long.

"While we were waiting for our vegetables and fruits to get big enough for eating, I went down to the shore and explored under the sea for towns. But I found only a few scattered farmhouses—no towns or villages. Again I got a bottle of wine or two—with a few gardening tools—and these I brought back to our hut. But what I had been hunting for was real solid food, to give the boy and girl a change. They had begun again to look sort of sickly on fish, with only a piece of otter meat now and then—and no vegetable stuff at all.

"On these trips I was forever hoping to find the old city of Shalba. It had been such a rich and well-fed town, as I knew it before the Flood. I felt sure there must still be plenty of good eatables among the wreckage of its shops—as well as good seeds in its Royal Botanical Gardens.

"But in this, too, I was disappointed. I could not find Shalba; and nowhere else, it seemed, could I find any solid food for menfolk to eat. I was very unhappy.

"However, on one trip I made a discovery. This time I went farther off than I'd ever done before. I was gone for twelve days and must have traveled several hundreds of miles from the hut.

"I had crossed one deep valley where the current, running

through it northward, was terribly strong. I suspected it to be the great River Nile, which drains most of Egypt. And, if it was the Nile, that meant I had passed over, underwater, from Asia Minor to the mainland of Africa. After going on a great distance, I became surer and surer this was true.

"Every once in a while I'd come to deserts and ranges of mountains that I could have sworn I'd seen before.

"Then suddenly I found myself on a long steep slope that stretched downward into much deeper water. Now, in my free days, before I'd been put into King Mashtu's zoo, I had traveled a lot through and around his kingdom—sometimes for big distances. But I couldn't remember ever having seen this steep slope before. I decided to go down to the bottom of it to make sure of where I was.

"Well, I never reached the bottom! For hours and hours I went on, skimming down, lower and lower. The light got so poor that at last it was black as night; and I could see nothing at all. No use to go on: you can't explore where you can't see. I knew, by the terrible cold and the great pressure on my shell, that I was now in enormously deep water.

"But I had found out something more. I only guessed at it then. Years later, when the waters settled still lower, and more shoreline showed, I knew that my guess had been right. This was a *brand-new ocean* I was in, one which had been cut by that wide and mountainous wave we had seen sweeping across the Shalba racetrack.

"You see, John Dolittle, the world before the Deluge had been made up of more land than sea; now it is more sea than land."

"Ah!" murmured the Doctor. "That explains a whole lot that geographers have been guessing at for thousands of years. But go on, please."

"Before the Flood," said the turtle, "Africa, Europe, and America were all joined—just one large continent. And Mashtu ruled as king over almost the whole of it. This new ocean, into which I had stumbled, was what you call now the *Atlantic*. America was a wild and distant country, with few or no people on it. Between the Old World and the New there was said to be a waterless desert of sand and stones. But later, when the Flood cut through, the ocean was simply full of islands. Most of them were soon washed away by storms and whatnot.

"And, as you know, today the only big island groups left are the Canaries, the Cape Verdes, the Madeiras, the Azores—with a few less important ones like the Bermudas and the Bahamas. The world was changed indeed! Even that little ocean you call the Mediterranean Sea, which used to be a large inland lake, cut the thin neck of land at Gibraltar and poured its waters through, to join the Atlantic."

"Most interesting," said the Doctor. "Don't miss any of this, Stubbins. It's terribly important to science."

"Very good, sir," said I. "I've got it all down."

"Tell me, Mudface," said the Doctor, turning back to the turtle. "The climates of the different parts of the earth must have been changed, too, by all this, eh?"

"Oh my, yes!" said Mudface. "In the good old days almost everywhere there seemed to be plenty of sunshine. Many good vegetables grew wild. A man need never starve, even if he wandered without tent or baggage; for almost anywhere the countryside would provide him with the food he needed. For this reason there was very little meat eaten—by civilized people, at all events. It was only after the Flood that man and beast had to struggle and fight one another for a living. Ah yes, it was very different then, keeping yourself alive!

"And it changed the lives of all creatures. Before, men had spent their days thinking of higher things, singing songs, playing games, and inventing poetry. Now everyone had to calculate and work and worry for *one* idea only: getting enough to eat."

"Do you feel," asked the Doctor, "that the world has not yet recovered—got over—that dreadful Flood?"

"No, Doctor," said the turtle. "Things got slowly better, of course. But this earth has never since been the same. What had been warm countries were now cold ones. Why, palm trees with dates on them, used to grow where the North Pole is now placed, in the frozen Arctic Ocean.

"But to get on with my own story: I swam up to the surface and started to go back to the hut. As I said, I had been gone from our home twelve whole days.

"When, after much hard swimming, I at last drew near to it, my heart was filled with fear. Gathered about the hut was a huge crowd of animals of every kind. How had they got here? Cats cannot swim. Then suddenly I remembered the birds who'd watched our gardening, and I knew. Those birds had led them here, over the land that had now grown so much larger with the lowering of the waterline. I cursed my stupidity in staying away so long.

"When I got closer still I saw the tigress, who seemed to be in charge—as usual. For weeks we had felt ourselves quite safe— thinking that, with so much water between us, the cats would never be able to follow. I could see nothing of Eber and Gaza—those children whom my wife and I had grown to think of as our own! . . . Were they killed? Had they been eaten?

"Tired as I was from the long swim, I broke into a run toward our home as fast as my legs would carry me."

THE SEVENTEENTH CHAPTER

Antelope and Grass-Eaters

TO MY SURPRISE, IT WAS THE PELICAN, AND not the raven, who came forward to meet me. Without waiting for any questions from me, he hurriedly told me that Eber and Gaza were still alive but in great danger. They had shut themselves in the hut and barred the door, but he feared they would not be safe for long, as the hut was so light and flimsy.

"But by the time I'd reached the edge of the crowd of animals, the bull-elephant had his shoulder against the shack's door. One shove from that great body could, I knew, lay the whole building flat. I cried out to the elephant to stop. Then I spoke to the crowd, asking the animals why they wished to hurt my friends.

"'Your *friends*!' cried the tigress, stepping forward and raising her upper lip in an angry snarl. 'Why do you call this man and woman your friends? Have not they and their kind made slaves of us? Did they not take away my cubs and put them in a cage to be looked at?'

"'Aye!' trumpeted the elephant, waving his trunk wildly in the air. 'Didn't they make a beast of burden out of me and walk me

"'Stand aside, Turtle!' yelled the tigress."

through the streets in circus processions? Did they not make slaves of the horses and oxen, setting them to plow the fields in the hot sun?'

"'Let them die!' snarled the tigress. 'Elephant, crush in the door and I'll swallow them in two gulps. We want no more men in the world. *We* are now the masters. This earth forever more shall be the kingdom of the animals. Smash the door, Elephant. They will make a juicy meal!'

"'Aye, aye!' they all howled. 'Break down the door!'

"The elephant drew back his shoulder in readiness, like a battering ram. I saw that this was the moment when I must act—and quickly. I put my head down and pushed my way through that crowd. The sharp edges of my shell knocked the feet out from under animals of all kinds, who fell to either side of my path in kicking, struggling heaps. I weighed eight hundred pounds, which made my shoving as destructive as that elephant's. I reached the hut; and while the elephant's shoulder was still drawn back, waiting, I slipped in between him and the shack and set my back against the door.

"'Stand aside, Turtle!' yelled the tigress. 'Your *friends* must die.'

"'Wait!' I cried. 'Wait and let me speak. You have told me why you think this man your enemy—that he imprisoned you and gave you hard work to do. Let me tell you that these things were done to me also. I, too, was a prisoner in a zoo. And yet I call those within this hut my friends. It was not they who made us slaves.

"'It was King Mashtu who did it—he who almost enslaved the whole world, man and beast. These two young people you wish to eat were also slaves—like you and me. Yet, in spite of his own slavery, the boy Eber did his best to make life more bearable for me and my companions in prison. And that is why I call him *friend.*'

"'What do we care for that?' asked a big black panther working his way forward to the front of the mob. 'If these two are allowed to live, they will have cubs, like ourselves, peopling the earth again with cruel masters. Give them to us, Turtle!'

"'Yes, yes,' the crowd yelled. 'We would rid the world of men now and forever. We want a free earth. Down with man! Let him and the woman be wiped out!'

"Then with ugly howls the crowd rushed forward. Once more the elephant, reaching over my back, put his shoulder against the door. I heard Gaza inside whisper to her companion with a sob, 'Good-bye, Eber. This is the end!'

"Then red floated before my eyes and a great anger boiled up in my heart. I shouted to the growling crowd. 'If any of you eat them, you're going to have to kill me first.'

"And suddenly, rearing up on my hind legs, I bit a piece clean out of the elephant's ear. With a roar of pain he staggered back carrying the others with him. And for a moment the space about the door was clear again.

"But I knew another rush would come. There were too many against me. Belinda, I guessed, was inside the hut, ready to put up a last fight for the youngsters' lives. If only I had the raven here to help me think out some plan! But he happened to be away seed hunting when that mob of animals arrived. I decided that the best I could do for the present was to keep them talking, hoping against hope that help would come to me from somewhere.

"'What of Noah?' I asked the crowd. 'Where is he? Have you eaten him?'

"'No,' barked the she-wolf. 'He's still back there at the Ark. Only the sheep stayed with him. There are two lambs; and Noah is trying to keep them alive with half a sack of dried rice out of his own stores. We came away and left him in disgust. For *us* he has no food. All he has given us for weeks is just promises. What was the good of saving us if we are to have nothing to eat to stay alive on?'

"'Maybe that was the only thing the old man could do,' said I. 'With no more than half a sack of rice left, he chose to save sheep instead of wolves. I'm sure I don't blame him.'

"'We would have eaten him and all his family,' said the tigress. 'But it was he, Noah, who saved us from the waters, so we let him live. But if his sons and their wives have any babies, we're going to eat them. And when Noah's grandchildren die, man shall disappear for good. Stand away from that door, Turtle! You have hindered us long enough.'

"'Fools, fools, *fools*!' I cried at the top of my voice—it was the best speech I ever made and that was the way I began it: 'Fools, fools,

fools! Do you suppose this Flood was an accident, like stubbing your foot against a stone? No. Someone—I don't know who—but someone *planned* all this. The king of Shalba made himself ruler of almost all the world. But his rule was bad—built on lies, slavery, cheating, and broken promises. Still he went on from power to more power. No country had the strength or courage to beat him down.'

"I saw that living skeleton, the she-wolf, shift restlessly, impatient at my talk. But many animals were listening with attention. I went on:

"'And had Mashtu become complete ruler of the whole world, nobody can say what bad things would have followed—nor how long that lying king and his children's children would have run the world to suit themselves and their friends.

"'Then this someone, whose name we do not know, but whose greater power controlled the rains, the tides, and the fires in the sleeping volcanoes, made up his mind that the world and its so-called civilization must start again from the bottom of the ladder. And even if some suffered, a new earth and a better civilization *must* be rebuilt.'

"'Oh twaddle,' I heard the tigress mutter. 'Words, words! We want food, not talk.'

"But most of the animals took no notice of what she said. Neither did I.

"'Now tell me,' I said to the crowd, 'do you think you can live without man? Well, look around at this land that the Deluge has given back to you. Has it grass or fruit or anything to eat on it? No. And more than half of you live on grass, not meat. When my two poor friends in this hut are killed, when Noah and his family are gone, what then? You'll start eating one another, won't you? Till there is no life left in a dead world. Look around you. The earth is naked—nothing but stones and steaming, rotting rubbish. Now go look behind this hut.'

"They went. There they saw the seedlings and young plants in the garden. In less than a minute every green shoot had been gobbled up by the hungry deer.

"So much for all of poor Eber's hard work, I thought to myself. But I did not interfere. I slipped back to the front of the hut, put my back to it again, and let them finish their meal.

"When they returned and gathered before me again, I said:

"'Now do you understand? It was not planned that man should pass from the earth—not in *this* Deluge anyhow. You need Eber's brains and skill if you want to live through this destruction. You need him to farm and plant, so that the earth may again give you food and pasture and cover.'

"Then from the expression in the faces of the deer and antelope—of which there were hundreds of different kinds—I saw that I had got them thinking. They began talking together in low tones. I knew that if I could get all the grass-eaters on my side, my battle was won; for the cats and other meat-eaters—although far more deadly fighters—were fewer than the animals that live on grass and vegetable food.

"'Listen,' I shouted, 'you who don't eat meat: Do you want this man Eber to live and bring the green earth back to life for you? Or will you give him to these cats to eat?'

"The deer, of course, were afraid of the tigers and leopards. They whispered together a moment longer, while I saw the scowling tigress talking to the lions a little farther off.

"Then suddenly those hundreds of antelope, deer, and chamois sprang to my side and lowered their horns like a row of swords to defend the door—to defend Eber, the gardener, against the meat-eaters of the world."

PART FOUR

Man Becomes a Servant to the Animals

THAT, I FANCY, WAS THE GREATEST SURPRISE of Mrs. Tiger's life. She was so furious at this unexpected turn that, very foolishly, she got her husband to make another rush at us at once. But the brave antelopes stood their ground. It was a bristling ring of horns that spread around the hut. They did not tremble; they did not give way—though I knew how they feared the queen of the jungle. And, within three paces of those spearlike points, the cats changed their minds and slowed down.

"The tigress muttered something—which I could not hear—to her husband. Then they turned and slunk back. Next, I saw her go through the crowd, whispering to each of the meat-eaters in turn. I guessed she was trying to get them all worked up to fighting pitch.

"At any time they were deadly brutes—now made more dangerous by hunger near to starvation. Again I grew afraid for Eber and Gaza; because it was plain the tigress was planning this attack upon the hut from several different points at the same time. Soon I saw the cats getting ready: they were forming up in gangs of six or eight in a bunch.

"'He is going to live, I say!'"

"But in the nick of time help came to me from a very unexpected quarter. I heard the cow-elephant whisper to the bull-elephant.

"'Husband, this moment is, I'm sure, one of great importance. If the cats should win this battle, much trouble—perhaps death for want of food—may come to us. I am for the turtle—and Eber, the sower of seeds. Where in all this devastated desert of a world are you and I—and our young ones later—going to graze, unless somebody gets the grasses started? The turtle is right. Let us take his part.'

"Then (you can imagine my relief!) just as the tigress opened her jaws to give the word for the next rush, those two great elephants tramped forward and stood, shoulder to shoulder, with the antelopes and myself. With them came the two hippos and a pair of rhinoceroses—also grass-eaters. All of them were heavy beasts whose trampling charge could knock a stone wall down. After that, there was no doubt whatever as to which side was the stronger.

"'Get away, you mangy cats!' bellowed the bull-elephant. 'Leave the man alone! We want grass. Eber is a good gardener. We need him. He is going to live, I say—to live and work for us. With food, we animals will be the masters of the world and he the slave. When his usefulness is done and the earth is green again, you may eat him if you wish. But until we have grass, he is under *my* protection. Do you understand? Good! Let no more be said.'

"Well, John Dolittle, that was how a short chapter in the history of the world began—the time when the animals were the masters, and man the slave. Alas! I had succeeded in saving Eber and Gaza from being killed, only to see their freedom taken from them a second time.

"When the door of the hut was opened, they were set to work at once in the garden, which was made larger yet. They were harnessed to the wooden plow which they had used for their own vegetables. And the elephant drove them like a team of horses along the furrows, cracking a big whip over their heads, the way he had seen the ringmasters do in the circus of Shalba. Many of the animals laughed and jeered at this sight.

"But to me, who remembered how kind Eber had been to the creatures in Mashtu's zoo, there was something terribly unfair and saddening in the whole business.

"However, you could not help noticing, after the elephant first defied the cats and took command himself of this new animal kingdom, how the creatures of every sort grew less afraid of the tigress. She couldn't boss them around the way she used to. A new leader had taken her place—a leader whose word was law. Many meat-eaters were now doubly dangerous. So near to starvation were they, they often fought, killed, and ate one another. Yet they were never allowed to touch Eber and Gaza.

"The birds and the little digging beasts, such as badgers, moles and field mice, were ordered to bring all seed, nuts, and acorns to Eber. And these creatures—though they, too, were ravenously hungry—did as their new elephant leader told them.

"For they all realized the importance of that first new crop of plants. This crop would of course, in time—as soon as the salt was washed away by the rains—spread its own seed over the world's naked soil. But it must be given a chance to come to full growth. So meanwhile, the grass-eaters were allowed to nibble only enough, here and there, to keep alive. And the leader elephant—who usually eats an awful lot in a day—he did the same.

"He was, in a way, the new Mashtu of the world—with this difference: *he always kept his word.* And though he worked Eber and Gaza terribly hard, he wasn't cruel or treacherous, like Shalba's king had been. All the animals respected and liked him.

"Those who stayed back with the Ark, were treated just as fairly. There, as the islands grew larger with the falling water, Noah's sons—Ham, Shem, and Japheth—were put to work, cutting the buds out of old uprooted trees and planting them in the ground to start new orchards. The patriarch Noah was not made to work because he was too old and weak. The elephant sent his own wife over to take charge of this part of his new kingdom—to see that Ham didn't loaf instead of work.

"I have often thought that if the beasts of the world were saved by Noah and his family from the Flood, the animals paid back the debt later. For they kept him and his sons alive by their good sense and planning when starvation—after the land began to dry, seemed to grip all creation with an iron hand.

"And so, for a while at least, things went along pretty well. But they did not suit that savage, selfish tigress. Although she pretended, like the others, to be obedient to the new Elephant Emperor, I—for one—did not trust her.

"She had always wanted to be the boss herself; and something warned me she had never given up hope of some day, somehow, again setting herself up as leader, now that man had sunk to slavery. Belinda and I talked it over; and we agreed that I was most likely right. So I made up my mind to watch that slant-eyed man-eater. For Eber's and Gaza's sake I did not intend to be caught napping a *second* time.

"I had to be most careful that the tigress should never learn I was keeping an eye on her. At last I became certain that, in spite of all her show of obedience, she was a traitor, jealous of the Elephant Emperor and working secretly for his downfall.

"And this was how I found her out. Eber and Gaza slept in the hut. But every night two animals were posted as sentries at their door, to make sure they did not escape. A short distance away a sort of stable-shelter had been rigged up for the Elephant Emperor to live in. Still farther off I knew the tigress had made a den for herself and her husband, out of a tangle of dead trees.

"It became a habit of mine every night to rest close to Eber's hut. I used to half bury myself nearby, so I could see but not be seen. One night, when Eber and Gaza were sleeping inside, tired and worn out with hard work, I saw the dark shape of the tigress lurking around the shack. The sentries on duty that night were two giraffes. But they did not see that great cat. Indeed the beast, in that poor light, sneaking slowly over the ground on her big padded feet, was more like a shadow than a living creature.

"Soon I made a discovery: she had not come to attack my friends tonight. She just wanted to make sure they were still safely locked up. And—what's more—she was, herself, most anxious that the giraffe sentries should not see *her*. She did not go up to speak with them. But, after sniffing round the hut a bit, she moved off in a direction quite different from that by which she'd come. So, after she'd gone, I followed her, making no more noise than she did herself.

"Now, at the bottom of a big hollow to the south there was a cave in the rocks, where the animals often went to enjoy the cool when the sun was especially hot. Mrs. Tiger was headed toward this cave. I reckoned it was about midnight. She came to the mouth of the cave and I saw her glide down into its dark depths without a sound.

"I was about to do the same. But on second thought I decided to hang back awhile. Lucky for me I did! Presently while I watched and waited—crouching low behind a stone—down into that hollow crept more cats: cheetahs, leopards, black panthers, lions, and many other kinds. It began to look like a gathering of our old enemies. Still I waited on, to see if there were more to come. After about a quarter of an hour I thought it would now be safe for me to move. I wasn't going down into the cave; but I was going to get as close to the entrance as I could.

"So, first, I went to a mud-hole nearby and caked myself all over with mud. When I had finished, I looked just like a lump of messy earth. Then I went and placed myself as close as possible to the cave's entrance, drew my head and feet into my shell, and kept as still as a stone.

"Well, I heard every word that was said at that meeting—which was what I'd come for. I learned every detail of the great Revolution of the Cats, which later overthrew the Elephant Empire.

"The tigress told them she thought the lion should be set up as leader in the elephant's place. The others all noisily agreed to that. But I, at least, was not taken in by her talk. I was still certain the tricky old cat meant herself to be the boss—even while she told the rest of them that in the lion they had chosen a good leader. All she really wanted—for the present—was to set them against the Elephant Emperor."

The Revolution
of the Cats

"WELL," MUDFACE BEGAN, AS WE SAT down next night, "the tigress told the meeting she had the whole revolution planned out and arranged: tomorrow, Saturday, I think, but—"

"Revolution indeed!" Jip growled in a low and angry voice. "What that old she-cat needed was a nip on the ear. But it certainly sounds exciting!"

"It was," said the turtle, "though not exactly as the tigress hoped. Her idea was this: the next night, as soon as the elephant would be fast asleep, she and the lioness, the leopardess, and the she-panther were going to surround the leader's shed and force him to give up his empire and go away. If he refused, it was agreed that they would kill him—which they could have done, so long as they attacked him in a band, unexpectedly. In the meantime the lion, the tiger, and the leopard would kill Eber. Gaza was to be kept for the women-cats to eat.

"You see, during all this time when the big meat-eaters were short of food, they had kept themselves alive by devouring other creatures who were too small and weak to fight back. Noah was not with them now to keep order. And so, John Dolittle—the same as with the trees—we lost many kinds of animals who were completely wiped out and never seen again. And as soon as the tigress spoke to that ravenous pack inside the cave of eating Eber and Gaza, I heard them all lick their chops and grunt with appetite.

"A little later I guessed, from the racket down below, that the meeting was over and the party was breaking up. And before I had time to get away from the mouth of the cave, all the big cats came trundling out, talking together in low whispers. For a moment I was scared I would be discovered, spying. But my disguise worked perfectly. With my head and feet drawn in and my back all plastered with mud, I looked like a part of the ground itself. Those great beasts walked over or around me, never suspecting I'd heard every word of their plot. Many of them actually stepped on me with their large padded feet.

"The last to leave the cave was the tigress. On her face I could see, by the dim moonlight, a grin of cunning conceit. She was thinking of the great plans she had set afoot to make herself queen of the animal kingdom. I watched her long muscular body creep up to the rim of the hollow, where she stood for a moment against the sky.

"'All right, you slinky old witch,' I whispered to myself. 'It's queen you're going to be, eh? Wait and see. I, Mudface the turtle, know now what you mean to do.'

"As she moved off the skyline, toward her den, I brought my head all the way out of my shell and shook off most of the mud in which I had caked myself. At first it seemed to me best to go at

"Many of them actually stepped on me."

once to the Elephant Emperor and warn him of his danger and the Revolution of the Cats.

"But on thinking this over a bit, I could see it wasn't such a good idea. It would only mean that fighting among the animals would break out sooner; for I felt certain at last the tigress would put up a fight to a finish, to be made the leader of the beasts.

"Besides, I myself partly agreed with the animals of the world in their not wanting to become once more the slaves of man. That is, I did until I saw how, through their everlasting separating and squabbling among themselves, they showed that they had not the sense to rule the earth—even as well as man had done. And that isn't saying much. But anyway, whether the animal kingdom succeeded or not, my mind was made up that neither Eber nor Gaza was going to be eaten.

"So I sat there awhile, wondering what was the best thing I could do. And presently I said to myself: '*Tonight!* That's it. Get them out of it—beyond the reach of the cats—before the dawn comes. It's the only way to be sure of saving them. If I wait till morning, all sorts of animals will be awake to tell the tigress what I'm doing. I won't stand a chance then. While now I have only two sentries to deal with—giraffes—who are not very bright. Eber and the girl must leave tonight.'

"I got busy, I can tell you. It was about an hour past midnight. First of all, I followed Her Majesty Mrs. Tiger to her den, taking care she shouldn't hear or see me. I lingered near her home till the sounds of a grunting snore told me she was safely asleep. Then I hustled off and woke up my wife, Belinda, who lived not far from Eber's hut. I told her the whole business as fast as I could. When I'd finished, she said:

"'Mudface, you're right about getting those two young people away immediately. But as for the giraffes, the sentries on guard at the hut, you'd better leave them to me. No use trying force, because they'd raise an outcry and we'd have the whole camp around our ears in two seconds. You keep out of sight a minute and let me go talk to the guards. I'll tell them of a place where the wild rice is sprouting.'

"'Where's that?' I asked.

"'Nowhere, so far as I know,' said Belinda. 'Yes, I grant you it's a dirty trick to play on those simple grass-eaters. But the boy and the girl come first. The giraffes are hungry enough to believe, and do, anything. I'll offer to lead them to the growing rice. Then, as soon as they and I have left, you burrow in under the wall of the hut and get Eber and Gaza to run off with you!"

"'Humph!' said I. 'That may take time, you know.'

"'True,' she answered. 'But we've got some hours before the sun rises. Get as far away as you can and I'll try to pick up your trail as soon as it is safe to give the giraffes the slip. But don't forget that those cats have dreadfully sharp noses for following a scent. You better make for the nearest water. And, again, remember that the nearest water is much farther off than it used to be, now that the seas are dropping lower every day. But once you reach the big water, you'll be safe from the cats—with Eber, anyhow. You may not be able to swim with the two on your back. . . . If you can't, hide the girl in a cave or something till I catch up with you. Now I'll go and talk to the guards.'

"'All right, Belinda,' I said. 'Lead them off to the westward for the rice, and I'll take Eber and the girl toward the east. Good luck to you!'

"'Good luck to both of us!' she answered."

THE THIRD CHAPTER

The Escape

I WATCHED MY WIFE AS SHE CREPT TOWARD THE hut. The long necks of the giraffes stood up like flagpoles before the door. I wanted to hear what was said, but I remembered Belinda's advice and stayed back out of sight.

"Just the same, I knew she must be finding it hard to get them to go away. For minutes and hours passed, and still the low murmur of their talk went on. I began to wonder how much more of darkness I had left to make the escape in.

"At last, to my great relief, the giraffes lowered their long necks and slunk away into the shadows, led by Belinda. Much time had been wasted; and as soon as they were gone I hurried to the door of the hut. I could not undo the latch and I was afraid to knock, lest the noise should wake the Elephant Emperor whose sleeping shed was quite near. So I started at once to scratch my way under the door.

"By working like a madman, I soon dug a hole big enough for me to get through into the hut.

"Inside it was pretty dark. The tiny window was covered with

"The long necks of the giraffes stood up like flagpoles."

sacks. I moved gently round the little room till I found Eber and Gaza sleeping on the floor. They were scared when I nudged them awake; but the boy's hands, touching my shell as he got up, told him it was I, Mudface—his friend.

"Then came another delay to waste still more of the remaining darkness. *I was unable to tell them what I'd come for!* You see, although I could understand most of their language, I could not of course speak it. I had to use signs and acting. And you've no idea what a time I had getting it into those people's heads that they were in the greatest danger and must fly with me immediately.

"At last, after I'd run back and forth between them and the hole I'd made under the door, they caught on to what I meant.

"'Eber,' the girl whispered, 'the turtle is telling us to leave the hut, I think. Perhaps if we follow him we may escape from slavery.'

"'What chance is there of that?' asked Eber. 'There are the giraffes outside, on guard. How could we get past them?'

"Then I grabbed hold of him and tried to drag him to the door. He came. He knelt down and peered out through the hole I'd made.

"'Why, Gaza!' he said. 'The sentries are gone! We can escape. . . . Good old Mudface!' He patted me gently on the head.

"As soon as they fully understood that I had come with a plan—and a chance for them to get away—it was not so hard for me. On all fours, both of them followed me out, scrambling under the door.

"Eber knew as well as I did that their great danger was the big cats (who can follow a trail, when there is meat to kill, better than any animals living).

"And he now did a very bright thing. He told Gaza to wait with me just outside the hut; while he himself ran all around it and went off short distances in every direction. This was to leave his scent all over the place, to confuse the cats when they would try to follow. As soon as he had finished, he came back to us. Then we started off.

"I led them to the eastward, as Belinda and I had arranged. But alas! We had scarcely gone more than a mile when I saw the sky ahead of us turning gray with the first show of morning. Most likely, I guessed, the giraffes had already returned to the hut from their wild-rice chase; and any moment now the whole camp would be warned of our escape.

"I was not far wrong. Soon, as we scrambled and tumbled forward, I heard in the distance behind us the howling of wolves and the bark of hyenas. Our flight was discovered.

"I blessed Eber's good sense then in leaving his scent on false trails before we came away from the hut. For, without that extra time, we would have stood a mighty poor chance. I reckon a good hour was spent by Mrs. Tiger, shooting off on wrong tracks, before she struck our true trail eastward.

"Now, I had hoped by this time to have found water. But, in spite of Belinda's warning, I had no idea how much more land had been left dry since last I'd gone exploring. The country spread out flat in all directions with not a drop of water in sight.

"Suddenly behind us I heard the first roar of the lion. He had pulled a little ahead of the other cats in the hunt. At that terrifying noise, poor Gaza clung to Eber, begging him to find some hiding place.

"Indeed I was beginning to think of that myself—bad though the chance of cover was. Still, I knew there was no hope of outdistancing our enemies in open country, now that they had got our scent.

"I clambered onto a big uprooted tree and looked in every direction for rocks or a cave—anything to put my friends in. There I might at least be able to defend them till Belinda's help arrived— or the elephant caught up with the faster cats and called them off. That would mean going back to slavery at the plow for the boy and girl; but at least it was better than being eaten.

"Suddenly Gaza screamed and pointed to the west. And there, just coming in sight over the skyline, was the whole pack of them— with the tigress now in front—traveling at full speed. Eber picked

"I clambered onto a big, uprooted tree."

up a rock and got in front of the girl. But of course for him to stand and fight such enemies as that (there were a good two dozen in the leading gang) was just madness.

"At my wit's end—with no other plan except to get them farther away—I scrambled down from the tree, made a sign to Eber to follow me, and stumbled on."

Mudface stopped a moment; and that same kindly grin passed across his aged face.

"*Stumbled* is the right word," he said presently. "I don't believe I ever ran so hard in my life. I tripped and fell and bumped my nose a hundred times. The roaring and the snarling of the cats grew nearer and louder every minute. I really thought it was all over for these human-folk.

"I could hear the elephant now, too, a long way behind the cats, bellowing to them to stop. But the revolution had broken out and they took no notice of the Emperor's orders anymore. As I glanced back over my shoulder, I could see that savage tigress leaping toward us at a truly terrific speed. Her husband galloped at her side—with the two lions close behind. And still, because there was nothing else to do, I stumbled on, gasping encouraging words to those two terrified youngsters—but with no real hope left in my heart.

"Soon the tigress, as she now saw her prey almost within grasp of her wicked claws, started jeering and laughing at us—calling me a clumsy fool every time I stumbled or fell.

"But she jeered—and laughed—too soon. The change in my luck was near."

The Fall of the Elephant Empire

A T THE LAST MOMENT, WHEN I WAS IN COM- plete despair—expecting to see the boy and girl torn to pieces before my very eyes—a miracle happened. The ground suddenly gave way under my feet; and I found myself wallowing in a bog!

"The country, which had looked so flat and dry for miles in all directions, was really one large marsh. I had not reached real water; but I had reached mud, which suited me even better.

"Eber and Gaza were up to their waists already. They scrambled onto my back. With the weight I began to sink— almost out of sight. I could carry one, but not both.

"Eber understood and got off at once, back into the mud. But I knew he couldn't last long there—exhausted as he was. So I sig- naled to him to take a hold on the shoulder of my shell and cling to it with one hand. In this way I could keep his chin above the mud.

So, with the girl on my back and the man in tow, I plowed on deeper into the bog. Presently I turned my head and shouted to the snarling, disappointed tigress behind us.

"'Come and get them now, you she-devil—from the mud, where *clumsy fools*, like turtles, are at home! Follow us here, if you dare!'

"And, would you believe it, John Dolittle," (again that half smile flickered in the eyes of Mudface) "the tigress was so mad she did try to follow us, as I had challenged her to do? She drew back for a spring and leapt out into the marsh after us, reckoning I suppose, that she'd land on my back in one leap and kill the youngsters before I could get them farther away.

"But, great jumper though she was, she misjudged the distance that time. And with an awful splash she landed two feet short of me. Down she went in the swampy mire, right up to her ears. It nearly cost her her life, that leap. For in the deep mud she was as helpless as a kitten. Her big paws stuck fast; and the harder she struggled to get them free, the deeper she sank.

"Finally her husband and the other cats formed a living chain from the dry land; and, little by little, they pulled her great body out onto the solid ground. But oh, how she looked! You know cats hate to be wet and dirty. Well, her beautiful striped coat, of which she was so proud, was plastered in slush from head to tail. She reminded me of an enormous drowned rat.

"So now for the present we were safe—but by no means in a pleasant situation for Eber. While I could, even with Gaza on my back, drag him slowly along in the bog, such traveling was dreadfully tiring for him. And I knew that to go any long distance would be quite impossible without the help of Belinda.

"For some time now I had wondered why my wife had not shown up. Where she was I had no idea. Eber, I could see, was already near the end of his strength. I stopped where I was for the moment to rest him.

"Meanwhile I watched the crowd of cats on the shore of the marsh. They were talking together—I suppose about what they could do next.

"Presently the elephant arrived and started storming and scolding the cats for not waiting when he called to them. It was a great surprise to him when the meat-eaters, after they'd whispered to one another some more, suddenly turned on him in open rebellion.

"'We will obey you no longer,' snarled the tigress. 'You are big, but too stupid to lead the animals of the world. I have been chosen to take your place. Go now—while still you can. You are emperor no more.'

"Then was it seen how that poor, good-natured elephant was never meant to be a leader. What he should have done, of course, was to talk pleasantly to these rebels till the rhinos, the hippos, and the other big grass-eaters should come to his help. But instead, he gave the tigress such a box on her ear with his trunk that he knocked her over on her back.

"She suddenly turned into a four-legged firecracker. From the safety of the mud, I watched her get to her feet. She was positively cross-eyed with rage. She sprang upon the elephant, biting, scratching, and tearing like a fury.

"The other cats joined in. And if it had not been for his thick leathery skin, he would have been torn to ribbons. As it was, he was soon bleeding badly from many places. He seemed covered in fighting animals—who had tasted blood. Then he suddenly lay down and rolled, killing some of his attackers under the weight of his enormous body. Those who were only wounded by the crushing were immediately eaten by the others, now they could no longer defend themselves. . . . Gaza covered her eyes to shut out the picture. So much, I thought, for a world run by animals alone!

"At last the elephant arose, shook the rest of them off him and, bellowing with pain, galloped across the country as fast as he could. Some moved to follow him; but the tigress bade them stay. The Elephant Empire had fallen; and that strange chapter in the history of the world when man was the servant of the animals was drawing to a close."

THE FIFTH CHAPTER

Meeting an Old Friend Again

"TELL ME, MUDFACE," SAID THE DOCTOR, "AFTER the elephant ran away from the cats, did mankind take hold again and run things?"

"Not exactly—or, I should say, not yet, John Dolittle," said the turtle, as he settled down to his storytelling the next evening.

"It is true of course that for a while many of the hunting creatures were led by the tigress. But the grass-feeders just kept away from her—out of fear mostly.

"The bull-elephant, for instance, went off and joined his wife in the country where Noah was. From there, later, the pair of them drifted still farther away, seeking better fodder.

"The same thing happened with the meat-eaters, too, in the end. They grew tired of that old she-devil, of her conceit, of her bossiness—as well as of her savage temper. Then another split came. They wanted a chief whom they could respect, who would rule by something more than fear and trickiness.

"The lion was a good fellow. At least he was honest, even if he, too, was a killer. They elected him. And, as you know, the lion is spoken of to this day as the *King of Beasts*.

"But as for man's return to the mastery of the world, that did not come about till many years after Eber escaped from the hut.

"And I, the clumsy turtle, did a great deal to make that third big revolution possible. I did not realize this at the time—being only concerned in saving the lives of my human friends from the cruel hunger of a ruined world.

"I will tell you more of that last revolution soon. Just remember for the present, Doctor, that in the story of Eber and Gaza I am going on from where the tigress is still more or less mistress of the animal kingdom, determined to destroy mankind altogether. And we three hunted creatures are waiting out there, in the mud, hoping Belinda will join us any moment. You follow me?"

"Oh, quite, quite," said John Dolittle. "And now tell us, please, what happened next."

"The cats at last," Mudface went on, "began to straggle back toward their camp. Anyone could see they were discontented over the tigress's failure to give them meat—as she had boastfully promised.

"As soon as the last of them had disappeared over the skyline, I got Eber and the girl out of the bog onto solid ground—for a more comfortable rest. But I did not as yet go far from the marsh's edge, lest our enemies return unexpectedly.

"By now I became really worried about Belinda. Surely she must know how much I needed her help! Where *could* she be?

"Well, it was twilight, with a rising moon, before she showed up.

"'What kept you so long, Belinda?' I asked.

"'Oh dear!' she sighed. 'I thought I'd never get free of those stupid giraffes. I took long enough to coax them away from the hut,

"I got Eber and the girl out of the bog."

but longer still to get rid of them afterward. I had to keep making up new excuses for not finding that wild rice. But after hours of fooling around, we heard behind us the alarm that meant your escape had been discovered. Then I thought the time was come when I might shake them. Not at all: they stuck to me tighter than ever. Better stay with me, they said, and get some rice out of it, anyway.'

"Poor Belinda was almost in tears.

"'Well,' I said, 'never mind. You got here—that's the main thing. Take the girl on your back: I'll carry the boy. And let's be going. I'm afraid of more trouble from Mrs. Tiger any minute. Now that darkness is near, attack will be easier for her.'

"As we waded into the marsh with our passengers aboard, I told Belinda about the elephant's downfall and flight.

"'But what on earth is your idea,' she asked as I ended my story, 'in taking these young people out into the mud-lands? What are you going to put them on? How are you going to feed them?'

"Belinda nearly always asked her questions in threes—I suppose to make three times sure she'd get *some* answer. I, as usual, picked out the easiest question, knowing she'd likely forget the other two."

"Huh!" grunted the London sparrow. "That, my old Mudlark, is somethin' I *really* understand." Becky pretended not to hear; while the Doctor whispered:

"Hush, Cheapside! A little more respect, *please.*"

"'Belinda,' said I,'" (the turtle's voice grew tired and I glanced at the watch) "'my idea is to put them on dry land—when we reach it—the other side of this swamp.'

"'But how do you know there *is* any other side?' she asked. 'What if this marsh is the end of the land? How can you be sure, Husband?'

"'My dear,' I said, 'I'm not *sure* of anything, except our need to go on. This is the only direction we can take to escape the cats. And if, later, the bog turns into open water, so much the better: our travel will be easier and faster when we can swim. Come along.'

"That ended the discussion for the moment. All night long we traveled on in silence, while our weary riders slept on our backs. I took a course, still eastward, by the stars. And as I gazed up from this clinging desert of mud into the free and spangled dome of the sky, I was reminded again of Shalba.

"I thought of the nights when I used to stare into the heavens from the water of our prison-pond. Then those twinkling, distant lights had somehow seemed company for my imprisoned loneliness of heart. And the stars tonight looked exactly as they had above the zoological gardens of Shalba in the dry season of the year.

"You see, Doctor, before the Flood we had no spring, summer, autumn and winter, the way we do now. The year was divided into two halves only: the dry season and the rainy season. I have met animals who say it was the changing of the earth's spin at that time—as much as the forty-days' rain—which caused the spilling of the oceans, the Great Wave, the rumbling noises underground, and all the curious things that happened with the Deluge. But whether this is so or not I cannot tell.

"Anyway, that night as Belinda and I churned our way along, I fell to wondering again what had become of the proud city of Shalba and the spot where it had stood—under water or above.

"As the day was breaking, our flat landscape of swamp showed signs of changing. Wisps of fog appeared ahead. Eber on my back turned and muttered in his sleep, as the chill wind of dawn swept fitfully across the marsh. I sniffed at it and turned to my wife.

"'Belinda,' I said, 'I think we are coming to a lake. See the wide puddles dotted about in front of us. Look how oddly the gray light plays on them, between the shifting banks of mist. I wouldn't be surprised if we are near a real big lake.'

"'How do you know it's a lake? Why can't it be the sea? What if we've come to the end of everything—but mud?' she asked.

"'Belinda,' said I wearily, 'whatever it is, I'm going on. We can't go back. I think it's a lake we're coming to. . . . *Please*, no more questions!'

"Little by little, the mud gave place to water deep enough for swimming. And by the time the sun was well risen we found ourselves right out in open water, with no land in sight to the eastward. We were on the broad bosom of either a large lake or a sea.

"'This water tastes salty,' said Belinda.

"'You can't be certain of that,' I snapped back at her.

"I admit I was a bit peeved, after stirring soupy mud all night (and remember, Eber was no lightweight to carry). 'Not even you can be sure of that, my dear,' I repeated. 'All water tastes more or less salty now, since the oceans and the rivers got mixed up. I don't suppose this water itself knows whether it's fresh or salt. And as for the rivers, one half of them have forgotten where they're flowing *from*; while the rest are still trying to make up their minds where they'll flow *to*. Very confusing business, a deluge.'

"'That's true, anyway,' Belinda grunted. 'And *this* Deluge, I believe, Husband, has made *you* a little crazy in the head.'

"'Maybe so,' I said. 'Ah—oh, but isn't it a relief to feel your legs free, where it's deep enough for swimming?'

"'I suppose so,' was all she answered.

"But even she was cheered out of her grumbling when, in the afternoon, we chanced to meet our old friend the raven. He was flying in the opposite direction, low down over the water. It had been long since we saw him last. He settled down upon my shell. And I told him of the revolution led by the tigress, and the reason for our present flight.

"'Humph!' he grunted. 'I'm sorry about the poor old elephant. A good sort, in his way—even if he wasn't a born leader. But, believe me, that big striped cat will mess things up for the animals far worse than ever he did. . . . Hulloa, Eber! . . . How are you, Gaza?' They smiled at the raven, guessing that this was a greeting from him.

"'Wonderful how they understand me!' he said proudly. 'And me so out of practice in their lingo I can hardly remember a word of it. . . . Well, thank goodness my work's over for this year!'

"'What work?' asked Belinda.

"'You know,' said the raven, 'the mating season. It used to be easy: hen-bird sits on the eggs and cock-bird sits on a limb nearby, singing: *tra, la—tra, la!—Twiddle-dee—TWEET!*—Oh gracious!' He broke off in a cough. 'I declare my voice is getting worse. All this dampness, you know. But if you think you're the only one who's had troubles, Brother Turtle, you ought to try and find enough worms to satisfy a large family of fledgelings. O' course we *would* have to have one extra egg in a flood year! What beats me, though, is how earthworms learn to disappear in a deluge. Like looking for needles in a haystack.

"'The wife says it's *my* fault—I've been off gadding instead of attending to my proper job. I'd like to see anybody *gad* since the Big Rain fell! Well, job's over now. The nippers are flying around on their own, bumping into everything, bless 'em! . . . But tell me, Mudface, where are you all going now?'

"'Anywhere—to get away from that tigress,' I answered.

"'What is this water, Raven?' asked Belinda. 'Is it the sea?'

"'Oh no!' croaked the black bird. 'This is only a lake. If you keep on swimming for two or three hours more, the way you are now, you should come in sight of land on the other side.'

"'What is the country like on the other side?' I asked.

"'Nothing to boast of,' said he. 'Low-lying and swampy, till you get away back. But then every place is pretty bad now. Got to expect that. I've been trying to catch fish—a fellow must eat something. But I'm no good at the game—never came so near drowning in my life. Wish I had old Shovelface Pelican here to teach me how. Somehow I lost touch with him ages ago.'

"'But where *is* the sea, then,' asked Belinda, 'if this is only a lake?'

"'Well,' said the raven, 'at the farther shore of this lake there's a river running out of it. It flows through a big drowned forest; the trees are all dead—but still standing, like ghosts. It's a gloomy place. If you follow that stream it will bring you out to the sea, a brand-new ocean. I've just come from over there. Turned back at the shore, because the ocean looked most awful large. But I suppose there must be more land on the other side of it—if anyone had a mind to go and explore. Once there, your troubles should be over. No cats ever crossed *that* piece of water, I'll take a bet.'

"Our traveling companion seemed really glad to see us after his lonely wanderings over the sad landscape of a deluged earth. He prattled on a while longer about the things he'd seen; and at last we asked him would he care to come along with us. He thought a moment and then he said:

"'That's not half a bad idea. Can't see much sense in my going to join the other animals now—so long as that mean-tempered old tigress is the boss. I never could stand that sneaky snooper—and she doesn't like me either. . . . Yes, I'll come with you. We always had good luck when we voyaged together before.'

"So he joined our party and we went forward again. And somehow on the wide waters of the lake both Belinda and I felt safer and more hopeful, now we had the company of our re-found, chatterbox friend, the raven."

How Lake Junganyika Got Its Name

T HE SUN WAS SETTING IN THE WEST WHEN WE reached the farther shore. Here again we found land difficult for travel. But we didn't stop. With the help of the moon and the raven's guidance, we pushed straight on till we came to firm ground, about six miles farther inland.

"Now at last we could let our passengers get off our backs and move around on their own feet. Such a relief for Belinda and myself to be free of our loads! Too weary to bother about a proper camp or anything else, we settled down at once to sleep.

"But next morning the everlasting question of food bothered us once more. Eber and Gaza hadn't had a thing to eat in two days. So I thought I would go back and explore the bottom of the lake. If luck was on our side, who knows? I might find the homes of men a second time—and food for the youngsters.

"Well, the lake's floor, to my surprise, was gravelly, instead of muddy—at least it was then. And somewhere under the middle of that wide water I ran my nose into—you'd never guess what: the bent and twisted railing of my old prison-pond! I had found the City of Shalba at last! And here before you, John Dolittle, you see the same lake that hid it then and hides it still.

"I knew every scratch, every chip in the paint on it. It was strange, as I sniffed at that railing beneath the water, how the picture of my bitter, unhappy days of captivity flashed again before my eyes. The smell of the iron reawakened a hatred in my heart for Mashtu, Shalba's cruel king.

"I left the railing, crossed the park, and made my way through the crumbling doors of the royal palace. And there, among the silent, lofty halls of marble and porphyry, I threw back my head and laughed.

"'So,' I said, 'Mashtu the king passes! But Mudface the turtle lives on! Now will I go down into the cellars and bring royal food to them who were a king's slaves!'

"My luck was not bad. Dainties and rare things for eating, brought from all over the world, were there in plenty. But only the stuff sealed up in jars and bottles was any good now.

"I picked out one medium-sized jar—with no idea what was inside—swam up to the surface and carried it to the shore. I had a terrible time getting it over the few miles to the camping ground where we had spent the night.

"With hungry cries of delight, Eber and Gaza set to work on the cover of the jar and had it open in a moment. Inside there were spiced dates in syrup, a dainty brought from China.

"'*Junga!*' cried Eber, clapping his hands. You see, that was his native word for dates.

"'*Nyika, nyika!*' laughed Gaza, shaking her head at him; for such were dates in *her* language.

"'*Junganyika!*' they cried together, cramming the fruit into their starving mouths. So it was that the word passed into their new language, both as the name for dates as well as for the lake in which I found them; and Lake Junganyika men still call it to this day.

"We searched the country about us for fresh food also. But we found nothing, absolutely nothing, for man or beast to eat.

"So I asked the raven how long did he reckon it would take us to go on to the seashore, traveling by the river he had spoken of. And he said we ought to be able to get there in a week.

"For a journey as long as that, Belinda thought we should rest up the young people a little; and it was agreed that I should make several more visits to the palace cellars and get them all the food I could.

"It was hard and slow work, hauling up the stuff, in small quantities, all by myself; for I always left Belinda on guard each time I went down under the water. And so, this way, we spent all of a week not knowing if we could get them any more food at all, after we should set out on our trip to the sea.

"The motherly Belinda of course pestered the raven and me to death with her fears that, even after reaching the sea, we'd still find nothing for these humans to eat. But the raven said that around a regular ocean beach we could surely hunt up diving seabirds, who would at least get fish for us.

"Yet, before we were ready to go, once more the long, threatening arm of danger reached across the desolate, starving world to us. One day—I think it was a sun—"

"Excuse me please," (this time it was the polite voice of little Chee-Chee, the timid monkey, who interrupted the story) "but the day of the week makes no never mind. Be so kind as to tell us what happened. Yes, please?"

"Oh, certainly," the turtle answered. "Anyway, it was when our whole party was on a food-hunting trip; we had come to a place where the dry land around us changed to the mud-swamp of the lakeshore. We were strung out single-file, and this time Gaza happened to be in front. Suddenly we heard the girl give a scream. All of us hurried up to her. We found her pointing with a trembling hand at a mark in the soft ground. It was the footprint of an enormous cat!

"'The tigress!' whispered Gaza through chattering teeth. 'See, she has followed us even here!'

"'How on earth did she get across the lake?' asked Belinda.

"'Never mind how she got across,' croaked the raven. 'She's here. No mistaking *that* footprint. We hadn't planned to leave for the seashore before tomorrow. But this changes things. We've got to get on our way *at once*. And we won't stop even at the seashore to build sandcastles on the beach. We'll go on. We'll cross the sea. Never mind food or the craft to sail in. We've managed before—somehow; and we'll manage again. But, once you're on that ocean I saw, no cat will follow us any farther. Step lively and let's get out of here, everybody!'"

The Graveyard
of the Giants

FROM THEN ON WE HUSTLED, AND NO MISTAKE. No more questions, arguments, or worries—even from Belinda. We turtles, who up to this had led the whole escape, were now quite satisfied to leave everything to the raven. It was he who told us what he wanted done: it was we who obeyed. Not one of us went back to the shelter where we'd lived—even for the blankets and the poor bits of things the youngsters owned. At Commander Raven's orders, we just left and raced at once for the river he had spoken of—the one which flowed out of the lake down to the sea.

"We guessed of course that the tigress and most of her man-eating gang would be following us by scent, hoping to cut us off. But they never caught sight of us again, after the raven had seen that big footprint in the mud. Because his speed didn't give them a chance—either to catch up with us or to cut us off. He knew what danger we were in; he knew of a shortcut to that stream; and, above all, he knew that once we were traveling in water, no cat could follow us by scent.

"Well, we got to the river. And *were* we glad to see it? At the spot where we struck the stream, it was running wide in flood. We took the youngsters on our backs again, plunged at once into the fast water and headed downstream. Meanwhile the raven flitted back and forth through the dead trees on the banks, keeping a sharp lookout for enemies behind us and troubles ahead.

"Along the first few miles the going was easy, while the powerful current swirled us on our way. But farther down, the river began spreading out into many branches that led nowhere. And if we had not had the raven to lead us, we would surely have been lost.

"That was the last dash that poor Eber and Gaza had to make to escape from the tigress. I told you: we never saw her again. Yet that journey was, I believe, the most terrible one that human beings ever lived through.

"It took us seven days in all. The line of it, from the lake to the ocean, was almost exactly the same as you, John Dolittle, followed in coming here from the ocean to the lake. But oh, how different was the country then!

"As we went forward into the district that the raven had spoken of as a dead forest, the main stream kept shrinking narrower—and shallower—till it was little more than a muddy dribble that no one could swim in.

"And often it was choked and barred by the big stuff swept down and stuck between the banks. Then we had to set our passengers off, to wait till we found a way for them around, under, over, or through the jam. Truly the raven had been right when he called it *The Land of the Dead Jungle*.

"No words of mine, Doctor, can draw you a picture of the dreary gloom of that drowned forest through which we fought our

"He called it The Land of the Dead Jungle."

way to the sea. Some of the trees were of immense size—many still standing upright, but now dead, gaunt, leafless, and broken. In other places they were fallen or leaning crisscross in great tangled masses—like walls of crazy shipmasts as high as heaven.

"And all this dead vegetable growth was steaming, rotting, and stinking in the terrible African heat, a Graveyard of the Giants. While before, it had been lovely greenery; bright with brilliant parrots; with gorgeous butterflies; with bright orchids in bloom.

"No birds or creatures of any kind could be seen then. In the jungle, always so full of life, life had stopped.

"We were unable to find one single scrap of food, in seven

whole days, to feed our human friends—only dirty, bad-smelling water, half salt and half fresh. In many places moving forward at even the slowest pace, while keeping track at the same time of that trickle of a stream, was so difficult that Eber and Gaza had to work too—hungry and worn out though they were. The raven stayed aloft in the trees, keeping watch; for he still feared that some prowling band of meat-eaters might by chance cross our path.

"Once Belinda, passing close to me, whispered, 'Husband, I fear the youngsters cannot hold out much longer. Don't you think we should rest them a spell while we send a scouting party forward to seek food?'

"But all I answered was:

"'Leave that to the raven, Belinda. He is a good leader.'

"But again, I did not tell her how hopeless I felt, myself.

"Yet, sure enough, an hour or so later I came upon the body of Gaza lying in the mud where she had fainted away from exhaustion. While I was trying to bring her to, my wife came up. I sent her to find Eber—who had before shown us he knew how to bring back life into a half-drowned human.

"In less than ten minutes I heard my wife calling to me from the other side of a tangle of fallen trees: 'Here he is. I've found him. I'm not sure if he's dead—but unconscious, anyhow. Husband, come! *I can't wake him up!*'

"I hurried around to her side. The boy was lying across a fallen log. No amount of shaking brought back any sign of life. I put my ear down against his chest and heard a regular thump—though very slow and faint.

"'Good boy, Eber!' I muttered. 'You're tough—you're tough, thank goodness!—Belinda, we must get the raven here.'

"'He's downstream ahead of us, I think,' said my wife. 'But what can he do here? Oh, Husband,' she sobbed, 'we'll never get these poor children to the sea! I believe the sun has burnt out and the very earth itself is dying.'

"'Let's find out what the raven says to that,' I answered. Then throwing back my head I sent out a parrot's call—a signal we had arranged between us in case of danger—screeching downstream over the leafless treetops. It was answered right away by a like call. And two minutes later our guide fluttered down at our feet.

"For once in his life the raven-chatterbox had little to say. As he took a look at each of the youngsters, I could tell very plainly he felt this was a bad business.

"'It's my fault,' he croaked solemnly at last. 'I've traveled them too fast. But seeing the shortage of food, I thought it best to get this trip over and done with as soon as we could. Besides, having no other birds around to get news from, made it more difficult—not that I blame anything on wings for staying out of this mess of a country.'

"'But what are we going to *do*?' asked my wife, bursting into tears again. 'We can't sit by and watch death take them from us, after all they've gone through!'

"'Ah now, wait a minute,' said the raven in a kindly voice. 'Don't give up yet, old lady. Once we reach the ocean's shore, they'll be all right. Getting them across the sea to the land on the other side may be a longer trip, but it will be much easier. This is the bad stretch, the dead jungle.

"'I knew that—but what was the sense in my telling you ahead and getting you downhearted? The best we can do now is for you to rest them up here while I fly the whole way down to the beach alone. There's birdlife there; and I can likely get some fish. Just how long it will take me to get back here with food, I can't say. Maybe quicker than you think. Because—strange thing—up there in the treetops, I've felt the air changing lately: a damp wind off the sea, perhaps. Anyway, I've a notion that we can't be *very* far from the river's mouth.'

"And then with a flash of his blue-black wings he was on his way, up through the skeleton jungle, to the higher air.

"'Good-bye!' he called. 'Don't be downhearted. We're not beaten yet.'"

THE EIGHTH CHAPTER

Belinda Changes Her Mind

WITH UNEASY HEARTS, BELINDA AND I watched him disappear. We knew we were alone indeed now—with two desperately sick young-folk in our care.

"We found a sort of cave in the river's bank and brought both Eber and Gaza to it. Nearby its entrance the stream still flowed sluggishly. Then, with big dry palm leaves, we scooped the water up, threw it over them, and fanned them.

"But after hours and hours of this they still showed no sign of life.

"'It's no use,' said my wife. 'And what good would it do if the raven did return—with *raw fish*? While they're unconscious, we couldn't make them eat it. True, the heat and the work have been hard on them; but their main trouble is starvation.'

"I had to agree with that, of course. But what she said next fairly took my breath away.

"'Mudface,' she sobbed, dropping her fan, 'you can't ask me to stay and see these brave humans die. . . . My dear, I—I am going away . . . till it's all over.'

"Then, when she turned her back on us and slowly moved off, I saw that her mind was made up to desert the task. And of a sudden, something like desperate anger boiled up inside me.

"'Stop, Belinda!' I shouted. 'Stay where you are! Did we not despair once before of Gaza's life? Yet we pulled them through, didn't we? Stick on the job: I order you.'

"'I *can't* stay and watch them die, Husband,' she whimpered. 'I really can't.'

"My heart sank as again she started to go farther into the forest. Never in my life have I felt so hopeless.

"'Belinda,' I called after her, 'you know I cannot stop you. But if you leave me alone now, when I need your help so sorely, you will be sorry for it all your living days.'

"That halted her. Why, I cannot say. Slowly she turned around and came back toward me. And she had not taken more than two steps when a half dozen clams seemed to fall out of the sky upon the muddy ground between us.

"Both of us looked upward. A tall and leafless mahogany tree stood close by the entrance to our cave. In the bare topmost branches of this we saw twenty or thirty pelicans gathered—their great shovel-bills filled with fish to overflowing.

"Among the odd birds I easily recognized the raven, who wasted no time in coming down to us.

"'What ho, my hearties!' he croaked. 'How are the kids?'

"'The same,' said I, 'as when you left us. We've tried all we know, but no life have they shown yet.'

"'Well,' said he, 'we've *got* to get them awake somehow. No use stuffing unconscious mouths with uncooked fish—it was all I could find. And we can't afford to be polite: *slap* them awake, if that's the only way.'

"So, taking Eber first, I began slapping his face with soft stems of palm leaves. The raven signaled one of the pelicans to come down with some more clams. Then he explained to Belinda how to crack them up in her mouth till she had a couple of quarts of clam juice ready.

"Unmercifully I beat and slapped poor Eber for a quarter of an hour. And the treatment must have done something to get his blood circulating again. For presently he mumbled, as if in a dream, about my roughness. At that I put my front legs underneath his arms, lifted him into a sitting position, and shook him till his teeth almost fell out. Then he stumbled, all groggy, to his feet and started to fight me back.

"'He'll do,' snapped the raven sharply. 'Now give the girl the same. Both of them *must* be alive enough to swallow clam juice.'

"With the gentle Gaza I liked this business still less. But I had been given my orders. And after I'd broken six or seven palm stems over her, she, too, woke up—and tried to run away! Of course she did not get far before she fell from weakness.

"But things went much easier for us after we had brought both of them to their senses. Belinda trickled the clam juice into their mouths and they gulped it down hungrily.

"It was wonderful to see how quickly those youngsters changed with food and rest. I watched them talking and smiling together. Once more they had been saved from the very jaws of death. I was happy—happy for them and for myself. But I believe I was happiest of all for Belinda: that she had changed her mind and not deserted us. For had she left me at that terrible moment, I am sure she never could have forgiven herself. Poor, motherly Belinda! She was crying again now—but this time out of gladness and relief.

"In a few days, the raven said, he thought we could be on our way again—as long as we watched how the humans took it.

"'You know, Mudface,' said he, 'I was delighted to find what a short trip it is. I reckon we should see the ocean within three or four days now—even taking it in easy stages.'

"Then he gave orders to the pelicans to fly along with us overhead; and we started off again on our march to the sea."

THE NINTH CHAPTER

The Ocean at Last

O N THEIR WAY HOME TO BED THAT NIGHT, the Doctor's animal family seemed unusually talkative.

"Looks to me, Doc," said Cheapside, "as if old Muddy Pants was coming to the end of his story. Thanks be! . . . Just to see dear old London once again! Do you realize, John Dolittle, MD, 'ow long we've been listenin' to that antediluvian yarn-spinner in the middle of this foggy swamp?"

"No," said the Doctor. "But, anyway, it was worth it."

"Tee, hee, hee!" tittered the white mouse. "You should know, Cheapside, the Doctor never bothers about time—when he's interested."

"Ah!" cried Gub-Gub suddenly. "Home! The thought—the very thought—of a nice large English cauliflower! Um-m-m! I'm terribly tired of these African vegetables."

"I wonder," said Jip, "how old Prince is getting on—teaching those pups to be gun dogs—without losing their tails. I wouldn't want the job."

"Ah me!" murmured Chee-Chee the monkey. "Africa *is* a beautiful country, of course. But if you stay away from it long enough, losing touch with your old friends, it's surprising how your taste changes. It'll be wonderful to see dear old Puddleby again."

"It would be," muttered Polynesia the parrot, "if it wasn't for that awful English climate—rain, rain, rain!"

"The truth is, I suppose," said Too-Too the owl, "your real home is where your friends are; the Doctor and his stories round the kitchen fire o'nights; the freedom of his home and the rest. Well—"

"And then there's always something new popping up there," said the white mouse. "I don't believe I'd *want* to live any other place now. For instance—"

"I'm afraid those kitchen windows," said Dab-Dab, "will need new putty. I wonder if Matthew Mugg has kept out of jail. . . . And as for the house-cleaning! Well, as the Doctor says, 'Never lift your foot till—'"

And so they all chattered on, mostly about Puddleby and the old home, till we reached the office and I had the notebooks safely stowed in the vault under the floor. Then we went to the bunkhouse and turned in.

"You know, Stubbins," said the Doctor as he lay down and punched his hay pillow into shape, "I fancy Cheapside's right: Mudface's story of the Flood is coming to an end. I *do* hope Belinda, his wife, shows up before we leave. Mudface shouldn't be alone—with his rheumatism so bad."

I had been thinking the same thing. "I suppose he won't take his medicine regularly after we go if she isn't here to see to it," I said.

"That's what worries me," said John Dolitrle. "Oh well, we haven't gone yet. Perhaps she'll return before we have to leave."

"Do you mean to ask Mudface about those ruined buildings we saw at the lower end of the lake?" I asked.

"Very likely," he answered, "very likely. But I have millions of things I want to learn from him concerning the days of Noah, I'm not sure if I shall get round to it. That's always the way: no matter how many questions you ask—when you have the chance—you always forget the most important till after it's too late. Oh well, we'll do the best we can, Stubbins. Good night!"

"We took things much easier now," Mudface went on the next evening. "We had to think of the young people's strength. But toward the end of the second day Belinda asked:

"'Isn't the ground sloping all the time? The walking doesn't seem so hard—or is it just my imagination?'

"'No,' said the raven, 'the going's all downhill, gentlelike, from here on. This is the ocean slope. We're coming down off a high jungle plain to the beach level below. Don't you notice that the dead trees are thinning out—growing fewer?'

"'Yes, I do,' said Belinda, smiling and brightening up for the first time in seven days.

"And soon, the river became wider and deeper. That may not sound much to you. But for me, to feel my feet no longer touch bottom—that I could swim again, instead of that heartbreaking scramble over and around tangled timber, that—well, what's the use? It would be impossible to make anyone understand the joy of it.

"No longer did that dreadful, stagnant stench of rotting woodland-world cling about our weary, overheated bodies. The clean smell of an ocean wind blew freshly in our faces.

"Every one of us took new heart, straining his eyes ahead to

"'We took things much easier now,' Mudface went on."

the promise of a new climate. And presently we saw the river was spreading out more and more, into a regular lovely bay—miles wide.

"I signaled to our passengers to get upon our backs; and, with mighty strokes, Belinda and I churned the clean water to cross this natural harbor, the harbor of Fantippo. The raven flew on ahead of us and alighted in a tall tree upon the bank. What a tiny dot he looked! But he was not so small or far that we couldn't hear his bass, croaking voice, as he turned and shouted back to us:

"'Surf ahead! The beach is just outside the bar. I can see the ocean breaking on the sands. We've done it, my lads! Take your time: we're all right now. The *sea*, the sea at last!'"

THE TENTH CHAPTER

Boat-Building

O F COURSE," MUDFACE WENT ON, "JUST FOR two turtles and a bird, traveling over an ocean would have been easy. But with two weakened people to care for, the crossing was a very different matter—especially since it was a sea no one had ever crossed. The *Atlantic*, you call it now. But at that time, remember, it was newly cut, completely unknown.

"Said the raven, when we were talking over the long trip ahead:

"'This is such a tricky sort of a journey—I think it would be foolish for us to try to get prepared for every little thing. Goodness! No matter what we do, we're bound to run into surprises—things we don't expect.'

"'True, Raven,' said I, 'very true.'

"'What we *must* have first,' he said, 'is good, fresh water, till rains come—and supply us at sea. Next, enough food to get us started. The pelicans tell me there are groups of islands on the way across. And on them we'll hope we can find something more to eat. A few fishing birds have promised me to fly partway with us; so we might be worse off. Then—very important—we must build a boat that will stand storm and rough weather. While you're busy on that here, I'll go ahead and try to find the first islands for you to take a rest on. What do you think?'

"'Sounds like good sense,' said I.

"'Very well. Let's waste no time,' he said. 'I've a feeling speed is going to be important—in spite of my mistake before.'

"'We'll keep an eye on the youngsters while you're gone *this* time,' said Belinda. 'Don't fear.'

"So, taking a couple of pelicans with him, the raven flew off.

"As he disappeared, my wife said, 'Husband, let us make sure of the food, first. All of us will go hunting. The boatbuilding will be easier, when we get Eber and Gaza in better health to help us.'

"Right away we all went off exploring for food. The young people by now—while they still could not talk our language—were much better at catching on to our sign-talk. It took us barely a moment, by acting out what we wanted them to do, to make them understand almost anything.

"Their spirits, too, were much happier on this food-searching picnic. They also seemed stronger already—no doubt through the change in air. Truly, I thought, they looked a most handsome couple as they followed behind us, laughing and talking.

"'They don't seem to be hunting very hard for food, now, Belinda,' said I, glancing back over my shoulder.

"'My dear Mudface,' she whispered, '*eating* is not the only important thing—except when you're starving. Sh! That's just a little lovemaking, stupid! Don't stare at them so! It's *their* business, not ours.'

"'Quite, quite,' said I. 'Their business, as you say. For truly I never saw turtles make love like that—throwing seaweed at one another. Most peculiar!'

"Along the shore we gathered many kinds of shellfish. These were carried up beyond reach of the tide and stored in marked places, for picking up later.

"A little farther back from the beach, where trees still stood here and there, we discovered the edible tree-mushroom, growing in plenty on the dead trunks. These, too, we gathered.

"The problem of making something for carrying drinking water in was not so easy. But, luckily, the one thing that Eber had brought with him on our last wild flight from the tigress had been his stone knife—which he kept stuck in his belt. When we came across a dead seal, we used the knife to skin it. Eber spread the skin out on a frame to dry in the sun.

"'I hate to see dead animals,' said Belinda gazing thoughtfully at the spread-out skin. 'But we do need something to carry drinking water. When that hide is sewn up properly, with tough grass-thread, it should hold nearly a hundred gallons. Well, let's get to the boat-building. The raven may be back any day now, croaking with impatience to sail.'

"This part of our preparations proved the hardest of all. We made many kinds of boats and rafts from the dead poles of trees. But when we came to launch them in the sea, they rolled and tossed and cracked us on the head; and they all ended by falling apart in the rough surf. Here we were dealing with water much rougher than the lake.

"It was not till the raven returned that we had any success in our boat-building. Without delay, he explained that there was only one kind of craft for us to use on such a journey.

"'It's a sort of outrigger,' he said, 'and it is pretty nearly unsinkable. You make two pontoons—out of long sticks—pointed at their ends, and you lay them side by side on the beach. Then you get heavier poles to fasten across the tops of the pontoons, binding them firmly over the pontoons to form a deck.'

"'What are we going to fasten them with?' asked Belinda. 'We haven't any nails.'

"'Why, with ropes made out of bark-strips of course,' said the raven. 'We'll need yards and yards of it—for the pontoons and for fastening the cross-pieces, too. Where are the youngsters? That will be easy work for them.'

"It's a sort of outrigger."

"'Well,' I said, 'last time I saw them they were chasing one another around the sand-hills—a new game: throwing mud at one another. Belinda says it's a sign—with humans—they're in love, and that I should leave them alone.'

"'*Throwing mud at one another!*' snorted the raven angrily. 'Don't they know there's work to be done—and in a hurry, too. The seabirds on the first group of islands told me the wind may change any day at this season. Then it'll be against us instead of with us—cutting our speed in half. It's a long trip—and I've no idea yet what the farther islands may be like. And these kids are *throwing mud at one another*!'

"'But they're so young,' said Belinda. 'The better feeding has made them feel like new people.'

"'New fiddlesticks!' snapped the raven. 'We've got to be on our way before this wind changes. Go and get them for me at once, please.'

"So I went and searched out the boy and girl and brought them back to the job of boat-building.

"The raven, after one glance at their mud-spattered faces, told me to take them off and explain what he wanted about the ropes.

"There was only one kind of tree on the bay-shore whose bark was any good for rope-making. But I found it; and soon we had coils and coils of rope of different thicknesses—twisted, braided, and strong. With these on my back and the youngsters clinging to my shell, I swam across the bay again, out to the beach beyond the bar.

"'Good!' said the raven. 'I think you've got enough there. Let's go to work.'

"Under his directions, I soon saw the shape our raft was going to be. It was a sort of double-keeled canoe. The cross-pieces formed a kind of deck; and this was covered over with a shade-cabin in which we were to live and store baggage. It had a window on each side, a door at each end—and a roof of thatched grass. By the time it was finished we had stopped referring to it as a raft and had begun to call it a boat: it looked so nearly like one.

"'Now,' said the raven, 'the paddles are the next thing. Get some soft light wood, you turtles, and bite them into the shape of paddles—with good wide blades and strong shafts. How about the drinking-water supply? We must have enough for six days, at least.'

"And Belinda explained how we had made the sealskin water bag.

"'Fine!' he said. 'Then we're all set, as soon as you've made the paddles. Let's launch the boat empty, first, to see how she behaves in rough water. Afterward we'll bring her back and load her with the stores.'"

THE ELEVENTH CHAPTER

Island of Peace

WHEN OUR STRANGE BOAT WAS loaded up, the young people were delighted with her. The arrangements for paddling were certainly very snug and comfortable. The whole floor inside the cabin was lined with thick soft grass. And the paddlers knelt on either side of the boat and paddled out of the windows. When they grew tired, they could just lie down on the cushiony grass and take a rest.

"The deck-house took up only the center of the boat. *Amidships* I think you call it?" (The turtle glanced this question at Polynesia, the old sailor—who nodded in agreement.) "And the ends of the little ship were left unroofed, for storing the food, drinking water, spare rope, and so forth.

"We had a rudder—of sorts—a long sweep-paddle: but we meant to steer mostly by watching the raven and his pelicans, who knew the way to the first group of islands. And by night I had the stars to hold a course on.

"At the last moment, the raven said, 'By gosh! I almost forgot the sail.' And he sent me back into the forest to fetch a bamboo pole. We laced the upper part of this with dry palm leaves. It looked like an enormous, long-handled fan; and we fastened it in the stern, so it could be turned, and set any way you wished.

"'That'll come in handy—especially if the wind changes,' said the raven. 'Now, my hearties, say good-bye to Africa. All aboard!'"

The old parrot, Polynesia, had up to this looked bored throughout the whole of Mudface's story. But now she became so interested in the turtle's seafaring talk she suddenly broke out into one of her sailors' songs:

> "Sailing, sailing,
> Over the bounding main—"

Her voice was very scratchy. And Cheapside growled, "Oh dry up, me old Pollywog! Voice needs oiling. You won't never get back into opera again. What'll you bet me they don't run into rocks afore they've gone two miles?"

"Now, now," said the Doctor. "We want to hear the story, please."

"Well," said Mudface, "the rest is islands, you might say— islands, islands, and more islands. I've told you there were many groups in those times, John Dolittle, which have since disappeared entirely.

"We crossed the Atlantic Ocean at almost its narrowest point. We left from somewhere around what you now call the Bight of Benin, in Africa, and—as near as I can judge—we hit across toward the big bulge of Brazil, in South America.

"In stages the raven led us from one lot of islands to another. They were all different; but practically none had any life on it except seabirds, shellfish, crabs, and the like. One or two islands had high volcanoes still smoking in their centers; and on these islands not even clams or seaweeds were to be seen. Here we anchored offshore, only to get a rest. But underground—or undersea—rumblings kept us awake all night, reminding us of the Deluge earthquakes; and we were glad to get away from them as soon as we could.

"Some of these island groups were much farther than others. And on one tiresome stretch we crossed about eight hundred miles without seeing land. This was the only stage in the whole trip where our luck seemed to go back on us. First, the wind dropped altogether; only hard work at the paddles kept us going at all. Then the wind swung about and blew right in our teeth. A storm was gathering.

"Belinda and I got out and swam, towing the craft with ropes. But even that did little more than hold us still, where we were. One blessing was that heavy rains fell, which we gathered in palm leaves—and so partly restocked our drinking supply. But the seas became enormous in size—waves seventy and eighty feet high. And there were times when we thought our outrigger would fall apart.

"But on the third day the dirty weather suddenly cleared; the wind changed in our favor; and, as twilight came on, the setting sun showed us a single lovely island not more than fifteen miles ahead.

"During the storm, which we had come through, our pelicans of course had not been able to catch any fish for us. And even if they had, it is doubtful if Gaza could have eaten it. For she was again in a state of terrible weakness—from the wild tossing of our little ship.

In the half-dark we found a bay on the island's south shore where we could anchor in calm shelter.

"Next morning, leaving Eber to act as nurse for Gaza while she rested, we went ashore to hunt up any new sorts of food we might find.

"This island seemed larger than any we had seen so far. And we were very glad—especially the raven—to discover it was a regular homing place for seabirds. You have no idea how happy we were when they told us that the next lap of our journey would be our last—about three hundred miles, they said. Beyond this there were no more islands to rest on; but if we could make that distance in one trip, we would sight the continent of South America, the country which these birds came from in the early part of the year.

"We had arrived, it seemed, when springtime (a season new since the Flood) was beginning in those latitudes. Nesting was going on at a great pace. In the early sunlight the island's steep sides had seabirds, in thousands, sitting on nests built on the rocky ledges of the cliffs.

"Remembering that poor Gaza had not tasted an egg in months, we asked the mother birds to give us some. They refused. Then the raven explained that we were escaping from the cats (old enemies of all birds) and that we had been fighting them halfway across the world. On hearing this, the birds changed their minds and willingly gave us one fresh-laid egg from each nest. This amounted to many dozens.

"And so we were able to make a change in Gaza's diet, which got her completely well again in a very short time.

"On this island too we found a good spring of cold drinking water, bubbling up out of the rock. We emptied our waterskin of its last supply—which had grown stale and smelly—and refilled it with this sparkling flow from the spring.

"Fearing more bad weather or other delays, the raven hustled us on again. We stayed only a day and a half on the island while we repaired our boat.

"She had taken an awful battering from that storm. The best we could do was to unbraid the old ropes at the worn places and plait them over again. We had drawn the boat up on the narrow beach at the foot of the cliff, to make working around her easier for us. Said the raven, as we finished re-binding the pontoons:

"'Let's hope these lines will hold all right. Mighty important! If we run into tough weather again it'll be pretty near impossible to fix 'em in a rolling sea. Well, we'll hope for the best. Tow her out through the surf, Turtles. All aboard for the last lap!'

"After we had paddled out from the island and set our patched sail on a westerly course, we were given an unexpected send-off by the seabirds, which I, for one, will never be able to forget. The cliff must have been a good four hundred feet high—with nesting ledges in the rock all the way up. Suddenly those millions of birds rose onto their toes, flapping their wings to us and calling good-bye in their shrill voices. The noise was deafening. And in a flash those fanning wings, like magic, turned the whole island a spotless white, from sea to sky.

"I glanced at Gaza. She was sucking a raw egg at the moment. But when that cry of farewell broke forth, tears ran down her face. And I was near enough to hear her murmur:

"'Good-bye, birds of the sea, good-bye! May your nesting home stay forever yours—yours alone—an island of peace!'"

A New Land!

I T TURNED OUT THAT THE LAST LAP WAS TO BE the easiest of our whole ocean crossing. The wind never again blew against us—though it did sometimes drop altogether.

"We made, I reckon, something between a hundred and a hundred and fifty miles a day. Anyhow, in the middle of the second afternoon, I thought I felt some kind of a change in the air. The wind was now fitful—a sort of gentle breeze, blowing in short spurts from north, south, east, or west; sometimes deathly still; sometimes hot; sometimes chilly. There was complete silence in our little ship. To the westward, a light haze blotted out the farthest skyline. I was puzzled—expecting almost anything. Suddenly the raven croaked:

"'What are you jerking your head around like that for, Mudface?' (I had no idea he had been watching me.)

"'I don't know,' I said. 'I've never seen the ocean this way before. It's something new, anyhow, and I don't know what. The wind seems to have gone a bit crazy; even coming from the west. I calculate we should now be less than a hundred miles from land—if what they told us at the island is right. But that low mist ahead shuts off the last stretch we should be able to see. And there's a current, too, or riptide, pushing us along toward the southwest. What do you make of it?'

"'It *is* mysterious, all right,' he grunted. 'Feels like a new climate to me.'

"'And what in heaven's name does *that* feel like?' asked Belinda. 'Will you two stop chattering mysteries and talk a little sense for a change?'

"'Certainly,' said the raven, 'as soon as I can make sense of it myself.... Oh, look! Look at the girl!'

"Gaza was indeed behaving almost as peculiarly as the wind. She was drawing in deep breaths. She rose slowly from the floor like someone sleepwalking; and, coming over to Eber, grasped him firmly by the shoulder. He gave a startled jump and asked:

"'What is it, Gaza? What's the matter?'

"'Eber dear,' she whispered, '*flowers*! The wind is from the west—from behind that haze. What is it hiding, that mist on the skyline?' And again she breathed deeply. Her eyes sparkled. She seemed almost in a trance; and we could barely hear her words:

"'Jasmine,' she murmured at length, 'violets and sweet-brier ... lilies of the valley ... lilacs—all the flowers the queen loved— and, above all, magnolias. I had almost forgotten that they ever bloomed!'

"Then once more the wind's mood changed—not steadily blowing in any direction now, but swirling round in gentle cyclones. And the far-off mist began to lift and roll away.

"At last we saw it—*land*! But none of us spoke: we were struck too breathless by the picture slowly getting clear before our eyes.

Land growing higher and higher, and as we crept nearer, the curtain of haze lifted. From the level of the sea, upward and upward, to where the mountains sloped into the white clouds, it was all colors. Land, fertile land in blossom—land as it had been before the coming of the Flood!

"Still not one of us said a word—just gazed and gazed. Then suddenly Gaza sprang forward and, grasping the mast at the head of the boat, she began singing. . . . And oh, *how* she sang!

"King Mashtu had boasted that this servant, whom he had brought from foreign lands to entertain the ladies of his queen's court, had the loveliest voice in all the world.

"She began singing."

"She began very, very softly—little more than a murmuring hum. I had not heard her sing since we turtles listened from our prison-pond across the zoological park of Shalba. Now, as the mist kept fading and the strengthening wind blew us closer to the land that would one day be called America, we saw that this great land stretched to the right and left of our course as far as the eye could reach. And slowly Gaza's voice grew and grew to its full glory. Eber moved forward and put his arm gently about her waist.

"Presently the raven (who always wanted to be a singer himself) was so carried away by the beauty of her voice that he joined in. But his croaking was so dreadfully out of tune that we all, Gaza included, broke into laughter. Then we all sang, just anyhow. Gaza came back from the bow and threw her arms around my neck while Eber did the same to Belinda. The spell was broken and there was general hubbub.

"And so, laughing, singing and joking, we landed in a New Land."

The Raven Explores
a New World

THERE WAS COMPLETE QUIET WHILE MUDFACE stopped and took a drink of muddy water from his dish on the floor. I rested my wiggling pencil and stretched my hand to get the cramp out of it; meanwhile I glanced round at the faces of the audience.

They were not an easy crowd to talk to, by any means. (Those hundreds of monkey carpenters were a restless lot.) But it was clear that the turtle had gotten them all interested now—no matter what they might have been before. Even the rowdy sparrow, Cheapside—still of course pretending to be asleep—had, I noticed, one eye open and was listening with all his attention. As for the rest of them, they were clearly impatient for the turtle to go on.

"My, oh my!" the Doctor sighed as the turtle was finishing his drink. "What a thrill *that* must have been for you! To discover a new world."

"Oh well, Doctor," said Mudface, wiping his mouth with the

back of his right claw, "you must remember that what I am telling you came just after the Deluge.

We had barely landed before the raven took me aside and said, "'I'm off on a big trip, old-timer. You and your wife must take care of the youngsters for a while; because someone has got to find out if they've any enemies here, same as they had at home. "'Sure, we've seen no people as yet. But that doesn't mean there aren't any. There was supposed to be a desert where the ocean is now, eh? And Mashtu always claimed that this land belonged to him. But very few travelers, I think, got as far as this. And no one who set out to cross the Atlantic Desert *ever returned to Shalba.* . . . Sounds strange, what? Anyway, it's got to be looked into.'

"Well, he was gone some months.

"Before he got back to us I was beginning to be homesick for the countries I'd left behind. Can't say just why. But I suppose home is always home. I found myself wondering how everyone was getting on back there . . . Yes, maybe that was it: age. I belonged to the Old World—while these young people were interested only in building a new one.

"I talked it over with Belinda; and I found that she agreed with me—for once—completely.

"'Why, of course we can't stay here—for keeps,' she said. 'I, too, want to know how my friends are getting on. Gaza and Eber are doing splendidly here. Whenever you're ready, Mudface.'

"So we turtles had it all planned to say good-bye as soon as the raven showed up. We made no preparations at all. Seagoing turtles, when they decide to take a journey, just get up and go. It is only men who pack a lot of bags and things and lie awake nights before, trying to remember what they have forgotten. All *we* want is water and—or—mud.

"The raven came. And I have never known him to have so much to chatter about. You should have been there, Doctor. He was chock-full of science.

"Of course we *were* interested. But we were also anxious to tell him the news that we were going back home. However, he jabbered on and on. Why was this country, he asked, so much further recovered than the ruined land we'd left behind? Because, he answered himself, the Big Wave (when the poles of the earth shifted and the Mediterranean burst through the mountains at Gibraltar) cut the new Atlantic Ocean on its way. It didn't come straight across west. The Gulf Stream had something to do with that. And by the time the wave had cut right across the Atlantic Desert it had, it seemed, spent most of its strength. Never got far inland this side, on account of the big mountains—the Andes and the Rockies— but just continued along on a more or less north-south line and washed the poisonous sea salt *off* the land, instead of pushing it on inland and westward."

Mudface paused a moment, smiling. "Oh, that raven and his science! I couldn't get a word in edgewise."

"Well, well," said the Doctor, "I suppose it *was* exciting for him to have discovered why the land was undamaged by the Flood."

"Yes," said Mudface, "but he wasn't through yet. I asked him if he'd seen any cats."

"'There are a few native ones—like the lynx in the north and the jaguar in the south. But none of the deadly fellows, like Bengal tigers and African lions—no real man-eaters. Still it surprised me there were any at all.'

"'That's good,' I said. 'Now, there's something my wife and I would like to talk over with you. . . . Belinda, Belinda!—I'd swear she was here a minute ago. That's strange. . . . Belinda, *Belinda!* . . . Where are you?'

"No answer.

"'Wait here,' I said. 'I'll go to the beach-shack and see if I can find her.'

"Halfway to the shack I met Belinda—in a great state of excitement.

"'Oh, Husband,' she gasped. 'She's going *to have a baby*— Gaza! Isn't that simply lovely? I just found out. Ah, I'm not saying I didn't suspect it before. But now it's certain. You remember I told you that when human beings started throwing mud at one another, it's a sure sign they're in love. . . . Oh,' (she gasped again) 'I'm all of a twitter!—Glad I could give you the wonderful news alone, without the raven hearing it yet. Because of course we can't leave now—not before the baby's born, can we?'

"'Why not?' I asked.

"'Good gracious!' she cried. 'Who's going to look after the child if I'm not here? Gaza never had one before. And besides, it will be the first baby of this New Land. Men-folk don't know anything about raising children. What if anything should happen to it—colic, foot-and-mouth disease . . . ?'

"I thought heavily awhile before answering. For me, it had always been only Eber who must be saved from the Deluge, from the tigress—from the meat-eaters. The girl, well, she was only necessary to keep him company.

"I was still in favor of a peopleless earth. Man, with his wars and all, had made such a mess of the world! And now my wife was asking *me* to help build a new race of men!

"Belinda must have read my thoughts. For presently she said very gently:

"'Husband, have you forgotten your words to Noah? You promised we'd rescue Eber so that he could start a world of his own, a world of happiness. Tell me, how can that be done if Gaza has no sons. Have you forgotten that we risked our lives over and over again to keep these two young people safe from that she-devil tigress and a hundred other dangers?'

"But still, for a moment, I gave her no answer.

"And suddenly a picture glowed before my eyes: the picture of all we turtles had suffered that those two might live. What use would it be now if new dangers destroyed their sons as soon as we left. And I said:

"'Belinda, we'll see it through. Whatever may come of it, as your brother, Wag, warned us, none can tell. But, homesick as I am, I'll stay with you till this first child is born in his new land. . . . You're sure it will be a boy?'

"'Bless you, Mudface!' said she. 'What *else* could it be?'"

The Farm

WELL, THE GREAT DAY CAME, THE DAY when the first new human arrived in the New World. When I say *first* human, I mean of course, the first as far as we knew. Because who can tell, with all the history books swept away, how many deluges there were before the one I saw?"

"Quite so," the Doctor muttered thoughtfully. "A very interesting consideration."

"Nor can we say, John Dolittle, how many more world floods yet may come—to start earth's life all over again.

"Anyhow, this baby was no ordinary child. Yes, it was a boy, all right; a most charming young person. He was tough and strong from the start—like his father. And he had a smile that would charm the birds off the trees—like his mother. He was named Aden.

"We all fell madly in love with him—you couldn't help it. Even the raven, who said that children to him were nothing but a nuisance—even he, when he thought no one was listening, used

"A most charming young person"

to sing lullabies in that cracked voice of his over the cradle. And he did clownish antics to amuse the little one—who enjoyed the performance with no end of giggles and gurgles.

"And, I have to confess, I was nearly as bad, myself. The baby seemed to take as great a liking to me as I did to him. When he was grown large enough to crawl, he tried to climb up onto my back.

"So I told them how, by making a little fenced play yard with a sunshade over it and tying it firmly on top of me, the baby could be set safely inside it. This was done. And I would take him for rides around the country.

"Secretly, once in a while, I even paddled him out into the

shallower water; and took him on little exploring cruises round the lagoons and lakes that lay inland from the beach. He loved these water-trips most of all. And he came to feel that I was his personal property and slave—a sort of mixture of nursemaid, play yard, perambulator, and his own private boat.

"But it was Belinda herself who was the worst of all. The way she fussed over that child from morning to night, you'd think it was *her* baby instead of Gaza's.

"And it was really my wife's fault that we stayed in America for so long, instead of only the week or two that we had planned.

"At last the raven said to me in private:

"'Listen, I know how hard it is for you to leave all this. I mean, for instance, Gaza over there: a picture of contentment—calm and happy, eh? . . . But I'll bet you one thing.'

"'What's that?' I asked.

"'She's going to have another—and soon.'

"'Going to have another what?'

"'Another baby, of course.'

"'What makes you think that?'

"'Oh, I'm not talking any highfalutin stuff like Belinda,' said the raven. 'But I've just noticed that folks on farms always has lots of kids—maybe it's the fresh air or something. It stands to reason she'll have another. And when she does, Brother Turtle, where will *we* be with Aunt Belinda? I tell you, when Gaza has *two* babies to look after, well, we're here for life, if you don't put your foot down. Two years we've been loafing round here like nursemaids. The Old World may have changed a lot in two whole years. Have you spoken to Belinda yet?'

"'Oh yes, Raven. But I got nothing but the old excuses. I've argued and argued with her.'

"'Well, *don't* argue with her. She's a woman. Y'ought to know better, at your age. Bound to lose. *Don't* argue with her: talk to her. Just say: the party is leaving for Shalba on Wednesday at eight in the morning. That's all.'

"'Yes, I know you're right,' I said. 'I better speak to my wife tonight—firmly. Maybe it'll be too late if I—by the way, will you help me—to, er, persuade her?'

"'Bless your heart!' he laughed. 'Of course I will. Myself, I'm getting a little sick of the roses round the door here. . . . If it wasn't for that kid—'

"Well, poor Belinda! I fancy she'd been having some of those *suspicions* about Gaza again. In any case, I've no doubt that if I hadn't had my friend to back me up, I'd have given in once more. But the raven just said offhand-like—after we had talked a while of this and that:

"'Heigh-ho! It's my bedtime. Oh, I almost forgot: Mudface and I are leaving for Africa day after tomorrow, Wednesday. You care to come along with us? Oh, my Sunday tail-feathers, just look at the way that baby sleeps over there! My, but he's a healthy one! Good night.'

"And before Belinda had a chance to answer him at all, he was on his way down the stairs. I went with him to see him out at the farmhouse door. But before he left, we stopped in at the kitchen to tell Eber and Gaza.

"It took me only a minute or so to make them understand in our sign language that we were leaving for Africa. Gaza cried a little. But Eber told me that, although they would both miss us terribly, our news was not a surprise to him. He had told his wife many times that, sooner or later, we would want to go back to our old home. It was only natural.

"And that was that! I felt a great weight lifted from my mind as I bade the raven good night and arranged with him to meet again the following day.

"The time went quickly. A grand feast was prepared at the farm to celebrate our going away. Eber asked if we would come back sometime to visit them—and we said we hoped so. However, I'm afraid that no one at the party was very cheerful—except little Aden, who was hardly old enough yet to know what was going on.

"The next day we went down to the shore. My wife and I waded out into the swirling blue-green water of the sea, while the raven took to the air above. Eber and his family waved to us from the sands. I do not like good-byes. And I was especially glad that this looked like being a short one. I think everyone, including even the raven, felt the same way about that farewell.

"But it was little Aden—barely big enough to talk at all—who changed it into something different. Suddenly he realized at last that we were leaving him, that he was losing his old animal friends. He burst into tears and stretched his chubby hands out toward us.

"'Linda!' he called. 'Do not go! Aden wants you, Linda.'

"Then I noticed that my wife was crying silently as, beside me, she breasted the heaving swell of the ocean in a desperate kind of way. But she did not look back at little Aden—I think she was afraid to.

"And then, after all, I found myself wondering: *Why* did she weep? Suddenly, in the way she often did, she answered my thoughts aloud:

"'Oh, Husband, Husband,' she sobbed, 'they're so helpless— really! Even if they have more brains than we have, and so can run a world in what seems a better way, they have not our animal sense to know when danger is near—though it's true we cannot tell *how* we know. They're helpless against the stormy seas—which we can cross like stepping over a log; they're helpless against starvation, when we can go without food for weeks; they're helpless against the wild beasts of the jungle. And because, sooner or later, my Aden will go down—fighting—where you or I would come through alive, I am crying, Husband—crying, because I know we'll no longer be there to protect him with our—our animal sense.'

"It broke my heart to see the way she half turned to look back at the human family on the beach—then thought better of it and firmly plowed on, eastward, toward the Old World.

"'Somehow I feel certain,' she said, 'that we'll never see them again. Other men are bound to come and discover this great land. And what then? Some new Mashtu will arise and crush the little world of peace and friendliness they're building—crush all the kindly faith in justice and honesty that Gaza is teaching the little one.... Tell me, even if we came back, who could find my Aden for me then? My baby ...'

"For the moment I had no answer, no word of comfort to give her. But presently I said:

"'Belinda, my dear, I know we have never spoken openly of these things before. But perhaps it was all planned this way. Maybe the someone, whose power was greater than Mashtu's, never intended that man should die out in this Deluge; and he set you and me, the peaceful turtles, across the path to save man from complete destruction. If that's so, we succeeded, didn't we? ... Look forward to seeing Shalba's lovely countryside again. All's well, they say, that ends well. Come, come! Cheer up!'

"But she just swam on, giving me no answer—trying only to hide her tears. I, too, felt very gloomy.

"Our feelings—indeed the whole business—was strange, making no sense. The ocean, wide-spread before us, looked unhomelike now, bleak and dull. Could it be, I asked myself, that living with a human family had changed us? Yet was it not ourselves who had made possible the busy happiness of life for those people we were leaving behind? Had we, the independent turtles, become a little like the warm-blooded men-folk—through years of living with them? We had grown homesick for the Old World; yet this parting now seemed like leaving our own family.

"Suddenly a little cheerfulness reached us from above, from the after-sunset sky—where you could hardly pick out anything but the evening star. It was the hoarse bawling voice of the raven; but it made us feel less lonely.

"'Hulloa, down there, Turtles! Set the course southeast by east. Should be a fine night, by the look of it. You'll hear from me again in the morning.'

"And that, John Dolittle, is the end of my history of the Deluge."

No one spoke for nearly five minutes after the turtle came to a stop. The Doctor himself just stared at the floor, far away in thought, as though, it seemed, all the questions he had meant to ask had gone clean from his mind.

At last, with a sort of start, he pulled himself together and spoke.

"Pray excuse me, Mudface," said he, "for not even thanking you for the most interesting story I've ever listened to. There are many questions I would like to ask, but I will have to run through all the notebooks with Stubbins to recall them. That would keep you up too late now. You have already talked longer than usual tonight. Please take your medicine and go to bed right away. You know, I am sure, how grateful I am to you."

"I was glad to tell it, Doctor," was all the turtle answered. "Good night!"

We Paddle Down the Secret Lake

TURTLETOWN, AS CHEAPSIDE HAD CALLED IT, was closing up. Great quantities of medicine for Mudface had been mixed and stored in the bunkhouse. John Dolittle had asked our visiting monkey carpenters to pull down most of the smaller shacks, because he feared that with bad weather they would most likely fall apart and become unsightly wrecks after we had gone. But the turtle's big shelter-shed had been strengthened to last a long time.

The monkeys then became the street-cleaning squad: clearing away the rubbish of the old buildings, sweeping the trash from the roadways and tidying up generally.

"I can't see the use of going to all this trouble, Doc," said Cheapside. "There certainly ain't goin' to be no visitors coming up to see old Mudpie's Castle-in-the-Fog for quite a while yet."

"Never mind," said John Dolittle. "The turtle may be muddy, but he likes to have things orderly and neat. I know, because when I got my post-office birds to build the island for him long ago, he was delighted with the way they finished it off before they left."

"Yes, and the blinkin' earthquake nearly finished it off too," grunted the sparrow. "This may be the top of the world, all right. But in my 'umble hopinion, the Deluge ain't over yet in these 'ere parts. The earth still seems rollin' around, 'avin' tummy-aches, you might say. Remember them ruins of the old 'ouses we saw, comin' up 'ere? Why, what's the matter, Doc?"

"My goodness, I nearly forgot!" said the Doctor.

"Forgot what?" asked Cheapside.

"Why, his garden," said the Doctor. "Mudface loves nothing better than a nice garden—the same as I do. I must attend to it right away. . . . Excuse me a moment, please."

The Doctor hustled off and questioned many of the monkey leaders. Well, they not only brought kernels, which would grow into fine shady palms—and bulbs that would become plants—but they actually got all the seeds from which the turtle's medicine was made. So, when these were planted, John Dolittle did not have to worry about his patient ever running short of what he had ordered for him.

While all this was going on I was digging down into our fire-proof safe under the office floor. I was trying to sort out, from all those notebooks, the questions that the Doctor wanted to ask the turtle. But what a job! Were there *ever* so many notebooks—filled from cover to cover?

After three hours of work, I hadn't got very far, and Polynesia went to fetch the Doctor himself. He glanced through my work and said:

"The whole record does you great credit as a secretary, Stubbins." He sat on the floor almost buried in notebooks. "But great heavens, to weed all the questions I want out of this library would take weeks, maybe months! Let's just pick out the most important and hope for the best, shall we? I really don't see what else we can do."

So that evening, when we gathered once more in the turtle's shelter, John Dolittle fired off question after question; and Mudface, if he could, shot the answers back just as fast—or shook his head if he couldn't answer.

It was nearly all about science—about what changes the Deluge had made in the world. Some of the audience were deeply interested: others not at all. But we all stayed up till long past midnight. And everyone, by the end of it, was so weary that there was no talking whatever, after we bade the turtle good night and made our way home to bed.

In the bunkhouse we found a visitor waiting for us. It was one of those wild ducks that so often carried messages between the Doctor and his family in Puddleby. This duck had come to tell him that the old horse in the stable near the zoo had complained that his roof was leaking badly.

"All right," said John Dolittle. "We are leaving here for Puddleby right away. Thank you very much for your trouble. Remember me to the birds in my garden, please—if you get back before we do."

The next day, when all was in readiness for our leaving, Mudface asked the Doctor if he might swim down to the lower end of the lake to see us off. John Dolittle was delighted with the compliment and readily said yes.

"Who knows?" he laughed. "On the way I may remember a

few more questions that I forgot last night. I may not get another chance after this for a long time."

So, late in the afternoon we all left the landing at the foot of the long road that led down from what was left of Turtletown at the island's top and started off. The fog over the Secret Lake was not bad; though once in a while it would roll up thick and heavy, close to the canoe, and we were glad to have a guide with us. Mudface knew his way across this lake (hundreds of miles wide at the center) in the pitch-dark. He took no notice of the cloak of mist about us, just staying close enough to the Doctor's stern-paddle so that we should not lose touch with one another.

"Tell me, Mudface," said the Doctor after we had gone about a mile, "how did King Mashtu come to get all this power you spoke of?"

"Through the children—mostly," said the turtle quietly.

"The *children*?" cried the Doctor in surprise. "I don't under-stand."

"Well," Mudface answered, "King Mashtu was all in favor of education. But instead of educating the children in the right way, in honesty and fairness, this king saw that an easier way to power for himself was to educate them the *wrong* way.

"Oh, Mashtu was clever. He taught those youngsters never to doubt his word. Then, when they were old enough to vote for him, he slyly put over his scheme for a one-man government for Shalba. That is, a government run really by a single person. He knew that even though many were allowed to take part in run-ning the country, one and one only should be the head. *His* word must be the law. And he lived and dreamed of one plan alone: that he, Mashtu, should be that head. He counted the days till he should be elected not only the head of the government, but king of Shalba."

"Mudface," asked the Doctor through the clammy fog, "I believe of course every word that you are telling me—but how did *you* come to learn all this yourself? You were a prisoner in a zoo."

"Well, Doctor," said the turtle, "Noah spoke often of the times before the Deluge. You remember he was the only one, besides yourself, to learn animal language. He, too, was a prisoner; though, as the head zookeeper, he was treated well. The old man had a habit of talking to himself. But being afraid of spies, he always spoke in animal language—even in his sleep. So of course no one understood him, except the animals. . . . He did not like Mashtu or anything about him."

"Ah, I see," said the Doctor.

"Also," Mudface went on, "much of what I've told you I learned long after it happened—from Eber and Gaza, when they were building up their new language. Belinda and I got to understand it quite well. And we would enjoy, by the hour, hearing Eber and Gaza chat over past times."

"Of course, of course," the Doctor answered. "I just wondered how turtles who always—and sensibly—mind their own business, I wondered—naturally—how you came to know so much about public affairs in bygone days: government, politics and all that, you know. Your memory is marvelous. Thank you. Pray go on."

"King Mashtu!" sighed Mudface. "He could have done so much good had he wished. But he was a puzzle no one ever understood. . . . Ah well, he's gone now. Yet while he lived I don't suppose any man was more admired—or more hated."

And all of a sudden, just as I had expected, this strange story broke off; the turtle was silent; the fog, in true Lake Junganyika fashion, had lifted without warning. And there, quite close on our port bow, lay the ruined buildings we had seen before.

"There they are, Doc!" cried Cheapside. "The half-drowned slums we saw on our way in. . . . Jiminy crickets! I've run across some ramshackle waterfronts in me day: but never nothing like this. . . . Lumme, what a mess!"

I saw the Doctor in the stern (up to this he had been nothing more than an occasional voice behind a wall) look down at Mud-face who swam nearby. The turtle, treading water with his hind feet, stretched his neck up as high as he could to see the buildings better.

"*Shalba!*" he gasped. "I know every alley, every stone in it. But how comes it here at the surface of the lake? Last time I trod its streets it lay beneath two hundred feet of water—at the bottom of Junganyika! This is magic, John Dolittle."

"No," said the Doctor gently. "No, no magic, old friend. I'm sure it's just the earthquake, the same one that buried you. They do these strange things sometimes. It has heaved the floor of the lake up, at this end, in almost one piece, so the buildings show above the water. That is all."

"Shalba!" muttered the turtle again. "Shalba arisen from the past, arisen from the Deluge. . . . Shalba arisen from the dead!"

The Treasure Vault

I WOULD BE GRATEFUL, MUDFACE," SAID THE Doctor presently, "if you could show us something of the city before we leave. But I don't want you to overtire yourself, you understand."

"Certainly," said the turtle. "Come!" And he led the way.

On the poorer alleyways leading us into the town, the buildings were no different from those we had seen on our first and hasty visit. The streets were really canals, full of water, which lapped in and out of broken windows. The houses—small shops and the like—were nearly all of them partly ruined at least.

We did notice, however, as we paddled on, how many of them were at the same level. This, as the Doctor had said, must have been because the lower end of the lake's floor had been pushed up in one piece—without splitting the town in halves.

After winding through many side streets and narrow lanes, Mudface presently led us out upon a wide-open space. At first sight, it might have been a market, a public park, or something of the kind. The buildings surrounding it were in a much better state.

"This was called Victory Square," said the turtle. "Once the middle of it was filled with lovely flowering trees, fountains, and park benches.

"All the buildings you see around it now were put up when Mashtu came back from his last great war—against the Dardellians. It was built to commemorate that famous victory. Every house in this square was a part of the king's home. These on the left were the royal stables. Next to them were the quarters for the King's Guard; and, beyond, you see what is left of the royal kitchens—they were almost as big as a town in themselves. Most of the rest were offices and government buildings.

"And that big place, with the crumbled towers, facing us, was the royal palace itself, where King Mashtu lived in a splendor such as the world had never seen before."

I find it hard to give anyone a picture in writing of what the turtle was showing us. Certainly the man who laid it out was a true artist, a great architect. The square was unbelievably large—certainly, I would say, a mile from end to end; and more than half a mile wide. The stone used must have been granite, or some other very hard form of rock, to have lasted all those thousands of years.

Even now (though there were gaps of ruins here and there in the close, even rows of buildings which surrounded the pleasure-park) enough of the vast planning still showed a beauty and magnificence that simply took our breath away.

The Doctor knew a good deal about ancient architecture; but, he told me later, the style of these buildings was like none he had ever seen—and gave him no idea of their age. The palace at the far end of the Square of Victory particularly held our attention. The outside of it, at least, seemed perfect—except for one of the high, slender towers which had crumbled away a little, near the top. It still looked what it had been: the proud and splendid home of a king long dead.

"Stubbins," said the Doctor at last in a voice strangely hushed, "just *look* at that huge main doorway! Did you *ever* see such carved stonework?"

The palace seemed to stand slightly higher than the rest of the square. For, even at that distance, we could see a half-dry strip of ground showing in the front—and, above that, a wide terrace that ran completely round the palace.

Suddenly Mudface spoke again; and the way his voice startled us both, made us realize how long we had stared, almost in a trance, at this enchanted monument of the past.

"That piece of dry land," said he, "in front of the palace should mean that its ground floor will be all right for us to get in. Would you like me—if it's possible—to guide you through Mashtu's home, John Dolittle?"

"You took the words right out of my mouth," laughed the Doctor. "I'd like nothing better. Who would miss a chance of seeing the palace of a king who lived before the Flood?"

So the turtle swam across the square while we, very interested and all excited, paddled close behind him. Reaching the strip of land before the big door, we got out and tied up our canoe. A wide flight of steps led to the top of the terrace and the main entrance.

Mudface's great body (it looked like some big, mud-spattered van) was already scrambling up the royal steps—even before we had the canoe made safe by its painter rope. As we hurried to follow him into the palace, I noticed that all our company were very grave and silent. They reminded me—for some reason—of a company of children being taken into church for an extra-special service.

Inside, the light was very dim; and it took our eyes a moment or two to get used to the gloom—though we had by no means come from full sunshine outside. Presently, however, our surroundings began to take shape in the half-dark.

We seemed to be in a sort of passage. The confusion of the furniture and such was dreadful. A film of mud or slime covered everything.

The great turtle lumbered his way down the corridor. John Dolittle and I stuck close to his heels. Mudface, with his great muscles, shoved everything aside, no matter how heavy, making a pathway for the rest of us to follow.

We came out presently into a high, enormous room. The dim ceiling must have been a hundred feet above the ground floor level. The clutter and confusion were not so bad here—though in places a rafter or beam had fallen from the roof. At the end of this tremendous chamber a high-backed chair stood all alone upon a low, raised platform.

This time the Doctor went ahead of our guide. He took his penknife from his pocket and gently scraped the slime from the arm of the big chair. Beautiful green stone was at once uncovered beneath the thin coating of mud.

I was close enough behind John Dolittle to hear him whisper, "Good heavens, it's pure jade! I suspected, from the shape, it wasn't wood. Must have cost a fortune. Solid jade, the whole chair! And the polish and color are just as good as when it was first carved. . . . This seat, Mudface, was of course the royal throne?"

"Yes," said the turtle. "This room was called the Throne Room, or the Royal Hall of Audience. It was here that King Mashtu sat in council and in judgment. And often—but—oh my gracious! Look, Doctor—over there—the Treasure Vault! . . . Why—why, *it's open!*"

"A high-back chair stood all alone upon a low, raised platform."

Mudface was usually a very calm animal. It took a lot to upset or disturb him. That was why both the Doctor and I turned quickly at the excited tone of his voice. He was staring across the big hall at a door that led into another smaller room. The wall above it had a crack running from the Audience Hall's high ceiling right down to the top of this door's frame. Plainly the door itself had been damaged, instead of left open by chance. For we could see that the frame, into which it had fitted, had broken down at the top; it was this that had burst it open, inward. The door was enormously thick and strong. Six heavy hinges had once held it in place; but now, all askew, it hung by only one.

"Come, John Dolittle," said the turtle. "I think you will wish to see what lies within that broken door."

THE SEVENTEENTH CHAPTER

Crown of the World

GAIN, MUCH TOO THRILLED WITH EXPEC-
tation to talk, we followed our guide. He made light
work of the rafters that lay in our way. Some of the
stuff was terrific in weight. But, as Cheapside used
to say, once Mudface pulled his head inside his shell and shoved,
well, even if it was St. Paul's Cathedral, it *had* to move. And as he
worked forward, the turtle talked to us about the little room we
were making for:

"King Mashtu kept the crown jewels in there. That's why it was
called the Treasure Vault. Ten soldiers of the King's Guard kept
watch here every hour of the day and night. Mashtu had sent search-
ers all over the countries he had conquered to get the best locksmith
in the world. He was found and brought to Shalba, after the messengers had hunted for two whole years. He did a grand job for the
king—made the vault and its doors the strongest ever built."

"Yes," the Doctor put in, peering ahead, "I'd say he certainly did."

"No thieves could get in," the turtle went on, "even supposing they could go to work with ten soldiers on guard. This locksmith was an old man. The king promised him all sorts of pay and presents for his work—a fine house of his own to live in, in his old age and all that. But when the work was finished, Mashtu had him killed instead. You see, Mashtu was afraid the locksmith might give away the secrets of the vault, or keep an extra key to the locks, so his friends could help themselves to the treasure and money stored there."

"But," asked the Doctor, "where—how—did Mashtu get all this money and treasure? For a vault, that room should be fairly large, judging by the size of the door."

"Well," the turtle answered, "some came through taxing his own people. But most of it he took from the kings and princes he captured or killed on the battlefield. He was crazy about money—not for itself so much—but he needed it to make war—more and more wars. And he didn't care how he got it."

We were standing before the door itself.

"Here we are, Doctor," said Mudface. "The boy can crawl in under at the left-hand lower corner. I'll have to stay behind a moment till I can push the whole door down flat. Even then the entrance will be only just wide enough for my shell to pass through."

I got down on my knees and started to creep in under the door, the animals waiting in line behind to follow me. To say that I was "thrilled" would give you no idea of the tingle that ran down my spine. I was Captain Kidd and all the buccaneers of history rolled in one. For me it was the moment of a lifetime.

The light was poorer still inside; and I called back for Too-Too (the owl who could see in the dark) to come forward and help my groping steps. The Doctor, also crawling on his knees, took hold of my left foot so we should not lose touch with one another.

"But here again it was only a minute or so before we got used to the darker room—or at least could see well enough to make out most things pretty plainly. Against the four walls, all around, stood heavy chests. But within the vault—except for the broken door—everything seemed orderly, in place, and neat. Of course there was that thin coating of mud everywhere which told the story of long, long neglect. Ghosts seemed moving and whispering everywhere.

Soon the Doctor rose from his knees and examined the whole room with great care.

"My goodness, Stubbins," he murmured presently, "King Mashtu's Treasure Vault! Almost gives you the creeps, doesn't it? There must be no end to the secrets that have laid hidden within these four walls—for no one knows how many thousands of years. Because every paper that was important or valuable to the state would have been brought down here for safekeeping. . . . Er—er, I wonder what *that* is."

His gaze had shifted now from the strongboxes round the walls to the center of the room.

There, about the height of a man's chest, it stood all by itself; and it looked like a cabinet of some kind. It wasn't large; but its sides were solid, so you could see nothing through them. But the top was grated; and through this you could look down inside.

For the first time the Doctor took a box of matches from his pocket and struck a light. Cheapside was perched upon my shoulder. Silently the three of us peered in through the grating. The bottom of the cabinet was partly filled with sand that had sifted in. But, in a circle, points of some half-buried metal were sticking up. I wondered was my imagination working overhard in this spooky room; but I felt almost sure that that half-hidden thing down there might be a crown!

"Huh!" chirped Cheapside. "Looks like old King Mashtu's top hat, if you ask me, Doc. Heaven defend us!" he added, as the match burned out in the Doctor's fingers and a thunderous crash filled the room. "What's that noise? Sounds as if the roof was fallin' in."

We turned quickly. But it was only Mudface. Dimly we could see he had pushed the heavy door right down and was now trampling slowly over it into the vault.

Said he, as he came up to the Doctor:

"That old locksmith's work was better even than I'd calculated. I thought I'd never break that last hinge."

"Well now, old Muddy-puddy," said Cheapside, "how about tryin' yer muskles on one of these 'ere treasure chests? They look as though they might 'ave somethin' in 'em better than dried apricots."

At that, without a word, the turtle put the shoulder of his shell against one of the big chests. He took a good grip on the floor with his hind feet. And then he shoved. He was squeezing the heavy metal box against the wall.

Soon we heard a sharp *crack*. The lock gave way; the chest simply fell apart. And a great pile of gorgeous jewels and gold coins flowed over him upon the floor.

"Crikey!" muttered the sparrow. "Would you look at that? Golden sovereigns the size of saucers. Why, with just one of these 'ere trunks a bloke could buy out the Bank of England!—And look at the pearls, diamonds—rubies like hens' eggs—enough jools to give you the drools. Hold me up, Tommy, I feels a faintin' spell comin' on. Now, Doc, you can live on Easy Street the rest of your life."

"But it's papers I'm looking for, Cheapside," said John Dolittle, "documents, you know, which will tell me about the world in Noah's time. What would I do with pearls and rubies?"

"Oh, I wasn't digesting you should wear 'em round yer neck, Doc," said the sparrow. "But this is *real money*! There's a fortune lyin' at your feet."

Dab-Dab waddled forward across the room.

"Now, Doctor," said she, as though she were talking to a naughty boy, "I know I've been through all this with you before. But do try—for once—to be sensible. Have we *ever* had enough money for the housekeeping in Puddleby? You're always going broke. Now tie up a handkerchief full of those large rubies. The weight will be nothing in the canoe. Then we'll never have to worry about money again. *Please!*"

"No, no," said the Doctor quickly. "You don't know what you're asking me. All this treasure has been stolen, taken from conquered kings and murdered princes. These gold coins cry out with the voice of suffering—of innocent men, of women and even children slaughtered in war. Money! Bah, it is the curse of the world!"

His voice rose almost to a shout as he pointed to a string of glistening diamonds near his foot.

"No, no, Dab-Dab!" he repeated. "This treasure stays where I found it. These precious stones have *blood* on them!"

The white mouse crept forward and examined the diamonds with his microscopic eyes. Then he looked up at Dab-Dab and gravely shook his head.

"I don't see any blood on them."

The duck shrugged her wing-shoulders helplessly and turned away; while Polynesia the parrot, who was standing near, raised her old eyebrows and murmured wearily, "What else did you expect?"

"Too bad, too bad, Dab-Dab, me old darling," chirped the

ever-cheerful Cheapside. "But this little pile would sure have bought you a nice lot of sardines. Well, well, easy comes, easy goes."

"Mudface," asked the Doctor, "do you know what this is in the stand over here in the middle of the room?"

"Ah, that?" said the turtle. "Yes, it was called the Crown of the World. After the king's last victory—over the Dardellians—many false-hearted men came to Mashtu with a very gorgeous gold crown and asked could they crown him King of the World. They said he now owned pretty much the whole of the earth and therefore he deserved it.

"But there was still one people left unconquered. They were called the Zonabites; and their country—which wasn't large—was a long way off from Shalba. They were mountain-folk and tough fighters. Mashtu had had a try at them before; and found them a hard nut to crack. They had thrown his troops back—almost the first time that a Shalbian army had been beaten.

"Mashtu was a villain: but he was no fool. He knew that to make war on the Zonabites, so far from Shalba, would cost a terrible lot of money. Also, being no fool, he guessed that these men wanting to crown him King of the World were only trying to flatter him—to get themselves made generals, or something of the kind. So he spoke his mind to them in plain language.

"'No,' he said, 'I will not be crowned King of the World till the Zonabites are conquered and the whole world is truly mine.' (That was what he had always wanted.) 'Till the country of the Zonabites is under the rule of Shalba,' said he, 'what you offer me is nothing but a sham and a mockery. And you know it.

"'What's more,' he added, 'when I am crowned as ruler of the universe, I don't want any fancy gaudy thing like *that* put upon my head. I will have a simple crown, costing nothing, made of bronze, with no jewels in it! Thus, when I am truly Master of mankind, when the Zonabites are crushed, I will show how little I thought of them—these last miserable enemies who keep Shalba from our dearest desire.'

"All this, Doctor, is written, I believe, in the Shalbian language, around the headband of the crown in that cabinet.

"Then King Mashtu began to get ready for his war. In spite of the sneering way in which he'd spoken of the Zonabites, his preparations for *this* war were the greatest in all his history. He spent money like water, fitting out his armies with all the latest deviltries his inventors could think up.

"He built great fleets of ships, down at the mouths of the rivers, to carry his soldiers across the seas to the distant land of the enemy. He meant to take no chances. He had the biggest army gathered together that mankind had ever seen. For this time, he boasted, he was going to wipe the Zonabites out—man, woman, and child—so they could never rise again."

The turtle sighed and stopped speaking a moment. And even in the poor light I thought I saw that half smile play again around the corners of his wrinkled mouth.

"But five days," he said presently, "before the Shalbian army was to sail, the Flood came. It began, as I told you, with a gentle rain only. The king ordered the ships to put out to sea anyway, and the captains obeyed and sailed. But every single ship was smashed and sunk by that great wave we'd seen roaring across the Shalba racetrack."

Once more Mudface hesitated, deep in thought and memories. And soon the silence that hung over us there in the dimlit vault was broken by the voice of John Dolittle.

"And so," he said slowly, "Mashtu did *not* become complete

master of the earth? He never lived to wear this," (the Doctor laid his hand on top of the cabinet) "the Crown of the World? But it took a deluge to stop him from gaining his dearest wish. . . . I wonder what kind of a world we'd be living in now, if there had been no Flood and—and he had succeeded."

The Doctor's voice dropped and slowed down so we could only just hear him. It seemed almost as if he were in a dream, talking softly to himself, his eyes half closed.

"Thanks to you, brave Zonabites! And, despite all the suffering the Deluge brought, thanks be to heaven for the Flood, too! Mashtu all but wore it, the Crown of the World! . . . Could you get it out of this case for me?"

"Certainly," said Mudface. He threw his front legs around the slender cabinet and squeezed. The grating in the top popped off and clattered to the floor like a tin plate. The Doctor put his arm down inside and fished up the bronze crown. He cleaned it off a little with his sleeve and examined the strange writing cut into the headband.

"Dab-Dab," he said quietly, "we will take *this* back with us to Puddleby. It is worth nothing, as King Mashtu himself said—just bronze. So I do not feel I am taking stolen goods."

Without another word he turned and moved toward the door. Cheapside was still perched upon my shoulder.

"Tommy," he whispered in my ear as we all started to follow John Dolittle from the room, "that's the Doc all over, ain't it? Look at 'im: knee-deep in diamonds—and all 'e carries home out of a royal treasure vault is an *old brass hat*! Swap me pink, that I should ever see the day!"

Outside upon the palace terrace we found the sun shining gaily; but it was getting low down, for evening was coming on. We had no idea that we had stayed so long within King Mashtu's gorgeous home. Remembering the wild duck's message from the old lame horse in Puddleby, we wasted no time in unhitching the canoe.

The Doctor stowed away the bronze crown with care. He fastened it, like the precious packages of notebooks, to the canoe's bottom.

"That, Stubbins," said he, "is in case we have an upset. If the rest of the baggage is lost, the floating, wooden canoe will still save the most precious things for us, as long as they are tied in. No, no, Gub-Gub, we can't go back to the palace cellars for your preserved dates, now. Sorry, no time."

Then the Doctor, before saying good-bye, gave the turtle his last instructions about the medicine; the foods he should, or shouldn't eat; and all the things he should do to keep well.

"No, Gub-Gub, we can't go back for your preserved dates."

"You *will* take care of yourself, Mudface, won't you?" said he. "Don't forget that the wild birds will always bring your messages to me, if you fall sick again or anything. As for your story, old friend, I don't know how to thank you enough."

"I am only too glad that I had the chance to tell it to you, John Dolittle," said the turtle. "As for thanks, you have done far more for me than I did for you. My heart is sad indeed to see you go. But I know you must."

The Doctor nodded. "Alas, old friend, I must," he agreed.

Mudface gazed down into the lake where the evening shadows of the palace towers were beginning to stretch out into the gloom of coming night.

"And yet, Doctor," he added, "if you do write what I have told you into a book, for all the peoples of today to read—who knows?—maybe war may stop altogether and no leaders like King Mashtu ever arise again."

The Doctor, silent, thought a moment before he answered.

"Indeed I hope so," he sighed at last. "At least I promise you the book shall be written and I will do my best to write it well. How many will take any notice of it: that is another matter. For men are deaf, mind you, Mudface—deaf when they do not wish to hear and to remember—and deafest of all when their close danger is ended with a short peace, and they *want* to believe that war will not come back."

He turned suddenly and looked down into the canoe. Everyone was in his place, waiting. The Doctor slipped into the stern and took up the long paddle.

"All right, Stubbins," he called. "The painter's free. Shove off!"

And as I pushed the canoe's bow out from the steps, I saw

Mudface start lumbering down toward the corner of the terrace, where there was a grand view of all the south end of Junganyika. The old fellow meant to see the last of us from the best place.

Hereabouts, where the Secret Lake began draining itself into the river, a strong current swept us on our way. Once clear of the stonework, we let the canoe drift pretty much, saving our strength for the harder work that would come later.

As the lake narrowed still more we saw a sharp bend ahead of us. We knew that, after we had passed that bend, we would no longer be able to see the palace, or the waiting turtle. The Doctor and I turned and looked back.

There he was still, his giant shape standing up on the terrace corner, black and clear against the evening sky. He waved a right foreclaw at us in farewell. We waved back.

"Good-bye, Mudface!" muttered the Doctor. "Who knows how much you changed the history of the world—in gratitude for the kindness of one man, Eber. . . . Good-bye to you, good health and good luck!"

I glanced at the mangrove-covered shores; they were nearer. We had rounded the bend. I looked back no more. I knew the turtle was now out of sight.

"You're right, Doctor," said Cheapside suddenly. "May—may good luck stay with 'im for—for the rest of his days."

I glanced quickly at the sparrow. It was not what he had said that made me look at him. But I heard an odd, choking catch come into his voice. And I knew that this vulgar little rowdy of London's streets—Cheapside, who always made a joke out of everything—was, for perhaps the first time in his life, very close to tears.

In fact, we all had that "let down" feeling which so often follows great excitement. The twilight had become almost real darkness now. A few big stars had appeared, and their light made shimmering paths on the gloomy water. We still rested our paddles, knowing that the powerful current would carry us into the river without the help of any guide.

So this was the end of the "lucky voyage." We had done what we came to do. By rights, everyone in that canoe should have been talking gaily of a well-done job behind us and a well-loved home ahead. But, instead, we were thinking, glumly—all of us, about the same thing: our leaving Mudface behind and alone.

It made no difference that we couldn't take the great beast with us. In any case the English climate would have been too cold for him. But he had been sick here in his native Africa. . . . No, it was impossible to feel happy about our lucky voyage when we were leaving him this way.

The mangroves on either side were closing in now, as we drifted nearer to the river. I knew without him telling me, that John Dolittle felt the most uneasy of us all. Suddenly he spoke:

"Stubbins, what's that ahead of us, near the opening to the stream? Seems to be coming toward us. Watch, you'll see the starlight glint on its wet body every once in a while."

I had long since given up being surprised at his truly marvelous eyesight for long distances. All I answered was:

"Yes, Doctor, there's *something* there—and moving. But goodness knows what. Hard for me to make out anything in this light."

A moment later he gasped: "By jingo! It looks like a turtle. . . . But what a size! I'd swear it was Mudface himself, if we hadn't just left him behind us on the terrace."

It was plain soon that the creature could see us. It was making straight for our canoe with no shyness or fear at all. It swam swiftly, but so low in the water that little more than its head showed.

Motionless, we all gaped over the side till this strange thing out of the night was practically alongside our bow. Then I saw that it was indeed so like Mudface I could easily have mistaken it for him in full sunlight. It raised its dripping head slowly out of the water and said in turtle language:

"Could you, by any chance, be John Dolittle?"

"Why, yes," the Doctor answered. "But—"

"Thank goodness!" the turtle interrupted. "I hardly dared to hope that I would find you. Is it true that Mudface met with some accident? Is he still alive? Can you tell me where to find him, please?"

"Yes, Belinda," said the Doctor, "he is still alive—and very well, too."

"Bless you, John Dolittle," said the turtle. "When the seabirds told me you were here, I prayed I'd be in time to meet you. But, tell me, how did you know I was Belinda?"

"Well," said the Doctor, smiling, "you always ask your questions in threes—your husband told me so. I've never been so happy to meet anyone in my whole life."

At that, the turtle looked aside, down into the black water. "I'm so ashamed, Doctor," she whispered.

"But, why?" asked the Doctor.

"For leaving my husband," she said. "I meant to be gone only a few weeks instead of all this everlasting time. You see, even after years and years away from Gaza and Eber and my baby Aden, I still longed for the human friends I'd left. And when news reached us that wars had started again, even in that beautiful America, I got so upset that, well, I couldn't sleep.

"I kept thinking of my baby Aden—or his children's descendants, as it would be by now. Still they were mine. They were fighting the foreigners from Asia. Eber and Gaza must have died of old age. Would the Eberites be beaten and wiped out after all? That tribe, too, was mine and Mudface's.

"My husband was too sick for such a journey. I thought it over a long while. Would my animal sense be of any help in saving the tribe—as it had in the past, rescuing Gaza and her husband? At last I made up my mind I'd go and see."

She started to cry a little.

"And so," she went on through her tears, "when poor Mudface was asleep one night I sneaked away and crossed the ocean once more. I left a message with the snipe who lived near us to tell my husband why I simply *had* to go."

"I understand. Cheer up," said the Doctor.

Belinda went on: "When the seabirds told me that the giant turtle had disappeared, I was almost frantic with worry: I had left the kindest husband in the world alone when he was sick! . . . I came back here as fast as I could possibly swim."

As the turtle stopped for breath, I could see she was almost too weary to stay afloat. "But," she asked the Doctor, "you're sure he's all right? He wasn't injured by this earthquake or whatever it was the seabirds told me about? Which way did you say I should go to get to him?"

"Straight ahead, Belinda," said the Doctor. "We left him a few miles back. I imagine, by now, he is on his way to the island my post-office birds built for him a few years ago."

"Thank you," said she. "I'll hurry on now, if you'll excuse me. I seem to be the only creature living that never met you, John Dolittle.

Even in America every bird, beast, and fish still speaks of you and your kindness. I hope I'll see you again soon."

Mrs. Mudface was already churning the water like a steamboat, away from the canoe's side—headed for the island.

"Thank goodness for that," sighed the Doctor. "I feel better now. Somehow I hated leaving him all alone this time. But Belinda will take good care of him."

And all of a sudden our own family brightened up. Cheerful chatter broke loose fore and aft and amidships. Cheapside even popped up to the masthead and shouted after the fast disappearing swimmer.

"Three cheers for Belinda! Hooray!" He was joined in his noisy outburst by all of us. And at the end of the cheering, Polynesia's voice could be heard singing alone:

"For she's a jolly good fellow.
Yes, she's a jolly good fell—Hello!
Oh, Belinda's a jolly good fell—Hello!"

The Doctor and I broke into outright laughter. For the parrot had set the words to the tune of a sailor's hornpipe.

Then, like one man with one thought, John Dolittle and I plunged our paddles into the starlit water at the same moment. The canoe shot forward into the river like an arrow (upsetting most of the merrymakers in a laughing heap on top of the baggage). We were on our way downstream, toward the west, toward Puddleby and home.

The End

GUB-GUB'S BOOK

AN ENCYCLOPEDIA OF FOOD

IN TWENTY VOLUMES

BY HUGH LOFTING

NOTE: Prof. GUB-GUB Announces that Owing to the High Cost of Living the other 19 Volumes of this GREAT WORK have been Temporarily Postponed.

Contents

INTRODUCTION

Tommy Stubbins, the son of Jacob Stubbins, cobbler of Puddleby-on-the-Marsh, explains some things about this book and Gub-Gub the pig

I NEVER THOUGHT THAT I WOULD FIND A BOOK about Gub-Gub a more difficult task than the books I have written about Doctor Dolittle. Yet this is true.

With the Doctor, although the work of being his secretary often kept me up very late at night, taking notes full of arithmetic and science, there was this to make it easier: I nearly always had the great man himself there, to ask questions of, if I should get stuck.

But with Gub-Gub it was difficult. There wasn't much arithmetic or deep science about what he wanted written; but he was very little help to me when we got to a difficult place. Whenever there was any question or doubt, it was I who had to do most of the deciding. John Dolittle was himself a very good author with a lot of experience; while Gub-Gub—although he wanted everyone to think him the greatest author in the world—had no experience at all.

Yet for whatever faults this book may have, Gub-Gub must not be held entirely to blame. Perhaps I am by no means the best person for the work. Maybe I am not what is called a good editor, that is, one who is clever at arranging, and putting in good, understandable words, the writings and sayings of others. But at the time that this was written, there were very few people besides the Doctor and me who could understand animal languages. Someday, no doubt, there will be many more.

John Dolittle himself, of course, could have done much better; and I had hoped that he would undertake the work. Gub-Gub had asked me to go and speak to him about it. But Dab-Dab the duck overheard our talk. And although she was only a duck, she took wonderfully good care of the Doctor and his home.

"Tommy Stubbins," said she to me—severely—"if you bother John Dolittle with putting that silly pig's nonsense-scribble into human writing, there is going to be trouble. You know very well the poor man is far too busy with really important matters to fuss around with a stupid hog's gabblings about food."

"Oh, but, Dab-Dab," I said, "eating and food are very important to the human race, too, after all. I have looked over what Gub-Gub has written in pig language, and much of it is quite good—and quite amusing."

"That's just it, Tommy," said she, ruffling her feathers. "He has told me some of the things he wants to have put in his book. He is trying to be funny most of the time. Eating is not a matter to be played with and joked about. It is a serious subject."

"Oh, well now, Dab-Dab," said I, "I'm not so sure. Eating should be a jolly business. I admit it's serious enough when you're starving. But you yourself take life too seriously altogether."

"Well," said she, shrugging her wings, "I have plenty of cause to—with this family. But the Doctor's too busy. There are no two ways about that. If Gub-Gub's book must be put into English, why don't you do it yourself, Tommy?"

After thinking this over, I decided the housekeeper was right. Poor John Dolittle, with all his work in doctoring the creatures that flocked to his doors morning, noon, and night—together with the many books he was writing on animal medicine and natural history—certainly had no time to spare.

And so that was how I came to take on the job myself.

Gub-Gub was delighted, when I told him, to know that his work, on which he had labored so long, was at last going to be published, printed on a real printing press, and sold in the bookshops.

He was a little disappointed when I told him I feared I could not use his own drawings as illustrations. I would have liked to. But—well—Gub-Gub's pictures were distinctly piggy pictures, and I doubted if any printer could have printed them. Gub-Gub was no ordinary artist. He did not often use pencil or ink or paint. He liked much better to do his illustration in mud, drawn on the stable walls. He even painted one picture (the portrait of the "Picnic King") in strawberry jam and mint jelly. He said that no paint or chalks, nothing, could give him just the beautiful green he needed, except mint jelly. I told him I was sorry, but I thought perhaps it would make things easier for the printers if I did the pictures and left out the mint jelly.

I cannot say that I think my own illustrations nearly as striking and unusual as Gub-Gub's. But at least this much must be said of them: I have tried my hardest to carry out Gub-Gub's wishes in every picture. The pig watched over my shoulder while I did them, grunting out remarks and orders until they looked exactly the way he wanted them to be.

But alas! When I came to go over what he had written (in the Dolittle Pig Alphabet), I found I had a much bigger task to deal with than I had reckoned on. To begin with, the pages were very hard to read. Turning written Piggish into English is not easy at best. The spoken, or grunted, language is fairly simple—if you have had plenty of practice. But Gub-Gub, although he had had many lessons from the Doctor in writing Pig signs in copybooks, was a very untidy author. The pages were full of blots—large, messy blots. Many of these were caused by his eating ripe tomatoes when he was at work—tomatoes gave him ideas, he said. And of course the juice of the tomatoes was always running down onto the paper and getting mixed up with the ink.

And, oh, what a lot he had written, to be sure! He used wrapping paper instead of ordinary writing paper. He hated to write in what he called a small, finicky hand. And one whole attic in the Doctor's house was filled, from floor to ceiling, with sheets and sheets of brown paper a yard square and all covered with his bold, untidy handwriting—foot-writing was what Dab-Dab called it.

Some people who read this will remember that the pig, when he first spoke to the Doctor's animal family about his book on the art of eating, said he was going to call it, *A Short Encyclopedia of Food—In Twenty Volumes.* But alas, we must not forget, Gub-Gub knew so much about food that twenty volumes would seem by no means long to one as learned in the art of feeding as he was.

And so I had to give him a second disappointment when I told him I would have to cut it down in order that we could print a book about the ordinary size that most books are.

More than that, when I had sorted out from the great mass of his writings those parts that I thought people—human readers—would like best, I saw it would help a lot if I added something about how he collected his information for the book, and, well, a few other little things that will be read and understood later on.

I do not mean that any of Gub-Gub's book is not strictly his own. It is only that I had to change the form as well as the length of it. It took me a long time to think of this best form or arrangement. And this was how I at last decided:

The pig author was in the habit of reading what he had written to anyone who would listen to him. As soon as he got a new chapter finished, he would try it out on the other animals of the Doctor's household. He nearly always did it in the evening, when the animals usually clustered round the fire before going to bed. It became almost a regular thing to have the whole family—Jip the dog, Too-Too the owl, Dab-Dab the duck, Cheapside the London sparrow, the white mouse, and sometimes myself—gather in that comfortable kitchen of the Doctor's after supper while Gub-Gub sat at the table and read to us from his sheets of wrapping paper. He often also lectured to us, explaining his book as he went along. He called it "author's readings."

The other animals, of course, gave their opinions, saying which parts they liked and which parts they didn't like—sometimes not very politely. A good deal of what they had to say, for and against, struck me as being important and worth putting into the book. The author's readings, however, spread over many weeks—some months, in fact. Therefore, I found that again I had to cut down. And, as will be seen, in the form in which I did give the book to the printers I have taken ten of these evening gatherings, or readings, and made them into chapters. In each of them I have set down everything as it happened and every word as it was said, whether it came from Gub-Gub himself or from those who were listening to him.

And so we will begin with—

THE FIRST EVENING

MY-GOODNESS-GRACIOUS-MARY-AGNES!" cried Dab-Dab, flouncing into the room. She threw down a tray with a great clatter upon the table. "That pig will be the death of me yet."

"Why?" asked Jip. "What has he done now?"

"What has he done?" squawked the duck. "I thought the end of my patience was reached when he started calling himself *Doctor Gub-Gub, D.S.D.*, but—"

"What does D.S.D. mean?" asked the white mouse.

"Doctor of Salad Dressings, if you please," snorted Dab-Dab. "That was bad enough. But now he has gotten hold of a pair of John Dolittle's spectacles. There's no glass in them—just the tortoiseshell frames. And he's wearing them. Thinks they make him look like an author. At this moment he's traipsing around the house with those spectacles on his snout, spouting passages from his own silly book."

"Tee-hee-hee!" tittered the white mouse. "What a picture! But you know, Dab-Dab, I think his book ought to be lots of fun. An encyclopedia of food. I've no idea what *encyclopedia* means, but it sounds like something awfully good to eat—something that would last a long time, too. I do hope Gub-Gub has plenty about cheeses in his book."

"Oh, you *would* like your books to be cheesy," growled Jip. He was lying on the hearth, his nose between his paws, stretched out toward the fire, his eyes shut. Anyone would think he was asleep, but this was only his favorite way of listening to the conversation after supper, and he never missed a thing.

"Huh! And you would like your books to be beefy, I suppose," smirked the white mouse, turning up his pink nose.

Too-Too the owl, the great mathematician, was seated on the back of my chair, still and quiet as the furniture itself.

"That pig, Gub-Gub," he said presently in a thoughtful voice, "reminds me of a boy I knew once. A small boy with a large appetite—lived on a farm where I had a nest in the barn. One day a visitor asked him what was his favorite sport. 'Eating,' he answered. 'Well, but what is your favorite outdoor sport?' asked the visitor. 'Eating outdoors,' said the boy."

"Yes, that sounds like our Gubby, all right," chirped Cheapside the London sparrow. He hopped up onto the table and began his usual job of helping Dab-Dab to clear away by picking up the crumbs on the tablecloth.

"Tell me, Tommy," he said, "'ow does our Perfesser Bacon manage about 'is spellin'?"

"He doesn't, Cheapside," said I. "You see, the Dolittle Pig Alphabet is made up of signs, not letters. Each sign stands for a word, sometimes for a whole sentence."

"Huh! Something like Chinese?"

"Yes," I said, "something like it—only much simpler."

"It would have to be that indeed," said Dab-Dab. "The simpleton! He's forever nosing into the Doctor's books about gardening and cooking. But of course he isn't reading really—just pretending. It's my opinion that pig couldn't spell the word *ham*—not if you promised him a seven-course meal."

"Just the same," chuckled Polynesia the parrot from the top of the grandfather clock, "it is wonderful how much information he has managed to collect for his book."

Chee-Chee the monkey slid across the floor and threw another log on the fire.

"Yes," he said, "and he doesn't get it all from books. He pesters me all the time to tell him about the African jungle fruits, and the vegetables too—like yams and wild mangoes, palm kernels, dates, ground nuts, and whatnot."

"Well, you're all going to get a dose of him very soon, I fancy," muttered Dab-Dab. "When I was washing the dishes just now, he passed through the pantry, and he said something about giving us an author's reading tonight. So those who would like to go to bed had better go—oh, goodness! Here he comes."

There was a knock upon the door. Gub-Gub's only difficulty in getting about the house was the doorknobs. He had to use both his front trotters to turn them, and he always knocked when he could get anyone else to let him in.

"It's he, sure enough," giggled the white mouse.

I rose and pulled the door wide. In the opening stood a strange figure: Gub-Gub as an author. Under one arm he carried a large, untidy bundle of papers; behind his ear there was an enormous quill pen; upon his nose there was a pair of tortoiseshell spectacle frames; and upon his face there was a look of great weariness.

"In the opening stood a strange figure."

"Dear, dear!" he sighed. "No one has any idea how fatigued I am."

"Fat you may be," snorted Dab-Dab. "But what should make you *fatigued*?"

"Research," the great author groaned. "Untiring, endless research."

"Where did you do your research," asked Jip, "in the strawberry bed?"

"What is research?" asked the white mouse.

Gub-Gub pulled a chair up to the table beside my own and sat down. Then he wiped his spectacles carefully—although they hadn't any glass in them—upon the tablecloth and put them back on his nose. "Research?" said he. "Well—er—research is—er—bibliography."

"And what is bibliography?" the white mouse asked in a meek voice.

"Oh, you go to libraries and you read their books. Then you know what to put in your own."

"Ah, I see. Just copying," snickered the white mouse.

"Not at all," said Gub-Gub with an annoyed look on his face. "It isn't copying at all. It's very hard to describe. There are some things in the life of a great writer that are beyond your understanding, Whitey. Research is one of them, it seems. All afternoon I have been trying to make sure of the exact spot where King Alfred burned the cakes. My head is so tired. I am beginning to wonder if there ever was a King Alfred—and certainly if he ever burned the cakes. I have just come from the library now. My study—the attic upstairs, you know—is just piled to the rafters with the books I brought back with me. And presently I will have to return to my labors, my—er—bibliography. But first I thought you might like to hear a food sermon that I wrote last night."

Chee-Chee's eyebrows went up till they disappeared into his hair, while Polynesia broke out in whispers of her usual and dreadful Swedish swearing.

"Holy cats!" growled Jip. "A food sermon?"

"Yes," said Gub-Gub brightly. "It begins this way:

"'Dearly Beloved Brethren,
Is it not a sin?
To eat a roast potato
And to throw away the skin?'

"That is a well-known quotation, first used as a text, I believe, by His Grace the Archbishop of Batterby. And—"

"'Ere, 'ere, 'ere! 'Alfa minute," put in Cheapside. "I don't think we quite feel like a sermon this evening, Your Reverence. But what was you digging round after Alfred the Great for?"

"I wanted to put him in my food map."

"And what's the use of a food map?" asked the sparrow.

"Oh, it's a lot of use," said Gub-Gub. "'The Geography of Food' is a very important chapter in my book. And the food map is an important part of that chapter. I have made several maps and thrown them away because I wasn't satisfied with them. It is so difficult to get the writing small enough to put in all I want. The map should be not only a great help in learning the geography of food but also for the history of food. I would like it to show all the towns where the great events in food history happened—the place, for instance, where Alfred is supposed to have burned the cakes that the old lady had set him to watch while they were cooking. But also the map should mark all the towns and countries that are famous for different kinds of eatables. Such as Melton Mowbray, where the pies come from; the river Neva in Russia—caviar; Yarmouth, famous for its sausages; and Banbury, where the well-known cakes are made—that same Banbury, by the way, where we were invited in our childhood to:

"'Ride a cockhorse
To Banbury Cross
To see a fine Lady
Ride on a white horse.
With rings on her fingers
And bells on her toes.'
Tra-a-la-la, et cetera."

Gub-Gub finished by waving his two front feet in the air as though he were beating time to music.

"You mean with bells on your trotters and rings in your nose, more like," snapped Dab-Dab. "What a tiresome pig!"

"Still, I don't see what you're going to *do* with this map when you get it finished," said Cheapside.

"Do with it! Why, it will be most valuable," said Gub-Gub. "It tells you where to go to find different things to eat. Supposing you got up in the morning and felt like spending a nice, quiet banana weekend. All right. You just look at the map and take a boat for Central America. Perfectly simple."

"I see what he's getting at, Cheapside," said Jip. "He's going to have a sort of bill of fare take the place of timetables. All you've got to do is go to a booking office and say, 'I want a ticket to the best pudding you have. First class, please.' Yes, it's simple, all right."

"Tee-hee-hee!" tittered the white mouse.

"I'm afraid none of you are taking me very seriously," said Gub-Gub. He glanced at the clock. "I'll tell you some more another night. It is the hour for my bibliography. I must go and bibble."

And with great dignity he gathered up his papers and left the room.

THE SECOND EVENING

*The great food author speaks of his research
into history and invention concerned with
the art of eating; and the white mouse adds
something for the book*

N OW, WHEN WE COME TO TAKE UP THE HIS-
tory of the discovery of food," said Gub-Gub after the
animals were gathered round the fire another night,
"we find ourselves faced with a big problem. Many
people have written on this subject, but not all of them seriously.
Some you might call just food philanderers. And much that is generally believed to be true, I found in my—er—research, was not
true at all. Take the potato, for instance—a tremendously important article of food. What would we do without it?"

"You'd grow thinner," muttered Jip.

Gub-Gub took no notice of the interruption and went on.

"Take the potato: its discovery, most people think, was made by
Sir Walter Raleigh. Wrong, all wrong. It is true that Sir Walter, in
1586, first introduced it to Ireland, where it is still quite the favorite
vegetable—known under the various names of spud, pratie, potat-
ter, etc. But Raleigh wasn't the first to discover it. He only brought
it over from the Carolinas and had it grown on his estates—in

Cork; and very soon the Cork potatoes spread over the rest of Ireland."

"Tee-hee-hee!" tittered the white mouse. "Cork potatoes! How splendid! Then they'd float in the stew and you wouldn't have to go fishing for them with a spoon."

"Dear me!" sighed Gub-Gub. "What a lot of things I have to explain to you, Whitey! Cork is a county in Ireland where Sir Walter Raleigh had his estates."

"Well, who did really discover the potato?" I asked.

"An adventurer named John Hawkins," said Gub-Gub. "It was he who first brought potatoes to England in 1563. He found them in common use among the people of South America—at Quito, in Ecuador, to be exact. And that's rather curious, too, for in Quito it is almost impossible to boil potatoes."

"Why?" asked Too-Too the owl.

"Because the city of Quito is way up in the Andes Mountains— very, very high. And the water all boils away long before your potatoes are cooked."

"Ah yes, I've heard of that," murmured Polynesia, who had been a great traveler in her time.

"I don't like potatoes anyway," Jip muttered, turning over on the hearth with a deep sigh.

"Oh, but, Jip," said the white mouse, "did you ever try them mashed and then baked in the oven with grated cheese over the top?"

"That is called *pommes de terre gratin*," said Gub-Gub with a superior air. "Then take the parsnip, that queen of all vegetables, known in botany as *pastinaca sativa*. It is found in the wild state on the roadsides in England and throughout Europe and temperate

Asia. It has been cultivated since the times of the Romans. Being, as it is, part of the natural order of *umbelliferoe,* it was always—"

"Can't you stick to the English language?" said Jip. "What's all this foreign stuff, the umbrellery-thingamajig and the rest?"

"Oh, don't take any notice of him," snapped Dab-Dab. "He's just trying to make us think he knows some Latin or Greek—and botany, too! *Bottomy* would be more to the point, for him—judging from his figure."

"Pardon me," said Gub-Gub politely, turning to the duck. "But no one could think of you as a judge of figures in pigs—in poultry perhaps, but not in pigs. Now, supposing you had ever seen that famous beauty Patricia Portly. I don't suppose you'd have thought hers a good figure."

"Who on earth was Patricia Portly?" Chee-Chee put in.

"She was a very well-bred lady pig," said Gub-Gub. "Came from one of the best families. And ah, there was a figure! Such grace, such curves! She was always spoken of as the Venus of the Berkshires. I must confess"—here the great author smiled a little over memories of bygone days—"that I was quite a bit in love with her myself at one time. I found her friendship most inspiring—for my book, I mean. I had had great difficulty in choosing the best eatables to inspire an author. Someone said that olives were good. But I did not find them so. They upset my temperament."

"What might that be?" asked the white mouse.

"I'm not quite sure," said Gub-Gub. "But it is something that all authors have. Don't interrupt. Well, to go back to Patricia Portly. She helped me a great deal in trying out the best foods for a writer to work on. Her drawing room was quite famous, and only the most refined pigs were invited to her parties. It was a pleasing

"Patricia Portly, the Venus of the Berkshires"

sight to see her lolling on a couch surrounded by pigs of importance, pigs whose names were known everywhere, pigs who had really done things. I have quite a piece about her in my book. For she, too, made a name for herself in the history of food discovery. Yes indeed, she will be known to future students as the inventor of food perfumes. A real pioneer, you might say. At every one of her parties she wore a different perfume: sometimes it was prune juice; sometimes essence of caraway seeds; or nutmeg or barley broth; and she had one that I thought was particularly lovely, a mixture of vanilla and horseradish—very delicate. But perhaps her greatest work of art in this kind of invention was first made public when she got married. She lay awake many nights trying to think up a new scent to be used at her wedding. You see she wanted a nosegay and—"

"A nosebag, you mean," Jip put in with another grunt.

"She wanted a nosegay," Gub-Gub went on, "which would be something that had never been used by a bride before. And finally she decided on a bunch of Italian forget-me-nots."

"I never heard of the flower," said Too-Too.

"Well, they're not exactly flowers," said Gub-Gub. "They are those long green onions that come in the spring. You see, the very refined pig society in which Patricia moved did not like to call them onions. So they changed the name to Italian forget-me-nots. They became very fashionable after that and were nearly always used at pig weddings. Patricia's wedding was a very grand affair. The only thing that spoiled it, slightly, was that some of the guests, instead of throwing ordinary rice at the happy couple, threw rice puddings. They meant well, thinking that the bride and groom would like cooked rice better than raw. But I must say it *was* a little untidy."

"That porker's imagination," said Dab-Dab. "Well—" She shrugged her wings in despair and said nothing more.

"My chapter on the history of food discovery," said Gub-Gub, "turned out to be a much longer one than I had expected. Because not only did it have to take in all those naturalists and travelers who had first found new things to eat, but I found that besides the famous Patricia Portly, there were quite a number of others who had invented very clever things connected with eating.

"For instance, there was the man who first thought of, and used, the soup thermometer. He was an Inuit chief. When this gentleman was invited down south to meet the governor general of Canada, many dinners and parties were given in his honor at Ottawa. And he had to eat lots of dishes that were quite new to him—among them hot soup. And of course he had been used to eating his food cold up in the Arctic Circle—raw seal steak and that sort of thing. Well, he thought the soup was fine, but he burned his mouth very badly on it. And he never seemed to learn the trick of telling when it had cooled down enough. Then one day he saw a thermometer hanging up somewhere. He asked what it was for. And when he heard that it told you how hot or cold the weather was, he said to himself, 'Ah, why not have one for soup?' And he bought himself one—it was really a bath thermometer. And he kept it always on a cord around his neck when he went out to parties and he never burned his mouth anymore and lived happily ever after."

Jip groaned but said nothing.

Gub-Gub turned over some of the papers that lay on the table before him.

"Here's another very clever invention," said he, after glancing down a page of his notes. "The gingersnap hygrometer."

"What's a hygrometer?" asked the white mouse.

"A hygrometer," said Gub-Gub, taking off his spectacles, "is an instrument for telling you if the air is damp or dry."

"No need for that in England," said Polynesia. "It's always damp. Beastly climate! Now, in dear old Africa it is—oh well, never mind. Go on, Professor."

"Well, there was a man once who suffered greatly from coughs and colds and asthma and all that sort of thing. And his doctor had told him that he should never go out when the air was damp. Now, you know how gingersnaps get sort of tired and soggy when the weather is damp—they bend instead of breaking with a crack. So this man always kept one on his windowsill and he used to try it every morning. If it bent, he stayed indoors; if it broke, he went out and took a walk."

"But what did he do with all the ones he broke?" asked the white mouse.

"He ate them," said Gub-Gub. "He had plenty of gingersnaps. He was a baker. But let me tell you about the invention of pebble soup. In Russia, many years ago, when Napoleon was making a nuisance of himself spreading wars all over the place, a very hungry soldier called at a farmhouse to see if he could get something to eat. The farmer's wife, who was alone in the house, had had so many soldiers coming to her door for food that she told him at once she had nothing. She closed the door on him and he sat down outside in the sun and began to think. The soldier felt sure that there were things in the house to eat; but the problem was how to get the farmer's wife to part with them. And suddenly he had an idea. He knocked again at the door. The woman opened it and told him that if he didn't go away, she would set the dogs on him.

"'Excuse me,' said the soldier, 'but are you interested in cooking?'

"'Why—er—yes,' said she. 'That is, when I have anything to cook.'

"'Well, did you ever hear of pebble soup?' asked the soldier.

"'No,' she said. 'I never did.'

"'It's very delicious,' he told her. 'I wonder if you would care to have me show you how it is made?'

"'Yes, I think I would,' said she. 'I'm always interested in new dishes.'

"You see, her curiosity was aroused to find out how on earth anything good to eat could be made out of pebbles. So the soldier put down his pack and gathered up from the yard before the door two large handfuls of pebbles. These he carried into the kitchen and washed the dirt off them with great care. Then he asked for a saucepan, and when he had half filled it with clean water and pebbles, he set it over the kitchen fire. He stirred it from time to time with a spoon. And when it had come to a gentle boil, he tasted it and smacked his lips.

"'Ah,' said he, 'splendid!'

"'Let me try it,' said the woman, thinking that some magic had been performed before her eyes.

"'In just a minute,' said the soldier. 'It needs salt—and pepper.'

"So the farmer's wife went and got salt and pepper, and these were added to the soup. He tasted it again.

"'That's better,' said the soldier. 'But you know, the last time I made this dish—just before we entered Moscow—I found that a little onion, just a trifle for flavoring, made a great difference. It is too bad you have nothing in the house, as you say.'

"'Oh, well, wait a moment,' the woman said. 'It is just possible I may find one—one that has been overlooked—in the cellar.'

"She was all interested now to see how this mysterious cooking was going to turn out, and she didn't want it spoiled for the sake of a scrap of onion. She brought one and the soldier sliced it up into the saucepan. Presently he tasted the soup again.

"'What a difference a good carrot would make now,' said he, 'if we only had one!'

"So next a carrot was brought and added to the pot. And once more the soldier tasted.

"'There's no doubt about it,' said he, 'that I have the touch of the true artist when it comes to cooking. I really should have been a cook instead of a soldier. When this war is over, I may change my trade. Who knows? Much better to feed people well than to kill them!' He took another sip. 'There now,' said he, throwing down the spoon, 'I have done better than I thought. I have no hesitation, good woman, in saying that that is a dish fit to set before a king. But do you know what a really first-class cook would do now?'

"'No,' said she.

"'Well, he would add one more flavoring—a bone. The soup is practically perfect as it is. But a really great cook would put in just a bone, or perhaps two—any kind would do, beef bone, veal bone, mutton bone—only for flavoring, you understand, just to give it body, as we say. Well, it is unfortunate that there are no bones in the house. But it can't be helped. Put the plates on the table and I will ladle out the soup.'

"'The plates are on the sideboard there,' said the woman. 'You can set the table. I've just remembered that I have an old beef bone in the larder. I'll go and get it.'

"'Oh, in that case,' said the soldier, 'I'll let the pot simmer awhile longer. The pebbles are not quite as tender as they should be yet.'

"So the farmer's wife went and brought a nice beef bone, which was put into the saucepan. And after a little, the soldier ladled out the soup, carefully, from the top, and the two sat down at the table to try it. The woman found it so delicious that she got a loaf of black bread out of the pantry to go with it, and the meal was a great success. It was only some hours later, when she came to wash the dishes, that she discovered the pebbles where they had sunk to the bottom of the saucepan, just as hard and uncooked as they were when they were put in. But by that time the soldier was well on his way to the next town, where there was plenty of food to be had."

"Well," said Chee-Chee, "the farmer's wife wasn't very clever, was she?"

"No," said Gub-Gub. "But the soldier was."

"Where did you get that story?" asked Too-Too.

"From the library—in my research," said Gub-Gub. "But to this day, I understand, it is still told in Russia. And it is supposed to be true, too."

"It is too bad," said Dab-Dab, "that you can't find something useful to do with your time."

The white mouse twirled his long, silky whiskers with both his front paws. There was a thoughtful look in his pink eyes.

"I don't know," said he presently. "It must be rather fun to write a book. I'd like to write one myself. But the only thing I could write would be short stories about cheese, and I suppose they might be tiresome to any readers but mice. Would you like to put me in your book, Gub-Gub?"

"Why?"

"Well," said the white mouse, "it just occurs to me that I myself have added something to food inventions."

"What did you invent?"

"Well, I wasn't exactly the inventor. I was rather the invention, one might say. I was—er—a pea fielder."

"A *what*?" asked Jip, looking up from the fire with a scowl.

"A pea fielder," the white mouse repeated in a small voice. "Long ago I told you how, before I came to live with Doctor Dolittle, I was a pet mouse. I was owned by a boy, eight years old. Whenever there were peas for dinner, this boy, although he was very fond of them, had great difficulty in eating them properly. He would try to lift them into his mouth on a knife instead of a spoon. And of course they spilled and ran all over the place. For this he was often scolded by his parents, who hated to have them trodden into the carpets. So the boy used to bring me to the table in his pocket. And he got me to run after the peas when they spilled, catch them, and eat them. And very busy it kept me too. For you have no idea how clever peas are in running away and hiding themselves—under the piano, down rat holes, behind the grandfather clock, everywhere. The boy called it fielding peas; so he ought to be put down as the inventor, although I did the work. I was to get an extra piece of cheese for supper if I left no peas uncaptured. But the boy was an awfully good spiller. And by the time I had caught and eaten them all, I never had any appetite left to eat the cheese. My figure was absolutely ruined. And while the beastly vegetable was in season, I was so round I could roll almost as well as a pea myself. Would you like to put that in your book, Gub-Gub?"

"Oh yes," said the great author. "I think it's very important. Certainly I'll put it in."

"You would!" snorted Dab-Dab in disgust.

The Third Evening

The Doctor of Salad Dressings, after a few words about a certain anniversary, tells the family circle the story of the wars of the tomatoes

THE NEXT TIME THAT GUB-GUB GAVE THE FAMily an author's reading there was a wintry wind blowing around the house. Chee-Chee, being of African blood, usually found the English weather rather trying, as did Polynesia—only, unlike the parrot, he was not always grumbling about it. Instead, he made himself an excellent wood collector and fire tender. The lively little monkey used to climb the trees in Doctor Dolittle's garden and take down all the dead branches he could find. He also kept the walks and lawns tidy by gathering up the fallen twigs. These he stacked neatly into boxes beside the kitchen fireplace.

Tonight he had a merry blaze roaring for us. But even with this, the room was none too warm for comfort until I had pulled the heavy curtains over the windows and most of us had gathered close around the hearth.

When the great pig author entered the room, we noticed he was wearing the old green coat that had been part of his costume when he had acted in *The Puddleby Pantomime.* In the buttonhole of this in days gone by he had worn a carnation or geranium to show that he was a smart pig-about-town. But this evening, instead of a flower, the once popular actor was wearing a piece of red silk ribbon.

"What's the decoration for, Perfesser?" asked Cheapside.

"That," said Gub-Gub, seating himself at the table, "is for the anniversary."

"Let's see," said the sparrow. "Today's the third of September—no, don't tell me—well, I give up. What anniversary is it?"

"Today is the anniversary of Yorkshire pudding," said Gub-Gub.

"You should have known better than to ask him, Cheapside," Jip growled.

"Decorations are always worn on great anniversaries," said Gub-Gub, looking over his spectacles toward the dog. "All people who are really well-educated eaters wear a red ribbon to celebrate that day when, many years ago, that great institution, Yorkshire pudding, was invented and placed upon a British dining table for the first time. It is a very important date in history. What did you ask me for if you are only going to be flippant and silly? After all, I do my best to enlighten your ignorance."

"Our *pignorance*, you mean," said Jip. "Nobody likes a good meal better than myself. But how on earth you manage to write and talk so much about food is more than I can understand."

With the manner of a patient, weary schoolmaster, the great author took off his spectacles and laid them beside his papers on the table.

"Now, what is the use," he asked, "of anyone pretending that eating is not important?"

"The Perfesser is quite right there," said Cheapside. "A bloke can't get far without grub. Wasn't it Napoleon what said, 'An army marches on its stummick'?"

"Maybe that's why camels can go so far," said Chee-Chee. "They are supposed to have two stomachs, aren't they? Or is it some other animal?"

"Tee-hee-hee!" tittered the white mouse. "Two tummies! What a wonderful idea! Still," he added, growing suddenly serious, "maybe it wouldn't be so good—always. Fancy having two stomach-aches at the same time. Oh my!"

"But don't forget, my friend," said Gub-Gub, "that if you got one stomach out of order, so long as you had two, you could always use the second one to carry on with. But can't you see"—he turned and waggled his enormous quill pen at Jip drowsing on the hearth—"that the story of food discovery is the history of the human race—the history, in fact, of the whole animal kingdom? Ask Doctor Dolittle himself—and even geography. How do you suppose the different races of people came to settle down where they are on the map today? Because they could get what they wanted to eat there. Or because they got pushed there by other people who wanted the same things to eat."

Gub-Gub got up and waved his pen still more wildly at his listeners.

"Many of the greatest wars in history, ladies and gentlemen, have been fought over nothing more than wheat to make bread with, or oatmeal to make porridge out of, or lands where the best grass grew to feed sheep and goats on. The sheep's wool was used to make clothes to keep people warm and the goats' milk was used to keep them from starving. But they couldn't get along without

"'Tee-hee-hee!' tittered the white mouse."

having first the grass. Food! And drinking water—another form of food, after all: tribes have fought tribes for hundreds of years over who should own wells and rivers that meant life itself to them. Whole nations have disappeared from the face of the earth because of famine—nothing to eat. Great kingdoms have tottered and fallen because the larder was empty. Mighty empires have risen to power and glory—on full stomachs. This book I am writing will show that there is nothing, ladies and gentlemen—absolutely nothing in this world—of greater importance to all of us than food."

The pig author sank heavily into his chair, seemingly weighed down with the earnestness of his long speech and the terrible importance of food.

"Did he say something about goats' milk?" murmured Jip sleepily. "Horrid stuff! Never could stand it."

"Your ideas ain't 'alf bad, Gubby—for the most part," chirped the cheerful Cheapside. "Nobody's denying that it's grub what makes the world go round. But what Jip 'ere meant was: Why be talkin' about it all the time?"

"Well, why not?" asked Gub-Gub. "It's nothing to be ashamed of, is it?"

"Oh no," said the sparrow. "Go on with yer lecture, Doctor Hog."

"Please don't call me 'hog,'" said Gub-Gub peevishly. "I wish you would remember that I have a pedigree—a long pedigree."

"A short tail and a long pedigree! Tee-hee-hee!" whispered the white mouse, tittering over his own joke.

"Well," Jip grunted, "I'd rather have a short pedigree as a fox terrier than a long one as a pig."

"There you show your ignorance some more," said Gub-Gub. "There have been knights of old who were proud to bear upon their shields and crests the sign of a boar's head."

"What is a boar?" asked the white mouse.

"A pig who talks too much," growled Jip.

"Don't mind 'im, Perfesser," said Cheapside. "'E 'as to 'ave 'is little joke, yer know."

"Well, now," said the great author, "you have heard of the Wars of the Roses—where one side wore the white rose of Lancaster and the other the red rose of York when they went into battle?"

"It was a little before my time," said Polynesia, who had led a very long life. "But I do remember hearing about them."

"Very good," said Gub-Gub. "But did you ever hear about the Wars of the Tomatoes? No? Well, I'll tell you about them."

The white mouse polished his long, silky whiskers again and settled down to listen. "The Wars of the Tomatoes! That ought to be good," he giggled.

"In a certain country," Gub-Gub began, "many years ago, the regular dish for Christmas dinner was roast goose stuffed with tomatoes. For as long as anyone could remember, this had been a national custom. People would no more have thought of going without roast goose with tomato dressing on Christmas Day than they would of flying. Fine, round red tomatoes were grown on the sunny hillsides of that fair and peaceful land specially for stuffing the Christmas goose, and all would have gone well with the happy simple folk if, one evil day, a certain gardener had not come to visit them from a neighboring country.

"The gardener was not himself a bad man, and although his coming caused no end of trouble, he meant well. He considered himself a great expert in growing new sorts of vegetables and fruits, and he brought with him a new kind of tomato. It was a yellow tomato— that color when it was ripe, I mean. And he told the people it was the latest and most fashionable thing—that nobody who was really up-to-date would dream of using the old red tomatoes if he could get yellow ones. Well, you know how folks are: they always think that anything that comes from a long way off, from a foreign land, must be better than that which is made or grown at home.

"So many of the richer families started to grow yellow tomatoes, and very soon the new fad spread and was taken up quite widely. And when the next Christmas came around, many a roast goose was stuffed with yellow tomatoes instead of red ones. But in every land there are always people who are called conservatives—that is, those who believe in keeping to the old ways of doing things. And the conservatives in that country began to get annoyed when they found that the Christmas geese were being stuffed with something new. They made speeches in the marketplaces. They called on all good citizens to take a firm stand against yellow tomatoes. Red ones, they said, had always been good enough for their fathers and should be good enough for them and for their children. It was a nasty foreign custom, they felt, creeping into their homes from enemy nations beyond the border, and if yellow tomato dressing was allowed to spread farther, their beloved native land would never be the same again—the country would just go to the dogs."

"The dogs would not have taken such a silly country as a gift," sniffed Jip. "We don't care for tomatoes anyway."

Gub-Gub raised his quill pen for silence and went on.

"On the other hand, the wealthy people—not the older families, but those who had just become rich and wanted to make a name for themselves as fashionable and up-to-date—they stuck to the idea of the new goose dressing. Soon they, too, began getting up at street corners and making speeches to the people. No end of a fuss was raised. The whole country was divided. Arguments and rows went on all over the place.

The government was upset. Ministers lost their jobs. All sorts of unexpected things began happening over this question that looked as though it would never be settled. At last real war broke out, the worst kind, civil war—a people fighting among themselves."

"Were there many killed?" squeaked the white mouse in a hushed voice.

"No," said Gub-Gub. "Fortunately not. It is perhaps the only case of its kind in history. For the Wars of the Tomatoes were indeed peculiar. Although they lasted a terribly long time, spreading over many Christmases—so that people began to wonder if they were ever going to stop—not a single person was killed. That was because they used tomatoes instead of bullets and cannonballs. One side called themselves the Yellow Party and the other the Red Party.

"But perhaps the most peculiar thing about the whole struggle was that the Red Party threw yellow tomatoes, and the Yellow Party threw red tomatoes. You see, they thought it would be more insulting to bombard the enemy with his own stuffing, so to speak."

"Well, who won?" Chee-Chee asked.

"Oh, the Yellow won," said Gub-Gub. "They at last managed to corner the Reds in a steep valley between two high hills. And there, on the bank of a stream, they simply smothered the enemy under a perfect mountain of tomatoes till they begged for mercy, and peace was declared. But it is said that long after the war was over, the river ran red with tomato juice."

"So the yellow tomatoes were used for stuffing after all, eh?" asked the white mouse.

"Oh no," said Gub-Gub. "You see, there wasn't a tomato left

in the country after the fighting stopped. They had all been used up in those terrible battles. Next Christmas, in fact forever after, the roast goose was stuffed with onions."

"Humph!" said Cheapside. "A very juicy bit of 'istory, Perfesser—still, if you must 'ave wars, I reckon that's as good a kind as any. From what I can make out, there ain't been none of 'em what's brought much more profit to either side than that—just a valley full of ketchup. Heigh-ho!"

"Ah, but the loss in vegetable life," sighed Gub-Gub, shaking his head sadly. "All those tomatoes! A race wiped out. Terrible, terrible!"

"Never mind," said Chee-Chee, putting another log on the fire. "Just think what a good thing it was that the people weren't arguing about coconuts."

THE FOURTH EVENING

After explaining the various things that his encyclopedia contains, Gub-Gub begins his famous "Food Mystery Story"

BEFORE YOU BEGIN AGAIN, PERFESSER," SAID Cheapside, "suppose you give us a general idea of the layout. I mean, what else 'ave you got in this bloomin' encyclopediddy of yours besides 'istory and geography?"

"Oh, lots and lots," said the author. "There are chapters on food poems; food music; food fables and nursery rhymes—'The Fox and the Sour Grapes,' 'Plum pudding Hot, Plum pudding Cold,' 'Miss Muffet and the Curds and Whey,' the Real Story of 'Little Jack Horner,' and so on. And food romances—that's quite a big section. It gives you, among other things, the love stories of famous cooks and the food life of famous heroes. Then there's a chapter on food fantasy, but I must warn you it's rather highbrow stuff— needs lots of imagination, you know, and—er—soul to understand it properly—pure food fantasy, very whimsical. So is the part on food fairy tales. Oh, and there's lots more: food detective stories, cooking crimes, and kitchen mysteries; food comedies; food trage- dies. I have even started a food Shakespeare."

"Lord save us!" gasped Dab-Dab. "Of all the impudence, of all the outrageous cheek I ever heard in my born days, that takes the cake. A food Shakespeare! What are you going to do—write the man's plays over again for him?"

"Er—well, not exactly that," said Gub-Gub. "But, you see, I thought it might encourage the education of young people—and of young pigs even more so. Very little has been done to make learning of any kind attractive to young pigs. Even now that John Dolittle has invented a Piggish alphabet, they don't do much serious reading. The works of William Shakespeare—or Shakespoon, as I call him in my encyclopedia—are very important to a good education. And I felt that by putting a little more about food into his plays—just changing words here and there—I might give young pigs a taste for good books."

"I knew a goat once who ate books," said Cheapside. "But 'is taste wasn't very good. 'E liked the cheap magazines best. Read us some of your new Shakespeare, Gubby."

"Well, I haven't gotten very far with it yet," said Gub-Gub. "I'll just give you a few quotations from it, and then you can see the sort of thing I'm trying to do."

He turned over a page or two of his notes.

"Ah, here we are," he said presently. "This is from the tragedy of *Macbeth*: 'Lay on, Plumduff! And burst be he who first can't hold enough!' You see the alteration is very slight. And here's another. This is from that beautiful and romantic play *Roly Poly and Juliet*: 'Oh, Roly-o, my Poly-o, Wherefore art thou, Roly-Poly-o? A dumpling-o by any other name would smell as sweet.' Isn't that nice?"

"A bit doughy and oh-y," muttered Cheapside. "But I get

your idea. Now, 'ow about these food detective stories you was speaking of?"

"Yes, let's have another food story," said the white mouse. "I liked that one about the pebble soup. Maybe you have one about a piece of cheese?"

"Not among the detective stories," said Gub-Gub. "Those are what is called a series, that is, they have many of the same characters, the same people, in all of them. The chief character is a man called Sherbet Scones, the famous Icebox Detective. He runs through the whole collection of mystery stories."

"Well," snapped Dab-Dab, "I hope he keeps on running and doesn't stop. I don't want to meet him."

"This detective was very clever," Gub-Gub went on. "Whenever things were stolen and the police were unable to find out who did it, Sherbet Scones was nearly always called in to catch the thief. It was the case of the missing eggs that first made his name known. That was when a certain very important Indian rajah was traveling around Europe to see the different countries. He had with him, besides his son, a great number of servants and a terrible lot of baggage. His favorite dish was curried eggs, and he had brought along with him three cases of eggs. Ordinarily a case of eggs is not very expensive. But these were awfully valuable. They were a special kind of seabird's eggs that could be found only on the shores of this rajah's own native state—and even there they were nearly priceless.

"Sometime after he got to England the first two cases were all used up. And one day when the rajah had invited a lot of people to lunch, and was going to treat them to his famous curried eggs, the cook came running to him in a frantic state, crying out that the third, and last, case of eggs had been stolen. There was a great commotion. Not only was the rajah dreadfully upset over having to disappoint all these guests in his house—most of whom were looking forward to his famous curried eggs—but the police, as soon as they heard about the business, were extremely angry. What would the world think of England now, they said, when important visitors had their very lunches snatched from them? Well, two rewards, both of them large sums of money, were offered. One was offered by the rajah to anyone who would get back the stolen eggs, and the other was offered by the police to anyone who could find the robbers and bring them to justice.

"Well, this cunning Detective Scones found out who it was. And you'd never guess. The rajah had been stopping at the university town where he planned to have his son go to college. Now, this university had a secret eating society, or fraternity, called Sigma Eta Apple Pie—after the Greek letters, you know. They used to hold secret meetings once a month, very jolly affairs, at which each member in turn had to supply some entirely new dish that had never been eaten by the society before.

"Sigma Eta Apple Pie was formed, I understand, because many people felt that the British, usually so brave and adventurous, were very unadventurous in eating. And it's true, we are, you know—no doubt about that—always eating the same things, very few dishes, when you think of France and other countries—no eating courage at all. And one of these lighthearted college boys, when it came around to his turn to think up something new to eat, had been very puzzled where to find it. Then he had heard about the visiting rajah and he thought curried seabirds' eggs would be just the thing. So he broke into the house and stole the rajah's last case of eggs. The young man had a very rich father, and he had meant to get the money to pay the rajah for the eggs afterward. But when he found that the eggs were worth almost a fortune, and that the police were after him, he decided to hide—both himself and the eggs. The great Sherbet Scones tracked him down and found him."

"Where?" asked the white mouse.

"In the secret icebox of the secret society," said Gub-Gub. "It was marvelous because no one knew where it was, nor even that it existed, except the members of the society. But Scones got only one of the rewards, the one offered by the police."

"Why, who got the other one?" asked the white mouse.

"Nobody got the rajah's prize for the return of the eggs because the young man had eaten them. And he was nearly frozen, too, when they took him out of the icebox. So that was how Scones first came to be known as the Icebox Detective. And after that he was called in on a great number of robberies, particularly those connected with food in any way; he was spoken of as a specialist in that kind of work. Police departments of other cities came to him for advice and help, and food robbers in every corner of the earth trembled at his name.

"But what I really started to tell you about was the hardest detective job that Sherbet Scones ever did. For the day came when the great detective found himself working against a mastermind— brains, daring, brilliant brains almost equal to his own. A whole string of robberies had suddenly broken out, like the measles, you might say. Nobody seemed able to find out who had done them, or how they were done. No clue was left behind which—"

"No glue was left behind, did you say?" asked the white mouse.

"No *clue*," repeated Gub-Gub patiently. "That is, no trace or other thing that would give anybody an idea who the thief might be.

HUGH LOFTING

"Scones, the 'icebox detective'—in disguise"

Please don't interrupt. No footprints could ever be found around the houses robbed; no fingerprints ever gave the clever thief away. After several of the robberies had been written about in the newspapers, people set guards around their houses, who stayed up all night with loaded shotguns. They put special bars and locks on their doors and windows. They rigged up all kinds of tricky alarms— wires strung across the floors so they rang bells if anyone should sneak in and trip over them in the dark. And still, all the time, houses were broken into and things were stolen."

"What sort of things?" asked the white mouse.

"Wait. I'm coming to that," said Gub-Gub. "Night after night Scones the detective lay awake in bed gnashing his teeth in despair—when he wasn't gnashing them through the silent streets, trying to find out who it was who so outrageously defied the law. You see, as I told you, he had built up a great name for himself. And as the weeks went by and no one was caught, he felt that his reputation was at stake—that he would no longer be considered a great detective, the greatest specialist of his kind in the world, unless he caught somebody soon and put an end to the chain of robberies.

"And then, too, the newspapers were so mean to him. They kept saying what fools all the police and detectives were and how poorly they protected honest people against evildoers. One newspaper—it was a food newspaper called *The Daily Meal* with offices in Grub Street—was particularly mean to poor Scones. As the robberies were all connected with food, *The Daily Meal* was very interested in them, and it told one of its men to give all his time to them.

"This man's name was Hamilton Sandwich. He was called Ham Sandwich for short, and just Ham by those who knew him very well. He was considered by his paper to be its very best and smartest reporter, for he was simply marvelous at getting food news ahead of anybody else. Well, Ham Sandwich followed Scones around wherever he went and made a great nuisance of himself, pestering the detective with questions, trying to learn what he had found out. And when Scones wouldn't tell him anything, he went back to his office and wrote sourcastic remarks for his newspaper to print about the stupidity of detectives in general and of Sherbet Scones in particular.

"But the Icebox Detective had not been idle—not by any means. By carefully examining all the houses broken into, be began to put certain things together in his mind. For instance, he noted that the thief, or thieves, always got in by the pantry window. That was at the beginning of the robberies. Later, when most pantry windows were protected with special locks, they got in some other way—often without leaving any trace at all as to how they had done it. Most mysterious! But Scones noticed also that no matter by what way the robbers got in, they always *visited* the pantry and apparently they always ate a light meal there before they went away. Because every time there were dirty plates and knives left lying around, showing that food had been eaten. And also *there was always one plate left on the floor of the pantry.*

"On discovering these things, Scones set to work to find what kinds of food seemed to be the thieves' favorites. And he found that whenever the pantry contained strawberry jam, a pot or two had always been opened. 'Ah-hah!' he snarled. 'A thief with a taste for strawberry jam, eh? This must be investigated.' And he hurried off on the scent, with the tireless Ham Sandwich close at his heels.

"He went to police headquarters and started looking through the records. Now, these records, as they are called, are drawers and drawers full of cards that are kept by police departments, showing a history of every thief who is known from past robberies. But though Scones spent a whole day hunting through thousands of cards, he could find none that told him anything of a thief who always helped himself to strawberry jam when robbing a house. He was puzzled, baffled. But presently he had a thought. 'Ah-hah!' he said again. 'No record here? Must be a foreigner, then. A foreign criminal with a taste for strawberry jam. No matter, he shall never escape the Icebox Detective!' And he hurried away again, tiptoeing past Ham Sandwich, who had fallen asleep among the records.

"Then he sent messages all over the world to the police of

other cities, asking if they knew anything of a daring thief who was fond of strawberry jam. But though he got many answers, none of them gave him any information of such a person. Scones was baffled again. Meanwhile new robberies almost every night were committed right under his nose, you might say. And he went on gnashing his teeth—while Hamilton Sandwich went on writing nasty things about him in *The Daily Meal.*

"Now, about the kind of things that were stolen: at first the great detective noticed that all sorts of different plunder were carried away—though never very much at a time—clocks, silver spoons, a little jewelry, suits of clothes, walking sticks, telescopes, cigars, and such. This also made it hard to tell who the thief might be or what kind he was. But one thing the police nearly always do when they are puzzled in this way is to watch the shops kept by receivers of stolen goods."

"What are they?" the white mouse asked.

"Receivers of stolen goods are men who buy things that have been stolen. They are careful not to ask where the things have come from because they know, or guess, that they have usually been taken from other people's homes. They pay a very low price for the goods and sell them for a much higher price. It is a regular trade but a dangerous one and certainly not honest. I had a pig friend once who was a well-known receiver of stolen vegetables. He was looked down upon by the best people in pig society as a very shady character. But it must be said for him that he never sold the plunder over again. He—"

"He ate it all up," Jip put in. "I'll bet a ham bone on that."

"Exactly," the great author agreed.

"That's what you call 'playing safe,'" Polynesia remarked. "Clever rascal."

THE FIFTH EVENING

The Food Mystery Story is continued
—and ended

WELL, TO GO ON WITH MY STORY," SAID Gub-Gub, "by keeping an eye on the receivers of stolen goods, the police are often able to run down an umbrella or a banjo or a hot water bottle or some other thing that has been stolen. Everywhere he went, Sherbet Scones carried with him a list of missing articles taken in the robberies. But he could never find a trace of a single one of them at the receivers'. He set some of his assistant detectives, disguised as chimney sweeps and tax collectors and whatnot, to call at their shops every so often and nose around. But nothing came of it. Nevertheless, this time, instead of being baffled, he learned something—or, rather, deduced something."

"De-juiced something?" asked the white mouse mildly. "You mean with a lemon squeezer?"

"Oh dear, dear, dear!" cried Gub-Gub. "*No!* 'De*duced.* That's a word used a lot in the best mystery stories. It means using your brain, if you've got one. Reasoning. You notice some small thing and you chew it over in your head for a while and presently it leads you to a new idea. For instance, suppose you came into the room here with your whiskers all gummed up with treacle. I would look at you a moment and then start thinking, and finally I would deduce that you had been to the larder. Is that clear?"

"Well," said the white mouse timidly, "maybe. But it seems to me that you would have deduced that I was just as untidy an eater as yourself. Which I'm not. But never mind. Go on."

"Now, Sherbet Scones deduced this way: He said to himself, 'If the thief is not taking the things to the receivers, what *is* he doing with them? He must be shipping them out of the country so his friends can sell them for him abroad. Ah-hah! Another link in the chain. No record with the police here. Friends abroad helping him. Why, he *must* be a foreigner—a nasty foreigner. Yet why have I not heard something about him from the police of other countries? A criminal as clever and experienced as this one must have a record somewhere. Strange! Strange!' He felt another attack of being baffled coming on and, hoping to shake it off, he went home to write a letter to his grandmother with rheumatism.

"The dawn was just coming up in the east when he let himself in with a skeleton key. The cat came out as he opened the door and began to drink the morning milk on the doorstep. But Scones didn't care. His mood was reckless and disgruntled.

"He went straight to his study and flung himself into a chair. On his desk he noticed a pile of letters, the morning mail that had just come in. Glum and brooding, his thoughts far away, he began idly turning over the letters. He came to one with a foreign stamp on it. Savagely he tore it open with his teeth. He hated everything foreign that morning.

"But as he read the letter his mood changed. His eyes popped. His mouth dropped open. The scowl on his features turned slowly into a wide grin. For the letter was from the chief of police in Venezuela, in South America. You see, Scones had forgotten to count all the answers he had gotten to his own letter, and this one, from a country such a long way off, had taken many weeks to reach him. It said:

"'We feel almost certain that the man you are after is one whom we have had on our records here for three years past. He usually enters houses by the pantry window. Always stops to eat strawberry jam on his way out—that is, if he can get it. But any jam will do. In fact, seems fond of all kinds of food. Not a native of this country, but well known here as Chillibillibeano, the Texas Pantry Bandit. Chilly for short. Does he use a dog to help him? If so, you can be sure it's Chilly.'

"Sherbet Scones sprang up from his chair. He sprang so suddenly and so high that he banged his head on the ceiling. But he was so excited he never even noticed it.

"'A dog!' he shouted. 'Why, of course! The plate on the floor. What else could it be for but a dog?'

"At this moment one of his assistants rushed in to say that another house had been robbed just down the street. The great detective quickly disguised himself in a long white beard and hurried away to examine the scene of the crime. As soon as he got to the house he questioned everybody in it. But, as usual, no one had seen the robber getting in or getting out, and, as usual, there were signs of a meal left in the pantry—jammy knives and spoons—*with one dirty plate left on the floor*. Scones then searched around outside the building for tracks of a dog. And, sure enough, he found them in the kitchen garden under the pantry window. So he was now quite sure that Chillibillibeano was the gentleman he was after. And the first thing he did was to put a piece in all the newspapers:

> "WANTED FOR ROBBERY
> Chillibillibeano, known as the Texas Pantry
> Bandit. Tall, dark, and thin. Slippery customer.
> Fond of jam. Works with dog. Anyone
> knowing anything that may lead to the capture
> of this desperate character will please write to,
> or call upon, Mr. Sherbet Scones, detective.

"And now everybody knew the thief's name and what he looked like, and there was a great deal of talking and guessing everywhere. But just knowing a robber's name and a few things about his looks doesn't mean you've caught him. In bygone days Robin Hood and Captain Kidd were well known and famous many years without being captured. And now in spite of all the chatter and gossip and everything, no one came forward who could say he had ever really seen this mysterious man whose long list of thievings had caused such a stir.

"And presently Scones began to wonder and doubt. Could it be Chilly after all? Surely a stranger would be suspected when everyone in the neighborhood was looking for him. Houses were broken into just the same as before, almost every night. But now the things stolen were always food. No jewelry or umbrellas anymore—just food. And such quantities! Careful housewives who had laid in large stores when things were cheap would have their whole supply carried off—sacks of flour, barrels of apples, a dozen jars of chutney in one night—which puzzled the great detective mightily. Because this was more than any one man could eat or want for his own use. It almost looked as if some gang—and not a single robber—were at work.

"So Scones said to himself: 'Very well, then. Suppose we *are* mistaken. And if we can't find the man, let's see if we can find the dog.' And he went back over the dog tracks and examined them all carefully through a magnifying glass. Then he made sketches of them. These he took to the dog breeders and dealers. They said they had never seen paw prints like them before and had no idea of what kind of dog it could be. Which was not surprising, because, just as Chilly was a brand-new kind of robber, so the dog he was using as a helper was a brand-new kind of hound."

"What was the breed called?" I asked.

Gub-Gub smiled to himself in a superior sort of way.

"It was a Sneakinese," he said.

"A what?" yelped Jip, starting up.

"A Sneakinese," the author repeated. "It was a cross between a Pekinese and a sneak—a sneak thief, you might say. Very rare. You see, for robbing pantry shelves and iceboxes in the dead of night it is terribly important not to make any noise. A clumsy hand reaching in to get a jar of pickles or a can of salmon can cause enough clatter to rouse the Seven Sleepers. Now, the Sneakinese had a very sharp, thin nose and a long, wormlike body. He could thread his way between bottles of vinegar and tins of tea and fetch out a bunch of asparagus without so much as a tinkle. He had been specially trained; and he never ate the things he was sent after because he knew that when his work was done, his master would prepare a nice midnight supper for him on the pantry floor before they made their escape.

"All this came out afterward. The dog remained unknown, unrecognized, and uncaptured up to the last, because, like Chilly himself, he wore a number of different disguises. Sometimes he was dressed up like a cocker spaniel; sometimes like a dachshund. And he always acted the character to go with the particular disguise he was wearing. Some days he would hobble about town dressed as a thoughtful Scotch terrier, very old, puffy, grizzled, and feeble. Other days he'd be a friendly Airedale puppy, frisking all over the place and talking to everyone. He could bark and growl in six different tones of voice. He could look cross-eyed if necessary. He could do everything. And of course no one got wise to him since he was never the same. There is no doubt about it that both Chillibillibeano and his dog had brains, great brains.

"The Texas Pantry Bandit, after his description appeared in the papers, became more daring and cheeky then ever. It almost looked as though he didn't care what he did. He took a mischievous delight in leaving notes behind him, at the houses he stole from, deliberately signed with his own name: 'Thanks for the nice supper. Your guards are too stupid for words. Anyone could get through them. Yours truly, Chilly.'

"He loved to tease Scones by calling him a flatfoot and a fathead. And he would actually tell him in these notes which houses he was going to rob next. And even when the Icebox Detective went to the houses and stayed up all night with two assistants and a dozen policemen, the best and most expensive food was found mysteriously missing the next morning.

"Then the police rounded up all the dogs in the town, every one, and had them claimed by their owners. And out of sheer devilment the Sneakinese came too. But he came dressed as a stray cat—

half Persian and half starved—frightened, soft-footed, and mean. And the disguise was so perfect, no one knew him from the real thing; and after getting a good square meal free, he spat at the other dogs and took his leave.

"Meanwhile, folks were getting more and more annoyed and indignant that the thieves were not caught. And Sherbet Scones went on gnashing his teeth. He had gnashed them so much that they were nearly all worn away, and he was very miserable because he couldn't eat properly. The papers went on making fun of him, and Ham Sandwich brought out a comic poem on the front page of *The Daily Meal*—at least Ham thought it was comic:

> *"When the night falls, deep and stilly,*
> *Through the pantry window Chilly*
> *Grabs great joints of beef and bones.*
> *What's the use of Sherbet Scones?*

"At last, however, Chillibillibeano went too far. He had stolen the most precious kinds of foods; he had made a laughingstock of the best detectives; he had thrown defiance in the teeth of the police; he had puzzled the world with his daring, brilliant villainy. But now he did something he had never done before, something that, perhaps, no one had ever done before: he stole a cook."

"What on earth for?" asked Chee-Chee.

"Why, cooks are very valuable," said Gub-Gub. "That is, good ones. And this one was marvelously good. She was famous for her pastry—for her rhubarb pie in particular. Her name was Vanilla Verbena. Her employer used to say that she was worth her weight in gold—and in her case that meant a good deal, because she was as big as a house and weighed a ton. Now, a strange thing began happening at the house where Vanilla Verbena worked. It had been broken into and the pantry robbed several times. The family was a large one to cook for: mother and father and six children, all with hearty appetites.

"Ordinarily they had been a very plump, well-fed-looking lot. But suddenly they started to get thin—especially the cook herself. That good woman's figure, which had been as round as an apple, shrank and shrank till it got positively scrawny. People said that maybe it was because her pantry had been robbed so often and that the worry over losing all that beautiful pastry as soon as it was cooked was making her thin.

HUGH LOFTING

"She was as big as a house."

"But be that as it may, suddenly she disappeared. Her bed, which had specially strong springs to carry her weight, was found empty one morning. Sherbet Scones at once got busy, busier than he had ever been before in his busy life. The seriousness of Chilly's new crime was not the only cause. Scones had a private reason—a romantic one—as well.

"You see, while he had been working on the robberies at this house before, the Icebox Detective had met Vanilla Verbena when she was still plump and comely, and after tasting her wonderful pastry he had decided it would be a good idea to marry her. He had even had the kitchen in his own home made larger so there would be ample room for her to work in. You can therefore imagine his rage, his furious indignation at Chillibillibeano, who had now added to his long list of evil deeds the unpardonable one of cook snatching. And he swore by his worldwide reputation, by his long false beard, that he would neither rest nor close his eyes till his precious Verbena was found and the wicked foreigner was thrown into prison.

"Well, he nearly died for want of sleep, but he did it.

"And this was how: First he did a lot of deducing. He asked himself, why should a man steal a cook? Because he liked good food? Of course. But after the robber got her, he couldn't put her to work in any house of his own because she was known by sight and would be recognized. He must be planning to use her to run a restaurant for him. And of course it would be a new restaurant, one just opened within a short time.

"So Scones set out and traveled all around, asking everyone about new eating places. And he went to all these restaurants and ordered rhubarb pie. He knew, of course, that Chilly would keep Verbena out of sight. But Scones remembered the taste of her famous rhubarb pie, and he was certain he could tell it from all others.

"In his travels he ate so many helpings of pie that he often felt he could never look another one in the face. But he kept bravely on. And sure enough, at last he came to a restaurant where the waiter served him rhubarb pie that he at once knew could be no other than Vanilla Verbena's very own. At once he had the owner of the restaurant arrested and handcuffed by one of his assistants. It was Chilly himself beyond any doubt. Then Scones made a thorough search of the place, and in the kitchen he found his darling cook chained to the pastry board, still making rhubarb pies—also there was a strange-looking dog eating out of a plate on the floor. And that was the end of the wicked career of the Texas Pantry Bandit."

"Did he get sent to prison for a long time?" asked the white mouse.

"No, that is the odd part of it: He never went to prison at all," said Gub-Gub. "While Scones was taking him to the police station in a cab, he began questioning the robber about several matters. For one thing, he wanted to know what Chilly had done with all the food he had stolen. And he found that the Texas Pantry Bandit was really a sort of Robin Hood in disguise. He had been robbing the rich to pay the poor. Whenever he found out that one wealthy family had large stores of food and kept a particularly good table, he would make a point of breaking into that house and feeding the poor people, who hadn't enough to eat, with the food he stole. Even Vanilla Verbena, the famous cook, he had carried off for the sake of the poor. He wanted to have a restaurant where tramps and hungry people who had no money could come and get good meals for nothing.

"But he was indeed a clever rogue. Seeing that Verbena was too big to push through the pantry window—or, in fact, to carry off by any man at all—he got a lot of reducing pills, medicine for thinning people down, and every time he broke into that house he put some into all the food in the larder. And that was how the whole family as well as the cook had lost so much weight.

"Now, when the Icebox Detective heard why his great enemy had done all these robberies, a great change came over him. He could not bear to think that a man who had been so noble as to spend all his life in the service of the poor should be sent to prison. On the other hand, he at least had to make it look as though he meant to bring him to justice and punishment. So after thinking silently for a while, as the cab rolled along, he said to his prisoner:

"'You would no doubt like to have a smoke. I will take off your handcuffs so you can get your cigars out of your pocket.' This he did, and Chilly thanked him. Then he said, 'Supposing you were a free man now instead of on your way to jail, would you lead an honest life or would you go on robbing houses?'

"And Chilly said, 'I would lead an honest life. At this robbing game one is bound to get caught sooner or later. Besides, I owe it to the Sneakinese. He was a perfectly honest dog when I first got him—from the circus where he learned to be so clever at disguises. But it was I who led him astray and taught him to steal.' He sighed sadly. 'If I were a free man now, I would take the Sneakinese and go on the stage. I can play the guitar very well. Alas, that it is too late for me to turn over a new leaf!'

"Again Scones became strangely silent, chewing on his false mustache, wrapped in thought. Suddenly he said, 'Excuse me a moment, I want to get out and speak to the cab driver.'

"He knocked on the window, stopped the cab, and got out. He was careful to leave the door open behind him. Pretending to give some orders to the driver, he watched Chilly out of the corner of his eye. And he noticed the Texas Pantry Bandit sneak away into the bushes, followed by his faithful dog. But Scones made no attempt to run after him.

"He got back into the empty cab and drove to the police station. There he asked for the officer in charge and said, 'I'm very sorry. I caught the thief and had him all handcuffed and everything, but he escaped from my clutches while I was bringing him to the jail. However, I feel sure you will be bothered with no more food robberies.'

"Then he went off and married Vanilla Verbena. And she got her beautiful plump figure back, and they both lived happily ever after."

How Quince Blossom saved
her father's life

T HIS IS A FOOD FABLE," SAID GUB-GUB. "IT'S
from the Persian."

"What is a fable?" asked the white mouse.

"Gracious me!" said the great author. "Sometimes
I think I ought to change your name to Mr. Whatsit! Every time
you open your mouth you begin with, 'What's a this?' 'What's a
that?' A fable is an old story that is sometimes meant to teach a lesson but is not necessarily strictly true. A fellow called Aesop wrote
fables. Aesop was, I believe, a cousin to Milksop, but of that I'm
not sure. Anyhow, he was a member of the well-known family of
Sops—all writers, poor fellows.

"Well, in the days before Persia was formed into a regular
country, there was a very warlike people that lived in those parts,
called the Bashibaloukas. They were great horsemen. They lived in
the saddle, you might say. In spite of being a very wild tribe that ter-
rorized the whole of the Eastern world, they were also a very clean
lot—most particular about taking regular baths. But they didn't

have to worry about it. Their horses took care of it for them. Living in the saddle, as they did, they also slept there. And the horses were so well trained that as soon as daybreak came they made straight for the nearest water. So, if you were a Bashibalouka, you usually woke up before breakfast, swimming in a river full of ice, or treading water at the bottom of some nice deep pond. This made the people very hardy.

"Well, the shah of the Bashibaloukas decided to go to war with his most powerful neighbor, the sultan of Kinkidoo. He got all his army washed and fed and set out for battle. For several months neither side won or lost much, because the shah could not seem to draw his enemies into a good businesslike fight. The soldiers of Kinkidoo kept to the mountains, where they could not easily be followed. And one day the shah called his commander-in-chief, General Pushpoud-ul-Pish, into his tent and said, 'General, in mountain fighting the sultan is too clever for me. I can't get near him. I have therefore decided what I must do.'

"'Yes, sir?' said the general. 'What is your plan?'

"Now, I should have told you at the beginning that this is a fable about poisons—a poisonous tale, you might call it!"

"Poisons!" said the white mouse in a very shocked voice. "I don't think I like that. What has poison got to do with food?"

"Oh, a great deal," said Gub-Gub. "There is a long chapter in my book on poisons. A knowledge of food teaches you what is good to eat, while a knowledge of poisons teaches you what is good *not* to eat. Both are important. You have all most likely heard that old saying, 'One man's meat is another man's poison.' Ostriches can eat things that would kill you and me—tennis balls, pebbles, and whatnot. But all poisons are not deadly. Some just give you a pain or make you sick for a while. In ancient times, when people studied poisons a good deal more than they do now, you could buy all sorts: a half-hour stomachache, a two-days-in-bed pill, or a few drops of innocent-looking tonic that could kill you dead in five minutes.

"Well, in those wild times, long, long ago, all kings and queens and people who were really important kept regular poisoners in their pay, and they lived in the palace along with the rest of the household. They were something like the royal doctors of today—scientists, regular chemists, you know. Anyhow, to go back to where I was: the general of the Bashibaloukas said to the shah, 'What then, O Mighty Monarch, is your plan?'

"And the shah answered, 'General, since I cannot draw the sultan into open battle, I think it would be a good idea to poison him off. Once the army of Kinkidoo is left without this very smart leader, my men, I feel sure, can knock it silly in no time. Go you therefore and bring me all the royal poisoners, in order that we can have a comfortable chat and decide the best means to dose the sultan in such a fashion that he will never again lead his troops in war.'

"At these words the general turned deathly pale. And I'll tell you why in just a minute.

"'Great shah!' he cried, falling on his knees before his master. 'We brought no poisons with us. The day before your army marched away from the capital, they had a grand feast. It was sort of a club dinner to which all the professional poisoners were invited. And somebody thought it would be a good joke to give them a little of their own medicine. Anyhow, something was put in the soup, and all the poisoners were so sick the next day they couldn't travel with the army!'

"The shah frowned a terrible frown. 'What, no poisoners!' he cried. 'I never heard of such a thing!' And he started stamping up and down the royal tent like a crazy man.

"Now, the reason that the general had turned so pale was not at the thought of poisoning off the sultan of Kinkidoo. To the hardy cavalrymen of the bloodthirsty Bashibaloukas that was a mere trifle. But besides being commander-in-chief, Pushpoud-ul-Pish was also the shah's grand vizier. And in those days if you were a shah or an emperor, and anything went wrong, the first thing you did was to chop off the head of your grand vizier, throw him away, and get another one—for anything at all. If the horses went lame, or the hens stopped laying, the grand vizier paid the penalty with his life. That's how you showed you were an important leader and not to be trifled with.

"The poor general started to sneak out of the tent, but as he left, the shah shook his fist at him and cried, 'Before the sun goes down, you shall pay for this with your head!'

"Miserably Pushpoud-ul-Pish made his way to his own tent. There he found his wife and his beautiful daughter, Quince Blossom, both fast asleep. He woke his wife and told her the sad news. 'Alas!' he cried, wringing his hands. 'This is the end of me!'

"But the general's wife was a very bright woman. In fact, some people said she was a much better general than Pushpoud-ul-Pish himself. Instead of getting excited, she went into a long think. She was looking at this beautiful daughter, Quince Blossom, sleeping peacefully on her couch of Bokhara embroidery.

"'Listen, Push,' she said presently, 'it is a poor head you have, but it is the only one you possess, and we can't afford to lose it. Even in this great army, husbands are scarce. Yonder maiden may yet save your life. Right well you know, for all her beauty and her innocence, she is the worst cook in the world. Ever since she nearly killed His Majesty's sacred elephant when she prepared his rice for him, has she not been forbidden, by royal command, even to boil water lest she burn it and injure the hardy manhood of our army? Very well, then: the shah's poisoners have been left behind. I propose to use our little Quince Blossom instead. If we can only smuggle her into the sultan's camp, to be employed as cook for him, I'll warrant he will die of indigestion before the setting of the sun.'

"Then very gently she woke up the beautiful damsel and explained the plan. She told her daughter that their family could not well afford to lose its head, and it was clearly the girl's duty to save her father, even if the work were by no means to her taste. Now, Quince Blossom was born what you would call a homebody—domestic and housewifey. The thing she most desired in life was to raise a family and cook good meals for a good husband. So Fate had been very unkind in making her the most terrible cook that every swung a saucepan. And when she learned what it was her mother wanted her to do, she broke down in sobs and her tears ran all over the Bokhara embroidery of the couch.

"Nevertheless, for her father's sake, in the end she gave in and said she would go. The best of the Bashibalouka scouts was summoned at once. And in a large fruit basket, covered over with pineapples for sale, she was carried up through the mountains and smuggled into the sultan's camp. There the famous scout left the basket in the marketplace while he went around and did some scouting and spying.

"He found out that, luckily, the sultan was in need of a new cook. Good! Also he learned that the sultan that same day had

planned to poison the shah. Poisoning was altogether too fashionable about that time. The scout could not afford to waste any time
because he had to introduce the new cook as soon as possible and
then hurry back to the shah to warn him of the plot against his life.

"But he was a good scout and knew his business. He hustled
back to the marketplace, got Quince Blossom out from under the
pineapples, and took her before the sultan. He boasted that she was
the finest cook in the world and was especially good at pancakes.
The sultan said he would try her and see what her cooking was like.
The girl was put in the royal kitchen and the scout hurried away.

"Well, she killed her man, all right. After the first pancake
the sultan was carried to his bed and never left it again alive. Two
of the best generals in the enemy army also died from the same
meal. Poor Quince Blossom! She thought she could never forgive
herself. She knew she wasn't a good cook. But she hadn't really
tried to make the pancakes specially bad. They just turned out
that way. For her, bad cooking came naturally. It was a kind of
a gift, you might say. Nor could anyone feel very sorry for the
sultan, since he had himself planned to poison off his enemy also.
Nevertheless, Quince Blossom, as soon as she knew her dish had
turned out unsuccessfully, wept all over the kitchen and ran away
back to her own people.

"There she found the shah's court holding a big holiday, and
everybody was very happy. Her father, the grand vizier, was given
presents and honors by his delighted master. The shah himself sent
for Quince Blossom to thank her, and he told her she had won
the war for him. Because, with the death of the sultan, the army of
Kinkidoo was already in full flight before the swift and hardy cavalry of the Bashibaloukas. He offered her the post of chief poisoner

to the royal household. But she refused, again bursting into tears at the thought of what her pancakes had done.

"The shah took the maiden on his knee to console her. And then he noticed, when she removed her veil to wipe her eyes, what a very beautiful girl she was. The shah was a bachelor himself and he promptly asked her to be his queen instead of his poisoner. She said she would be glad to if he would promise that her father's head would never be chopped off whether the hens laid or not.

"This promise he gave her—he even said she could do all the cooking she liked, too—so long as he and his army never had to eat it. He said it had better be buried, so the horses and dogs couldn't get at it.

"And so they were married amid great rejoicings and they both lived happily ever after."

THE SEVENTH EVENING

*The pig author, after a few words about diet,
tells how a beautiful sunset once inspired him
to writing something truly his own*

AGAIN THERE WAS A FINE FIRE ROARING up the Dolittle kitchen chimney—to keep away the chill of the year's early days that so often lead us into believing that summer has begun when winter hasn't really gone.

The good Chee-Chee was dragging broken boughs across the floor, and those too heavy for him to carry he rolled before him like a barrel. Much dust and bark were left behind on the way, but the monkey looked after that with the hearth broom. And when he took his seat to listen, the kitchen floor was clean and spotless enough to satisfy even Dab-Dab herself.

John Dolittle was fiddling with an aquarium up in his study— where he was trying to make rare water plants take kindly to indoor life. The housekeeper never permitted anyone—on any account— to interrupt his work.

Everybody else was gathered in the kitchen. We had now come to make a pleasant habit of listening to Gub-Gub's readings. Dab-

Dab still treated his writings and discussions with the contempt she felt they deserved. But we noticed that she nearly always came to listen, and we had begun to suspect that she thought the encyclopedia of food not quite as rubbishy as she had at first declared. Besides that, she no longer shooed us off to bed at the regular hour. So that sometimes the pale blue of the morning sky was glimmering at the windows before Gub-Gub had done talking to us about the art of eating.

Too-Too the owl and Polynesia the parrot never said a great deal about anything at any time. And for this reason they perhaps earned a reputation for being very wise without much work. I myself was always interested, because I never knew what surprise the great pig author would spring on us next.

Cheapside, the London sparrow, and the white mouse enjoyed quite openly Professor Gub-Gub's lectures, roaring with laughter or giggling like schoolchildren when some particularly crazy passage took their fancy.

Even the grouchy Jip interrupted less and less, and when he did, it seemed as though he was rather pretending to criticize—because he thought it was perhaps his duty—than giving his real opinions.

The Doctor of Salad Dressings was this evening somewhat late in appearing. And when he at last showed up, the white mouse, who had for half an hour been twirling his sleek white whiskers impatiently round his pink nose, demanded the reason for his lateness.

"Well, for one thing," said Gub-Gub, "I've been reading over *The Book of Food Dreams*."

"What's that for?" asked the white mouse.

"Oh, it's not a very important work," said Gub-Gub. "Rather trashy. But I thought I would look into it just the same. It pretends to tell you the meaning of dreams about food. For instance, if you dream you are eating broccoli, it says you can be sure that some calamity or accident will happen to you. On the other hand, if you should dream you have had a hearty meal of turnips, you are likely to be successful—very soon—in business or love.

"But the thing that delayed me most this evening was my visit to Doctor Pillcrank. Doctor Pillcrank had been advertising in the papers that he could reduce people's weight by mental treatment instead of by dieting."

"What is dieting?" asked the white mouse.

"Dieting," said Gub-Gub, "is doing without all the things you like to eat and eating all the things you *don't* like. I had been getting rather stout, and I thought I would try this mental treatment, which sounded so much better than the usual one of dieting. But I was very disappointed. The main part of Doctor Pillcrank's treatment is to make you say to yourself over and over again the same thing: 'Tummy, tummy, go away and don't come back another day.' It seemed to have no effect upon my figure whatever.

"Provided you said this to yourself several times a day, he let you eat anything you wanted *mentally*—that is, in your mind. He wrote out for me beautiful meals—artichokes, potatoes, spaghetti, stuffed dates, Welsh rarebit, etc.—which I was told to *think of* at breakfast, lunch, and supper. And that was supposed to give me all the nourishment I needed. But it didn't. It merely gave me a terrible appetite. And all I was allowed to take was a little barley water at morning and noon. The rest of the time I was just to think about eating. And if I hadn't had the presence of mind to put three or four apples under my pillow at night, there is no knowing what would have happened to me. I don't think I'll go back to him anymore.

He charged a lot of money and called it Dr. Pillcrank's Mental Treatment for Obesity."

"Obesity?" asked the white mouse. "Is that the same as obeastliness?"

"Yes," growled Jip.

"Before you came in," said the white mouse, "we were having a little discussion about your book. I was taking your part. I said I liked the food stories best. But Chee-Chee said that he expected a good deal of the book was just made up out of your head. Jip said he didn't believe anyone could make anything out of your head—except perhaps packing cases. But Chee-Chee was sure he was right, because most of your stories ended, 'They all lived happily ever after.' And that's the way that fairy stories usually end, isn't it? We would like very much to know how much of the book you really did make up."

Gub-Gub cleaned his glasses carefully. He was silent a moment. And we were all sure that a very important announcement was coming from the Doctor of Salad Dressings.

"What you say brings me to a special part of my book," he began, "which I have purposely kept till the end—that is, till the end of my readings. You see, I felt that beside the bibliography, the library searchings into food history, geography, legend, and so forth, I would like to do a little something that would be entirely my own. I have done it—and I am very proud of it."

"Is it a food story?" asked the white mouse.

"In a way, yes, it is," said the author. "It should perhaps be called a 'food novel.' And yet that isn't quite the word either. I didn't know what to call it, so I invented a word for it myself. It is an *epicnic*."

"And what may that be?" growled Jip.

"An epic," said Gub-Gub, "is a poem—a poem of importance, or a history tale in poetic language. The story of Helen of Troy, by Homer, for instance, is an epic. But this work of mine, to make it more foodish, more appetizing, you might say—I called an epicnic: the word *epic*, scrambled with *picnic*. It is the story of King Guzzle the Second, or the Picnic King.

"The way I came to begin it was peculiar. Most people have an idea that we think only of food. This is not strictly true. When you see a row of young pigs with a wistful look upon their fresh faces, you must not always suppose that they are daydreaming merely of potatoes. Well, one lovely afternoon I was myself gazing out over a beautiful summer landscape, bathed in the crimson light of an August sunset. I was chewing thoughtfully on a horseradish root, but my mind was full of poetry—chockful.

"'After all,' said I to myself, 'I am a country pig—a country gentleman. That city life is all very well for a short spell—for a change, you might say. But when everything's said and done, there is nothing like the country. Consider this lovely scene before me: rolling, grassy hills; lush meadows fringing the mere.' You see, that's where the poetic part comes in: to say just 'lush meadows' wouldn't mean much, but 'fringing the mere' at once draws a living picture for us. A 'mere' is a sort of lake; 'lush' means green, well-watered, and grassy—but not squdgy or muddy—splendid hunting ground for sweet lily roots and the like.

"Well, to go on: 'shady copses; the cool, slow river wandering and wiggling down the broad valley; plump, nutty-tasting acorns, lying in bushels beneath the spreading oaks, with little mushrooms popping up like buttons in between; gorse clumps with friendly rabbits running in and out; tall clover in full bloom waving to the gentle breeze; ripe blackberries hiding coyly in the hedges; crab apples crabbing around all over the place.' A scene to delight the heart of any poet—a scene, in fact, of which someone said, 'Where every prospect pleases and only man is—'

"'But hold!' said I to myself. 'Do I smell truffles? By my trotters, indeed I do! But I will not dig for them. I will not be tempted. Earthy thoughts shall not interrupt my mood sublime.' You see, I was getting more and more poetic as I went on. I leaned back among the cowslips on the grassy bank and half closed my eyes. Quite possibly I might have starved to death from sheer poetry. Such a thing has happened—to truly great writers—before today.

"But a bee came and stung me on the nose. I suppose he smelled the clover I had been eating. But such was my feeling of friendliness to all nature, I did not even allow this to interfere with the gentle spirit of my thoughts. And besides, my snout is tough, and not even an angry black hornet can affect it greatly when I am filled with verse and fantasy. I merely raised a cool dock leaf and laid it on my face. Presently I ate it—even poets have to have some nourishment.

"'Yonder pleasant prospect,' said I, 'needs only a little of my masterly imagination to make of it the opening scene to a great play, a food opera, a poem of good taste—what you will—something that shall be read and recited by good eaters for all time to come. Here is the first act laid out before me. For is not this the "Picnic Kingdom" itself?'

"I leapt to my feet, burning with the fire of inspiration. Two more bees stung me as I got up—for it appeared I had been sitting on a nest of them. But I took no notice. Grasping my notebook, I set to work. I wrote and wrote and wrote. After I had finished the notebook I began on dock leaves. When there were no more dock leaves, I wrote on anything that came to hand. I even ran after a cow who was browsing near and made notes all over her. I was full of ideas.

"And as I worked, the story of King Guzzle the Second came to life before me in that beautiful scenery that might have been made for him. Darkness fell without my noticing it. And with the daybreak a farmer's boy arrived to milk the cow. I tried to make notes on him, too, for I was now roused to a perfect frenzy of inspiration. But he wouldn't let me. So I did my last lines on the trunk of a tree instead.

"When the sun rose in all its glory, I stopped at last—tired, worn out, thirsty, and hungry, but happy—happy as only an author can be who knows he has done his work and done it well. I fell fast asleep—while the cow ate up all my dock leaves and rubbed the notes off herself by rolling in the grass.

"But it didn't matter. The great epicnic was safe in my mind. I went home and wrote it out on wrapping papers. And I will now, with your permission, read it to you."

There was much rustling and shifting of chairs. Chee-Chee rolled a large log on the fire. And the white mouse gave his whiskers an extra twirl before settling down to listen.

THE EIGHTH EVENING

The Life Story of Guzzle the Second, known as the Picnic King. Of the strange court he held; the curious manner of his life; of his tremendous wealth. Here the author begins the epicnic (which he hopes will live as long as Shakespeare). He describes the greatest of the king's famous picnics and the peculiar guests who were invited to it from all parts of the world. He speaks of the king's friendship for the great Christophe Plantin. And of how the Frenchman's sonnet came to be engraved on the Golden Saucepan with which Guzzle himself cooked on his birthday

NOW, THE GUZZLES, EVEN BEFORE THEY were kings, had always been a family of noble high degree, second to none in the land. The old man, spending his days in fighting, had been widely known, and feared, as a most powerful prince. Later, when he was crowned as Guzzle the First, he made his country very rich by adding to it conquered lands. Long after he passed away his skill and cunning in warfare were spoken of and remembered. His reign was looked back upon by high and low alike as the Age of Chivalry, when knights were bold, ladies were fair, and soldiers were proud to be numbered in his army.

"Therefore when his son, Guzzle the Second, came to the throne, there was much talk about what manner of king he would turn out to be. With his respected father's memory to follow as an example, it was quite clear from the outset that he'd have to be a great man indeed to come up to the expectations of the people.

"Most folks thought he would start his reign off with a nice big war, so as to make a good impression with a lot of victories that would add still more lands to the Realm of Guzzledom.

"But they were greatly surprised to find that he did nothing of the kind. Instead of calling up his knights in armor and having war trumpets blown all over the place, he sent for his lord treasurer and hundreds of clerks who could tell him how much money he had in the banks and what the condition of the royal treasury was. He knew that his father had left the country well off, but even Guzzle the Second was astonished when the bankbooks were looked into and examined. He found that he had become king of the richest realm in all history. Old Guzzle the First had been very economical, and never let a cook buy a new apron without a special order from the lord treasurer, signed with the royal seal.

"'Why, then,' said the new king to himself, 'have any more wars, when the royal treasury already has more money than it can spend?' Buying gunpowder to blow off, and new armor to get cracked, seemed simply silly in the circumstances. Instead, he at once gave orders that all the cooks should have new aprons, and caps as well; that all the royal gardeners should have new suits of clothes; that new dishes of gold and silver be bought for the royal dining hall; that new sties be built for all the pigs; new stalls for all the cows, with milk pails of solid pewter, etc., etc.

"You see, he had decided that it was no use trying to earn a reputation as a soldier to match his father's, and that he would therefore make a new kind of reputation for himself. His father had been known as Guzzle the Warrior; he meant to be famous in history as Guzzle the Spender.

"And oh, how he did spend! At first the lord treasurer and the chancellor of the exchequer would come running to him five or six times a day with bills a yard long, saying that he must be careful, that this kind of thing couldn't go on. The country would be ruined, they said, rich as it was. But Guzzle the Second would just wave them aside and order a set of new silver horseshoes for his favorite horse.

"And after a while—as things turned out—they began to see that perhaps he was right. To be a king or queen in the eyes of the world, you had to have money in those days, the same as you do today. It cost an awful lot to run a country that was at all important. And very soon folks the world over decided that Guzzle's kingdom must be the richest of all because it spent the most. Traders came from every corner of the earth, anxious to open shops and to do business. And instead of getting poorer, the kingdom of Guzzledom seemed to grow richer and richer the more it spent.

"Now, King Guzzle took to eating in a serious way. Not that this was anything new, of course. Kings must eat, the same as farmers. And many great princes have become famous for the wonderful dishes that they invented. Cardinals and grand dukes have not thought it beneath them to go into the kitchen and attend personally to the preparation of meals that carried their fame to all corners of the civilized world.

"But King Guzzle the Second was greater than all these. After he had made the country prosperous and famous everywhere by his wild extravagances of every sort—so that it became a saying common abroad to speak of a man as being 'as rich as Guzzle'—he settled down to the serious matter of good food in a way that surprised the world. And the world was beginning by now to be surprised fully and often by that monarch.

"Eating was never raised to a higher art. Fortunes were given to a scullery maid who thought of a new sauce. The chef, that is, the head of the cooks, became so important a personage in the royal household that ministers from foreign lands usually went to the kitchen first, to have a chat over the pots and pans, before making their official bows in the Royal Chamber of Audience.

"And then the dinners and luncheons that he gave! He would be second to none, he said, in the magnificence of his dining room. But he liked best of all to eat *al fresco.*"

"Al *who*? asked Cheapside.

"*Al fresco,*" said Gub-Gub. "That means, 'out of doors,' in—er—Italian."

"Oh, just something furrin," said the sparrow. "I thought for the moment you was referrin' to my old friend Al Freshface. Great old bloke was Al! Always saved the crumbs of 'is bread and cheese for me. 'E was a cab driver. Go on, Perfesser. I didn't mean to hinterrupt."

"Well, it was from this pleasant habit of feeding outdoors that Guzzle the Second came to be known to future generations as the Picnic King. He had many other titles of great distinction: Grand

Master of the Order of the Golden Fleas, Knight of the Garter and Suspenders, etc. But throughout his long and busy life he would always rather hear his subjects speak of him as the Picnic King than under any other name.

"He formed what was known as the League of Rations—a sort of international club devoted to good food. It became famous in history.

"But the picnic that King Guzzle considered his greatest work of art, and that will probably be remembered for all time, was given in the month of July, when the much-loved king had passed that time of life called middle age. Nothing of its kind had ever happened before. Guests were invited from every corner of the earth.

"The Grand Picnic took place in that lovely spot I have already described to you. The Great Sward was thronged with chefs, footmen, and serving maids waiting on the guests, who are said to have numbered not less than a thousand persons.

"It would be absurd for me to try to give you here every name from a list so long. However, the complete Roll of Honor was written down in a special book in the library of the Royal College of Cooking. Many foreign names appear, because the royalty and nobility of other lands were most eager to do King Guzzle any compliments they could, since he was so rich and his money such a power in the world.

"Very well, to begin with, there was the Queen of Blenheim-Orange with her daughter, Princess Mignonette of Marjoram and Rue; there was Prince Pudge, heir apparent to the throne of Greece and Gravy—his father was very desirous he should attend the Grand Picnic. And it must be said that Prince Pudge certainly did his father's kingdom great credit: He ate so much, his war horse was quite unable to carry him home, and special arrangements for a coach drawn by six span of oxen had to be made.

"Vladimir, chief of the Don Cossacks—you can imagine how a man from such a distant territory would be thought highly important—even if he did throw a ham bone at another guest he didn't like. Such would be a small matter in Vladimir's own country—but created a mild sensation at the polite court of King Guzzle.

"Many other kings and queens flocked from east and south and west and north, and when, on account of family matters at home or affairs of state, they were prevented from attending in person, they sent important ambassadors in their place. For example—Belini Anchovy, dictator of the Republic of Rhubarb, had a revolution on his hands; but his uncle, Don Castro Castor Oil, came in his stead. Good-looking he was—very, but not at all popular. The Duke de Barleduke, always bothered by the gout, was represented by Ambassador Linseed. And so on.

"But by far the greater part of the guests were made up of the landed gentry; those who, while of noble blood, were famous for their country pursuits rather than for being descended from this royal line, that grand duchy, or from the other reigning house. Men of the land they were; and it was with them a matter of greater pride that the whole world knew the excellence of their cattle, the quality of their asparagus, or the honey raised by their bees than all the knightly deeds in Morte d'Arthur or the families of the Domesday Book. And it was for this reason—because they were, so to speak, specialists beyond compare in their particular line—that they had been invited to the Grand Picnic of Guzzle the Second.

"To mention a few: There were Sir Lancelot Lollipop, famous

rescuer of Distressed Damsons. The Dutch naturalist Viscount van Veal, whose work on vegetable botany had caused such a stir. Conrad, Earl of the Marshmallows. Gumbo Goulash, of Budapest, whose Danube dairies supplied the finest butter in the world. Sir Cinnamon Bunn. The two Scottish lairds of high renown, both heads of their clans, Sir Benjamin Butterscotch and Sir Haggis McTavish. Lady Viola Vinaigrette, who raised the finest melons in the country. Madame O. Gratin, the best-known hostess in Paris.

"Sir Simeon Sausagely was there too—he who was supposed to know more about the raising and training of water spaniels than any man living. Her Grace, the Duchess of Doughnut, specialist in French pastry—specialist in eating it, that is. Sir Marmaduke Marmalade, direct descendant of the House of Orange. Fatima, the Sultana of Chutney. The Countess of Curd, who had given her whole life to cream cheese. Young Nubbin, the Brussels Sprout, of noble lineage. Judge Juniper, who was later to marry Lady Dredful Manners—a very charming young person—and there was much talk about the difference in their ages. The Dowager Countess of Caramel Custard. And that highly important person in the eating line, the Marchioness of Cling and Cloy.

"The king himself had lately given more and more of his time to the farm, the country, the fish and game preserve, etc. The business of state, which he had found very tiresome, he was content to leave to his ministers—and notably to his nephew, of whom we shall have more to say later.

"The ladies were indeed well represented. Some folks said that it was because they were fonder of food than men—which started a terrible argument—while others claimed it was because they had less business to attend to and were naturally keen about picnics and parties.

"Be that as it may, certainly a terrible lot of them came, and they seemed to enjoy themselves heartily. Among them was that charming little debutante Sticky Fudge—equally good at lace making and riding horses. She had only just been presented at Court, so her mother came along with her.

"Another girl who was very popular with the young men at the food dances was Pepita Pancake from Madrid. She had a regular chaperon. Played well on the harp, too, did Pepita Pancake, but only simple songs; but after all she was only a flapper, you might say.

"Last, but by no means least, there was Squire Squab of Squelchley-on-the-Squeam, renowned for the raising of pigeons. So worldwidely important was his fame in this respect that the king considered it a compliment that he honored the Grand Picnic with his presence.

"It was generally feared that the beloved king might eat more than was good for his health, and some other monarch be elected to take his place. However, for the present, Guzzle the Second seemed sound and hearty, and he liked nothing better than to go into the kitchen to try his royal hand at cooking. He was indeed quite good at it. He would put on a silken apron and, with the chief cook acting as assistant, he would prepare special dainties in the Golden Saucepan.

"The Golden Saucepan had a history to it and became an institution of wide fame and importance. The king remained a bachelor all his life; otherwise it would have been presented on the fiftieth anniversary of his wedding. But instead, when his fiftieth birthday came and went, and he was still unwed, his loving subjects all subscribed what small sums of money they could afford and gave him a saucepan of peculiar design, wrought of solid and pure gold.

"Now, as it happened, the king's birthday was also the day when that great dish, steak and kidney pudding, was invented. This the Court took to be a happy sign of fortune and good luck. Just as some people are born under the sign of the lion and Venus, so it could be said that King Guzzle the Second was born—in a manner of speaking—under steak and kidney pudding. And that is how His Majesty's birthday, which was celebrated throughout the land with great rejoicing and ceremony, came to be known not only as King's Day but also as Steak-and-Kidney-Pudding Day.

"So important did the king consider this odd happening in connection with the date of his birth, that he issued a royal decree that so long as he lived he would act as cook in his palace kitchen on that day, serving his people with the famous dish prepared as it had never been prepared before.

"Thus, year after year, when his birthday came round, the king's henchmen, high and low—foresters, falconers, gardeners, gamekeepers, and whatnot—foregathered in the lofty dining hall and made merry while the greatest monarch of his time served them steak and kidney pudding with his own royal hands from the Golden Saucepan. They held high wassail—"

"What's wassail?" asked the white mouse.

"I'm not quite sure," said Gub-Gub. "But it is something you always held at great feasts in ancient times."

"Oh," said the white mouse. "A napkin, very likely."

"About this time there was in France a great printer and poet of the name of Christophe Plantin. The king much admired this man, and had him specially invited to the palace. Among his works is a sonnet called 'The Happiness of This World.'

"King Guzzle the Second, at fifty, had given up many of the wild extravagances of his early days, and he meant to spend the remainder of his reign in teaching his people how to live—not just eating and drinking, but the true art of living, sauced with good sense and a knowledge of things real and worthwhile.

"Christophe Plantin seemed just the man to help in this, and the king, when presented with the Golden Saucepan, summoned the court engraver and bade him chisel on the sides of that noble vessel, just as it was written, that poem 'The Happiness of This World.' Of course it was in French—and Old French at that. So I will not bother you with foreign wording."

"No. You'd better not," growled Jip.

"In translating it into English I have been most careful to stick to the sense," said Gub-Gub, "almost word for word. All I have done is to change the position of a line or two here and there."

The great pig author cleared his throat and started his recitation. And though the white mouse tittered at the beginning over the idea of a mere pig turning French into English, he and the rest of them were oddly solemn when the poem ended.

THE HAPPINESS OF THIS WORLD
Sonnet

TO HAVE
A comfortable house, beauteous and clean;
   A garden where the well-pruned, scented
      branches lean;

Some fruits; some vintage rare;
 A little group of children; servants few;
Cherishing, without boast, the faith
 Of helpful housewife fair.
To have no debts, nor pride,
 Nor quarrels, nor fussings with the law;
Nor business disagreements with relations over
 money.
 Satisfied with little,
Expecting nothing of the Great,
 All planning built in faith upon a model fair.
Reposefully awaited in this house of mine,
 The knowledge of the value of these things,
Shall make the Coming of Life's End,
 Instead of something dark and grim
The pleasant Visit of a Gracious Friend.

THE NINTH EVENING

*The Truffle Troubadours, the River of
Lemonade, the Jamming Contest, and other
things brightening the Grand Picnic,
which lasted many days*

MANY ARE THE TALES TOLD OF THE KING'S wild junketings. But most of them I am much inclined to doubt—especially after the coming to the Court of that great naturalist, poet, and philosopher, Christophe Plantin. No man ever lived with more sense and peaceful beauty.

"But I ought, however, to give you some idea of a few of those peculiarities of King Guzzle that set tongues to spinning strange yarns in odd corners of the earth.

"For instance, it was he who invented the Alarm Clock Menu. On retiring at night he never gave such orders as, 'Wake me at six o'clock' or 'Let me sleep till nine.' He would say, 'Wake me with fried eels' or 'I would be aroused tomorrow's morn with griddled wheat cakes, garnished with chervil—be careful not to omit the chervil.'

"Now, ordinarily it would be supposed that these were the dishes he meant to eat for breakfast. Not necessarily, at all. In the morning he was quite likely to send the food down to the royal kennels, or make a present of it to one of the cottagers. All His Majesty had wanted was the *smell* of the cooking to wake him up by.

"He didn't care to have fussy valets come and tell him what hour it was. Hours meant very little to His Majesty, whereas smells did. The fragrance of a perfect kitchen—that was different. You could lie in bed an extra twenty minutes or so, pondering over whether you really felt like fried eels; or making up your mind if griddled wheat cakes with chervil garnishing were truly worth getting up for. He had a long list of dishes for this purpose, and before he said good night to his company, the first lord of the bedchamber always came to him and said, 'Shall the lord chamberlain arouse Your Majesty with grilled kidneys tomorrow, or mushrooms on toast?'"

"Why, I never heard of anything so stupid!" said Dab-Dab. "What a scandalous waste!"

"Not at all," said Gub-Gub. "I've already told you that the food was always given to the dogs or the peasants. Besides, it is so much pleasanter a way of being woken up than having someone tugging at the bedclothes, yanking up the blinds, and gabbling about how late it is."

"But," said the white mouse, "I don't see how you could be sure that just a smell of cooking could wake you up."

"Ah," said Gub-Gub, "that shows that you are not what is called a real genius in the art of eating. Once I took a furnished apartment to live in—well, it wasn't exactly an apartment—they were too expensive. I hired a clothes closet with a hot water pipe running through it. Quite comfortable and much less expensive. And the woman across the hall used to wake me up every morning at six o'clock by cooking hot gingerbread. Regularly to the minute. I never—never in my life—could sleep through hot gingerbread. I suffered agonies of insomnia. It was no use. I had to leave and go to live somewhere else.

"Well, another thing that must be put down to the credit of King Guzzle the Second is the institution of the Truffle Troubadours. In those days, you must understand, all great courts had troubadours. Sometimes they were just wandering minstrels who picked up a little money here and there by singing a song at a feast. And yet other times they were regularly attached to the household of a king as court musicians, poets, and songsters. Their special job was to make up long lays, as they were called—historical poems that would last through eight or nine courses—usually about the warlike deeds of the king or other great person who kept the troubadours in bread and butter.

"Guzzle the Second had not much use for war or deeds of military glory. And though he was probably the richest man in the world, he was, by and large, a very modest man and withal a gentle soul. He therefore thought it would be a good idea to have his troubadours, instead of spouting long lays about the bravery of his ancestors in battle, sing songs of food and compose poems about things to eat. He hoped in this way to give good appetites to his guests. Nothing upset him so much as to have a perfect dinner prepared and then to find that no one was hungry enough to eat it. By good kitchen music he often made languishing ladies quite peckish and the heartiest of his huntsmen ready to eat the battlements off the castle walls.

"Again I must restrain myself, for the songs and poems and roast-beef roundelays he ordered composed were many. One piece that was very popular began:

> "'The Tripe-and-Onion Troubadours
> Came traipsing through the gate;

For Lady Popsy Peppermint
Was dancing very late.'

"It had twenty-five stanzas. Another was a very touching little thing about the jealousies of Apple Charlotte and Brown Betty. Then there was a rollicking song concerning the Legend of the Milksop and the Hard-boiled Egg. Another: 'Gather Ye Radishes While Ye May' was always being called for. The chief of the troubadours was often sent for to recite a series of delicacies in verse that gained great favor with the ladies—when they were busy at their tapestry before luncheon—called *The Salad Sonnets*.

"But enough of that. The palace of King Guzzle the Second was peculiar in more ways than one. The royal artists, instead of decorating the halls with portraits of kingly ancestors in full dress, painted the walls with what is called *still life*—that is, pictures of fruit and cold salmon on platters, onions and peaches in full bloom, and the like. And I must say it added greatly to the brightness of the royal dwelling. Castles are too often made unnecessarily gloomy with pictures of sour-faced dowagers with curses and pimples, and cross-eyed princes on horseback in full armor. Above all things, the king liked to make life cheerful for his fellow men; and no one could blame him for putting peach trees in full bloom and boiled salmon surrounded by lifelike cucumbers in place of sour-faced dowagers and gloomy, cross-eyed princes.

"And then, architecturally speaking, the palace was quite out of the ordinary, too. Usually in the castles of kings the various parts of the building are given such names as the Bloody Tower, Traitor Hall, the Haunted Chamber, and such like. Noble families are proud of these names—though why, no one has ever been able to find out.

"King Guzzle changed all this. He gave orders that no matter what a particular part of the castle had been known as in his father's day, cheerier names would be used in future. That is how folks came to speak of the main gate, with the drawbridge over the moat, as the Gate of the Heavenly Noodles. The great dining hall was known as the Hall of the Crystalized Ginger. The winding steps leading to the keep were called the Macaroni Staircase. The long, flagged walk, where kings and queens had paced and pondered, became the Terrace of Tittering Toffy. And so on.

"Well, to get back to the Grand Picnic:

"Delicious dishes decked the length and breadth of hillside, heath, and meadow—acres and acres of elegant eating. Most of them were fancy things that had rarely been seen before, such as pickled samfire from the fenlands of Lincolnshire; mangoes sliced with strips of anchovy; curried prawns from Bombay powdered with dried ginger; lampreys steeped in nutmeg and old wine; grapes of Muscatel stuffed with cream cheese and powdered sugar; medlars pounded into a thick paste with pomegranate syrup; bamboo sprouts dressed with the juice of wild sloes. All these recipes, also, were set down with the most exact care in the great library of the Royal College of Cooking.

"Then there were the jamming and pickling competitions. Dame Gwendolyn Goosebury got the prize for jam, while Mistress Sourly Dill carried off the pickle honors. A special pavilion for children was set up. No one was put in charge; and sailing toy boats in the soup was permitted, and the diners let the chops fall where they may.

"Candies and sweetmeats were hung from the trees, and the king had even made the main stream into a River of Lemonade, from which the people—especially the youngsters—drank their fill. But this turned out, however, to be not altogether a success. The trout did not care for the lemon juice put into the river. It did not kill them nevertheless. It merely turned them into a new species. Instead of speckled trout, they became the far-famed *sour-faced trout*. And this most unusual fish was considered a great delicacy from that time on.

"Then there were food games and gambols—such as the potato race, ducking for apples in the tub, tossing the pancake, etc.

"But the most important feature of the picnic was the prize given for a new vegetable. The Marchioness of Cling and Cloy brought out an edible rose—a tea rose that could be used in place of chamomile or coffee. And everyone thought she would surely win the prize. But the judges declared this was not truly a vegetable, and therefore the marchioness's rose could not be considered. However, Squire Squab, who had spent much time in his vegetable garden, produced something that no one had ever heard of before—a cross between a leek and a sea kale. This caused quite a sensation, and the judges felt sure that the seeds of this unusual vegetable would turn out the prize winner.

"And Squire Squab was a very proud man."

The Tenth and Last Evening

*How Prince Nastibozo, the king's own nephew,
plotted to overthrow his well-beloved uncle and
reign in his stead. Revolution is brought upon the
land through the wickedness of the chancellor of
the exchequer. Guzzle the Second is exiled. The
counterrevolutionists throw out Nastibozo and
try to bring back the old king to the throne. The
Golden Saucepan and the Picnic King's last
promise to his people*

BUT AT THIS POINT IN MY STORY I HAVE TO bring in a very unscrupulous villain, no other than Prince Nastibozo, the king's own nephew. This man, without conscience and without shame, had been in partnership for some time with another rogue, but one of a very different kind. He was the chancellor of the exchequer and his job was to see to the expenses of the palace and the royal living. He had a very bad digestion, had the chancellor—so bad that a mere custard or the lightest soufflé could give him a violent stomachache.

"This did not improve his disposition, which was bad enough

already. He was very much against the king's spending money for food—which he couldn't eat—and especially against the new Vegetable Competition and the whole of the Grand Picnic. Therefore when Prince Nastibozo came to him with a wicked plan, the chancellor of the exchequer was very pleased.

"You must understand that the seeds of Squire Squab's new vegetable were as yet very scarce and very hard to get. There were only four in existence, and the squire, in order to make sure of a good plant to show the judges, intended to plant them all. He was a real sportsman, and if no good plant came up from all four seeds, he would take his loss and misfortune like the gentleman he was.

"So when Prince Nastibozo came to the chancellor of the exchequer and told him he knew where the seeds were hidden, the chancellor shook with fiendish laughter—in spite of having a bad stomachache at that very moment. For he saw at once that if Nastibozo only poisoned the seeds with acid, no good plant could possibly grow up for the judges to consider. Chuckling with glee, the chancellor complimented Nastibozo as a clever prince, worthy in all things of his uncle's throne, that someday before long must be left empty.

"You see, there was double wickedness in the black heart of the chancellor. He hoped, as we say, to kill two birds with one stone. Not only would he beat the worthy Squire Squab of Squelchley-on-the-Squeam, but he trusted he would do something more important as well. For years he had been going to the doctors with insides desperately upset by the rich dishes devised by his master, the Picnic King. Moreover, he did not by any means approve of spending the country's great wealth in such frivolous ways. He hated King Guzzle the Second. And would have been glad to see anyone take his place.

"Here, then, was a grand chance for a revolution. Guzzledom in those days was an Elective Kingdom—that is, a king's son did not necessarily follow him. But the new monarch was chosen by the people, and if troublesome times came along, you never knew who might rule the country.

"Now, at last, the wicked chancellor saw his star of hope rising. Everything was right—and ripe—for the overthrow of King Guzzle the Second. Even though that monarch had changed his ways somewhat of late, the people could still be told that the greater part of the country's money was spent in food and extravagant living; the brave days of Guzzle the First deserved to be brought back.

"Nastibozo was an important prince with a big following. Even if the people did not cry out for a new king, a revolution could be arranged, the chancellor was sure. All he had to do was to send messengers to those foreign countries who had lent money to the Picnic Kingdom, and tell them all to insist that their loans be returned to them next Monday noon and not an instant later.

"This would be sure to throw all the business of Guzzledom into a great mess, and almost certainly cause a revolution. For anyone to find money in a hurry to pay his debts with is always difficult, but with regular merchants it gets them so worked up they are ready to do almost anything.

"And so there was a revolution in Guzzledom—the first and the only one in that kingdom's history. People ran around in all directions, did a great deal of talking, and acted in a perfectly crazy manner. The king's nephew, Prince Nastibozo, aided by the chancellor, was busy as a bee, everywhere plotting and stirring up hatred against the king and the king's friends. There were many shootings and blowing up of public buildings. Nobody seemed to know quite what he was doing, or what might happen any minute. Business came to a dead stop. Shops were closed. It was a terrible mess.

"All this saddened the heart of the good king. It was not that he was afraid of Prince Nastibozo and his other enemies; it was not that he was greatly worried about the danger of losing his power as monarch. But after years of kingship he had come to think of the people always as his children. And now to find that they would turn against him just because a stupid popinjay like Nastibozo had done a lot of low-down gossip and backbiting was something very bitter and hard for an old man to bear. It must not be forgotten that His Majesty was no longer a young man.

"He felt pretty sure that by fighting his nephew, he could beat him. But this he did not want to do. It would mean retraining the army and calling to his help all the noblemen of the countryside with their men-at-arms and archers. Thus, most likely, he would stay on as king. But before he could be victorious over his enemies he knew he would have to spread the horrors of war over his beloved land—a war in which many innocent people would suffer and be killed, just because they had been silly enough to listen to Nastibozo and his lies.

"'No,' said the king. 'Whatever happens, there shall be no war. I spent my days teaching the people what the good things of life and peace are: Shall I end my days by shooting them like dogs? No!'

"This his nephew and the chancellor felt quite sure would be the king's decision. Guzzledom had been for many years a country of farming, stock raising, and the sensible, useful arts. The chancellor knew right well that by getting the foreign powers to call in their loans, the kingdom was not really made the poorer at all. It only gave the appearance of this; and the whole world believed hard times were now coming to every land upon the earth because the richest of them all seemed suddenly to have gone poor.

"Nastibozo and the chancellor took advantage of this also. They told the people that great poverty had come upon them because the arts of war had been neglected. The cure for this, they said, was to make the country what is called an industrial one. Factories must be built everywhere—never mind about the farms—they needed especially the kind of factory that made swords and armor and cannon and those other things that are used for fighting.

"Thus they persuaded the poor, ignorant people that evil days had justly come to Guzzledom because the arts of war—by which the king's brave father, Guzzle the First, had made his reign so rich in victories and successful campaigns—had been laid aside and forgotten.

"Their idea also was to prepare for a revolution against the king that was sure to bring them success—when Prince Nastibozo was to grasp the crown and the chancellor be made his prime minister.

"Clever in politics, these two.

"And at first they succeeded. Such was the terrible confusion that came over the peaceful land, nobody knew which party to join, and the king was nearly killed more than once. But quiet, kindly old gentleman that he was, Guzzle the Second was above all things a brave man. And where many monarchs in like position would have hidden themselves in the cellar or fled from the city, he walked the streets without even a guard.

"'My children'—as he always called the common people—'will do me no harm,' said he to the anxious ministers who wanted him to stay indoors when guns were going off in all directions. This had the effect of making the people, who had always liked him, think it would be a good idea to keep him as king instead of setting up Prince Nastibozo, whom, for all his clever talk, they disliked and suspected without knowing why.

"Thus the country was sadly divided. The wealthy merchants and the army were all for Prince Nastibozo. So were some of the more powerful nobles, dukes, and the like. But the common people, the country gentlemen and the farmers, they were solidly for the king. And certain they were that given a proper chance, he would bring back good times and make Guzzledom once more the richest land in all the world.

"And so to decide what should be done about the matter, a kind of meeting was held. The king was put on trial. It was a tremendous affair. Nastibozo came with the wicked chancellor, and both of them talked themselves blue in the face. They hoped that if they could only make things look black enough for the king, they'd get the judges to order his head chopped off and then everything would be easy.

"But this the judges would not consent to do. Even if they had wanted it, they were afraid of the people. However, Nastibozo and the chancellor made some very clever arguments, and after six hours of talk it was decided that His Majesty's life should be spared but he should be sentenced to exile—that is, he must leave the country and give up being king. Prince Nastibozo was elected in his place to rule the land.

"And so Guzzle the Second packed up his trunks and with a few servants and a dog or two he set off for a foreign country, while King Nastibozo settled down to be monarch in his place.

"But after a week he found that the business of being a king was not so easy. For one thing, he was not popular at all. As soon as the people had time to become quiet and could think straight, they made up their minds that the last thing in the world they wanted was a lot of factories to make swords and armor and guns. They straightway set fire to these and burned them to the ground.

"King Nastibozo turned the soldiers on them and many were killed and wounded. Then it leaked out that the wicked chancellor had asked the foreign merchants to call in the debts, and this made everybody perfectly furious. In the middle of the night two hundred farmers called on Nastibozo and told him to get out of Guzzledom before daybreak and take the chancellor and his bad digestion with him.

"By daybreak they were gone and were never seen in Guzzledom again. Thus the kingdom was left without a king. And there followed what is called a counterrevolution—that is, a new lot of rebels set to work to undo what had been done by the first lot. The army was dismissed and put to digging potatoes.

"Then there was much discussion as to whether they should try to get King Guzzle the Second to come back. The counter-revolutionists won easily. And the same two hundred farmers set off to find him and bring him back.

"Well, they found him after a good deal of search in foreign lands, but they couldn't bring him back. He didn't want to come. He gave them several reasons; for one thing, he said, he was probably too old now to make a good king; for another, he was a little disappointed in the people of Guzzledom. The country would perhaps do better as a republic than as a kingdom.

"Finally he told them that the task he had set out to do was done—he had taught his people the true value of the things worthwhile in living. He wanted now, he said, to settle down as a country gentleman to breed trout, to raise pheasants, and prune peach trees. And besides, as one of his dogs was going to have puppies in a few days, he couldn't possibly be absent for that, even for the ruling of a kingdom. Let them try a republic, he said, and see how it worked out.

"The farmers were very disappointed. But before they left they made him promise that once a year he would visit his old kingdom to celebrate the anniversary of steak-and-kidney pudding. The famous Golden Saucepan, which he had so often used in years gone by, would be kept glittering and bright against his coming, and the silk apron he always wore in the royal kitchen would be specially laundered. He could not refuse this, they said, wiping their tears on red handkerchiefs—republic or no republic. He could come as a private gentleman visiting the state.

"This he swore solemnly he would do, insisting only that he bring his own dough with him—since the old pastry cook, the only one who could knead it to his taste—had refused to be left behind and had come to share his exile with him."

The End

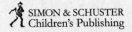 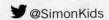